# UNreal

# gods

by
SP Clarke

Buko Publications • Portland OR

The reader is hereby reminded that all characters, locations and events mentioned herein, including those whose names may seem familiar, are products of the author's imagination, and any resemblance to actual persons, living or dead is purely coincidental

The author wishes to offer his profound gratitude to Lesley Lathrop, Celeste Johnson-Pugh, Steve Hettum, Houston Bolles, John Leonard Rancher, Astrid Rancher-Hanke, and Buko for their invaluable assistance, without which this project never would have come to fruition.

For Billy...

was falling. Falling. The snow was falling, soft and white upon the ground. The snow was falling. Mounding into soft, round tufts and cold, still drifts. Transforming the hard red bricks of the surrounding buildings and the cloud gray pavement into an amorphously soft, white, shifting pile.

The snow was falling for no reason and falling all around. Lulling the pavement and the air and the ground with a soft and cold, white falling sound. A hush.

Softly down, the white snow rushed. Falling. The snow, white and rounded and hushed upon the cold hard ground, was falling. Falling down. Still.

Inside a bar in northwest Portland a din sloshed sloppily.

Trudy Verducci stood with Billy against the wall at the side of the stage, carefully assessing the other contestants. Most of them seemed to represent a David Bowie era, but none really looked like Bowie—not, as they figured anyway, as much as Billy did.

To a round of impatient applause from a good-sized crowd of around two hundred and fifty, Rockin' DJ Connie Pony took to the stage of the Earth Tavern.

—Hi gang. I'm Connie Pony, rockin' drive time DJ for radio K-N-O-W. We're in the know, y'know.

She lightly chuckled at the levity of her oft-repeated remark.

—And tonight, we're here for the nineteen seventy-eight Portland City David Bowie Look-A-Like contest.
A smattering of sarcastic hoots and hollers rose up from the rowdy crowd.

—The winner of our contest, and a guest, will be chauffeured by limo, courtesy of Regal Limos, and transported to the David Bowie concert at the Memorial Coliseum on May twenty-seventh, riding with none other than David Bowie himself! After the concert, the winner will be given a backstage pass, where he or she will meet the members of Bowie's band and entourage and hobnob with the groupies and hangers-on!

Somewhat inspired by the prospect—the crowd vaguely shouted half-hearted approval. Soldiering on like a trooper and a true veteran of such crazy promotional skirmishes, Connie Pony continued her highly polished spiel.

—That's right people, an evening rubbing shoulders with the stars, brought to you by the happenin' DJs at K-Now. If we don't play it, the record isn't happenin' *now*! It looks like we've got a lot of contestants here tonight.

Connie Pony shaded her eyes from the glare of the stage lights, surveying the motley crowd, of whom many purported to be contestants, though few even remotely resembled David Bowie.

—So let's get the festivities started!

Bowie's *Ziggy Stardust* album blared distortedly through the PA speakers, as the crowd began to whistle and whoop in nervous anticipation, inside the large low, dark area that was the Earth's main hall.

—Our first contestant will be...uh, Just Jeremy. Ladies and gentlemen, from Beaverton, Oregon, Just Jeremy.

The crowd noise neither rose nor fell in volume. Apparently the audience was anticipating some specific favorite contestants, who were further back in the line, awaiting their opportunity to cavort.

An awkward-looking Just Jeremy walked stiffly out onto the stage, sporting a sort of *Hunky Dory* Bowie look—platform shoes, bell-bottom pants, a slight spare tire oozing over his belt, with unfashionably long, permed hair. Half-heartedly Just Jeremy attempted a couple of well-known Bowie poses, but the crowd mostly ignored him. Microphone in hand, Connie Pony moved closer to the hangdog contestant.

—Tell us, Just Jeremy, what period Bowie are you? Looks like kind of an early Bowie, *Space Oddity* thing. Am I right?

—Uh, I don't know nothin' about David Bowie. My girlfriend made me do this.

—His girlfriend made him do it! He don't know nothin'. Just Jeremy, ladies and gentlemen. Just Jeremy. Good job Just, it's always hard to be first!

With a flourish, Connie Pony bade Just Jeremy adieu, as he trudged to the far side of the stage and stood, awkwardly attempting to find something to do with his hands.

The crowd tittered mildly, as Connie Pony shuffled to the next index card, which bore the name of the contestant who was to follow Just Jeremy.

—Next here on our stage

Connie Pony poorly feigned an impression of Ed Sullivan.

—Mister Lewis Hallman! Mister Lewis Hallman from Northwest Portland, ladies and gentlemen.

Again, the restless crowd, buzzing incessantly, seemed not to notice the announcement. Arrayed in a fine cream-colored silk suit—his hair close-cropped, dyed brown, Lewis slid to center stage as a reasonable representation of the "Thin White Duke" Bowie.

Though Lewis did not much resemble Bowie, at least he had a slender physique. He struck a few angular poses in time to "Soul Love" as it blared through the speakers, executing a quick, faultless exit—to no reaction whatsoever from the crowd.

Connie Pony returned to center stage, smirking and laughing, as if she had just been sharing a private joke with a few members of the audience—which she had not really been doing at all.

—Oh thank you so much, Lewis Hamlin...

She checked her index card.

—uh, Hallman. Sorry 'bout that, Lewis.

She waved at him daintily.

—Next up is Leslie Flynn from Northwest Portland. Leslie...?

Leslie Flynn seemed to somewhat resemble Bowie from the Ziggy period. Her short yellow-blond hair and garish blue jumpsuit heightened the similarity, to some extent, though her space boots seemed too large for her feet. She clomped around as if navigating the moon. The horde chuckled collectively.

Leslie performed an awkward lip-sync to "Star Man," which was met with ripples of laughter and derision. Disconsolately, she stomped from the stage.

Connie Pony announced.

—Ladies and gentlemen, Miss. Leslie...Miss. Leslie. Flynn. Miss Leslie Flynn. Let's give her a big hand. She's awfully brave to come up here and make a fool of herself like that, in front of you bozos.

The assemblage snickered and cackled.

Thrusting a finger at certain individuals within the throng, Connie shot back.

—She's braver than any of you guys.

She laughed.

—Maybe not as smart...

3

The gaggle rowdily hooted and crowed. Connie Pony continued.

—Anyway, let's get our next contestant up here. Let's see, who's next?

She searched for the next index card.

—Reza Khouri. Reza Khouri. That's what it says. Are you here, Reza? Let's have a look at ya.

Reza, a dark-skinned middle-eastern looking lad, approached center stage—wearing a shiny red, green, gray, and blue nylon shirt, broad-striped with a long collar, a brown sports coat, gray slacks, and brown wing-tipped shoes. He did not seem to discernibly represent any known incarnation of Bowie—more resembling a disco dancer who might have taken a wrong turn on Northwest 21st Avenue.

Billy casually leaned against a wall, just off stage, waiting with the other remaining contestants. He was tall and beautiful, his hair dyed blood red and shaped into an enormous sculpted flat-top shag, swept up and held into place on top by a large quantity of hair jell.

In the back, his hair was long and straight. His girlfriend, Trudy Verducci stood in front of him, carefully applying red paint across his forehead. Then, in a sharp zigzag across Billy's cheek, she contrasted it with highlights of blue. He was heavily made up, dark red eye-shadow setting off his eyes and cheeks.

—Don't move, silly. This is the most important part.

He watched her, amused. She stood back from him and smiled

—You look really weird, Billy. You look just like Bowie.

Trudy held up the cover of *Aladdin Sane* next to Billy's face. She glanced back and forth between Bowie's photo and Billy's face. Distracted, she directed him.

—Now close your eyes and tilt your head down—like that.

She steadied the angle of his head.

—Perfect. You're perfect. You're an identical match.

Proudly, Trudy stood back again and gazed intently at Billy, brushing wavy auburn hair away from her face.

—God. That's pretty amazing. The flash even looks identical.

She grabbed a compact out of her purse. Expertly flicking it open, she aimed the mirror at Billy. Eyes wide, Billy smiled enthusiastically.

—Wow! Is that me? It doesn't even look like me. God! Great face-streak, Trude. It really does look just like the album.

Billy moved toward Trudy, to kiss her.

—Smear that face and you're history. Let's save the kissing for afterwards.

She playfully pushed him away.

Looking nothing like Bowie from any era, Reza Khouri lip-synched "Hang On To Yourself" with amazing expertise. His stage movements were those of a middle-eastern Buddy Holly, but the unruly throng, seemingly aware of the odd incongruous exhibition to which they were witness, clapped in time to the music.

—Alright now, Reza! Far out! That was amazingly cool.

Connie Pony awkwardly clapped her hands, holding fast to her stack of cue cards.

—Reza Khouri, ladies and gentlemen. Give him a big hand. Next up, Richard Stark...Richard Stark? Isn't that *Ringo's* real name?

Trudy gave Billy an admiring smile.

—-Well, it looks like you're up next, big boy. You remember all your moves?

Billy nodded, a determined expression on his face. Trudy grinned assuringly.

—You're a shoo-in. Just flash the moves, stay in time and try to remember the words. Do you remember the words to 'Suffragette City'?

Billy nodded again. Solemn.

—Yeah, I remember 'em, Trude. I'm gonna win this thing goin' away.

He gazed in the direction of Richard Stark, who, at that moment, was gyrating helplessly on the stage, to the strains of the song "Ziggy Stardust."

—These people are turkeys. I've got star quality.

He puffed his skinny bare chest out slightly, with half-mocking pride. Connie Pony took center stage next to Richard, confiding.

—Oh Richard, you took my breath away. How's about a big round of applause for Richard Stark everyone. The fifth Beatle.

Silence.

—Next up, from southeast Portland, we have Billy Granger. C'mon people, let's give Billy some encouragement. Put your hands together!

As the first strident chords of "Suffragette City" rang though the PA system, Billy strutted to center stage in silver spandex pants and silver platform shoes, shimmying his shoulders and rhythmically sliding his hips. The audience erupted in excited cheers.

—Yay, man...

Mouthing the words Billy trotted and frugged around the stage, his lissom frame taut and sinewy. Coos and moans swelled from among the female contingent of spectators. He did the cool jerk, thrusting his arms down and away from his chest, while suggesting a shing-a-ling skating motion with his lower limbs. Screams and shouts met his every move.

He froze into hard, angular stances through the chorus.

—Hoo ha!

And he strode from the stage, arms and legs akimbo. Obviously buoyed by the performance, Connie Pony shouted.

—Alright! Billy Granger, everybody. Billy Granger. Let's hear it for Billy Granger. He out-Bowied Bowie, I'd say.

As Billy stepped from the stage, Trudy ran up to him, arms open wide. She kissed him passionately, placing her tongue deep into his mouth. But he was distracted.

—God, you were so good, Billy. You were so great! You had the crowd in the palm of your hand.

Hugging him, she ran her hand up and down his sweaty naked back.

—You win the prize here, big boy and I'll have a little prize for you back in the car.

She jammed her tongue deep into his ear, circling and massaging it suggestively.

Billy yanked his head away from her ministrations, never allowing his gaze to stray from the stage. It was as if he could see his own ghost dancing beneath the lights. He shivered slightly, as he hugged Trudy—absently fondling her ass.

## II

Billy and Trudy waited in the rear of the spacious limousine, sipping champagne in a callow caricature of supposed elegance. Parked outside the Benson Hotel, the couple was dressed casually. Trudy wore a bright-green pleated miniskirt and a black cardigan sweater over a pink blouse. She highlighted the ensemble with day-glo pink ping-pong earrings, an oversized black leather motorcycle jacket and pink ballet slippers.

Billy wore a half-unbuttoned white shirt, which bore faint, multi-colored abstract designs upon it, black jeans and white slip-on boating shoes with no socks. He too wore a black leather jacket.

David Bowie seemed to be in no hurry to leave the hotel and proceed to his engagement at the Memorial Coliseum. Billy and Trudy were isolated from the warm summery night by the thick smoked-glass windows of the limo, bathed in cool air-conditioned luxury.

—Billy, I'm so excited, I think I'm gonna pass out. What if he's sick and has to cancel the show? What if I get sick? Oh my God, I'm gonna be sick.

Oblivious, Billy peered out the windows to the entryway of the hotel. He watched the doorman anxiously march back and forth in front of the glass entry doors. Trudy rummaged through her purse, nervously searching for her lipstick.

—Is he coming? Can you see him?

—No, not yet, Trudy. I don't see anybody comin'.

Muttering to himself, he glanced away from the window, turning his gaze to Trudy.

—Why don't you calm down?

He feigned a cockney accent.

—Why'n't ya' just calm down? 'e's just some bloomin' little Bri'ish bloke. Like my baseball coach always used to say…

Trudy had heard it before.

—I know. I know 'He puts his pants on the same way you do, one leg at a time.'

She smiled, a mischievous glint in her eye. She began massaging the fly of his jeans, inquiringly.

—But what about this leg, Billy boy? What did coachie tell you about this leg, Billy? Huh?

She nuzzled his neck affectionately.

—Hey, knock it off, Trude. What's Bowie gonna think if I shake his hand and me with a huge boner?

She continued to stroke the squirming young man.

—He swings both ways, doesn't he? He'll probably be flattered.

Billy grabbed her hand.

—Will you cut it out? We're gonna meet a big star. I don't need you beatin' me off. Let's just watch him and see how he does it.

—What? Beat you off?

Pouting, Trudy sat up and returned to searching her purse for her lipstick. She whined.

—See how he does what?

—See how he acts like a star? Try to figure out what he's got. He's not God. He's just a guy. I know I could do what he does...

At last, three men emerged through the glass doors of the hotel. Two grizzled looking men in black leather jackets led a slender man of medium height toward the limo. Bowie's mauvre silk shirt and puce-tinted suit coat glinted in the lights at the hotel entry.

One of the grizzled men opened the door to the limo. First the other grizzled man got into the vehicle. Then Bowie and the other grizzled man followed. The three of them sat in the seat opposite to Billy and Trudy. The limo pulled away from the curb. In a dignified British accent, Bowie said.

—Hello, I'm David Bowie.

He extended his hand upright, in a European handshake. Billy grasped his hand awkwardly, as if to kiss the star's ring, giving it a gentle squeeze. Trudy did the same. Bowie gestured to the grizzled men. He quickly glanced sideways to the right and then to the left.

—This is my road manager Mick Lamb. And this is my bodyguard, Goat. A goat and a lamb. Can you imagine that? I often tell Goat to go to hell and yet he never does.

Numbly, the two grizzled men smiled, sharing what was obviously a longstanding private joke. Bowie carefully observed the young couple—his blue eye trained on

Billy, his brown eye on Trudy.

—And you are?

Initially, Billy did not realize that Bowie was asking him a question. He was busy watching how Bowie did Bowie. Billy smiled a sheepish grin, nodding his head nervously.

—What? Oh. I'm Billy Granger

—And...?

Bowie prodded, in Trudy's direction.

—I'm Trudy Verducci.

—And a lovely Trudy Verducci you are, indeed. Is this the first of my shows that you have attended?

Trudy blushed faintly.

—No. We saw you up at the Kingdome, about three years ago for the *Young Americans, Station to Station* tour.

Bowie's face lit up with glee.

—Oh, how nice. A delightful personae. I'll have to bring him back for an encore one day, eh?

With animated vigor Trudy gestured to the affirmative. The star then turned his attention to Billy.

—So. They tell me you won some look-alike contest or other. It's rather funny, really. I don't think you look at all like me. You're so Nordic and I'm so Middle European. You're very tall, aren't you? How tall are you?

Answering shyly, Billy replied.

—Six-four.

—Oh. Well that wouldn't do! Much too tall for European girls.

Bowie flashed his toothy crooked grin toward Trudy, asking Billy:

—And what is your age?

—Twenty-two.

—Oh my. When I was twenty-two I wasn't half your size. I couldn't have weighed seven stone in those days. So, how did you portray me at the contest?

9

Proud of her artistic acumen, Trudy trumpeted.

—We modeled him after your *Aladdin Sane* period and he looked just like you. We got the makeup just right.

—I hope so. It took Duffy and the make-up team five hours to get me looking just right for that shoot. So, Billy. Are you a musician?

—Not yet. But I'm gonna be.

—Oh. I love that drive. That's what it takes, you know. Can you sing?

—A little. But I'll learn to sing better. I want to learn to control a crowd like you do. I want to be like you.

Bowie was a bit taken aback by Billy's determined forthrightness.

—I certainly want to wish you all the luck in the world on that.

The trip across the Steel Bridge to the Coliseum did not take long. The limo arrived at the stage entrance. Mick and Goat led Bowie, Billy, and Trudy through the wide doors—steering them in the direction of the dressing rooms.

With every step they took, more and more people gathered around the entourage. They were seeking photos. They were seeking interviews. They were seeking autographs. They were seeking, simply, to be seen by and with Bowie, to touch him, to catch his attention in some way. Mick and Goat expertly pushed their way through the crowd, in the direction of the dressing rooms, which were located to the side and just below the main stage.

They arrived at a reception area, filled with tables littered with catered food and drink: plates of fresh vegetables, bowls of nuts, a rack of lamb, a cooked turkey, a baked salmon. Loaves of various kinds of bread and dishes of condiments were strewn about the tables. Iced-tubs with bottles of Perrier, soft-drinks and drink mixers, various brands of beer, white and red wines and champagne were filled to overflowing, placed against a table—bottles of liquor lined up at the tables edge, with a variety of plates, silverware and crystal.

Wide-eyed, Trudy seemed in awe of the magnitude of the banquet. More relaxed, Billy simply took in the luxuriant splendor. Bowie put his arms around the couple's shoulders.

—Well, I must be off now. Time to put my face on and all that. Please help yourselves to anything you see here. Anything you might like to eat or drink. If you get to it early enough, it won't be all messed up by the staff and crew. I hope you enjoy the show.

And with that, Bowie wandered off in the direction of the dressing rooms, a gaggle of toadies following in his wake. They disappeared behind a door with a sign that said 'Private. Do Not Enter'.

—God, Billy. He was so nice. Wasn't he nice?

—Yeah, he was nice. I guess.

—You guess? He knew about you. Knew you had won the contest. He didn't just stare out the window. He actually spoke to us. Didn't that impress you?

—Yeah. I was impressed. That's how I'll treat fans when I'm as big as he is.

—Aren't you taking a little bit for granted? *When I'm as big as he is*? He's been at this for a long time, Billy. More than ten years. You've never, like, written a song or sung in front of a crowd. You don't know how to play an instrument or anything.

—Well, I'm gonna learn, Trudy. Watch me now. I'm gonna learn. And I'm gonna learn real fast. Wait and see. I'm gonna be a star. Just like Bowie. It's not that hard to learn guitar. It's just six strings and a bunch of lines. I can learn chords. I can write songs too. And I'm not afraid of being in front of a crowd. That's the easiest thing in the world.

The concert congregation slowly began to gather, finding their seats in the auditorium and chattering nervously in anticipation of David Bowie's arrival on stage. Billy loved the sound of the mounting excitement in the rush of the crowd. He loved the way Bowie's entourage had fawned over the star, scurrying about to fulfill his every whim—the attention they had bestowed on him.

Billy and Trudy grazed and nibbled at various food items. Trudy drank a Perrier. Billy had a Heineken. Mick ambled over to where the couple was standing.

—There's a place just off to the side of the stage where you can watch the concert, if you'd like. It's right up those stairs over there.

Motioning with his head, Mick indicated where they could stand.

—David will be starting his show in about twenty minutes or so. I only ask that you be cognizant that there will be various people with jobs to perform, and that you not interrupt them, nor interfere with their duties. David is very particular about that. He's very precise you know.

Billy and Trudy bobbed their heads acquiescently. Trudy crunched on a carrot stick, gawking blankly at the road manager. Billy was staring at the backstage curtains at the top of the stairs.

The excitement of the growing throng steadily increased in volume, becoming more animated and intense—as Billy savored the idea of thirty thousand eyes watching only him on a stage. He pictured himself strutting beneath the bright, colored lights in a leopard skin jumpsuit, a mic cord carefully coiled around his left forearm. He thought of himself as Mick Jagger. He thought of himself as Bowie, controlling the response of the hordes with a flick of his hair or the set of his chin.

Trudy interrupted his flight of fantasy.

—Hey, Billy. Are you still with me here? Billy? Hello-oo. Ground control to Major Tom.

—Yeah. Yeah, I'm here. I was just thinkin'.

—Thinking about what, pray tell?

—Thinkin' about the future. How things are gonna be in the future. Who I'm gonna be.

—Billy, this is a side of you I've never seen before and I don't know what to make of it. What's gotten in to you?

—I've seen the future, Trudy. I've seen my future. It's standin' right in front of me like a ghost or somethin'. It's right there.

Trudy looked off in the general direction of where Billy had fixed his eyes— somewhere toward the backstage curtain.

—I wish you luck with that, Billy. I really do. But I'm not sure I can see it.

Suddenly David Bowie appeared above them. With catlike grace, he paced at the side of the stage, just out of view of the roaring horde. He ran his hand through his carefully coiffed blond hair, with a slight smile. Jumping up and down, his feet barely left the ground. He trotted without effort, pumping his elbows, as if in a brisk, happy jog.

With a quick thrust of his hand, he swept aside the curtain and moved in a dash toward the center of attention, the flock screaming hysterically. Billy and Trudy moved up the stairs, to the curtain at the side, where Mick Lamb said they could stand.

The band launched into "Panic In Detroit" and the mob lost all sense of decorum. They howled in heat, as Bowie pranced and preened before them, his careful baritone careening God-like from the PA system.

Billy stood transfixed. He catalogued Bowie's every move. He memorized each inflection, every nuance. It was all so easy. Billy was convinced that it was so very easy. It wouldn't be long and he would be out there too. Just like Bowie

# III

Casey Avon and his namesake band finished up their set at the Long Goodbye, opening for the rowdy Malchicks. An amiable fellow, Casey led his group through several original songs and a few cover tunes. On the final number, lead guitarist, the rooster-haired Col Duquesne, contorted his body into a pretzel-like clump as he struck his final power chord.

—Thanks, everybody. The Malchicks'll be up in a few minutes.

A raucous cheer went up.

—We'll be at Dusty's Corral next weekend, so c'mon over. We'll see ya' then.

A smattering of applause rose up from the dance floor.

As Casey Avon moved their gear off the stage, a boisterous crush of drunken Friday night revelers anxiously awaited the appearance of the Malchicks—the brash, new young band who were commanding so much attention in the scene. As always, the crowd was predominantly female. Word had already spread that the Malchicks lead singer Billy Granger was indescribably gorgeous—and likely to do almost anything on stage to garner attention. The band supposedly bore some resemblance (in spirit) to the young Rolling Stones. And they played several Stones cover songs in the context of the ten or fifteen songs they actually knew.

In only six previous performances, it was rumored around Portland that Billy and his brother Denny had pissed on the dance floor from the stage—while spewing beer from pitchers in a spray across the audience. They had already been in two fistfights with each other. One time, at Sacks, they knocked over drummer Pete Johannsen's cymbals while rolling around on the stage, pounding each other's faces with their fists. Band followers loved the mayhem, and their numbers increased exponentially with every show.

As always, hawk-faced bassist Gib Stryker was the first to set up—as the band's de facto roadie, leviathan Bam Bam, hefted the musician's bass cabinet onto the stage. Tall, with close-cropped, wiry brown hair, Gib had what seemed like a perpetual frown strewn across his serious face. With his fingers, he methodically slapped at his bass. He was the most reliable and experienced member of the band, having played in a couple of country bands before he joined the Malchicks. While Pete Johannsen completed his drum set up, Gib expertly executed various runs up and down the fingerboard of the bass. Pete performed a series of drum fills and various rhythms.

The other more consistent band associate, Pete was quiet and responsible, with a sense of determination. He had married three years earlier, at age twenty, when his wife had their baby. The most business-like of the quintet, Pete generally handled band finances and the distribution of funds.

Rhythm guitarist Rod Castro carefully tuned his finicky Rickenbacker guitar with Gib's bass. Broodingly handsome, dark haired Rod acted as reckless cohort in Denny's drunken debauches. Funny, glib, solipsistically cruel and lecherous, he played the Brian Jones role in the Malchicks' Stones-like configuration.

Billy and Denny took the stage together. Slender, gawky Denny wore a light blue workshirt and black spandex pants His spiky, straw-colored hair—modeled somewhat after Keith Richards—poked out in a porcupine.

The Apollo the girls had come to see shine was tall, lanky Billy, with his incredible good looks, feminine features and piercing blue eyes, rimmed heavily with mascara. He was dressed in a blue plaid western shirt, tucked into skintight jeans, which were pushed inside light brown cowboy boots—a thin chain draped around his right boot. A red neckerchief around his neck, two more were wrapped around either wrist.

Billy and Denny tuned their guitars in haphazard fashion. Billy did not really play his guitar much during the course of a Malchicks set. He mainly used it as a prop. Denny was the lead guitarist, though he could not play much better than Rod. He had lead-guitarist moves. He would crouch effectively at vital moments during his lead lines, snickering and grimacing with a determined urgency.

Billy stepped to the mic and huskily announced himself to the unruly mass of flesh that stood on the dance floor below him.

—Good evening, ladies. And you too, sir. Welcome to the Long Goodbye Milkbar. I'm Billy Granger and we are the Malchenky Malchicks. These are me droogs, Pete, Gib, Rod and Dim. Uh, I mean, Denny.

Denny glared at Billy. He had heard that reference one too many times within the short history of the band's existence.

—We hope you'll settle in with your favorite variety of moloko and give us a listen. Our set isn't very long, but it should be fun.

With that, Rod swung into the familiar chord progression of the Kinks' "All the Day and All of the Night." Billy sang the lyrics staccato, playing coyly with the girls who stood at his feet. He marched happily, with a sense of boyish charm. Every time he flicked his golden blond hair, an audible sigh emanated from the females below him.

They immediately followed that song with a loose version of the Stones' "Honky Tonk Women" and then launched into a particularly sloppy intro to the Who's "Pinball Wizard." Conjuring Elvis, Billy drawled.

—This is for all you Pinball Wizards out there. Thang yuh veruh mush.

14

Billy and Denny began bumping into each other, each time more fiercely, as Denny attempted the chord sequence that led into the vocal section of the song. Denny speared Billy with a familiarly sharp, bony elbow. Billy retaliated with a rough shoulder shot to Denny's ribs, which were exposed beneath his left hand, fretting his guitar.

Walking away from the fray, Billy strutted smartly back to his amp, drawing a huge swig from a pitcher of beer that sat upon it. He swallowed mightily, then took another quick gulp, before sprinting back to the mic to perform his vocal duties. As Billy sang, Denny smacked him in the back with the neck of his guitar.

The mass of young women—and the occasional male—who moved to the mess on the dance floor, were oblivious to the inter-familial infighting that was taking place above them. Instead, they shouted into each other's ears and swayed to the music in careful sensual movements. Meanwhile, the band swung into Van Morrison's "Gloria." Billy quizzed the flock.

—Is there anybody named Gloria out there? Anybody? No? Well this is for you, Gloria, wherever the hell you are.

On the dance floor, the clutch of girls moved more feverishly to the familiar rhythm, undulating suggestively. As the band created the mood, Billy wandered back to his amp to consume another large quantity of beer.

As the band swung into the chorus, Billy nudged Denny gingerly, before resting his arm on his brother's shoulder. Billy crooned the second verse.

—She come across town

He lowered his voice to a provocative whisper.

—Strollin' up the street

The dancing young women began to jump up and down orgasmically, as the band swept into the final hesitating chords of the song, hammering away with boisterous exuberance. Rod Castro leered at two girls in front of him, licking his lips seductively. Gib Stryker stood at the back of the stage, positioned motionlessly next to Pete Johannsen. Meanwhile, Billy and Denny continued their wrestling match.

Behind the bar, club manager Tommy Demeola smiled and slowly shook his head in wry disbelief. Tommy was older than his constituents. His dense, curly black hair was puffed up into an Italian bramble. His heavy-lidded, dark eyes peered out at the world with a sleepy, casual indifference. A full, black moustache gave him the look of a Mexican outlaw from the old west. A slender man of medium height, he nonchalantly leaned on his elbow against the counter of the bar taking in the Malchicks' show.

During the break between songs, Denny dashed back to his amp and swallowed the contents of an entire pitcher of beer. Billy finished off his pitcher, then stepped back up to the mic.

—Say, Tommy, would you be so kind as to send one of the lovely Long Goodbye waitresses up with more pitchers of beer for us poor workin' lads here on the stage. We work up a mighty thirst underneath these hot, hot lights.

Several girls in the audience reached up to Billy to hand him their drinks.

—No, no. Thanks anyway, ladies. We earn these beers and you pay enough money to see us. The beer is part of our pay. How're we comin' with that beer out there, lovely Long Goodbye waitresses?

Tommy Demeola leaned on the beer tap, drawing four large containers of Budweiser. A big-breasted girl with shoe-polish black hair in a white blouse and black skirt hoisted the tray of pitchers over her head and dutifully advanced toward the stage, as the sea of onlookers parted respectfully.

She arrived at the stage, setting the tray down in front of the brothers. Billy and Denny each grabbed a pitcher, and they chugged them down thirstily, handing the empty containers back to the waitress. Then they grabbed the other two pitchers she had brought and ran them back to their amps. They returned with the two empty pitchers they had consumed earlier and gave them to her, as well, as she turned to trek back to the bar.

—How's about a big hand for Francie, everybody.

The crowd bellowed.

—That's, Francie. And she's my girlfriend. Well, she's my girlfriend tonight anyway. Anybody out there wanna be my girlfriend tomorrow night?

Amidst a sea of raised feminine hands (and, curiously, one male), came shouts in affirmative reply.

—Well then. That's encouraging. But, I'm sorry sir...

He looked at the young man who had raised his hand.

—I swing, but I don't swing that way.

The dance floor girls cheered vehemently.

Rolling up in her red Mustang in the cold fall night, Trudy searched for a parking spot somewhere near the Long Goodbye. She had just finished her four-to-midnight shift at Quality Pie, waiting tables and tending the counter. She reeked of Crisco and cigarette smoke. Finally, she found a space about two blocks from the club and hurried to catch what was left of the Malchicks' set.

She stood at the table at the entry, paid her cover charge, got her hand stamped, and began moving toward the bar at the back of the club. She immediately caught Billy's eye.

—Hey, Trude, glad ya' could make it. How're the banana cream pies at QP tonight?

Embarrassed, she ignored him and rushed through the crush of people, intent upon getting a drink and hiding from the curious eyes that she felt were directed at her. At the bar, she ordered a rum and Coke and turned to watch the band.

The Malchicks shifted into the routinely customary chords of "Louie, Louie." Billy dutifully recited his tale.

—Here's a little ditty that the Kingsmen recorded right here in Portland, Oregon, back in nineteen sixty-three just around the corner at Northwest Recorders, for fifty-eight bucks. The record sold millions. Not a bad return on that investment, I'd say.

Halfway through the song, the band changed the rhythm of the chords and began playing "Wild Thing," to an excited distaff response.

Billy and Denny began to slam against one another again. Each impact jarred Denny's grip on his guitar, frustrating him by the mistakes it caused. The girls on the dance floor seemed unmindful, writhing and coiling like a den of agitated vipers.

Frustrated by all the attention Billy and the boys were receiving, Trudy left her drink at the bar and moved across the dance floor to the front of the stage. She was wearing a black skirt and blouse and knee high black boots. She stood right below Billy. Pulling up her blouse, she exposed a black-lace bra and proceeded to flash him—partly out of lust and partly out of frustration

—Buffalo wang, you make mah mouth stang.

Billy winked at Trudy seductively, with a big smile on his face. She turned and trotted back to her drink. A smattering of applause arose from the males sitting at tables near the bar. Not to be outdone and picking up on Trudy's lead, other girls began to flash Billy too. Billy and Denny abruptly quit smacking into each other to stare wide-eyed at the show on the floor. "Wild Thing" ended rather inattentively, with the two brothers entirely distracted by the unexpected show. Billy shouted.

—Well alright! Looks like we got a whole roomful of wild things tonight. Don't let us hold you back, girls. Don't let us hold you back. We've got a little original tune we want to play for ya' now. It's called 'Girl Over There'.

With a mood and setting reminiscent of the Stones' "Play With Fire," Billy sang the simple lyrics, while eyeing Trudy from his perch.

—Girl over there, she's sittin' in the corner
Girl over there, she's all alone I see.
Girl over there, somebody oughta warn her
She's lookin' for trouble when she's lookin' at me.

17

Trudy had heard the song before and didn't much care for it. She took the lyric personally, sensing that it was a thinly veiled reference to her relationship with Billy. Even though they often got together, she wasn't prepared to say that they were even dating, exactly.

Often, Billy only wanted gratuitous sex from her, without a lot of talk or social interaction. She felt used, but she realized that she was using Billy, too. She used Billy to be near the charisma that he exuded and to be close to the fame she thought was soon to descend upon him.

Their relationship was mutually convenient on many levels. Trudy enjoyed her sexual escapades with Billy. He was a good lover. But there was a decided lack of an emotional exchange between them. Wham bam thank you ma'am. In Trudy, Billy had a reliable and compliant lover to whom he did not have to commit himself on an emotional level. In his heart, he knew she was not his girlfriend, nor would she ever be. Nevertheless, he was happy to hang out with her until the real thing came along.

As the band wrapped up its original tune, Denny jostled Billy with a hip check, which Billy returned with an especial verve, almost knocking Denny off his feet. Denny returned the blow and the two began skirmishing yet again. It was never obvious whether the two of them were just having good-natured fun, or whether they truly hated each other.

—'Girl Over There' everybody. We wrote that song. Pretty cool, eh? Now we're gonna do a song by the Animals, called 'It's My Life'.

Gib moved through the sinuous bassline of the song, as Denny interjected the Eastern-flavored modal lead guitar intro. Billy seductively mumbled the first few lines of the song.

—It's a tough world to get a steak in
All my meat's been shaked and baked in

Again he stared at Trudy, as if to reinforce the sentiments of the previous song. To Billy, even though he forgot the lyrics, the song was the truth and a prediction of his future. The band swung back into the bass and guitar intro. Billy smiled implacably and sang the second verse.

—Yeah that girl she's got her value
And you can bet she's gonna tell you…

As the chorus rolled around again, Billy began to pogo with ecstatic enthusiasm.

—She's my wife and she does what she wants
I ain't seen her in seventeen months

The girls on the dance floor mirrored his movements, some of them exposing their breasts to the players on stage.

Rod Castro jumped off the stage and began to pump up and down with one of the dancers, simulating, none too subtly, the sex act. His partner met his motions with urgent thrusts of her own. The crowded dance floor parted, the two of them gyrating primitively. As the song concluded, Rod ripped one last power chord on his Rickenbacker, then fell to the floor, still quivering spasmodically. His partner fell on top of him and he slid his hand up and down the neck of his guitar as if masturbating. Billy quickly chimed in.

—Okay then. This is a song by The Who and it's a true story.

The band whipped into "The Kids Are Alright," as Rod continued undulating on the floor with the girl from the audience. The rest of the dancers encircled the pair urging them on. At the bar, Trudy ordered another rum and Coke, smirking slightly at the antics of the band. Several males in the audience were whistling and howling riotously—happy for the free show they were getting for the mere cost of the cover charge.

Probably the most appreciative of the display was Bam Bam. Despite his belief to the contrary (he thought of himself as being something of a ladies man) the opposite sex feared Bam Bam as a potential stalker, at best, and probably someone far more dangerous than that. He stood tall, perhaps six-foot six, weighing nearly three hundred pounds, massive and strong as a stevedore. He had a face like a piece of raw meat, pock-marked, with a cruelly sadistic sneer permanently slapped upon it. His viscous brown hair cascaded down in sweaty rivulets around his head.

At their third gig as a band, Bam Bam appeared after the show, announcing to the group that he was their roadie. Then he proceeded to remove all the equipment from the stage as if he were carrying extra chairs from the dining room table. Denny made the mistake of referring to Bam Bam as Godzilla. Bam Bam picked Denny up from the floor by the collar of his shirt and said.

—Don't ever call me that again.

Hanging in mid-air, choking, Denny acceded to Bam Bam's demand. From that point on, everyone in the band called him Bam Bam, and nothing else—even behind his back. In truth, it was possible that Bam Bam had simply intimidated his way into the entourage. No one among the band members had the courage to tell him he could not have the position.

As the band wrapped up "The Kids Are Alright," Rob Castro finally rejoined his band mates on stage, hanging his head, wearing an embarrassed grin. Bam Bam sidled up to Trudy at the bar under the impression that she, like most other women, was deeply attracted to him. With a lascivious leer, he arrogantly inquired of her.

— Hey, how're ya' doin', Trudy? The band sounds pretty good tonight, don't ya' think?

Trudy did not want to talk to Bam Bam—or even to be seen with him. But she knew he was not going to go away, so she resigned herself to continuing the dialogue. With a heavy sigh she said.

—Yeah. They sound real good.

—Quite a show going on tonight too, right? Man, Billy knows how to get the girls worked up. Does he get you worked up like that, too? I bet he does.

Not wishing to discuss the topic with Bam Bam whatsoever, Trudy looked him in the eye.

—I don't think that's any of your business, Bam Bam.

Temporarily humbled, Bam Bam was at a loss for words. Scanning the bobbing heads of the excited crowd, he elected to suspend the conversation.

—Well, set's almost over. I better get up there and get ready to, like, get the gear off stage.

—Yeah, Bam Bam, you better do that.

With a sense of inflated, self-importance, Bam Bam swaggered off into the undergrowth of writhing bodies. Shoulders squared and head held high, as if he were preparing to defend a military installation, Bam Bam strode toward the stage—where Billy and Denny antically windmilled their guitars, imitating Pete Townsend. Concluding the song, Billy announced, Elvis-like.

—Thang yuh. Thang yuh veruh mush. Thank you everybody for comin' tonight. And a special thank you to the Malchicks' dancers. You guys really heated up this joint tonight. We're gonna finish up with a song I'm sure everybody knows. And we've all been there. I know that for sure.

Denny buzzed into a reverential simulation of Keith Richards' classic riff for "Satisfaction." With a devilish grin, Billy began to intone a lyric in a hypnotic drone.

—I can't get my panties action.

The girls on the dance floor frantically erupted into a hot, tribal dance, swinging their arms and gyrating their bodies with unbridled abandon.

—And I cry and I cry.

Billy spotted Trudy among the throng, still standing back at the bar, and smiled broadly.
Meanwhile Denny rammed into him at full force and Billy attempted to karate-kick his brother in return. Denny staggered drunkenly, attempting to avoid Billy's foot, messing up his moment with the riff.

Once again, girls began flashing Billy. He smiled wider at the sight then glanced at

Trudy, who wore a disapproving frown. Billy began jumping up and down again, as if to try and wrest Trudy from her foul mood.

Trudy eyed Billy with a look of sadness and contempt. Grabbing her purse, she headed for the door and out into the crisp fall air. She proceeded toward her car in frustration and mortification. She didn't know what to do about Billy. He was slipping away from her and there was nothing she could do about it. Nothing at all.

Billy had watched Trudy leave the club, and tried to catch her attention. But she would not make eye contact. He shrugged haplessly and went back to his ministrations. An overtly sexual electricity charged the air.

—My my hey that's what we say.

Billy and Denny began to dance, haphazardly punting their legs out to their sides.

—I can't get my
Panties action
My panties action
My panties act-shun
My panties action!

With a drunken flourish, Denny polished off the riff. At the song's conclusion, Rod and Denny surrounded Billy at the middle of the stage, where each swung his arm around his partners' shoulder. The females in the crowd screamed in appreciation, and the males cheered heartily.

Dipping their legs at the back of Billy's knees, Denny and Rod attempted to make him collapse. In a move reminiscent of the Three Stooges' Moe, Billy good-naturedly grabbed the pair by their necks and squeezed their heads together in front of his chest.

He let the two of them go, as Bam Bam hopped up onto the stage, making sure the approving multitudes were aware that he performed some function for the band. He quickly unplugged all the cords from the guitarists' amps and began to lug the equipment to the side of the stage.

The band mates hopped down and began to engage various audience members in idle conversation. Billy was talking to a tall, cute blond girl with exceedingly beautiful breasts, whom he had noticed through the course of the night, when he saw Tommy coolly signaling him from behind the bar. With a twinge of regret, Billy excused himself and went to the back of the room to join Tommy.

—C'mon, let's go back to my office and I'll getcha paid.

The pair traipsed down a narrow hall that led from behind the bar to a small room painted a sickly shade of yellow. The room was barely big enough to hold the government-issue gray desk and three chairs it contained. Tommy opened the door and motioned Billy in, closing the door behind them. Billy plopped down on one of the folding chairs, as Tommy sat down in the office chair behind the desk.

—I got yer money here. You guys did pretty good tonight.

Shrugging indifferently, Billy was well aware that they had drawn a large crowd.

—You brought two hundred and twenty-seven people through the door. That's six hundred and eighty-one bucks. Take twenty off to pay for Al at the door and thirty to pay Concert Sound for the PA. Twenty to pay Tom for doing the sound. That's pretty cheap to get Tom Robinson and his PA for fifty bucks. And Casey Avon gets fifty.

Billy nodded affirmatively to the familiar litany of deductions that would come off the top of the evening's take.

—So that comes out to five hundred and sixty-one dollars. That's not bad for an hour's work.

Tommy tossed a rubber-banded roll of bills to Billy. Billy briefly looked at the handful of money, before stuffing it into his jeans pocket, for Pete to count later on.

—Y'know, I like you guys. Ya' remind me a lot of the street punks I knew when I was a kid back in lower Manhattan. They were troublemakers. Not real violent or nothin'. They just liked stirrin' up trouble. Bored, I guess.

As he spoke, Tommy's New York accent began to creep into his speech. With serious attent, Billy eyed Tommy carefully, for he liked and respected him as a mentor and a knowledgeable source of information about the music business.

—You guys do good at the door. Really good for a new band just startin' out. And your crowd really drinks a lot. That always makes a bar manager happy.

Running a hand through his sweat-matted hair, Billy smiled. He crouched forward, leaning his elbows on his thighs.

—And you guys really draw the chicks. That's a good sign. Great. 'Cuz it's a well-known fact that where the chicks go, the guys'll eventually follow. That's always true. Never fails.

Billy replied.

—I trust what you say about the girls. About everything. They don't call ya' the Maltese Falcon for nothin'.

Tommy chuckled, for he had not heard that nickname before.

—You guys have a chance to be a good band. Popular. You can make some money in this town. But…

Waiting for the other shoe to drop, Billy sat quietly.

—But you guys need to quit screwin' around up there. That punky stuff can only work for so long. You're young and energetic and I know you got some kinda thing goin' on with yer brother, but ya' need to refine yer show. The girls will still show up even if yer not bouncin' into each other and guzzlin' beer. Shit, man. You don't even know the words to any of the fuckin' songs!

Bent low, Billy listened intently to Tommy's words.

—You don't have to be wild men up there. You guys got charisma. You especially. You don't need that other shit. That's just window dressin'. That shit was old with the Sex Pistols and they were, like, *over* years ago. Besides, you guys aren't punks anyway. Yer not the fuckin' Rollin' Stones, or The Who. Ya' got too much breedin'. Yer more like the Knack or somethin'.

Billy frowned at the comparison. He wanted his band to be edgy and unpredictable, not the flavor of the month.

—Hey, sneer if ya' want, but those guys have made, like, a ton of money in the last year. They're not so bad. They've got their shit together. They're not goofin' around. And they write pretty good songs. Maybe Elvis Costello or Joe Jackson, if that'd make ya' feel any better.

Billy brightened slightly at the new allusion.

—But you guys need to figure out a sound and start writin' some songs. That 'Girl On The Corner' song is okay, but it sounds old. Stale. You need a sound that's new. Somethin' new. Ya' oughta think about it.

Billy stood up from his chair and flashed a knowing grin at Tommy.

—I know you're right. We've talked about writin' more songs. We've got a couple of new ones. 'Wrong Number' and 'Bonnie Jo'. And we know about our sound. But we don't rehearse much. Right now, we're just sort of ridin' the wave and diggin' the party.

—Maybe so. But every party's gotta end sometime 'r 'nother. Where're you guys gonna be when the lights go out?

Billy's expression firmed as he stood to leave.

—Well, you've given me a lot to think about. I respect your opinion. I don't know if these guys'll ever listen to me, especially Denny and Rod. But I'll give it all some thought.

Tommy flicked his head slightly to signify that the conversation was ended. Billy pointed at him, fired a finger gun and slowly closed the door behind him. Resolutely he strode down the hall and toward the band, who were collecting their gear on the Long Goodbye stage.

23

# IV

It was a Tuesday night at the venerable Sack's Front Avenue. Sack's had been a bastion of the local rock music scene for many years. The building was a remnant from Oregon's pioneer early stages in the mid-eighteen hundreds, when it had been a landmark on the Portland waterfront.

The interior of Sack's was less than hospitable to the patron of loud music. High brick walls and a raw beam ceiling enclosed two large rooms with coarse-grained wooden floors. The larger foreroom, held an elaborately ornate bar with about twenty stools for seating at the counter. Polished brass spittoons were bolted to the floor. A large, aged mirror reflected the glowing, dull, brown interior.

Opposite the bar, a stage occupied the south wall. It sat about three feet above a wide, worn dance floor. It was a clapboard plywood stage with enough give and play to provide a trampoline effect if a musician took to bouncing or leaping upon it—which Billy often did when the Malchicks took the room. Small, stately oval brown tables surrounded the dance floor, with round-backed chairs encircling each. Two wide, brick archways partitioned the music area from the bar.

It was at Sacks that Billy sprayed beer on an overflow crowd, before grabbing the pillow that Pete used as a muffle on his kick drum and emptied feathers all over a drenched crowd.

Tuesday being Dollar Beer night, the club was packed with boisterous revelers shouting above the uproar, as the Gulloons played a set of peppy pop rock. Even at midnight, the crowd showed no sign of subsiding.

Billy had been drinking cheap beer in the large anteroom all evening. The room was decorated with recycled pine siding haphazardly tacked to the walls, littered with ten or fifteen large, round tables, each encircled by disheveled chairs. Because it was out of the line of sonic fire, people would gather in the area for a respite—or just to be able to hold a conversation without screaming.

Along the east wall stood a long row of pinball machines that blinked and buzzed and chimed and clanged. Billy and Denny were playing the *El Dorado* machine. Earlier, he, Denny, Rod and Col Duquesne had played the *Spirit of '76* and *Eye of the Tiger* machines, with Billy winning nearly every four-way match. Rod and Col eventually drifted away and Billy and Denny squared off on the *El Dorado*.

Billy had no difficulty outscoring Denny at every turn, wracking up many free games along the way. Billy knew every nuance of most of the machines in the row. He knew the special shakes and bumps that would maneuver a ball away from the drain and into the firing line of one of his flippers. But, the *El Dorado* was not his favorite.

Denny pulled the plunger on his final shot of their tenth match. He smacked his flipper violently, knocking down a series of drop targets, returning the ball to the top of the machine, where he finessed the ball to engage a number of the bumpers. He was having a hot round, and he would need it, to score another forty thousand points to catch Billy. His ball returned down the launch lane, and he pulled the plunger as if to start the round all over again.

But, at thirty-eight five, Denny's ball skittered down the middle of the playing surface and quickly slid down the drain. Denny slapped the machine smartly. He had lost yet again.

—Shit! I almost had ya' that time. I can't win against you.

—They don't call me the Pinball Wizard for nothin'. C'mon, I'll buy us another round of beers and you can try again. There's still plenty of free games left.

But Denny had had enough of defeat for one night.

-—Nah. I think I'll go check out the Gulloons and see if there's any action going on out on the floor. You're on your own now, Bro'

Denny wandered off into the other room. Meanwhile, Billy scurried up to the bar to order another beer. Then he strolled back to the pinball area with a pint. Because there were yet many free games left, he was compelled to continue playing the *El Dorado*, the game he liked least. For some reason it was not as willing to cooperate with him compared to the response of the other machines. He had trouble navigating his ball in the lanes, and the flippers seemed slow and unresponsive. Still, he drunkenly slapped the button on the side of the machine, and it rang to action. No pinball game could get the best of him. He was invincible.

On his first two balls, Billy racked up seventy-five thousand points. A decent run on his last ball would win for him at least another free game, maybe more. Well within his reach. The metal ball rapidly bounced against the top bumpers as Billy expertly joggled the machine in order to move the ball into position to be able to use his flipper to re-engage for another approach. Using extreme body english, he carefully maneuvered the ball, smacking his flipper, firing the projectile against a row of drop targets to the right.

Approaching the one hundred thousand-point mark, Billy shoved his body hard against the machine, intending to redirect the ball toward his left flipper. Suddenly the game went dark, but for a "Tilt" light blinking on the screen before him.

—Shit! Shit, I had it. I was right there. Goddamn machine. What the fuck?

Billy began to carelessly rock and teeter the *El Dorado* machine, so that it was swinging back and forth on two-legs. Suddenly the machine toppled to the right, smartly striking the *Spirit of '76*, which dominoed into the *Pioneer* and on down the line, until all the machines were skewed on two legs, balancing precariously, against the next machine over.

Furious, he stomped the *El Dorado* in a rage, and the entire procession of pinball games slowly slid to the floor. Somewhat surprised by the turn of events, Billy grabbed his beer from the table behind him and hustled out of the gaming area into the main room.

He found Denny on the dance floor and stood next to him, staring blankly at the Gulloons' onstage show.

—You're here pretty quick. What's a matter? *El Dorado* get you again?

—Yeah. Pissed me off. I don't know what the hell's up with that fuckin' game. I kicked it pretty hard.

—Kicked it? Wha' d'ya mean?

—I kicked it. I rocked the shit out of it and tipped it over. Then I kicked it.

—You tipped it over? Holy shit. Lee's gonna be pissed about that.

—Oh he's gonna be pissed about a lot more than that. I knocked over all the machines.

Denny muttered in Morse code.

—Knocked-over-all-the-machines? How the fuck did you do that?

—I don't know, I shoved the *El Dorado* and they all fell over. Probably screwed 'em up pretty good. At least threw all the stool pigeons out of whack. Those machines'll probably need to be repaired a little bit.

—Hey, Lee's gonna want ya' to pay for that. What're ya' gonna do?

Billy shrugged in reply. He didn't have much money. Certainly not enough money to repair four pinball machines.

—I dunno.

Feeling a tap on his shoulder, Billy whirled around to see the club manager, Lee Heyward, with a grim look on his face. Lee was an imposingly robust hippie-type fellow, with wire-rimmed glasses, rust-colored hair that ran to the middle of his back and a long, bright red beard.

—I need to talk to you, Billy.

Lee was not kidding around. He motioned to Billy to follow him up to the bar.

—Let's go into the game room.

Billy anxiously followed the older man, as if his dad had come back to read him the riot act. The pair stood in front of the mayhem of machines. Billy hung his head as Lee stood staring disbelievingly.

—What the fuck did you do, Billy? How the hell did you knock over all the pinball machines? Are you crazy?

Shoulders hanging defensively, Billy stood—silent.

—What the fuck am I supposed to do now? These games are a good source of revenue for the club. How am I supposed to replace that money? And where am I supposed to get the money to fix these goddamned machines?

Billy was wordlessly piqued with embarrassment. With great effort, Lee righted the *El Dorado* game, which teetered unevenly on its four legs.

—Well, this one's fucked up for sure. Shit. What am I supposed to do?

—Get 'em fixed, Lee, and I'll pay for the repairs.

—You'll pay for the repairs? How're you planning on doing that?

—You can have the money from our next couple of gigs until we...uh, I, get it all paid off.

—Wishful thinking, Billy. Wishful thinking. I don't want your band playing here anymore, and I don't want to see you in this club again.

With a shocked expression, Billy gaped uncomprehendingly at Lee.

—But...

—No buts, Billy. I've had it with you guys. You got no respect for the club. You got no respect for your audience. You've got no respect for anything as far as I can tell, and I don't want you guys in here anymore. Get your brother and your buddies and get out of here. And don't come back.

Billy felt an accustomed roiling in his stomach, rapidly rising to his throat.

—Okay. Yeah. I will. But I need to get outside pronto. I think I'm gonna puke.

—Well, don't puke in here. I don't need that. Yeah. Go ahead and go outside. But when you're done, I want you guys out of here and I don't want to see you again.

Already moving quickly toward the front door, Billy faded to a paler shade of yellow with every step. He emerged from the building and staggered toward Yamhill Street at the corner of Southwest Front. There, into the gutter, he began to puke profusely. He briefly wiped his mouth with the sleeve of his black cotton jacket, before heaving heavily, once again.

—Ah, Grasshopper. To overindulge is to lose the path.

Billy turned slowly to see Incomparable John Dailey moving in his direction. Billy had met Incomparable John a time or two, in passing, as the Portland music community was rather small and incestuous. Incomparable John's reputation preceded him. He was quite the character.

Several years before, Incomparable John had been a national hang-gliding champion. He was renowned for his dangerous dives from precipices that no one else would go near. He would trot off the edge of a cliff, cackling maniacally in a high-pitched squeal.

He once jumped from a promontory in Oahu, and the updraft instantly tangled his chute—impelling him to drop abruptly. He laughed like a crazy man as he plummeted toward certain death on the jagged ocean rocks below him. At the last minute, another updraft caught his chute and spun him in the opposite direction, instantly freeing his lines. Incomparable John skillfully rode the updraft back to the top of the cliff, reappearing before a startled crowd of onlookers—who were thinking that they were seeing a ghost.

Thin and wiry, of average height, Incomparable John had a head of medium-length fine, brown hair, a wispy fringe of bangs hanging down his forehead to the tops of his eyebrows. His almond-shaped brown eyes glistened ferally. He almost always wore a wry grin, as if he knew something, a secret perhaps—but he wasn't telling. Incomparable John was wearing a blue plaid, cotton shirt with a tan, denim jacket and light-brown corduroy pants. He stood above Billy, shaking his head.

—You'd never catch anyone in my band getting all drunk and stupid.

—Well, I guess not, John. There are advantages to being a one-man band. Bhyakk!! Chaim. Chaim. Hawkkk.

—It's the Boom Chuck my son, the yin and the yang. My band is the chief proponent. We all get along. Drummer, bass player, guitarist, and vocalist. We never argue, and we don't drink. We are the purveyors of Boom Chuck. That is our mission.

—What the hell are you talkin' about? Boom Chuck. Sounds like what's goin' on in my stomach right now.

Incomparable John reached into the breast pocket of his jacket, producing a fat joint. He sat down next to Billy, carefully avoiding the vomit in the gutter.

—Here, slide down this way and smoke some of this. It'll make you feel better. And I'll tell you a story.

Incomparable John took a big hit and passed the joint to Billy.

—It all started with 'Papa Oo Mow Mow'. Then it was Desmond Dekker, Grasshopper. Desmond Dekker.

—Who?

—Desmond Dekker, my son. He recorded the first real Boom Chuck record. 'Papa Oo Mow Mow' was an accident. Back in nineteen sixty-five, Desmond Dekker recorded 'The Israelites'. He was the inventor of ska. Rude boys know the ska, eh? Are you a rude boy?

He grabbed the joint back from Billy—who had begun choking and hacking from the overpowering smoke.

—What the hell you got in that shit?

—Never mind that for now, Billy Boy. I'm telling you about Desmond Dekker and 'The Israelites'. The Boom Chuck.

—I don't know what you're talkin' about. The Boom Chuck. I never heard of it.

—The Boom Chuck. The yin and the yang. The up and the down. The in and the out. The black and the white. The on and the off. The over and under. The tick and the tock. The dog and the cat. It only takes two chords to play. That's all.

—Maybe it's 'cuz I'm drunk, but I'm still not gettin' it.

—Guitar, Grasshopper. It's all right there on the guitar. The upstroke. You've gotta get your upstroke down. All you need is two chords. The one and the four.

He took a long drag on the joint and handed it back to Billy.

—Don't dawdle with that now, Billy Boy. That stuff is primo. It's not cheap. Two chords. The one and the four. All the rest are filler. All the rest are jazz chords. They don't mean anything to a song. They're filler.

Billy screwed up his face as he took another long hit, muttering.

—I think I know what you mean. Like 'Satisfaction'.

—Well, sorta. But 'Satisfaction' doesn't have the upstroke. It's a down stroke song. That's what all rock songs are. Downstroke. I can play 'em all with the upstroke and just two chords. And they all sound a lot better. Upstroke is the rhythm. That's the key. Two chords and you can play any of the classic rock or blues songs. That's all there is to it. Even you could learn how to do it. It's Boom Chuck

Again Incomparable John grabbed the joint from Billy and smiled. He took a drag and continued.

—Boom Chuck is the sound of the kick and the snare. That's all you need. That's why I'm a one-man band. I can get the Boom Chuck with my left foot on the hi-hat and comping with my guitar. The rest is hairspray and window dressing.

Incomparable John smiled as if he were joking—but he wasn't. He eyed his acolyte carefully. He was testing Billy to see if he was paying attention. Billy was paying rapt attention, even through the dense haze of his abject stupor.

—So it's a drumbeat. I got it.

—Ah, but, Grasshopper, it is so much more than just a drumbeat. It is the heartbeat. The beat of life. It's the rhythm of the planets. It's the rhythm of the gods. It's all you need to know. It's Boom Chuck.

Billy shook his head dazedly. Between the alcohol and the pot, he could not be certain whether or not the entire conversation was real or just a hallucination. Incomparable John dug around in his shirt pocket, producing a small package. He fished a pocket knife from his pants. Opening the packet with great care, he scooped a generous quantity of fine white powder onto the blade of his knife.

—Here, have a little coke. It'll sober you up.

He held out the knife blade to Billy, who leaned over it, plugged one nostril with his finger and snorted hard into his other nostril.

—Hoo ha! That hit the spot.

Incomparable John took another measure of the coke and held the blade out to Billy.

—Now the other one, my son. You cannot have the Boom without the Chuck.

Chuckling, Billy sucked the coke into his other nostril, sitting up a little straighter on the curb.

—Shit. That's some good shit too. Where do you get this stuff? The pot. This coke. It's all the best stuff I've ever had. Who the hell *are* you anyway?

Billy squinted at Incomparable John as if he had met up with a brujo, like Don Juan, or some other magical being.

—I come from a land far away, Grasshopper. I have come to teach you the ways of the Boom Chuck.

—Yeah, yeah. I get all that, but what's your story? You're not from Portland. That's obvious. You're too crazy to grow up in this town.

Incomparable John shoved a couple hits of coke up his nose, sniffing deeply and refolded the small parcel, placing it back in his shirt pocket. He snapped his knife closed, slid it back into his pants, and relit the joint they had been smoking. Breaking his facade for a moment, he spoke without affectation.

—Ah, I grew up in pretty weird circumstances. My dad was a diplomat in Brazil. I lived in a mansion with a governess and maids and servants and attendants and shit. My mom wasn't around much. She was drunk all the time. The governess and the maids pretty much raised me. I had the run of the place.

—You grew up in Brazil? Wow. What a trip!

—Yeah. It mostly sucked. I didn't have any other kids to play with, except when one of the other diplomats from, like, France or Germany came over and brought their kids with them. The kids weren't any fun. None of them spoke English.

—So, how'd you end up here in Portland?

—My old man moved back to the states when I was eighteen, and we lived in Santa Barbara. Then he kicked off about five years later. I started going to Claremont College down there. But I got interested in hang-gliding, so I decided to become a bum. Money wasn't a problem. My dad left us plenty of money. I got my girlfriend Donna pregnant last year, and we got married and moved up here so she could have the kid near her family. They all live up here. Our daughter Jilly was born last Fall.

—Amazing.

Billy began to sober up. As they finished off the joint they had been smoking, Incomparable John tossed the butt into the gutter drain. He produced another joint from his jacket pocket and fired it up, puffing on it with great force, in order to get it burning properly. He offered the joint to Billy, who snatched it up vigilantly.

—Where'd you get this shit? I've never smoked pot this strong. It tastes a lot different than, like, any Mex or Columbian I've ever smoked. It's even stronger than some Maui Wowie I smoked a couple of months ago.

Billy sloppily inhaled the joint, holding it between his thumb and forefinger. Incomparable John wrested it away from him.

—Here. Give me that. You're making it run. Ya' gotta turn the joint as you smoke it, so it doesn't run. See?

John gave the joint a quarter turn with each puff.

—See? It burns nice and even. And don't go getting spit all over it. I hate slimy joints.

He handed it back to Billy, who carefully practiced his new smoking routine.

—So, you didn't answer me. Where'd you get this shit anyway? How can I get a hold of some of it?

—You can't get a hold of it unless I say it's okay. I grow it myself, in my garage.

—You *grow* this shit? How the hell do you do that?

—With lights. Big halogen and sodium lights. To simulate daylight. I clone the plants from a mother plant and plant them in soil, and I grow the plants. And if you ever tell anybody about it, I'll cut off yer nuts.

31

Incomparable John was dead serious and he bore a stare into Billy's watery blue eyes and continued.

—You grow these big fat buds under the light. They're huge. Bigger'n my arm. And they're the best stuff. Funny you mention Maui Wowie, because it was Maui Wowie seeds that I grew to be the mother plants. But this stuff is better than Maui Wowie. It's fresher and stronger and tastier. Controlled environment.

—No lie! It's the best stuff I've ever had.

Billy handed the joint back to Incomparable John, waving his hand.

—No mas. No mas

Incomparable John returned to character.

—Ah. Grasshopper has partaken of the magic plant, and now he knows the secrets of the Boom Chuck. That is enough for one night. You must rest now.

Incomparable John took a long last drag from the joint then heaved the roach out into the street, where it sparked and flared briefly, a ghostly wisp of smoke rising in the November air.

—We will meet again, my son. And we will see if you have learned anything from me. Whether you got the message.

—Oh I got the message. I got it alright.

—That is good.

Incomparable John began to walk away, up Yamhill Street. After a few paces, he turned.

—And you better not tell anybody about me growin'. I'm warnin' ya.

Billy nodded solemnly at the strange man and stood up. Then he suddenly remembered—slowly staggering back into Sacks to find Denny and Rod and to escort them from the club—to which they would never again return.

# V

The crowd began to collect in the late morning at Terry Schrunk Plaza, across the street from City Hall. Bewildered, people sat on the steps, which surrounded the square in a semi-circle. A small stage had been constructed at the end of the plaza where the circle broke. The mourners stared at each other with hollow, empty eyes. Nothing seemed real. A light snow fell, white and soft, on the assembled grieving mass.

It was an impromptu event, organized at the last minute by a few distraught fans. By early afternoon, several thousand distressed faces gazed toward the stage, awaiting words of comfort or reassurance. The Malchicks gathered together, as Bam Bam, aided by the band's new soundman, Billy Dreier, handed equipment up to them. They quickly set up and began to tune their instruments. It was by far the biggest audience the fledgling Malchicks had ever been in front of. Near the stage, a gaggle of fans quietly sang "Give Peace A Chance," which others around them began to join.

The snow continued to fall like a fine veil of ash, as Billy stepped to the microphone. He was not nervous in the least, but emboldened by the magnitude of the multitude.

—Okay. Hey, Billy, are you ready back there?

Billy cupped his hand above his brow to see if Billy Dreier was at the sound board. Billy Dreier was hard to miss. He was massive, with shoulder-length blond hair, over which he wore a navy blue stocking cap. A dark blue workman's jacket was draped over the immense, baby-fat girth of his mid-section. Billy Dreier even vaguely resembled Billy Granger, in a way—except that he was three times larger. The literal equivalent of three Billys.

Through the stage monitors, Billy Dreier murmured.

—Yeah. Go ahead.

—Hey, everybody. My name's Billy Granger and, as some of you know, we're the Malchicks. I guess we all know why we're here. John Lennon was a hero to a lot of people. He stood for peace and love, and I guess those are things that everybody can understand.

Billy smiled wryly, for John Lennon had never been his hero, particularly—although he admired the Beatles' success and hoped to replicate it one day.

—It's so weird that a man who believed that *all you need is love*, could be gunned down on a sidewalk in New York. Instant karma I guess.

He did not understand the insensitive severity of his words.

—John Lennon was so loved and admired. It doesn't make any sense that one crazy guy with a gun could end it all. Just like that. But that's what happened and there's nothing we can do about it now, I guess. It's sad, but nothing can bring him back. We'll just have to live with that. And we'll have to carry on, in the spirit of peace and love and respect for our fellow men. Make love, not war.

Many members among the throng began to sob in anguish.

—Well. We're here to make things a little brighter if we can. Even though it's overcast and snowing, we hope we can cheer you up a little bit.

Billy counted off the first of several Rolling Stones songs that the Malchicks played during their short set, which also included a couple of Who songs and a Kinks song. They were typically sloppy in their performance. While not drunk, Denny had downed a few shots of Wild Turkey before taking the stage, ostensibly to ward off the chill. Rod was morbidly quiet and still. As usual, Gib and Pete, sober and stoic, steadfastly held down the structure of the shifting rhythms.

Despite the sadness of the day, the bleakness, it was apparent to many that Billy had a great deal of charisma, an ineffable star quality. It was hard to take one's eyes off him. Tall and boyishly good-looking, he had the high cheekbones of a model—brashly flashing a big, toothy grin. His elegant stature and youthful demeanor were captivating. Females among the crowd simply gawked—openly gaping at the grace of his movements.

Billy delighted in showing off for the crowd. It was the easiest thing he had ever done. Natural. His every movement drew the attention of all eyes and he basked in the light of that mutual attraction. For he loved looking back at them, too.

As Carrie Deeds stepped out from the office of the water bureau, which bordered the west end of City Hall on the bus mall, she could hear music echo and reverberate from all the buildings around her. She circled the block to see what the source of the music was and saw a flock of people over-spilling the city block perimeter of Schrunk Plaza Park.

Carrie wandered in the direction of the stage—drawn not so much by the music, as by the handsome young man who was singing. She plunged her hands into the pockets of her black ski parka and hugged herself to ward off the chill of the cold December day. She maneuvered her way to the foot of the stage, where she stared admiringly up at Billy.

Spotting her instantly, Billy was attracted to her slim build and beautiful green eyes, which he could see even from a distance. She was quite lovely, like a pretty schoolteacher or a sexy attorney. She looked smart and thoughtful. He smiled at her; she shyly averted her eyes. For the rest of the Malchicks' set he did not stop staring at Carrie. And though her head was lowered, she never lost sight of him either.

She was charmed by his off-handed sincerity. He seemed like a young boy, innocently acting out—just to be noticed, parading confidently back and forth across the platform in front of her. Hoping to impress her, Billy was even more exuberant than usual.

The Malchicks concluded their set with an inspired version of Buddy Holly's "Not Fade Away," a song that the Stones performed in their early days. Billy announced respectfully.

—Alright. Alright. That's it for us today. We're very sorry about John Lennon's murder. It's a heartbreaking thing. All we can do now is imagine a better world and carry on the best we can. Thank you all. Thank you very much.

The audience, though far from enthusiastic, given the somber nature of the event, were appreciative nonetheless and offered the band a warm round of applause.

Wearing a green crew neck sweater with a white diamond pattern on the front and a pair of tight blue jeans, with white athletic shoes, Billy immediately jumped down to introduce himself to Carrie. Several other girls approached him, but his intent was locked on Carrie.

—Hi. I'm Billy Granger. What's your name?

—My name's Carrie. Carrie Deeds

—In*deed* it is!

Billy chuckled to himself at the cleverness of his pun, one with which she was entirely familiar, having heard it regularly since the sixth grade. He held out his hand to shake hers. In her presence, he became slightly nervous and tongue-tied.

She was very cute, with a permanent deadpan smile on her mouth and eyes as green as the hills of the coast range. She had faint dimples and perfect teeth. Billy especially liked her hair. It was a very light shade of brown, with bangs brushed away from her forehead. She was tall enough, chin high to him. Awkwardly, Billy continued.

—It's a real pleasure to meet you, Carrie Deeds. Did you come here for the John Lennon memorial?

—No, actually. I came down here to pay my water bill and when I came out of the water bureau office, I could hear music. So I just followed the sound.

—I'm glad you did. Really glad. Have you heard us before?

—What's the name of your band?

—The Malchicks.

—No, I'm afraid I've never heard of the Malchicks. It's a nice name, though. I don't go out much to hear music. I'm pretty busy with school.

35

—Yeah? Where d'ya go to school?

—PSU. I'm in the pre-nursing program up there and my apartment is right in that neighborhood, so I thought I'd walk down and pay my water bill.

—Pre-nursing, huh? That must you keep you pretty busy, alright.

—Yes, very busy...a *lot* of reading.

Billy looked over to see Bam Bam and Billy Dreier carrying the band's amps and gear in the direction of Billy Dreier's van, which was parked on the lawn behind the makeshift stage.

—Shit. I really need to go. We're gettin' ready to leave. Can we meet for a drink or somethin' sometime?

—Yes. I guess so. Sure.

—How's about tonight at Geraldo's?

Knitting her brows, she looked puzzled.

—Where's that?

—It's just around the corner from here, actually. Over on Second and Taylor. Middle of the block on the east side of the street. I'll meet you there at eight. I'll be upstairs. I'll save a booth for us. So, are we on?

—Okay. We're on. I'll see you at eight.

With that, Billy turned to join his band mates who were piling into the van to head back to the band house over on Arthur Street.

—I'd offer you a ride, Carrie, but I don't think we could fit another body in there.

Carrie dismissively waved her hand at him and smiled. She walked away into the lightly falling snow.

It was snowing even harder, at eight-oh-five, when Carrie walked through the doors of Geraldo's. The lower room had a nice wooden bar at the left of the entry and wrought iron tables, with glass tops, spread out around the room. There were high white ceilings and a staircase to the right that led to the more intimate, second bar up above.

Seeing no one she recognized downstairs, she climbed the steps to the upper bar. Reaching the top, she looked around for Billy—finally spotting him sprawled out in a large half-circle booth, red, with tuck and roll naugahyde upholstery. He was talking to an older looking fellow with frizzy black hair and a dark Fu-Manchu moustache, dressed in a black sweater and black jeans. She walked in their direction.

—Man, that sucks. Sellin' the Long Goodbye. When did you find out about it?

—This afternoon. I didn't even know they had the place up for sale. Jack just came up to me this afternoon and said 'hey, we're shuttin' down the club, sellin' it to some *restraunteur*' or whatever 'and we aren't goin' to be havin' music in here anymore.' My jaw just about hit the fuckin' floor. We were really startin' to do good in that room.

Billy looked up to see Carrie moving toward them. He sat up straight.

—Oh hey, Carrie. I'm glad you made it. I wasn't sure if you'd show up.

She sat down next to him, and he helped her off with her jacket.

—I wasn't sure if I was going to make it either, but here I am.

—So, uh Carrie, this is Tommy Demeola, the 'Maltese Falcon.' That's what everybody calls him. He is, or was, I guess, the manager of the Long Goodbye.

She looked at Billy quizzically.

—The Long Goodbye is a club over in old town around Tenth and Everett.

She nodded, vaguely apprehending the location. Billy continued.

—Tommy, this is Carrie Deeds. I met her this afternoon at the John Lennon rally.

Smiling slyly, Tommy extended his hand as if to shake hers. But when she extended her hand, he took it and kissed the back of it, with a continental flair.

—It's a pleasure to meet you. You're a cute couple. When're the two of ya' gettin' married anyway?

Carrie and Billy both blushed.

—It's a bit early for that, Tommy.

Billy beamed at Carrie. Then he began to explain.

—Tommy just found out this afternoon that they're closin' the Long Goodbye... How soon Tommy?

—Right away, I guess

—So they're closin' the Long Goodbye and Tommy's sort of out of a job. That's really too bad, because the Long Goodbye was one of the best clubs in town and gave a lot of bands that were just startin' out a chance to get their shit together. Tommy nodded in agreement.

—So, what are ya' gonna do now, Tommy? Have you even thought about that?

—Well, as a matter of fact, I've been thinkin' about openin' my own club for a while now. I've had my eye on a hall down the street, over by Burnside, Ankeny actually, on Third. It used to be the Medieval Inn. It's a pretty good sized room, good sight lines, and it wouldn't take much to get it up and runnin'. I've talked with Frank, the owner of the building, and he's open to it. The place has sat empty for over a year now. So I think he'd be happy to have somebody in there payin' rent, as long as they weren't tearin' the place up or anything.

Billy smiled at Carrie and said.

—Sounds like it could be a good place.

—Yeah. It could be. It's got a full kitchen in the basement. The basement's kinda weird. It's all cut out of stone and shit. Looks like a dungeon from the Middle Ages or somethin'. We could have some wild parties down there. It's pretty big, with lots of nooks and crannies. It's a good hideaway.

Tommy slid out from behind the table and stood in front of the couple.

—Well, I need to head outta here and figure out what I'm gonna do about things. I should give up this space here anyway, so that other folks can come over and kiss yer ring.

Billy chuckled at Tommy's acknowledgement of his rising popularity.

—Ya' oughta buy this girl a drink, before someone else does and steals her away from ya'.

Tommy seductively beamed at Carrie. He stuffed his hands in the front pockets of his black jeans and ambled off.

—Tommy's a real cool guy. He's given me a lot of good advice over the past year and he helped the Malchicks get off the ground. The Long Goodbye was, like, our home base. I hope he gets the new club up and running soon. After gettin' kicked out of Sacks, we're running out of places to play all of a sudden. What would ya' like to drink anyway?

Carrie ruminated on the question. She was not a big drinker. But because it was so cold outside, she thought about a hot drink.

—Do they have Spanish Coffees here?

—Yeah, sure they do.

Flagging down a waitress, Billy ordered Carrie's Spanish Coffee and another rum and Coke for himself. Carrie inquired.
—What's Sacks? Is that a club or something?

—Man, you really don't get around do you? Yeah, it's a club—around the corner on Front and Yamhill. I kinda had a *misunderstanding* with the club manager a while back and we got eighty-sixed from the place.

—What did you do?

—Oh, I got all drunked up and did a stupid thing. We've acted up there before and I guess Lee, the manager, had had enough of me...us. I don't blame him, really. For some reason, we can't seem to get our shit together. Too much drinkin' on stage and not enough rehearsal.

Carrie nodded, only indistinctly understanding what Billy was saying. But she got the drift that he and his band might be a little wild.

—Were you guys drunk this afternoon when you played in the park?

—No. Well Denny, he's my brother, he might have had a couple of shots of whiskey, but otherwise we were pretty sober. It was weird to be sober and playin' in the daytime, outside: in the snow. That was a first for us in all those categories. Pretty weird. Especially under the circumstances of John Lennon gettin' shot and everything.

—Were you a big fan of John Lennon?

—No, not really. But I dug, well I still dig his message. It was all about love. There's just not enough love in the world.

Dipping her head in agreement, she glanced down at the table. The waitress appeared with their drinks. A blue flame clung to the rim of Carrie's Spanish coffee glass. Slowly, she sipped the warm, sweet liquid.

—That tastes good. It hits the spot on such a cold night. So what did Tommy mean when he said something about people 'kissing your ring'?

—Oh, he was just jokin' around. We've been drawin' pretty good crowds at Long Goodbye lately. That's why it's such a bummer to have it go down like this.

The pair continued talking into the night, exchanging their life stories—only occasionally interrupted by a fellow musician or a fan of the Malchicks. Around one a.m. Carrie decided she should go. She was a bit tipsy and wobbled a bit when she stood to leave. Billy got up and grabbed her by the elbow.

—Whoa! Maybe I oughta help ya' home. Where'd you say ya' live?

—I live up on Tenth and Jefferson. Right by PSU.

—Oh yeah. That's right. Well, that's not so far. I could walk up there with ya'. I don't live that far from your place.
He helped her on with her jacket and slipped on his brown tweed overcoat. Holding her by the arm, he guided her down the staircase, out the door of Geraldo's, and into the snowy early morning darkness.

—Where do *you* live?

—Just down on Third and Arthur, down at the south end of Third, over by the Ross Island Bridge. We live in a big old house. There's six of us there now.

—Wow! It must be hard to get any privacy there.

—It's not too bad, really. The place has five bedrooms and one of the guys is stayin' in the basement. We have a rehearsal space down there, too. The tough part is that there's usually music blastin' out of somebody's stereo at all hours. And it's tough to get any time in the can.

Carrie laughed at the thought. Billy moved his arm around her shoulder and squeezed her close to him. He stopped and kissed her softly. She returned his kiss and they hugged, walking in silence the rest of the way to her apartment.

It was Valentine's Day and the Malchicks were headlining the grand opening of Luis' La Bamba club, Tommy Demeola's new project. The wide, expansive wooden beams supporting the high ceiling of the main hall were bedecked with red streamers, pink and white bunting, balloons, and other decorations. It was a spacious room with a legal capacity of three hundred and fifty patrons.

The stage, roomy, wide, and deep, was framed by two broad pillar supports, with a decorative border above the curtains. An array of formica tables, liberally strewn around the room, surrounded the sizeable parquet dance floor. Over to one side stood a compact, modern looking bar. There were no stools at the bar. Standing room only. Males stood at the bar. Females did not.

Backstage, the band was revving up for its first really important gig. For the occasion, Billy had dyed his hair a bright Valentine-heart red. He had painted his face bright red as well, with white hearts punctuating his cheeks and jaw. He wore a white headband, a kimono-like red-striped tiger print silk shirt, unbuttoned and tied at the waist, black leotards and tan cowboy boots. Not to be outdone, Denny was clad in a red and white plaid suit that he had bought at the Salvation Army store in Old Town. His hair was teased into a wheatfield-like bale at the top of his head.

Rod, Gib, and Pete were less spectacularly adorned. Rod had red construction paper hearts stapled all over his sports coat. Gib wore a red rayon dress-shirt with black slacks; Pete had on a red duffer's cap and a torn pink t-shirt with "Turning Japanese" scrawled across the front.

The party was on in the green room. The band, Bam Bam, Billy Dreier, and a few hangers-on, downed several pitchers of beer and passed around a series of joints in preparation for their set. Denny moved up the steps and peeked out from behind the dark maroon curtains at the Nuo Males, an all-girl band who were wrapping up their performance with a series of punky-pop original songs. Denny scrambled back down the stairs.

—Jesus Christ, the place is fuckin' packed! I hope the fire marshal doesn't show up. There's way more 'n three-hundred people out there, easy. Prob'ly four. This is gonna be hot shit.

He sat down on the wooden bench against a wall and began gulping beer from a pitcher.

—Easy on that, Denny. I thought we were gonna try and stay sober for this one.

—I'm sober, Billy. Don't worry. I'm sober.

—I just don't want to be sloppy tonight. I told Tommy we wouldn't get too messed up for this show.

—Don't sweat it, Bro'. Everything's A-OK.

Denny circled his thumb and forefinger and flashed it at Billy. Billy shook his head disapprovingly.

—Hey, so where's your girlfriend tonight? I haven't seen her around

—Oh, she's gotta study.

—That girl sure studies a lot.

—Yeah. Well, I think she wants to make somethin' of herself. She said she'll try to make it down a little later.

The Nuo Males concluded their set and quickly moved their gear off to stage left, which was the cue for the Malchicks to assemble stage right. Billy Dreier made his way through the crowded audience, to the back of the room, and up a couple of stairs to a little crow's nest platform, where the soundboard was installed.

Bam Bam stepped down from the stage and positioned himself right next to one of the large PA speakers on the floor—his arms folded in an admonitory fashion—as if to let whoever needed to—know that the sergeant-at-arms was on hand for any potential high jinks.

The guitarists plugged their instruments into their amplifiers, which had already been placed on the stage in advance of the Nuo Males' set. Pete Johannsen performed runs and rolls across his drums, as Billy Dreier adjusted the volumes of the mics placed around his kit. He then slowly brought up the volume of each of the other instruments, starting with Gib and Rod, finishing with Denny and Billy. He waved his hand above his head to signal that everything was ready to go.

—Okay. Alright. Welcome to Luis' La Bamba club, the newest, coolest place in town to be. Looks like plenty of you folks already knew that.

The crowd rustled in anticipation, hooting and hollering, whistling and yelling. At that point in time, the local male population had learned that the females were fond of the Malchicks, so the ratio of men to women was much closer to being one-to-one.

—I'm Billy Granger and we're the Malchicks and we're here to rock your asses off.

With that, Billy counted off the song, and the band swung into "Louie Louie," to honor the fictitious "Luis" to whom the club ostensibly belonged. The females of the audience crowded near the stage, and the males were quick to follow, jamming up close in an enthusiastic herd.

The band continued on, playing familiar portions of their regular set. A row of pitchers of beer sat in front of Billy and Denny. Denny freely guzzled from them, but Billy was not drinking. He was intent on giving the audience a good show, and he didn't want the slipshod effect of alcohol to get in the way.

As the Malchicks swung into the Stones' "Heart of Stone," Denny wobbled clumsily and slipped on the sloshed remains of beer that he had spilled on the stage. He fell flat on his butt with a shrill *thwang*, his guitar loudly registering the sudden impact. Billy turned away from Denny, ignoring him as best he could, furious at his brother's slovenly behavior.

With all due haste, Denny righted himself, but he staggered slightly and had some difficulty getting back into the flow of the song. Billy did his best to pretend that Denny was just goofing off, but he knew his brother was sloshed—yet again. The band proceeded through the next several songs with no further incidents. The Malchicks managed a stalwart rendition of the Yardbirds' "Heart Full of Soul," managing to regain some respectability, in Billy's mind.

They made manifest a decent interpretation of "Wild Horses," though Denny decided to dance inanely during the verses, grinning crazily at a couple of girls in the front row, and showing off in a sloppy, juvenile manner.

Frustrated, Billy did his best to keep the momentum going.

—Alright, we're going to do a Kinks' song now, and it goes like this.

Denny managed to get right the opening two chords of "You Really Got Me," in the launch of the song, while Billy willed the band through a satisfactory rendering of the rest of the number.

—This is gonna be our last song for the night. It's another Stones song, and as you can see, it's a true story.

Grimacing slightly, Billy glanced at Denny from the corner of his eye. The band then embarked upon a muscular version of "You Can't Always Get What You Want," moving through it without much trouble.

—I go to Rexall pharm'cy
To get my little yellow pills
And there stands Mr. Dimmy
And he smells just like a still

As the group concluded the song, Billy popped the cord from his guitar, and severely aggravated, stomped off the stage. The crowd began its usual call for an encore, but it was obvious to the band members that there would be none. Denny stepped to the mic.

—Thangks a lot ever'body. We're the fugkin' Malchicks and we'll see you again rull soon. Happy Valentine's Day and g'night.

Denny bowed awkwardly, belching, smacking his head on the mic stand as he unplugged his guitar, and headed for the green room.

An air of disappointment palpably descended upon the hall. The revelers were in no mood to end the evening so soon. But, as the rest of the band trudged from the stage, it became abundantly apparent to the audience that there would be no encores.

When Denny appeared in the green room, Billy was wiping red-stained sweat from his body with a white towel. His smeared makeup gave him the indefinite look of a bleeding Picasso painting. Denny demanded.

—Wha' the fugk was that, Bro'?

—That was nothin', Denny. Nothing. I told you I wanted to make this show somethin' special—for Tommy. For the band. But, as usual, ya' just fucked it up.

—*I* fucked it up? You were the one who split when the chicks were screamin' for another song. How professional was that, Bro'?

—I wasn't gonna stand up there and make a fool of myself any longer. Maybe you don't care how this band sounds, but I do. I want to see us make it.

—Make it? Make it where, Billy? All we are is a cover band. We've about made it as far as we can, I'd say. And who appointed you fugkin' king of the band anyway? I thought our band was a d'mogcracy. Wha' the hell happen' to that?

—Even a democracy needs a leader, Denny. You can't just have five people voting five different ways.

—Well, it started out as *our* band, and now it's startin' to sound like *your* band.

Billy grabbed a jar of cold cream from his duffle bag and slathered it onto his face, methodically scrubbing with the towel.

—Nothin' to say Billy? Why shouldn't we fugkin' go out there and have a good time? Tha's what it's all about. That's about all that we got.

—It's not *what it's all about* for me, Denny. I wanna be the best I can be. I want to be the best band in the city.

—Best band in the city? That's fugkin Dollarshine's territory, son. They've pretty much got that whole fugkin thing locked up. And we are definitely not Dollarshine.

—There's room for our band. Dollarshine's out on tour now. They're not playin' around town anymore. There's an openin' for some other band to fill the spot, and I want to fill it.

Denny laughed at his brother, with a belittling cackle.

—Dream on, Bro! Dream on.

Denny sang the words, aping Aerosmith.

As the rest of the band came down to the green room, followed by Billy Dreier and Bam Bam, Billy said nothing. He sat on the bench and fumed. Everyone else began popping beers and lighting up joints. The party was on.

Billy dressed quietly, without losing his temper or lashing out at the group. But his impulse was to do just that. The others noticed that Billy was unusually silent after the show, but largely they did their best to ignore him.

He sauntered up the steps and out to the bar, where Tommy was talking to the bartender.

—Hey Tommy. How'd we do at the door?

—A new record, Billy. The best we've done so far.

—Smartass. This bein' the first show and everything, I would expect we'd have the record. Bijou, could I get a rum and coke please?

The cute little bartender with long, straight, shiny brown hair, hustled away to make Billy's drink

—I think it was around fifteen hundred. It was headin' toward two grand I know. It was a real good night. How ya' doin'? You seem a little down.

—Oh, me 'n Denny had a fight. I'm gettin' real tired of him fuckin' around on stage. I took what you told me at the Long Goodbye that night to heart. I really do want this band to make it and be one of the best.

—Well maybe yer tryin' it with the wrong band, Billy. There's no reason to be forcin' it if it ain't gonna go.

—Mmm. Maybe you're right. Maybe so. Thanks, Bijou.

Billy grabbed his drink and took a couple of quick gulps.

—I feel responsible for Denny. I feel responsible for all the guys. But for as long as I can remember, Denny and me have fought like cats and dogs. It's why we couldn't make our landscapin' business happen.

Tommy snickered slightly.

—Ya' can't be responsible for anyone else, Billy. You can only be responsible for yerself. Maybe you'n Denny aren't s'posed to be in the same band. Did ya' ever consider that possibility?

Billy looked up, trying to remember a time when he wasn't attempting to include his younger brother—or to protect him.

45

—I hadn't thought of that. It never occurred to me. I'll think about it. I really will.

He patted Tommy on the shoulder and wandered in the direction of the stairs that led to the restaurant in the basement, stopping every couple of steps to talk with a friend or fan.

In the cavernous, hewn-stone basement, the First Annual La Bamba Underground Arts Festival was fully underway. There was a large, gray, stone fireplace that separated the dining area from the more distant chambers in the back of the cellar space—little hollows in which patrons were making out or snorting coke. For the Arts Festival, some of the alcoves were utilized as separate display areas for the various artists involved.

Next to the fireplace, in the corner, at the nexus of the two sections, Incomparable John Dailey was in the process of wrapping up a fourteen-hour, one man band marathon stint—in the final minutes of his incredible medley: Papa Oo Mow Mow meets Peter Gunn at Gloria's House of The Rising Sun to do the Hanky Panky. Peggy Sue's singing Hi-Ho Silver, I got a Whole Lotta Love. Help I need somebody, but I'll get by With A Little Help From My Friends on a Stairway To Heaven. Tommy Can You Hear Me, Let Your Lovelight Shine and Bring It On Home to Me, yeah yeah yeah and just call me Angel Of The Morning. Baby Love, Come See About Me, In The Midnight Hour. Wooly Bully, Mustang Sally.

With his left foot clapping a hi-hat and his right foot dancing on a Moog Taurus pedal bass, Incomparable John kept everything going by droning on his low E guitar string in between songs, never losing for a moment his upstroke, Boom Chuck sense of momentum.

To break things up, he would occasionally drift into rambling vocal monologues, perhaps blow abstractly into the harmonica wired to his shoulders, or he would launch into extended guitar excursions, punctuated by numerous effects attached to his guitar strap and to a large board, placed directly in front of him. He broke into a wide smile at seeing Billy enter the room and nodded at him faintly.

Billy sat down at the long table nearest Incomparable John's tiny performance niche. The table and benches were crafted out of rustic wood planks. Billy began scanning a menu, as the waitress approached.

—Hi. How many are gonna to be in your party?

Billy quickly estimated seven, unsure if the whole band would be coming down or not. The waitress deduced.

—Okay. I'll bring seven waters then. Are you ready to order? Or would you rather wait for the others.

—Nah. I'll order now. I'd like the chicken enchilada dinner and a Dos Equis, please. Why don't ya' go ahead and bring over four pitchers of Bud. That should get 'em started. You can put everything on one tab.

46

The waitress hustled off, returning briefly with chips and salsa, waters and beer, and Billy's Dos Equis.

Billy kept an eye on the staircase, hoping that Carrie might appear. After a while he was joined by Rod Castro and Billy Dreier. Then Denny, Bam Bam and Pete Johannsen moved in next to them. Gib had already gone home.

As Denny walked toward the table, Incomparable John imitated the sound of a machine gun with his guitar and aimed it at Denny. When Denny sat down at the table, Incomparable John executed a loud farting noise. Denny briefly considered getting up and punching the guy out, but he thought better of it. He curled his lip and muttered.

—That guy's a real asshole.

As if not hearing Denny, Rod Castro asked,

—What're you havin', Billy? I'm thinkin' of tryin' their chicken mole. I don't think I've ever seen a Mexican restaurant in Portland that serves mole.

—The chicken enchiladas. Tommy says they're supposed to be real good.

The rest of the crew ordered their meals, and the waitress quickly brought them over on a big tray, setting it down on a folding server. The entourage attacked their meals with great ferocity, downing the fare in colossal mouthfuls, washing everything down with huge gulps of beer from the pitchers that Billy had ordered for the crew.

Incomparable John wrapped up his set with an ominous original song called "Dance Class," which he claimed was based on the song "Papa Oo-Mow Mow." Turning off his instruments, he walked toward the Malchicks' table. He sported a dark brown cowhide gaucho hat with a military green army jacket and blue jeans. He smiled warily at Billy, having never actually met the other members of the band.

—Ah, Grasshopper. Here for the post-gig sustenance. I've heard their food is supposed to be pretty good here. Jim Goodwin, the cook, used to work at a high-class Mexican restaurant in LA, I guess.

Amused to see his newly made friend, Billy motioned for Incomparable John to sit down next to him on the long bench—lightly shoving Rod Castro over to make room for him.

—Hey, John. It's good to see ya'. Everybody, this is Incomparable John Dailey. Incomparable John, this is everybody. Incomparable John is the greatest one-man band in the world.

Doffing his hat in a feigned cavalier fashion, Incomparable John plunked down next to Billy.

The one-man band grabbed a menu, thumbed through it, and snapped it shut, convinced that all the dishes looked relatively credible. Billy put his arm around Incomparable John's shoulder and inquired.

—You want anything to eat? How's about a drink?

—Nah. Thanks. I'm not hungry and I don't drink. Drinking makes you messy and careless. It ruins the weed high.

The other members of the group stopped eating for a moment to consider what Incomparable John had just said.

—This guy has the best weed in the world, I'm tellin' ya'.

Incomparable John glared at Billy, as if to remind him of the consequence of loose lips.

—It's the best weed I've ever smoked. The best in the world.

The others' eyes lit up in anticipation, as they shoveled down mouthfuls of their meals with great rapidity. Incomparable John demurred sheepishly.

—Yeah, it's pretty good I guess. It brings on the rasta vibration.

Quizzically, Billy looked on as Incomparable John continued.

—You know, it might do you guys some good to lay off the booze and do more weed. You're not a bad band, but the booze makes you careless.

Incomparable John shot a look in Denny's direction. Denny noticed, sneering slightly.

—Booze is okay after the gig, if that's what you're into. But drinking before the gig is a big mistake. It's for losers.

It occurred to Billy to interrupt, but Incomparable John was on a roll.

—It probably wouldn't hurt you guys to rehearse either. And you really need some original material.

Denny began to breathe heavily, munching on the last of his taco. With his mouth full, he complained.

—How do you know so much about our band? And who appointed you the fugkin' band guru? We've been doin' just fine without your help. Did ya' happen to notice that the room was full tonight, smart ass? People seemed to be havin' a good time.

—Ah, I hit a nerve, my son.

—I'm not your son. You couldn't fugkin' hold a candle to my dad. You're just another know-it-all who has it all figured out what our band should do and who we should be. Form your own goddamn band, asshole.

—I *am* my own band. And none of us drink. And we all get along fine. That's more than I can say for your band.

Denny began to get extremely agitated. Billy saw it and said.

—Take it easy, Denny. He's just tryin' to be helpful. He doesn't mean any harm.

—Helpful? Who the hell is he to be makin' comments like this about our band?

—Shut the fuck up, Denny. You're embarrassin' yourself.

—Look, pretty boy, you may be the golden son of the family, but you're just about ready to get your ass whupped.

—Yeah, that's your answer for everything, eh Denny? Get drunk and beat some heads.

Denny pointed his finger at Billy threateningly.

—I've had about all I'm gonna take from you, dickweed…

Billy violently swatted Denny's hand from out of his face. Drunkenly, Denny took a fierce swipe at Billy from across the table, knocking over food and drinks as he clumsily lunged at him. The other members quickly stood up and vacated their positions at the table, backing away in fear and curiosity. With a clenched fist, Billy hammered Denny on the top of his head, as if it were a nail.

Crawling through the spilled beer and smeared refried beans, Denny lurched wildly at Billy, who deftly sidestepped the slurred movements of his besotted sibling. They briefly scuffled on the floor, but Billy was careful not to hurt his brother. Denny was much too drunk to do any real damage, except to himself.

Billy stood up from the grime and grabbed Denny by the back of his shirt. He pushed him down on the bench.

—That's it, Denny. We're all done. I've had enough of this bullshit. This isn't a band, it's a good ol' boys club for poor, dumb losers.

—Losers? I'll show you who the loser is. Fuck you, Billy. You don't know shit.

Storming from the room, Denny hopped up the stairs to the main floor, refried beans dripping from his jacket. The rest of the cadre soon followed him out of the chamber to assemble the band's gear and haul it back to the band house. Billy looked at Incomparable John and shook his head in disbelief.

—Jesus, you really know how to clear a room. What brought that on?

—Don't blame me. You were the one who broke up the band. But I hate to see a band take advantage of an audience. And that's what some of your band members, including your brother, are doing. They owe people a show for their money—not a fucking drinking display.

Billy couldn't argue with that. He had already come to the same conclusion himself. He pursed his lips tightly and sighed. He decided to change the subject.

—What's this rasta vibration thing you were talkin' about? What's that?

—The rasta vibration is what Boom Chuck is all about. It's the upstroke. Have you ever heard of reggae or ska music?

—I've heard of it. Like Bob Marley and those guys from Jamaica. I've heard they smoke a lot of weed. Is that the connection?

—It's only partly the connection. Weed puts you in the headspace to appreciate the hypnotic effects of the upstroke and Boom Chuck. It's almost like a religious experience. C'mon out to my truck and I'll give you a few tapes to check out.

The pair moved up the stairs to the main room and out of the building. Incomparable John's red Toyota pickup truck was parked on the street near the front of the hall. Incomparable John unlocked the passenger door and reached into the compartment between the seats.

Fishing out a few tapes, he handed Billy a cassette of Toots and the Maytals, a compilation of the original Wailers, with Bob Marley, Bunny Wailer and Peter Tosh, including some of Tosh's solo work. He also gave Billy a compilation of recordings by Jimmy Cliff, and Sly and Robbie.

—Check out Sly and Robbie. They have the Boom Chuck down. They call it 'rocker's beat,' but it's Boom Chuck all the way. Study these and I'll check your progress some other time.

Billy stuffed the tapes into his jacket pocket and stood staring at Incomparable John.

—Why're you, like, doin' all this for me anyway?

—Because I think you could be a star, man. A real star. I think you have the looks and the moves. You've got a good voice, and you know how to get people to look at you and pay attention. Not everybody can do that. Here, c'mon.

Incomparable John flashed a mighty spliff, and the two walked down the sidewalk around to Ankeny Street, where they ducked into a doorway. John lit the monstrous joint. Turning it slowly as he had prescribed in their earlier meeting, he sucked in a tremendous lung full of smoke and handed it to Billy, who did the same. Incomparable John continued his sermon.

—Your band doesn't have to be a reggae band or a ska band...

—What's ska?

—Ska's reggae, speeded up a little bit, with a walking bassline. Where was I? Oh yeah. Your band doesn't have to be a reggae band or a ska band. In fact, that would be a bad idea. The purists would hate you. But if you can incorporate elements of those styles into some of your songs, man, that would be hot.

Billy took a second hit, nodded and handed the joint back to Incomparable John. Incomparable John sharply drew in his breath and continued, with smoke rising above him, as if he were some ghostly apparition

—And you've gotta start writing your own songs, man. You're not going to get anywhere singing old Rolling Stones songs. Here, take this.

—Yeah, I know. I know you're right about that. Tommy was kinda sayin' the same thing to me. We *have* written a few. But I don't know what to write about.

Billy seized a long drag from the joint and handed it back.

—Write about anything. Write about your life. Write about someone else's life. Make shit up. It doesn't matter. But you gotta start incorporatin' what you know into some kind of new sound.

Incomparable John inhaled one last enormous puff and gave the joint back to Billy.

—Okay. I gotta take off. You need a ride or anything? Or are you still driving that lime-green piece of shit Caddy around town?

—Nah, I finally couldn't get it to start. It's parked over in front of the band house. I was thinkin' I shoulda, like, just left it runnin' all night. It was always a little funky startin' anyway.

—Yeah. Yeah. Somebody told me that you'd leave that car running for hours at a time. Lock it up and walk away.

—Yeah. That's true.

—So do you need a ride then?

—Nah. Thanks. I'm cool. I'll just hike home. The walk'll do me good.

Gesturing dismissively, Incomparable John began walking in the direction of his truck.

—Okay then. You listen to those tapes now.

—I will. I'll figure out what the reggae is all about.

—I'm sure you will.

He waved over his shoulder at Billy and turned the corner, back onto 3rd Avenue and his truck. Billy leaned back against the stone exterior of the New Rose Theatre building and finished off the joint, reviewing in his mind all that had transpired that night.

It was at that moment that an ephemeral form appeared from out of the gathering fog. To Billy it looked like an angel floating in his direction. He squinted into the mist trying to accustom his eyes. Suddenly, Carrie appeared, walking directly toward him. Billy brightened considerably.

—There you are. I'm glad you could make it.

—It doesn't seem like I made it for much. Is the show all over?

—Yeah. Short night. Show's over. But I'm glad you're here.

He hugged her tightly and kissed her on the forehead. She asked.

—Where's the rest of the band?

—They all left a while ago.

—How were you planning on getting home?

—I was gonna hoof it. It's not that far.

—Well, I parked my car around the corner.

She pointed vaguely in the direction of her car.

—You drove down here? I didn't think you ever drove that car of yours.

—If I had walked, I would have missed you. I guess I was supposed to drive down, so that I could pick you up. Do you want to spend the night at my place tonight?

—Yeah, sure! Let's go.

Billy tossed the remains of the joint onto the sidewalk, and the couple walked along the sidewalk in the direction of Carrie's unremarkable gray Toyota sedan.

As they drove the twenty blocks or so to her apartment, Billy began to talk about the problems he was having with the band. He tried to describe his relationship with Denny and the other members of his family, especially his father.

—My dad was a big influence in my life. When I was a kid, I wanted to be a baseball player, just like him. I know dad was disappointed that I didn't go on and play pro ball—or try anyway. When me and Denny started gettin' into music, just before he died, I know he was a little disappointed. He tried to back us up all he could, but I could always see the regret in his eyes, and I felt bad.

They arrived at Carrie's building and took the elevator up to her apartment, on the third floor. Billy wandered into her bedroom and plopped down on the bed, exhausted from the strenuous night he had just undergone. Carrie helped him off with his clothes, removed her own and joined him. For the first time in their relationship, Billy let down his emotional guard.

—Carrie, I don't know where I'm goin', y'know? Everybody's got an opinion about what I should do and how I should be if I want to be successful in the business. Everybody's got a ton of advice. And I've just about had it with Denny and the others in the band. Well, Gib and Pete are okay really, but Denny and Rod just wanna party. They don't wanna be serious about our music. I'm afraid I'm gonna hafta start all over with another bunch of guys.

Carrie stroked his head as he lay on his back.

—And I'm worried about me and you.

—You're worried about us? Why?

—I feel like I'm not good enough for you. You're a Westside, uptown girl. You went to Lincoln and hung out with all the other rich kids. I come from a middle-class family, living in an eastside neighborhood and I went to an average high school with a bunch of kids who weren't even as well off as my family was.

Heaving a huge sigh, he became quiet.

—I don't care where you're from, Billy. It's how we were brought up, not where. You must be from a good family to be such a good person. The person I see. You're smart and handsome and sensitive and everything I want in a boyfriend. You're more than good enough for me.

She rolled onto one shoulder to see his reaction and noticed that he was asleep and beginning to snore. She smiled at him and turned off the lamp next to the bed.

When Billy awoke in the morning, Carrie had already left for the day, with a full schedule of classes. He got up, dressed, quietly left the apartment, and sauntered down the sidewalk in the direction of the band house, which was about a mile away. He passed an outdoor intramural basketball court, where six young men were playing three-on-three on the uneven asphalt surface, steam rising from their bodies.

Cocking an ear, Billy heard a familiar voice from the past. He wandered over to the chain-link fence surrounding the court and peered at the guys out on the court. One of them was Mak Poppin. Billy was certain. Billy had not seen Mak since high school, but no one else in the world looked like Poppinfresh.

Mak was of medium height and round in every aspect of his body. He was bow-legged, his trunk was round and his face was round. Mak had a ruddy complexion, with a high forehead and bulging blue eyes. He always wore a very earnest expression, which may or may not have been legitimate.

—Hey, Doughboy. Nice shot.

Scowling, Mak looked up in Billy's direction. Then, recognizing his old friend, he brightened and ran over to the fence.

—Nobody calls me that anymore, Billy. How're you doin', man? What're ya' doin' around here?

—Aw, my girlfriend lives over in those apartments over there and I was just on my way home.

—Where ya' live?

—Down on Arthur with the rest of the band.

—Oh, right. The Malchicks. I've been hearin' about you guys. You all live in the same house?

—Yeah, for now. Most of us. What're you up to?

—Well I dropped out of school last term—accountin' major, and I've been livin' with my parents. But they're gettin' ready to kick me out. I'm not sure what I'm doin'.

Without hesitation, Billy offered.

—You could, like, stay with us if ya' need to. I mean, we can fit another person into the basement. It's a little chaotic over there right now, but I think things are gonna be changin' pretty soon.

—Changin'? Ya' got personnel changes in mind?

—Yeah, I guess you could say that. Maybe so. Why don't ya' come with me and you can check the place out.

Running back to the court, Mak fished out his sweatshirt and jacket from a pile under the basket. He joined Billy and the two of them walked down in the direction of the band house. Mak wanted to know.

—It's a pretty old house, I bet? They're all old down there in that neighborhood aren't they?

—Yeah, it's old, eighteen ninety-eight, or somethin' like that. That's what the mark on the sidewalk says, anyway. It's got three floors and sort of a converted attic. The attic is my room. It's pretty nice up there. Privacy. It's hard to get much privacy in that place. I will say that.

—Must be hell to heat the place.

—Nah. Bam Bam—he's our roadie—he rigged up the gas meter so we get our heat for almost free. He's got some way of movin' the electric meter back, too, so we hardly pay anything for electricity either. It's, like, really cheap to live there with everybody payin' rent. Like, about seventy-five a month each. And it's hardly anything for the utilities. I guess that's obvious.

Mak's eyes widened.

—Well, that sounds pretty good. I could probably come up with that kind of money.

—Maybe you won't have to. I've been thinkin' my band would be needin' a manager pretty soon and then you show up, accounting major and everything—like karma or somethin'. So I was thinkin' maybe you could, um, do the job.

—Uh, wait a minute. Slow down. Slow down. You're movin' too fast here. Your band? What d'ya mean?

—I mean I'm probably gonna start a new band with new players and you could, like, manage the band.

—Gee, I don't know Billy. I've never managed a band before. That's kind of a tall order, don't ya' think?

—Oh, it's not that big a deal. Ya' just, like, book us gigs. Most of the rooms know who I am. And ya' collect the money at the end of the night. I'll give ya' ten percent. Last night we made around fifteen hundred, so that woulda meant a hundred and fifty for you.

—I could live with that I guess.

Mak was being facetious.

—That could definitely help pay the rent. When would I start?

—I want to get started on the new band right away. But I could let ya' coast on rent until we got up and runnin' again.

—Okay. That sounds great.

The two arrived at the big, old gray house and traipsed up the stairs to the front door. The two of them entered to the thick smell of the smoky stale and moldy moist old building. They stepped into the living room, where Denny was plunking on an acoustic guitar, absently watching television with the sound off. He ignored Billy, pretending he was not even there.

—I'll be goddamned. If it ain't fuckin' Poppinfresh the goddamned Doughboy.

Mak's face turned an even deeper shade of apple red.

## VII

That evening, without telling him what was going on, Denny solicited a ride to Geraldo's from Billy Dreier. At Geraldo's, Denny began to drink a long series of beers, becoming increasingly more plastered and remorseful with each glass he downed. Later on, the Irish-eyed Indian Jim Finity came up to the bar and introduced himself.

—Hey, you're Denny Granger aren't you?

—Yup, that's me.

—My name's Jim Finity. I opened for your band a couple times. Last time was at Euphoria. It was some five band night, and my band, the Grown Men, opened up the show.

Denny nodded, feigning recollection of the event.

—I played solo at the Lennon Memorial concert in Schrunk Park too, but you guys played ahead of me, and I think you took off before I got to play.

Denny stared off into space, without answering.

—I really like your band. You guys are a lot of fun.

—Tell that to my brother. He's not so into fun these days.

—Billy? How's Billy doing anyway?

—Oh, he's great. Just great.

Denny started to well up, but he caught himself.

—Well, tell him I said hi. We've never met. I wouldn't imagine he'd remember me from the times I've played with you guys.

Gloomily, Denny swirled the remnants of his beer in the glass.

—You're right. He probably doesn't remember you.

Detecting that Denny was not in a talkative mood, Jim Finity ever the good-natured gentleman, made an offer that Denny couldn't refuse.

—Can I buy you a beer?

—Sure, sure. You can buy me a beer. Thanks.

Denny really didn't want to continue the conversation, but he was running low on funds and he was not nearly as drunk as he wanted to be—despite the fact that he was already trashed. His mind wandered to Billy and what the future might hold. The bartender slid them two drafts of Budweiser from the tap, and Jim Finity slapped a five-dollar bill down on the counter.

—Sorry, Jim. I'm not very talkative tonight. I've got a lot on my mind.

—Hey, I've been there. Too many times to count. You don't have to apologize to me.

Denny stared at his beer.

—You know, Jim, I'm not Billy...

Jim nodded, unsure where the conversation was heading.

—I'm not a performer like him. My brother would do anything for press. Anything for attention. He knows how to be a star. He wants to be a star. Who'd ever want to be a fuckin' *star* anyway?

Jim Finity gazed straight ahead, unable to answer.

There was a sudden commotion in the room and the crowd sluiced aside. It was Billy, trailed by a desperate Bam Bam. The entire bar fell silent as Billy entered: blue jeans tucked into his red, pointed-toed cowboy boots, a black leather jacket and teardrop blue Elvis shades. A visible charisma field surrounded him.

Jim Finity did not even recognize Billy. He no longer resembled the kid Jim had seen at the John Lennon Memorial Rally in December. He asked Denny.

—Who's that?

—Oh, it's Billy. Being a star again.

Unnerved, Jim Finity finished his beer quickly, sensing that Denny was not feeling particularly sociable.

—I gotta go, man. It was nice to meet you, Denny.

Jim Finity got up from his barstool and walked away. Denny mumbled.

—Yeah. Yeah. It was nice to meet you too.... Hey, thanks for the beer.

Jim Finity did not hear him. He melted away into the Geraldo's crowd, outside of Denny's field of vision and soon left the premises. Denny finished his beer and quickly exited the bar, as well.

As he sat down in a booth, Billy spread his arms magnanimously. A pack of fawning followers soon encircled him.

Within weeks, Billy began the formation of a new band. He recruited bassist Gib Stryker from the Malchicks. Gib, who was serious about the music business—perhaps even more so than Billy—was eager to move up in the local scene, and Billy was nothing if not upwardly mobile.

After searching around for other members, Gib mentioned that Col DuQuesne was leaving Casey Avon. Before the Malchicks, Gib and Col had played together in a couple of country bands. Billy always liked Col's approach to the guitar—a little country, a little classic, Chuck Berry rock 'n' roll, with some Keith on the side—so they decided to meet at Café Vivo late one afternoon.

The two hit it off right away. Billy thought Col looked right for his vision of a new band, and Col knew that Billy was going somewhere. Fast. They discussed drummers for a while, as drummers were the key to the success of any band, and Billy did not know that many good drummers in town. As they talked, Gilly Walker began his regular happy-hour gig at Café Vivo as a solo pianist.

Billy was immediately taken with Gilly's style. Col knew Gilly and knew that he had a synthesizer, which few keyboardists in town had. Not only that, it was one of the best synthesizers made. Col told Billy that Gilly was pushing forty and hailed from New York. Billy was not dissuaded by Gilly's age. He wanted him in the band.

So, during a break, Billy approached the pianist, introduced himself, and asked if Gilly would be interested in auditioning for his new band. Gilly said that he would and they made a date for him, Col, Gib, and Billy to get together to jam on the following day. In Billy's mind, it was a foregone conclusion that Gilly was in the band.

The rehearsal in the band house basement only confirmed Billy's initial sense that he was on to something new and different. The four of them created a sound that was far removed from the sloppy barroom din the Malchicks had managed to fashion. The musicians played parts, rather than just banging away on their instruments with every beat.

Col invented clever licks, utilizing simple, efficient effects. And he proved to be an adequate singer, good enough, at least, for backup vocals. Gilly was primarily interested in adding single-note orchestral sorts of lines, reminiscent of Greg Hawkes of the Cars. The fact that Gilly was no great techno whiz was a plus in Billy's mind. As for Gib, he was as solid and stable as a tractor. Billy was satisfied that he had in place the right components for his new band. They lacked only a drummer—and original material. Then they would be on their way.

Col said he knew of a drummer, Ian Autry, who was available and not bad. However, on his way over to their first rehearsal, Ian ditched his motorcycle and badly tore up his right leg. He was going to be down for at least six weeks, and Billy had no intention of waiting six weeks to get the band rolling. He wanted to be playing out in the clubs by then. Seeing it as an omen, Billy decided that another drummer was in order. Billy Dreier, who had also thrown in his lot with Billy's new venture, mentioned that his best friend, Dawson Fellows, was a fine drummer. Billy told him to get the drummer over right away.

At the band's first rehearsal, he knew that everything was in place for his new band. Billy was convinced that he had found a better drummer than Ian, the original choice. With the band set, Billy summoned a meeting at Quality Pie.

Quality Pie, where Trudy worked, was a classic '40s soda fountain, a place from another era altogether. It had become the late-night, post-show hangout for Portland bands and fans alike. From the entryway to the right-angle turn of the room, there were numerous chrome swivel stools with maroon naugahyde tops facing a long, white formica counter. On the opposing wall were typical booths of the period. The second section of the room, around the corner, was all booths. That was where all the cool people hung out to laugh drunkenly and converse at the top of their lungs, smoking furiously.

In the florescent-lit ambience of Quality Pie, a thick nicotine haze, as always, hovered in the air like some cancerous specter. Billy, Billy Dreier, Mak, Gilly, Col, Gib and the new drummer, Daw, convened to discuss the future of the band. The five band members crowded into one booth, while Mak and Billy Dreier sat behind them in another booth.

A haggard looking waitress ambled by to get their orders. They all requested coffee. Billy asked.

—Have ya' got any of that banana cream pie tonight?

The waitress nodded.

—Is it fresh baked?

The waitress shrugged her shoulders, apathetically.

—I'll have the pie. And we'll all have coffee.

Col and Mak lit cigarettes, adding to the smog of the room. Gib stared intensely at the ashtray while Daw lit matches from the book he had picked up at Cassidy's earlier in the day. Blowing them out one by one, he watched the smoke of each curl up into the air.

Billy took command of the conversation from the start.

—I want you guys to know right off. This is, y'know, gonna be my band. I'm in charge. I learned from havin' a band with my brother that democracies don't work for a band. There has to be, uh, a leader and I'm the leader of this band. Y'know, that doesn't mean that ya' don't, like, have a say in things. You will... you do. It's sort of like a modified democracy, I guess you'd say. But I make the final decisions.

The others hesitantly agreed, unsure whether they might be signing on with Captain Bligh. The waitress brought Billy's banana cream pie, and he dug in, forking off a big mouthful

—We're gonna have the best band in town. We'll be the coolest band and everything will be done right. Y'know? We're ready to start giggin' right now. We've got, like, a set's worth of songs and we've got 'em down real tight. Now we just have to come up with some kinda gimmick to get our name out there.

From the next booth, Mak interjected.

—How's about puttin' up posters around town that say, like, 'band is coming'? Kinda get peoples' curiosity fired up?

Somewhat confused, Billy asked

—What do you mean, 'band is coming'?

—Well, not *band* is comin', whatever the name of this band turns out to be. Like 'The Beatles are coming,' or 'the Rolling Stones are coming'. Um, somethin' like that, y'know?

—That's not a bad idea, but what should the name of our band be? The name has to be, like, bigger than life, but also something that would be, like, a, a *contradiction in terms*. Like Hell's Angels or somethin' like that. I mean, Hell's Angels is already taken, of course. So, we wouldn't wanna go there.

Col suggested several names.

—How about Devil's Angels? Maimin' Angels? Or the Killer Angels? Or how about Killer Gods? Tender Giants? No. I guess that's too close to Gentle Giant.

—Naw. Those suck. They're, like, totally unreal. We need... No! Wait. Unreal. How about Unreal Gods? That's perfect for us. Billy Granger and the Unreal Gods. That's a name that sounds like us. Sounds like where we wanna go.

Dusting his cigarette into the ashtray, Col retorted.

—To heaven?

—No, not heaven exactly, but out of this world, you know? An unreal god. That sounds easy enough, but what is an unreal god when you, like, think about it?

The band members shrugged. Gilly chimed in.

—What's a *real* god, when you think about it?

The metaphysical aspects of his question silenced the crew momentarily. Finishing his pie, Billy persisted.

—Unreal Gods is just right. It'll get people thinkin'. We have to be good with a name like that. It'll look good on that poster Mak's talkin' about: the Unreal Gods are comin'. Sounds like a Salvation Army show or somethin'. People will wonder about that.

The band seemed amenable to the name—or at least unwilling to contest it, given the circumstances. Billy continued with his agenda.

—We have to have like a special look on stage, too. I don't mean, like, we all wear the same outfits or anything. That would be stupid. But we need a look.

Giving serious thought to the issue for a moment, Mak said.

—Well, how about we have band colors like red and black or black and gold, and we paint all the equipment that color? Like school colors. Like a team.

Billy brightened at the thought.

—Or blue and yellow, like the Swedish flag. My mom would like that.

The rest of the band looked at Billy quizzically, trying to understand what his mom had to do with anything.

—We'll paint everything blue and yellow, like the Swedish flag. Stripes. Everything will have a look. We'll all look like we play in the same band.

Concerned, Col asked.

—You mean like uniforms or somethin'? If I wanted to, like, wear a uniform, I'd join the Boy Scouts. No. Maybe the Girl Scouts would be more fun.

—No, I already said that. Not all the same, like uniforms. But like we all belong together, that's all. Like the Stones or something, y'know?

Daw looked up from a burning match and chuckled.

—Maybe we need cheerleaders too. Like that 'Hey Mickey' chick. What's her name?

Gib supplied the name.

—Toni Basil.

Replying to Daw's suggestion, Billy said.

—Yeah, that's not bad. But cheerleaders would be too frou-frou. We need somethin' a little tougher. A little more street. Bad girl cheerleaders. Like a street circus comin' to town.

Mak exclaimed.

61

—How's about go-go dancers? We could put 'em in white boots and short little skirts and hang 'em in cages above the stage or somethin'.

Billy knitted his brows briefly, trying to conjure up the image in his mind.

—Yeah, I like it. That's good, Poppy. Billy Granger and the Unreal Gods and the Goddesses A Go-Go. That sounds like a real circus, alright. I can, like, see it in my head and it looks pretty cool. Girls doin' the Cool Jerk in cages above the stage. That'd be a real spectacle. That's good. That's real good. But I don't know if we could, like, hang cages from the ceiling, man. That's probably not very practical. No tellin' where we'll be playin'. But maybe put 'em in cages up on pedestals or somethin'. I like that.

Billy thought for a second, then wondered.

—So, where are we gonna find dancers?

Gilly suggested.

—My girlfriend Marie dances down at the Mocambo Club. Maybe she could get one of her friends down there to be a dancer with her. Maybe Candy. I know she'd do it. They'd love to dance in front of a big crowd, and Marie doesn't mind heights. I know that.

Billy pictured the scene as he spoke.

—We wouldn't have them dance on every song. Just on certain songs. Make it a special occasion. They'd be like trapeze artists or somethin'. We'd have to find a way to get 'em in and out of those cages on the platforms. Maybe black covers or somethin'. I want 'em to just, like, appear out of nowhere—like magic. Like, 'where the hell did *they* come from'? I don't know...

He pinched his chin.

—That seems like a pretty tough production to, like, uh, pull off at every gig. Maybe the cages for our first show or somethin'. And the platforms, we could maybe use them when we played on larger stages.

Soon, there were posters all over town. "The Unreal Gods are Coming. The Unreal Gods are Coming." The band did not have its first gig secured, but they had posters on every telephone pole promoting the appearance, whenever it did finally happen.

Gilly's girlfriend Marie did not last long as a Goddess. In fact, she did not even make it to the band's first performance. She had a bad attitude. And she constantly complained that the seventeen-fifty per show wage the band was offering was much too low. She could make that much in an hour at the Macombo Club.

Actually, Gilly was happy about that turn of events. After thinking about it, he was not that keen on Marie being around all the time at all the gigs—impeding his side action. As far as he was concerned, it all worked out for the best.

So the Goddesses needed another dancer. Candy, who at thirty-three, was actually older than everyone in the band except Gilly, said she might know of a girl. Besides dancing at the Macombo Club, she intermittently modeled clothing for the Jantzen Corporation.

Candy sometimes worked with a young woman, Colette, who also occasionally modeled for Jantzen. Colette would be perfect for the job. Candy knew she had had many years of dance training—so she would easily catch on to the undemanding, basic changes the band's songs required.

Unbeknownst even to Candy, Colette was very young. Underage. Auditioning for a band was a very big deal to her. A little nervous, a little unsure of what she was doing, she arrived at the old, dilapidated two-story house, uncertain, that she was at the right place. But as she walked up the steps to the front door, she could hear the band pounding away in the basement, playing a catchy song.

—I used to hang around
With all the other boy boys
We went to all the crazy places
We made all the same noise.

In order to find the entry to the basement—in the kitchen—Colette walked into the house, as Candy had instructed. She was deeply alarmed by what she saw.

The place smelled like stale beer, garbage, smoke, and man-stink. In the living room, she first noticed a whiskey brown woodstove made out of a fifty-five gallon oil drum, fitted into the chimney of a gray stone fireplace. The mantel was crowded with arcane mementos and memorabilia; such as a bowling pin autographed by the members of Journey and a thirties vintage photograph of Bing Crosby in an old, ornate gold frame.

In addition, there was a complement of empty beer bottles on the mantle—some of an exotic brand or of expensive quality, other were merely reminders of particular subsequent conquests. There were odd trophies, for golf and bowling. There were several colorful blobs and dribbles of once molten glass: souvenirs from the days when Gib had worked at a glass factory.

There was a worn, brown, overstuffed sofa along one wall with a homemade coffee table in front of it, littered with beer bottles, notebook paper, books, pencils, cigarette papers, empty baggies, smoking pipes, small cellophane wrappers and corners of pages from Penthouse magazine. There was a smudged mirror, with a small length of a straw on top of it. Two coffee cups, one empty, one left half full for several days. A broken reclining chair was positioned next to the couch. A mauve overstuffed chair, in surprisingly good shape, sat angled opposite the coffee table.

A low stand, with a plant on it, was situated near the window, next to the armchair. A wooden birdcage, with a peyote cactus growing inside, hung from the ceiling, above the armchair. On the wall behind the couch was a poster of John Travolta, arm raised, locked in *Saturday Night Fever* strut. Behind the armchair on the wall, next to the window, was a poster of Frank Zappa, a Groucho phony moustache, nose and glasses obscenely stapled to his crotch. There was a mired brown carpet laid upon the hard wood floor.

Two pair of stereo speakers were stacked on either side of the fireplace. Next to the speakers on the left was a six-month old heap of newspapers piled in a large cardboard box. A large color TV, with serious color problems, was positioned on top of a small end table next to the column of speakers on the right. Littered around the room were old chocolate milk cartons, chunks of wood and nails, sawdust and mummified dust curls, a layer of soot and dust. An old rickety chandelier hung in the center of the room, with only two of the five lights working.

Faded dirty yellow curtains bordered the three windows in the darkened room. The stereo ran along the wall abutting the anteroom leading into the kitchen. Several crates of albums were neatly stacked around the equipment. More crates of albums were lovingly arranged around the anteroom—which had probably been a dining room in better days. There were at least four or five thousand albums. The collection was the pride of the band household.

The kitchen lay beyond the anteroom. From the entryway, Colette could see that it was buried in dirty dishes—the sink was piled high. Empty cereal boxes, milk cartons, tableware—thick with left over meals—were packed onto the counter. Empty Burger King sacks. There was a tuna can filled with cigarette butts. Strands of uncooked spaghetti were strewn all over. A half a kettle of popcorn sat on the stove, which was crowded full of mucky pans and skillets. The formerly fern-green floor was filthy and sticky black. There was a round table in the corner, with three mismatched chairs. It was littered with paper and poster supplies, cereal bowls and plates with bits of toast and egg remnants.

Colette shuddered, wondering what she had gotten herself into. She had never seen anything like those rooms. She knew that males were pigs, but she did not know that anyone could live like that.

When the music died down for a moment, she walked into the kitchen and rapped authoritatively on what appeared to be the door to the basement. She heard footsteps bounding up the stairs. It was Candy. Relieved and horrified, Colette breathed a heavy sigh. Candy grabbed her by the hand and led her down to the basement.

At the bottom of the basement stairs, Colette could see that there was a bedroom directly opposite from where she stood, a sheet hanging in the doorway. Billy Dreier would disappear and reappear from the room.

The main area was a rehearsal space, with one portion, just to her right, walled off into a separate little area. It served as a control room, where an array of tape recorders, sound boards and effects devices were scattered—and into which Billy Dreier would enter after coming out of the bedroom. A plate glass window faced the rehearsal space so that Billy D. could maintain eye contact with the band during recording sessions.

Surrounding the main rehearsal space, the basement was a bone yard of broken and discarded musical equipment. In one corner sat an old Lowry organ, bordered by electric guitars in various states of decline. Several gutted guitar amps lay around, as well as a couple burned out PA heads.

The rest of the floor was littered with broken drum sticks, broken drum cases, broken snare drum heads, mangled guitar cases, broken guitar strings, dead cables, raw speakers, wheels and hardware for road cases, sheet music, notebook paper with lyrics and chords scrawled upon them. There were empty guitar string packages scattered everywhere—beer cans and bottles, ashtrays and trash.

Colette stood with Candy, frozen in place at the bottom of the stairs. Candy pulled her over to the only clear space in the room, an area about six feet square. As the band started to play another song, Candy shouted to Colette.

—Just do what I do. I'll show you the moves.

Candy demonstrated for Colette the Twist, the Monkey, the Swim, and the Frug, the Hitch Hike, the Watusi, the Shimmy, the Shing-a-Ling, and the Boogaloo. None of those dances were at all familiar to Colette, who had been an infant when they were popular. Candy was just entering her teens when most of the dances were all the rage. At first Candy was confused as to why Colette was having trouble. But Colette soon picked up the steps.

—That's it. Just do what I do. That'll be our choreography until we work out some moves of our own.

The band finished up rehearsing "Stereo Area," when they finally noticed Colette in the room. Candy spoke up.

—Everyone, this is Colette. Colette, that's everybody. That's Billy and Col in the front. Gib on bass back there, Daw on drums, and Gilly on the synthesizer. And that big guy in the recording booth is Billy Dreier. Everybody calls him Billy D.

The members nodded faintly as Candy introduced them.

—It'll take you a while to learn who everyone is. I'm just now figuring it out myself.

Preoccupied, a harried Mak Poppin came down the basement stairs, his round red face rounder and redder than usual. He looked at Colette balefully. Candy said.

—That's Mak

—This the new girl? Must be the new girl, I guess. It's gonna be awful crowded in the van with you two in there too.

Colette spoke up.

—It's okay. I have my own car. A little purple Bug. I can drive myself to the dates.

I can drive Candy too, if that helps.

Mak softened slightly, but remained officious.

—Well, okay. But I want you to know upfront, we can only pay ya' seventeen-fifty a gig. That wasn't enough for Marie. But we've got a lot of mouths to feed and thirty-five bucks for the two of you is all we can afford for now.

Colette shrugged her shoulders.

—That's okay with me. I didn't come here for the money.

Colette ran a hand through her straight, shoulder-length copper hair. She was quite a bit shorter than Candy, who was leggy and nearly six feet tall. Colette was around five-foot-six. She had a fuller figure than blade-thin Candy. A pretty, girl-next-door face compared to Candy's long black hair and more striking features.

Mak Poppin continued to lay down the law.

—I don't want a lot of, uh, mind games and head-trips. You guys need to, like, take care of yourselves. Me and the band'll have other things to do at gigs. We can't be lookin' after you.

The girls nodded their heads in agreement. Candy spoke up.

—We can take care of ourselves, Mak. You don't need to look out for us. I'm a brown belt.

Pissed off at Mak's rude behavior, she turned to Colette.

—Look, I'll show you the dances later. We need to go looking for costumes. Billy wants a go-go girls get up, and I have some ideas. Let's go hit the second-hand stores and see what's out there.

Somewhat relieved at the thought of leaving, Colette followed Candy up the stairs to the kitchen as the band began to play another song.

To promote the band, Billy called in all his markers. He gave interviews to every music writer in town. His big coup came in securing a conference with John Westman, the *Oregonian*'s chief music critic. Westman had always been a fan and supporter of the Malchicks—of Billy in particular—and he was more than enthused at the prospect of Billy forming a new band, one that might help the young musician to realize his enormous potential. He also relished the opportunity to break the band in his column. To get the scoop.

Westman published a sprawling review in the Friday Arts and Entertainment section of The *Oregonian*. He gushed like a schoolgirl over Billy and the possibilities the new band possessed. In a long, rambling interview, Billy revealed the direction he intended for his new band.

—The Malchicks were basically a copy band. With the Unreal Gods, it'll be like night and day. This band is devoted to my sound. I'm writing the music and the music direction has changed drastically. It's contemporary, but very relative to our past influences.

And the new band's sound?

—I think it's prophetic of what rock 'n' roll will be in the eighties. We're coming from ska but will fuse rockabilly with a faster rhythm from ska and reggae. Some of that sound is pretty big now in England, but we're making it an American sound in our arrangements.

Is this a new direction for you then?

—When me and my brother Denny formed the Malchicks, we were in it for the music and the fun of it. The Malchicks lasted a full year. I learned a lot in that time, especially since practically none of us were musicians before the band got started. We found out it wasn't that hard. But I'm committed to it now, the music and the profession. This band will have a much stronger professional outlook.

In what way?

—We're relating to older times, like the sixties, in a different way. We're looking at a recording career and we'll have help coming in that direction. And I'm even investigating the video thing that's coming on fast.

Just that article, alone, did much to summon the hatred and jealousy of all the other musical acts in Portland—many of whom had struggled for years, never to receive a single accolade.

Billy's ability to curry such immediate favor with Westman, without the Unreal Gods having played even a note, only further provoked the animosity of everyone within the tight circle of Portland musicians, many of whom thought that the Malchicks received too much unwarranted attention as it was. They hated the Unreal Gods and hated Billy for being so attractive and controversial as to receive an interview with Westman, having done absolutely nothing. The public, however, were very curious.

Soon, with Mak in tow, Billy approached Tommy Demeola, pleading for a show at La Bamba.

—C'mon, Tommy. We can pack the room. We got that great article from Westman. We've got posters up all over town,

—Well, just the same, I don't think people fuckin' know who ya' are. An article and a few posters don't make you guys household names or nothin', y'know? I can't give you a weekend. Not for a new band. I can't afford for you guys to tank. I've gotta have good nights every weekend to make ends meet right now. To pay the bills, y'know? How 'bout I give ya' a Tuesday night and we'll see how ya' do.

—A Tuesday? That's the worst night of the week!

—Naw, Sundays and Mondays are worse. I've got too many good bands with guaranteed draws wantin' in here on the rest of the nights. We'll give ya' a Tuesday night and see how ya' do. If ya' do good, then we'll get ya' in here on a better night. That seems fair. Don't ya' think? Even you gotta work your way up, y'know.

In no position to argue the point, Billy took the next open Tuesday, electing to make the most of the opportunity.

The next day, Billy and Carrie were walking in Washington Park, down a deserted path that was once the zoo railway, when the zoo was in that location. Billy absently kicked at stones that were lodged between the old ties. He told Carrie.

—When I was a kid, I wanted to be famous. I wanted to be number one. The first to do everything.

—Why do you think that was?

—I guess because I was the older brother. I always wanted to get there before Denny did.

—Don't you think that sort of ruined things for Denny?

—Yeah, I guess so. But I didn't think about that back then. I was just better than Denny, anyway. Better at tennis and swimming and baseball. Remember? I told ya' I wanted to be a pro baseball player, 'n' all? I wanted to play for the Dodgers, just like my old man. Only better.

—So, why did you give that up anyway?

—Aw, I got sidetracked by music, and the idea of bein' a star.

Carrie stopped walking and looked at Billy, bewildered.

—Why is being a star so important to you?

—It just seems like what I'm supposed to be. I look ahead and it looks easy. I'm supposed to be famous. I don't know if I'll ever get rich, but I'm gonna be famous. I'm sure of that.

She tried not to let her disbelief show.

—You know, I don't care if you're rich or famous. You'll always be a success to me. I love you just the way you are.

—You don't get it, baby. I'm *supposed* to be famous. I can feel it. I need you to help me get there, wherever it is I'm goin'. I need your support and encouragement. I can't do it alone.

—But it seems like you have all the support you need right there in your head.

What do you need me to do? And what about *my* hopes and dreams?

He became quiet and peered off toward the forest below them.

—Never mind. Let's just forget it.

Suddenly concerned that Billy was referring to their relationship—to just forget it—she grew apprehensive and hesitant.

—But, Billy, I'm afraid too. That's just a part of growing up, I guess. I need you to help me too.

—But I can't, Carrie. I can't. I've gotta focus on me. I *have* to be famous. I can't be a failure. I've got my own work to do. For me. A full-time job.

—Where is this coming from, Billy? I don't understand.

—I don't know, but I can't deal with *your* doubts right now. I have to be famous. I've got too many worries of my own. I need total support.

They walked a little farther and then turned back. In silence, Carrie drove Billy back to the band house. After dropping him off, she drove back to her apartment, mulling his words, her face wrinkled in concern and confusion. With renewed purpose, she spent the rest of the night studying for an upcoming mid-term in her Health Sciences class.

At home, Billy turned on the TV and sat down on the old, dilapidated brown sofa in the living room, as if he were leaning against a sleeping camel. After lighting a joint rolled from the stash kept in a box on the coffee table, he picked up a guitar that was leaning against the arm of the sofa, and began to strum it, puffing heartily. Almost immediately, what seemed like familiar chords reverberated from the guitar and he began to write a song. "I'm walking down a rocky road for you."

The song seemed reminiscent of something else. Maybe Johnny Cash? He had it mapped out within minutes and relatively completed within half an hour. Immediately recording the song on the small cassette recorder on the coffee table, he determined that the band would learn it and play it at their first gig.

That night, Jim Finity was hosting an open mic at the Dirty Duck on Glisan in Old Town, at the foot of the Steel Bridge. Mak Poppin walked into the tavern and sat down on a stool at the bar, watching Jim open the evening playing a short set of his original songs, accompanying himself on acoustic guitar.

After his set, Jim walked up to the bar and sat down next to Mak, on the only available stool.

Mak proffered.

—Hey, man, I like what you do. That's some cool stuff.

—Thanks, I've been doing it for a while now.

—My name's Mak Poppin.

He held out his hand.

—I'm Jim Finity. Poppin? Are you related to Jak Poppin? From Madison? You look like him, now that I think about it.

—Yeah. He's my older brother.

—Sure, I remember you. We used to get you to play basketball with us on Saturdays.

—Naw, that was my brother Zak. I was just a little kid back then. Zak's the middle brother and I'm, like, the little brother.

—Yeah, sure. Mak. I remember you. So what's Jak up to now?

—He's a photographer and lives in Woodstock, New York.

—Woodstock huh?

—Yeah. He's a nature photographer. He met a girl from up that way and they, uh, got married and now they've got, like, three kids.

—Jak never seemed like the kind of guy to settle down. He was kind of a wild man.

—Yeah, that's what everybody tells me. But he's real settled down now.

—Kids'll do that. I've got a young son myself. He'll be four in October.

Mak nodded, staring blankly at the bartender.

—Hey, here's my card. I'm managin' a band called Billy Granger and the Unreal Gods.

—Oh yeah. Billy. I had a couple of beers with his brother a while back.

—Denny?

—Yeah. Denny. So Billy started a new band? They're calling themselves the Unreal Gods?

—Unreal Gods. Yeah. I just found out that they're playin' a Shriners Benefit show at La Bamba in a couple of weeks. It's on a Tuesday. Would you, uh, be interested in openin' the night? You'd be the perfect opener. I can't pay you much, maybe like twenty bucks. But you'd get to play in front of a packed house.

—Well, yeah. Sure. That'd be great. I'd love to see the new band, too. From what I've been hearing, they're going to be something else.

—Yeah. They've been gettin' a lot of press lately. Pissed a few people off.

—Aw, you can't please everybody all the time. Yeah, sure. I'll do it. Let me know when and I'll be there.

—It's Tuesday, June sixteenth. You could start around nine and play for half an hour or so. That would be great. I've got a couple of bands lined up to play after you, before Billy comes on.

—The sixteenth? Okay. You're on. That should be fun.

# VIII

Tuesday, June sixteenth, nineteen eighty-one, was a perfect, beautiful, Oregon near-summer day, with the temperature in the low eighties, and not a cloud to be found in the sky. The Rose festival fleet had just left town, and there was a general atmosphere of *party* in the air.

The evening of the Unreal Gods' first gig was warm and friendly, and the house at Luis' La Bamba Club was packed. There was hardly room to move. Whatever promotional opportunities the band had explored seemed to have worked perfectly. Tommy Demeola marched around the club as if Luis himself were imparting a blessing on the proceedings. The crowd was excited by the mood, waiting in anticipation of Portland's next big thing.

Backstage, before the gig, Jim Finity wandered around nervously. People were running around crazy, in gaily-colored leotards and heavy eye makeup. It was a true circus. Jim spotted Billy in the corner of the dressing room. He seemed oblivious to all that was going on around him, leisurely smoking a joint.

Jim eyed him carefully.

—So you're Billy Granger.

Billy appeared to Jim like a thoroughbred horse, sleek and majestic. He was delicate looking, but young and strong. He was very slender, with long, elegant arms and hands. The two musicians greeted each other respectfully.

—Hey, Billy. I'm Jim Finity. I'm opening tonight.

—I've heard of you. I heard you went to Madison High. That's where I went to school.

—That's true, but I went there about ten years before you went there. I graduated in nineteen sixty-nine. My best friend was Merv Moss.

—You mean Merv Moss of Dollarshine? Gold record Merv Moss?

Jim nodded reverently.

—Merv Moss went to Madison too? Wow! That's really somethin'. We were always known for havin' all the baseball players. Like Rick Wise. I didn't know we had so many musicians. That's pretty amazing.

Becoming more animated, Jim said earnestly.

72

—I hope you make it all the way, man. I hope you make it to the top. You've got all the tools.

—Well, thank you, Jim. That's really nice of you to say.

—So Billy, does it matter which mic I use on stage? The one on the right or the one on the left?

—Gee, I don't care. It doesn't matter to me. Mine's the one on the right and Col's is on the left. Take your pick. Billy'll get ya' dialed in.

Satisfied with that response, Jim stood up and began to climb the stairs leading out of the dressing room. Billy shouted after him.

—Good luck out there, Jim. Go get 'em, man.

Jim performed his brief set with customary elan and professionalism. "Watching Rome Burn To The Ground" met with an unusually dramatic response, despite its weighty subject matter. "Sweet To My Eyes" kept the audience engaged. "Rain On The Marshland," the title track from his most recent album, met with reasonable approval. Jim's ode to the Terwilliger Bridge brought more than a smattering of applause. And he was gone.

Incomparable John Dailey quickly followed, with a brief collection of some of his most inflammatory one-man-band material. He seemed mostly intent on infuriating the listeners. It was as if he were baiting the crowd, trying to agitate them in some way.

But the happy throng would not allow even him to spoil a joyous evening. In some respects, Incomparable John Dailey had fallen miserably short in his mission. He had failed to attract attention to himself. That displeased him beyond measure. If he could not get an audience to react, even negatively, Incomparable John felt that a performance was a complete and utter defeat. His night was ruined.

The Ids were up next, with a set of their typically peppy pop songs. Lead guitarist Duane Rogers looked like a twelve-year-old boy beneath the La Bamba lights. His carefully trimmed shaggy haircut gave him the look of the Kinks' Ray Davies as a youngster, his silver braces gleaming in the red and green glow.

Duane's brother, the drummer, Kevin, drove the band with an incessant beat. Sullen lead vocalist Zen Gable nervously trolled and stalked the stage, urgently grasping the mic stand with both hands, as if they were at the throat of a disloyal lover. Bassist Jim Palmer, short and muscular with an angular face and curly blond hair, stood planted motionless in one spot, perhaps to quell the roiling sense of seasickness Gable sometimes imparted.

The Ids were not a thinking fan's band, but were cute and entertaining, which was precisely what the crowd's mood called for. As always, Duane oversold his lead guitar playing, displaying tremendous effort and emotion fingering a simple G-chord or executing an elementary run up the fretboard.

73

Kevin Rogers rhythmically threw long brown bangs away from his forehead without missing a beat—as did Zen Gable, who looked more like Kevin's brother than Duane did. But Zen's motions gave the impression he was sweeping the hair from his face out of some sort of uneasy desperation.

The Ids wrapped up their set with amiable promptness, in part because the crowd was not really paying attention to them. They were bobbing in anticipation of Billy Granger's new band. The Ids knew that, and were in no mood to forestall the proceedings.

Backstage, in the deserted green room, Colette and Candy quickly changed into their costumes for the evening. They had no dressing room of their own, so they just stripped off their street clothes and dressed in the middle of the room. Colette was a bit embarrassed, but she followed Candy's lead and acted as though it were an everyday experience.

Just as they were applying their make up—large blue and glitter triangles above their eyes, lined with heavy mascara, and lipstick on over-sized deep red lips—Mak Poppin came rushing down the stairs.

—Are you guys just about ready?

The girls nodded.

—Good. I think we're rollin'.

Suddenly Mak was stuck by a frightening thought.

—Look, I don't want you guys drinkin' durin' the gig. We don't allow that.

Candy began chuckling.

—I don't drink, Mak and Colette's too young to drink. I thought I told you she's only nineteen.

Mak's red face visibly blanched pale.

—She's what? Nineteen?

—Yeah. She'll be okay. She's with me.

Speaking as if Colette was not standing right in front of him, Mak said.

—Well then she's not allowed in the bar area at all. She'll have to stay backstage at all times. If we get Tommy busted, that would be the end of our giggin' here, and we can't have that. You'll have to keep her backstage at all times.

Candy laughed at him.

—Everything will be fine, Mak. Don't you have something better to do?

Mak ran back up the stairs, sweating profusely.

Billy Dreier rocked a mix tape through the speaker mains of old Stones, ska and new wave hits by Joe Jackson, Elvis Costello and others—as the Ids removed their gear from the stage with great haste. Mick Noyes, the Unreal Gods' new stage manager and monitor man, arranged everyone's equipment precisely, having earlier marked each location on the platform with neon duct tape.

Mak came back down the stairs.

—Are you guys ready?

Candy sighed

—Yes, Mak. We're ready.

He carefully led them up the stairs to their positions in the cages, and helped them in. The two large cubicles, four-foot square and seven-feet high, were enclosed in a cell of tall, white doweling, connected at the top by inter-locking two-by-fours. They were mounted atop two-foot-tall platforms, located at either side of the stage, draped with black felt covers, that were to be removed when the musical cue came.

Fashioning a giant megaphone, Mick held on to one end of a long piece of corrugated plastic piping, hanging it over Billy's mic, while Mak unwound the other end to far off-stage. Mission completed, Mak ran back to the green room to change clothes—donning a white tuxedo jacket, black bow tie and black slacks.

The stage lights darkened, with only single spotlights trained on each of the felt-draped cubicles. In the wings, the band gathered. Gib wore his customary black dress shirt and gray slacks, with dark brown cowboy boots. For the event, he was wearing a bit of mascara and his cheeks were slightly rouged.

Daw wore a sleeveless powder blue t-shirt, jeans and white gym shoes. He had modest makeup applied to his eyes, and his long brown hair had been fluffed in ornate curls. He methodically twirled his drumsticks like two flaming batons.

As if windblown, Gilly's dyed midnight-black hair swept around the front of his head. With heavy eye makeup, blue eye shadow and intense rouge, he was dressed completely in black, perfectly appointed with a long dark purple scarf. His floppy black velvet boots gave him the look of a transvestite elf—only heightened by his impervious grin.

Col looked like a star. His hair was teased and sprayed high above his head. He was cosmetic perfection: every aspect of his eyes and face expertly turned out. He wore around his neck a black and white Arab keffiyeh. A black Levi jacket and skin-tight black jeans were offset with studded black leather wristbands. An array of chains and several silk scarves were neatly threaded though the belt-loops of his jeans. His pants were tucked into black-velvet, chain-adorned cowboy boots, offset with red and blue bandanas tied to each calf. He looked the consummate rocker.

Clearing his throat, Mak began intonating, from thirty feet away, through the far end of the plastic tubing, into Billy's vocal microphone onstage. His voice sounded as if it were coming from far away, down a long hallway. The great and powerful Mak.

—Ladies and gentlemen, for the first time anywhere on the planet earth...or in the known universe...Billy Granger and the Unreal Gods and the Goddesses A Go-Go.

In the dark, the band took their places and began the intro to their first song. At last, Billy appeared in the wings, his light blond hair held in place with a red skiers headband. He was heavily made up. Thick mascara, heavy blue eye shadow and intense rouge gave him the look of some strange, cross-dressing puppet.

He wore his customary gold and black leopard-skin top, tied off at the waist, two leopard-skin wristbands' black leotards and his favorite red cowboy boots. A single gold bandana was tied as an accent to his right boot.

Mick handed him his blond-brown Stratocaster, and Billy scooted and skanked onto the stage, knees crooked, head bobbing. Suddenly the lights went up and the band exploded into the first verse, their blue and yellow striped color scheme given a 3-D effect from the shifting colors.

As Billy stepped up to the mic, the black felt slipped from the cubicles at each side of the stage, exposing two white-trimmed cages, a go-go dancer in each. They both wore white leather mini-skirts with swaying fringe and knee-high, white, patent leather boots. They began to rhythmically Cool Jerk in time to the music.

Col's tremolo guitar wobbled expertly as Gilly, with a cherubic grin plastered on his face, manipulated his synth, creating tinkly sounds and rushing swoops. Daw accented every fourth beat with a shotgun blast snare/tom smack. Over a hard driving chord progression, Billy began to sing.

—Go-go boots are coming back
Don't throw yours away
Go-go boots are coming back
And they'll be here to stay
And mini-skirts are coming too
And they blow men away
Go-go boots are coming back
No don't throw yours away.

The audience rushed the stage, suffocatingly squeezed together at Billy's feet, as he shifted from side to side in a skating motion. The males in the audience cocked and craned their heads at the dancers in an attempt to look up the their skirts, a tactic for which Candy and Colette were discreetly prepared. Candy had seen it all at the Mocambo Club. She knew how guys were, and she had warned Colette.

—The girls in all the fashion mags
Making all the scenes
The other girls are wearing rags

Livin' off their dreams
Come and see Vanity Fair
It really is a scream
There's so much beauty everywhere
Their fingernails are clean.

Searching the room for Carrie, Billy finally spied her standing uneasily at the side of the stage nearest the bar, nursing a Greyhound that one of her girlfriends at school told her about. It was rumored at school that grapefruit juice contained enzymes that helped one to lose weight. Despite the fact that she was slender as a colt, she always worried about her weight, a vestige of childhood issues.

Billy caught Carrie's eye and smiled at her, somewhat bashfully. She smiled back, watching him move on stage—extroverted and talkative—almost a completely different person from the one she knew. The Billy she knew was quiet and contemplative, if a bit full of himself.

—My go-go boots are made for walking
And that's just what they'll do
One of these days these days these go-go boots
A gonna walk all over you

Go-go boots're coming back
Go-go boots're coming back.
Go-go boots're coming back
Go-go boots're coming back.

Gilly manipulated his keyboard to sound like a semi-truck rolling down a highway, as the song wound down. The crowd responded with overt glee, shouting and cheering wildly. Two girls jumped on the stage and tried to smother Billy with hugs and kisses, but Mick caught them in full stride and deposited them off the stage and into the teeming multitude.

Before the mob could quiet down, Billy shouted into the mic.

—It's called a *Boom Chuck Rock* now.

The horde began screaming and shrieking. Col snapped into a hyper upstroke reggae-ish theme on his black Stratocaster, with Gilly accenting the alternate beats with a ringing Farfisa-like sound on his synth. As the band turned the corner on the opening riff, a hint of old-fashioned rock and roll crept into the ska arrangement.

—Well it's Boom Chuck a rock
And it's a rockin' sound
You hear it in the country
And in every town
They call it Boom Chuck
And it's the Boom Chuck sound
The Boom Chuck rock
It's the only kind of rock around.

The dance floor was a pool of quicksand. Coiled snakes leapt and hurtled from the quagmire, into the air. Candy and Colette hopped and shimmied in time to the music, their cages swaying improbably from side to side. The tassels on their skirts whirled hypnotically. Not a trace of fear crossed their faces. No situation could ruffle their sleek feathers. They were ready for the show.

—Yeah, let's go boys
Oh yeah yeah yeah, let's go old women
Oh yeah yeah yeah, let's go boys
The Boom Chuck-a rock is the only kind of rock I know.

Finishing her drink, Carrie left her glass at the bar and turned toward the entryway, where the restrooms were located, bracing herself against the twisted thicket of drunken high humanity in the opposite direction of the flow.

In the crowd to Billy's right, he saw a familiar head of curly red hair, parting the crowd in the direction of the stage. It was Trudy. She made her way to the front of the stage, laying a dozen red roses at Billy's feet. Wincingly, Billy smiled and continued singing.

—Boom Chuck-a music ain't no heavy sound
Boom Chuck-a music, it's the up and down
The call it Boom Chuck
It's just the Boom Chuck go
The Boom Chuck-a rock
It's the only kind of rock I know.

Without hesitation, Trudy pulled down the scooped bodice of her black blouse, exposing her breasts to Billy. He tried hard not to pay attention, but he could not help himself. Trudy's tongue traced a familiar path around her lips. Billy became distracted, transfixed, but fought his urges and continued singing. He saw Incomparable John Dailey standing near Trudy. Billy allowed his concentration to drift toward Incomparable John, as he sang.

—Well the Boom Chuck-a rocker he's a one-man band
Go Boom Chuck chuck, you Boom Chuck man
He never stops a boomin', always chuckin' around
'Cuz the Boom Chuck rocker
Wants to Boom Chuck-a rock around 6the clock around.

Incomparable John smiled with glee at hearing himself referred to in song— even if the rest in attendance knew nothing of the allusion. Trudy noticed Billy's attention wander and became nervous as to how she could win it back. Short of taking off all her clothes, she had no ideas.

The band finished up the song, and Mick and Mak opened the doors to the cages, whereupon the two go-go girls skipped back stage. The males in the audience groaned in disappointment, but the general hysteria in the room remained heightened.

They swerved into "Rockabilly Queen," a vaguely rockabilly number, as Carrie returned to her perch at the far left of Billy's view of the stage, another Greyhound in her hand. Upon seeing her, Billy began to have a sick feeling in the pit of his stomach, unsure as to how he would keep her and Trudy from becoming entangled. His band's first gig was not the situation in which he had hoped to reconcile his former and current lovers.

—Rockabilly Queen she got you
But she won't get me
I'm spoken for.

Three deep in impatient patrons, Tommy Demeola was behind the bar, trying to help his staff keep up with orders. Jim Finity hunched near the waitresses' station, nursing a beer. Incomparable John Dailey wandered by, belting out a Mexicali cackle to no one in particular, but adding to the crazed atmosphere in the room.

Billy kept an eye on Carrie, watching her closely to see if she had observed that there was another woman trying to capture his attention. Trudy noticed and followed his gaze toward Carrie. Comparing herself to the slim, pretty girl with tawny-blond hair, standing at the other side of the dance floor, she felt a jealous rage wash over her.

The keening crowd, packed far in excess of the house limit, expanded and compressed as if it were breathing a single breath, though there was actually very little actual oxygen left in the room The Unreal Gods had already proven themselves to be far and away much better than the Malchicks.

The Malchicks were a band of boys, who played cover songs and screwed around on stage. The Unreal Gods were pros, controlling every aspect of their performance—building their momentum. The band had measured up to their advance press. The Unreal Gods were coming. And they had arrived, in a big way.

The band swung into one of their more dramatic numbers, "Psylocybin Doll Faced Child," building in intensity as they moved to bring the set to a close. Billy placed a sense of drama to the song, singing about a mushroom trip he took, while watching television at Carrie's apartment.

Carrie had known that he had taken something, but she was not sure what it was. He did not seem particularly freaked out, so she didn't worry about him. She figured that as long as she was with him, he could not get too far from earth. Together, they watched a video tape of *Logan's Run*.

Gilly Walker produced interstellar fills on the synth, as Col DuQuesne power-chorded his way through the stirring verses. Gib and Daw were tightly wound, producing an undercurrent of rhythm that sounded like a single low reverberating heartbeat, punching and throbbing at an accelerated pace. The audience began tripping to the song, swirling in a contact high.

Because it was a Tuesday, Carrie could not stay for the entire set. She had an eight o'clock class in the morning. She gulped down the last of her drink, and waved daintily at Billy, as he lifted his head in acknowledgement. Dropping her glass off at the bar, she made her way through the crush, out into the warm, sweet air of almost summer.

She could not help but notice a 1969 Red Ford Mustang parked in the space directly in front of the club. She mused as to how it was that the hot cars were always afforded the best parking opportunities, as she made her way to her own car, three blocks away.

The Unreal Gods finished their final song of the evening, spotlights flashing wild, strobe-like, before going abruptly dark. The band left the stage to towel themselves off, before returning for the customary encore.

While the unruly pack whooped and howled, Mak and Mick guided the go-go girls back to their places, having earlier draped the black velvet covers over the cages again. Trudy peeked over to where Carrie had been standing and noticed she was gone. Her eyes remained trained to the spot, hoping that Carrie would not return. Then she could have Billy all to herself. Just like the good old days.

Suddenly the lights went up and the band retook the stage to a tumultuous response. Col DuQuesne began "Symmetry" with a rapid ska upstroke, a little rock riff decorating the turns in the progression. Billy imitated a prancing Mick Jagger dance, hopping and skipping. His arms were extended in front of him, as if running in slow motion. He puckered his lips in insouciant smooches; his guitar slung behind him like a six-string backpack.

Just as Billy stepped to the mic, the black felt covers were again pulled from the cages to expose Colette and Candy, imitating Billy's Jagger moves.

—I need some symmetry symmetry symmetry
In my play in my play in my play
I want it perfect in my theater now perfect in my theater
I need some symmetry in my play.

Billy squared his thumbs and forefingers like a director framing a crucial film shot.

—And when I'm walking with you by my side
I want it perfect now perfect now perfect now
I need some symmetry in my play in my play in my play in my play
Hoo hah.

Col Duquesne whipped into a fiery solo, as Trudy, satisfied that Carrie would not be returning to her spot at the other end of the stage, flashed Billy again. Billy snickered good-naturedly.

—'Cuz I'm watching the best show
That I ever seen
But the leading Bozo
Drives a real Boraxo team.

The human swarm was packed together tightly, abuzz in nervous hive agitation. Trudy gave her full attention to Billy. She performed her own go-go dance just for him. He was not indifferent to her efforts. He watched her out of the corner of his eye.

—I want the two notes that I play on my guitar
To be perfect now, perfect now, perfect now
Watch me now. Hoo-ha.

With that, Billy massaged the fretboard of his guitar, coaxing a moaning note, bending the string up and down until it writhed—like the mob in front of him. Trudy undulated with the note, her body wriggling and squirming beneath the urgent motion of his finger on the string.

—'Cuz he's watching the best show
That he's ever seen
But the leading actress
She's crying tears that he can't see
She needs some symmetry...

The stage lights again blacked-out in an instant, leaving the pack on the dance floor in a furious frenzy. Without hesitation, the band left the stage, as Mick and Mak again escorted Colette and Candy down from their cages. Billy Dreier brought the break tape up in the mains and despite the requisite demands from the audience for just one more, the stomping and the chanting, the band was gone. The evening had been a complete success.

Backstage, the band and their frenetic delegation of newly devoted camp followers fired up joints and guzzled beers and liquor. With the switchblade he produced from the back pocket of his jeans, Dealer Walt cut a dozen long lines of snowy coke onto a large mirror from the "dressing table" and, along with a rolled up dollar bill, passed it around to the band members, as the gathered contingent watched on enviously.

Snorting two lines, an immediate rush nearly bowled Billy over. He felt his head begin to swim in a jubilant surging reverie. Taking a deep hit from one of the joints being passed around, he drew a long swig of beer. His body was drenched in sweat.

Colette was somewhat taken aback by what she saw. She had not been around drugs much—especially not in the quantities to which she was being exposed backstage.

Looking around the room, Billy saw many familiar faces. Incomparable John Dailey was there, hooting and chortling, lighting up a succession of thumb-sized joints. Denny was in the corner, nursing a bottle of Jack Daniels—mumbling and slurring. Bam Bam was there, attempting (and failing) to include himself among the inner circle.

Disheveled and perspiring, Trudy appeared, looking entirely ravaged from the

81

excitement of the band's performance. Mak, Mick and Billy Dreier joined the party, adding to the escalating merriment. But there were many people that Billy did not recognize. They were laughing and shouting wuthered in the secretion of adrenaline in the room.

The mirror came around again and Billy snorted another two lines of coke—his nose and throat suddenly growing thick and numb. He could barely speak. He peeled off his leopardskin blouse, briskly toweled himself off and threw on a dry, gray PSU sweatshirt; still wearing his black leotards and red cowboy boots.

—I'm goin' out to talk to Tommy.

Alerted to possible business transactions in the offing, Mak took one last, long hit from one of the joints being passed around and followed Billy out of the dressing room.

Tommy Demeola was totaling up the night's bar receipts as two barmaids bussed racks of dirty glasses to a little room behind the bar, where a sink and two dishwashers sat.

—So, hey, Billy. Pretty good night we had here.

Tommy tossed a banded roll of bills to Mak.

—That oughta make you guys happy. There's over four grand there. I guess ya' won't be doin' any more Tuesdays. You broke the bar record, too. We did almost twelve thousand at the bar. That's a record, by a long shot.

Billy beamed, proudly.

—I told ya' we needed a weekend.

—Yeh, yeh. I know what ya' told me, but I hadda find out for myself, y'know? You proved yourselves. That was a great show tonight. And it seemed like you were payin' attention to that little discussion we had over at Long Goodbye that night.

Billy nodded silently. As Mak began to thumb through the wild wad of cash, Billy grabbed his hand.

—Hey, don't do that, man. Don't be countin' the money in public. You either do that in the office or wherever, or wait until you get home. Tommy wouldn't screw us anyway, so you don't need to count any money he gives us.

Shamed, Mak jammed the cash in his coat pocket. Billy turned to Tommy.

—He's new. Hasn't learned all the ropes yet.

—It's okay. I know how it goes. Anyway, you guys did great tonight and we'll get you back in for a weekend as soon as you want. I got openin's next month. So let me know.

Tommy slapped Billy on the back and went back to finish running the numbers from the cash register. Billy and Mak began to walk back to the dressing room.

—Hey, Mak. I'm gonna want you to do somethin' you're not gonna wanna do. But I want ya' to clear all the goddamned hanger-ons out of the fuckin' dressing room. You know, our personal friends and guys like Denny and Bam Bam. They can stay. Trudy. Even Dealer Walt. But all those people none of us know, they gotta go, and we can't be havin' that going on backstage again.

Mak began to protest.

—But I...

—No, it's okay. It's not your fault. This is our first gig and all. But if we don't know who they are, they gotta get out. It's just like a Bowie concert. If they don't have a backstage pass, they don't get backstage, and it's gonna be your job to make sure that's how it goes. On second thought, maybe a few chicks, if they're really cute...

As Billy eyed him askance, the manager nodded. He understood. He had a serious look on his face. Billy knew he could count on him. Mak had the guts to do the things he didn't want to do himself. They stepped back downstairs to the dressing room and Mak got after it, clearing the small room of anyone not closely affiliated with the band.

Grabbing his jeans, Billy stepped behind a screen in one corner of the dressing room to change out of his leotards. He took off his red cowboy boots, pulled off the sopping wet garments, slipped on his pants and put his boots back on.

As he reappeared from behind the screen, he saw Trudy staring at him with a look he had seen many times before. Temptingly raising an eyebrow, she massaged her chest in a slow, sensual motion. Unsure how to proceed, Billy knew what Trudy wanted, but he felt obligated to his relationship with Carrie. He was in a bind, but he was too high to really give anything much serious deliberation.

—Can I give you a ride home, Billy?

Locking Trudy in with cool, squinting eyes, Billy nodded slowly. He threw his stage clothes into his gym bag and got up to leave. As they were climbing the steps out of the dressing room, Incomparable John bellowed.

—Hey, Billy. I'm going to paraglide off of Crown Point tomorrow at eleven. You really ought to be there to see that.

Billy laughed.

—*Paraglide*? Shit. I wouldn't miss that for the world. I'll be there. I'll be there.

Trudy led Billy out to her red Mustang, parked directly in front of the club. She unlocked the passenger side door and he slipped into the seat. With animal urgency she moved to the driver's side, sliding in behind the steering wheel.

She leaned over and kissed Billy hard, her lips and tongue moving in a familiar manner. She placed her hand on his thigh.

—Do you want to take the short way home or the long way home?

—The long way, I guess. That'd be okay.

Starting up the car, Trudy pulled away from the parking spot.

She drove them up Burnside turning left on 23rd, heading south and up toward Washington Park. She circled around the lower gardens a couple of times before parking just above the reservoir, near the path where the old zoo railway used to run. They each clicked their seats back, reclining as far as they would go.

Trudy wasted no time in unzipping Billy's fly. As she leaned toward him, he snaked his hand under her blouse and began fondling her breasts, toying with her nipples. They kissed passionately. With abandon, Trudy moved her tongue around in Billy's mouth.

—Long time, no see, big boy.

Billy said nothing, but proceeded to move his hand under her skirt, his fingers tracing a slow path up her thigh. Trudy moaned softly, flicking her tongue in his ear. He placed his fingers on the fleshy opening and found it moist and slick; inserting two fingers and moving them in a steady, repetitive motion—as if he were massaging the two strings on his guitar.

Reaching her hand inside Billy's jeans Trudy began to purposefully stroke his cock in a way that was entirely familiar to him. She knew what to do. He continued fingering Trudy, as her breathing became rapid and heavy. Within only a few moments she cried out, continuing to caress Billy's cock with indefatigable determination.

After a brief respite, she moved her head down to Billy's cock and let her lips slowly slide around it, moving up and down with expert conviction, her tongue slipping and gliding around the shaft. Without warning, he suddenly came in her mouth, hardly making a sound. It was almost as if he were performing a duty, rather than an act of love or pleasure.

Trudy raised up her head and smiled hazily, and then kissed him again, very hard and very fervently. He could taste himself in her mouth, but he did not respond to her kisses. It was as if he were in a trance. After a few minutes, he noiselessly readjusted his pants and zipped them up and shifted his seat upright. Trudy was still breathing heavily, reclined in her seat, staring out the windshield at the stars. Billy broke the silence

—Well, I guess we better get goin'. I need to get home.

Trudy looked at him with an odd expression on her face, feeling no passion from him, just an authoritative coolness. She replied curtly, trying not to sound upset.

—Yeah, we better get going.

Raising her seat upright and smoothing out her skirt and blouse, she fired up the Mustang and maneuvered down the hill from Washington Park, cutting over to Salmon at Southwest 21st Avenue.

As Trudy guided the car down Salmon, Billy was silent, until they passed 10th Avenue. He said, matter-of-factly.

—I'll just get out here, you don't have to take me home.

Trudy looked at him, a terrible, hurt expression on her face.

—Here? What's here?

—Oh, I just wanna walk the rest of the way.

She pulled over to the curb. He opened the passenger door, and hopped out with great alacrity.

—Well, I guess I'll see ya' then.

—Yeah right...

She sneered.

—*See ya'*

He slammed the door shut behind him and Trudy sped off—tires squealing, leaving a patch of burnt rubber in the street. Billy watched her peel out and sighed. He didn't feel good about their escapade. In fact, he felt nothing at all. He walked the short distance over to Carrie's place on Jefferson Street, ringing her apartment. After a while, she buzzed him into the building.

He gently tapped at her door, and she let him in. She was wearing her pajamas and fluffy pink slippers.

—I didn't know you were coming over. I have a class at eight tomorrow—or this morning, or whatever it is. What time is it?

—I'm not sure. Probably two or three.

Billy grabbed Carrie and hugged her close to him. He kissed her hard. But she protested.

—You smell funny.

He kissed her again.

—You taste funny too. You taste like booze and pot and something else. What is that taste? Sweat and something else, too. Musk or something.

Billy innocently shrugged his shoulders. But Carrie saw a faint look of guilt trace across his face.

—Why do you look guilty? What did you do? Where have you been, anyway?

Mumbling unintelligibly, he tried to hug her and kiss her again, but she pushed him away.

—You taste like *you*. That's what it is. How could you taste like you? You taste like somebody else, too. Have you been kissing somebody else tonight?

Billy turned red with shame, but he said nothing.

—You've been kissing someone else. What else have you been doing? Did you have sex with someone else?

He shook his head, but he was not very convincing.

—You had sex with someone else!

—Well, it wasn't sex exactly.

—It either was or it wasn't, Billy. Which was it?

—Well...

—I can't believe you. We've been together six months. I thought we were a couple, an item or whatever. How could you? Who was it? No forget it. I don't want to know.

—It was an old girlfriend. She sort of kidnapped me.

—Right. She sort of kidnapped you. You were powerless to escape. I don't believe it. I don't believe you could do this. Why would you put our relationship in jeopardy, Billy? Don't you care?

Overcome with remorse, he sighed.

—Of course, I care. It just happened. That's all. It just happened.

—How would you like it if it *happened* the other way around? How would you feel? What if I had an *affair* with someone else? You would be hurt.

He hung his head.

—Well, I'm hurt. I'm broken-hearted. You told me you needed my help. Is that how you treat someone who tries to help you? Is it really all about you and what you want and when you want it?

Carrie was furious.

—No it's not like that. It's…

—It's what, Billy? It's what? Is this the sort of thing you meant when you said you couldn't help me, that you were too busy *trying to be famous*, or whatever you said. Is it really all about you?

She whimpered.

—Well, if that's how it is, you can get the hell out of here. Go on home! I don't want to see you.

Billy looked shocked. No female had ever said that to him.

—But I love you…

—Love me?

She mocked him.

—Love me? I don't think you even know the meaning of the word. Do you love anyone or anything besides yourself? I think you should leave.

Opening her apartment door, Carrie motioned him toward the hallway. As he walked out the door, he said uneasily.

—I'll call you tomorrow.

—No, Billy. Don't. Don't call me. Don't come over. Just leave me alone. Maybe you'd be happier with that other girl—whatever her name is.

With that, she closed the door in his face.

He slowly walked the mile or so back to the band house. It was warm outside and the first rays of dawn light were beginning to appear over Mount Hood in the distance. The sky in the east was turning a vivid shade of red. He felt ashamed and confused and disappointed with himself. As he walked he began to sing a song softly to himself.

—I'm walking down a rocky road for you. It's all that you have left me to…

# IX

Later that morning, when Billy and Billy Dreier drove up in the van, a small crowd of about fifteen or twenty people was already gathering in the parking lot at Crown Point. Incomparable John Dailey was dressed in a white jumpsuit, checked the blue and white striped paraglider spread out on the pavement, carefully inspecting the rigging.

As they approached, Incomparable John smiled cunningly at Billy.

—Oh, so you made it! I thought maybe you'd be sleeping in today. It looked like you had a long night ahead of ya'.

—Uh, it was a long night. But not like you think.

—No, eh? Well, I'm a little shocked. But I guess you can't win 'em all.

Smiling half-heartedly, Billy bobbed his head in agreement.

—Well, it's a perfect day for gliding. A nice, light breeze—but no gusts.

Acknowledging the idyllic Oregon blue-sky day, Billy said.

—Yeah. It's a perfect day alright.

Incomparble John grabbed the paraglider and tramped up the steps to the Crown Point rotunda. He quickly slipped on the harness around his shoulders and thighs and double-checked every connection. He climbed up the small wall at the far side of the rotunda and steadied himself with skilled self-assurance. He smiled and said with a hint of sarcasm.

—You know, Billy, your luck can only hold out for so long. You shouldn't take things for granted. That Carrie's a real cool girl. Maybe she deserves better than you. Maybe you're too self-centered for someone who wants to be a nurse or whatever.

The small crowd scrutinized Billy, attempting to ascertain his complicity, and wondering if Incomparable John was about to commit suicide. Incomparable John strutted back and forth atop the wall, desiring to be the center of attention. Even though the jump he was about to undertake was relatively simple by his standards, Incomparable John milked his moment for all he could.

—Well, here I go folks. It's not too late to stop me. Give my love to Donna and Jilly. I will all my belongings to Billy. He'll know what to do with the stuff. I want to donate my body to science.

88

A County Parks official, who was working inside the Crown Point facility, rushed toward the gathering and hollered.

—Hey. Hey! You can't do that. It's against the law to jump here. Hang gliding off the Point is totally illegal!

Suddenly, without notice, Incomparable John unfurled the silk wing of his paraglider and lightly leapt off the wall into the soft warm breath of the sun, high above the Columbia River gorge. The glider immediately filled with air as Incomparable John, crowing maniacally, briefly hovered at eye level, about thirty feet out in front his audience. Then a thermal updraft caught him and he began to soar above the rotunda and parking lot—a vantage point from which he could see several County Sheriff patrol cars arriving onto the scene of the crime.

Incomparable John cheerfully circumnavigated the congregation as one of the county cops broadcast through a loudspeaker for him to come back down. He was violating the law. The audience clapped and cheered as the Sheriff deputies returned to their cars, trying to determine where Incomparable John intended to land.

Incomparable John put the craft though a series of maneuvers, arcing and twirling, spinning and looping—showing-off as only he knew how to do. Finally, he aimed the wing away from the cliff, and sailed out high above the freeway, moving in the general direction of Rooster Rock State Park, a few miles to the west, north of Highway 84.

The contingent of onlookers quickly ran to their cars. Billy D. and Billy were first out of the parking lot. They were followed by about five or six other cars, and, bringing up the rear, were three County Sheriff cars, their lights and sirens blaring.

The group quickly descended from the Crown Point, down the scenic highway, toward Lewis State Park—on the south side of Highway 84, across from Rooster Rock—where it had been agreed upon in advance that Incomparable John would land his craft.

As the excited party arrived at Lewis Park, there were already two State Police cars parked in the lot, waiting. Incomparable John lazily circled in for a landing, but after catching sight of the awaiting troopers, he took off again, across Highway 84 toward Rooster Rock. The state cops and county mounties swiftly raced after him, but there was no easy way to get over to Rooster Rock by car from their location. They had to drive east several miles up the highway all the way to Multnomah Falls before they could turn around and head west toward Rooster Rock. The entourage gleefully followed.

Incomparable John flew directly to Rooster Rock Park and circled the area, looking for an opportune spot to land. He decided to put down on the nude beach at the west end of the grounds. Landing on the beach, he quickly slipped off his glider rigging, swiftly spooling the sail into a ball. He then peeled off his jump suit and rolled it up. Finally, he slipped out of shoes, brown jeans and black tee shirt and stood completely naked on the shore.

After grabbing three joints and his lighter from his shirt pocket, he then stashed the incriminating bundles in a crevice in the cove among the river-worn boulders. He covered the evidence with a few grapefruit-sized rocks and several handfuls of sand. Then he turned and walked back toward the beach, where he laid down among several other sunbathers, supporting himself on his elbows.

He fired up one of the joints and took a long hit, offering it to anyone around him who was interested. There were several takers. After that joint was exhausted, Incomparable John lit a second, taking several powerful drags on it before passing it on. He then pushed the third joint and his lighter into the sand next to him. He laid his head back on his hands and stared up at the blue sky, smiling happily to himself, satisfied with his accomplishment. The other bathers were somewhat stunned, attempting to fathom the man from the sky who got them high.

It was at least twenty minutes before the cops showed up. They came down to the beach and started questioning the bathers, their nude reflections glaring brightly off the officers' mirror sunglasses. The patrolmen asked each person, if they had seen some guy on a glider flying around.

Softened by Incomparable John's righteous weed and friendly demeanor, all of the bathers shook their heads no. They had seen nothing of the sort. A state patrolman, dressed in dark blue, including a short military style jacket—considerably overdressed, given the milieu—stood directly in front of Incomparable John, blocking his view of the river.

—How about you? Did you see a guy on a hang glider fly by here?

Screwing up his face, Incomparable John feigned ignorance. As if he had never heard of such a thing. Hang glider? No (a paraglider, perhaps). The officer glowered at him for several moments. The fellow did seem to resemble, somewhat, the character he had seen fly over Lewis Park, but he couldn't be certain. And Incomparable John appeared to have nothing in his possession or about his person that they could search for evidence.

Regrouping, the cops wandered around the sandy beach and into the cove, but they found nothing out of the ordinary. Frustrated, they left the nude beach. After checking the opposite side of Rooster Rock—the less popular side—the police gave up and returned to their cars. They drove off at accelerated speeds, as if they had somewhere to go—but in fact, their haste was from maddened aggravation at not apprehending the malefactor.

As the law stormed away, the support team finally arrived. They hopped out of their separate vehicles and ran toward the nude beach to see what they could find out. Seeing the cops leave without him, they feared that Incomparable John had perhaps gotten lost, or worse, to have possibly drowned.

Billy was the first to arrive at the beach from the parking lot. He immediately spotted Incomparable John, lying in the sun, smoking a big spliff.

—Ah, grasshopper. At last, you arrive. You have a worried look on your face. Did you doubt your master's ability to outwit the mindless constabulary? I fly through their nets like an invisible butterfly. Sting like a butterfly, float like a bee.

He handed the joint to Billy as the others arrived, all feeling a bit awkward wearing clothes. Billy took the joint and shook his head in disbelief at his mentor's exploits. What a guy.

On the trip home, in Billy Dreier's van, Billy suggested to Billy D. that the time had come for the band to record an album. Billy Dreier replied.

—Jeez, Billy, the band's only been together, like what, six weeks or so? And you've only played one gig.

—Yeah, but we're ready. I know we are. We have all the songs down. Besides, by the time we get into the studio, we'll have, uh, like, thirty or forty more to choose from. Easy. I'm workin' on tons of new stuff, and we should have it all down in the next couple months. Plenty of gigs to get 'em down. I'm figurin' September we'll go in.

—Man, do you realize how much money that's gonna cost? Probably, like, ten thousand. Minimum. Maybe more. Maybe a lot more. Where're we gonna get that kind of money?

—We'll get it. We'll get it from giggin'. I'll take out loans. Whatever it takes. We're gonna be big. The world's waitin' for us to show up. We've *got* to do this. What's important is the recording. We've gotta do it.

Billy D. shook his head in disbelief. But he had no doubt that Billy would get what he wanted. He always did.

Billy stared out the windshield of the van—envisioning the future he was certain lay just ahead. It was a bright future, full of promise. And it was right there in front of him.

Not more than a couple of weeks later, Billy and Daw were sitting in the waiting room of the office of Rexford Fellows, Attorney-at-Law. The office of Rexford Fellows was located downtown, on the third floor of the Corbett building, a popular home for prominent law and accounting firms. It was well appointed, looking like the sort of place in which a successful attorney would work.

Daw and Billy entered the room as Mister Fellows shuffled important piles of paper into smaller piles on his big cherry-wood desk. As they came in, he looked over the top of his glasses in their direction.

Billy thought that Mister Fellows resembled an older version of John Candy, one of his favorites. He was overweight with wild sandy-colored hair, bristly thick and flecked with gray. He had big lips and a smirking smile. Mister Fellows motioned toward two chairs opposite his and they sat—awaiting interrogation. He asked, somewhat sarcastically.

—So Dawson, what is it that I can do for you today?

—Dad, this Billy Granger. He's the guy I told you about. He's the leader of our band.

—Yes. Yes. The Surreal Lords?

—Dad. The *Unreal Gods.*

Billy stood up, extending his hand.

—Mister Fellows. It's a pleasure to meet you. I'm Billy Granger.

—And so you are.

Mister Fellows quickly sized up the young man. He determined that Billy appeared to be of decent breeding and that he carried himself well. He seemed to have manners—somewhat impressive for a musician.

—Then what is it that I can do for the Unreal Gods today?

Daw started to speak, but Billy, still standing, took over the conversation.

—We're here to ask you for a loan, Mister Fellows.

—Please. Call me Rex.

—We're here to ask you for a loan, Rex.

Shifting his weight in the chair Mister Fellows scratched at the side of his cheek.

—A loan? What would your band do with a loan from me?

—We want to record an album of our original material and we don't have all the money together to do that, just yet.

—Well, I don't know.

Unfazed, Billy continued.

—Our band is one of the top bands in town. We make a lot of money from our shows. But we have a lot of overhead. We have ten people on the payroll. Manager. Roadies. Dancers. We could come up with the money ourselves within the next year, but I would like to record right away. While the iron's hot.

—Yes. While the iron is hot. That's important, I suppose. What would you do with this album, once you have it recorded?

Billy looked directly into Mister Fellows' dark brown eyes and answered forthrightly.

—Well, first of all, we'd sell it. To get some of the money back. But I want to send it to the major record labels. I think we could get a recording contract from one of them.

—You'll have to explain to me. Why would you record and produce an album in order tó secure a *recording* contract?

Billy understood that the concept of how the music business worked was difficult for outsiders to comprehend, even an attorney. He had the same difficulty explaining it to his mother.

—Well, we need a lot bigger budget than what we can put together. If we can get ten or twenty thousand dollars, we can record a good-sounding demo album that might attract a major label. A professional, big-league album that you see in the stores, that may cost a hundred thousand dollars. Maybe two hundred thousand.

Mister Fellows arched his eyebrows at the figures that Billy was tossing out.

—I see. Tell me. What is a *demo*? And why does it cost so much to produce a professional sounding album?

—The deal is, Rex, the whole band would have to go down to LA or to New York to record the album. That's where all the good studios are. Those studios cost hundreds of dollars an hour. We'd, or uh, the label would have to hire a major league producer. Producers don't come cheap. The label would pick up the cost for all that and a place for us to stay and for the production and promotion of the album after it was recorded. They'd make sure it got distributed to all the record stores in the country. They'd make sure that it got played on the radio.

Mister Fellows was confused.

—I don't understand. Can't you record that sort of album in Portland?

—Ya' see, there's only one decent studio in town. That's High Tech. That's where Dollarshine recorded their demo. Jack Barnes, the guy who runs the place, he's a good engineer. He can make sure we sound as good as we can. But a producer has input into the songs. Sort of a vision, I guess. Arrangements.

Shifting his weight uncomfortably in his chair, Billy spoke frankly.

—And to tell you the truth, Rex, Jack's studio can't really compete with the LA and New York studios. There's a reason why all the pros record in them, and sound the way they do.

Mister Fellows nodded, appreciating the complexity of the whole affair. He artfully directed the conversation back to the topic at hand.

—And as for the production and promotion you spoke of?

—That's it. Besides recording time, ten or twenty thousand dollars, it'll cost us another five thousand to get the album made, the covers printed up and all that. And none of us know how to promote an album to the national press or radio. We'd either have to hire someone or just try to do it on our own.

Mister Fellows was beginning to understand the financial gravity of what the boys were requesting.

—So how much money are you asking from me?

Billy looked over at Daw, who had been sitting silently though the whole conversation.

—Well, Dad. We were thinking of a loan of about ten thousand dollars.

Billy jumped in.

—We can match that, so we'd have a budget of twenty thousand dollars to get everything done. That's flying on the cheap. But I think we can cut corners by recording live in the studio.

—Is there any other way to record an album, Mister Granger? You certainly can't record an album dead.

—No. No. But there's a lot of overdubbing and sweetening that usually goes on—adding layers over layers on extra tracks. That's what makes albums sound professional. Lots of layers.

—Okay, so you would record live in the studio and that will save money.

—Yeah. And Jack said he'd give us a deal if we booked a block of studio time. We'll probably need four weeks, maybe five. He said he'd do a hundred dollars an hour. Eight hours a day. Forty hours a week. Four weeks. That's eight, twelve thousand...sixteen thousand. We can get the whole project in for around twenty thousand, maybe a little more, if we keep up a good pace.

Mister Fellows was impressed that Billy had done his homework and had all his facts and figures together. It did not seem that they were trying to get the money for some wild weekend at the coast.

—Okay then, say I lend you this money. What could I expect to get out of it?

—We'd give you twenty percent.

—And how soon would you pay me off? That's twelve thousand dollars.

—We'd pay you a thousand a month, every month, next year, startin' in January. If we get signed to a deal, which I know we will, we'll just pay you the whole she-bang at once.

Feeling somewhat reassured, Mister Fellows thoughtfully replied.

—Alright then. I suppose I could enter into this. But we would have to draw up a contract, of course.

Billy became excited.

—Of course. That's how we work. A contract, for sure. That'll make it all legal.

—Yes. Legal. That's how I work, too.

Billy and Daw proudly left the office with a check for ten thousand dollars in hand. Although their first impulse was to throw a big celebratory party back at the band house, they knew they'd need every penny if they were going to make the project work.

Back at the band house, Billy Dreier shook his head incredulously.

—You guys got ten thousand bucks out of Rex? How the hell did you do that? Hold a gun to his head?

A little put out, Billy replied.

—No, D. I just laid it all out for him. What we needed and how much it would cost, and we drew up a contract, and he gave us a check.

—Are you going to pay him any interest?

—Yeah. Two thousand dollars. A thousand a month for all of next year.

Billy Dreier whistled loudly and blew one of his long blond bangs up above his head..

—Whoo. That's a lot of cash.

—Well, we're gettin' three thousand pressed. If we sell a thousand albums for twelve dollars each, that'll pay him off. And we'll still have two thousand left to repay the band and send copies out to all the press and record companies. We can do it. I know we can.

—You're the boss, Billy. I hope you're right.

Billy had been trying all week to get a hold of Carrie on the phone. But she wouldn't pick up. All he got was her answering machine.

—Hi, I can't come to the phone right now, but if you leave your name and number, I'll call you back as soon as I can.

—Carrie, uh, hi. It's Billy again. I really want to talk to you. I want to tell you how sorry I am. I never meant to hurt you, but I know I did. I know I was, uh, selfish, and I was only thinkin' of myself. I was weak, and I know you need me to be strong, just like I need you to be strong. I've learned something this week.

He hesitated for a moment, then continued.

—We're gonna record an album. Daw's dad is lendin' us the money. I gave him a sales pitch and he drew up a contract. So we're gonna to do it. I want to see you. I miss you so much. I...

The phone beeped the end of his message. Billy called her number in order to continue his one-sided conversation.

—Hi, I can't come to the phone right now, but if you leave your name and number I'll call you back as soon as I can.

Hi. It's me again. I wanted to tell you I love you and that I don't want to be without you and...

—Hello?

—Carrie?

—Yes, I'm here. I heard your last message. Congratulations on making a record. I know how important that is to you.

She was cool and distant.

—Well, yeah, Carrie. That's important to me. But not as important to me as you are. You're my whole world. None of this means anything if you're not here to share it with me. I need you.

—Are you sure, Billy? Are you really sure? I don't want to be jacked around anymore. If you want to be free, if you don't want a committed relationship, then fine. We'll go our separate ways.

—Baby, I've learned my lesson. I don't want anybody besides you. I never have. Not a day, not a minute since last December, when we met at the John Lennon memorial at Schrunk Plaza.

—I feel the same way about you sweetheart, but...

—No. No buts. That's all I need to hear. I've made a lot of mistakes. And I have a lot to make up to you for what I've done. I owe you.

—Oh, you don't owe me anything. I just want you to be sure about what you're doing. We have to be able to trust each other. Without trust, our relationship means nothing.

Billy shamefully replied.

—I know. I know you're right. I know you have to be able to trust me. I already trust you, baby. I'm the one who has to clean up his act.

The phone grew quiet.

—Carrie? Carrie are you still there?

She was crying.

—Yes Billy, I'm here.

—I'm sorry I made you cry. I don't ever want to do that again.

# X

The next gig the band was to play was a return engagement at Luis' La Bamba club. They determined that they wanted to charge seven dollars a head at the door—an unheard of sum—nearly double what any other band charged. Tommy Demeola had scheduled them to play the second weekend in July, both Friday and Saturday nights. Mak Poppin was in the club, one afternoon, with Billy at his side, arguing the necessity of charging such an exorbitant amount at the door.

—We got ten mouths to feed, Tommy. And we got time in the studio booked for September. People will pay whatever we tell 'em they hafta pay to see our shows. Especially at this club. It's the coolest place around.

Flattered, Tommy momentarily forgot his train of thought. Then he tugged himself back to reality.

—Ya' don't understand, Poppy. We're competin' with every other club in town for the customer's dollar. I took a big risk on you guys last month when I let ya' charge five at the door. I know that worked out okay, but people're gonna be reachin' their limit here. We're headin' into a recession. People don't have that kinda money to be throwin' around.

Billy jumped in to the discussion.

—Tommy, man, our people will pay whatever we, like, tell 'em to pay. They know we're the coolest thing goin'. Everybody wants to see us. They'll pay seven at the door.

—I wish I had your confidence. I'm takin' a big enough chance givin' ya' both nights of the weekend. If both nights suck, I'm in some deep shit. Ya' know?

Billy countered.

—We know. Look, if your bar receipts aren't what they were last time we played here, we'll make up the difference from our take at the door.

Mak looked at Billy.

—But Billy, we need that money if we're gonna make that record.

—I know we need it. But I know we can make more at the door than we did last time. I think we can pull in, like, ten grand over the two nights. Easy. That would make the recording thing a lot smoother.

Mak nodded solemnly. Tommy was not so sure.

—I think yer makin' a big mistake, Billy. Yer a new band, ya' don't have a loyal following, yet. Mostly it's a buncha people wantin' to know what the big deal is. If ya' charge too much, they're just gonna go check out somebody else.

—Then they'll be missin' the best show in town. And next time they'll come to see us, even if we charge *ten* bucks at the door.

Reluctantly, Tommy conceded that the band was going to charge whatever they wanted to charge. His ass was covered by Billy's promise. He gave in.

—Okay, man. It's yer funeral. I'm not gonna try 'n' talk ya' out of it. Okay. Seven bucks a head. But I sure hope yer right about this.

—I'm right about it, Tommy. Don't you worry about a thing.

The band took in nearly eleven thousand dollars over that July weekend. In addition to the recording money, the take helped to pay for new equipment for all the members, as well as a quarter ounce of coke—a substance of which the band had become enormously fond. They also bought an ounce of Incomparable John Dailey's killer bud. When all was said and done, they had a little over a thousand dollars to put toward the recording.

Still, it was a good summer for the group. They were invited to play prestigious gigs as the opening performers for several national acts—Stray Cats at Euphoria and Bow Wow Wow at La Bamba. With every performance, the troupe garnered increasing attention and another tier of fans, rabidly willing to pay any price to be among hip local music aficionados. The Unreal Gods could, indeed, name their own price, and fans would still come through the door.

As the summer began to draw to a close, the recording date arrived. It was late August and it was very hot. The band had no upcoming gigs booked, as they were prepared to spend all of September in the studio recording their album.

But they ended up spending not only all of September in the studio, but most of October, too. Billy had written more than fifty songs for the project and all were possibilities for inclusion on the finished album. They had rehearsed all the songs dutifully, because they could not choose the final ten that would be selected for the finished product. Thus, they recorded all fifty as well.

Having run so much longer than expected, they greatly exceeded their budget. In order to complete the undertaking, Jack Barnes the owner of High Tech Recorders, gave them the studio time in exchange for ten percent of the sales returns.

Ever the perfectionist, Jack recorded every track with dogged determination. He was truly the best engineer in Portland and, doubtless, the only person who could give the band the professional sheen they were seeking. Although he was not getting paid nearly the full amount for the studio time the band had used, he realized he had a stake in the action, which only heightened the intensity of his perseverance.

Billy narrowed down to twenty songs the list of possibilities to be included on the finished album. When the final mix on those twenty was completed, he arrived at the final ten songs. The band crowded into the engineer's booth to hear the chosen tracks in the order they would be heard on the album.

They all were incredibly impressed with the finished product. And they were very pleased with themselves and their individual performances. They also complimented Jack Barnes for the great sound he had captured. It sounded totally pro. But Jack protested.

—Billy, man, ten songs is too many. You'll crowd the grooves on the album. It won't sound as good as if you only lay down eight or nine. You'll lose fidelity. It won't sound like it does in here.

—I understand that, Jack. But we have to give people their money's worth. I don't wanna cheat the customers.

Jack looked at the others for some sort of support, but they all agreed with Billy. Col said.

—If Billy says ten songs, then ten songs is what we'll put on the album. We'll have the master. If the album does well, we can make, like, a *multi*-record set or somethin' later and get all the other songs on there too.

—That master is mine until you guys pay me off. You realize that don't you?

The band was a little taken aback by Jack's bluntness, but they understood the deal they had made with him. Col replied.

—Yeah, okay, we get the picture. We'll pay you off, don't worry.

Billy agreed.

—We're not gonna have any problem sellin' the first three thousand copies. Well, maybe twenty-seven hundred. We need to give a lot of 'em away to the press and radio and such. But twenty-seven hundred is still twenty-seven thousand dollars or so when they're all sold.

Daw fretted.

—Don't forget my dad, Billy. We've got twelve thousand we need to pay him for the loan.

—We've got all next year to pay him back, Daw. Don't worry. How much more do you figure we owe you for the time we used?

Jack Barnes quickly jotted down a series of figures on a sheet of paper.

—Well, you owe me another eleven-five for recording and mixing. And if you sell twenty-seven hundred for twenty-seven thousand, you'll owe me twenty-seven hundred. And, like we agreed on, we're good for the first ten thousand copies sold. So if you do a re-press, I'll get ten percent of that too.

The band members had not fully considered the amount of money they had guaranteed Jack for his time and expertise. The impact of the deal they had made with him started to sink in. It was beginning to dawn on them that he was a pretty shrewd guy.

They were going to pay him almost twenty-three-thousand dollars for the whole recording process—and then they would owe him a buck on every album they sold, up to ten thousand copies. He was going to make more out of the album than they were.

And they still had the mastering and pressing to pay for, before they would even have the finished product in hand. That was going to cost another five grand. The Unreal Gods were broke.

They quickly scheduled a couple weekends at La Bamba and a single gig at Euphoria. Euphoria was a great gaping converted meatpacking warehouse, situated near the Willamette River on the inner eastside, between the Morrison and Burnside bridges.

The club was set amid a stand of warehouses and storage vaults that were deserted at night. Railroad tracks scuttled past, embedded in the street in front of the massive building. The club, with a capacity of around five or six hundred, had the acoustics and ambience of a concrete cattle arena.

The band cleared nearly ten thousand dollars from that single performance at Euphoria. Mak thought there should have been more. But the Gods were able to acquire the necessary cash to replenish their coffers and to finance the mastering and pressing of the album.

With apparently no audible imperfections, the master tape was quickly approved. The album was to be delivered within three weeks from Bob at Northwestern. Just in time for Christmas. Because of the uncertainty in their recording schedule, Mak did not book any shows until the middle of November, blowing off Halloween, even though it fell on a Saturday.

During the down time, Billy decided he would take his share of the gate from the La Bamba and Euphoria gigs and travel with Carrie to England for two weeks. It was an impulsive move, but not unlike him. The rest of the members stayed behind at the band house waiting for the major label interest to arise.

England did not offer the warm reception that Billy had expected. He thought the nation would embrace a budding American star. Instead, he was met with suspicion and derision. He and Carrie enjoyed traveling the countryside, even visiting Liverpool. But London had no interest in him.

He played a cassette of the new album for many musicians in London—and was roundly ridiculed for the poppy lightness of his band's sound. The Unreal Gods were not the Clash. They were more like Adam and the Ants. And for that, Billy received no respect at all—only mockery and scorn. Tosspot. Poofter. He was discouraged, but his resolve became more strong.

The day after the couple returned from the UK, Billy D. delivered the finished albums from Northwestern. He and Mick unloaded sixty boxes of records from the van. Once inside the house, the boxes took up most of the living room—astonishing the band members. It had never occurred to any of them just how much space three thousand albums would take up.

Annie Fisher was a known doer and shaker within the Portland music scene. She was freckled and plain looking, reed thin, with wiry blond hair. She did little to make herself attractive to the opposite sex. However, that did not dissuade her from pursuing every eligible male in every band that caught her fancy. At the time, she was tracking Billy Granger and the Unreal Gods, even though all of the members of the band were more-or-less spoken for. Mak and Billy D. were available, but they were of no interest to her.

Annie desperately wanted to manage the Unreal Gods on a national level. She had good connections on the circuit from her many years working at Double-Z: the agency that booked most of the national rock acts into Portland venues. She tried every way she knew to insinuate her way into the Gods' inner circle, dangling opening gigs with major acts and assuring them that there were more where that came from. It was through Annie that the band got the Stray Cats gig at Euphoria.

In attempting to prove herself, Annie found many occasions for the band to serve as openers for national acts. The Bow Wow Wow show and Adam and the Ants soon followed. Annie got them their first Seattle gig, opening for John Cale. But as badly as she wanted to manage the band, Billy would hear nothing of it. Mak was the band's manager, come whatever.

However, Annie was not easily discouraged. She found an opportunity for the band to open for Peter Tosh at the Paramount the following March. The Unreal Gods had never played in a venue that large or prestigious—and all were rightly impressed. Not so much with Annie, as with the stature in playing the Paramount. Billy, especially, was excited about the prospect of opening for one of the reggae greats. Peter Tosh.

## XI

Eric "H.E." Carus had been a writer in the Portland music scene for two years. He wrote for Loose Screws—the best known music publication in the area. Owing to the fact that Eric's sister was close friends with his wife, Cindy, Jack Barnes was familiar with H.E., as a writer for Loose Screws. Jack was rightfully proud of the work he had done for bands in the Portland area. And he invited Eric down to the studio to hear the just finished mix of Billy Granger and the Unreal Gods' new record—*Boom Chuck Rock Now!*

Loving a scoop, Eric was quick to agree to head down to High Tech Recorders to audition the album. He was very much impressed and wrote glowingly of the album in his review.

*Here I am, under the phones. It's Billy and the Unreals' new LP Boom Chuck Rock Now! Not bad, eh? Well keep listening. Yeah it was done over at High Tech Recorders. Wha'? Oh yeah. Sorry about the yelling. I forgot I had these things on. But yeah, isn't it just the way you expected their record to sound? Isn't it perfect now? You think the guys are going to be kicking around this backwater burg with this making the rounds in LA? Wha'd'ya think is the thing Billy saw he never saw before in his girlfriend's drawers?*

*OK. OK. So who really is the leading Bozo that drives a real Boraxo team?*

*Do you realize how much talent this guy has? He's the Elvis man, the absolute Elvis. Hell, besides sounding like Elvis and himself, too, he alternately sounds like Paul Mc, David Bowie, Tom Petty, Lou Reed or the Mick. Who does he think he is anyway? It's weird but "Symmetry" sounds like David Bowie fronting Wings with Ringo on drums, around the Venus and Mars period. And "Upstroke Down" sounds like Lou R., David B. and Joe Jackson from around his Look Sharp days.*

*Gilly's synth work is really effective, wouldn't you say? Simple, understated, but spot on. He's alternately a guitar, a sax section, steel drums, a cello or, hey, even a piano. And he's in the mix real subtly. In fact, I like Jack Barnes' mix in every way. He does Billy's voice real justice. Caught Billy's and Col's guitars real nicely. He doesn't overdo the panning, like most of these local jokers do. And Gilly is always right there in the background, off whistling in the distance like a lonesome train.*

*Like on "Rocky Road." God, I love that song. See, I've got it figured out. It's a rewrite of "I Walk The Line." He's got all the railroad imagery going. Sing in a low register, then an octave higher, just like Johnny Cash does. Col's guitar's got a real country thunk going on. But the main thing is that Billy is a dead ringer for Mick in the verses, early Mick, "Tell Me You're Coming Back To Me" Mick. And then, just like Petty on the choruses. You think the big guys down South'll see similarities in Billy and Col and Mick and Keith twenty years ago?*

*"Uptown" is a nice vehicle for Stryker's bass: doing that little Motown shuffle thang. Meanwhile, that vintage vibrato gives the guitars a real '60s sound. And Billy sounds like Lou Reed in lots of places too, wouldn't you say? You know, I don't think it's a rip to sound like someone else, as long as you've got some of yourself in there, too. Billy's definitely got plenty of himself,*

*"English Boy" reminds me of the current Who. Gilly's prancing synth line is well organized and proficient. I hope the boys realize this is a hit single. Col's power chords really muscle the song in a rock direction. And I love the take off the Unreals do of the Beatles doing the Beach Boys: 'The Soho girls really drive me wild...' And Col's little "I Feel Fine" riff at the end. Nice touch. The guys really pay honest homage to their influences. And they do it really well.*

*"Something New" gets back to the band's ska roots, with a great Stone's sound ala "19ᵗʰ Nervous Breakdown" layered on the top—with Dawson Fellows' hypnotic, Watts-like drumming. It's that Boom Chuck accent on the second and fourth beats. It's on every song. Boom chuck rock, you boom chuck band."*

H.E. Carus was not the only critic to laud the band he was simply the first. He reviewed the album before it was released, even as a promotional recording. All through the winter months, the Unreal Gods' album was the talk of the town. As had been the band's plan, *Boom Chuck Rock Now!* hit the stores a couple weeks before Christmas.

For New Year's Eve, the Unreal Gods were placed on a bill at Euphoria with Dollarshine, whose debut album was a national hit. The Unreals were to open the evening, with Dollarshine taking the stage in time for the traditional New Year's countdown.

Jim Finity had just finished playing a solo acoustic gig at PC&S tavern and he was excited to see the Unreal Gods in the big room of Euphoria. He was not looking so forward to seeing Dollarshine. His perception was that his old high-school friends, Merv and Mindy Moss, had become distant in the years leading to their success—as if he were no longer an equal, but somehow beneath them in station.

This struck Jim as particularly odd as they had all shared a house in college, less than ten years earlier and had been very close for so long. But he had come to accept his new position in their lives, and, though saddened by the damages success could sometimes impose upon the lives of old friends, he had moved on with his life. And all the same he had more interest in seeing Billy and the Unreal Gods than he did Merv and Mindy anyway.

Upon entering the huge riverside warehouse that was Euphoria, Jim was amazed to see the room packed with at least seven hundred in attendance. They were young and drunk, coked up and strung out. Billy was in the midst of singing "Coca Cola," his ode to the real thing *Coke*—in all its various permutations. Jim felt ill at ease. Success had changed the band, since the previous summer when he had last seen them. In that time, their fan base had doubled and re-doubled, attendance at their shows growing consistently.

The recent release of their album had only intensified their popularity. In Portland, the Unreal Gods were becoming an unlikely household name. They could do no wrong. They were number one in Portland. No other band could touch them—not even Dollarshine.

To Jim, the Gods seemed to be taking their success for granted, acting differently than they had in the beginning. Arrogant. Somehow entitled. All of the band members seemed to have a certain cocky haughtiness about them. Billy was shaking cans of beer and squirting them into the gaping maws of Col and Daw, as well as into the open mouths of the writhing bodies below him.

Billy hated Euphoria. He was convinced, not without reason, that the club manager, Bob Shore, and his assistant, Jonathan Dixon, as well as the door men and many of the staff, were ripping off a piece of the admission to Gods' shows and the shows of other bands as well. There had long been a rumor among local musicians about Euphoria.

On New Year's Eve, almost to spite the club, Billy ran around the stage like a divine bad boy satyr reigning at a pagan ritual rite celebrating decadence and excess. His shirt was off. He was drenched in sweat. And he was taking the band's performance to the point of the absurd.

But, over the months, the crowd had changed too. As the band got more fried out on success and its trappings, the audience was frying too. Coke-addled and moneyed kids with cash to burn and their brains in flames. Immolating. To Jim, the up and down merriment of the Unreal Gods seemed calculated and a sham. They had become caricatures of themselves: grooved-out rock guys.

The hour was getting late, drifting toward midnight. Dollarshine should have been setting up their equipment. But Billy showed no signs of being aware of the time, nor indicated any intention of yielding the stage. He had created a near-riot of debauchery—drunkenly urging the smashed mob with a phony Jamaican accent.

—Potty to the rasta vibration that is within us all. Do you all feel the rasta potty vibration?

The herd screamed back in the affirmative, with raucous approval.

—Oh, tell your brother and your sister. Tell the person dancing next to you of the joy you are feeling deep inside your soul. It's quivering in your soul—the rasta potty vibration—say yeah!

The throng shrieked in assent.

—Now potty on the floor with your brothers and sisters and feel the rasta vibration.

The swarm on the dance floor collapsed to the ground in a writhing heap. Jim was appalled at the display. It was as if the Malchicks had returned, but had become smug and ugly, rather than just stupid.

The band segued into "Upstroke Down," and all hope that Dollarshine may have had of ringing in the New Year was abandoned. Never even announcing the arrival of the midnight hour, the Unreal Gods did not leave the stage until twelve-thirty—their minions demanding an encore, with rowdy screams and riotous rasping catcalls. The band bowed haphazardly and strode from the stage.

Jim Finity was curious, indeed, to see how the headliners would comport themselves. Instead of leaving after the Unreal Gods' set, as he had planned, he decided to stick around for a while and watch the carnage.

By the time Dollarshine finally did take the stage, the sweating mass of music lovers was worn out. And despite the fact that they were national stars, the band was unable to attain the fever pitch the Unreal Gods had established. They simply were not the same sort of act. They were slick and polished and not terribly accessible.

They were a listener's band, not a partier's band. After five or six songs, the crowd began to thin out. By the end of their set, only sporadic huddles of diehard Dollarshine fans remained, the Unreals' contingent having long before departed to find their party elsewhere. Jim felt embarrassed for his old friends. He slipped out of Euphoria, certain Merv and Mindy had not seen him in the audience, even as sparse as it had become. At that point, they probably would have welcomed his familiar face.

Backstage, after the show, Billy tried to strike up a good-natured conversation with Merv Moss. Billy wanted to bring up the Madison High School connection. But, as Billy approached, Merv merely scowled at him.

It was at that very moment that a sodden Denny arrived backstage, with a bottle of champagne in one hand and a cute little drunken blond girl in the other.

—Merv Moss!

Denny slurred.

—Fugkin' Merv Moss. I can't believe it. Fugkin' millionaire *Merv Moss*. Fugkin' Merv Moss. Fugkin' king of Dollarfugkinshine. How the fugk are ya', Merv? Written any fugkin' hit songs lately? Hey Merv, has ennybuddy ever tol' ya' yer band sucks the big green weenie? Has ennybuddy ever tol' ya' that, Merv?

Billy, who tended to have a similar propensity for not being able to tell when he was pissing someone off, could tell his brother was pissing off Merv Moss and the other members of Dollarshine. Billy was embarrassed for Denny, as much as by him. He tried to guide his brother away, but Denny wanted to talk to Merv some more. Billy shoved Denny out of the dressing room.

—Denny, what are you back here for? Just to cause trouble?

—I wanna inner duce ya' t' m' l'il fren' here. Her name is...wha' the fugk is yer name?

Denny looked at the blond, a confused look on his face.

—I tol' yuh, it's Blue. Can't you remmemmer anything?

—Oh yeah. Blue, you good dog you.

Reaching around beneath her arm he squeezed her breast roughly, and she swatted his hand away. Denny continued.

—Yeah, Billy, I wanned da innerduce ol' Blue here to my famous rock star brother. Famous rock star brother, this is Blue. Blue, this is my famous rock star brother. Say hi to Blue, rock star Bro'. Maybe it'll get me laid.

Billy just stared in disbelief at his brother. Denny's appearance had a sobering effect on Billy.

—Billy, don' be a rude boy now, say hi to my fren' ol' Blue.

Billy sighed.

—Hi, Blue. How are ya'?

Blue made an attempt to tell Billy how much she loved his band, but Denny kept singing snatches of Gods' songs, while trying to fondle her tits and ass. Finally, sensing that she might be more interested in his brother than him, Denny dragged the girl from the backstage area. Billy swiftly packed up his guitar and left the club, as quickly as possible. As he walked out into the cold winter night, a light snow began to fall from the starless sky.

Shortly after the holidays, *Boom Chuck Rock Now!* sold out and the band was obliged to re-press another three thousand copies, which, after Jack Barnes had been paid off (including his percentage of sales), took nearly all of the money they had made on the first pressing. But, more than making money for themselves, the goal had always been to impress the moneymen in LA.

If they were to sell ten thousand copies, a magic number of sorts, the record executives in Los Angeles would sit up and take notice. The Gods wanted a major label record deal. They were as good as the popular bands on MTV and they knew it.

A week and a day later, at Mak Poppin's behest, Jim Finity attended a party at Carrie's apartment, though Carrie was not to be found. In the kitchen, where the keg was, Jim stood chatting with Billy. Adjacent to the kitchen was the bathroom—which seemed to be the hub of activity, for some reason.

From out of nowhere, Bam Bam appeared, and intentionally interrupted the conversation. Bam Bam, absent from most Unreal Gods functions, had managed somehow to invite himself to that party. And he had his eye on Jim. And he was giving off all kinds of bad vibes. Jim became acutely aware that Bam Bam wanted to prevent him from obtaining something from Billy—like a dog that might guard another dog with a bone, fighting for its place in line. Jim was naïve as to what was going on.

Bam Bam informed Jim how important he had been to Billy's career, how much he had done for Billy, and all the money he had made. Jim did not notice that, at several points, Billy slipped away into the bathroom with a number of other people. It eventually dawned on Jim that Billy was off snorting coke.

At one point, after Billy had returned to the conversation, sniffing and clearing his sinuses, Jim said to him.

—Billy, man, I think you're great. I think your band is great. You're going to make it, I can feel that about you. I hope you'll be a great leader.

Billy looked at Jim, somewhat puzzled, as if he had never before given consideration to the fact that he might become a *role model*. Billy replied.

—Well Jim, I listen to what you say, because I know when you talk that it's from the heart.

Then Billy excused himself and returned to the bathroom. Bam Bam resumed his dissertation, as Jim tried to figure out how to get out of the mess. During a momentary lapse in Bam Bam's monologue, he saw Mak Poppin in the living room and walked over to him, quickly engaging in small talk and other innocuous time wasters, merely to keep from having to listen to Bam Bam for another minute.

Later, as the party began to break up, Jim left Carrie's apartment and headed for his car. As he walked down the sidewalk, he saw Billy getting into the back seat of a new BMW. He yelled.

—Hey, Billy.

Seeing Jim, Billy paused and shouted back.

—Hey, Jim, it was nice talkin' to ya.'

—Yeah, you too, Billy.

As Billy slipped into the car Jim called behind.

—Billy!

Billy looked up, the driver of the car gunning the engine impatiently.

—Watch out for the fringe benefits!

108

Jim wasn't sure if Billy had heard him. The car sped away with a toot of the horn.

The following Monday, the band began to prepare for the Peter Tosh show at the Paramount. They were tremendously excited at the prospect, rehearsing diligently. Billy was a taskmaster. He wanted everything to be perfect. Symmetry in his play. The leading Bozo of a real Boraxo team.

# XII

About two months later, as he showered, getting ready to head over to Carrie's, Billy noticed a strange lump under his left arm—about the size of a golf ball. He hadn't noticed it before. It seemed to have appeared overnight.

He had been feeling a pain in his groin for quite some time, but ignored it, thinking it was just a reaction to all the coke and booze. A chill washed over his body, but he did his best to put it out of his mind. Determining that he must have injured himself, strained something lugging his guitar or amp up and down the basement stairs at the house, he reckoned all would be well in a couple of days.

That evening, at Carrie's apartment, Billy disguised the lump as best he could, wearing a loose fitting work shirt and relying upon his right arm to hug her and hold her. Later, in bed, he hid the lump by lying on his left side and holding her close to his right. Even as they made love, Billy kept his left arm tucked close to his body, forcing Carrie to keep her arms on his shoulders or hips. She noticed nothing out of the ordinary.

But within the next few days, the lump had tripled in size and the pain in his groin had only gotten worse. He began to feel pangs of nausea and fatigue. Something was wrong and it was not getting better. He knew he would have to tell Carrie about it. When he did, she registered unrestrained alarm—counseling him as to the severity of his symptoms.

The next day, after consulting with some of her teachers at PSU, she made an appointment for Billy with an oncological specialist, recommended by the head of the nursing department. Billy was reluctant to go, hoping that the whole situation would just go away, but he knew that it would not, and he resigned himself to getting everything checked out.

At Providence Hospital, he underwent numerous tests, which included a battery of blood workups, x-rays, a biopsy on the lump in his armpit, and other tests on his right testicle.

The head of the oncology department, Doctor Morton Todd, visited with Billy and Carrie. Doctor Todd was a solemn looking man, middle aged, with wispy black hair. He had a prominent skull beneath his brow, deep-set eyes—watery, of no color—aquiline features. He was tall and slender, gaunt and pale. He had cold, delicate hands, which he clasped, as if to sing an aria. His nails were ivory white.

Wearing a dull, gray lab coat, the physician seemed detached, obsessed with his work, dispassionate, clinical, but direct and forthright. Speaking in a slow, soft monotone, Doctor Todd delivered the shocking news that the lump under Billy's arm was a malignant lymphatic tumor. What's more, the cancer had spread to many of the surrounding lymph glands and nodes. And his right testicle would have to be removed. Surgery would be imperative and necessary immediately. He was grim, glum and mordantly seductive.

Doctor Todd's prognosis was not encouraging. Billy suffered from MCL—Mantle Cell Lymphoma—a particular type of cancer usually found in older men, in their fifties and sixties. Billy had an acutely virulent form of the disease and surgery was required without delay. Todd was pinch-faced, but he did offer some hope that if they were able to remove all of the cancerous glands and nodes chances were good that Billy could recover. He cautioned that, in addition to surgery, Billy might have to undergo chemotherapy—but that they would know more after the surgery. Billy asked.

—So is this terminal, Doctor Todd? Or do you think I can I beat it?

—You know, Mister Granger—in medicine, all cases are eventually terminal.

He smiled a large, rectangular grin that resembled a skull and cross bones. Billy refused to believe the doctor's diagnosis.

Doctor Todd sent Billy home. Surgery was to be performed in three days. On the way to Carrie's apartment, both he and she were silent—staring out the car windows at some distant abstract image. Carrie spoke first.

—Of course today would be the Ides of March. That seems perfect for the situation.

Billy had heard the term.

—What is the Ides of March anyway?

—Oh, it's from the old Roman calendar. It refers to the fifteenth day of the month. Back then they had a different way of counting the days of the month. But what we call the fifteenth of March—or any month for that matter—was called the Ides by the Romans.

Billy was looking at her, completely confused as to where she was going

—In Shakespeare's *Julius Caesar*, a fortune-teller tells Julius Caesar to 'beware the Ides of March' and it turns out that Caesar ended up getting murdered on that day. So, it sort of means a bad luck day.

Billy stroked his chin with his thumb and forefinger.

—So you think this is a bad luck day?

—Well, I wouldn't call it a good luck day. Would you? But it's okay, we can make it through this, too.

111

—You're damn right we can. I've got too many things to do to kick off now. I've got you and the band and music and everything else that I have to work out. It's too soon for me to die.

Carrie gravely scowled at the utterance of the word.

—It's okay, baby. Don't worry. We'll just have to be strong. I'm probably gonna have to lean on you for a while. But I'll bounce back. Just watch.

—I know, I know. If anyone can make it through all this, it's you. But it's all so scary.

—I'm not scared. It's just a bump in the road. Or a *lump* in the road, maybe. But it's nothin' to worry about. And besides, we've got the Peter Tosh show next week.

Staring at Billy in disbelief, Carrie shook her head slowly, not completely understanding what he was telling her. He smoothed her hair with his hand, pained in his armpit at the motion. Carrie laughed, still shaking her head.

—You're something else, Billy. You really are something else.

—Yeah. I'm somethin' else. They threw away the mold when they made me.

Carrie smiled.

Later that evening, Billy called Mak at the band house and told him about the situation. Mak became silent at the news. Billy tried to calm his friend's trepidation. Mak advised.

—Billy, man, we'll have to, like, cancel the Tosh show.

—No. It's alright, Poppy. We're gonna play that gig at the Paramount.

—That's totally fuckin' crazy.

—Maybe so, but if I live through the operation, we're gonna play that gig.

—Yeah, right. That's, like, a week from Wednesday! You're an amazing guy, Billy, but even you ain't superman.

—No, maybe not. But I've got things to do. And one of them is playin' that gig, so you better tell the other guys to rehearse and be ready, because I'll be comin' out smokin.'

—Okay, Billy. Okay. Whatever you say.

Billy chuckled.

—Sorry, Poppy. You're not gettin' rid of me that easy. I'm gonna be around for a long time—just to torture you.

—So what do I tell Tommy? And Bob and Jonathan? We're gonna have to cancel some shows, even if you do manage to play the Tosh show, which I don't see how that's possible. You'll be down for a month or so, no matter what.

—Don't tell 'em anything. Make somethin' up. I don't want it gettin' around town I've got cancer. The majors might get wind of it and decide they don't want to give us a contract. I'll be back to normal in no time. Don't worry.

The night before his surgery, he lay in bed next to Carrie, dreaming.

Coach Newman: corny motivational. Lean bat, flip ball—*Gentlemen, not say life. Do.* Newman hit ball—fly high to left. *Life guys. Just a fly ball sky. Don't know land, fairfoul. What do, land you fair. Work hard, fly clear fence a four-bagger.*

Billy awoke in a bewildered state, sweating profusely. He did not understand the meaning of the dream. He swung his arm around Carrie and went back to sleep. He would not remember it when he woke up.

The next morning, he was operated upon.

As Billy was being cut open, Mak Poppin had the unenviable task of canceling the Unreal Gods' gigs at La Bamba and Euphoria. When he called Tommy the Falcon was beside himself.

—Mak. Yer pullin' the rug out from under me at the last minute. What's tha deal? It better be a death in the family. That's about the only excuse I'm takin' on this. Who'm I supposed to get in here on two week's notice? Nobody who can fill the room. That's fer sure.

—Tommy, man.

—I think maybe you guys are gettin' too fuckin' big for yer britches. Where's the gig?

—What gig, Tommy?

—The gig you're throwin' me over for...where is it? They must be payin' you guys a lot to fuck me up. Maybe yer forgettin', I'm the guy who hooked up the Malchicks in the old days at the Long Goodbye. I gave Billy's band their first gig. I thought we sort of had a partnership goin'.

—Tommy, man, you don't understand. It's not like that.

—How is it then, Mak? How is it? What the fuck's goin' on?

—A band member's sick, Tommy.

—Band member's sick? Two weeks in advance? Man they must be pretty fuckin' sick, man. Pretty fuckin' sick.

—It's bad, Tommy. Real bad. Billy's got cancer. He's gettin' operated on right now.

—Cancer? Are you fuckin' shittin' me? Why didn't ya' just tell me that?

—Billy didn't want me to. He doesn't want it gettin' around town that he's down with cancer. He's afraid it'll screw up the majors being interested in the band. He doesn't...he didn't want anyone to know.

—Well, ya' coulda told me. I won't go spreadin' it around. I know how to keep my mouth shut. You should know that.

—Yeah, Tommy, I know. I'm just doin' what Billy told me to do.

—How bad is it? Is he gonna be okay?

—They're gonna cut him from his shoulder down to his belly button. Plus, they're gonna cut off one of his balls.

—One of his balls? Man, that's tough.

Tommy whistled hard.

—That's real tough. Well, when can I see him? I mean when is he gonna get out? Or when is he gonna be able to have visitors and all that?

—I don't know, Tommy. I just found about this a couple of days ago. I've been tryin' to figure out a way to tell ya', without gettin' ya' pissed off. Billy's gonna be upset when he finds out I told ya'.

—Aw, don't worry about that, Mak. I'll take care of it. I'm sorry I came unglued at ya', but the Gods are my big moneymaker. You know that. A weekend with them, and I make my nut for the whole month. I kinda depend on them for that. Ya' know? Nobody I could hire can make that up.

—I know and I'm sorry, Tommy. I know Billy didn't want to screw things up. He just found out about this a coupla days ago himself. It's not like he's been keepin' it a secret for a long time, or anything. I don't know what we're gonna do. He says he's gonna play the Paramount on Wednesday. But I don't see how he's gonna do that. I think he's crazy. Wishin' on a star—or somethin'.

—Okay then, Mak. Yer secret's good with me. Tell him I hope he pulls through okay and that I'll be up to see him as soon as he can have visitors.

—I'll tell him, Tommy. Thanks.

Mak's call to Jonathan at Euphoria did not go quite as well. When Mak told him that the Gods would have to cancel their gigs at the club, Jonathan irately demanded to know why.

—Jonathan, man, one of the guys in the band is sick. Real sick.

—Well get a fuckin' replacement for him then. There must be a million guys out there who'd love to play with the band.

—This isn't a goddamn basketball team we're talkin' about here, Jonathan. It's a band. You can't just run some guy in and expect the band to be able to give people their money's worth. It doesn't work like that.

—Shit, other bands have done it plenty of times.

—Well, not our band. It doesn't work like that.

—So *whoever* must be pretty fuckin' sick.

—Yeah, real sick, Jonathan.

—What the fuck is going on?

—I can't say, man. I've been told to cancel the gigs. That's all. I had to cancel our dates at La Bamba, too.

—So how'd Tommy take it?

—He was pissed, just like you.

—I'll bet he's fuckin' pissed. That leaves us in deep doo-doo. We're screwed. I hope Billy knows that.

—Oh, he knows it. Don't worry about that. He knows.

—Well, I hope he's not plannin' on playin' here again.

—Jeez, Jonathan. Don't be cuttin' off your nose to spite your face. That's not a very good business move. You know damn well the band would play if they could. We need the money just as fuckin' bad as you do. We've got a lot of bills to pay too.

With that Jonathan relented. He told Mak to tell Billy he was pissed. Then he hung up on the hapless bearer of the bad news. Mak felt like shit, but he had done what Billy told him to do.

A team of surgeons worked to eradicate the cancer from Billy's abdomen. Carving him up on his left side from the armpit down to his groin, they sliced out forty-seven lymph glands, while collapsing his left lung in the process. His right testicle was removed. Carrie did not leave his side throughout his recovery. Sleeping next to him in his hospital bed.

He woke up with no pain, woozy from a morphine infusion he had received post-surgery. His mouth was dry. His tongue was thick and dry; his voice a weak croak.

He tried to talk to Carrie, but he was unable to formulate the words. He was extremely frustrated by the condition. Even in his groggy state, he knew he needed to shape up. He was going to play that Paramount gig. One way or another. And, as he drifted away again on the morphine, he merely smiled beatifically and began to grope Carrie. Then he passed out.

The afternoon of the day after his operation, Billy spoke to Denny by phone. He hailed him feebly

—Hey, Denny, it's Billy, man.

—Hey Bro', how're ya' doin'? Are you okay?

—Yeah, I'm fine. Never felt better.

Denny chuckled.

—Hmm. Well that's good. So, are ya' ready for the Paramount show on Wednesday?

—Oh yeah. I'm playin' that gig. No matter what. Don't worry about that one. I ain't missin' that for the world.

Despite the severe circumstances, Billy felt responsible for Denny. He did his best to put on a brave face to assuage Denny's profound depression.

—Do ya' think that's such a good idea, Bro'? I mean, do ya' really think you're gonna be fuckin' well enough to play? I don't want ya', like, dyin' on stage or anything. Y'know?

Subconsciously, Denny feared that he was murdering his family from within, slowly poisoning them with his bad blood and debauched behavior; his failure to live up to expectations. First he'd killed their father, now he was killing Billy.

—Naw. I'm not gonna die on stage. Don't worry about that either. I feel a lot better than I did. At least I don't feel like I'm gonna heave. I'm just real sore. That's all. I've been worse

Billy lied.

—Okay, man. There's nothin' I can say that'll change your mind. I know that better'n anybody. Y'know?

—It's what you do in life that matters, Denny. And I'm goin' for, like, that long, fair ball.

Denny was entirely perplexed by that statement. And so was Billy, for he did not remember the dream he'd had the night before.

—Okay, Bro'. It's your life. Long, fair ball. Right. Whatever you want. You're the Rock Star.

Later that afternoon, Doctor Todd came into Billy's room and informed him and

Carrie that, although it would seem to be fairly miraculous and too early to really know for certain, nevertheless it appeared that the cancer had been eliminated. They'd gotten it all.

Dr. Todd cautioned that the prognosis would only be borne out over time, but that Billy's white blood cell count had recovered to a level that was highly satisfactory. Very encouraging. Still, only time would tell. Billy smiled knowingly at Carrie. It was that long, fair ball.

Shortly after Doctor Todd left the room, a nurse appeared with a full IV drip bag.

—Time for some more pain medication, Mister Granger. I've got another dose of morphine here for you. It might make you a little loopy, but it will take care of any residual pain you're experiencing.

—No. Nuh-uh. I don't need any medication. I'm not feelin' any pain.

Billy lied. Carrie put her hand on his head and said.

—Sweetheart, you must be having some pain after everything you've been through. Why don't you let the nurse give you something? It'll make you feel better.

—I feel fine, Carrie. Besides, I don't wanna be all doped up for the gig at the Paramount. That morphine really fucks me up. No way.

—You're not still planning on going through with that, are you?

The nurse interrupted.

—Going through with what, may I ask? You have a lot of recuperating to do, Mister Granger. You went through six hours of surgery this morning. You don't recover from that in a couple of days.

—I'll recuperate after Wednesday. But Wednesday, me and my band're playin' the Paramount and nothin's gonna stop me.

Billy sounded determined. The nurse looked horrified.

—But, Mister Granger. You've got to rest. You won't be anywhere near healed by Wednesday. You'd be risking infection or some other severe complication.

—Listen to what she's saying, Billy. She knows what she's talking about. You're not out of the woods yet. Not by a long shot. Don't be so stubborn. Let her give you some pain medicine.

—I'm not gonna let the band down, and I'm not gonna let myself down. I don't want to be all messed up for the show. And I'm playin' it. After that, I'll get all the rest I need. We cancelled all the other gigs for a month after the Paramount, and I'll rest then. But I'm playin' the show on Wednesday, and I'm not gonna be all messed up and cotton-mouthed on morphine for that. No painkillers. No.

117

The nurse indifferently shifted her shoulders and took the bag of morphine from the room. She was confident that Doctor Todd would never let Billy leave the hospital six days after critical major surgery. Doctor Todd would flip out.

Doctor Todd did flip out. But it did not do any good. Billy was going to play the Paramount concert, and he was not going to be talked out of it. Not by the nurse. Not by Doctor Todd. Not by Carrie. Not by anyone.

# XIII

The stately Paramount stood in downtown Portland on Southwest Broadway. It was one of the oldest venues in Portland—originally a vaudeville house, before becoming a movie theater. The ornate filigree trim surrounding the stage and along the flanking walls, gave every impression of some forgotten era.

The theater had become a rock music venue in the late seventies, hosting a wide array of new wave acts—Talking Heads, Elvis Costello and the Attractions, Blondie, as well as innumerable other, lesser known, bands.

The Unreal Gods' dressing room was just next to that of Peter Tosh's group. They could smell right rude rasta blunt smoke wafting in from next door. Good stuff, indeed.

A decent spread of drinks and food had been laid out on a table for them. Probably nothing compared to the Tosh allotment, but far better than that to which they were accustomed in the Portland clubs. They were very impressed. Gilly gushed.

—This is the life, man. It must be great to be the headliners. A lot more space and all the good food and booze. The girls…

Daw agreed.

—Yeah, it's a long way from Euphoria.

Col concurred.

—Dig it. It'll be great when we go out on tour as headliners and we get, like, the big dressing room and all the good hotel rooms. That's what I want. That's what it's all about.

Everyone nodded.

Except for Gib, the band members were dressed in their best stage clothes. Gilly had donned his knee-length black leather SS coat, with black dress slacks and a wing-collared white shirt. His eyes were heavily made-up, thick with mascara. Gib Stryker chose a different tack, dressed in light brown slacks and a bright gold unbuttoned golf shirt, with white vertical stripes.

Daw wore his customary tight jeans and new, white tennis shoes, offset by a powder blue sleeveless t-shirt. His hair, tousled high above his head, was carefully jelled to keep it in place. Garbed in tight jeans, high-top black Converse and a turquoise blue sport shirt, Col had on a blue, jeans jacket, with the sleeves turned up mid-forearm. Several strings of colorful beads adorned his neck and wrists.

Billy was clad in a tie-dye t-shirt tucked into black parachute pants and a thin red belt, set off by white high-top leather gym shoes—a multi-colored, harakiri-style headband holding back his shock of honey-colored hair.

The entourage was squeezed into the green room. Besides the members of the band, Mak, Billy D., Mick, and all the go-go girls were jammed into the space. Colette and Candy got ready in a small restroom in the back of the dressing room..

In addition to the Goddesses, two other go-go girls were added—for better visual appeal on the massive Paramount stage. Jane and Wren were casual friends with Candy, and they anxiously awaited their turns in the restroom.

A color-scheme inspired by the Ethiopian flag—for the rasta Tosh show— Candy and Celeste had decided the dancers would wear snug-fitting sleeveless red, yellow and green striped one-piece polyester tops, yellow hot pants, offset by red nylon tights, with black and yellow striped leggings. Their look was provocatively hot.

The band brought along plenty of their own bud, with the intent to be properly buzzed for a show with Peter Tosh. And they were well on their way toward achieving a righteous rude mood. Billy and Mak conferred quietly in a corner, while the rest of the team nervously chatted—laughing and bellowing—high and excited. Mak asked.

—Billy, are you feelin' okay, man? Are you sure you're not, like, makin' a big mistake doin' this?

—Aw, I feel alright. Just a little sore, that's all. No, mostly I'm frettin' about havin' my right nut cut off.

—Wha'd'ya' mean?

—Well, y' know, I feel like it makes me into some kind of freak or somethin'.

—Hey, Hitler only had one nut, and look how far he got.

Billy smirked.

—Well, I guess that kinda makes me, like, the anti-Hitler.

The two of them chuckled, which broke the tension.

—Look, just don't do anything stupid out there. I don't want to see you makin' all this worse than it already is.

—It's alright, Mak. I'll be fine.

—Well, I hope so. I hope so.

Swinging his arm around Mak's shoulder, Billy gave him a friendly squeeze. Mak recoiled.

—That's not your bad side is it? No, I guess not.

—Mak, man. I'm okay. I'm *okay*.

—Alright, Billy. If you say so.

The audience was still filing in as longtime Portland stalwarts Opopo opened the night—good-naturedly playing their set of strange r&b tinged rock. They received little acknowledgement—but carried on nobly, despite the lack of support.

Van the rubber band man, adroitly maneuvering his thumbs, coaxed a vague saxophone-like sound from his strange "instrument." Paul McCartney look-alike J. Mitchell Kelly was locked in tight with drummer Oily Moon. Opopo were a household name in Portland, but apparently not to Peter Tosh concert-goers.

To a response of little more than silence and loud conversation, Opopo concluded and quickly scurried from the stage: mortified. They were not accustomed to being ignored. The Unreal Gods could hear the dispirited voices of the Opopo members trudging down the hall to their adjacent dressing room. They knew it was their turn on the stage. Ever the apprehensive manager, Mak remarked.

—I hope they're not, like, throwin' us to the lions out there. I'll have some choice words for Annie if this doesn't work.

Billy answered confidently.

—You worry too much, Mak. It'll work. Just keep it together. Everything'll be fine.

—It's my job to worry. I wish I was as optimistic as you, Billy.

Billy merely smiled self-assuredly.

The band took the stage to a round of mild applause from the still-gathering spectators. The members took their positions on the expansive stage, with pairs of go-go girls flanking at either side. They warmed up and casually tuned their instruments, preparing to kick off the set with "Symmetry."

—Good evening, lady and gentlemens, I and I be Billy Granger and we be de Unreal Gods and de Goddesses A Go-*Go*.

A faint stir rippled over the onlookers.

—Here at de wunnuhful Par'moun'. A wan irie likkle place. Lawd have muhseh. We be here to entertain 'fo Peter Tosh be cum out.

Amidst a decided grumble, a much louder cheer went up at the sound of their hero's name.

—This be a little song called 'Symmetry'.

Instantly the Goddesses launched into vigorous gyrations, swimming and ponying with a fierce lack of restraint.

The band played a spirited version of their hit song, the lively ska rhythms pumping energetically. At the conclusion, they were met with half-hearted clapping.

—Tank yuh so much. We be honored to be here wit' de great Petah Tosh. He be a rasta giant of the fust degree. We be here to lively up de potty and to brang you to a righteous rude mood. This one be called 'Upstroke Down'.

And they kicked into another ska-driven number, influenced by Bowie and Joe Jackson.

—Walkin' down the boardwalk San Francisco Bay
All the boys are happy least that's what they say
Why there he goes again over by the record machine
He told me he's Prince Valiant
But I think he's really Valiant's queen
You know—he thought he had it made
When he got his upstroke down
He got his upstroke down
Watch him now.

At the instrumental section, Billy began pogo-ing furiously—forgetting entirely that he had undergone serious surgery only three days before.

—Sitting at a bus stop in downtown LA
So many funky people I don't know what to say
I got a little record, I want to show around
You Hollywood producers, I got the upstroke down.

The band worked intensely, attempting to elicit some sort of reaction from the sober pack. They were unfamiliar with playing to a passive crowd. Billy began to try harder. Bending his knees, he crouched toward the mic.

—Well I've seen the rotten apple
The city of decay
Let me tell you something gorgeous
Don't believe a word they say
You know New York's got the Yankees
The red, white and the blue
And it's a lovely place to live
Aside from a muggin' or two
The mayor said we'll all have it made when
We got our upstroke down
We got our upstroke down la-la
We got our upstroke down
Watch us now.

Col leaned into a tightly constructed riff to conclude the song. They all bowed faintly.

Silence.

—Tank so much kin' peoples. We hope yuh be feelin' de vibration. We be a band of de true rasta vibration, mon. And we be here to potty strong, good brothuhs and sistuhs. This be a song called 'Rasta Rhythm'.

It was during that song that Billy felt distinctly a sense of unease washing over him. The crowd seemed surly and the band sounded far away. His stitches began to hurt. His groin felt sore. Faint traces of sweaty blood began to seep through his tie-dyed shirt.

At the conclusion of "Rasta Rhythm," Billy continued his Jamaican patois.

—Ah de rasta rhythm. Yah, mon. Praise be. Jah de lion be de huntah of de world. Weh yuh honor an respec him. Bring de rasta vibration to all de peoples of de worl. Di wola yuh a me fambly. We nuh dun yet.

Billy turned and counted off the next song—"Black Man"—another reggae shaded number. The crowd began to become unruly, with some people booing and shouting as the band played. Billy thought that, perhaps, the sound system was malfunctioning. He could not understand the audience's bitter reaction.

Once they had finished the song, the Gods were supposed to play two more. But the crowd was so aggressively belligerent toward them Billy decided to end the set immediately—after only twenty minutes.

—No worry, no cry. No bodda bawl, we soon cum bak.

He was met with the sound of hoots and jeers. A beer bottle skipped across the stage, nearly hitting Colette as the girls left the stage. A half-eaten hotdog quickly followed.

Walking past the Peter Tosh contingent in the wings as they exited, the Unreals were met with antagonistic glares and outright animosity. Chagrined, the band moved through and continued backstage. In the green room, Billy wiped his hair with a towel and took a deep breath. Sitting across the room Col stared at him and, horrified, exclaimed.

—Billy, man. Look at your chest. You're, like, all bloody!

Billy looked down to see that his t-shirt was drenched in sweaty blood, the outline of his stitches showing through clearly.

—No big deal. It's mostly just sweat.

—It looks like fuckin' blood to me. Are *you okay*?

—Yeah, yeah, I'm fine. What the fuck happened out there? Those people hated us. And the Tosh bunch looked like they wanted to kill us. What was that shit all about?

Frustrated, the other members gestured haplessly, shaking their heads in disbelief. Gilly offered.

—It was a tough crowd, man.

—They were beyond tough. They were, like, downright hostile. Even with the Malchicks I don't think I ever saw anything like that. I thought we played real good.

Col rejoined.

—Yeah, we were tight. No screw-ups. The girls looked great. I don't get it. I wasn't nervous out there or anything. Nobody else seemed nervous.

The other band members nodded in agreement.

Furious, Mak burst through the door, followed by a dejected Mick and Billy D.

—What the hell were you guys tryin' to do out there?

He looked at Billy.

—We shouldn'ta played the gig tonight after all. What's wrong with you? Are you, like, tryin' to ruin your career?

Mystified, Billy could not fathom.

—What are you talkin' about, Mak? What'd we do?

—You humiliated the Tosh people. They thought you were makin' fun of 'em—the way they talk and their lifestyle in general. That was absolute bullshit, man.

Embarrassed, Billy hung his head.

—Jesus. I never meant to humiliate anybody. I was tryin' to, like, pay tribute to 'em or somethin'. I wanted their crowd to like us.

—Well they fuckin' hated you. They were ready string you up after 'Black Man'. What the hell were you thinkin'? You gonna talk with a fake British accent openin' for the Stones? That was stupid, Billy. Really fuckin' stupid. Wha'da *you* know about rasta vibrations or Jah or any of that crap? That's their fuckin' religion man! You shat all over that.

Billy had never seen Mak so angry. His round head looked like a red rubber ball, bouncing up and down. Sweat was pouring from his forehead. He was clearly mortified at having to try to defend the band when there was no defense he could offer.

—Jeez. I'm sorry, man. I'm really sorry. I didn't know.

Billy's mood soured as he weighed what Mak had said. He resented the dressing down that Mak gave him in front of the others. He felt bad about offending anyone. But he had not done it maliciously. It was all in fun.

His bandmates would not meet his gaze, staring off in various directions as Collette and Candy undressed in the rest room. Jane and Wren helplessly stood by, shivering, huddled in the corner. The pre-gig warmth had turned decidedly chilly.

—Hey, Billy, no big deal. It's not like you're gonna be playin' the Paramount or any more reggae shows any time soon.

Billy was not cheered in the least by Mak's snide declaration. He leaned back against the wall and studied the crimson pattern soaked into his t-shirt.

The following day, Drew Thomason, the *Oregonian*'s new music critic, brutally sliced up the band's performance. He called it "shameful" and "misguided." "Wrong-headed" and "just plain dumb." The band was stung. They had never received negative criticism before. It was a new and uncomfortable experience—one they wished never to repeat.

It was only a month after his surgery that Billy and the band were back playing the clubs. Billy's strength had returned. He felt completely healed—as if nothing had ever happened to him. Doctor Todd considered it a minor miracle—as did Carrie. But Billy just took the situation to be business as usual. By May, he was playing pick-up games of basketball with Mak and others at the court near Carrie's apartment.

In early June, the Unreal Gods celebrated the seventy-fifth anniversary of the Rose Festival at La Bamba, playing seventy-five different songs over two weekend nights. Mak hired Wren—one of the extra dancers at the Tosh show—to wear a skimpy maid's outfit and carry placards across the stage, counting down the songs from seventy-five to one. Meanwhile, Candy and Colette danced atop their two-foot high platforms at either side of the stage.

H.E. Carus' band Ticky Tacky opened for the Gods on the Friday night portion of the weekend. It was their first gig ever. They played to a packed house, which, in addition to the generally unruly crowd that the Unreal Gods typically drew, consisted of a large contingent of drunken sailors—in town as part of the Rose Festival fleet. La Bamba was packed to nearly double the legal capacity. Every song Carus' band played was met with uproarious approval.

Tommy and La Bamba were suffering somewhat from the effects of a turf war he had gotten into with Barry Hurrvitz and Starry night, which lay about five blocks away on the other side of Burnside, at 6th Avenue. The conflict, an epic battle of egos, was unrelenting.

Not content to run the most popular club in Portland, Tommy was always looking to expand his empire and thwart competition. Ever the impresario, he kept trying to convince Billy that he should manage the band, feeling that he was the don of a Portland rockaroll mafia. But Billy remained loyal to Mak. He was doing a good job. He was the Unreal Gods' manager.

For his part, Mak began to expand the Gods' territory from the downtown venues to the suburbs—from the Faucet on Beaverton-Hillsdale Highway and the Orange Peel on Capitol Highway in the west to Tippers on Powell on the deep eastside. The band began to make trips down the Willamette Valley to the college towns of Corvallis and Eugene.

They were finding new fans with every performance. Each show was standing room only, each better than the last. Still, though Mak tried diligently to find gigs for the band in Seattle, he met with little success.

Mak's greatest achievement was booking the group into Lung Fung on the eastside at Division and 82$^{nd}$ Avenue. Lung Fung was an expansive Chinese restaurant complex that had a large dance floor and stage at the end opposite to the massive dining area, with a full-sized unused bowling alley outstretched between.

Besides getting the band into a room with over eight hundred capacity, it was Mak's intention to stage all-ages shows on Sunday afternoons. The under-twenty-one set was a demographic that no other band in Portland had yet exploited, and Mak wisely surmised that the city's youth would jump at the opportunity to see Portland's hottest band—even if it was on a Sunday afternoon. He was absolutely right.

And it was not just teenagers present at the shows. Hundreds of adults were also in attendance—possibly in an attempt to avoid the wild, hedonistic revels that the band's evening performances had become. The Unreal Gods regularly sold out their Sunday afternoon shows at Lung Fung—sometimes playing to nearly a thousand patrons.

The Fourth of July fell on a Sunday in nineteen eighty-two. The Unreal Gods threw a righteous all-ages holiday bash, drawing their largest crowd yet at Lung Fung—more than twelve hundred people. Not only was the ballroom area filled to capacity, but the bowling alley, even the individual lanes, was packed as well.

The opening act, the Consequentials, were another top-tier Portland band, a muscular punk/pop trio led by singer and guitarist Harold Meek. Meek was a tall, bony lad with a prominent nose, somewhat resembling Pete Townsend in his youth. His kinetic energy was not dissimilar to Townsend's either. His songs were angst-filled paeans to young adulthood.

The underage crowd fully identified with his material. The front of the stage was encircled by a gaggle of young girls, who peered up at him with unfettered adoration. Most of the Consequentials' female fans were of the burgeoning Goth persuasion, dressed in schematic black, with heavy eye makeup and depressed dispositions.

Harold Meek's disheartened songs were like anthems for the dispossessed, and suited the distaff sensibilities of his audience accordingly. The girls would sway from side to side, with downcast eyes and blank, emotionless expressions.

The Consequentials' set lasted about an hour. Because it was Sunday afternoon, there was not the tightly scripted pressure of a weekend night. Time frames were estimates, and the Unreals were not concerned about when they were to take the stage. They were abundantly confident that they would take their young legions by storm.

During the break between bands, a whole new coterie of young girls rimmed the stage, five deep and vibrating with nervous pubescent tension. Fashion-wise, they were a far more divergent confederacy. Some of the girls were dressed in typical summer wear—tank tops and shorts, with flip-flops on their feet.

Others were more ornately decked out. Some were clad in punkish schoolgirl attire with black skirts and ties, white blouses and funky black Converse high tops. A small number were clothed as new wave Tinkerbells, with sheer scant green silk skirts, and diaphanous green and yellow flower-print chemises.

A few chose flashy pink petticoats with full-length black bustiers and volumes of beaded necklaces and flamboyant rosaries, set off by copious rings of brightly colored bracelets—exotic elbow-high gloves, adapted from pink and black striped leggings—worn over the arms.

When the Gods and Goddesses took the stage, an entirely different atmosphere erupted, as each member of the band (except Gilly, who was attired in a midnight blue Marine Corps dress coat with a choker collar) had crafted individually different adaptations of the old red, white and blue.

His hair teased as high as the comb of a Rhode Island Red cock, Col wore a carefully torn American flag t-shirt over tight blue jeans and red high top tennis shoes, with a red and white striped neckerchief headband. Gib dressed in a red patterned white bowling shirt, with black slacks and blue leather bowling shoes. Daw's garb consisted of a red sleeveless t-shirt, blue jeans and white high-top leather athletic shoes.

Billy arrived on stage looking like Uncle Sam—long vertically red and white striped silk slacks, American-blue coat and tails, a matching blue top hat with a dumb white wig underneath, white chin patch and eyebrows affixed with spirit gum. Candy and Colette were resplendent in matching metallic red camisoles, very brief light blue silk gym shorts and red, white and blue striped tennis shoes.

They stepped onto the two black, two-foot-tall dance platforms, at either side of the stage and stood motionless, poised like puppets.

As the band swung into the introduction to one of their most popular songs, and the Goddesses began to break free of their imaginary strings, cool jerking athletically, Billy addressed his followers with typical good-natured aloofness.

—Well alright. Good afternoon music lovers and happy Independence Day. I'm Uncle Sam Granger and these are the Sons of Liberty and the Daughters of the American Revolution.

With his arm elegantly extended, he gestured around the stage.

—And we're gonna start off this show with an oldie but a goldie called "I Used To Hang Around."

Daw counted off the song with a propulsive kick, a quick fill, then matched Gib's driving eighth note bass line. On keys, Gilly provided shimmering upstroke chords, while Col wove his guitar into the mix, an onrushing Spaghetti Western sort of figure, vaguely reminiscent, in its urgent forthrightness, of Ted Nugent's lead line on the Amboy Dukes' sixties gem, "Journey To The Center of Your Mind."

—I used to hang around
With all the other boy boys
We went to all the crazy places
We made all the same noise

Me 'n' Billy's boy boys
We used to love the same girl girl
And I remember one night
We loved her from the wrong side of town

What happened to you now
You used to be my friend
C'mon little Queenie
Let's get together again.

The young girls at the foot of the stage swooned in sheer delight at Billy's husky voice, his tall slender body, his boyish good looks and his unbridled charisma. They stared up at him, hands held up as if to reach him, to grab him, to selfishly steal him away.

Billy loved the attention and began to hop around the stage on one-foot—like a scarecrow Chuck Berry—as he pumped a hard rhythm on his guitar, smiling broadly at his brethren band mates, his tongue tucked coyly into his cheek. He stepped back up to the mic, mimicking Elvis.

—Thang yuh. Thang yuh veruh mush. Yor tew canned.

With his back to the audience, Billy beamed at the band, turning again to announce the next song.

—This one is called 'English Boy'. Uh one-two, uh onetwothreefour. Col swung into windmill power chords, reminiscent of Pete Townsend, as the band launched into a Who-like number.

—Oh-oh English boy
Don't I know you
I'm from America
And I'm true blue

English boy
Please come quickly
Your British friends
They're scarin' me

I can shake
Watch me shake watch me shake watch me shake
Shake just like you
You don't have to show me
Some old tattoo.

Then the band swung into the bridge, modeled after the Beatles' "Back In The USSR" facsimile of the Beach Boy's "California Girls."

—The Soho girls are really wild
Watch 'em smile
As they leave ya'
English boy
Well the London girls are really wild
When they cut your hair
They got you in mind
But all I'm asking of her majesty
Is stop and take a good look at me
English boy.

Col churned out a classic rock 'n' roll lead to drive the song headlong into the final verse, before ending on a Harrisonesque riff reminiscent of the Beatles' "You Can't Do That."

Excited, the young girls began to squeal—moaning with excitement and cooing woozily.

—Yes, yes. English Boy. Well, I hope you're all havin' a good time.

The girls screamed their approval with uninhibited enthusiasm, inspiring the rest of the crush to whoop and shout with glee.

The Unreal Gods and Goddesses worked the crowd into a heated frenzy, each contingent sensually charming the opposite sex with well-rehearsed efficiency. It was not just the young girls who were getting stirred up. Their unfettered energy had all the teenage boys stimulated, as well as many of their elder brethren, who openly lusted after the young women.

As if not to be outdone, the women who were of age, and who had consumed a suitable quantity of alcohol, began to behave in an overtly sexual manner, for

129

whoever would pay attention, which only further agitated the teen boys who were paying very close attention. It was a sexual circular firing squad.

Gilly openly leered at the young females—his tongue hanging out of a maniacal lipstick grin. He fluttered his cosmeticized lids blackly thick at them, his beady bat eyes glowing like two dark marble orbs set in a strange, cartoon, aging-facial landscape. Despite his age he had his share of groupies who called to him and waved affectionately.

The youth were sequestered from the adults by a maroon felt rope suspended on short chrome stanchions. The grown-ups stood between the kids and the promised land, which lay at the bar at the back of the room. The lure of alcohol was enough to prompt a contact high, and the under-agers staggered drunkenly up front.

The felt cord barrier only separated the kids from the booze. It did not prevent the sometimes sloppily inebriated patrons from freely mingling with the juniors. The merged combination created a very heady atmosphere in front of which the band found a great deal of inspiration and motivation. It was a slightly perverse soft-porn love fest.

The band quickly whipped through more of their most festive material: "New Wave Redneck," "Rockabilly Queen," and "Go-Go Boots." The spectators loved the dumble entendre of "My Girlfriend's Drawers." They bobbed and wove to the crazy upstroke rhythm and Gilly's glossy synth accents. Billy was waving lit sparklers in each hand.

—In my girlfriend's drawers
In my girlfriend's drawers
You don't mess with mine
I wont mess with yours
I found everything
Inside her drawers
I found it in my girlfriend's drawers.

The show ended in a climactic crescendo generated by an unimpeded abundance of frantic human voltage, which had been collecting in the room all afternoon. When the troupe finally left the stage, it was almost as if a discharge of static relief had swept over the space.

As the band toweled off backstage, engaging in their usual post-gig festivities, a drunken underage little blond with a messy mouth appeared and sat next to Billy, attempting to strike up a conversation. Billy needed many things in life, but he did not need teeny-bopper jailbait in his life. Maybe some other time.

With the husky voice of a chain-smoker, the girl emptily chattered away in clattering monologues. Mid-sentence in one of them, Billy impolitely stood up and wandered back out to the stage where Mak stood talking to Mick as they moved gear from the stage.

Billy approached them with a distressed expression upon his face.

—Hey, Mak. Can I talk to ya' a second?

Mak gladly quit pushing equipment around.

—What's up, Boss? Ya' need somethin'?

—Yeah. Yeah, I do. There's this groupie-type chick backstage. Blond. Underage. I think her name's Courtney. I'm pretty sure she's Chris Oldman's girlfriend. Or she lives with him, or somethin'.

—So what'cha need me to do?

—I need ya' to go back there and chase her out. She's like stalkin' me or somethin'. Scarin' the shit out of me. Get her out of there. And I don't want ya' lettin' her backstage again.

—Well, shit, Billy. Ya' told me to let the good-lookin' ones back. I didn't know she was an underager.

—It's okay, Mak. I don't blame ya' for anything. But just keep her away from me, that's all.

—Okay, Billy. I'll get her out of there. Just give me a minute or two.

Breathing a sigh of relief, Billy hid behind the curtain at the other end of the stage until he was certain she was gone. Talk about a chick with an agenda.

Billy Granger and the Unreal Gods and the Goddesses A Go-Go owned Lung Fung. It was their room. No other band in Portland could hope to fill it or even come close. Only the Gods were capable of making the expanse seem intimate. Only the Gods commanded a room of that size by the sheer unmatched capacity of their draw.

It was Tommy who proposed having a battle of the bands between the Unreal Gods and the Cowboys—the most popular young band in Seattle—with a local notoriety there not unlike that of the Gods in Portland. The Cowboys had opened several times for the Unreal Gods at La Bamba and once each at Euphoria and the Last Hurrah.

Actually, Tommy and the Cowboys' manager, Norm, had cooked up the idea: a battle between the two biggest bands in the Northwest. Mak couldn't see the value in it. The Unreal Gods didn't need the Cowboys to fill Lung Fung to overflowing. They could well do that on their own. And besides that, the Cowboys had never extended the favor back to the Gods. The only gigs the Gods had scored in Seattle, they had gotten through Mak's patience and persistence. Or Annie.

But Billy thought the idea was brilliant. And though Mak couldn't understand why, he had no say in the matter. It was out of his hands. Since Tommy and Norm

131

were promoting the event, he was relegated to putting up posters and running menial errands.

Late in July, on a Sunday afternoon, the battle of the bands took place. Both bands outdid themselves. The athletic Gods reacted well to the competition. They were obviously the superior outfit, which the crowd that evening fully sanctioned, with a loud, riotous response when their name was announced in the judging of audience response.

The Cowboys didn't mind losing to the Unreal Gods. It was a payday for them either way: as Norm and Tommy had agreed that the Cowboys would be guaranteed two thousand dollars, win or lose. And Tommy and Norm had taken forty percent to promote the event.

The Unreals took home more than six thousand dollars after expenses, most of which was the four thousand dollars Tommy and Norm took as commission. The two of them and the Cowboys had walked away with as much as the Gods had. For whatever reason, Billy decided they could afford to be magnanimous.

Mak was furious for several reasons. For one thing, he could not understand giving the Cowboys anything more than five hundred dollars. It was the Unreal Gods' regular gig, and they were doing the Cowboys a favor just by letting them play in front of fifteen hundred Portland music fans, who far preferred their hometown Gods over the overblown cowpokes from the North. Secondarily, he lost out on a twelve hundred dollar payday himself.

And though he didn't know the details, he had no doubt that Tommy and Norm had pulled down far more than his customary ten percent of the take. Though he was not certain, Mak figured it was closer to thirty, maybe forty, percent—and that Billy had probably gone along with the deal because it was Tommy, and he owed him some favors. Everybody made plenty of money, except for Mak.

Mak felt betrayed. In the past, Billy had always turned down such production proposals, vowing that Mak was the band's manager and all engagements went through him. But suddenly Billy's allegiance seemed not to be quite so strong, his devotion not so deep and abiding. It worried Mak. It worried him greatly.

XIV

The next weekend, at La Bamba, after the show, Colette was visiting with her boyfriend Frank. He was a part-time cook in the club's kitchen. She followed him all around the busy galley, carrying on a disjointed conversation as Frank rushed past her, preparing various meals. Pivoting sharply as he passed by her, Collette slipped on the slick floor.

On impact, she knew she had broken her arm. It was numb, but she could feel a deep radiating pain in her elbow. Frank was unable to take her to the emergency ward, so she had to drive herself. She did not get home until four in the morning.

She had been giving some consideration to leaving her position as a Goddess. While she loved the excitement of being with the biggest band in town and relished the attention she always received, she had other things she wanted to do with her life. She was young, still not yet twenty-one years old. There was much still undone, unaccomplished..

The couple had discussed moving to the coast and opening a shop of some sort. Or a restaurant or something. They just wanted to get out of Portland to some more relaxed atmosphere, with a slower pace. The coast seemed like the logical choice.

She talked with Candy about the possibility of leaving the fold. Candy had told her that she understood. Being a Goddess was not the end-all and be-all of life. Candy, too, had goals outside the band. Being older, she had already done a lot in her life.

Candy had once lived on a commune with no electricity and no running water—growing her own natural food. She had been in the army for two years. She had lived in Hawaii giving tours to statesiders. She wanted to become a professional jeweler—another of her vocations was as a silversmith. Her brown-belt.

It was her intention to produce film documentaries. She had even thought about possibly documenting the rise of the Unreal Gods, but she had determined that she was too closely tied to the band to give an honest portrayal. Still, a documentary about the business of rock and roll was not out of the question. She was independent, smart and very attractive, and she could pretty much do whatever she wanted in life.

The emergency room staff placed Colette's right arm in a plastic partial cast that immobilized the fracture, without the bulk of a full plaster cast. Her forearm was reinforced with a purple splint, which she wrapped with an ace bandage—as much to camouflage the injury as to protect it.

133

The following week, the band journeyed south to Corvallis to play for the frat rat regulars who weekly attended the shows at Mother's Mattress Factory. The bands who played the Factory on weekends were almost always Portland-centric, and the Unreal Gods were the most popular of all. Their good-natured attitude and appreciation for white powder substances ingratiated them to the college bunch, who had a penchant all their own for drugs, as well as copious quantities of alcohol.

The dressing room at Mother's Mattress Factory was small and cramped. There was barely room for the band members, let alone Candy and Colette. The girls decided to dress in the women's restroom at the front of the building, near the bar. While the conditions there were not substantially more spacious, they were better than the dressing room.

Because of her arm, Colette required Candy's assistance in getting into her costume—a tight, strapless, sort of one-piece bathing suit with vertical purple and red stripes. The pair wore purple ballet slippers with the ribbons tied, crises-cross around their calves up to their knees.

A dense thicket of hard-core fans surrounded the Mattress Factory stage. They raged as only college students can rage—not going gentle into that good night, but partying, partying against the dying of the buzz. They surrounded the band like a pack of wolves.

The ceiling was so low that the Goddesses did not perform on their platforms, but merely on the stage, next to the band. That the stage was only a couple feet off the ground and members of the audience were massive, athletic scholarshipped offensive tackles gave to the Unreal Gods a looming sense of being on a sidewalk, far below tall towering skyscrapers.

About midway into the first set, things went off the track. It was during the song "Upstroke Down," that a possible fullback, a long-necked bottle of Bud in hand, drunkenly lurched forward toward Colette, just as she was pumping her buttressed right arm forward in an energetic march. The possible fullback went down hard, as if in a goal line helmet-to-helmet collision with a seasoned middle linebacker.

He fell back into a coppice of happy merry makers, who themselves fell backward into others behind them, as the weight and rolling thrust of the possible fullback was absorbed by about twenty human bowling pins. Colette stood motionless on the stage, bewildered.

At almost the same time, on the other side of the stage, a tumult occurring behind them shoved a regular guy and his uptight girlfriend in the front row forward. The regular guy was pitched ahead just as Candy was kicking her leg to full extension. It was an unfortunate event of great impact, especially—her toe to his temple—for the regular guy. At first, he seemed to be okay. He took a step or two to his right as if nothing was wrong, but then he began to stagger toward the back of the room. He fell to the floor after his third or fourth step. Out cold.

His uptight girlfriend screamed in horror. She reflexively tossed her gin and tonic all over Candy, and awkwardly flipped her empty glass in Candy's direction. Candy began to leap toward the uptight girlfriend, but caught herself mid-stride. Among her many other attributes Candy was availed of profound good judgment. She had had worse shit thrown at her and on her in her career as a dancer. There was no reason to make a bad situation worse.

The uptight girlfriend immediately ran to the side of her regular guy boyfriend who was attempting to stand up, as decorously as possible, despite having just been beaned by the square wooden toe of a tall, muscular dancer wearing ballet slippers. Candy continued to dance until the song ended when both of the dancers bowed and left the stage on Colette's side, stepping back into the dressing room.

Colette was the first to speak.

—Wow. That was too weird!

—I never imagined...

Candy replied, stunned. Colette continued.

—I don't understand what just happened out there. It was like 'kung fu masters' or something. '*Kung Fu Masters Meet the Three Stooges*'. It's the perfect night.

Candy quizzically looked at her partner.

—The perfect night? For what?

—The perfect night to leave the band. It just couldn't get any weirder or any better than this. This was a classic. One for the ages.

Candy nodded, understanding the rationale behind the young girl's line of reasoning.

—We took out, like, twenty-five people out there. They never had a chance. You could have killed that girl who threw her drink on you. She doesn't know how close she came to getting her ass whipped.

Candy laughed aloud. She knew Colette was right.

—No. You know I've been wanting to get out of this for a while now. This is the perfect time. It's the night. It's like a lightening bolt from the gods. Change course. Move on. Next!

—I know you're right. It's time for you. But I'm sure gonna miss you...

She hugged the younger girl.

—You're like a little sister to me.

The two of them began to bawl. The Goddesses would never be the same.

On the way home, in Billy Dreier's van, Billy and the band briefly weighed the impact of losing one of their dancers. Gilly, Col and Mak didn't think it would be a huge deal to replace her. Billy was rather cheerless at the prospect. It was like the first chink in the wall. He shook off a brief shiver of dread.

Then, to break the gathering silence in the van full of Gods, Billy conjectured aloud.

—I think we need to record another album. I think it's time.

Caught unexpected, the band members sat gaping.

—We've got a ton of material. Too much. Like, what? Almost a hundred songs now? And maybe we'll need to write some more. But we've, like, y'know, improved. The sound of the band is changin'—we're almost soundin' like a rock band sometimes. We need to, y'know, get that sound down on tape.

The rest of the crew were in no position to argue. It was under Billy's leadership that the Unreal Gods had become as big as they had. It was under Billy's direction that they had attracted as much notoriety as they had. And if he said they should record another album, even though their current one had come out only six months earlier, then they would record another. But it was going to cost a lot of money. Money the band didn't have.

It was Gilly who approached everyone a couple days later with a plan he had hatched with Tommy.

—My brother Angie lives in Jersey City, in New Jersey, just across the Hudson from New York City. He's got a close friend who own a club called the Trappe D'Or. It's a real popular spot where we could play whenever we wanted.

The band members leaned in close. Billy said.

—Yeah. Go on.

—Well, Angie also does some work at the Power Station in New York.

—I've heard of that place. The Stones and Aerosmith record there.

Gilly lit up, relishing the details.

—And Springsteen and the Talking Heads and the Ramones. Angie does some work for Tony Bongiovi. Tony designed the fucking place. It's got the best sound in the world. We need to record at a legitimate studio, if we're going to take the next step.

Slightly bedazzled, Billy scratched his nose and exhaled, sighing deeply.

—So what are you drivin' at, Gilly?

—Well, Angie says we can come out and stay at his place. He'll set us up with gigs at the Trappe D'Or and get us a good rate if we want to record a few songs at the Power Station. We could stay out there three or four weeks or whatever.

The band immediately became excited by the possibilities such a trip might confer. A trip to New York, New York. Make it there, anywhere, it's up to you.

But, ever the pragmatist, Mak wondered about the nuts and bolts of such a large scale operation.

—So how many people are we gonna take along with us? The band and me and Billy D. and Mick. Are we takin' Candy and Colette's replacement out too? That's ten...

Mak raised his hands helplessly.

—How're we supposed to finance all that? Then come up with the cash to record at the Power Station. Like, how much money do you think we'd need to record, uh, four songs there, Gilly? Even if your brother got us a great rate?

Angelic grin turned tight-lipped and serious, Gilly became pragmatic in an instant.

—Oh, probably around ten thousand bucks.

—Ten thousand dollars! Ten thousand dollars? How're we supposed to come up with that kind of money? We just gave forty-five hundred away on Fourth of July.

Billy was silent as Mak indignantly continued his tirade.

—You *guys*, we don't have any money saved up. It's gonna cost at least another three grand to take care of everyone out there. And, like, another thousand just to get us all out there and back. If we're lucky. We'll need a minimum of, like, uh, fifteen thousand dollars! It's way out of our range.

Gilly brightened again.

—Well, I was at La Bamba last night and talking to Tommy, you know, and I was telling him about this opportunity we have. And I mentioned that we were going to need a lot of money to make this trip, and he said he'd be willing to loan it to us.

Mak's face reddened in frustration

—That's big of him. Givin' us our own money back—at ten points interest, no doubt.

Billy scowled.

—Just listen to him, Poppy, and we'll make up our minds later.

Elbows balanced on his thighs, Mak rested his head on his fisted hands.

Gilly continued.

—Okay. So Tommy said he'd lend us ten thousand. Maybe more if we need it.

Billy's face screwed up.

—Well, what's he gonna want for that much money?

—Twenty points.

—Wha'd'ya mean twenty points?

—Twenty percent of whatever the band makes.

—Forever?

—No. Maybe not forever, but, like, for three or five years.

Billy rubbed his hand on his chin.

—Jeez, Gilly. If we hit it big in the next three years—like a million bucks or somethin'—he'd be in for, like, what? How much, Mak?

Mak looked up dejectedly.

—Two hundred grand.

—*Two hundred grand*? Are you sure?

Mak glowered, frustrated.

—Yeah, I'm sure. That's my job.

Gib interjected.

—Yeah. He's right.

Wincing, Billy complained.

—Two hundred grand is a pretty good return on ten or fifteen thousand bucks. Nice work if you can get it.

Gilly rebutted.

—Well, it takes money to make money, man. We need to take the band to the next level if we're going catch on with a major. We need to have all our ducks in a row.

Worriedly, Billy slowly wagged his head back and forth.

—Maybe we should make him, like, a counter offer or somethin'. Two hundred grand is a lot of money.

Gilly challenged that line of thought.

—Billy, man. It's only two hundred thousand if we get a million. But if we get a hundred thousand, he only gets twenty grand.

—Yeah, twenty grand until we make the million. Then he'll have two hundred and twenty thousand and we'll still have two years to go.

Frustrated, Gilly put his fingers to his temples.

—You're jumping to a lot of conclusions.

—I'm not jumpin' to fuckin' conclusions, man. We're gonna make millions. I don't wanna give it all away for, like, a fifteen thousand dollar bet. We've gotta talk him down to five percent or somethin' like that. Even that's a lot of money. What's five percent of a million dollars, Mak?

—Fifty grand.

—Fifty grand sounds a lot better than two hundred thousand. And that still gives him a good return on his investment.

Gilly was becoming perturbed.

—But if we only make a hundred thousand, then he only gets like…

He looked in Mak's direction.

—Five thousand?

Mak nodded.

—Gilly, man, I just told ya'. We're gonna make millions.

—Yeah. Yeah. Millions. But we're not going to make anything unless we can get Tommy, or somebody else, to lend us the money.

With nothing to say, Mak slowly shook his head, disbelievingly. Gilly persisted

—Well?

Billy sounded resolved.

—I'll have to think about all this, and I'll have to talk to Tommy.

Gilly frowned.

## XV

It was soon decided that Tommy would lend the band fifteen thousand dollars and the entire team—dancers included—would make the journey east. A contract was drawn. It was agreed that Tommy would at least receive his money back, plus twenty percent interest, which resulted in a figure of a minimum of eighteen thousand dollars that he would pocket, no matter what.

If the band were to hit it big—a huge hit single or some other unforeseen lucky break—Tommy had three years to make up to five times whatever the amount was that they finally ended up borrowing from him. Fifty, seventy-five grand. Then he would be officially paid off. No piece of the action if he was paid back in full within two years with interest.

Mak was still dubious about the deal. But Billy overruled him. That did not stop Mak from trying to convince him not to go through with the plan to go back east.

—We don't have to go to New York to record. We can do that here. We can go back to High Tech and let Jack record us. He'd do us right. We've almost paid off the money we owe him.

—Mak, man, we have to go to New York. We *have* to. We need to show the labels we're upwardly mobile. World-class. We need to come up with a world-class recording, even if it's just a four-song demo.

—I don't think that makes any sense. We're spendin' money we don't have—just to do this. It's crazy.

—Mak, you don't understand. There's bands that would give their right nut to be where we are right now...

Billy chuckled at the irony of his statement.

—Okay. I mean, there's bands that would just die to be where we are. But we've gotta take the next step. We hafta prove that we're major league, if we want to play in the major leagues. I know it's a lot of money. I know it's a risk. But we can do it. And when we get it all done, there's gonna be plenty of money around for everybody.

Mak was not so certain. He felt a sense of unease about the whole project. But he knew Billy was not going to be dissuaded, so he finally relented.

—Alright Billy. It's your ballgame. You're the coach. You're the boss. If you say steal third, then we're gonna try 'n' steal third. If that's what you want, we'll do it.

So, the plan was hatched that the Unreal Gods and Goddesses, Mak, Billy D. and Mick would head out to New York City in the first week of October. Annie Fisher would accompany them (at her own expense) as some sort of liaison, between the band and any hotshot industry type she knew—who might come around, blowing smoke

Mak set about booking the band for every date available in the six weeks before they were to leave town. He figured that he might be able to whittle down the size of the loan that they would have to get from Tommy—maybe cut it in half, or more.

Meanwhile, Candy was frantic, struggling to work out routines with Colette's replacement, Mary Jane, who went by the name of MJ. MJ was a muscular woman of moderate height, with long, kinky-brown hair that suited her Hungarian-Mexican heritage. She had beautiful jade, green eyes, with spectacular, rust shaded eruptions for irises that spun out from the volcanoes of her pupils.

And while she was a good enough dancer and had the body to keep the guys watching, MJ was not Colette. Candy had gotten used to working with Colette. Colette had a dance background—dance instruction. Even at such a young age, she instinctively knew all the moves they had worked out. MJ was a good dancer. But she did not have the training. She was innately talented, and certainly attractive enough—young and supple. The two of them got along well, with similar tastes in stage-wear. But teaching her all the moves wore Candy down. Her stress level was extreme. MJ seemed not to notice. Or if she did notice, she wasn't letting on.

The band played four nights a week for those remaining six weeks—from August, through September and into October—at every club they could worm their way into. They played Eugene one night and Corvallis the next. They played the Orange Peel and the Faucet. They played Tipper's, the Foghorn and Lung Fung. They played La Bamba and Starry Night, the Last Hurrah and Key Largo. They even scheduled a gig at a little club—the Fat Rooster—on the Eastside, at 16th on Hawthorne Boulevard, on Friday, the night before they were to leave for the east coast.

In all they made over forty thousand dollars from their gigs. Because of its limited size, the Unreals charged twelve dollars at the door at the Fat Rooster. Despite the exorbitant door charge, there was still a line stretching around the corner and a block and a half up 16th Avenue.

The club had a capacity of two hundred, at most, but there were at least three hundred people crammed into the room. There was literally no room to move, but every time someone left the building, the doorman would let one or two people pay their cover charge and enter—if they were able to wedge themselves in somewhere.

The Fat Rooster had a small, sunken dance floor that could comfortably hold about fifty, but it was swimming with one hundred people or more on that night. Above the stage, to the right, there was a balcony that had room for maybe twenty or thirty, in which more than fifty fans were jammed. Behind the dance floor was

141

the community area—with tables and booths scattered around the room.

Every available seat was taken. And people were stacked in, standing shoulder-to-shoulder, holding before them, like alcoholic shields, their glasses of beer, to keep the lions at bay—to prevent anyone from encroaching upon the remaining non-space.

Still, the waitresses, Bev and Barb, had little trouble patrolling the floor and taking orders for refills. They expertly hoisted their trays of empty or full pitchers and glasses. They were like runaway trains, as the spectators clutched together to get out of their way.

At the bar, the owner, Dave Concannon, a short, pudgy fellow, with a scruffy moustache, manned the bar, drawing beer from the eight taps as fast he could. As the foam was settling on one glass of Heineken, he stood filling another from the Guinness tap. Glasses of Coors, pitchers of Miller and Bud—an endless conveyor of beer.

Behind him, his wife, Carol, a tiny woman with curly brown hair and severe black-framed glasses, staffed the cooler, fishing out bottles of popular beer and the occasional jug of red or white wine.

As he schlepped up the hill on Hawthorne, tall, Irish-eyed Indian, Jim Finity could see the animated bunch waiting to get in the door at the Fat Rooster. He stopped on the sidewalk and gave serious thought to turning around.

But he really wanted to see Billy and the band before they left for New York—to assess how much they changed by the time they came back to Portland. Jim knew the doorman, Rob Rolfe, so he was sure he could slide into the place without waiting in line or paying cover. He just wasn't sure he wanted to join the madness inside.

He slowly passed the Snowdrift Sleeper futon shop and stood outside the emergency side exit of the Fat Rooster. He could see a figure moving in the shadows of the narrow alley between the buildings.

It slowly dawned on Jim that the ghostly entity he spied was actually Billy Granger. He was partied up to the max, and secretively smoking a joint. As Billy pitched toward the light of the streetlamp, Jim exclaimed.

—Hey, Billy, it's great to see you, man! I've listened to your *Boom Chuck* album a hundred times, and I don't care what they say, it's a great record.

—Oh, hey. Hi, Jim. That's nice of you to say. I know the critics call it corny and wimpy. But that's just the kind of band we are. You can't make a tiger change its spots. 'Scuze me a sec.

Billy stuck the joint between his teeth and ducked back into the alley between the buildings, proceeding to take a leak on the futon shop wall. As he pissed, he continued his train of thought.

—This town's a joke, man. Euphoria and the club owners are fuckin' gangsters. I'm, like, willin' to take bullets for what I believe. People say we're corny. I know we're corny—that's what we are all right. Well, we may be corny, but we're not phony, and neither is our record.

—That's great, Billy. Don't ever listen to what anybody says.

Billy looked out at Jim, a bit defensive.

—Thanks, Jim. I'll think about that. Sometimes I think I, like, listen to too many people. And everybody's got their own opinion. Sometimes I've just gotta, like, y'know, trust my own judgment about this shit.

Billy reappeared from out of the alley, tossed away the remnants of the smoldering roach and quickly swung open the supposedly locked, jimmied side door into the club. The band had already launched into the intro to "Go-Go Boots Are Coming Back."

Billy quickly leapt on to the stage, strutting up to the mic, hiccupping like Buddy Holly.

—Go-Go boots are comin' baah-yuck,
Don't throw yours away-ee…

Jim momentarily thought about following Billy into the club to join the teeming masses, but he decided against it. He'd had the sort of interaction with Billy that he had hoped. It wasn't going to get any more intimate than the setting they had just shared. He turned and walked back down the hill on Hawthorne Boulevard.

The next afternoon, the travelers were to assemble at Portland International Airport at around four, with only the barest of clothing and costume essentials. Carrie drove Billy to the airport in her little gray Toyota. She was apprehensive about Billy's trip—for inestimable reasons. It would be the longest they had been apart since they met.

Carrie was just beginning the first term of her second year in pre-nursing. There was no way she would be able to visit Billy in New York. They were going to be apart until Thanksgiving, maybe later. Storm clouds gathered on her face.

—Billy…

Vacantly staring out the window at the late day gray sky, Billy was trying to wrap his mind around the mission he was about to undertake. He hoped he was bringing enough weed along: only twelve ounces of Mex and a couple ounces of John Dailey's homegrown super bud. He was figuring an eighth of the Mex a week, per person, for two months. And around half a gram of the good stuff per person per week. That sounded reasonable.

—Hey.

She nudged him on the shoulder as she drove up 82nd Avenue toward the airport.

—Billy!

He shook himself free of his flighting thoughts.

—Yeah. *Yeah.* What do you need?

—Can I trust you?

Confused by the incongruity of the question, he asked.

—Can you trust me to do what?

—Can I *trust* you? Are you trustworthy? Can you be trusted?

Billy glared at her with resentment and embarrassment.

—What's that supposed to mean?

—I just want to know if I can trust you. You could be gone for two months. You're going to be in New York—one of the biggest cities in the world. Can I trust you? Trust you with our relationship? Trust you to hold our relationship in your hands? Carefully? To hold it dear...?

—Yeah. Yeah. Well, sure. I'm not going to New York to, like, meet girls. I'm *going* there to get a step closer to bein' where I'm supposed to be...

The pair crossed Northeast Sandy at 82nd. She glanced at him hopefully as they cruised through the intersection.

—I'm *going* to record at the Power Station. The Power Station! You can trust me with doin' that. I'll always have our relationship with me—right here in my heart. In my shirt pocket...

He patted his chest. Apprehension welled in Carrie's eyes.

—And it doesn't matter where I am. Portland, or New York.... Anywhere...

They arrived at the airport, where the others were transferring their belongings to a large baggage cart. Billy removed his bags, his guitar, and a backpack from the trunk of Carrie's car. With the engine idling, Billy and Carrie awkwardly kissed goodbye in the din of the airport departure area, with the rest of the band looking on.

Carrie drove away from the airport in tears.

After a time, the lot of them excitedly boarded an United Airlines 757 and flew away from the city, east, to find their fortunes in New York City.

Well, Angie's apartment was in Jersey City, it was true. But as far as the band were concerned it was just like the two sides of Portland: only separated by the Hudson, instead of the Willamette. Manhattan was just across the river from Jersey City. No big deal.

Their flight arrived into Newark at four-thirty in the morning east coast time. They searched the airport for a familiar face, but found none. Gilly was dispatched to look around the airport to see if he could locate his brother.

At the baggage claim area, the rest of the group, sacked out atop their carry-on gear, waiting to retrieve their possessions from the flight's checked luggage. Grim-faced, Gilly returned.

—I didn't see Angie around, so I tried calling his place. I woke him up. So, I guess he overslept.

Col was sitting on the floor next to Candy, his head in his arms leaning against the chair in which she sat. He sprang like a startled cat at the sound of the word "overslept."

—He wha'?

—He overslept. I guess he got in late last night. And it's the middle of the night here, not like…what time is it? Like one o'clock or whatever it is back home.

With a sense of profound frustration, Col further addressed the issue.

—But he was supposed to be here waitin' for us. You told us he'd be here waitin'.

—Well, he got in late and overslept. He'll be here as soon as he can.

—And how long would that be?

—An hour or so, maybe. As soon as he can.

—Well, that's a great start to our fuckin' little adventure. I wonder what other surprises we can expect.

Mak stared at Billy, who feigned sleep with his head resting on his backpack. He knew Billy knew he was staring at him. Mak looked for some sort of sign that Billy was watching back, but saw none. He glanced over at Col, who with teeth clenched was narrowly peeping back at him from the corner of his eye.

His head humbly bowed, Gilly pronounced.

—Well, he'll be here as soon as he can.

Eventually, the ten of them sorted through the incoming baggage at the claim area, assembling a much bigger pile of personal property. Billy and Col fished out their guitars and started jamming intensely, though their electric guitars were nearly silent without amplification.

Daw and Gib sat silently. Daw drummed his thighs with bored enthusiasm. Gib bobbed his head rhythmically, in time to Daw's beats. Billy D. and Mick lay dozing, sacked out on the floor of the deserted claim area. The Goddesses sat on their luggage, inspecting every item in their mound for signs of damage.

As time stretched inexorably on, with every second a drip of water on the collective forehead of the entire crew, Gilly became increasingly nervous, while Mak and Billy continued their avoidance game.

The girls read. They immodestly talked to each other about their lives—laughing out loud at times. The rest of the delegation was mostly silent. Col and Billy, having tired of their jam session, were absently staring off in opposite directions.

Mak gave up on eyeballing Billy, reconciled that whatever point to be made was not lost on the leader. He gaped out the window, waiting to see a pair of headlights that were the pair of headlights that would drive them away from there.

It was a long time, an interminable time. Universes were born. Eons passed. Histories unfolded. Lives whisked desperately by. Finally, Angie showed up, driving a beat-up white, extra-long, eight-person Dodge transport van, with all the back seats ripped out to carry music gear.

It was a tight fit, intolerably tight, but they were able to get all the equipment and other stuff loaded into the compartments at the rear of Angie's van. And, with Billy and Gilly piled up in the front and eight more in the back, shoved up right behind them, the ride from the Newark Airport to the west side of Jersey City, where Angie had his pad, was stiflingly uncomfortable. Every bump or turn induced an audible group gasp.

Angie was a year or two older than Gilly, maybe a little over forty, about five-foot-five, stocky, with a thick, black beard and long, wavy shoulder-length hair. He was an animated character, about four cups of coffee ahead of everyone else. Acting as the tour guide, at six-thirty in the morning, he pointed out familiar landmarks, giving a brief history of every attraction—addressing correct pronunciations for the newcomers' benefit.

Eventually, they arrived at Angie's apartment at Carbon Place, just off of Westside Avenue, which was actually the upper floor of a large, converted warehouse. It looked like a warehouse, too, as Angie was not one for interior decoration. There was a beat up couch and a couple of old overstuffed chairs placed over dirty oriental rugs in what served as the living room. A couple of semi-living house plants were positioned on tables around the room.

There was a sixteen-channel soundboard, half taken apart, on the dining room table. Various other recording decks and stacks of effects were strewn around the rooms. The visitors huddled together in the middle of it all, trying to figure out where they would stay, where they would sleep.

It turned out that there were three makeshift bedrooms down the hall toward the can—a lavatory, which could only hold one person at a time, a military-style shower, with a curtain wrapped around a circular frame, a primitive tin drain on the floor.

One of the rooms was Angie's and the other two were used for storage. One would go to Billy, and the other to the Goddesses. As Angie pointed out, there were no beds in the spare bedrooms, but with a bit of maneuvering of certain articles, they would probably be satisfactory quarters for Billy and the girls—at least providing them a degree of privacy.

The seven remaining guests would be left to fend for themselves. Col called the couch, early on. So the other members of the tribe were afforded spaces to sleep in the overstuffed chairs or on the hard wooden-slat floor. A couple of them had thought to bring sleeping bags. The others were given blankets. Angie turned the heat up to sixty degrees. A big deal. The sun was shining through the cold gray clouds on the morning of Sunday, October tenth, as they all settled down to get some sleep—as best they were able.

That afternoon, Angie took the group in his van down to the Trappe D'Or, to check out the facilities and to get a feel for the place. It was a single rectangular room, bigger than La Bamba—maybe six or eight thousand square feet—with a low stage at one end and the bar at the other. There were several stools abutting the bar. A few circular tables were placed around the area. Booths were arranged on either side of the open space in front of the stage. But for the most part it was standing room only in the Trappe D'Or.

As the others walked around the club, inspecting the stage and the PA system, Angie and Gilly introduced Billy to the owner, Larry Giufreddi. Larry was a gruffly terse individual of medium height and build. He had long wavy, wiry black hair and a short-trimmed black beard, which he shaved on a neat line around his neck to demarcate his beard from the dense black body hair that sneaked out from under his shirt.

Larry and Angie had known each other since junior high school, so they spoke in a kind of shorthand. Gilly was familiar with the language.

—Hey, Alfredo, how the hell are ya'?

—It's Gilly. I'm called Gilly in Portland.

Larry chuckled at Gilly.

—Yeh, yeh. Fuckin' Gilly Walker. Yeh sure. I heard about it from Ang. Don't worry Alfredo, yer secret's safe wit' me.

Larry grabbed Gilly by the shoulder and shook him good-naturedly

—I swear ya' look more 'n' more like yer mom every day. Ya' both fuckin' look like Howdy Doody wit' dyed black hair. Ya' got the same goofy grin as Antonia. It's really fuckin' weird, man. The older you get…

Gilly immediately reverted to the fourth grade, in awe of his brother's junior high buddy. Larry sized up Billy, who towered over him by more than half a foot. Larry asked Angie.

—S's this the guy yer tellin' me about?

—Yeh. This is Billy.

Larry and Billy shook hands.

—Billy's gonna be the next big thing.

—Yeh? I wish I hadda nickel for every time I heard that one!

—Well ya' never heard it from me, Larry. If I say it, I mean it. I ain't just blowin' smoke up yer ass. You know that.

—Yeh. Yeh. I know Ang, but things change so fuckin' fast in this business. One day it's disco balls and DJs and the next it's a bunch of kids who can barely tune their shit, drawin' all kinds of other kids to watch 'em. They're all the next big thing, until they ain't no more.

—Well, wait'll ya' see this guy and his band...And the go-go girls.

—Yeh. Those girls look pretty cherry. Do they take their clothes off?

Billy jumped in.

—No. They keep their clothes on. Leaves more to the imagination.

—Well, my imagination's workin' overtime on that long, dark haired one. Shit oh dear! That's a pair of legs on that bitch.

It's quite possible, had she heard his assessment of her appearance, that Candy would have karate kicked Larry in the throat. But she and MJ were busy trying to figure out how they were going to fit on the undersized stage—and what moves they could perform without getting in the band's way.

—I like the idea of dancers. We haven't had that in here before. That oughta liven up the guys who come in.

Angie interjected.

—Yeh. They really warm up a room fast. The band ain't bad either.

Angie elbowed Billy in the ribs and laughed self-consciously. Billy smiled reflexively and tried to figure out where he was and what he was doing. He felt like he was on another planet.

—Well, you tell that long one if she needs any spendin' money, I gotta few things that need lookin' after around the club. A coupla things.

He muttered lewdly. Billy merely stared off at the bar taps, ostensibly oblivious. Larry turned and engaged Billy directly in the eye.

—Look. I'll tell ya' what I'm'onna do. I'm'onna give you guys Thursday nights, to start. Ya' don't hafta have an openin' band if ya' don't want, or I can scare up a band to open for ya'. No problem.

Billy set his head thoughtfully as Gilly and Angie nodded in agreement.

—And then on Friday and Saturday, for the next coupla weeks, anyway, I'll let you guys open for Moby Dickens. They're about the biggest band in the area. So you'll have a good crowd. People'll see ya'. Then we'll see about what happens after that. We'll see how ya' do.

The four of them stood there, silent for a moment, before Angie spoke up.

—Okay, Larry. That'll be great, man. Just wait 'n' see. These guys got somethin' goin' on. Even with Alfred in the band. They're good.

Larry raised his eyebrows in suspicious disbelief. He knew Angie had never seen the band play.

—Well yeh. Okay. We'll see what happens.

The band piled back into Angie's van, and they stopped to eat at the Miss America diner, located not far from Angie's apartment. A variety of dishes were served there—breakfast, burgers and fries, steaks and chicken. Not a bad joint.

After dinner, they trundled back to Angie's apartment, where the entourage lounged around and watched television. Angie, Billy and Gilly conferred in Angie's bedroom for quite a while—presumably discussing matters of great importance to the Unreal Gods' future.

Mak was uneasy with the secretive nature of Angie's consultations. He felt that he should be included in all band business. That was his job and he was being left out. He began to wonder why he was in New York at all, if not to manage the band's affairs. As usual, the rest of the group did not care about the business operations of the band. They left that in Mak's and Billy's hands. Mak knew this and fumed.

The next day, Angie and Gilly took Col and Billy down to the Power Station to have a look at the studio where they would record. The other band members, and Billy D., Mick, and Mak felt excluded—as if they were some sort of second tier. Billy and Col were definitely the chief members of the organization, but Gilly was only along because Angie was his brother.

Billy D. did not understand why he wasn't being included in the technical aspects of the recording process. He was under the impression that, in addition to live

149

sound engineering, he would be working with Angie behind the board in the studio, too. He thought he was going to assist and learn some studio tricks. He felt let down.

Mick, Gib and Daw, and the girls were simply bored. They had expected that there would be a lot of down time, so they weren't surprised. They smoked weed, watched TV and drank the beer that Billy D. bought down at the corner market.

Back in the control room of Studio Four, Angie's quiz began

—So, how many songs ya' plannin' on recordin' here?

Billy thought that Gilly had cleared that up ahead of time. He didn't really want to bring Angie up to speed on the whole project. He expected that Angie would hit the ground running.

—Well, we've got four we wrote. We want to do four. More if we can.

—Four songs? They gonna be demos or are ya' gonna be tryin' to record the real deal? Somethin' you or somebody could release?

Col was the first to reply.

—We want it to sound pro. We want it to sound like records on the radio.

Billy searched the board as if there was a word written on one of the faders..

—We want the drums and the guitars to sound major league. We want to sound like the real thing, because we are.

Gilly put it more literally.

—We want to sound like Tom Petty and the Cars and U2 and, like, who are they? Duran Duran. They recorded here didn't they?

—Yeh, sure. Some. They're supposed to be comin' back in in a coupla months.

Col asserted his vision.

—Like Simple Minds, or the Specials, or Boomtown Rats.

Billy sensed that the presentation was losing its focus.

—We wanna sound like those bands and the Stones and Springsteen. And the Psychedelic Furs and ABC and Adam and the Ants. We wanna be big as all of those bands. But, mostly, we just wanna sound like ourselves. You'll hafta figure that part out yourself, Angie.

Ever the pragmatist, Angie returned to his primary line of thought.

—Well, see, the reason I'm askin' is, I want for you guys to have some clue about how much this is gonna cost ya'.

Billy understood the economic logistics, but he was a little put out that Angie cut to that chase so quickly. Still, it was the cruel reality of their intentions, and Billy decided they needed to hear it. Angie continued.

—So the studio's gonna cost ya' two hundred an hour, and I'll do the engineerin' and producin' for fifty an hour.

Taken aback by the estimate, with wickered brow, Billy crocheted a silent message of alarm toward Gilly, who had implied that the cost would be substantially less.

—Well, Gilly said you might be able to get us some kind of deal. Record on off-days in off-hours.

—Well, there *are* no off-hours here. Not really.

—Or maybe get us a rate on a block of time.

—Yeah, me 'n' Gilly did talk about that. That's true. I'll see what I can do. How much did ya' have budgeted for this?

—Ten grand. Ten grand to record—and a few grand to keep us goin'...while we're here. That and whatever we make playin' shows.

—Well, you guys do the math. Even at a good rate, it's prob'ly gonna cost a thousand a day. Five hours a day, five days a week, two weeks and there goes ten grand.

Looking at Gilly suspiciously, Billy wondered if perhaps Gilly had his own cut in all of it. He knew Angie did, but he expected as much. Nobody does anything for free.

Still, he wanted to make sure the band had the time to get the job done. The Gods had borrowed all that money from Tommy to record a solid demo EP. That was what he wanted to do—whatever the hell it cost.

Sensing all that, Gilly proposed to Angie.

—Well, can you see what you can do? We really want to do it, and we want to do it right.

Snorting brusquely, Angie shook his head. He got it.

# XVI

That afternoon, Angie took the band members into the city, down to Sam Ash, to rent the equipment they would need to perform and record. None among the four Oregonians had ever been to New York City before, but they weren't particularly impressed. Col remarked that New York City looked just like Portland, only taller. For the most part, they were interested in where the hot venues were, but not much else.

Arriving at Sam Ash, Gib, Col and Billy headed over to the guitar amp area. They had brought several of their guitars and effects with them. Billy had taken his trusty blond Strat. And Col brought his three main guitars—the Gretsch, the Les Paul Standard and the SG Standard.

But they were going to need to rent amps, the amps to which they were accustomed. Billy and Col would be fine with Fender Twins. Gib needed a Kustom amp with two fifteens in the cabinet.

Daw had brought along his cymbals, but he needed to find a kit he could work with, one with a good tone, both in a live setting *and* in the studio. That was going to be a very difficult task. His drums were crucial to the outcome of the band's recording. He wanted a seven-piece Tama set with a twenty-two-inch kick and a rack of steel mini-tymps. They were the foundation to the band's sound. The way he and Gib interacted, rhythmically and sonically, was as important as all the digital delays and tube amps with tremolo in the world. He knew it. And he willingly accepted the responsibility. He was very proud of his drumming and the quality of his drum sound. He wasn't going to let anything slide.

Gilly had his synth, a late-seventies Oberheim OB-X. He was of the opinion that the OB-X was the greatest synth ever made. No two were alike. Each one had a sound to itself. The OBX was renowned to become warmer and more harmonically dynamic as time went on.

Hot-rodding his model, Gilly got the pots replaced on each individual voice card, which made the instrument much easier to keep tuned. For that reason he was less reluctant than most to use his synth in live situations. And he was not afraid of shipping it across the country. He knew it was imperative to the band's sound that his keyboard settings were specific and exacting. All he needed was a good amp—a Roland Jazz Chorus would be fine.

It took several hours for the Gods to arrange their affairs at the equipment dealer. Their salesman, Rick, whom Angie called Ricky—though he had warned the others in advance, that they should not—made the band a great deal, renting them the whole set up for two hundred and fifty dollars a week. That really was a great deal, even by Portland standards, where the Gods could get pretty much any piece of equipment they wanted from any dealer for next to nothing.

By the time they finally left Sam Ash it was dark outside. With all the gear capably stashed in the back of Angie's van, the trip back to the apartment was crowded for the five band members and their host, but not as bad as the insufferable trip from the airport.

When they arrived back at the apartment, they were greeted by a lethargic bunch, who had spent the day smoking weed and drinking beer, watching game shows, and soap operas on TV. Billy, Gilly and Angie immediately retired to Angie's bedroom for chalk talk.

Even Col and Daw were a little put out over that. There wasn't the usual team BS session that typically followed such excursions. Instead, Billy and the two brothers were plotting the band's next step with no involvement or input from any of the others. It didn't exactly foment a sense of comraderie. The eight of them spent the rest of the evening wondering what would come next.

The following day, the band set up their equipment at the Power Station. It was ten o'clock in the morning, and the employees walking around the facility looked like zombies. There were no other musicians wandering the halls at that ungodly hour.

The studio was mostly deserted. According to Angie, the place didn't start hopping until after four, and really cranked up after ten at night. That was somewhat contrary to his previous inferences that there was always an abundance of activity—there being "no off hours" and all.

But the Gods were too wound up to pay attention to such details. Mak was along for the trip, as were Billy D. and Mick. The Goddesses had stayed back at the apartment with the intention of getting out and hitting the second-hand stores in the neighborhood.

They made contact with Annie Fisher, who had arrived from Portland and was staying at her brother's apartment in Greenwich Village. She was only a quick cab-ride through the Holland Tunnel away. She could come over and join them and show them around a bit. She'd grown up in Rego Park and she knew the area pretty well.

Mak, Mick and Billy D. hung out in the control room, staying out of the way, as Angie paraded around the recording area, guiding the band members to specific locations, hooking up direct boxes and microphones. Occasionally he would impart learned suggestions regarding the finer points of recording in a major league studio. The boys listened reverently.

In the control room, Angie sat behind the thirty-two channel Trident board and began to fine-tune each input, as the musicians warmed up, becoming accustomed to the space. Angie took careful notes as he set everything up, knowing the band would have to break down their set-up on Thursdays for their gigs at the Trappe

D'Or and then start all over again on Sunday afternoons. Angie wanted to make sure problems were kept to a minimum.

After a couple of hours, everyone was finally ready to try something with the tape rolling. Through the talkback channel Angie asked

—Billy. How ya' wanna do this? Basic tracks on all four songs and then come back and add the overdubs on the second pass, or what?

Billy thought about his options for a moment.

—Nah. I think we should record the whole song—basic tracks, overdubs, effects and everything. Then we'll move on to the next one...

Pensively, he peered at the studio walls.

—Rough mixes. We can sweeten 'em afterwards. But that way, we'll come out of here with some kinda demo, even if it's only a couple songs—like 'Police Told Me' and 'Made In Hong Kong' or somethin'—that are on the money.

—Well, that oughta give yer songs some momentum. We can do it that way if you want. I ain't guaranteein' it'll be any faster. In fact, it probably won't.

Angie eyed Billy through the thick soundproof glass between the control room and the studio.

—But it'll make things a lot easier in some ways when we hafta keep breakin' down and settin' up. Maybe we can get all the important stuff done on a song one day and come back and do the overdubs on another, so we ain't tryin' to catch the same sound as we had the last time.

The Gods nodded in agreement. Angie finished his thought.

—Yeh. I was worryin' about that, actually. That was gonna be a real bitch. That takes care of that.

The band kicked off their studio set with "Police Told Me"—one of their most ambitious songs yet—which Billy had written during the summer. Over Gilly's symphonic synth violins, Col added bubbly, echo-laden flurries of guitar.

The basic instrumental tracks went down fairly smooth. It only took seven takes to record a version they were all happy with. Billy, cost the band several extra takes. But he was alert for a sound he wanted, and he wanted the band to sound live, not canned.

Mak and Billy D. watched Angie closely. Mak was assessing the actual amount of effort Angie was putting into the project. He was reasonably satisfied that the band was getting its money's worth. Billy D. was absorbing as much tech information as his brain could hold.

Their time was up at three in the afternoon, and they had just finished listening to the chosen take for the fifth time. As they listened, Angie started rough-mixing the tracks, to get an idea of the balances he wanted. The band was happy with the results. It didn't sound like Portland. It sounded big and thick and shiny.

On Wednesday, the band overdubbed instrumental flourishes: Daw fluffed up a few fills; Gilly added string pads; Gib worked with Angie to get the bass tone he wanted in the mix; Col added a second layer of effervescent guitar figures.

Billy made his first stab at a lead vocal, adding a little cry to the end of his lines.

—The poh-lease told me-uh
The poh-lease told me-uh
The poh-lease told me about yo' plan.
It's the same old story
The same old story
You ended up coke in your hand.

The band had decided to load their gear out of the studio after the session. They were going to have to set up and sound check a new room, the Trappe D'Or, on Thursday. They figured they wouldn't get any more work done on the song until Sunday, unless Billy and Angie were able to make it in sometime over the weekend, to work on the vocals or something.

They arrived back at Angie's apartment around seven, and the girls were not back yet. Everyone opened up beers from a case Mak had bought Tuesday night. They fired up a couple of joints and talked about their experience in the big league studio. There was a lot of joking and laughing. Things were more like normal— more so than at any time since the trip had begun.

But it was just then that Angie motioned with his head, toward his room.

—Hey, Billy, come on back, I wanna talk to ya' a sec.

Billy followed dutifully, and Gilly was right behind him. Mak stood up from the couch, with some notion of tagging along—as much to make a point, as to listen in. Still, he was curious and more than a little hurt that he had not been included. He felt as if he had been demoted from his position as band manager. He had been relegated to the role of toady and beer hauler.

The others did not fail to notice Mak's actions, did not fail to share his same sense of frustration and unease. Billy D. and Mick felt like roadies and guitar tuners. Billy D. especially, was upset that he had no input on the recording process, nor on the selections of the track they kept. He thought the band should have kept the strongest version of "Police Told Me," the fourth take, and dubbed over the minor miscues that had come up. It was a much better version—much better energy and execution. But Billy didn't even ask his opinion—decided the issue on his own, without any input at all. They went with take seven.

Col, Gib and Daw felt like reserves on the band team. They were well aware it was Billy's band. It had always been Billy's band. But there had always been an overriding intimation of democracy and a feeling of shared contribution that was suddenly, sadly missing from the discourse. It was upsetting.

Back in his bedroom, Angie was addressing his young adherent. Billy listened seriously to Angie, believing him to be a source of knowledge that could not be found back in Portland. Angie knew the professional recording studio process. He knew a lot of important people who could be valuable down the line.

—Okay. Now Billy. You guys did pretty good fer yer first time in a real studio. You handled yerselves pretty well in there. I think ya' got a good take and some good dubs, and I can hear the finished version in my head now. It's real good.

Giving the matter some serious thought, Billy said.

—I think it sounds good too. I mean, y'know, there's still a lot of work to do on it and everything, but it sounds real good.

Angie took the praise with a modicum of modesty. Billy was not telling him anything he did not know. Billy speculated.

—Maybe we can get back in there sometime over the weekend and get the vocal part finished up.

Angie did not respond right away, but weighed Billy's request.

—Yeh. We'll see how it goes. See how ya' feel. A lot goin' on in the next few days. We'll see how ya' feel. Say look, there's somethin' I gotta talk t'ya' about.

Gilly nodded faintly, as though he knew what Angie was going to say.

—We gotta do somethin' about the population in this place. It's too crowded around here. Ya' can't even take a decent shit in the can, without someone walkin' right into yer fuckin' fumes. There's no hot water. The place is a fuckin' disaster area, with bodies everywhere. We gotta move some people outta here.

Billy's eyes widened at another unanticipated turn.

—Look. My mom...

Angie briefly looked at Gilly, confirming,

—*Our* mom...lives in our old family townhouse a coupla miles from here. It's a brownstone walk-up. Two floors. Four bedrooms. Three upstairs, with a second bathroom. There's a little attic where people could sleep. A little garden in the back. My...*our* mom lives there with our brother, Augie.

It sounded pretty nice to Billy. He started thinking about making the move.

—I think me 'n' you and 'Fredo and the girls should stay here. We can all fit in the bedrooms and nobody's sleepin' on the floor or the couch. That just sucks, man. It looks like a fuckin' flophouse around here.

Billy silently acknowledged Angie's concerns.

—If we move some of the guys over to my, our mom's, it'll be easier to talk business.

Billy winced. He dreaded telling the other band members that they would need to move to another place. He was aware that there had been a little distance between him and the band since they had gotten into town. And he knew the move being contemplated would not help that situation. But he felt he really did not have much choice. Angie was doing them all a big favor. He had to pretty much go with what Angie wanted.

—I'll talk to mom and Augie tomorrow. We'll have to give 'em somethin' like rent, ya' know? But I need to charge ya' a little bit here, too—just to cover my water and electricity and shit.

—How much ya' thinkin'?

Billy felt his temperature rising.

—Aw, maybe like fifty or seventy-five a week. I'd be all right with that and I think our mom would be okay with that much too. Maybe a little more. She's a nice lady—a little high-strung sometimes.

Giggling, Gilly chided his brother.

—Aw c'mon Ang, she's not that bad. She's cool. She puts up with you and me and Augie.

Angie just shrugged.

Feeling helpless, Billy resolved himself to the terms.

—When should we tell 'em?

—Aw, let me talk to ma and Augie, and we'll see what's up.

The meeting broke up with the three of them returning to the front room. Billy saw eight sets of eyes staring at him—each face with a slightly different expression. All of them seemed glum and grim.

The next day, the entourage and Annie Fisher woke up late and went to breakfast at the Miss America diner. They ate quietly, with not a lot of chitchat to liven things up. After the meal, they all piled into the van—which was just as uncomfortable as ever.

They arrived at the Trappe D'Or at around two. Larry was there with a couple of mixologist-looking guys, who were cleaning up around the bar area in the back. Mick and Billy D. helped Angie and the band move their gear in and get it set up.

Billy D. headed back to the soundboard in the middle of the room, to inspect the equipment he would be using. There was a decent sixteen-channel board, a couple of Crown PA amps and a few effects mounted in a rack. Angie brought some of his own effects too.

Angie ambled back to the area.

—Okay stuff, yeh?

—Yeah. It'll work okay, I guess.

Angie slid in behind the board.

—Well why'n't ya' go up and get all the mics and direct boxes set up, and when they're ready, we'll get to work on a sound check. You can do the stage monitors.

Shocked, Billy D. gawked disbelievingly at Angie. The guy was going to try to muscle in on the live sound engineering job. That was Billy D.'s position. He was the only soundman the band ever had. He had never missed an Unreal God's gig.

He walked away from the board and headed toward the stage, directly to where Billy was setting up his guitar and amp.

—Billy, man. Angie's tryin' to push me out back at the board. What's the deal? I thought I was the band's soundman.

—You *are* the soundman...

Billy emphasized.

—But Angie wanted to do it for a couple of gigs to get a feel for the band. He's never really heard us.

Billy D. was beside himself. He had not anticipated Billy's indifference. He couldn't understand why Billy wasn't stepping in. Frustrated, he moved toward Mak, who was standing off to the side of the stage. Billy D. quietly whined.

—Billy's gonna let Angie do the sound. I don't get it. If I was good enough to do my job in Portland, how come I'm suddenly not good enough to do it here?

Mak lowered his head in shame. He had been asking himself the same question. He felt completely cut out of the picture. Now, so did Billy D. The two of them stood, with shoulders hunched, commiserating like confused children. They felt lost and far away from home.

After the sound check, Billy placed his guitar on a stand and wandered back to the bar, where Larry was sitting, smoking a cigarette.

158

—Hey, Larry, how are ya'?

—Hey, kid. I'm awright. It's a little early in the day for me. But I wanted to be here on yer first day settin' up and everything, in case ya' needed somethin'.

He ticked his cigarette on a black plastic ashtray, flicked off the ash, and sucked down another breath.

—So what'ya' think of the fuckin' *Big Apple*, so far, kid?

He briefly changed character.

—Have you *formulated* any impressions?

Billy was caught off guard by Larry's suddenly refined demeanor.

—Uh. Whuh? Uh, yeah, everything's pretty big, and things move really fast here. It kind of like takes my breath away. But it's exciting, and I think I'm gonna learn—and the whole band's gonna learn a lot—while we're here. We've already learned a lot in just a few days.

Pulling profoundly on his cigarette, Larry slowly nodded in agreement, trails of smoke leaking from the corners of his mouth.

—Yeh. Things move faster around here, maybe. I've heard that before. Seems pretty fuckin' normal to me. It's the only speed I know.

Billy tried to angle the conversation back to its intended objective.

—So, what did you decide about an opening band tonight? Are you havin' anybody come down? We're fine playin' the whole night. We've got three sets of great stuff.

As he tapped his cigarette on the rim of the ashtray, Larry addressed Billy with his glossy gaze.

—I was gonna ask ya'. It's up to you. If ya' want somebody ta' open up, then I can call any number of bands. They'd be right down. Any of 'em'd love a Thursday openin' slot.

—Nah. I think we're fine playin' all three sets. We need to go through our material to keep it fresh, and we'll see if any of your regulars like us. Maybe catch the ones who just stop in for a beer or two.

—That's good thinkin'. If they like ya' it'll get around the whole neighborhood pretty fuckin' fast. We'll know by tomorrow or Saturday night. If people start showin' up to catch yer shit....

Larry looked in the direction of Candy and MJ, who were intently chatting with Annie in the middle of the dance floor.

159

—And I'm pretty sure there's a few guys'll be comin' back a time or two to check out that Candy chick... The other one ain't bad either. She's fuckin' cherry. But that Candy gets me goin'.

With his thumb, he rolled his cigarette between his fingers.

Delayed by the fine-tuning required to dial in the rest of the band in the sound check, afterward Angie walked quickly up to the two of them—as if he might have missed something crucial. Larry noticed.

—Hey, Ang. What's up, man? Y'afraid yer missin' somethin' back here, or what?

Taking a long last deep drag from his cigarette, Larry crushed it out in the black ashtray. Defensive, Angie spoke up.

—Nah. It's not like that, y'know? But I need ta be in the loop with all this shit.

—What? You their fuckin' manager now, all of a sudden?

Peering at the mirror behind the bar, Angie searched for the precise words he wished to articulate. He wanted to be prudent.

—Larry, man. I gotta take care of these guys. Look out for 'em. Make sure guys like you don't lead 'em down the fuckin' *primrose path*. Show 'em the ropes. Y'know?

—Who the fuck 'r' you? Saint Angelo of the Wandering Bands all of a sudden?

—Look. I just wanna make sure they don't make a bad decision talkin' to the wrong people, that's all.

He innocently smiled at Billy. Then, predictably, Gilly walked up with an asinine grin on his face.

Observing the activities transpiring back at the bar, Mak decided the only way he was going to remain informed about anything was to insinuate himself directly. He strolled back, to join Billy, the club manager and the brothers.

With his hands in his pockets, Mak approached, shyly smiling at the four of them.

—Hey. How's it goin'?

The quartet suddenly became silent. Billy spoke up.

—Hey, Mak. Me 'n' Larry were talkin' about whether or not to have an openin' band tonight, and I said no. We don't need one: we need the workout.

Mak sniffed, bobbing his head in assent.

—I think you're right about that. That's a good idea.

Angie and Gilly raised their shoulders in vague agreement.

Holding his hand out toward Larry, Mak said.

—Hey, man, I don't think we've met. I'm Mak Poppin, the band's manager.

—Oh, *you're* the manager. I was startin' to wonder if Angie wasn't takin' over the job. Yeh, hey, I'm Larry. Nice ta' meet ya'.

They shook hands. Ignoring what Larry had just said, Mak maintained his straightforward approach.

—So, have we got the money thing figured out?

Billy and the rest were caught off guard by the abruptness of Mak's query. Billy replied.

—Nah. We haven't talked about that at all. What d' you guys think?

Billy's expression sought answers from Angie and Larry. Larry took up the subject.

—I got no fuckin' idea how much we're gonna draw tonight. It's kind of a crapshoot. When you're openin' for the Dickens guys, I'll give ya' a hundred and fifty. That's about the best I can do with that. We'll just hafta see how the Thursdays go. But I'll take care of ya'.

With gloomy faces, Mak and Billy met each others' furtive glances: money was going to be a problem. It wasn't going to take very long at all before it became a huge problem.

Billy D. ambled up to the congregation gathering at the bar.

—What's happenin', guys?

Billy smiled uncomfortably at his soundman.

—What's happenin' D.?

Billy D. stared directly at Angie, with as much enmity as he could muster, which was hardly any at all, even by Portland standards. He was a big, round baby duck. Angie sensed the hostility, all the same, though he wasn't in the least intimidated by it. But Angie was Angie—as Gilly had warned, before the band left home for the trip east—and he was gonna do what he was gonna do. Billy D. answered.

—Not much. Just hangin' out. Catchin' the vibe.

Something was weird. Even for Billy D., he was uncommonly laid back. Calm as Mount Saint Helens in the moments before it blew.

—Groovin' on down.

Billy knew Billy D. as well as anyone, and he had never seen him act so strangely. It was as if he was getting ready to erupt and the boss was not sure what he would do if that were to happen.

With nothing more to say, the five of them stood in an uncomfortable semi-circle around Larry, who was sitting at the bar, lighting up another cigarette. He blew a smoke ring as Mick and Col, Gib and Daw, hands in their pockets, gathered with the group as well. Larry loved an audience—no matter how ill-at-ease they were—but he felt like he was surrounded by a bunch of stiffs.

—Well. Ya' sounded pretty good up there. I think my crowd's gonna like you guys. They might like ya' a lot. We'll just hafta see.

Col and Daw waved in tacit concurrence and moved over to order beers from the bartender. Gib and Mick quickly joined them. The four of them stood about six feet away from the powwow and talked quietly between themselves.

The Goddesses were in the middle of the room, unselfconsciously practicing various moves, stretching and twirling around, as they limbered up, laughing and talking to Annie. Larry undressed the two dancers with his eyes, redressed them in sexy lingerie and then undressed them again—the flaccid cigarette hanging from his distracted lip.

—Man. That tall skinny one is one really flexible bitch.

Everyone smiled warily.

—Who's that flat chick with the blond hair?

In a quandary, jacking his face around, Billy attempted a response.

—Who's the wha'? Oh, Annie. That's Annie.

—She a dancer too?

—Nah. She's just a friend of ours. From Portland. She came out here to visit her family and hang out with us in New York.

With an edge of concern in his voice, Larry confirmed.

—She *ain't* a dancer, though?

—No.

Puffing on his cigarette, Larry breathed an audible sigh of relief. Not a dancer. Okay.

The flock of them flew back to Angie's apartment, where they called out for pizza. Mak was elected to go to the corner bodega for another case of beer, and Billy D. volunteered to accompany him.

The troupe was excited and even a little nervous. Billy had not been nervous before a gig since some of the Malchicks' first shows. It was an entirely foreign sensation for all of them. He hoped that the nerves were a portent: a positive one.

On the sidewalk, alongside Mak, Billy D. sauntered toward the little grocery store. He was worried and he was fretting.

—Mak. Man, this is fucked.

—What's fucked? Havin' to go get the beer?

—No. Well...sorta I guess. No. It's all fucked. What the hell is goin' on? It hasn't even been, like, a week out here and everything's changed. It's total bullshit.

—D., we can't let it get to us. We know what our jobs are and we gotta do 'em, as best we can. Under the circumstances. We gotta try. We can't, like, let ourselves get pushed out of our jobs.

—I get that. I saw what you were doin' back at the club. I think it's a good idea to stay in the mix, even if Angie and Gilly are tryin' to crowd us out.

—Yeah. I can't figure out what's goin' on. It's like we're not even here. Or we don't know what we're doin' or I don't know what. It's crazy. But I'm just gonna hang in there. I'm not gettin' pushed out of *my* job. Not without a fight.

By the time the pair returned to the apartment, the pizza delivery guy's car was double-parked outside the warehouse, with the motor idling. They hustled up the stairs to the second floor, just as the delivery fellow was retreating down. Walking through the door, they found everyone in the kitchen, tearing at the pizzas on the counter. Mak announced.

—Beer's here.

He gingerly set the box down on the kitchen floor. Billy D. opened bottles with the bottom of a Bic lighter, efficiently handing them out. He slipped one to Mak and grabbed one for himself. Then the two of them grabbed a piece of pizza and sat down at the kitchen table, vying for space with the dismembered sixteen-channel board.

After eating, and working on a second round of beers, Billy produced a big spliff, which he lit with the lighter that Billy D. had been using as a bottle opener.

—This is some of Incomparable John's shit. It's kind of a special occasion—first gig in New York and all. I figured I should break it out.

He took a big hit on the joint and passed it on.

—No matter what happens, nobody can take this gig away from us. We made it. Now all we have to do is play as good as we can play and blow these assholes away.

Raising his arm in a small cheer, Billy smiled confidently.

—And we're gonna do it.

# XVII

The band arrived at the Trappe D'Or around seven. The five Gods, two Goddesses, and Annie crowded into the small dressing room, located through a door behind the stage. To their surprise there was a cooler waiting for them, stocked with bottles of Rolling Rock, cans of Coke and 7-Up, a quart of orange juice, a bottle of vodka and a bottle of rum.

With only a small partition in the corner for privacy, the guys hurriedly slipped into their outfits, so that the girls could dress in private. They traipsed around the stage, toting their bottles of Rolling Rock—not certain as to what they should do with themselves. A little lost.

Hopping off the stage, Billy wandered over toward Mak.

—What d'ya think, Pop?

Unsure how to answer, Mak twisted his mouth ruefully.

—Wha' do I think about what?

—What d'ya think about all this? Bein' here? The whole deal?

Mak knew it was not the right time to have it out with Billy. Yet he wondered if the time would come again.

—Oh, it seems okay. It's all a little chaotic. I think some people are feeling left out.

—Left *out*? How?

—This probably isn't the best time to go over it, Billy. Maybe tomorrow before the show.

—Yeah. Maybe so. So, who's pissed off?

—We'll go over it tomorrow, man.

—Yeah. Okay. Tomorrow.

Somewhat fuddled, Billy moved toward the bar at the back of the room, briefly chatting with Larry and Angie, before he rejoined the rest of the Gods up on the stage. The Goddesses emerged from the dressing room, wearing skin-tight, silver one-piece hooded-jumpsuits, with sexy, cat-faced cardboard masks and white Batman panther boots wrapping their calves, up to the knees. They looked like characters from *Tron*.

164

Once the women had finished dressing, everyone reconvened in the green room to hang out and prepare, but mostly so that they could make a grand entrance when the show was to begin. The males each drank a couple more beers and were properly lubricated when showtime rolled around at nine-thirty. Candy, MJ, and Annie sat in the corner blathering anxiously.

There were about one hundred people in the room when the Unreal Gods took the stage. Those in attendance were not particularly interested in the band's goings on. They were at the Trappe D'Or on a Thursday as part of their week's social activities line-up. If the band was okay, some of them might stick around.

As was often the case, Mak introduced the band, parroting Ed Sullivan.

—And now, right here on our stage, it's Billy Granger and his Unreal Gods— featuring the Goddesses a Go-Go. C'mon. Let's hear it for 'em.

There was no reaction from the attendees hanging out back at the bar. In the threatening quiet, Billy and the band swept into the intro of the first song.

—Good evening, ladies and gentlemen. I'm Billy Granger, and these guys here are the Unreal Gods.

Candy and MJ took to the stage.

—And these are the Goddesses a Go-Go.

A small, raucous cheer went up from the back of the room.

—And we're here to tell ya' that 'Go Go Boots Are Coming Back'.

The band slipped comfortably into the tremolo thickened first verse.

Almost immediately, several people in the back of the room made their way closer, to check out the band. They stood about fifteen feet away from the three-foot-high stage. Billy swung into overdrive as the Goddesses churned and wriggled at either side. Another Gods show was under way. Another show just like the other shows. All was right with the world.

They finished the first set with "Symmetry," playing to one hundred and fifty people standing on the dance floor, holding drinks, and intently watching the band. Whenever the Goddesses came out, the crowd would inch toward the stage; they would recede on the songs whereupon to which they did not perform.

Billy's energy may have been a little too intense for a first set. That did not deter a gaggle of young women from huddling near him deciding amongst themselves what they liked most about him. Some liked his blond hair; others his Nordic water-blue eyes. Still others adored his boyish grin and guileless charm. He was rapidly acquiring fans and all was well.

The Gods concluded the night with "English Boy." The audience, which had swelled to maybe two hundred and fifty demanded an encore. The band followed with an inspired version of "Police Told Me," which the crowd seemed to love. The Unreal Gods were on their way at the Trappe D'Or.

After the show Billy, Mak, Gilly and Angie went back to talk to Larry, to see how they had done. Larry handed Angie twelve hundred and seventy dollars.

—Ya' had two hundred and fifty-four paid at the door.

Grimacing, Mak and Billy looked at each other warily. Mak had, from a distance, been casually counting the number of people who had paid the cover charge at the door, and it was easily far more than two hundred and fifty patrons.

—Ya' did real good up there. I betcha ya' do great this weekend. You'll scare the shit out of Moby Dickens.

Peeling off six twenties, a five and two ones from the door money, Angie handed the rest of the stack to Mak.

—Hundred and twenty-seven bucks. That's my ten percent of the door.

Incredulous, Mak asked.

—Ten percent? For what?

—Commission. For bookin' the gig. I gotta get my ten percent commission. That's one of my gigs. I gotta make a fuckin' livin' too, man.

He defensively glared at Mak. Billy jumped in.

—Yeah, sure. Ten percent. No problem. Thanks for everything you've done for us, Angie.

Disarmed, Angie ducked his head, jamming the commission into the pocket of his jeans. Mak slid the remaining money into the inside pocket of his coat. Eleven hundred and forty-three dollars. It wasn't nearly what they should have gotten. They lost at least three hundred at the door. That was Larry's "commission," most likely. Everyone was always getting paid for something in the City. There were no free rides.

It was three in the morning by the time they made it back to Angie's. Everyone was exhausted. Gilly followed Angie back to his bedroom. Candy, MJ and Annie went back to their room. Billy remained out in the living room with the rest of the band and staff.

They turned on the TV, a repeat of the Joe Franklin Show on WOR, smoked a series of joints and ran through a round of beers from the case Mak and Billy D. had bought earlier in the day. Billy spoke up.

166

—That was a good show. We won 'em over.

Lolling his head in spaced-out accord, Col said.

—I wasn't sure if it was gonna happen, at first. That was a new one for us, I think, wasn't it? First time we didn't have a crowd automatically goin' nuts over us?

He looked to Mak for confirmation.

—Yeah. I think you're right. I don't remember anywhere where we didn't have 'em pretty much eatin' out of our hands. Maybe up in Seattle, openin' for John Cale.

—Oh yeah. John Cale. And there was Peter Tosh, of course.

Mak's eyes widened in surprise. He stealthily juddered his fingers, shooshing Col. Billy did not need to be reminded about *that* one. Mak followed-up, artfully dodging the subject

—Yeah. It was pretty good for a first night in a strange town. We did okay.

Between themselves, Daw, Gib, Mick, and Billy D. discussed nuts and bolts rhythmic and sonic nuances, sorting things out, especially on some of the newer material. Col lost interest in trying to talk with Billy and Mak, who were really rather quiet and withdrawn. He joined in the conversation with his comrades.

Though each knew what the other was thinking, Billy and Mak said nothing. Both were considering certain unhappy members of the band. Both were doing quick arithmetic, calculating that the band would earn fifteen hundred dollars from their first weekend in the city. It was something.

But Mak knew it was not nearly enough to support the band and to pay for recording. And Billy knew it wasn't even enough, just to support the band, especially if they were going to be split up and housed in two different locations. Both heaved frustrated sighs, but for slightly different reasons.

Everyone slept in late on Friday. Except Angie and Gilly, who were up by eleven and out the door, and Annie, who ended up taking a cab back to her brother's place. The rest did not stir until nearly two in the afternoon—their first real opportunity to sleep-in since they had arrived in Jersey City.

When they finally began to stir, they all were hungry and had nothing to eat. So Mak was again selected to go down to the store and get beer. The decision also was made to order take-out from the Chinese restaurant down the street from Angie's pad on Westside Avenue. So it fell to Mak to retrieve that as well. Billy D. again volunteered to go with him.

Antonia had always been the matriarch of the Belladro family. But after Egidio died, when the boys were all in their teens, she became exalted, ruling with an iron hand. Her word stood. To incur her wrath was to invite real physical pain and severe psychological torture.

167

For Angelo, Alfredo and Augusto, she would at various times call up their dead father, conjure the body of Christ and the hand of god, or invoke the eternal suffering of a soul in hell. The boys lived in mortal fear of their mother—especially the youngest, Augie, who had never really recovered emotionally from the loss of his father.

He was a hermit and not likely to ever depart the family house. He had a bedroom upstairs at the other end of the house from his mother's, whose was at the front on the main floor. When he wasn't listening to top forty radio, he played a limited collection of records on a dilapidated portable stereo, with a nickel taped to the tone arm to keep the record from skipping.

He usually carried a baseball bat with him and was known to occasionally mutter "no meat!" for no particular reason. He had yet to do anything with the baseball bat, so it was unclear why he carried it (possibly to club to death anyone caught eating meat in his presence). It was a good deterrent, though his mother freely ate meat, apparently with no repercussions.

Angie and Gilly unlocked the front door and stirred about the entryway of the family house. Angie called out.

—Ma! Augie! Anybody home? Ma?

There were rustlings in two different parts of the house. Mrs. Beladro shuffled in from the laundry room in back of the kitchen.

—Angelo, what'sa matta, yer yellin'? *Alfredo*! Little Alfredo. Come 'n' kiss yer mama.

Dutifully hugging his mother, Gilly kissed the top of her head.

—Fredo. Yer so skinny. Aren't ya' eatin' no more? And what's all over yer face? Is that make up, or what? Ya' look so strange. I hardly reco'nize ya'. A mother don't reco'nize her own kid, it's a sad day.

Gilly wordlessly shrank away.

—We hafta tell yer brother.

She scurried to the base of the staircase leading up to the second story, shouting out.

—Augusto! Come down stairs. I gotta surprise for ya'. Angelo's here.

Again, there was a stirring up above.

—Augusto!

More rustling.

—Yah. Ma. I hear ya'. Stop yellin' I'll be down in justa second.

Soon after, Augie came down, with his trusty Reggie Jackson model Louisville Slugger hanging over his shoulder. He noticed Gilly standing in the hall.

—Hey Fredo. It's you! It's good to see ya'. Ya' look like a fuckin' fairy. But it's good to see ya'. Who're ya' supposed to be anyway? Johnny fuckin' Rotten or somebody?

—Well no. Johnny Rotten, actually...

Gilly cut short his clarification. Augie wasn't listening. His mind had wandered off somewhere.

Augie was built like Gilly, slender and sickly, but he was hairy like Angie. He had long curly black hair and a thick, heavy beard and looked older than thirty-eight years. Weary and defeated. He was bleakly unkempt—seeming not to have bathed for several days.

He snapped back to the present.

—Yeh. Yeh. Johnny Rotten was what?

—A punk. I'm not a punk.

—What *are* ya' then?

—I'm a musician and I dress like a musician. It's just a costume.

Bashfully, but determinedly, Gilly continued.

—Punks dress like punks. I don't dress like a punk. Punks have leather jackets and safety pins and purple Mohawks. I dress New Wave. New Romantic. The lipstick and mascara...It's just a costume. I'm still the same person.

—Yeh, sure. Maybe.

Laughing, Augie finished his thought.

—But ya' look like a fuckin' fag.

Mrs. Belladro agreed. But she summarily moved to another line of questioning.

—So how long ya' in the city, Alfredo?

—Three or four weeks. Anyway.

He fixed his eyes on Angie, who stood expressionless in front of his mother and Augie.

Angie picked up the thread.

—Yeh, Ma. That's what we came over to talk at ya' about. Wha'd'ya' think about havin' some of the band people stay here with you and Augie for a few weeks? In the spare bedrooms upstairs and maybe in the attic.

With a worried look, Mrs. Belladro replied.

—Well, I dunno, Angelo. They gonna be noisy and up takin' drugs all night?

—Nah, Ma. They ain't like that. Maybe they'd smoke a little weed. But that's it. They're good guys. They'd pay ya' some rent. Ya' wouldn't hafta cook for 'em 'r nothin'.

Giving the matter some serious consideration, Mrs. Belladro said.

—Yeh. Yeh. Go on.

—They'd be out of the house all days from Sunday to Thursday, and out all night on Thursdays, Fridays and Saturdays.

—Would they make a lot of noise comin' in so late?

—Nah, Ma. They're quiet, normal guys. Like I said, they drink a few beers and smoke a joint. No big deal. They can do the weed up in the attic, so it don't smell up the house. They'd be good with that.

—How much ya' talkin' with the rent thing?

—Maybe seventy-five a week? They can't afford much. They're destitute musicians. They got no money.

—Yeh. I suppose it'd be okay. That's an extra three hundred a month…

—Thanks, ma. It's pretty crowded with everybody stayin' at my place.

—How many are there of ya'?

—Well, there's me...and ten?

He looked over at Gilly for confirmation. Yes.

—Yeah. Me and ten people with the band. That's too many to crowd into my place, even as big as it is.

—How many ya' thinkin' of bringin' over here?

—Six I guess. Five? Mak, Billy D. and Mick. Col, Daw and Gib. Yeh. Six. Two in each bedroom and a couple in the attic.

—Well, there ain't enough beds.

—We can get the cots out from the basement. We'll figure it out.

—Well, I guess okay, then. I hope I don't regret it. They aren't like those three guys are they?

—Guys in Grand Funk Railroad? Mark, Don and…what was the bass player's name? Mel? Yeah Mel. That was it.

Mrs. Belladro looked at Angie expectantly.

—Nah. These guys're a lot mellower. That was a long time ago. Different era, Ma. Those guys in Grand Funk was trouble. They were fightin' with their manager, and they were feelin' pretty sour.

—Yeh, but I never forgot it. Swore I'd never do that again. Now look at me. Ya' got me wrapped around your little finger, Angelo.

He kissed his mother on the forehead.

—Okay. Well, we'll prob'ly bring 'em over Sunday or Monday sometime. We gotta load gear into the studio Sunday afternoon. So it might be early evenin'. Like six or seven. Not too late.

—Alright. But I hope it's not like yer Railroad buddies. They was a real headache.

—Ya' won't even know these guys are here.

It was pushing six o'clock, and the band was finishing up the Chinese food, and a second and, in some instances, a third round of beers when Angie and Gilly finally returned from their mother's house (with a stop for lunch on the way back). They both looked a little ashamed, knowing that they had just sold much of the band down the river and across town to Mama's house.

Angie and Gilly wrangled Billy and led him back to Angie's room. The others determined that it was more secret hocus-pocus and there was nothing they were going to know about it until they were told.

Back in Angie's room, he let Billy know the outcome of the meeting with Mama Belladro.

—So Billy, our mom said okay. We can move everybody over on Sunday. Sometime Sunday afternoon, or Monday. Whenever.

Saying nothing, Billy dispassionately weighed the situation.

—I told her we'd be bringin' six of 'em over. She's okay with a hundred bucks a week rent. That's a good deal.

Billy maintained his stoic silence. He had no idea that Angie had tacked an extra twenty-five dollar finders fee onto the weekly rent. But if he had really thought about it, he would have realized that there was no way Angie was going to miss out on any chance to make a little bit more money, no matter where the opportunity fell.

It was left to Billy to break the news to the rest of the band that they would be splitting up, as least as far as their living quarters were concerned. He determined that he would either tell them after the show that night, or on Saturday, after everyone woke up. Or maybe on Sunday. Maybe Sunday would be best.

After the meal, everyone relaxed for a couple of hours, before heading down to the Trappe D'Or to open for Moby Dickens. When they arrived at the club, they were surprised to find it packed with Dickens fans—even before nine o'clock. Larry wasn't kidding when he said they were popular in the neighborhood.

When the Unreal Gods walked in, an audible hush crept over the room. Apparently the portion of the crowd that had seen the Unreals the night before were enlightening the uninitiated in attendance as to what they might expect.

That sense of suspense filled the air with certain electricity. Even Larry noticed. He had never before experienced that kind of a *rush* before a Moby Dickens show, in the three years they had been playing his club. Clearly, many in the crowd had come to see Billy and the Unreal Gods. Nothing moved faster than word on the street.

The Gods played forty-five minutes, opening with "Go Go Boots Are Coming Back," with the Goddesses instantly interesting the male contingent in the proceedings. They ended the set with "Symmetry." The crowd, won over early on, demanded an encore and the band did "Police Told Me." It was a wonderfully successful night. It seemed likely that they would do well on the following Thursday—and they still had another night to promote that show.

They hung around for the whole night, catching both Moby Dickens' sets. They were a reasonably proficient bar band. Good-natured rock. Their original material mostly dealt with lonely Friday nights and drunken Saturdays. But the crowd knew all their songs, often singing along with the choruses.

The two bands bonded at the end of the night, communing with the true fealty of fellow rock musicians, while slugging back shots of whiskey with beer backs. Everyone got sloshed.

The Dickens' leader, Anthony Hudson told Billy stories about playing the Trappe D'Or and opening some shows around Jersey for Bruce and the E Street Band. One night, he even came in and jammed with Moby Dickens.

Angie handed Mak one hundred and thirty-five dollars for the evening's show. Mak looked at the money briefly, and noticed.

—Hey, there's...

Then he remembered that Angie was taking his commission out of the receipts.

Mak shrugged dejectedly and put the money in his pocket. Another couple days of pizza and beer.

It was three before the band got back to Angie's place. They were all worn out, but feeling good that hey had succeeded in winning over a large part of Moby Dickens' crowd. Billy told everyone they had done a good job and then went off to his bedroom. He'd save the discussion about moving until tomorrow. Or maybe Sunday.

Candy and MJ huddled on the couch, trying to warm up. Both had gotten chilled on the ride home in the van. Candy, especially, seemed to have difficulty in shaking off the October cold. She shivered uncontrollably as MJ put her arms around her, sharing body heat. After a while, the two of them wandered back to their room, to cover up with a couple of blankets.

Without saying a word to the others, Angie and Gilly headed off to Angie's room. Mick, Mak, Billy D., and Gib, Daw, and Col moved quickly to select new seating arrangements—and then spent half an hour silently staring off into space. The bunch of them nodded off, sleeping as best they could under the conditions.

Waking up around noon on Saturday, Billy wandered out to the front room to find Mak and a few of the others starting to stir, as well. A little hungover, he sat dozing at the dining room table, mumphy head cradled in his hand. Mak approached and handed Billy the wad of bills that he had received from Angie, the night before.

—It's one thirty-five. Angie took his ten percent. Fifteen dollars.

Billy stared at the money as if he did not recognize it as coin of the realm. Mak continued his thought.

—It's not much, but at least it'll buy us all breakfast and dinner, or *somethin'*.

Jamming the money in his jeans pocket, Billy said.

—Yeah. Okay. Cool.

Billy briefly thought about discussing the new living arrangements with Mak, but chickened out. Maybe later. Tomorrow for sure.

The others started to wake up as well, mouths thick with the booze of the night before, heads fogged by the long slog that was their first week in the Big Apple. Each of them considered that they would be there for many more weeks to come, and all surmised the toll that the expedition might take on their individual psyches.

As Candy and MJ meandered out from their room, it was instantly obvious that Candy did not feel well at all. She was congested and hoarse, her voice nearly an octave deeper than normal. MJ had her arm wrapped around the shoulders of her partner. Candy asked.

—Is there, like, any coffee or soup in this place?

Gawking at her heedlessly, the others sat dumb. Mak stepped forward.

—Let's look around.

He casually opened the cupboard over the counter.

—There's some canned soup here. Split Pea and Cream of Mushroom..

Making a sickly face, Candy's eyes urged Mak to keep looking. He checked another cupboard. Dishes. What there were of them. The next cupboard did contain coffee.

—Coffee. Folger's instant. Lipton's chicken noodle soup mix.

He tossed Candy the jar of coffee and flashed the box of soup.

—OK. I guess that's the best I'm gonna do. Could you hand me that can of mushroom soup then?

He fished the can from the first cupboard.

—Oh. Toss me the soup mix too. I might as well stock up while I have the chance.

Gently, Mak tossed her the box of soup, as she moved toward the cabinets under the counter, seeking a pan in which to boil water for the coffee and chicken noodle soup. Candy had determined that she would save the cream of mushroom soup for later when she was hungrier. Mak proposed.

—Hey Billy, maybe we should hike up to that All-American place, Miss America— whatever it's called. Where we ate...Go up there and get something to eat.

The rest of the group perked up at the suggestion. Col piped in.

—That sounds good to me.

Chiming in together, Daw and Gib agreed simultaneously.

—Yeah. Sounds good.

Billy was in no mood to argue. He agreed.

—Okay. Let's get it together, then, and we'll head on down there.

The troops quickly assembled. Billy was the last out the door. He looked back at MJ and Candy.

—Can I get you two anything? Candy? You want a couple burgers or some French fries?

—Oh yeah. French fries!

Raising her eyebrows, MJ smiled.

—Me too. French fries. And a chocolate milkshake. Please.

Billy replied.

—Check. Got it.

And he closed the door behind him.

# XVIII

A distinctive voltage hovered in the air, when the band arrived at the Trappe D'Or that Saturday evening. Even at eight, the club was full. There were five or six hundred people in the room, with wound-up revelers already engaged in serious motivational therapy. It was obvious to the Gods that the people were there to see them.

For one thing, it was a different crowd from what the Moby crew drew. Moby Dickens' crowd was more of a neighborhood thing. The audience awaiting the Unreal Gods was more "cosmopolitan." Younger. Hipper.

The other clear indication was that such a large crowd had even gathered at all. There was no other reason for them to turn up so early, so far in advance of Moby Dickens' starting time of eleven or so. Instead there was an excited throng, anticipating a crazy brush with burgeoning greatness.

It was an atmosphere to which the Gods had become accustomed—even begun to expect. The Thursday night show was the only time they had ever played to anything less than a packed house. They were used to being adored. They were inured to being treated as stars. They were stars.

Squeezed into the green room, each band member dressed carefully, adopting a look that would play to the room. Billy had a red bandana wrapped across his forehead, heavy eye shadow and mascara. He wore a white dress shirt, with the sleeves torn off at the shoulder, the collar turned up, with the tips crisply ironed in neat little wings. Blue jeans and his red cowboy boots.

With his hair ratted up into an angry nest, an elaborate single earring dripping down from his left ear, Col had on a sleeveless black cowboy shirt with the ultimate in western floral designs—embroidered scroll-work across the chest, smiley pockets and mother of pearl snap closures. Jeans, with scarves and chains woven through the belt loops.

Gilly, Daw and Gib were within their typical costume parameters: grinning Gilly, a black-leather clad twenty-first century gypsy; Daw the enigmatic gym-rat; the inscrutable Gib in black slacks, pink bucks and a brown golf shirt with ornate converging pink stripes.

The Goddesses wore sequined one-piece bathing suits and snug hats, with sequined dance shoes. Candy was fighting her cold, and MJ helped her to get dressed and made up. Then she covered herself with her coat, snarking and sniffing in great misery.

Mick and Billy D. arranged amps and tuned instruments on the stage as Angie tweaked the sound for the full room. Mak stood to one side of the stage, counting heads. He wanted to know how many in the crowd that were there to see the Unreal Gods would hang around to watch Moby Dickens launch through their effective sets of predictable barroom rock.

Smiling faintly, Larry Giufreddi stood at the back of the bar surveying, with satisfaction, the mass of people spread out before him, secure in the fact that he was going to make a lot of money that night. A big payday.

Since the Unreals were only getting a hundred and fifty dollars to open, with Moby Dickens receiving their usual five hundred dollar guarantee, Larry stood to make at least a couple grand, twenty-five hundred at the door. Maybe more.

The band kicked into the intro to "Go-Go Boots Are Coming Back," the room instantly congealed into a writhing mass of bodies at the foot of the stage, sensuously moving to the beat. The Goddesses took the stage, swimming in the green and red light of the spots. Shimmering mermaids floated before the transfixed males in the audience.

—Go-Go boots are comin' back.
Don't throw yours away-ee.

And so the hypnotic Unreal Gods experience began to casually unfurl, lulling the crowd into a goofy, good-natured daze. They were a peculiar musical object, theretofore unseen and unheard in those faraway parts. They were west coast, all the way.

"Girlfriend's Drawers," "High School Degree," "Boom Chuck Rock," "Upstroke Down," the band ran through their tried and true material, slowly gathering momentum. As they wound through the set, Billy noticed a beautiful young woman in the undergrowth gazing at him with flirtatious intent.

She was incredibly pretty—young looking, with straight, silver-streaked, auburn hair that draped around her shoulders and hung to the middle of her back; skyblue eyes, which flickered out from beneath thin brown eyebrows; a full mouth with a heart-shaped upper lip. She was supurely statuesque, with an incredible figure—graceful and poised. She saw Billy staring at her and smiled broadly back at him. He nearly forgot the words to "Something New," just from the distraction.

The band eventually finished the set and Angie revved up a break tape—Duran Duran, Bruce, Culture Club, the Stones, Tom Petty, Adam Ant, The Cars, et cetera. The spectators stood in groups on the dance floor, smoking and shouting above the din.

Billy hopped down from the stage and immediately moved through the throng toward the woman in the crowd. He smiled at her with a big, boyish grin, batting his eyes coyly as he approached her.

—Hi. I couldn't help but notice you from the stage.

—No?

—Oh, yeah. You're, like, the most beautiful woman in this place. Possibly the most beautiful woman I've ever seen. How could I *miss* you?

She blushed a little.

—I like your band. You guys are a lot of fun.

He ran a hand through his sweat-drenched hair.

—Thank you. That's nice of you to say. We have a lot of fun on stage.

—Yes, it certainly seems like you do.

She held out her hand.

—I'm Happy.

Gripping her hand, Billy corkscrewed a brow.

—Well, I'm not doin' too bad myself.

—Yeah, like I haven't heard that one before. No, Happy. That's my name. Happy.

—Happy, huh? I don't think...no, I *know* I've never known anyone named Happy before. Well, are you?

—Am I what?

—Happy?

—Yes, I'm Happy. I'm always Happy. Even when I'm sad.

It seemed to Billy that he was talking to an exasperated parrot. But he realized, too, that, with such an unusual name, she probably had been having the very same conversation, five times a day, every day of her life.

—Well, you'll have to tell me. I mean, you don't have to, but I'd like to know how you came by the name Happy.

That, too, was familiar territory.

—It's more boring than you might think. There's no spinster aunt or welling of great joy by my parents when I was born or anything. It's like this. My name is Hailey Ann Paterson...

—Like Floyd Patterson? The boxer?

She stared at him uncomprehendingly.

—I don't know who Floyd Patterson is. Paterson, like the capitol of New Jersey. Paterson.

Then it was Billy's turn to look perplexed, geography not being among his most favored subjects. She continued.

—Paterson, with one 't'. Paterson is the capitol of New Jersey. Hailey Ann Paterson. One 't'.

Billy nodded vacantly, a little bewildered by the mesmerizing depth of her blue eyes and the sculpted opulence of her cheekbones, the dewy translucence of her skin.

—Yeah. I got it. Continue. Please.

—So, because my initials are H-A-P, I'm Happy. I guess I was a good-natured little tyke, with a cheery disposition. So that pretty much meant that it was a given that I would be Happy.

She half-shrugged.

—It's not the worst name in the world to have. It could have been Maddy or Saddy or Fraidy or Stressa or something like that. Joy. Joy's okay, I guess. Sunny. I could have been Sunny. I think it's easier to be Happy than Sunny...

—Does anyone call you Hailey?

—*No one* calls me Hailey. No one has ever called me Hailey. I'm just Happy. That's all.

—Then, I'll call you Hailey.

—No. You better not do that. I won't know who you're talking to. I've always been Happy, and I'll always be Happy. You'll get used to it. I did.

From the stage, Moby Dickens began to bring their instruments up to show volume as their soundman faded Angie's break tape out of the mix. Billy covered his mouth with his hand, to mute his voice, and hollered into Happy's ear.

—I'd like to talk to you some more. You wanna come backstage with me, and we can talk back there?

She did not directly reply, but only looked him straight in the eye.

—Well, I don't know. Can I trust you?

Billy cringed—a chill ran up his spine. That word. What was it with chicks and that word?

—*Trust* me? Trust me how?

—You know. Can I trust you not to trample all over me? I just got out of a relationship like that.

—Well, yeah. You can trust me. But, I mean, we're only here for, like, a month or so. Then we have to head back.

—Head back where?

—Portland. Portland, Oregon. That's where we're from.

He laughed.

—We're big stars back there.

It was her turn to laugh.

Looking around as the volume in the room began to increase exponentially, Billy yelled.

—C'mon, Happy. We can talk backstage, and we won't have to scream at each other. You can trust me.

He gently grasped her by the arm and led her away toward the green room.

Backstage, Candy and MJ were changing out of their stage clothes behind the partition, Candy's voice becoming huskier and more hoarse by the moment. A few of the Gods shared a joint, joking about some of the strange people they saw in the audience, as Billy and Happy entered the room. Happy shyly averted her eyes, while Billy wrapped an arm around her. She curled her nose, retracting slightly from his sweaty clutches.

—Smells good in here. You guys this is Happy. Don't ask why her name's Happy. But that's her name. You can believe me on that one.

He smiled at her genially and motioned toward the guys.

—That's Col over there. He's the guitar player. And Daw, there, is the drummer. Gibby is the bass player. And that's Billy D. His name's Billy too. He's our soundman. It looks like Candy and MJ are gettin' changed back there. And Mak and Mick and Gilly are floatin' around out there somewhere.

—They're back at the bar with Angie and that Larry guy—guardin' the treasure.

Handing the joint to Billy, Col belched a big cloud of pot smoke, chuckling and coughing. Billy took a solid hit and offered it to Happy. She snatched it from him carefully: as if she were pinching a butterfly's wings, and noisily overdrew a short, hot puff—swiftly blowing off the acrid smoke, as only an amateur would.

Moby Dickens began to tune-up on stage, preparing for their first set. Curious, Happy picked up the conversation from where they had let off out on the dance floor.

—So out there you were saying you guys are big stars back in Portland?

The other members laughed derisively at Billy. He glared back at them and continued. Defensive.

—We *are* big stars. We're the biggest band in Portland. We get thousands of people showin' up to our shows. We're gonna record a great demo out here and we're gonna get signed by a major label.

Somewhat impressed by Billy's bravado, Happy reticently batted her eyes at him, purring.

—Really, dahling? Do tell me more.

Billy pulled away from her slightly, eyeballing the young woman with careful scrutiny. A little embarrassed.

—Well, it's true. If you ever come to Portland, we'll show you. It doesn't matter, really, you'll be hearing us on the radio soon enough. We're gonna be as big as Bowie, or the Stones. Wait and see.

Smirking vaguely, she smiled at him.

—I'm sure it's true. No really, I'm sure.

Looking down at himself, Billy noticed he was still wearing his sweaty stage clothes.

—Hey, Happy. Give me just a second. I gotta get out of these wet clothes. Are you girls decent back there?

With Candy sniffling and wheezing, MJ replied.

—Yeah, we're changed. It's all yours.

The two women emerged from behind the partition. MJ stepped toward Happy.

—Hi. I'm MJ, and this is Candy. I think Candy is catching the flu or something.

She grinned at her cohort, who was bravely attempting to smile: miserably.

—Hi. I'm Happy. Nice to meet you. You two really add a lot to the show. I've never seen a band with—*cheerleaders*—before. I mean, I don't mean you're not great dancers. You guys are real pro. A lot of energy. But you're also kinda like cheerleaders, cheering the band on. I think that's cool.

Candy spoke in a raspy ghostly whisper.

—The original idea was along those lines. We're supposed to be cheerleader go-go dancers. That was always the idea. That's how people respond. It's not a bad thing.

Col, the only one among the stoned-out crew who was able to assemble his thoughts into cogent, coherent sentences inquired.

—So, Happy. Or whatever your name really is. Do you live around here? Are you a local?

—Yeah. I live fairly close-by. I have an apartment that's not too far from here.

—What do people do to have fun around here?

—Well, for one, they come here. There's an arcade pub-like affair down the street where you can drink and play games like pinball and video stuff like *Donkey Kong* and *Pac-Man* and, what's it called? Those Super Mario guys? We hang out there. There's a couple of coffee shops, and a lot of little spots around the university. There's the Hudson mall about a mile from here, up by the Lincoln Highway. And we go into the city a lot.

—Sounds like what we do in Portland.

It was Happy's turn to be defensive.

—Well, there's restaurants and art galleries, movies, tons of music clubs and plays. Fashion. You can go over to Liberty Park and look at the Statue of Liberty if you want. What are you looking for?

Col was not prepared to actually be challenged.

—Oh, I was just kiddin' around. Don't mind me.

With disheveled resignation, she turned her attention back to Billy as he came out from behind the divider dressed in a black t-shirt, blue plaid flannel shirt and a well-worn denim jacket, faded jeans and white leather basketball shoes. He tousled his hair dry with a white towel.

—We've sorta got our own tribal sort of outlook on things.

—Yeah, I got it.

—Well, just don't, like, you know, take it *personally* or anything.

She was disarmed by his childlike ingenuousness.

—No. Not at all. Don't worry, I've hung out with bands before. My ex played in a band. I can take shit and give it right back.

Billy's face straightened slightly.

—That's cool. I just didn't want you to...Hey, you wanna go have a beer or a drink or somethin'?

She stood and began moving toward the green room door.

—No. I should get going before it gets too late.

—Aren't you gonna hang around for Moby Dickens?

—I've seen Moby Dickens, more times than I care to remember. I came to see you guys again and that's about it.

—Again? Have you seen us before?

—Yeah. I saw you on Thursday night. I was in here for about half an hour or so. I hung out back by the bar. You guys seemed kind of different, so I came back tonight to see if I still thought so.

—And...?

—And, yeah, I still think you're kind of different. And pretty good too, you know?

Billy nodded smugly.

—But, anyway, I should get going.

Waving at the others, Happy turned to leave, with Billy right behind her.

—Well, so I'll walk you to your car.

—I don't have a... I didn't drive. I rode my bike.

—Well, let me walk you out to your bike then.

Amused, Happy headed out of the room, waving at everyone. She moved toward the building entrance, but sidetracked as she neared the bar.

—Hold on a sec. I have to get my stuff.

She went over to the busy bar and flagged down one of the bartenders, who went into the room behind the bar, shagging her coat and purse. Billy helped her on with her coat.

—Thank you, sir. Such a *gentleman*!

She steered her way toward the exit, with Billy in tow close behind. They walked outside into the cool autumn air. Happy sauntered toward her bike: a blue, twenty-four inch boys' Schwinn, with white plastic handle-bar grips, red white and blue streamers cascading from the holes, a bouquet of plastic flowers in the basket and a crucifix mounted to the top of the steering pinion.

—Okay. Well, it was nice to meet you.

She extended her hand, to shake his.

—Look, I'll tell you what. Maybe I should walk you home while you ride your bike. It doesn't seem that safe out.

—It's completely safe. I live over by the university. But that's why I'm leaving at eleven at night. I know my way around this neighborhood. Besides that, I have this.

Happy fished around in her purse and held up a small, cylindrical container.

—What is that?

—It's mace.

With a hint of repugnance, he twisted up his face as she placed the canister back into her purse.

—Well, I just think I should walk with you anyway. I'd feel better about it.

She really didn't want to argue.

—Okay. Well, c'mon then.

She slowly rode up Westside and then down Audubon Avenue in the direction of her apartment, with Billy trotting alongside, his breath fogging rhythmically. He gulped.

—So...So wha'd'ya' do, Happy?

—What do I do?

She pedaled a little harder.

—I don't know if you wanna know what I do.

He puffed.

—Sure I do. Unless you're, like...like, a psycho killer or somethin'.

She braked her bike to an abrupt halt.

—I'm a librarian psycho killer. You're right.

—No...No, really...Wha'd'ya do?

—I'm a stripper.

—A stripper? You're not a stripper.

—I'm a stripper, an *exotic dancer*, and I take off my clothes in front of men, and they give me money to do it. Crazy world, eh?

—You're a stripper? I don't believe it. I mean you're pretty enough and...sexy enough to be a movie star.

—Oh, I don't know if I want to be a movie star. That would be awfully high maintenance. I think I'd like to be like you. Maybe in a smaller way.

She tried to blow a smoke ring in the fog.

—Like me? What do you mean?

—I'm a singer. And a songwriter, too. I've written some pretty good songs. Well, I wrote the lyrics; Paul wrote the melodies. They're good songs. A couple of them are really good, I think.

—So why are you a stripper?

—I've got to make ends meet, too, Billy, dear. It's not cheap around here, even to live in just a studio apartment. It's not cheap to live anywhere, I suppose.

Leaning the bike against her hip, she rolled her eyes skyward.

—Besides, I don't make any money singing with Paul around here. Paul plays guitar and sings harmony sometimes.

She explained.

—But we just play coffeeshops and small bars and restaurants. Places like that. We don't make thousands of dollars when we play, like you guys do.

There was a trace of indignation in her voice.

—I think it's great that you're a singer. And that you write songs too. That's great. How long you been doin' that?

Hiking her leg over the frame, she deftly remounted the bike, pedaling only fast enough to keep it upright.

—I've always written words. Lyrics, or poetry, or whatever. Since I was a kid. But Paul—he's a friend of my girlfriend Marissa—he's played with lots of people. He started working with me about a year ago. And we've been singing out for about three or four months.

—A singer, songwriter, stripper. Wha'd'ya' know? So where do you work, anyway?

—You don't know where anything is around here, why do you want know where I work?

She could see the corner of Bostwick Street up ahead. Billy was getting winded.

—I...I just wanted...to know. That's all.

—It's called the Electric Kitten. It's up at the north end of town. It's a couple miles from my place, sort of in the other direction from Trappe D'Or. Up north.

—Electric Kitten...I like that name.

—Yeah, well, it's just another dive, but the clientele are nice, and they're upwardly mobile—generous. That's my building up there.

She coasted to a stop in front of a gray stone apartment building. Propping herself against the wrought iron railing adjoining the entry, she waited for Billy to catch up.

—Well, I guess this is where I get off.

—So, you're not going to invite me in?

—No. I don't know you well enough for that.

—But I don't think I know how to get back to the club.

—You didn't leave a trail of crumbs, Hansel?

She clucked.

—Tsk tsk.

—Maybe I could sleep on your couch.

—I sleep on my couch. Didn't I tell you it was a studio apartment? I thought I did.

—I could sleep on the floor, then.

—No. I don't think so. I think you can find your way back all right. You seem to be a guy who knows where he's going.

Wheeling her bike down the steps behind the railing, she looked over her shoulder.

—Good luck.

—Wait a minute. You live in the basement?

For some reason, Billy was found dumb by the thought.

—*Yeh-us...*

She said impatiently.

—Yes. I live in the basement. Someone has to live in the basement, and I guess it's fallen to me. Besides, the rent is a lot lower than for the other apartments in this building. This is a good neighborhood, you know.

He inspected the other buildings on the street where Happy lived.

—I guess so. But isn't it kind of a pain livin' in the basement of a building?

—Well, if some asshole pisses in front of my door, or someone pukes—that's inconvenient. But I have a couple of plastic buckets that I can carry water in, and wash it all down the drain there. And that's only happened a couple of times the whole time *I've* lived here. Anyway...

—Well, I hope I get to see your place sometime.

—Maybe you will. But not tonight.

Happy unlocked the door, blew Billy a warm kiss and quickly wheeled her bike inside the apartment. She flipped the door shut behind her, nimbly locking it tight. Billy stood befuddled, staring at the entrance to the wood nymph's lair. He stepped away from the building and turned around, slowly making his wayward way back to the Trappe D'Or .

# XIX

Moby Dickens were wrapping up their last set by the time Billy finally made it back to the Trappe D'Or. He could feel blisters forming on his feet, and he was sweating profusely, even though it was quite chilly outside. He searched the club for the rest of the crew, but saw no one, so he headed toward the dressing room.

Inside, everyone was gathered around smoking weed, except for Angie and Gilly, who were off somewhere talking to Larry. Col spotted Billy first.

—Hey, Lancelot, what the hell are you doing back here? What'd ya' do, like, fuckin' piss her off or somethin'?

Grabbing the joint Col was passing, Billy plopped down next to Mak. He took a deep hit.

—No. She's just no pushover. That's all.

Confused, Mak asked.

—Who're you guys talkin' about?

Col replied.

Oh, Captain Romeo met some chick. You musta missed her when he brought her back.

With a chuckle, Daw volunteered.

—That girl was beautiful. What was her name? Happy, was it?

Col grunted lustily.

—Yeah, Happy. She made my dick happy. I fuckin' know that. She looks like, what's her name, Ginger from *Gilligan's Island*. The movie star. With a silver streak in her hair.

Gib, who rarely spoke, seemed confident in the answer to that conundrum.

—Tina Louise. But she looks a lot like Veronica Lake too.

Col screwed up his face.

—Veronica Lake? Who the fuck is Veronica Lake?

—Uh, she was an actress in the forties. *Blue Dahlia*?

—How do you know this shit, Gibby? *Blue Dahlia*? What the fuck?

—Aw, my mom was a movie trivia freak when I was a kid. We always used to watch old movies in the afternoons and I remember Veronica Lake. I had a thing for her, the hair over the eye thing—and Loretta Young.

Impertinently, Col needled Gib, snickering

—Did ya' have a boner for 'em?

Gib ignored the question.

—Anyway, Ginger's name is Tina Louise.

—Yeah, Ginger. That's it. She kinda looked like Ginger. Same tits!

Gib firmly set the record straight.

—Tina Louise.

—Okay. Yeah. Tina Louise.

The subject being something he knew about, Gib spoke up.

—You know who she really looks like? Sharon Tate.

Col was flummoxed.

—Sharon Tate. Sharon Tate. Why does that name sound familiar?

—She was one of the people Charlie Manson murdered.

—Oh, yeah. That's right. Manson.

—Sharon Tate was exquisite. I swear she made film stock turn blurry. She only made a few flicks. I saw her in *Fearless Vampire Killers*. That was a Roman Polanski flick. They were married.

Daw rebutted Col and Gib's contentions.

—Well, I don't know about any of those chicks. Personally, I thought she looked like Marilyn Monroe, only with darker hair.

Billy agreed.

—I think she kinda looks like Marilyn Monroe too. She's, like, gorgeous. I know that. And jeezus, what a body!

With a great sense of appreciation for the subject, Col raised the question.

—How do you know what kind of body she's got? Did you get a look at it?

Billy wanted to tell them all that Happy was a stripper and that they could all get a look for themselves. But a sense of modesty or chivalry or possibly possessiveness prevented him from doing so.

—Nah. I didn't see her naked or anything. But it was pretty obvious she's got, like, a hot body. I mean, didn't *you* notice?

Col rejoined.

—Fuck, yeah. I noticed her body alright. That girl's built like a shick brithouse. You always spot the hottest chicks. I swear ya' got radar or somethin'.

—Maybe so. But she's also incredibly smart and cool and talented. She's a singer and a songwriter.

—And she's fuckin' gorgeous and she's got a spectacular rack...

—There's that too, I guess.

Billy flashed a shrewd grin.

—So when're you seein' her again, Loverboy? Are you gonna to be AWOL for the rest of the trip, or what?

Astonished regret crossed Billy's face. He slapped his forehead.

—Shit. I forgot to get her phone number. Maybe I might be able to find my way back to her apartment, but I don't know. I made a lot of wrong turns gettin' back here from there. Shit. I guess I'll just have to wait for her to turn up again.

—You better hope she comes back, man. Maybe you'll never see her again.

—Oh, I think I'll see her again. I'm pretty sure.

About an hour elapsed before the band could get loaded out of the club and into Augie's van. It was nearly three before they were settled in back at Angie's apartment.

Angie tossed a roll of bills in Mak's lap.

—Hundred and thirty five. One-fifty, minus my commission. That asshole Larry's makin' out like a fuckin' bandit.

Uncomprehendingly, Mak looked at Angie for clarification.

—He gives Moby Dickens five hundred, you guys one fifty and pockets the rest.

You do the math. That's, like, a couple of grand, easy. Prob'ly three.

Mak made a mental note of what Angie was saying with the intention of applying the information when the money was distributed at the end of the night on the following Thursday.

Followed closely by the ever-more remote Gilly, Angie headed toward his bedroom.

—Okay, then. We'll get set up in the studio tomorrow and get back after it, take a few listens to what we got down last week and figure out what we're gonna do Monday. Hey, Billy...C'mere. I need to talk to ya'.

Billy self-consciously tagged along.

Back in Angie's room, the elder brother rapidly began his interrogation.

—So Billy, man. Didja tell those guys about movin' yet?

—Nah. I didn't get a chance. First thing tomorrow.

—Yeah. We should get rollin' on that. I'm sure everybody'll be a lot more comfortable with the new arrangement. Maybe we can get 'em moved over tomorrow night, after we get everything loaded in.

—Well, I'll see what I can do.

With a profound sense of remorse and dejection, Billy slipped out of Angie's room—and headed down the hall to his own.

It was around ten when people began to stir, rustling around, prowling for something to eat. Col found a box of saltine crackers and doled them out to his compatriots. Candy searched the cupboards for any kind of tea to help to soothe her enflamed throat, which made of her voice a husky croak.

It was not long before Billy came out from his room. There was a serious look on his face, as if there were bad news to deliver. Col prompted.

—Hey Billy, we're all starvin'. How's about we go get some breakfast somewhere? There's that Miss America place up the street, or that cafe over on Mallory. We could eat there.

There was a general tumult over the subject, rolling across the lot of them like thunder in the valley of empty bellies.

—Yeah. Yeah. We'll get somethin' to eat in a little while. First, there's somethin' I've gotta talk to you guys about.

Just by the tone of his voice, the others knew Billy had something important on his mind.

—You guys, I've been talkin' to Angie, and he thinks it's too crowded in this place, with all of us here, and that we need to split things up.

Frightened, puzzled eyes met his gaze. Mak spoke up.

—Well, who's goin' where? And where're they gonna go, Billy?

—Angie's got that covered. You can move in with him and Gilly's mom and their younger brother. It's a nice big house, with bedrooms and room in the attic. It'll give everyone a little privacy and a real place to sleep. It's not that far from here. It won't be hard meetin' up or anything.

Bafflement—with a tinge of hurt.

—Look. It'll take a coupla days to get squared away. But I really do think it's for the best.

Again, Mak took up the thread.

—So who's goin' where Billy?

—Me 'n' Gilly and the girls're gonna stay here and the rest of you are goin' over to Gilly's mom's place.

Col raised an objection.

—Ya' know, I called the couch when we first got here, and I'm callin' the couch now. I'll sleep here on the couch. It won't be a problem. I'm comfortable with the couch.

Not in the mood to argue, Billy acceded, with a wave of his hand, while Mak maintained his line of questioning.

—Well, Billy, when are we gonna do this move?

—We were thinkin' maybe later this afternoon, after we get loaded into the studio.

A cloud of gloom quietly collected in the room, with everyone seemingly on the verge of tears or at the threshold of screaming, or both. They gathered themselves together and wordlessly walked in the rain to the Paradox Café about five or six blocks away on Mallory and Yale. A gray pall followed them as they moved.

It was a silent breakfast. Occasional whispers could be overheard, flapping and flicking like flags in the wind. But, generally, the mood was grum and glibless. Mak absently studied the waitress, who was forty-ish, brunette, kind of frumpily cute, but well within her element at the café. She was efficient and effective at her job, guilelessly ebullient in a somewhat subdued way.

Peeling bills from a roll, Mak solemnly paid the bill, with a generous gratuity for the pleasant waitress, who was possibly the only bright spot in an otherwise dismal day.

The group arrived back at Angie's place at around one o'clock. Angie and Gilly were sitting at the dining room table, drinking coffee, when the bunch of them trudged through the door, scowling at the brothers. They sat down around the living room, as Billy said.

—Well, Angie, I told everybody about the idea of splittin' us up.

—Yeh? Well, I think that's the best idea. Don't you guys? It'll give us all a little room to move, room to breathe.

He surveyed no response.

—So, maybe you guys can get yer shit together and we'll pack up before we head over to the studio. Then after we're done downtown, I can take ya' over to my...shit.

He looked at Gilly.

—*Our* mom's place and you can meet her and Augie, and get settled in.

The others peeked at each other from beneath pinched, sorrowful brows.

—So really. You guys. It's gonna be okay. You'll like it over there. We got beds and cots for all a ya.' You'll have a little privacy. You won't wake up to this...every fuckin' morning.

He casually waved his hand in their direction, where they sat cramped and crowded on the couch and the chairs, and the arms of the chairs and on the floor.

Mak was convinced that nothing was going to change in the scenario, and that the situation was possibly for the best. He thought splitting everyone up was a huge mistake, but it was also readily apparent that it was too crowded for eleven in Angie's apartment. There was no sense fighting the inevitable.

But his mind also crawled toward the swampy inevitability of his own current situation within the band. He had been rendered useless in practically no time at all—reduced to being the treasurer and chief aide de camp, a gopher. Still, he sullenly soldiered on—because there was really nothing else he could do.

—Okay, that sounds like a plan. But we oughta get goin' down to the studio. It's gettin' late. We've got a lot to do.

Standing up abruptly, as if a bug was biting him, Angie snorted.

—All right, man. Let's get to it then.

It was just after three when they finally finished loading the equipment into the studio. The girls had remained back at Angie's place. They weren't going to be moving anyway and Candy was in no condition to be running around in the rain.

Mak, Billy D. and Mick sat in chairs in the studio control room, while the band got their settings adjusted out on the floor. Billy D. watched intently, as Angie dialed in the band at the big board. Billy D. wished he could get a crack at it.

Once they were set up for recording basic tracks the following day, the musicians filtered into the control room, to review the work they had done the previous week. From the first play, Billy wrinkled his nose as if there were a terrible smell in the room.

—Is this the same cut we did? It sounds all fucked up. It's too slow. It's not edgy enough. What happened?

Dithering slightly, Angie reacted.

—Well, it's all the same man. I didn't change nothin'. All the tracks're there, the overdubs. Everything's mixed pretty much the way...

—No, Angie. It's not you. Everything *sounds* fuckin' great. It's us. We're just playing terrible.

Billy looked at Billy D.

—Wha'd'ya think, Billy?

—You want my honest opinion?

—Well, *yeah*. I don't, like, want your *dishonest* opinion.

—I really think take four was the best. It had a lot better energy.

—Well why didn't you say somethin' at the time, man?

—Nobody asked me.

They listened back to take four and all agreed that it was the better one. More fluid, more vigorous than take seven. But, ultimately, Billy was not totally happy with that take either and elected that they would start all over the following day.

After a few more reviews of take seven, the assemblage resolutely exited the studio, to transport Daw and Gib, Mak, Billy D and Mick over to Mrs. Belladro's house.

It was a mournful trip for the forlorn quintet. They sat crowded with their suitcases, bags and bedrolls in the back of Angie's van, with expressions of disenchantment written across their faces. Because the trip to Mama's house was on the way back from the Power Station in the city, not one of them had the slightest idea where they were, or where they were going.

They were going to the northeast end of town, over toward 8$^{th}$ and Monmouth to Mama Belladro's tall, two-story row house on Pavonia—precisely between Jones

Park and Hamilton Park, around four miles away from Angie's place. A nice area, but foreign and forbidding, all the same.

Angie pulled up in front of the brownstone townhouse where he and his brothers had grown up. He swung around in the drivers seat, facing the back and called out.

—Well, this is it. Nice place. Like I told ya'. Look, before we go in, I need ta go over a coupla things with ya'. It's gonna be a hundred bucks a week for rent for all five of ya'. Twenty bucks apiece. That ain't bad. I'm chargin' the rest of 'em rent for stayin' at my house too.

The five huddled together in the back of the van like a bevy of orphaned ducklings, cheeping softly to themselves.

—And my mom is a little worried about havin' ya' stay. She's worried about drugs and booze and wild women, and you guys comin' in late and makin' a lot of noise and shit. I told her ya' wasn't like that, that you were pretty quiet guys. She had a bad experience with Grand Funk Railroad during their *turbulent* years way back when.

He was met with a thralled hush.

—I told 'er you were cool. That ya' might smoke a joint up in the attic or drink a few beers, but ya' weren't wild party guys. She's cool with that. There's also the issue of our brother, Augie.

The tenor and tone of Angie's voice frightened them further, as if he were about to tell them about a ghost in the house.

—Augie's a little, uh, different. He ain't been quite the same since our dad died. That was, like, twenty-five years ago. Anyway, he's got a few *peculiarities* ya' need to know about. First off, he carries a bat around with him at all times.

Billy laughed out loud.

—You mean like Ozzy Osbourne?

—No. I mean like Reggie Jackson. Mister October?

Catching on immediately, Billy went along. Angie continued.

—Augie idolizes Reggie Jackson. Even with him playin' with the Angels this year. A lifelong Yankees fan and he switches to the Angels when Reggie does. Some kinda loyalty, I guess. Loyal to the man, not the team.

A wistful moment of baseball veracity passed between the two of them.

—Anyway, he's been carryin' that bat around non-stop since Reggie autographed it in seventy-eight. The year after the year, ya' know?

Not as familiar with New York Yankee lore, Billy's head fluttered obliviously.

—Where am I? Yeah. Okay. So Augie carries that bat around with him.

Billy asked.

—How does that work out in, like, restaurants and theaters and stuff?

—Aw, Augie don't really get out that much. He's kind of a stay-at-home kinda guy. Y'know? I know I'm forgettin' somethin' here. What else, Alfie?

—I can't think of anything.

—Well. I'll probably think of it later.

Angie, Gilly, Billy and Col accompanied the fivesome into the house. The nine of them crammed into the hallway, as Angie bellowed.

—Ma. Augie. We're here. Hey, Ma! Hey, Augie!

They could hear activity in different parts of the house, with the sounds of footsteps moving in their direction. Mrs. Belladro came in from her bedroom, in front of the living room.

—Oh hi, boys. Wow. There's a lotta ya'. You're not all stayin' here are ya'?

—No, ma. Just five of us. Them.

He introduced everyone to his mother, while the sound of Augie rushing around upstairs echoed down the staircase.

—Augie. Ya' comin' down?

A muffled voice called back from a distant room.

—Yeh. Yeh. I'm comin'.

Augie rushed down the second story hallway and down the stairs, baseball bat slung over his shoulder, shouting.

—No meat! No meat!

Angie suddenly remembered. He explained to the guests

—Oh yeh. That's what I forgot. Augie will occasionally get on this *no meat* kick. We're not exactly sure where that came from. Ma eats meat. Hell. *He* eats bacon.

Disheveled Augie shambled toward the group.

—Hey, Augie. This is that band I was tellin' ya' about. Band, this is Augie.

Like a cornered possum, Augie engaged them with a wincing glare of frightened menace.

—No meat.

—Yeh. Yeh. No meat. That's great Augie. Ya' want these people ta think yer a complete fuckin' mo-ron? We'll get to the meat thing later. Say hello ta everybody

Augie calmed down, pensively smiling. He held the bat before him as if it were Excalibur on a silk pillow.

—Hi. Hey. You guys wanna see my bat? It's autographed by Reggie Jackson.

—Nah. Aug. They don't want to see yer fuckin' bat right now. Let's get 'em situated here and then you can tell them all about Reggie Jackson. Right guys?

Eyes wide in nervous apprehension, the new boarders nodded bleakly.

—Yeh. See? Let's get 'em figured out where they're gonna be bunkin' and I'm sure they'll be fascinated by your *expertise* on the subject of Reggie Jackson.

—Okay. But don't forget: no meat.

—Yeh, yeh. No fuckin' meat. Jesus Christ Augie, give it a rest will ya'?

Angie led Gib, Daw, Billy D., Mak, and Mick upstairs, showing them their quarters. Fortuitously, Augie's room was at the very end of the hall. Next to it, on one side of the hall, was a small bathroom, with just a toilet, sink and shower.

Across the hall from the bathroom were the stairs up to the attic. And the two available rooms were set in opposition, next to the stairs at the other end of the hall from Augie's room. Maybe Billy was right. Maybe they really would have a little bit of privacy after all.

Because Billy D. probably would not fit on one in order to sleep, Mick volunteered to take the cot in the attic space. Billy D. and Mak selected one bedroom and Gib and Daw took the other. Neither room could have been called spacious, but it afforded the guys some seclusion.

It was obvious that tensions were mounting within the organization. In only a week's time, confusion and disconnection had set in—creating a rift within a group that had always been so tight. Though opportunities for reflection were few and far between, it was possible that the five of them could develop measures to counter what they perceived to be a division within the ranks.

The most troubling aspect of the new living arrangements was that the members would be surreptitiously separated by distance, as well as by the loss of esprit d'corps. It was at least six miles from Mama Belladro's place to the club. A long walk. There were restaurants and grocery stores nearby. That would not be a problem. But they were stuck out in the middle of nowhere with no transportation.

That was a problem.

Looking around the musty attic, Mick decided that it was not too bad a deal. There was an old cot with a canvas cover, near the window at one end of the rafters. He would be comfortable on that, squeezed inside his goose-down sleeping bag.

And there were two, forest green overstuffed chairs and an old wooden coffee table tucked away in the corner—perfect for making a little entertainment den— for hanging out to drink beer and smoke the occasional joint with the other band lodgers. Even an old portable TV they could watch. Mick wondered if it worked.

Mak and Billy D. were content with their accommodations. It was a modest room, but reasonably capacious. The bed and cot were located near the door, against either wall, at one end of the room—an antique cedar chest at the foot of the bed.

A small desk abutted the window at the other end of the room, which looked down upon the backyard of the building next door. There was a tall bookcase standing at one side of the desk, a tiny closet at the other, with two straight-backed wooden chairs neatly propped against either wall.

Billy D. was assigned to the bed, while Mak inherited the cot, which had been moved into the room. There were a sheet and a couple of wool blankets in which he could wrap himself—a far cry from sleeping on Angie's floor, with nothing for covers other than a moldy old sheet and a dusty, gold brocade curtain.

The two of them continued with the sporadic conversation they had been having for the preceding week, attempting to ascertain their roles within the new dynamic that the trip had created within the band. Was Angie going to take over as the band's soundman and manager? If that was the case, what place was there for Mak and Billy D?

The other bedroom, where Daw and Gib were quartered, was slightly larger, with a bigger closet, but similarly appointed. Daw was given the bed, and because he also had a sleeping bag with him, Gib drew the cot.

As they were getting settled in, Daw confided in Gib his unhappiness.

—So, Gibby. Wha'd'ya think about how things have been goin' since we came out here? Kinda sucks. Don't you think?

—Yeah. It's not quite what I expected. I thought things were going to be planned a little better.

—Or at *all*! I don't think that Angie guy gave this whole thing any thought at all. And I don't know where the hell Gilly's head's at. This totally sucks.

—Well, I guess we'll just have to make the best of it. There's not much else we can do.

It was nearly ten o'clock before Angie arrived back at the warehouse with Billy,

Col and Gilly in tow. Billy felt a profound sense of trepidation, augmented by the sneaking suspicion that he was forgetting to do something. It had been nagging at him for several days, but because of all the turmoil, he had not been able to pause long enough to figure out what it was.

Without the rest of the band in the way, there was plenty of room in Angie's apartment. The remaining six inhabitants were able to sit on the couch, or in one of the chairs, while watching TV. It was not the madhouse that it had been But Billy worried about splitting them up, even though the others were just a phone call away.

A phone call. In the week they had been gone, he had never even once thought of Carrie. She had been given no phone number by which to contact Billy, who had forgotten completely that she even walked the planet. He was embarrassed and afraid—embarrassed that he had forgotten her, and afraid that she would know he had.

Resolutely, but with great consternation, Billy dialed Carrie's number.

—Hello?

—Hi, Carrie, it's me.

—Billy? Did you finally remember me? I was wondering when you would.

—Carrie, it wasn't like that. It's, like, really complicated. We've been really busy and runnin' around all week. And some of the guys had to move and we had recording and gigs. I just haven't had the time till now. What time is it back there?

—Don't try to change the subject. It's a little after seven. You were so busy that you couldn't call me? Call me and talk to me for ten minutes? You didn't have the time? After the conversation we had on the way to the airport? About trust?

She reminded him, sarcastically, for which he was thankful, because he couldn't remember the conversation all that well. He was confusing the conversation he had with Carrie with the one he had had with Happy. It seemed to him that they were very similar. He thought to himself how insecure women could be.

—Yeah, yeah. Trust. I remember. Am I trustworthy? That stuff. It wasn't like I wanted to make you mad. It was always three in the morning when I was free to call.

He lied.

—Then you could have called me then. It never slowed you down back here. You always seemed to feel free to call anytime at all.

—But the time's different.

—So what? If you called at three back there, it would only be midnight here.

He winced.

—That's *right*, we're the ones three hours ahead. I keep thinking it's the other way around. That it's one in the morning back there, when it's really seven at night.

—I'm disappointed that's the best excuse you could come up with.

—It's not an excuse. It's an explanation. It's been nonstop out here. One thing right after another. I haven't had one second to even sit and think. Just, like, blam, blam, blam.

—Blamblamblam? You amaze me Billy. Blamblamblam.

The phone clicked in his ear. She had hung up on him.

He considered calling her back, but thought better of it. He knew she wouldn't answer.

## XX

As had been arranged the previous day, the plan for Monday morning was for Angie and Billy, Col and Gilly to pick up Daw and Gib and whoever else among Mak, Mick and Billy D. wanted to go over to the studio.

The Goddesses stayed behind at Augie's place, to meet up with Annie Fisher. They had the intention of making the tour of Manhattan: Greenwich Village, the West Village, Wall Street, the theater district, and Central Park. Annie knew a music attorney downtown, whom she hoped to interest in Billy and the Gods. But, mostly, it was a sightseeing trip.

Mak had talked to Candy on Sunday night, and it was settled that he would go along with them. That was not an inconvenience for the ladies, necessarily—but perhaps just a change in itinerary.

So Mick and Billy D. accompanied the band into the studio, while Mak, Candy and MJ went with Annie. It was Mak's intention to take along posters, promoting the band's Thursday night shows to post in any appropriate-looking locales. Annie also suggested that she might have a little surprise in store for Mak.

Gathered together in the studio once again, a weight of great tension was lifted from the group's collective shoulders. It was their natural habitat—playing together in an enclosed room, looking directly at each other, without distractions. This time, they felt comfortable in the studio, as though it were a shelter from the dreariness of the world outside.

They resumed attempting to record a basic track of "Police Told Me," one with the crackling energy and lightning execution for which the band had won its acclaim.

But things quickly bogged down. First Col broke a string during a crucial part of the song. Then Gib broke a string on his bass, a rare event among bassists, and something that had never happened to him before. Col had plenty of replacement strings, but because breaking a string was such a rare event for a bassist, Gib did not.

So Gib and Angie set off in the van searching for a nearby music store. Meanwhile, the others sat around in the studio control room chatting aimlessly—sharing a couple of joints of decent Mex.

As he mulled the previous night's exchange, Billy tried to resolve for himself how to move forward with Carrie—given that they were over three thousand miles apart and likely to remain that way for the foreseeable future.

He sensed that she was not going to trust him, no matter what he did with himself in New York. In some ways he felt liberated and free to pursue Happy without guilt. Carrie was going to indict him anyway. He really had nothing to lose.

He was going to have a lot of making up to do with Carrie when he got home. There was no way around that. He wondered if he should try to call her again right away or wait a few days for her to cool off. He was unable to decide in the moment.

Driving her brother's Honda Civic through the chilly gray, foggy fall air, Annie arrived at Angie's place at around eleven in the morning. She picked up MJ and a still very sick Candy. Despite her condition, Candy was not about to miss a chance to go into the city. With some uncertainty as to where their destination lie, they made their way over to Mama's house to pick up Mak.

The three of them knocked at the front door of Mama's house—Candy feeling absolutely terrible, with a voice about two-octaves below normal and gritty as sandpaper on a microphone. They rang the doorbell several times before Mrs. Belladro came to the door. She peered out at them guardedly.

Annie spoke up.

—Hi. We're here to pick up Mak.

With a slightly horrified expression on her face, Mrs. Belladro looked at them as if they were the wild women that she had feared would start showing up if she were to take boarders. She didn't know who was upstairs hence she called up to Augie, so that he could investigate.

—Augusto! Come down. I need yer help here.

They heard Augie rumbling around upstairs, before he bounded down, with his bat comfortably cradled against his neck. He engaged them with a sense of fear and hormonal curiosity. It occurred to him to mention his stringent meat stipulations, but for some reason, he elected not to—brevity being, perhaps in his case, the better part of valor.

—Augusto. These girls are here looking for one of the band guys. Which one is it?

—Mak

—Yeh. Mak. Ya' know if he's up there?

He shrugged. Augie had no idea which one of those guys was Mak.

—I dunno.

—Well, can ya' go up and check for me?

—Yeh. Okay. But remember, *no meat*.

Annie and the Goddesses eyed each other warily. Mama Belladro muttered.

—You and your meat Augusto. These girls're gonna think yer nutty.

Augie shrugged apologetically and trotted back up the stairs knocking at both of the spare bedroom doors. When Augie rapped upon the second door Mak answered.

—There's some girls downstairs wanna see Mak. They're pretty cute too.

Mak smiled. Annie and the Goddesses would, no doubt, be flattered to know that Augie thought they were cute. He grabbed his coat, a stack of posters promoting the Unreal Gods' Thursday night shows at the Trappe D'Or and his industrial-gauge stapler.

He stashed it all in his backpack and dug around in his duffel bag on the cot searching for a couple of cassettes and a VHS video tape, among those he had brought out with him from Portland for just such an occasion. He tossed them in his backpack, as well, then headed downstairs to join the girls.

From Mama Belladro's house, Annie hopped onto the Pulaski Skyway and took the Holland Tunnel into the city. She transported her tourists to the usual sites, driving them through Greenwich Village, past the Bitter End to CBGB on Bleecker and Bowery.

Mak made Annie double-park outside CBGB while he stapled posters to telephone poles and walls around the club. They might have been at an unknown club on the other side of the Hudson, but Mak felt a twinge of proud satisfaction in promoting the shows at such a landmark as CBGB. It was as if Columbus were pitching his flag in Hispaniola.

Continuing the sightseeing mission, Annie drove her guests to the north, past the Empire State Building, over to the Peppermint Lounge, where Mak again had Annie double-park, so that he could poster the nearby walls and phone poles.

They circled Times Square, the theatre district and Central Park, before Annie found a spot to put the Honda, on East 57th Street near 5th Avenue, where she announced that they were going to journey, on foot, to Park Avenue, to the office of Jordan Archer, the music attorney friend of her family. She was hoping Jordan could advise Mak as to plotting the future of the Unreal Gods. Mak was pleasantly startled by the Annie's surprise. A New York music attorney. Cool. Privately, Annie still clung to her own desires to one day manage the band. She knew she could do the job. But she needed to prove herself to Billy.

In an office that was considerably larger than Angie's apartment (and much better appointed), the four of them sat in firm, shiny, brown leather chairs awaiting their consultation with Jordan Archer. Mak watched the gatekeeper as she assiduously went about her business. He found her somewhat attractive—in a prim, proper, passive-aggressive sort of way.

Under different circumstances they might have made a cute couple. Her face was even rounder than Mak's. As a couple, they would have looked like the Campbell's soup kids. Their children would have looked like koala bears. None of this occurred to Mak as he sat daydreaming about what it would be like to have a girlfriend who was the office manager in a big swanky law firm.

Jordan Archer looked like someone who should be named Jordan Archer. He was handsome and dark-haired, with a distinguished touch of gray at the temples, a cleft in his chin and narrow square-shoulders. He wore a dark blue, dot-stripe, wool, three-button Gucci suit, and he looked extremely at ease in it. It was his uniform, his customary attire.

He graciously invited the four of them into his office, bidding them to sit in burgundy leather chairs near his desk. Annie introduced Mak and the Goddesses as Mister Archer maneuvered himself behind his high-backed cherry wood and black leather antique chair. It purportedly had been Adlai Stevenson's chair when he was the Governor of Illinois. Jordan interlaced his fingers, resting his hands on the back of the chair.

—Angela, it's been several years since I've seen you, isn't that right?

—Yeah. I think it's almost four years. When I was out for Christmas in seventy-eight. How're Lila and Lyn?

—Lynettes's graduating this year from Columbia University's School of Business. She wants to be a stockbroker or possibly a business lawyer. Just like her old man, I guess. As for Lila...Lila is taking a little more time to find herself. She lives in Stamford with her boyfriend, Lanny. They make jewelry and sell it at fairs and farmer's markets and such.

—Lila's always been so artistic.

—I suppose so. I just wish I saw a little more art in her artwork.

—How are your parents? And Tim?

—Uh, Mom and Dad just headed down to Fort Lauderdale for the winter.

—So they still have the winter house? I was wondering about that. Marlene and I should try to get over and see them this winter. We have a winter place in Miami. You'll have to give me their number.

—Yeah, and Tim lives over in Greenwich Village. He does editing for a book publisher. Simon and Schuster.

—That sounds like Tim. Always so studious and exacting. I remember when he was a kid, his room always looked like a museum. All of his baseball memorabilia and everything, all in its proper place.

—Oh, he's still like that. He makes you take off your shoes before you can go into his apartment.

Jordan Archer stood shuffling some papers on his desk as if to signify that the chit-chat was finished. He stepped around his chair and eased himself down.

—All right then. Now, you had mentioned a successful band from Portland you're working with.

Still acting as the band's manager, Mak dragged his chair towards Mister Archer's desk.

—Yes, sir. Billy Granger and the Unreal Gods. They're a great band, and there's somethin' very special about Billy.

From his backpack he produced the cassettes and videotape he had brought along. As he handed them to Mister Archer, he explained.

—These here are cassettes of the band's new album, *Boom Chuck Rock Now*. On the back of that tape are home demos of the stuff we're out here to record.

Mister Archer inspected the parcels with curiosity, cracking.

—Is your intention to buy Manhattan from the Lanapes with these items?

For a moment, Mak engaged Mister Archer with not a windy thought in his head, before he managed to pull himself together, continuing.

—The other cassette is a bunch of live stuff we've collected over the past year. And the video tape there is sort of a greatest hits package of live shows. It'll really give you an idea of what the band looks like on stage. Bobby Lester recorded those. He's a very well-known video guy in Portland.

Remembering who he had accompanied, Mak resumed his pitch.

—The Goddesses are on stage, too, dancin' of course. They're a big part of the show.

He half-turned and thrust a thumb in the direction of Candy and MJ. Jordan smiled smartly at Candy, who promptly sneezed.

—So, with that stuff you'll be able to see what sort of a, uh, a vision we've got. But we're at the stage where we need help.

Mister Archer sat forward in his chair.

—And how can I help you?

Annie pulled her chair forward.

—We just need your guidance and wisdom. The Gods and Goddesses are the hottest band in Portland, but they could be hotter, like, worldwide. Billy's magical. You'll see.

205

Leaning his elbows on the desk, Jordan grinned at Annie.

—Well, Ann, we'll see what I can do for you. Allow me a few days to sort through these items and I'll give you a call at the end of the week—and if the fit seems right, we'll have you in to talk.

Annie, Mak and the Goddesses stood up and, in succession, shook Mister Archer's hand. As they made their way toward his office door, Mister Archer called out.

—Oh, Angel...a

She gracefully spun around, intently staring at him with a bemused expression on her face.

—If you speak to them before I do, please do wish Delores and Chuck well for me.

Annie dutifully nodded.

—And let them know that Marlene and I will look them up this winter when we're down in January.

She smiled forthrightly and walked out the door.

The day in the studio had not been as productive, nor rewarding for the Gods as they had hoped. Gib and Angie finally returned with a set of bass strings at around one o'clock. For several hours they tried to make it through a good take of "Police Told Me."

But, as was to be expected given that Gib had just replaced all four strings on his bass, the instrument kept going out of tune, as the strings stretched and the neck re-adjusted itself to the stresses.

That situation caused tension within the band, as if there were not enough anxiety already. They tried hard to get some momentum going, but it was not to be. Finally, after a disorder of great frustration, they decided to scrap the session and try again on Tuesday.

After a quiet trip from the Power Station back to Jersey City, Angie dropped off Gib, Daw, Mick and Billy D. at Mrs. Belladro's house. The four of them exited the van, and without a lot of discussion between them and Billy, Col, and Gilly, they watched as Angie hurriedly drove away.

Mick assessed.

—Well, that was weird.

Daw added.

—We didn't even talk about tomorrow or the song or how fucked up everything was or anything. It was just, like, thanks for nothin' guys, bye.

Gib interjected.

—Something's going on with Billy. I don't know what it is, but he's, y'know, changing. He's not the same guy he was. He's, um, distant, faraway.

Daw replied.

—Well we're not going to get much done with that shit goin' on.

Billy D. tried to no avail to put a more optimistic spin on things.

—We just gotta hang in there and hope he gets it together pretty quick or this is just gonna be, like, a big waste of time and money. A real fuckin' fiasco.

Simmering just below fume, Angie drove the rest of the way back to his place without saying a word to Billy, Col or Gilly. He was not sure what he wanted to say to Billy. Things had seemed disjointed at the studio, which was to be expected given all the circumstances. But Angie knew the clock was ticking on the project, and it would not be long before the band would be out of money. They needed to get something in the can. Soon.

Standing on the front porch at Mrs. Belladro's house, the Power Station four realized than none among them had a key to enter the premises. It was quickly deduced that the doorbell was going to need to be engaged in order for them to gain entry. Mick took it upon himself to take responsibility for such an action.

Eventually Mrs. Belladro appeared at the door, more inconvenienced than upset.

—I guess I'm 'onna hafta get some keys made for you guys. But if I do, yer gonna hafta promise me that ya' won't be comin' in at all hours of the night, like those Funky Railroad guys.

The band members chuckled. Daw spoke up.

—Don't worry, Mrs. Belladro. We'll, like, keep all of that to a minimum, as best we can. We're not ragin' punks or anything.

Somewhat reassured, Mrs. Belladro turned and threw her hands up in the air, as she silently shuffled off in the direction of the kitchen. The next day she would have keys made for each of them

The boys hiked upstairs, spotting Mak, who was sitting on his cot, with a blank look on his face.

Daw remarked.

—Hey, Mak. You're back. How was your trip to the city? Did you go anywhere, or, like, see anything?

—Oh yeah, man. We drove all over. Annie took us by CBGB and the Bitter End,

Knitting Factory, Bottom Line. I put up posters for the Thursday night shows at all of 'em. At the Peppermint Lounge, too. Maybe somebody'll show up. You never know.

Mick suggested that the whole lot of them should adjourn to the attic rec room, where they could partake of a joint or two. They hopped up the stairs to the attic, whereupon Mick produced from his backpack three quarts of Old English 800 he had smuggled in the evening before when they had moved in. Mak and Daw plopped down in the chairs, while the others sat cross-legged on the floor.

After flipping on the TV to *Magnum PI*, Mick opened one of the bottles as Billy D. probed his shirt pocket for a joint and his white lighter. The joint and then the bottle quickly went around the circle in rapid succession. Mick encouraged Mak to continue the account of his journey into the city.

—Okay, Mak. So go ahead. Um, so like, what else happened?

—Oh Annie took us around to see all the regular tourist sights. The Empire State Building and Central Park and all that. Then we stopped and went up to an office on Park Avenue to meet up with a music lawyer who's a friend of Annie's family or somethin'.

Holding the bottle of Old English conch-like, with both hands, Mick quizzically inquired.

—A music lawyer? What was that all about?

—Aw, Annie wanted to see if the guy could give us any advice on how to plan for the future.

—And…

—And I gave him a couple of cassettes and a videotape, and he said he would check it out and get back to us. According to Annie, I guess he runs in a pretty tight crowd of big stars—like Jagger and Springsteen and guys like that.

—So when're you gonna meet with him again?

—I don't know, some time next week, I guess. He said he'd give us a call.

Daw tittered mischievously.

—Yeah, yeah. Don't call us, we'll call you.

—Naw, it wasn't like that. He seemed really interested in the band. Annie had told him some stuff. He knows we're big stars in Portland. He wants to come out and see the band sometime.

Hoping to avoid the cynicism, Mak changed the topic.

—So how did it go with *you* guys? How was it at the studio? Did ya' get anything done?

Gib, Daw, Mick and Billy D. hung their heads. Daw answered.

—It sucked, man. First Gib broke a string…

Guiltily, Gib lowered his eyes, as if he were somehow personally responsible for the broken string and the wasted session at the studio.

—Then everything was out of tune. And the energy was just totally sucky the whole time.

Billy D. added.

—Billy was actin' real weird, man. Quiet. And kind of sidetracked. That didn't help either. It was just a fucked up day.

—So did you get anything down?

—Uh, no man. Didn't even come close. We shouldn'ta even bothered going in there. That was, I don't know, like, five hundred dollars down the drain, for nothin'.

It was a little after eight-thirty when Billy, Col, Gilly, and Angie finally arrived back at the apartment. Candy and MJ had just finished watching *Facts of Life* on TV and were preparing for an episode of *One Day At A Time*. They looked up at the returning guys with a mixture of excitement and apathy. Somewhat disinterested, Candy acknowledged them.

—Hey. You guys. You're back. How did it go?

Trudging into the living room, Billy replied.

—It was a tough day at the office, honey. The boss was breakin' my balls.

Candy smiled faintly.

—That's nice, dear.

Crowding on the sofa in between the girls, Billy inquired of Candy.

—So how was your day, doll?

—It was good. We went into Manhattan and Annie showed us all around. She took us to all the clubs, and Mak put up posters for the Thursday night shows. He must have hit, like, seven or eight places. Then she took us to Park Avenue to see some music lawyer she knew.

Col and Gilly sat down in the overstuffed chairs. With a look of alarm on his face, Angie straddled one of the dining room chairs, his arms resting on the backrest.

—Music lawyer? What's his name? What'd you guys talk about?

—Oh, his name was Ashton Archer. Something like that.

MJ corrected Candy.

—I think his name was Jordan.

—Yeah. Right. Jordan Archer. That's it. He was a nice guy. Mak did most of the talking. He gave him some tapes and a video.

Agitated, Angie tried to pry deeper.

—So, what'd him and Mak talk about.

—Oh, nothing much. Just small talk really. The guy said he'd check out the tapes and he would give Mak or Annie, or one of them, a call sometime next week. He's a friend of Annie's family. He was talking with Annie about her parents and his kids. It was just a short visit, really. He was a nice guy.

—Give them a call about what?

His anger mounting Angie tried to contain himself.

—I don't know. About whether he liked the tapes, I guess. You'll have to ask Mak. It was really no big deal.

—Maybe not, but I need to be in on these kinds of conversations.

Suddenly sitting up rigid in his chair, Col frowned at Billy, who seemed oblivious— staring intently at Valerie Bertinelli on the TV screen.

—What do you need to be *in on these kinds of conversations* for? Mak's our manager. He's still our manager, isn't he, Billy?

Mesmerized by Valerie Bertinelli, Billy responded blankly.

—Yeah. Yeah. Our manager. He's our manager.

With eyes opened wide, like two exclamation marks, Angie made a hard left, ninety-degree turn in attitude.

—Well, yeh. Yeh. Manager. I just thought I should be in some kind of a fuckin' advisory role or somethin'. Make sure you guys don't get ripped off 'r nothin'.

—Y'know Angie...

In a contentious frame of mind, Col got ready to unload.

—We didn't exactly fall off of the pumpkin truck last week. We've fuckin' been

210

doin' this for years. We're no fuckin' hay bales.

—Nah. Nah, man, I didn't mean it like that. It's just...

—It's okay, man. It's just that we've been making our way pretty good without a lot of help from the outside. If we want it, we'll ask.

—Sure, man. Sure.

Again turning his attention to Billy, Col zeroed in.

—Hey, Billy. What's the deal with you and that Valerie Bertinoni chick?

—Valerie Bertinelli? I don't know. I guess I think she's cute or somethin'. I hadn't really thought about it.

—Isn't she a little young for you? What is she, like, fourteen?

—Nah. She's older than that. She's, like, in her twenties.

—She's the wholesome one. The other one, that McKenzie chick. She's the wild one. You like those wholesome chicks, don't you?

—I don't know about that. I just like girls. That's all.

—Aw, man, look at you and Carrie. She's about as goody-two-shoes as they come. You could bounce a quarter off her tight ass.

Billy glared. Col smirked.

—She's got you wrapped around her little finger. Admit it Billy. You're whipped.

Billy declared.

—I'm not whipped! What're you fuckin' talkin' about?

But then it occurred to him that he ought to try to phone Carrie to see if he could patch things up.

—I better go call her.

Col got in a final jab.

—Yeah. Better run along. But you'll miss Valerie Whatshername. Ya' gonna tell Carrie about Valerie Whatsername? Or how about that Happy chick?

Billy never heard him. And it was just as well, because there most certainly would have been a skirmish over Col's impertinence.

Everyone laughed with great enthusiasm to see Billy spring from the couch and hurry over to the phone on the dining room table. He yanked the long, long phone cord with him as he made his way down the hall and into his room, closing the door behind him.

With no response, Carrie's phone rang and rang. Her answering machine never came on, so Billy was unable even to attempt a conciliatory message. Disconsolately, he hung up, wondering if maybe she was out studying for a test. Or where?

## XXI

The band got nothing accomplished in the studio on Tuesday or Wednesday. Energy flagged, and the members were becoming overtly critical of their recorded performances, stifling all creativity. They were not a very merry bunch.

Mak, Mick, and Billy D. did not go into the studio with the band. They agreed that their services (or presences) really were not needed, so they elected to stay back at the house—with the intention to paper the nearby neighborhoods (and eventually all of Jersey City) with posters promoting the Gods' Thursday night gigs through November.

Stealing off with the Belladro residence upstairs phone, Mak spoke with Annie every day. The phone sat on a half-round tri-legged black walnut table in the hall, stationed next to the stairs up to the attic. The white and yellow pages sat on the floor, reinforcing the stability of the table.

Mak and Annie commiserated regarding the division within the band ranks. And everyday Mak would ask if she had heard from Jordan Archer. And every day she would reply that she had not. They agreed that if she had not heard from Archer by Friday, she would call him.

Mak had not spoken to Billy all week. Billy had presumably been too preoccupied with everything going on in his life, and Mak had simply been too busy. He was convinced that Angie was bad-mouthing him at every turn, attempting to usurp his position in the band. He was not far from wrong, though he probably underestimated the grand scale of Angie's Machiavellian machinations.

The three who remained behind decided that, for the first day or two of their postering expeditions anyway, they would travel together, hitting the most favorable locations within the immediate vicinity of Mrs. Belladro's place. In doing so, they would be allowed to become more familiar with the lay of the land; making it easier for the trio of explorers to find the way home, in future journeys farther afield.

The plan was that over the weeks that lay ahead, they would work their way concentrically away from her house, toward the rest of Jersey City—to the west and southwest toward St. Peter's College and Lincoln Park, and to the south—following the few arteries that would lead them into the greater city, in the general direction of New Jersey City University.

There had been many unseasonably warm and dry days that fall in Jersey City when the troupe arrived. An Indian summer. But over the weekend, the weather had turned. No rain. Just a chilly depressing gray. Gray. Chilly gray.

On Tuesday they made a first effort toward their goal of postering the entirety of Jersey City. From Monmouth, moving westerly, the intrepid trekkers soldiered down Pavonia to the corner at Brunswick.

While Billy D. and Mick papered every phone pole and properly available space on the blocks surrounding the intersection, Mak ducked into the Star Bar on the southeast corner.

It was Mak's custom to check out any bar that crossed his path—in order to establish for himself the viability of playing a show in the "venue." The Star Bar had a nice ambience, but it was mostly a video game parlor, and it was far too small for a band the magnitude of the Unreal Gods.

From the entry door, Mak could see beyond the bar a small stage, which was situated at the far end of the room—suitable for a duo or a small trio. A few intimate tables were randomly scattered around the stage. Mak estimated the Star Bar's capacity at around seventy-five patrons.

He considered hanging out at the bar and ordering up a beer until he remembered that his comrades were outside waiting in the gray, chilly gray and the team had only been on the job for about fifteen or twenty minutes—a little too early in the work day for a beer break. So he headed back outside.

From Brunswick and 8th they journeyed a mile or so east to Marin and Newport Centre Mall; then they took 7th back west, past Brunswick to Division. Next they tracked 6th, then 5th. In all, it took about five hours.

Their travels sufficiently wore them out. Heading back across 5th toward Monmouth, they spotted a small café and agreed they should stop for dinner—or, more to the point, their meal for the day. They voraciously consumed their victuals along with a few beers and returned to the Belladro house to meet up with Gib and Daw, smoke weed, and review the day.

The following day, Wednesday, it was warm and blue sky again, so they decided to split up in order to cover more ground. Billy D. and Mick followed Newark Avenue west. They parted ways at Tonnelle Avenue, with Mick covering the territory west and Billy D. east, moving south from there. Mak resumed traversing the numbered streets South of Mama Belladro's place. He checked the intersection of 5th and Monmouth and was surprised and gratified to see that none of their posters had been torn down.

The custom of band postering appeared not to be as rampant in Jersey City as in Portland—a promotional peculiarity Mak embraced as an inexpensive way to advertise the band's performances.

But, in Portland, a band would be lucky to have their posters up a couple of days, at most, before competing bands would tear them down or poster over them. Telephone poles existed as valuable territory and had to be protected with constant upkeep—some crucial poles had to be re-postered every day or so, some even more often than that.

But such diligence was usually rewarded, in that other bands would eventually acknowledge that certain spots on certain poles belonged to the Gods, and there was no sense in attempting to thwart such staunch authority. It was just a waste of paper and time. No such machinations were required in Jersey City.

Mak continued down Monmouth to 4th and began his journey anew. It took about an hour and a half to blanket 4th, and about as long for 3rd and 2nd. At 2nd & Coles, just a block from Monmouth, he spotted a club that seemed bigger than most, a good location for the band if the place hosted music.

From out of the perfect fall day into the dark, comfortable bar Mak stepped, immediately struck by a rush of heavy cigarette smoke. There was a stereo blaring an extended disco-mix version of "Hungry Like A Wolf" in the room in back of the bar. Even at three in the afternoon, it seemed like there was some kind of real action taking place. The joint was jumping.

He strolled past the bar toward the source of the commotion to discover a comely young brunette, nearly naked, her hair strewn with autumn leaves, collecting her costume and any remnant residual cash scattered around her before somberly exiting the stage.

As she maneuvered down the steps at the side of the stage, a heavy numbness seemed suddenly to seize her limbs. Her feet, so graceful and fluid only moments before, seemed almost stuck to the floor, like roots. She felt as if she were becoming a tree, her skin as rough as bark. Only her exquisite unclothed femininity remained.

She anxiously looked around the audience, spying, at last, a young man who was nervously smoking a cigarette. Blowing smoke rings into the shadows, he sat at a table some distance from the stage. She smiled at him somewhat desperately, relieved to see his presence. Juddering and jittering, she shivered and shuddered, quickly striding backstage to dress.

Snagging a waitress, Mak ordered a beer and sat at a table in the back, near the smoking guy. There were probably twenty-five or thirty men in the room—pretty-well dressed, like businessmen or something—most of them sitting at small tables rimming the stage. There were maybe six or seven women—one table of three, unescorted, and two tables where a few girls were sitting with a couple of men at each.

With a microphone in his hand, a stereotypical emcee leapt to the stage, with his hair slicked back sporting a blue brocade dinner jacket. And utilizing atrocious mic technique, he bellowed.

—Daphne. That was the lovely Daphne everyone. Give it up for Daphne.

A smattering of applause. A low, decadent tone crept into his voice. He spoke conspiratorially, muttering.

—And now, one of our most popular dancers ever. She's the one the guys come to see and the one the women come to glare at...Cassandra!!! Cassandra everyone. Let's hear it for *Cassandra*!!!

Palpable electricity abruptly filled the room with static excitement. She was beautiful. Mak was not sure that he had ever seen a woman so stunningly attractive. Not in-person anyway. She looked like a Playboy model. She began to dance around the stage, gracefully twirling around a shiny chrome pole off to one side. Mak could not stop staring at her spectacular body.

Willowy, yet muscular, she was of medium height. She had shoulder length silver-streaked auburn hair, a lock of which draped down across her forehead and over her right eye. She had a look of innocence, but her opulent blue eyes narrowed seductively as she glanced around the room.

Her face was incomparably pretty, symmetrical, with a wryly sly, sarcastic smile— as if there were a joke and she was the only one who knew the punchline. She had a truly exquisite body: long legs, a narrow waist, fine round ass and the large, firm breasts of a milk-maid Madonna, bountiful and fecund.

She looked vaguely familiar, but he could not recall any situation or event where he might have had any interaction with her. He would have remembered. Perhaps it was just that she looked like a movie star. Memorable. He was too transfixed to ponder such questions.

Not being a habitué of strip clubs, Mak felt self-conscious and a little embarrassed, but he could not avert his gaze—could not, even for a moment, look away from the gorgeous woman who was slowly disrobing before him.

After what seemed like hours that went by much too fast, she stood, magnificently naked; spectacular flesh exposed to the hot, sweaty, smoky air—currency littering the stage. She delicately scooped up the money, along with her diaphanous costume, entirely unashamed—almost proud—of her state of undress. Slack-jawed, Mak's mouth yawped open. She was a goddess. A real goddess, not a Goddess a Go Go. A goddess.

Feverishly mopping his brow, Mak stood with haste, anxious to be on his way back to the Belladro abode. It had been a performance he would never forget. But he wanted to preserve the memory fully intact without any extraneous material. The perfect retention of a sublime event. No interference.

He made his way up Monmouth back to Pavonia, where he turned right and walked the half block to Mama's place. Mick and Billy D., and Daw and Gib were hanging out in the attic, smoking a joint and drinking beers that the wayfarers had obtained on their path back from the hinterlands. They had been sharing tales of their wanderings.

Mick handed Mak a beer as he joined them, sitting cross-legged on the floor. Though he urgently wanted to tell them about his exciting discovery—the fantastically good-looking stripper at the club down the way—he also covetously wanted to keep her all for himself. Cassandra. He opted to remain silent about his exploits. Mick asked.

—Hey, Mak, so how did it go, man? Did you, like, have any, you know, adventures or anything?

—Naw, not really. All the posters we, uh, put up yesterday were still up.

Mick and Billy D. registered no real surprise. Billy D. said.

—Yeah, they don't seem to go in for the postering thing much around here. I didn't have any trouble with anyone, except some old fart, who wanted to know why I was defacing the phone poles. And I'm all, like, 'well, it's not like they're all that *scenic* in the first place, mister'. And he, like, got all up in my face, but I just walked away from him. I coulda squished him like a bug.

The others laughed, appreciating the reality that if Billy D. wanted to squish anyone like a bug, they would be splattered moths on a windshield. They all watched *Real People, The Facts of Life* and *Family Ties* without saying much, except for making fun of someone or something on the TV screen.

Then the party broke up. Gib and Daw headed off to bed, after another long hard day in the studio. Mak retired to the room he shared with Billy D., while Mick and Billy D. remained in the attic to watch *Quincy*.

On Thursday, the Belladro residence contingent hung out in their rooms all morning. Mak and Billy D. slept in, while Daw and Gib eventually left the house in search of a diner or restaurant of some kind. Anywhere they could find something to eat.

Mak needed to talk to Billy. He had not spoken to him since Sunday, and they needed to get on the same page about a lot of band business. He had Angie's number. He had not yet told Billy of his conversation with Jordan Archer— though Mak was pretty sure that the girls had told him all about it.

Nor had he told Billy of the postering operation. He wanted to get things straightened out with Billy before the weekend of live performances. Mak needed to figure out what to do with himself in his new secondary role. In just a few weeks, the structure within the band had become realigned. Mak wanted to know where he fit in.

It was around eleven when he called over to Angie's to speak with Billy.

—Yallo.

—Hey, is this Angie?

—Yeh. This is Angie. Who's this?

—Hey, Angie, it's Mak. Is Billy around? I need to talk to him?

—Wha'd'ya need to talk to him about?

—Just stuff, man. I haven't talked to him since, like, Sunday. There's stuff we need to go over.

—Like that lawyer guy? We heard about that.

—Yeah. That. And other stuff. Is he there?

—Yeh, yeh. He's here. Hold on.

Mak could hear Angie yelling down the hall to Billy's room.

—Hey, Billy. Ya' got Mak on the phone here. Ya' wanna talk to him?

From a great distance, he could hear Billy yell to Angie that he wanted to talk to Mak. And he could hear a racket as Billy hurried to the phone.

—Yeah. Hi, Poppy. Hey, how's it goin' over there?

—Aw, it's not too bad. We got it all figured out. How about you guys?

As he made his way toward his room, Billy suddenly sounded defensive.

—Wha'd'ya' mean?

—I meant how did it go in the studio this week? How're things at Angie's? How're you? What's goin' on, y'know?

—Yeah, sure. Well, it was pretty shitty in the studio, as I'm sure you heard. It was me and Col and Gilly. It wasn't Gib or Daw. Those two were rock solid the whole time. I'm, like, havin' a lot of trouble keepin' my head in this. And Col's just a little too wound up. And Gilly, I don't know what the fuck's up with Gilly.

—Well hey, man, this is, like, y'know, a strange situation for everybody. You can't expect much, out of the box. It's just too weird and new. It's like another world. I know it is for me.

—Yeah. Another world. Yeah, and I can't get through to Carrie. She's really pissed off with me.

—What's she pissed off about?

—Oh, I didn't finally call her until last Sunday, and she got all bent out of shape about it. Now she won't pick up the phone and doesn't even have the answering machine runnin'. The phone just rings and rings.

—Oh, fuck. You didn't call her for a week? I've only had, like, a couple of girlfriends in my life, man, but even I know that ya' gotta be callin' 'em every day. Especially when you're so far away and all that.

—Yeah. I know. I just lost track. That's all. I kinda forgot about her there for a while—with everything going on and all.

—Shit, man. No wonder she's pissed. Chicks are *all* fuckin' psychic, man. You think she doesn't know ya' forgot about her? She figured that out the first night. You're in deep, deep shit, bud.

—Yeah. I guess I am. Anyway, so I've been worryin' about that a lot and playin' in the studio has just been sort of unenergetic. There's no spark at all.

—Well, let's wait and see how it looks next week, after the band's had another three-day weekend to work things out. I bet they'll come in to the studio next week with a lot better energy.

—I hope you're right, man. So what's up with this music lawyer dude that Candy told us about?

—Aw, nothin's up with him, yet. I gave him the pitch and the promo package and he said he'd get back to me and that was about it. He's some friend of Annie's family, I guess.

—So, he hasn't, like, y'know, gotten back to ya' yet or anything?

—Nah. I haven't heard from him. I'll let ya' know when I do.

—Yeah. You know the number here. What's the number over there, anyway?

Sitting down at the kitchen table, Billy grabbed a piece of paper and a pencil.

—It's four-two-eight, five-seven one-four.

—Four-two-eight, five seven one four. Okay. Got it. Just in case.

—Just in case?

—Yeah, you know. Just in case I need to call you and shit like that.

—Sure. Makes sense.

—So what is it we're supposed to hear back from this guy? Is he going to like sign us? Or give us advice? Or will he just wanna bill us five hundred fuckin' bucks an hour and fuck us over?

Mak chuckled. Billy was more pragmatic than he. Mak knew that Billy was right. Nobody offered something for nothing in the music business. There was a catch to everything.

—Annie knows him. I don't think he'd screw Annie over. He was asking about her mom and dad, like he knew 'em. She set up the appointment. I think she thinks he'll like us. But I don't know if he'll like us or not.

—Of course he'll like us. We're the best band in the world!

It was good to hear some of Billy's cockiness again. Mak realized that there had been a profound absence of that since they had arrived. It was that arrogance that made the band as good as they were. It was like the Stones. Same thing. They were smart asses.

The Gods arrived at the Trappe D'Or around eight o'clock Thursday night, to a packed house, the room at capacity. There was no place for even one more person to squeeze. Whatever their difficulties were in the studio, the Unreal Gods were the hottest live act in all of civilization. Even as strangers in a strange land, they easily drew to a full house, after not even two weeks in town. Word had traveled fast.

Every member of the stage show had their own devoted following of fans out on the dance floor who huddled near them, watching their every move. The Goddesses had their customary delegations of male admirers, lathered up and hot for action.

Billy and Col were used to the gaggles of women, who typically pooled at their feet; but even Gib, Daw and Gilly had their own little clusters of devotees peering up at them with eyes full of lustful adoration.

All night, Billy searched the room to see if Happy was in the audience, but she was not. He performed with his usual panache and flair, but he was deeply disappointed not to see her. He had expected that she would be in attendance and was not familiar with the frustration and despair her absence generated. He took it personally.

She was not at the Friday or Saturday shows, either. Between her and Carrie, he was having something of a bad stretch with the female gender. He was completely out of his element in that regard. Women had always fallen at his feet. He neither understood nor enjoyed his predicament. He was merely confused.

Finally, on Sunday afternoon, Billy was able to get through to Carrie. She was cool toward him and not very conciliatory. She listened politely to Billy's meager attempts at appeasement, but his entreaties fell on deaf ears. Carrie had heard such things from Billy before, and she was not in the mood to believe his feeble excuses—especially with him three thousand miles away and not very communicative.

After that particularly unsatisfying conversation, Billy decided to go for a walk, hoping to clear his mind. It was cold outside and drizzling lightly. He strode south down West Side to Woodlawn where a brightly lit storefront pizza parlor drew his attention. The flashing colors attracted his eye, even in broad daylight.

Sensing it as his destination, he decided to go inside. Billy noticed an attractive dark-haired woman, probably in her late-thirties, sitting at a table near the counter. She was evidently awaiting a pizza to go.

Before he could see them, he could hear arcade games whirring, ringing and singing their siren songs in the room adjacent to the pizza parlor. He immediately moved toward the allure of the sound.

Since it was not yet noon on a Sunday, Billy pretty much had the gaming area to himself. The only other participant was a young boy, maybe ten years old, who was working his way through a game of *Asteroids*.

Billy gravitated toward *Pac-Man*, which he had heard of but had never played. He exchanged a ten-dollar bill for a pocketful of quarters, and he set about making the effort to learn the new *Pac-Man* game.

To begin, he was introduced to the protagonist, Pac-Man—a cross between a smiley face and a piranha. It appeared that the mission was for the Pac-Man to maneuver through an involved maze, consuming little dots along its journey. From time to time, the little yellow fellow managed to ingest some sort of power pellets which, for a time, afforded temporary extra strength.

Those higher powers became valuable when fighting or fleeing the perambulations of the nemeses. It was the responsibility of four ghostly figures—apparent "monsters"—to inhibit the progress of the hero. Ultimately, they had the ability to take his life (requiring another quarter in order to resurrect oneself with the intent of discovering hopeful redemption).

Working through his clutch of quarters, Billy slowly mastered the nuances of *Pac Man*, advancing to higher stages, with the inherently greater risks involved—prolonging the inevitable death that was always the eventual final outcome.

At around one-thirty, he ran out of quarters. With a sense of relieved satisfaction, he departed, back in the direction of Angie's place. Angie was upset when Billy returned. He did not know where Billy had gone and was worried that something had happened. As Billy sat down on the couch, Col warned him of the stormy weather.

—Hey Billy, uh, ya' better, y'know, lay low for a while—Angie's all Angietated.

—What's *his* beef?

—Aw, he thought you disappeared or some such shit. I think he was like afraid he was missin' out on somethin'. Anyway, he got all bent out of shape. I think he's callin' the other house to see if you're over there, talkin' to Mak or somethin'. It's totally off the wall.

—Oh, there you are!

With a troubled tinge to his voice, Angie exclaimed.

—Man, I was worried about you.

—Worried about what? I just went for a walk and ended up at a pizza parlor and played arcade games. I needed some time by myself. Y'know?

—Yeh. Yeh. I got ya'. I mean, it just seemed like one second you was here and the next you was gone. I just thought it was weird, that's all.

—Well, I'm a big boy. I can take care of myself.

Col chimed in.

—That's what I tried to tell ya' the other night, man. You don't need to protect us. We know how to handle ourselves.

—Got it. I guess it must be the big brother in me. I wanna take care of the family or somethin'.

With a wide grin, Gilly piped in.

—I can second that. He was a complete pain in the ass the whole time I was growing up. Always getting into your business...

A couple hours later, Angie, Gilly, Col, and Billy piled into the van, setting out to get things set up in the studio for recording the next day. On the way, they stopped at Mama Belladro's to pick up Billy D., Mick, Daw, and Gib.

At the Power Station, the team assembled their gear quickly and efficiently. Mick and Billy D. loaded the heavy items into the studio and smoothly got the instruments set up and everything plugged in and ready to go. It was nearing six when they left the studio.

After dropping off Gib and Daw, Mick and Billy D. back at the Belladro household, Angie maneuvered his van in the direction of the Trappe D'Or. Billy asked.

—Hey, Angie, what's up? Aren't we goin' back to your place?

—Yeh, yeh. But Larry wanted to talk to us, so I thought I'd swing by on the way home.

—What's he wanna talk to us about?

—I don't know. Prob'ly gigs 'r somethin'.

Silently, they drove the rest of the way to the club. As they entered, they could see Larry smoking a cigarette at the bar, Journey's "Wheel In The Sky" shrilled from the house stereo.

—Hey. There's my guys!

He crushed his cigarette out in a black plastic ashtray.

—I'm glad you guys stopped in. I been thinkin'. I wanna make ya' a offer.

Ever attentive to enhancing the band's income, Billy was ready to consider pretty much any offer.

—What kind of offer? I think we've proven that we can pack this room. And we're the ones doing it. Not Moby Dickens.

—Yeh, yeh, yeh. You ain't tellin' me nothin'. You guys are the best fuckin' thing to hit this place since I dunno when. I ain't gonna jack ya' around about that.

Furrowing fingers though greasy hair, he continued.

—I want you guys to play here every weekend 'til ya' leave town. You can keep Thursdays too, if ya' want.

Billy thoughtfully weighed the offer.

—Weekends seem like a possibility. We wouldn't want to be playing Thursdays anymore, though. We can use that extra day in the studio, and I don't want people to get sick of us.

—Sicka ya'? I don't think that's happenin' anytime soon. These people around here love you guys. They'll keep showin' up as long as yer playin' the club.

—We'll, we gotta make this thing pay, ya' know? What are you willing to offer us?

—Offer you? Shit, man, wha'd'ya want?

—Well I want, like, a guarantee, that's all.

—What kinda guarantee ya' talkin' about here?

—I was thinkin' a couple grand a night. More if we beat that at the door. Like a percentage or somethin'.

—Two-grand? Yer fuckin' killin' me here. I count on the door too, y'know.

—C'mon Larry. I've seen 'em five deep at the bar when we're playin'. You're doin' just fine with the tab at the end of the night.

—Yeh. Okay. Pretty sharp kid.

—Maybe we oughta be negotiatin' about us gettin' a percentage of the bar. We get that in Portland.

—Yeh? Well ya' ain't in fuckin' Kansas no more, kid.

—If we can make two to three grand a night then we'll be fine. I'd like to make more...

Quietly observing the transaction, Angie began to calculate his percentage of the take.

—We've got mouths to feed and bills to pay.

Unpityingly, Larry shot Billy a glance.

—Fuckin' five grand or so a weekend oughta help that out.

—Yeah? We'll see. We'll see. When's Halloween this year? A week from tonight? Shit. Next week. So for next Saturday night we'll want five. That sounds fair. We'll give you a great show.

-Fair? *Shit*!

—And we'll wanna blow off playin' Friday night. We wouldn't wanna spoil the show.

His back against the wall, Larry gave in without much of a fight.

—Awright. Awright. Five. We can do that. I'll find a band fer Friday night. Moby'll prob'ly do it. Be their last weekend night fer a while. They'll prob'ly fuckin' jump on it.

Billy confirmed.

—Then we'll do it.

As the group rode in the van, back to the warehouse, Angie began to follow a different thread of thought.

—Hey, Billy. Man. Fuck if ya' didn't get Larry over a barrel, man. That was pretty fuckin' impressive. Larry don't bend over for no one.

—Aw, we go through that shit all the time back home.

—So what the fuck do ya' need Mak for? I mean, you can do all this shit yerself, fer chrissakes.

—Mak takes care of the details. He makes sure all the i's are, like, dotted and the t's are crossed. I don't have the energy to take care of all this shit.

—Well, maybe y've outgrown him then, man.

—Wha'd'ya' mean?

—I'm just sayin'.

—Yeah?

—I'm just sayin' he probably did a good job for ya' back in Aw-ruh-gawn. But you guys're just about ready to move up to the next circle here. You're gonna need somebody who's been around that kinda shit. Somebody who knows how to play fuckin' hardball.

Sensing that Col was beginning to once again bristle at the topic of conversation, Angie astutely elected to shut up—for the time being. Mutely, they made their way back to Angie's place.

As they entered through the door, back at Angie's apartment, the quartet of voyagers found Candy lying on the couch wrapped in a blanket, looking pale and drawn. Billy was the first to notice.

—Shit, Candy. You look terrible!

—You don't look so good yourself, asshole.

—No, you know. I meant, uh, ya' look really sick.

—I *am* really sick! I can't get my fever to go away. And it seems like every time I dance at a show, I get even worse.

Curled up in one of the chairs, MJ delivered her prognosis,

—I think she's got pneumonia or something. I think she should go to the hospital.

While Gilly was following Angie to their bedroom, Col sat down in the other chair, frowning in concern. Billy's face wrenched itself in misery.

—Aw shit. Do you really think you need to go to the hospital, Cand?

—Probably. But I just want to go back home. The eastern seaboard thing just hasn't worked out very well.

—Yeah, it's been pretty tough for everybody. But we didn't even get you a ticket for the flight back home did we?

—No. I told Mak I didn't need a round-trip ticket. I was going to stay with Annie for a few weeks—see the sights and everything. I was thinking I might want to move out here someday. But now I'm not so sure.

—How were you gonna get home?

—Oh, we were gonna take the train back and see the county.

—Wow! Sounds like a real party. You girls are, like, a couple of wild-ass women.

—It's just something we both wanted to do when we were kids. And we found out we both had the dream of doing it, so this seemed like the perfect time, that's all.

—Yeah. Sure. That's your deal. Sounds okay to me.

—But, I don't think I can make the trip now. I'd be sick the whole time. It'd be even worse by the time we got home. It takes about six days by train.

Massaging his forehead with thumb and index finger, Billy mumbled.

—Well, we'll figure out somethin' for ya'. Don't worry about that. We'll get ya' home.

Angie emerged from his room and signaled with his finger.

—Hey, Billy. C'mere for a sec. I wanna talk to ya' about somethin'.

With a long sigh, Col shot a glance toward Billy—who somnambulantly wandered in Angie's direction. In confused frustration, Col's exhalation made a windy sound through his nostrils.

—There's somethin' weird goin' on around here. I don't know what it is, but it's really fuckin' weird.

A delirious daze swirled around Candy's eyes, as she lifted her head.

—Weird like what?

—Like I don't know. Like Billy's fuckin' hypnotized or somethin'. Like a zombie.

—Maybe he's just got a lot on his mind, with everybody out here and playing the shows and doing the recording. He *is* the leader of the band. That's a lot of responsibility. Especially with this band. And then he's got that thing going on with Carrie.

—Yeah, what's that all about anyway?

—I think she's mad at him for the same reason you're suspicious. Because he's preoccupied.

—Yeah. Preoccupied. That's good word for it. But, y'know, I don't trust that Angie guy either. It always seems like he's up to somethin'. Scammin'. I don't think he likes Mak.

—He's just New York Italian, Col. I swear, that's how they all are. A little manipulative.

—Manipulative. That's another good word. You should get sick more often, Candy.

—No I shouldn't.

Back in Angie's room, Billy sat down on Gilly's bed, as Angie delivered the next installment of his speech.

—So, Billy. I meant what I was sayin' back there in the van.

Deliberating his words carefully, he paced in front of his jury of one. Head slightly bowed, Billy eyed him with caution.

—Meant what?

—Meant what I said about the band movin' up to the next level. You guys're gonna need the right kind of fuckin' representation. I know all the musicians and producers in town. I know music lawyers and label presidents. That's the kind of management yer gonna need.

—Sounds like you're auditionin' for the job.

—Yeh. I guess it does. And maybe I am. That Mak guy seems like an all right guy. But I kinda think maybe you've outgrown him. Don't you? Ya' need somebody who can do more than book gigs and put up posters. But I'm good at that, too. I got you the gig at the Trappe D'or. I could do that anywhere.

—Well, maybe so. Look, I understand what you're sayin', Angie. But Mak's been with us since the beginning. Shittin' on him would be like shittin' on Gilly.

Sitting on Angie's bed, the keyboardist brother shifted uneasily.

—Yeh, yeh, yeh. I get it. That kinda shit's not easy. But ya' gotta do what's best for the band. The band's like a livin' thing. It's growin' on its own, and ya' gotta tend to it and keep it healthy. Ya' know what I mean?

Hesitantly, Billy nodded.

—I get what you're sayin', Angie. And maybe you're right. But that's somethin' I would really have to, like, think about

—Yeh. Yeh. I get ya'. Yer right. Think it over. Yeh. That's a good idea.

—Yeah. Sure. There's a lot goin' on right now. That's all.

With that, Angie rested his case—for the time being. Further voir dire would be required, of course.

On their way to the studio the next morning, while stopping at the Belladro house to pick up Daw and Gib, Billy hopped out of the van.

—I gotta talk to Mak about a couple of things for a second. I'll let Gib and Daw know we're here.

A slight look of worried surprise fell across Angie's face.

—Well here, let me help let you in.

—Naw, it's okay. I'll just knock at the door.

Billy ran up the steps to the house, smartly rapping at the front door. He could hear Augie sprinting down the stairs, shouting.

—I got it, Ma. I got it.

His Reggie Jackson casually nested at his shoulder, Augie thrust open the door—with a self-assurance that, perhaps, only comes to one armed with a baseball bat.

—Yeh?

—Hey, Augie. I'm Billy. I'm in the band with everybody? The guys stayin' here? We met the other day?

Jogging his memory with a severe degree of impedance, Augie could not recollect the precise event. But it did sound reasonable. He recalled that, indeed, there were guys staying upstairs.

—Yeah. There's Angie down at the van. See.

With a slight flourish, Billy pointed toward the van. Mortified Angie waved back half-heartedly.

—I'm here to get Gib and Daw. And I need to talk to Mak for a second.

Restlessly tapping the air with his finger in the direction of the stairs, Billy continued.

—Can I come in and talk to Mak. I'll send Gib and Daw down.

Somewhat disarmed by Billy's genuine charm, Augie backed away from the door and allowed Billy to enter. Billy quickly bounded up the stairs. Augie called after him.

—Okay. But remember...

Billy stopped and glanced back at Augie.

—No meat!!

—No. Of course not. No meat. Wouldn't think of it. Meat is, like, *murder.*

A grimace of abject horror spread across Augie's face like fingers of lightning.

—It's just a saying, man. Don't think about it.

Augie relaxed somewhat and Billy continued up the stairs.

—Hello? Anybody home?

Thumping on the bedroom door, Billy tumbled into the room that Mak and Billy D. shared. The two of them had been hanging out—Billy D. laying on his bed, reading a *Playboy* magazine and Mak at the desk, with the phone next to him, preparing to make a phone call.

With a snap of his head, Mak jumped up from the chair.

—Hey, Billy. All right. What's up man? You guys headin' over to the studio?

Teasingly grabbing the *Playboy*, Billy sat down on the bed next to Billy D. and began to thumb through it.

—Yeah. Headin' over. Hey, I wanted you to know that I set up a deal over at the club.

A chill went down Mak's spine.

—What kind of deal?

—Oh, we stopped by the club after we dropped you guys off last night and that Larry guy wanted to give us headliners on the weekends and I told him two-grand a night—and a percentage of the door over that.

—What'd he say?

—Oh, he said yeah. What else was he gonna say? He's never had anybody like us in there. I got five grand for Halloween, next Saturday.

—Well, that's a pretty good deal. You did real good. I couldn'ta done any better myself.

With a sense of some gravity, Billy eyed Mak.

—Well, I kept askin' myself what you'd do? How you'd handle it.

—Man, you did really good. We need that money. The shit's gonna hit the fan, money-wise, by next week, so gettin' some real money comin' in is a good deal.

—Yeah. That's what I thought.

Pulling out the centerfold, Billy gave Miss November the once over. She was a curvy blond—a good-looking Nordic girl—Marlene Janssen. He motioned to Billy D. with his head.

—Not bad.

Lasciviously wrinkling his eyebrows, Billy D. nodded in vigorous assent.

—I thought he was gonna wet his pants. I don't think any band's ever told him what the deal was gonna be before. He almost started cryin'.

With a chuckle, Billy playfully tossed the magazine into Billy D.'s lap as he stood up and walked toward Mak.

—So what're you guys up to today?

—More posterin', I guess. We're gonna cover the town. Especially with the weekend gigs now. Jeez, I'll have to get, like, a new batch of these printed up.

With his hand, he motioned to the pile of posters on the desk.

—Are we still playin' Thursdays? Or is it just the weekends now?

—Just the weekends.

—Are there gonna be openin' bands?

—Wasn't plannin' on it. I don't see why, do you?

—No, no. I just wanted to make sure we were on the same page with it. That's all. Get the info right on the posters. You know. All that shit.

—Yeah, sure. I know. It's okay. Have ya' heard from Annie about that lawyer yet?

—Naw. I was just gettin' ready to call her and see if she talked to him this morning. I'm feelin' like if we don't hear from him this week, then he's probably not interested.

—Well, if he's not interested, then I say fuck him.

He socked Mak on the shoulder. Mak snorted.

—Yeah, fuck him. Fuck him very much.

Aimlessly, Billy wandered the room toward door. Then he remembered, turning.

—Hey, Mak. You know Candy is really sick.

—Yeah, she seemed pretty out of it over the weekend.

—No man. She's *really* sick. Like, *pukin'* sick. Emergency ward sick. I think she's got, like, pneumonia or somethin'. I don't know what to do.

—What's she wanna do?

—She just keeps sayin' she wants to go home.

—But she doesn't have a plane ticket home. She was gonna go back on the train with Annie.

—Yeah, yeah, I know. That's what I'm sayin' man. I don't know what to do. Anyway.

231

I gotta round up Daw and Gib and we'll go see if we can record a hit song or two. I'll see ya' later. Let me know what you wanna do about Candy.

—What about MJ?

—We'll have to figure that out too.

Billy waved over his shoulder and started banging on the door to Gib and Daw's room across the hall.

—All right you two, get your lazy asses out here and let's go to work.

Briskly flinging open the door, Gib emerged from the room lugging his bass in its sturdy case. Daw followed closely behind, with a black suede quiver of drumsticks drawn over one shoulder and a canvas tote bag containing his cymbals slung over the other. Officiously, Gib glibly reported.

—Oh-ten hundred hours and reporting for duty, sir.

Wagging his head, Billy led the way toward the stairs.

—All right then. Okay. We need to watch out for Augie. He's lurkin' around down there somewhere.

Daw smirked cheerfully.

—Batman? Aw, Augie's just a puppy doggie. Don't worry about him.

—Augie Puppy Doggie. I like that

—Yeah? Well, I dare you to call him that to his face. Or *Batman...*

Billy registered a hint of sheer trepidation. Daw slapped his chest as he passed him, moving down the stairs.

—Just remember, man. No meat. No meat.

—Oh yeah. I got that. I got that loud and clear.

And with that, off they went in search of the perfect recording.

The new information that Billy had imparted temporarily derailed Mak's intentions to paper Jersey City with news of the Unreal Gods' appearances. He was going to have to design and print a new poster immediately.

He petitioned the expertise of Mick and Billy D. as to how to move forward. Together, the three of them crafted a reasonably attractive poster—one that contained all the pertinent data—including the Halloween show—that would look good in full-color and in black and white.

Purposefully, they resolved between them that, from the next day through Friday, they would redouble their efforts at postering—especially in the neighborhoods around the Trappe D'Or, and over toward New Jersey City University. Mak knew it was up to him to prevail upon Angie to act as the ferryman for those excursions.

They transported their artwork to Jedermann Reprographics down on 3rd and Newark, between Brunswick and Monmouth. After leaving their work at the printers, and with a few hours to kill before they could pick up the job, they decided to get something to eat.

For a moment, Mak gave some thought to inviting the team over to that club, as it was only a few blocks away, over on 2nd and Coles. But he decided against it, sensing that it would be a distraction at this juncture of their operation.

Wandering down Newark Avenue, they spent some time hanging out at Abandonment Music checking out gear. Mak chatted with Kerry, the owner of the shop, and mentioned the band's gigs at the Trappe D'Or. Kerry said he had never been there, but he had heard of the place. And he promised to come down for the Halloween show when Mak pledged to put him on the guestlist.

Then the trio continued down Newark to La Gramita, a little Mexican restaurant, where they ordered lunch and drank a few Dos Equis, with the intent of establishing a proper frame of mind from which they might proceed through the rest of the day.

Over in the studio, the Gods found the going much smoother. They were far more assured in their presentations. Confident and energetic. Their efforts toward recording a definitive version of "Police Told Me" came much nearer to fruition. The basic track seemed effortlessly exciting, exuding an easy electric intensity that had been missing in earlier attempts. Music was fun again.

Upon finishing their lunch, Mak, Mick, and Billy D. returned to Jedermann's to pick up the posters—one hundred color posters and one thousand black and whites. Stuck without band funds on his person, Mak paid the two hundred and twenty-five dollar charge out of his own pocket, with the intention of being repaid after the following weekend's gigs.

Satisfied with the quality of the posters, the three of them canvassed the neighborhood, liberally covering their earlier efforts as they made their ways back to the Belladro abode.

Mak wanted desperately to stop into the club at 2nd and Coles to see if the lovely Cassandra might be dancing that afternoon, but he had other, more pressing, matters on his agenda. Thus, he was compelled to blanket his third of the neighborhood with posters and return back to the house as quickly as possible.

With an indistinct sense of urgency, Mak dialed up Annie as soon he returned.

—Annie. It's Mak.

—Oh, I'm glad you called. I was going to call you.

—Did you hear from that Jordan guy?

—Yes. Yes I did.

He could hear her puffing on a cigarette at the other end of the line, exhaling with satisfaction.

—He likes what the band is doing. He wants to arrange for a live performance, at a club where he can get a few people down to see the Gods. You know, big shots. All that.

Her matter-of-fact manner confused Mak. He did not understand the meaning of her words. Her tone was ambiguous and he was not clear as to what she wished to truly convey.

—So wait a second. Are you sayin' he liked our stuff?

—Yeah, he seemed to. Yeah. I think.

Vibrating like a hummingbird, Mak could hardly contain himself.

—He liked it? That's what you said?

—Yeah. I think he likes the band. Yes. He wants to see them play. He wants to set up a gig at the Peppermint Lounge. Fairly soon. He said he wants to get moving on this.

His head whirling in a welter, Mak tried to fully comprehend what he was hearing.

—Well, that's great. That's great, Annie. Way to go. Peppermint Lounge. Billy's gonna fuckin' shit his pants.

—Oh, God! Let's hope not!

—No. No. He's just gonna be fuckin' knocked out, that's all.

Mak could barely wait to tell Billy the news. He knew that Billy would see it as a major deal and a chance to move up the ladder toward rock 'n' roll success.

Unable to contain himself, Mak ran around the bedroom, giving Billy D. pieces of the story from time to time. Billy D. was extremely confused. He could not establish exactly what had taken place, but he was relatively sure that it was good news.

Mick welcomed the information, as well—although he, like Billy D., was unable to make much sense out of what Mak was saying. It sounded like it was a pretty big deal however. And Mick was in the mood for a little good news. It had been a pretty miserable trip up to that point.

234

By the time Gib and Daw returned from the recording session, Mak could hardly control himself. As they jogged up the stairs to their room, Mak sprinted past them, hoping to catch Billy and the others before they left in the van to go over to Angie's house.

But he was too late. He could see the van turning left onto Monmouth. He would have to give Billy a call later in the evening. Mak spun around and dashed back up the stairs to give Gib and Daw the low-down.

Mak was pleasantly surprised by their responses. They actually seemed to comprehend the enormity of the offer that Jordan Archer had made them, and they understood that it was their big opportunity—probably the biggest they were likely to get while in New York. They were as excited as Mak was.

After Daw made a quick beer run, the five of them gathered in Mick's pad in the attic and chattered away about the possibilities. Lighting up a joint of Mex, Mak told them that Annie had said Archer would be bringing other dignitaries along with him when checking the Unreal Gods out at the Peppermint Lounge.

The Peppermint fuckin' Lounge. It was beginning to feel as though their year and a half together was paying off; they were on the verge of hitting the "big-time," in the myriad ways each of them had conjured the idea. Toys, drugs, chicks, status. *Making it.*

Later, Mak made his way down to the phone in the hall. He snatched it up and shuffled toward his room, dragging the long cord behind him. Ringing Angie's place, Mak knew that Angie would want to know what was going on and why did he want to talk to Billy and yadda-yadda. So he decided that the best defense would be a good offense.

—Yo!

-Hey, Angie. It's Mak I gotta talk to Billy.

—Yeh yeh. Wha'd'ya wanna talk to Billy about?

—I just wanna be checkin' in. Y'know? That's, uh, my job. Speakin' of which, I need your help with a project, Angie.

—Yeh? What's that?

—We need you to come over and pick us up some morning this week—before you guys head out to the studio—and bring us over to your neighborhood. We need to poster for the shows. I wanna catch the neighborhoods around the club and around the University.

—Yeh. Well, sure, I guess. Yeh. I could probably do that one of these mornings.

—Then, when you came back from the studio, with Col and Billy and Gilly, you could, like, take us back to your mom's place. It would mean a little extra drivin' for ya', but the three of us can get all of your part of town done in a day. We could pay ya' for gas and everything.

—Yeh. Okay, okay. So when were you plannin' on doin' this?

—Uh...Wednesday? How's Wednesday?

—Okay. Wednesday. I'll be over to get ya' at around nine, and I'll take you guys back whenever we get back from the studio.

—Okay. That'll work. That'll be great. We'll have posters up everywhere before next weekend. It'll be huge. Hey. Can you put Billy on?

—Billy? Yeh. Sure. Sure. I'll get him.

Satisfied with himself, Mak could hear Angie march down the hall to hail Billy. He could also hear Candy hacking hoarsely in the background, the television rattling *That's Incredible* in the background. It was in that moment that he determined what he was going to have to do for her.

—Hello? Mak? What's up?

—Billy man. Some good shit,

—Like what?

—Like that lawyer Jordan Archer called Annie back this morning and he likes our shit and he's gonna set up a showcase gig for us at the Peppermint Lounge.

Incredulous, yet not with complete surprise, Billy greeted Mak with droll nonchalance.

—Well it's about *fucking* time, man. We're like a goldmine here, waitin' for the first smart miner to stake his claim.

Taken aback a bit by Billy's aloofness.

—Billy, man. The Peppermint Lounge! The fuckin' Peppermint Lounge!

—Yeah, yeah. I heard ya'. So where else would he put together one of these wingdings for him and all his buddies?

—But it's a big deal for us, Billy. Don't you think? I mean it's the Peppermint Lounge! It's, like, one of the biggest showcases for a band like ours in the fuckin' universe, man.

Mak was bewildered by Billy's attitude. At first he thought he was joking, but it had become apparent that Billy meant every word he said. He was starting to sound like Angie. Arrogant. Assholy.

—Well. I'll let Annie know to tell this guy to eat shit, that we'll make our own fuckin' way.

—Hey, Pop. I didn't say that.

—Well, it kinda sounded to me like that's what you were sayin'.

—Mak, man. How come you don't, like, believe in the band?

Silence.

—No. Really. How come you don't believe in the band?

—I don't know what the hell you're talkin' about, Billy. Of course, I believe in the band.

—Then act like it, Pop. None of this should come as any fuckin' surprise to you. Not if you, like, really believe in the band. That Archer guy and his buddies would be goddamn fools to pass us up. That's right, isn't it?

—Yeah. I guess it is. But...

—*But* nothin', man. These guys are lucky to have us blow into their lives. They probably think we're a buncha hillbillies and that they can push us around. Well, that's not the way it's fuckin' gonna go down, man. I'm tellin' ya' that right now. I'm gonna be famous and you guys can come along for the ride if ya' want.

Befuddled, yet oddly exhilarated by Billy's strange speech, Mak had no reply for his friend. The Stones had made their names as snotty bad boys, and Billy was determined to have things his way. He was not a snotty bad boy. He was merely a snotty all-American boy. Mak tried to appreciate the difference, though he was unsure as to what that difference was, exactly.

—I won't argue with ya' about that, Billy. You're, like, gonna be a big star. Anybody who's ever seen ya' knows that. I believe in you, Billy. Whether you're in a band or in the movies, I know you're goin' somewhere. You won't get any argument out of me.

Appeased, for the time being, Billy changed the subject.

—So we did good in the studio today.

—Yeah? That's great.

—Yeah. I think we got a good, workin' basic track of 'Police Told Me.' It felt good. It felt like what we're goin' for on that one. Good energy and we played good.

—Cool. Very cool. I'm glad to hear it.

—So what did you guys do?

—Uh, let's see, first we designed some new posters, promotin' the weekends—and the Halloween show and everything. And then we took it down to the printers. And they were ready about one, and we postered the hell out of the neighborhood around here. I got Angie to come over on Wednesday morning and pick us up and we'll come over to your area and poster around the club and over around the college.

—Sounds good. Sounds good.

Mak could hear the *Mash* theme playing on the television in the background, while Candy unburled a croaking wheeze.

—Hey, Billy. I can hear Candy back there. She sounds like shit. Like you said.

—Yeah man, we're gonna have to like take her to the doctor or somethin'.

—Well, I was thinkin' maybe I'd give her my plane ticket, so she can fly home. I think she needs to get back to Oregon. Soon.

—That's a great idea. I don't want her dyin' or anything. That wouldn't look good. Ya' know?

Mak could not tell whether Billy was serious. Billy sensed Mak's unease.

—Fuck. I'm just shittin' ya'. It's a good idea, and it's real nice of ya'. I'll tell her about it and see what she, like, wants to do.

—Okay. Okay. Well, keep it up in the studio, man. Get some momentum goin'.

—Yeah, Mak. We'll try. You keep it goin' too.

## XXIII

Hanging up the phone, Billy turned to Col, who was watching *Mash*, just as Margaret was learning that Colonel Beatrice Bucholz was on her way for an inspection of the nurses' station.

—Hey, Col. That lawyer guy called Annie. He wants us to, like, play a showcase at the Peppermint Lounge.

—He what?

—He wants us to play a showcase at the Peppermint Lounge.

Either via masterly psychic abilities, some secret, hidden second phone line, or just an amazingly acute sense of hearing, Angie seemed to know and he came bursting out of his room as if the apartment were in the midst of an earthquake.

—Wha'd'ya' say, man? A showcase where? Did you say the Peppermint Lounge? Shit!

—Yeah. I guess that lawyer guy called Annie and she called Mak.

Hoping to steer the conversation in propitious directions, Angie asked.

—What'd she call him for? Why didn't she call you?

—Well, because it was her and Mak that went and saw the guy, I guess. And probably because we were, like, in the studio, and Mak was near his phone. I wasn't there. I don't know. I don't think it's a big deal, Angie.

—It's just. Ya' know. It's like we talked about.

Col squinted in Angie's direction, sneering slightly.

Knowing there would be better opportunities to speak directly to Billy about these issues, Angie decided to drop the subject. He inquired of Billy.

—So wha'd he say?

—Who?

—Mak! Wha'd he say the lawyer said?

—He said the lawyer said he wanted to set up a gig at the Peppermint Lounge, so he could bring in his buddies and check us out.

—Buddies like who?

—I don't know, you'd have to ask Mak.

—When's this s'pose ta happen anyway?

—This is all stuff to ask Mak, man. I don't know if he even mentioned it to me, to tell you the truth. Shit, I almost forgot. Hey, Candy.

Nearly immobile, Candy feebly lifted her head from a pillow on the couch. She answered wearily.

—Yes, Billy, dear. I'm right here.

—Yeah. Mak said you could have his plane ticket and fly home whenever you want.

—He said I can fly home on his ticket? You're kidding! Not really.

—Yeah. Really. He's all worried about you. We're all worried. He wants for you to get home and see a doctor. We don't want ya' dyin' out here.

His repetition of the jest did not go over any better the second time around.

—He said that about dying?

—No. No. I was just fuckin' around. But anyway, he's gonna give you his ticket.

—Oh, that's so nice of him. When do you think I should go?

—I don't know Cand. We got the Halloween show this weekend...

—Maybe I'll wait until the show at the Peppermint Lounge before I go. If it's not too far off. I'd hate to miss that one. As long as I don't die.

She stuck her tongue out at Billy and rested her head back down on the pillow.

—That's all really cool, Billy. Great news. I'm going home. Home.

She was happy for Candy, but wheels began to turn in MJ's brain.

On Tuesday, Mak, Mick, and Billy D. resumed their re-postering of the Hamilton Park area, as well as the surrounding environs and hinterlands. It just so happened that it once again fell upon Mak to cover the territory in the vicinity of the club over on 2nd and Coles. He postered the neighborhood with a great sense of urgent anticipation. He really wanted to see that beautiful girl again.

Cunningly, he managed to save the club as the last of his stops for the day, so that he could spend the time necessary to see that girl, Cassandra, or whatever she called herself. He was filled with a certain longing. He had a thing for that girl.

So, with Sniff 'n ' the Tears' "Driver's Seat" pumping at jet engine volume through the sound system, Mak moved right past the bar, grabbing a table in the back of the room. The performance seemed more lightly attended.

A different girl was dancing, a pleasant-looking, brown haired woman of indistinct heritage, with gargantuan, surgically enhanced breasts. The guys sitting in the rows of tables that surrounded the stage moved their heads in time to the swaying trajectory of those monsterous orbs, never taking their eyes from them even for a moment. Spellbound.

She leapt down from the stage and sat in one guy's lap, sensuously staring directly into his eyes. It was probably the greatest thing that had ever happened in his entire life. To the beat of the music, she began to rhythmically hump and grind against his groin, while grabbing him by the hair and driving his face between her massive boobs. They batted his cheeks on either side, slapping against his ears.

The music cut to a sudden stop and she froze, the lucky guy's face lodged between the bountiful provinces of her giant gazongas. He began to suffocate, but he didn't care—his friends would never believe him anyway. He just left his face there, nuzzling her breasts like a happy baby nestling at his mama's chi-chis.

The same emcee from the previous time, looking eerily identical to his preceding appearance—wearing the same blue brocade dinner jacket—hollered distortedly.

—The exotic Desiree. Desiree, ladies and gentlemen. Let's hear it for Desiree, the goddess of the Nile.

Desiree departed to the backstage area amid polite applause, marked by an especially effusive response from the recipient of the tit whipping. Apparently no one felt like correcting the emcee and mentioning to him that the goddess of the Nile was actually Anuket. Probably, no one knew or cared.

Mak was hopeful that Cassandra might be the next dancer. A fine moisture of anticipation misted his forehead. He wanted badly to see that girl again. He wanted to see her without her clothes on again. The image of her naked body had not left his mind for even a moment since he had seen her the week before. She was a true unreal goddess, not a hillbilly princess.

It was not to be. Desiree was followed by Tiffany—a slender young woman, with a slight build, heavy eye make-up, long straight bottle-blond hair and a certain detached expression that attracted only a few of the patrons, who sat at the tables at the edge of the stage. However, those few gave the impression that they were staunch supporters.

Searching the area with narrowed feral eyes, Mak did not see Cassandra anywhere in the room. He had no way of knowing if she was backstage, preparing to perform. Or perhaps, for all he knew, she was not even on the bill for that day.

Frustrated and not a little disappointed, Mak decided to leave. He had no idea how to find out what the schedule was or when she might appear again. He had returned on a different day of the week, at about the same time, but she was not performing. Nor was Daphne.

Fairly confident that the club regulars knew each girl's schedule with atomic precision, he opted to not engage anyone for fear that he might become perceived a regular himself—though it was entirely possible that he might become one.

Instead of waiting around—with the prospect of only more disenchantment looming large—he despondently plodded from the Electric Kitten, stepping into the sullen gray of the rainy Jersey City afternoon. He knew his thoughts would be haunted, presumably for the rest of his life, by the heavenly image of Cassandra's unclothed form.

The next morning, rain subsided, Angie arrived at Mama's house promptly at nine o'clock. Mak, Mick, and Billy D. were ready to go. They knew they were in for a long, arduous day. Gib and Daw were not as prepared.

Already pissed at the inconvenience of the assignment, Angie sat parked on the street, the engine of the van, idling rhythmically. The poster battalion came outside, Mak taking the front seat, Mick and Billy D. sitting on the bench in back. Angie looked up, a little put out.

—Where's the drummer and the bass player? I told 'em ta be ready. What're they doin' up there? Pickin' their asses?

Mak felt compelled that he should respond.

—Don't know, man. Didn't talk to 'em yet this mornin'. We were gettin' ready for our poster job.

Aggravated, Angie wagged his head in a slow boil. Finally, Gib and Daw dawdled from the building, trundling along without a care. The pair joined Mick and Billy D. on the bench in the back of the van.

With great haste, Angie transported the poster delegation back to the warehouse. Billy stood waiting out on the sidewalk with Gilly and Col, who was smoking a cigarette, his narrow shoulders hunched against the brisk, foggy, morning air.

The prisoner exchange concluded, Angie drove off in a huff of exhaust; the intrepid wayfarers left to wend their map of day by the devices of their own sails and the wind, reckoning true the unseen stars.

It was Mak's idea to knock at the apartment door to hail MJ or Candy. MJ came down, frazzle frizzed in morning muss, half asleep.

—You guys! What're you doing here? How'd you get here?

Mak took up the trail of the explanation.

242

—Angie came and got us so we could, like, poster the neighborhoods around here and the club, and around the area by the college, if we get that far.

He raised his brows expectantly in the direction of his mates.

—Well, c'mon up. Candy's still sacked out. But I can make some coffee if you guys want.

They marched up the stairs to Angie's space. The idea of coffee seemed like a good idea. Mak ventured.

—Yeah, coffee would be great. We're gonna need all the help we can get. It's gonna to be a long day.

While MJ was fussing in the kitchen, Candy yawningly wandered out from the girls' bedroom.

—I was wondering what was going on out here. I thought Billy and everybody had gone already. I couldn't figure out...

Pulling her hair back from her face, she twisted it in a thick knot behind her head. Dramatically, she pirouetted. Affecting a twang, she purred.

—Anyway...hello boys. What brings y'all 'round these parts?

With his hands jammed into his coat pockets, Billy D. was pacing around the kitchen.

—Mak wants to poster the area around the club and everywhere.

—Yeah. I wanna get it done before the Halloween show this weekend. We've got that show, like, billed on the poster.

Pulling one from a canvas sheath, he handed it to her. She nodded approvingly.

—And all the weekend shows after that—until we head back home.

Sighing, Candy whimmed.

—Home. 'Where my thought's escaping'.

Wearily, she trilled the syllables as if she meant them. She did.

—'Where my love lies waiting, silently for me'.

A wistful, dreamy expression crossed her face, as she dejectedly snuffled and sniffed.

—Well, Candy, you know you've got my ticket home, and you can set up that flight whenever you want.

Maintaining her brusque cowgirl manner.

—Tryin' to get rid of me, eh?

—No. You know. Whenever ya' want. I didn't mean…

—I know, Mak. I was just yanking your chain.

She smoothed his furry head as if he were a friendly bear cub and slumped down into the familiar consolation of the couch.

—I really appreciate that you're doing it for me. It's so unselfish of you.

Blushing, Mak scuffled his feet self-consciously.

—Aw. Y'know. That's what it's all about. We're all like brothers and sisters here. You'd do the same for me if the situation was reversed.

Pausing to consider, she smiled mischievously.

—I *suppose* you're right. Anyway, I want to give you my train ticket so you can use it. Or give it to someone else to use. I still don't know what Annie's going to do. I kind of screwed up our trip back.

With great difficulty, Mak attempted to stay on subject.

—I guess the train ticket would be good. Somebody could use it I'm sure. We could, like, give it to Angie, so he could come out to Portland.

—You're kidding aren't you? You can't be serious.

—No. Now I'm just yankin' *your* chain. I mean we could give the ticket to someone we like.

—That's more like it. You had me worried there for a second.

Shivering, she hugged her knees, huddled in a ball on the sofa. MJ called out.

—Who wants coffee?

Simultaneously, the three males responded like magnets, swiftly drawn in her direction.

—I wish I always got that sort of response when I spoke.

The guys grabbed mugs MJ had set out and began pouring themselves cups of coffee, adding sugar and creamer, milling in a pack-like circle, blowing on their brew as they sipped and slurped.

—I said, I wish I always got that sort of response…? I said.

She shrugged in mock-frustration.

—Well, there you go.

The two band contingents performed their functions admirably that day. Mak, Mick, and Billy D. nearly covered the entire south portion of Jersey City—from the Trappe D'Or to the University. They felt confident that the public was properly notified.

Meanwhile, in the studio, the band members were concisely performing up to their capabilities: finally. One by one, each member layered complex overdubs onto "Police Told Me," thickening and sweetening the sonic frosting with buttery finesse.

As that was going down, the others aimlessly lounged around in the control room, reading all available porn and music-related magazines—*Rolling Stone* and *Penthouse. Creem* and *Playboy*. They sloshed down beer after beer and lit a litany of joints.

Still, they were all tied into the music. Despite being blasted out of their minds much of the time they never seemed to lose sight of their artistic vision. Their shared intentions and musical goals remained in tact.

Once Angie and the band agreed that the instrumental tracks were pretty much in the can, it was Billy's turn to take a stab at capturing the lead vocals. He made a couple of passes that ultimately did not stand up to scrutiny. After taking a break, he tried it again and came closer to what they wanted, but it was still not the definitive take.

As it was getting late, the group decided to call it a day, agreeing that they would carry on the task of recording the lead vocals on the following day. They felt that they were finally making some progress and their old cockiness was welcomely beginning to return to the fore.

Mak, Mick, and Billy D. were exhausted when they finally reconvened in front of Angie's place. They knocked at the entry door, and MJ came down the stairs and let them in.

—You again? We have to stop meeting like this. So, how'd it go?

—It was colder than shit out there.

Mak opened his parka, allowing the heat of the room to quell his chill.

—I never did warm up. My teeth were chatterin' all day.

Billy D. agreed.

—Me either. My fingers were, like, numb in the first half hour.

Nodding, Mick concurred.

From the couch, Candy woozily lifted her head, resurrecting her tough-but-tender saloon-girl character from earlier in the day.

—Hello, boys. Back for more sugar? What kept you so long? It's not nice to keep a girl waiting, you know.

Inexplicably embarrassed, Mak moved from the entryway to the back of the couch. Peering down at Candy, he earnestly intoned.

—Well we went as fast as we could. We covered a lot of ground today. Everybody in Jersey City is going to know about the Unreal Gods now. We made damn sure of that.

—That's great, Makkie. You and your little friends did a good job. And if I wasn't so sick, I'd give you a big juicy reward.

With more than a hint of seduction in her voice, she arched her eyebrow at Mak, the gauze of a suggestive smile smoothed across her face. As she looked up at him, Mak uncomfortably shifted his weight from foot to foot. Eyes nervously averted, his face and neck slowly turned the color of ripe watermelon pulp. Candy delighted in making him blush.

The theme of the *NBC Nightly News* reassuringly hummed from the television. The latest network newscaster was running down the events of the day.

—*Good evening, I'm Tom Brokaw. Roger Mudd is on assignment. These are the breaking stories. Missing over seven weeks, there is still no sign of twelve-year-old Iowa paperboy, Johnny Gosch. Local authorities fear he has been kidnapped. The Worlds Fair in Knoxville, Tennessee, is set to close on Sunday. Over eleven million visitors have passed through the gates.*

Hypnotized by the warm, comfortable tone of the newscasters' voice, Mak distractedly ignored Candy and stared at the set.

—*The champion Cardinals paraded through the streets of downtown Saint Louis today after clinching the World Series in game seven last Wednesday, with a six to three victory over the Milwaukee Brewers at Busch Stadium in Saint Louis. Series Most Valuable Player, Cardinal catcher David Porter was the parade Grand Marshall.*

Momentarily daydreaming, Mak reflected on the vicissitudes of playing the position of catcher and the profound sense of fulfillment Porter must have experienced.

—*Sales by the Sony Corporation of the musical 'Compact Disc Player' have been modest since the US launch of the device on October first. Utilizing state-of-the-art 'digital technology', the first compact discs were released in Germany last August. Despite the cool initial response from the public and lovers of traditional vinyl recordings, Sony insists the advantages of compact discs far outweigh their shortcomings and that they will soon gain a foothold with music consumers across the nation and around the world.*

Compact discs. Computers. Billy had been talking about all that electronic stuff for quite a while. Gilly had a synthesizer that could sound like any instrument. Daw was playing around with *drum pads.*

To Mak, it all seemed too space age and strange. *Cutting edge.* None of it rang true to the essence of his own acoustic folk sensibilities. While he was excited by the notion of these new toys, the gadgets nevertheless frightened him.

The news broadcast had nearly concluded, when Angie, Gilly, Billy and Col, with Gib and Daw in tow, ascended the stairs to the apartment. Col drowned out the cigarette he had been smoking and threw the butt in the trash as he entered the living room area, Billy and Daw trailing him closely.

—What's happenin', gang?

Col was met with a silent wave of weary indifference.

—Don't everybody talk at once. What happened? You guys overwork yourselves?

Not particularly in the mood to deal with Col's sarcasm, Billy D. snapped back.

—Look, Col, asshole, we walked all over this town today, puttin' up posters for *your* fuckin' band. The least you can do is be thankful for it.

Realizing his error, Col prudently tried to remove his foot from his mouth, as he back-pedaled as fast as he could.

—D, no. No, man. I didn't mean it like that, man. I was just, like, givin' you guys a hard time. I know you walked all over for us, man. It had to be cold out there. I'm thankful for that. I didn't mean to piss ya' off.

Appeased, Billy D. sighed.

—Aw, it's all right. I just didn't want you pussies takin' us for granted.

From where he stood, next to the television, with his hands in his jacket pockets, Billy chimed in.

—Hey D! You guys are the fuckin' glue in this operation. You know that. You're right. We *are* pussies. We wouldn't even know how to set up our amps without you and Mick. And Mak, man, Mak—we're broke now, but we'd be pimpin' ourselves out if it wasn't for him. And some of you wouldn't be able to help the cause much, with the shit you're showin'.

They all laughed at the jest, which further helped to reduce the tension in the room. But Mak thought he heard something peculiar in what Billy was and was not saying.

247

—We're all workin' hard here and givin' what we've got. We're all, like, strangers in a strange land, y'know? We need to be pullin' together like a team and givin' each other support, with no fuckin' around and no bullshit.

Stroking his chin, Mak reasoned.

—There's a lot goin' on right now. A lot of changes comin' down. Billy's right—we need to be coverin' each other's asses. We're the only friends we've got.

Mak shot a look at Angie, who was sitting at the kitchen table with his head down, squeezing and massaging his fingers, listening fixedly to every word being said.

—If we can't keep it together now, we'll never be able to keep it together when the going gets really tough.

His eyes curtained by long, curly hair, Daw shook away his brown bangs, adding.

—We're all kinda like experts. If we didn't know what we were doin' we wouldn't be here in the first place.

Hastily rising and leaving the room, Angie had nothing to say, while Daw finished his thought.

—We just need to, like, keep doin' what we've always done. Y'know? If we all do our job, everything will be cool, and we'll be in the big leagues in no time. You all know how close we are. It's gettin' closer everyday.

Finally getting off the topic, Mak conjectured aloud to no one in particular.

—Everything went okay in the studio, then? Things are goin' smoother?

Gilly, who had been sitting mute at the kitchen table with his brother, tossed out his opinion.

—We've just about got 'Police Told Me' done; just Billy's vocals left and maybe a few final layers, harmonies and fills, over that for thickening and that should be it for that one. Sounds fuckin' great, man.

Brooding, Billy registered his impressions of the effort, thus far.

—This version sounds a lot better than the one we did when you guys were in there.

He watched the trio of worker bees humming quietly—as if communicating between themselves at some frequency outside the capacity of human hearing.

—This version rocks. Once I, like, get the vocals done—tomorrow, I hope—and we get the relish and mustard smeared all over it, it's gonna be one fuckin' giant weenie of a song. These big city boys're gonna eat it up. Just you watch.

# XXIV

—He wants to set up the show for next Wednesday. He thinks he can get that Cousins Vetter guy from Rough Edge Records to come down—and maybe even Bruce. He said he couldn't promise anything but that he'd try.

Still wiping the night from his too-early morning eyes, Mak attempted to assimilate what Annie was telling him at the other end of the call.

—Wait a minute...Wait. You mean that Archer guy is bringin' the guy from Rough Edge Records to the Peppermint Lounge show? And he wants to do it next Wednesday?

—Yeah. Is there a problem with that?

—No. No. I'm just tryin' to wrap my brain around it. I just woke up.

—'Cuz I could tell him we need to shoot for some other time.

—It's okay, Annie, next Wednesday's great. If that's when he wants to do this, then that's when we'll do it. Now what's this about Springsteen? Are you, like, shittin' me? Or what?

—No, really. I guess Bruce is in town and Jordan's been talking to him, and he invited him down to check out the band. He said he'd make it down if he could. That's all I know.

Mak nearly swallowed his tongue.

—Fuckin' Bruce, man! That's incredible, Annie. That's fuckin' incredible. You really came through on this one.

—Well, nothing's happened yet.

—It's just a matter of time, Annie, just a matter of time.

He heard himself echoing Billy's conceits, and he was mildly pleased.

—We've got it all, and it doesn't take a genius to figure that out.

—I hope you're right, Mak. That would be great. Wouldn't that be great?

—Yeah it would. No shit! And we owe it all to you.

249

Feigning modesty, Annie soaked up the praise, even if she would have preferred to hear it from Billy. She had always been confident she could do Mak's job—probably better. He did not seem to notice her attempts to encroach upon his territory. Or if he did, he was not letting on.

As he hung up with Annie, Mak was eager to tell Billy the news. He immediately tried to catch him over at Angie's place, before they set off to the studio. But they had already gone. He was a little surprised when MJ answered the phone.

—Mak. I thought it was probably the boys, or I wouldn't have answered. They just left about five minutes ago. I don't live here, you know? I don't like answering that guy's phone.

He told MJ about the show at the Peppermint. She began to hyperventilate and handed the phone to Candy. Mak gleefully repeated the account to her, and she too was euphoric, though soporifically. The conversation was short. Mak asked Candy not to tell Billy about the show—that he wanted to be the one to break the news. She said okay and they hung up.

Given the evolving circumstances Mak was unsure what to do with his day. His camp had already decided they would take Thursday off. They had made an impressive effort the day before, and all agreed they deserved the break, if only to rest the blisters on their tired feet and the tender blue squeeze-bruises on the palms of their stapling hands.

It occurred to him that he would need a costume for the Saturday Halloween show. So would Billy D. and Mick. So would everyone else, he supposed. He took it upon himself to initiate a search for a Salvation Army store or some other similar source. He hauled out the yellow pages from under the table in the hall.

But as he began to flail through the pages with no direction or aim, he became conscious of the fact that it was fruitless to conduct any sort of undertaking involving fashion without first consulting Candy, who was the undisputed group maven.

At first, he hesitated calling her back. He hated the thought of disturbing her again when she was feeling so shitty, but he was sure that she would understand. At the very least, she could point him in the right direction.

He dialed Angie's house but neither Goddess answered the phone. Mak figured that they were not picking up, because he had just hung up with them, so it couldn't be him and the band were not likely to be calling either. He hung up and called right back, then hung again up after two rings and tried once more. Hesitantly MJ picked up the phone.

—Hello?

—Hey, MJ. It's me again. I need to talk Candy.

She walked the phone over to her dance partner, who was more or less passed out again on the couch.

—It's Mak. He says he needs to talk to you.

The weight of the phone forced Candy's arm to the floor. With uncommon bravery, she lifted the receiver to her ear.

—Hullo? Mak? What's up?

—I forgot that we need to get outfits together for the Halloween show on Saturday. We'll need your help with that if we're gonna pull it off.

Cheered immeasurably by Mak's call, Candy's condition seemed instantaneously to improve. There was suddenly more vitality in her voice than Mak had heard since they had first arrived back East, almost three weeks earlier.

—Let me call Annie and we'll figure something out. Maybe some kind of expedition tomorrow. I'll tell Billy about that when they get home and see what he wants to do. We'll need everyone along for this, if we're going to make them all happy.

—Okay. See what Billy wants to do. I'll be callin' over there tonight at some point and we'll, uh, get it all put together. We got a lot goin' on here in the next week. It could be, like, the biggest week the band's ever had.

Candy vibrated at a very high frequency.

—You're right, Mak. This might be the biggest opportunity the band ever sees. Everyone will have to be at their best—for both shows—for Halloween, because it's probably the biggest show, as far as audience goes—and for the Peppermint Lounge show. It's just huge in so many ways.

Her enthusiasm was contagious. Mak became more and more excited by the moment. His anticipation of upcoming events was probably nothing more than fantasy, but there was, too, the likelihood that it would all play out as Billy had predicted. He was positively giddy.

While Billy D. dozed on the bed, Mak spent the rest of the day at the desk, sorting through various permutations of every possibility, viewing each from all angles, jotting down notes and ideas. He wanted to cover all the bases—to anticipate the unforeseen little details.

Within minutes of arriving back at Angie's apartment, Billy was on the phone to Mak. Candy had told him just enough to pique him inquisitive.

—Mak. Brutha. What's up? Candy said you had some kind of news.

Mak blurted.

—Well, that lawyer guy, Archer, called up Annie and said he booked the Peppermint Lounge for next Wednesday. So we're playin' there next Wednesday.

—Wednesday? That's so soon. What's that about?

—She said he was all hot to bring in Cousins Vetter from Rough Edge Records and maybe even Bruce.

—Bruce? *Springsteen*?

—Yeah. She kinda like laid the deal on me. She said we could back out if we wanted, but fuck, man, we never know when we might have a chance like this again. I told her we'd do it.

Miffed that he was being informed of the gig, rather than consulted, Billy became the type-A male bandleader.

—I guess that's all good. But I kinda would have liked bein' in on the negotiations.

—Well me, too, man. Annie just sort of dumped it in my lap.

—Maybe Annie and I should be talkin' to each other. What's her number anyway?

Mak's spine spasmed.

—Her phone number? It's actually, like, her brother's phone.

—That's okay. We should be able to talk direct in situations like this. I need to get her number from you.

—It's, uh.

He leafed through the black leather pocketbook he carried with him wherever he went.

—It's, uh, two-one-two area code. It's long distance over there, y'know.

—Yeah, sure.

—It's two-one-two, three-five-three, seven-seven-nine-three.

—Two-one-two, three-five-three... Seven-seven...nine what?

—Nine-three. Seven-seven-nine-three.

—Two-one-two, three-five-three, seven-seven-nine-three.

—Yeah, that's it. You got it.

—Good. Yeah, man. I probably would have reacted like you did. But I mighta told her we need more time, too.

—We don't need more time, Billy. What happened to that confidence you were spoutin' last time we talked? I thought we were ready for anything, so I said okay. I told her okay. This band is goin' all the way. Remember?

—Yeah, I did say that. I guess you're right about this.

—Fuck yeah, I'm right What's the band gonna do, anyway? Like, *rehearse* or somethin'? When was the last time this band rehearsed anything? It's not like 'from the page to the basement to the stage' anymore. It's 'from the page to the stage'. All the rehearsin' fuckin'gets done on stage now, man. During sound checks and in the middle of the third set. That's how it's been for six months, anyway. Think about it.

Weighing Mak's words Billy admitted.

—Okay, you're right about that. We really haven't actually rehearsed for a long time. In fact, now that you mention it, none of the songs we're recording here were ever rehearsed—we just started workin' 'em out on stage.

—That's what I'm tellin' ya, Billy. This Wednesday. Wednesday a month from now, what the fuck's the difference?

—I guess there probably wouldn't be any difference. We'd play some songs better and some songs worse, just like we always do.

—That's exactly what I'm sayin'. So look, we gotta get the costume thing figured out for Saturday. Candy said she can get Annie to come over tomorrow and they'd help us find stuff at all the thrift stores and what not.

Billy said nothing.

—So that would mean you guys wouldn't record tomorrow and we'd all head out in Annie's car and Angie's van and we'd get our outfits together. Wha'd'ya think?

—Man, Mak. I don't know. We didn't get my vocals done on 'Police' so that would be draggin' the song into next week.

—But I think Saturday will be too fuckin' late to get everything together. Don't ya' think? We gotta look really bitchin' for that gig. It's gonna be, like, packed out there. Fuckin' *packed out*. And we'll need Candy's help to pull this off. Annie's too. You know how brilliant Candy is with all the fashion shit. She just knows the places to go and what'll work.

—Yeah. You're right, Poppy. I guess we really don't have any choice. We'll hafta make it over to the studio sometime on Saturday to get our gear. But we do hafta look sharp for Halloween. We want for people to remember us. Remember the show. Always.

—That's *it*, Billy. You got it.

Mak moved the conversation toward more immediate concerns.

—So you, like, tell the boys and Candy and MJ about this. I'm gonna leave that to you.

—Yeah. Okay. I'll give 'em the update. I'll talk to Angie about drivin' us around. It'll probably totally piss him off. But the little fucker is makin' more money out of this operation than we are—we might as well put him to work.

Slightly uneasy, and a little defensive, Mak continued the conversation.

—Well, everyone should have a job, I guess. Seems like he's got plenty. But if we pay for his gas and his lunch and for his fuckin' outfit, I don't see where he's got any reason to bitch. Fuck him, if he can't take a joke.

Billy snickered.

—Yeah, fuck him if he can't take a joke.

After hanging up with Mak, Billy convened the other five members of the household and told them of the plan. Candy and MJ already pretty much knew about the Peppermint Lounge show and the Halloween costume scavenger hunt, so none of it was a surprise to them.

But the reactions of Col, Gilly and Angie were, each in his own individual response, as different from one another as a shovel from an onion to a penny. Col thought everything sounded totally cool. Angie was overcome with concern. Gilly flipped randomly between heads and tails.

Gilly was ecstatic over the turn of events, but fretful that the events were turning without his brother being in the position of band axle, around which the sprocket, and the wheel, with all its spokes, revolved. The conundrum created within him a familiar fuddle of ambivalence. But it occurred to him that either way, things sounded good. Real good.

However, as was his nature in the circle of all things, Angie felt the necessity to control the orbit of the planets within his solar system, maintaining a blackhole gravity of opposition, which rivaled even that of the sun. Or so it seemed.

And so, with all due haste, but with the sort of unflagging conspiratorial strategy for which he had so quickly become renowned, Angie summoned Billy to his room for a corporate tete a tete.

As the two of them stood to leave the room, Gilly rose, too, in hopes of fulfilling a role: such as CEO or VP of Musicology, or whatever was available. But Angie waived him off. Top-level conference. Need to know sort of thing. Never mind.

Even before the door to his room was closed, Angie began his quiz of Billy.

—Billy, man, it's too soon. Don't ya' think it's too soon?

—The Peppermint Lounge?

—Well, yeah, the fuckin' Peppermint Lounge. Don't ya' think the band needs a bit more seasonin' before playin' in front of the big brass?

—Seasoning? Naw. Mak and I talked about that. We're as good as we're gonna be right now. Maybe in six months or a year we'll be better, but right now, any show we do is about as good as we can do.

—It just seems like that kind of gig requires a lot of plannin', ya' know? Rehearsin'. Put on a show and that sort of shit.

—There's no point in us rehearsin', Angie. We're fuckin' rehearsed. We can run through a few things at the Crap Door if we need to. Monday or Tuesday or whatever.

Shrugging, Angie stood directly in front of Billy.

—Well, what's up with this Halloween costume thing? We're gonna blow off a whole day to go lookin' for fuckin' costumes? What's with that shit? It's gonna kill the momentum you got goin' in the studio. And we just got you finally up'n rollin' in there.

—Angie, fuck man, we were just now talkin' about a show! It's the Halloween show. We better look like a million bucks up there. It's no good lookin' around for shit on Saturday at the last minute—with our backs to the wall. We might as well spend the day tomorrow gettin' our shit together. With Candy and Annie along, they'll get us set up right. And they can fix whatever's fucked up. And another thing, we're gonna need you to drive us around tomorrow.

As if hit by a curare dart, Angie's face wrenched in paralytic discomfort.

—Man, if we're not workin' tomorrow, I got shit I need to do…

—We need the van. We need it for haulin' everyone around. We're not all gonna fit in the car Annie's got. Mak says it's some little Japanese car. A Toyota or somethin'. We need to all go together as one unit for this, so Candy can figure things out.

—What about the gear and shit?

—We'll pick up the gear on Saturday. It's no big deal. We'll get it. Saturday. We'll have lots of bodies to help lug the shit around.

—Okay, Billy. You're the boss. But it seems like yer bitin' off a lot doin' the Halloween show on Saturday and the Peppermint Lounge on Wednesday.

—We've played bigger shows closer together, and we've been fine. We'll be fine this time too. We're fuckin' pros.

—I hope yer right, man. I hate to see ya' blow a big opportunity.

Angie began to pace the narrow channel between his bed and Gilly's

—It wouldn't be us blowin' the opportunity, Angie, it would be the big wigs blowin' it.

—I hope yer right.

Momentarily halting the impetus of his mass, Angie shifted gears.

—So this fuckin' Halloween gig is gonna be, like, huge, eh?

—Yeah, it should be a big payday for everybody.

—Y'know Larry's fuckin' wettin' his pants over this one. Sometimes ya' can't tell with him. He's, like, a hard read. But this is the biggest gig he's ever had there. By a long shot. The help's tellin' me he's been spinnin' around the club like a fuckin' ballerina.

—It's gonna be packed in there. That's for sure. This'll be more like the shows at home. Standin' room only. Mak and Mick and Billy have postered the whole fuckin' town. People are gonna know about this gig. It's gonna be jammed.

With steadfast determination and arachnid patience in entwining his prey, Angie proffered.

—I'm not sure if posters do any good around here. Bands don't really do it much. So I dunno if that'll work or not. We'll see. Hard to tell, I guess. It was good for those guys to have somethin', like, constructive to do. Y'know? Keep 'em from goin' stir crazy. There's not really that much for 'em to do. Except for roadie-related shit, I pretty much got everything covered.

Sensing the drift of Angie's presentation and mostly ignoring it, Billy scratched his head and wiped his eyes with his open hand.

—Well, Angie, we'll just take it one day at a time. Tomorrow we'll go look for clothes and shit and we'll just see how everything plays out from there.

Intuitively, Angie grasped that he had run his implorations to their logical conclusions, and wordlessly he subsided. He smiled wanly at Billy and opened the bedroom door as if to signify that Billy was free to go. And Billy went.

Angie picked up the second team at Mrs. Belladro's house, and brought them back to the warehouse. Before they left to go shopping, Candy wanted to take rough estimates of everyone's measurements, ascertaining the approximate quantities of materials necessary in order for her to execute the concepts she had in mind for the characters in her play.

The field trip to the thrift stores was a grand experiment in mayhem, with the nine males riding in Angie's van and the three women in Annie's brother's car. At each store, the boys would tear around the premises like crazy, hopped-up kids in a second-hand store, while the three ladies would look on approvingly. Oh those boys. Being boys.

Candy had developed a vision for each member and acquired precisely the items necessary to properly adorn them all in their various roles. Unbeknownst to her, her subconscious was creating a sort of loose theme for the Halloween show. An amorphous organic fairy tale with no particular plot. Shakespearian. Grimm-like. A passion play.

For lunch, they dined at a famous White Castle eatery and there they discovered the gustatory grandeur of sliders, though they remained unconvinced they were at all superior to the greasy burgers obtained back home at Quality Pie.

As the day wore on, the boys grew tired and cranky. And, eventually, whenever they arrived at a new destination, they just wanted to sack out in the van. Yet Candy trooped them mercilessly onward and made them come inside each new location, so that she could properly judge the appropriateness and necessity of every article she considered.

It was early in the evening of what had been a heavenly October day—clear sky and blue and up in the seventies, a condition, at that time of year, mostly unfamiliar to the travelers from the west.

As night closed in, the fellas in the van mostly wanted to get to their various domiciles and sack out. Kick back. Drink a little beer, smoke a dube. Watch a little TV and call it a day.

Candy, riding with MJ and Annie, however, was just beginning to assimilate the magnitude of assembling everyone's costumes, a function she would have to perform within the subsequent twenty-four hours. Even with pneumonia clearly within her state of being, she relished the idea of staying up all night and creating the wardrobe for their little mystery play. She was in her element.

They stopped at an American Drugstore to pick up scissors, double-faced basting tape, thread and needles and any other available extra supplies they could think of. They took a trip down the Halloween-related product aisle. Candy carried a complete sewing kit with her at all times, but she needed to be sure there was plenty of backup materials. For her, the process was like a game of chess. She was one step ahead of the action, planning every move.

Though not as focused as Candy, MJ and Annie were heartily enthusiastic toward assisting Candy in her ministrations, helping her in any way to complete the tasks—and, thus, to attain her artistic ambition. Whatever it was. Possibly a fever dream.

They were already hard at work when Angie, Billy, Col, and Gilly finally turned up after taking the others to the Belladro estate. The boys were clearly exhausted by the day's endeavors, able only to wilt limply upon the couch and chairs.

As Billy fired up a couple joints of John Dailey's death weed, Angie flicked on the television. Winding down, they reflected quietly. And as a prelude to *Knight Rider* at nine o'clock, the four of them settled in to watching the *Dukes of Hazzard*. Billy had a bit of a thing for Daisy.

Meanwhile, at the kitchen table, according to Candy's stately decree, the girls busily collected together heaps of things they had acquired at the thrift stores. Some items were fine just as they were. They ripped the seams out of several pieces, cutting up others, making separate piles of the modified attire—one for each member of the band.

After *Knight Rider*, the guys were ready to turn in. The day had been much tougher for them than other typical days: where they would spend hours and hours in the studio, moving gear, or performing. Clothes shopping had been an extraordinary expense of energy. They were worn out.

It was left to Col to find his own means for sleep, sunk in the sofa, in the same room as the girls, who were kibitzing fastidiously like squirrels in a walnut tree. Col turned up the volume on the television—*Remington Steele*. In the meantime, the women set about their appointed obligations, with machine-like precision.

It was nearly four on Saturday morning and the apartment, with no heat to speak of, had grown quite chilly. Candy, MJ, and Annie had managed to put together Halloween apparel for all twelve of them—some outfits more ornate than others, some more imaginatively intricate. But each guise bore the mark of Candy's rampant ingenuity.

Around noon, the lot of them migrated to Mama Belladro's to pick up the others and head to the studio to haul the gear over to the club. With Mick, Mak, and Billy D. along the moving went quickly and efficiently with a minimum expenditure of effort.

Then at the Trappe D'Or, after the equipment had been set up and a quick sound check performed, Candy made everyone try on their duds in case any last minute alterations were required. Finally, after a great deal of tortured deliberation, Candy determined everything to be satisfactory.

Which came as a great relief to the male delegation, who were fussing uncomfortably—sighing and scratching, demanding to know when they were going home. None of them seemed to care what their roles were in Candy's passion play, which was fine with her. She wanted no complaints. She did not wish to explain.

A relative peaceful fog fell upon the dozen of them on their way back to Angie's place. It was decided that they would all return to his apartment, where they could drink beer, smoke weed, order out for a pizza and relax before the show.

Candy crashed severely after her whirlwind bout of activity. Her physical resources utterly depleted, she lay down on the sofa in an attempt to generate the energy to dance with the band later that night. Still, though she was thoroughly worn out, she derived a great deal of satisfaction from finally contributing to the band with her design talents.

Though he fretted about it, Billy had resisted the urge to try calling Carrie. Stubbornly, he wanted for her to call and apologize to him—for what, he was not sure. He had tried to apologize to her and she would not accept it. It was time for her to give a little and apologize to him.

But, by later that Saturday afternoon, he realized that Carrie might not ever call and that she would then be gone from his life. Though he was unsure of his feelings, Billy did not want her to disappear altogether. He required his freedom and his space—but in his case he was too free and too far away. And he had never been good at resisting temptation.

Lying on the bedding in his room, he apprehensively dialed her number, not knowing what he wanted to say—only that he missed her and had been thinking of her. The phone rang three times, and then she answered. Haltingly, he spoke her name.

—Carrie. It's me.

—Who?

—Me. Billy!

—Oh yeah. Hi.

Her indifference threw him. He was anticipating any number of reactions to his call, but sheer disinterest was not among them.

—Hi. How've you been?

—I've been fine.

—I've tried calling, but you didn't pick up and you didn't have your machine on.

—Yes. I know.

Silence. Billy's timing was all messed up. She was rushing the downbeat and it was throwing off his upstroke. Bum tick. Bum*tick*.

—You knew I called?

—No. I knew I didn't have my machine on. What's up?

—Well, I just wanted to call and say hi—let you know how much I love you and miss you.

—I miss you too, Billy.

—Do you? Do you really?

—Yes. I miss you.

—Do you love me?

—I don't feel like talking about that right now, Billy. I have a discussion group and a test on Monday and I have to study. I don't have the time or the inclination to get into a long discussion right now.

Puzzled by her reply—and a little humiliated—he mumbled.

—Oh. Okay. I didn't know it would be a long discussion. Well, I'll let you get back to it then, I guess. But I want you to know that I love you and miss you.

—Yes. I know. You already said that.

—Okay then, I guess I better go then.

—Okay.

—I'll talk to you later.

—Okay, Billy.

—Bye.

She hung up the phone without even bidding him farewell. Billy was stunned bewildered. No one had ever treated him like that before. Dismissive. He was surprised. And dispirited. Carrie was surprised and dispirited too, but Billy was far too immersed in his own blithering wuther to mull her state of affairs—three thousand miles distant and a world away.

# XXV

It was just getting dark when the band arrived at the Trappe D'Or, a little after seven. Early. But they had a lot of preparation yet to carry out. Getting into costume was going to be tedious and time-consuming.

As Angie searched unsuccessfully for a place to park the van, Billy and Gilly could see that there was a line of revelers—most dressed outrageously and behaving accordingly—that extended from the door of the club at Westside, far down Armstrong Avenue. It was going to be a packed house.

Mak spied Kerry, the owner of Abandonment Music, dressed as a bum. Recalling that he had told the fellow he would put him on the guest list, Mak invited Kerry to enter the club with the musicians.

After quickly parting with Kerry, the band discovered, once they had successfully made it inside the club, that it was already a packed house—of a suffocating density; that had become customary for the band, during their tenure in Portland. With great difficulty they sliced their way toward the dressing room, besieged by glad-handers and well-wishers of all colors, shapes, and species. It was going to be a wild night.

Backstage, the band members freely guzzled the beers that had been awaiting them splayed like green glass feathers over ice. They passed numerous joints around—both the good Mex and John Dailey's killer bud. Slowly, each member began the process of gaily donning their apparel.

Candy and MJ were matching angels: diamond blue ballerina tutus and dance shoes, ornate furry white wings and halos. Annie was a charming Little Orphan Annie, with a red sweater and a blue empire-cut dress, black patent leather mary-janes. Her thick wiry hair was colored bright, orange red and teased to maximum beachball volume, sprayed to a shellac-ian state that did not move.

Not surprisingly, Candy had created a big yellow baby duck motif for Billy D. At first, he was not especially enamored of the role. But he warmed to it after receiving a lot of positive feedback from the others, especially the girls.

Mick too found the part of convivial canine to be worthy of exploration, as he humorously trotted around trying to hump the leg of everyone in the room. He was far more enthusiastic in his machinations toward the females. But that was to be expected, boys being boys and all.

One of Candy's finest achievements was her creation for Angie. She fashioned for him an outfit of biblical proportions. Literally. From linen cloth, cotton sheets, and an old, dark, brocaded curtain she had tailored it. Initially, thinking it was a Merlin wizard like deal, Angie was okay with it.

But when Candy handed him the two large tablets she had made out of multiple layers of cardboard, Elmer's glued together and spray-painted gray, a list of five items scribbily inscribed with a magic marker on each one—only then did he realize she had cast him as Moses. He felt a wave of embarrassment tide over him. But he did not let on.

As for the members of the band, Candy reserved her most inspired efforts. Gilly was easy. It was almost typecasting for him to be a vampire, but Candy made certain that he was a smartly dressed vampire, with a beautiful black silk cape.

For Daw, she chose the character Luke Skywalker from the *Star Wars* movies. Even though *The Empire Strikes Back* was a couple of years old, a well turned out Luke Skywalker still drew rave reviews—and Candy's adaptation was especially faithful.

Over tight, tan stretch slacks, he wore thick, knee-high, rust-colored leggings and a thigh-length, white jujitsu gi, trimmed with a woman's wide, patent leather belt. He looked very dashing—as if he were Errol Flynn.

*Urban Cowboy* was the inspiration behind Gib's western-themed duds. There was also an element of Jon Voight's *Midnight Cowboy*, too, but Candy was the only one old enough to recognize the reference, so it was strictly a private joke. In addition, it was a bit of a stretch to think anyone might confuse Gib for John Travolta. But Gib loved his get up, just the same.

Col had been the most problematic. It was difficult to picture him as anyone other than Keith Richards. But, inspired by a beautiful white suit she had found at the Bargain Rite store, Candy opted for Colonel Sanders—which doubly tickled her in the wry play on Col's name.

The white wig, moustache and eyebrows had been easy enough to procure. Candy found them at the American Drugstore in the costume aisle, along with some basic stage make up, masks and other essential items. In costume, Col actually looked like a dignified, benevolent plantation owner who had freed all his slaves long before any of his peers.

Saving her most flawless ideas for Billy, Candy gathered together garments fit for a king. She matched together a loose fitting white toga chlamys made from a sheet and clasped at the right shoulder with an ornate brooch. To that, she added a short, pleated, white, silk cheerleader's skirt and a pair of brand new Fruit of the Loom briefs.

Candy knew that invariably, Billy would eventually strip down to just the skirt, so she planned accordingly, making the chlamys ready to doff with a flourish. To top him off, Candy found a battery-operated blinking Statue of Liberty headdress— the representation of sunbeams—to fulfill his Halloween destiny as the God of all things bright and mellifluous.

Confused by the depiction, Billy felt it was, perhaps, a little too feminine for his latently manifested macho rock 'n' roll personae. However, he was greatly reassured when Candy informed him that he was Apollo, the God of the Sun and Music. Billy confirmed that he was satisfied with such a representation. Yeah. He could dig being the Sun King. Candy thought to correct his mistaken notion, but decided to drop it.

A wave of fulfillment swept over Candy. She had conceived and overseen the fabrication of a dozen costumes in just a little over twenty-four hours—that included the scavenging of the materials required in order to enact the specifics of her revelations. They were good outfits that almost seemed to tell a story of their own.

The Chronicle of Candy's Subconscious Morality Play:

One afternoon, Little Orphan Annie Fisher is over at the Gods' house, hanging out in the living room, listening to the band rehearse in the basement, when she is overswooned by some especially powerful John Dailey killer weed. The room starts to whirl and she passes out on the couch.

The house begins to swoop and twirl beneath her and, while passed out, she is transported to a place far away. New Jersey. When at last the house crashes to the ground, Annie is jolted awake with a start. She steps outside the house into a foreign land, populated by humanoid creatures, who speak a strange version of English.

Upon exiting the house, Annie is informed by the inhabitants that, with her abrupt arrival, she has killed one of the evil "brothers" who run things in those parts. Sure enough. They lead her to a spot where there are just two legs extending from the foundation of the structure—a broken Louisville Slugger baseball bat at the side of the victim.

Annie inquires of the natives as to where she might find an airport or a train station so that she can make her way back home to Oregon. They tell her that they live in Jersey City and are incapable of doing much of anything. Maybe Apollo at the Power Station can help her. They gesture toward a skyscraper city in the far distance that glows and glitters like a neon sign.

They also point to a highway that winds its way over hill and dale in the direction of the Power Station: the New Jersey Turnpike. As a going-away gift, the citizens bestow upon her a gold record. They sing a farewell song, "Yer Off Ta See Apollo," and they send her on her way down the New Jersey Turnpike toward the Holland Tunnel.

But before she can leave the premises, Moses appears from out of the sky in a bale of burning weed, accompanied by his weasly vampire little brother, Christian, who is wearing a black silk cape and Foster Grant sunglasses. Moses wants to know who knocked off his middle brother, and all the townspeople immediately point to Annie. She says she didn't mean to and that, technically, it was the house that killed his brother, not her—she was merely a passenger—and that she smelled a potential lawsuit cookin.'

Moses checks his tablets for an appropriate citation among the ten inscriptions. "Yeh, okay, here it is: 'Thou shalt NOT fuck with Moses' family'. I believe that one's fuckin' punishable by death." Moses raises the tablets above his head to bash Annie, but before he can do it, Luke Skywalker and the Urban Cowboy guy appear.

Luke wields his light saber menacingly, as if to provoke Moses into battle. Apparently, Luke figures Moses' primitive tablet light sabers will never stand up to his highly technical modern equipment, which had been developed eons before the planet Earth was even formed. And Luke knows Moses' puny light sabers are just part of a long-standing joke for all those along the Force line: the legendary Jedi Mind-fuck versus Commandments. Heh.

Standing next to Luke, the cowboy looks super cool, with a mechanical bull at his side. His hat pulled low over his eyes, pointed-toe boots gleaming in the artificial sunlight. His thumbs are comfortably slung in the loops of his jeans, as he strikes a serious model pose. Luke points out to Moses that he can't do jack shit, because Annie's got a gold record—meaning she can pretty much do whatever the fuck she wants. With no repercussions.

Frustrated, Moses and his vampire brother take off, and Luke and Bud, the Urban Cowboy, tell Annie not to worry about her trip, they'll round up some livestock to protect her on the journey. So she heads out, with her gold record in hand, singing the Cars' "Let the Good Times Roll."

Along the way, she meets up with a bear, a dog and a baby duck and they sing songs about their needs: "If I only had a fish, if I only had a bone, and if I only had a pond," et cetera. Proceeding slowly, the allies make their way toward the Power Station, but they are repeatedly interrupted by several instances of hijinks sustained via Moses and his sidekick vampire brother.

Finally, they reach the Power Station. There is a great glistening white marble hall, with two angels hovering in the rafters above the scene. The tourists try to meet Apollo, but Colonel Sanders, his manager, and a contingent of bodyguards won't let Annie or her entourage anywhere near the god.

The next day Apollo is preparing to leave the Power Station to travel by limo up to nearby Honalee. On his way to the back of the limo, he briefly stops to autograph a girl's glossy photo, and in that fleeting instant, Annie finds a way to attract Apollo's attention—despite Colonel Sanders' vehement objections.

With great haste, Annie tells Apollo her story. She's from Oregon. She had a bad pot trip and ended up sailing clear across the country in the house, landing in Jersey City on top of Moses' brother. The one with the bat.

And she and her animal buddies all met up along the way from Jersey City to the Power Station and they formed a band and could he please help them get back to Oregon so they could record a single? She shows him the gold record that the New Jerseyians gave her. Apollo is fairly whelmed by that. So he gives her an EP demo deal and sends her on her way.

Her gold record and demo deal in hand, Annie is ready to go back to Oregon, with her newfound bandmates in tow. Shit. They miss the train. But Luke Skywalker and Bud, the Urban Cowboy, appear in the nick of time and tele-transport the group to the dining car of the departing coach. Annie sings her signature song, "Some Way Out of New Jersey." The End.

The Unreal Gods took the stage to a tumultuous avalanche of shouting and applause. As had become their custom, they immediately launched into "Go Go Boots Are Coming Back," instantly prompting the entrance of the Angel Goddesses.

Hopping up onto small platforms on either side of the band, they began frugging feverishly. Their wire-reinforced fuzzy white haloes bobbed and fluttered in the air. Diaphanous veils surrounded their bodies, only partly concealing form and skin. Their furry wings flapped furiously, giving the impression that the girls were about to fly away. Angels A Go-Go.

As a warmup for the evening, the band's first set consisted mostly of their "greatest hits," before they dug in for more adventurous material later in the evening. They whipped through "Symmetry," "My Girlfriends Drawers" "Uptown," "Rockabilly Queen," "English Boy," and "Rocky Road" before they stopped, even for just a moment, to take a beer tuning break.

The heat in the room began to rise dramatically. The oxygen was correspondingly sucked out by a rapid contraction in the density of the mass of all the partiers. Like a whole galaxy compressed into a pea.

Because of the costumes many were wearing, several people in the audience seemed as if they were on the verge of passing out after only a half an hour or so. Mak the Bear, Mick the Dog, and Billy D. the Duck stood off to the side of the stage, carefully watching the band.

Ever mindful that a situation might arise, Mak the Bear kept a close eye on the crowd for the first sign of a problem. Twice he was able to hale members of the club staff to rescue three or four young women who had fainted. Even in his bear suit he was able to command a sense of authority. He was clearly a *guardian bear*.

Standing aloofly at the monitor board at the side of the stage, Billy D. the Duck had a harder time earning any respect. Dressed as a huge, yellow, baby duck did nothing to augment any sense of menace or dread. Except for his size, he seemed to wield absolutely no power, even though he was clearly a member of the staff.

Mick the Dog faired somewhat better, but like Billy D. the Duck and Mak the Bear, with nothing really to do at the shows, he gave the impression as more of a hanger-on than someone who actually had his own position within the firm. Other than turning on amps and tuning guitars, there was absolutely zip for him to do—except put up posters, of course. And, back in Portland, that was something they paid some kid to do.

After a few more songs, the band ended the set with "Boom Chuck Rock." Backstage, they were all sweating copiously—downing beer after beer and passing around a series of spliffs. For possibly the first time since they had made the trip East, there was a sense in the green room of unity. And fun. Everyone embodied in their costumes and acting accordingly. It was fun.

Fun had been absent. It had been all work since they had come out. And as they soon discovered, work was no fun at all which was why it was called work, one would suppose. It took a night with a thousand absurdly dressed lunatics—who had begun to get very high and were starting to act quite insane—to retrieve for the regiment a faint recollection of fun. And they were having it. Fun.

The second set was even more so. Apollo was completely loose and warmed up, prancing around in his toga and cheerleaders skirt, and white underpants. His Statue of Liberty head dress blinked randomly above him. A part time sun god.

They joyfully spun through "Coca Cola," thick with Colonel Sanders' spaghetti western guitar intro and Latin percussion supplemented by Christian the Vampire's strange synth patch, underpinned with a weird disco beat from the kick and bass—the whole band chanting.

—Coca Cola…every night."

Apollo even referenced Paul Simon's "59th Street Bridge Song."

—Slow down, you're movin' too fast You got to make the Cola last.

It was one big happy party.

Happy…Was it? Apollo momentarily thought he saw her flicker among the onlookers about midway back in the room, but he lost sight of her. The band engaged in a sprightly version of the Stonesy/Chuck Berry-like "Neutral Stomp," Colonel Sanders' showcase lead guitar song.

Then they segued into the similar feel of the David Bowie-informed, "Upstroke Down," into a vigorous rendition of the lengthy "Rasta Rhythm," and finally, concluded the sequence with "Stereo Area." Meanwhile, Apollo continued to search the room for another confirming glimpse of Happy.

They were in the midst of wrapping up the set with the Stonesy "Madilyn's Rough" when he thought he had caught sight of her again. He spontaneously altered the lyric.

—Happy's so rough. Happy's so rough. On the edges.

And in the bridge he began to chant

—If you're happy and you know it clap your hands.

He saw her applauding sarcastically. It was Happy! Strange things began to spontaneously roll from his mouth.

—Happy she makes me
Happy she takes me
Where I wanna go.
When I wanna go there
Without her I am nowhere
Oh oh oh.

She disappeared again. Apollo was not wholly confident that he had not hallucinated seeing her in the first place. He hunted for her among the strange and contorted creatures amidst the spectators. She had been wearing a snake on her head and heavy eye make-up. Like Cleopatra maybe. Something ancient it seemed. But even from a distance, she looked strangely exotic and exceptionally beautiful.

Briefly, he surveyed the hall from the stage. Sweat soaked through the sheet that was his toga, and his hair was dripping. He could not see her out there anywhere. Grabbing a towel, he leapt from the stage and quickly moved toward the backstage area through a sturdy thicket of rapidly dementing wellwishers.

Nearly everyone in the company was fixedly smoking weed and drinking beer by the time he finally made it back to the green room. Billy D. the Duck and Mick the Dog, Luke Skywalker and the Urban Cowboy, the two Angels, Little Orphan Annie, Colonel Sanders, Christian the Vampire and Moses were all crammed together in a cylinder, like cartoon tamales in a can. A dense swirl of smoke spiraled in between them. Apollo sat down next to Orphan Annie, across from Colonel Sanders.

—It's, like, fuckin' crazy out there tonight.

With a flourish, Apollo flipped his wet towel on Mick the Dog. Billy D. the Duck. quacked up excitedly.

—Hey, Billy. Angie's gonna let me run sound for the third set. And Mick'll have the monitors. It'll be just like old times.

Well aware that Moses was in the mood for debauched bacchanalia, Apollo smiled scoffingly—reflecting on the fact that it had been only three weeks since they had left the "old times" to which Billy D. the Duck referred. Moses nodded.

—Yeh. I thought I'd put these fuckers to work so I can go out and chase some tail tonight.

Laughing, Apollo jeered.

—Yeah, and with this crowd, tail might be exactly what you'd get.

—Knock, knock.

Simultaneously, the whole retinue looked up toward the opening door, at the interruption. But it was Apollo who recognized her.

267

—Happy! It *was* you. I was wondering if I was ever going to see you again.

He rushed in her direction.

—I forgot to get your phone number that night we met and we've been so busy...

Drolly, she whirred and purred.

—Yeah. I've been busy too. Lot's going on.

He hugged her to him.

—Uhhgh. You're all wet!!

—I get all wet for you, baby!

Laughing lasciviously.

—I bet you hear that all the time.

She narrowed her eyes at him. He was the only one among them who knew her occupation.

—I hear it from chauvinist pigs now and then. What's your point?

Humbled, Apollo tried to make a joke out of it.

—I didn't see any of them out there. A couple of regular flat-nose porkers, but no chauvinist pigs that I saw.

She carefully assessed his visage.

—So who are you supposed to be anyway? Apollo?

—No, I'm the sun king.

—Um. I don't want to be the one to tell you, but you don't look anything like the Sun King.

Confused, Apollo looked in Little Orphan Annie's direction.

—He's supposed to be Apollo.

—Yeah. I'm Apollo the Sun King.

Cassandra sniffed loudly.

—It's called mythology, Bubba. Jeezus Christ. You really did leave it all on the field, didn't you? You may be the Sun King, but you look like a god to me.

Not grasping the sarcasm, the compliment, or the gist, Apollo skimmed along the surface of their exchange. A cloud passed.

—So who're you supposed to be? Cleopatra?

—No, oddly enough, given the circumstances...

She chuckled, though no one had the slightest idea why.

—I'm Cassandra.

The others in the room skewed their faces with startling unanimity. She was confusing them.

—Wow! Okay, so here's a little prediction. I predict your band is going to be huge. But beware of darkness. Keep a candle burning in the window. One for all and all for one.

Everyone regarded her as a some kind of nut job.

—*Okay* then.

She had brass snakes spiraled around her forearms, calves, and neck, coiled around each breast, with a single snake for a headband. Little makeup snakes perched in a hissing whisper at each ear.

Inquiring with real concern, Apollo kissed Cassandra on the cheek.

—So what's with all the snakes anyway?

—It's a long story actually, and I don't want to bore you guys on your break.

Everyone nodded in agreement, as Mak the Bear came rushing through the entry to the green room.

—We're killing them at the door you guys. We must be sittin' at almost ten grand out there. Still got a set to go. Larry's, like, doin' fuckin' cartwheels back at the bar.

With the breaking news of the great gate, Moses was out the door and off to the bar. Mak the Bear sat down across from Colonel Sanders, pulled the paw mitten from his right hand and looked around for the nearest joint. As he turned to his right to receive from Apollo, he absently reached out and sitting between them...

It was her. It was that beautiful girl from that strip club. Cassandra. It was her. Mak the Bear could not speak. He could barely breathe. He immediately passed the joint in the direction of Colonel Sanders on his left. That amused everyone.

—Hey, Yogi.

Colonel Sanders snatched the roach away, took a long drag and passed to

Christian the Vampire.

—Ya' forgot to, like, take a fuckin' hit, man.

Mak the Bear placed the mitten paw back on his right hand. He could not operate his mouth. His lips would not move. Helplessly, he sat muttering, staring at his left paw.

—Buh...buh...buh.

Apollo noticed.

—Hey, Poppy. What the fuck's goin' on? Are you okay?

Mak the Bear tried to nod, but his head remained motionless. It was her. The most beautiful woman in the world. The true goddess. And she was in the room. She was alive and breathing, with snakes crawling all over her body.

Her body. Mak the Bear remembered every centimeter of her body perfectly, though he could not bring himself to engage the form of the gorgeous creature before him. He averted his gaze toward the floor.

—Pop, man. Have you met Happy? I don't think you met her last time. This is Happy. She saw us at the very first show.

Apollo turned and regarded Cassandra proudly. She extended her hand to shake Mak the Bear's paw, but he could not raise it. His front paws would not function.

Ignoring the awkwardness of the moment, Cassandra took in the enclave with a sweeping glance and exclaimed to no one.

—It's a regular circus back here. Bears and dogs and ducks. Oh my! Who're you supposed to be?

—I'm Colonel Sanders.

Colonel Sanders replied, somewhat defensively.

—Oh yeah. I see the resemblance now. Do you, like, fry up the duck at the end of the night, or what?

Billy D. the Duck shifted uneasily, sitting at the end of the bench, next to Mick the Dog. No one was getting any of her jokes that night. They all stared at her blankly.

—Eleven secret herbs and spices?

Nothing.

—*Okay* then.

Embarrassed, she sidled up to Apollo without actually touching him, because he was unquestionably icky.

Mak the Bear sat motionless with his paws folded neatly in his lap. There was so much spinning through his mind in that moment, but there was no one else in the room, in the world, who could possibly understand his passionate sensations. And if his friends would not understand, then no one would—seeing as how his heroine was sitting in the room with them at that very moment.

After a time, Mick the Dog caught Apollo's attention and looked at his paw as if he were looking at a watch, authoritatively tapping his wrist. Apollo briskly stood up.

—You're right, Hound Dog. It's time to get back to it. We should get back out there everybody.

Candy the Angel who had been huddled, shivering, next to MJ the Angel the entire time they were backstage, moaned slightly, as MJ the Angel shook her lightly.

—C'mon, Canders. Last set.

Slowly, everyone rose to their feet. Despite Cassandra's obvious discomfort, Apollo hugged her tightly.

—So, are you gonna hang around until after the show?

Colonel Sanders cruelly mocked Apollo's boyish sincerity.

—Nora boo wanna bang a cow the hill affa thush oh?

Irritated at the insolence, Apollo sneered at him grumpily. Then he redirected his attention toward Cassandra.

—No. I mean it. Are you gonna hang around?

—Well, I was planning to. Do you have any objections?

—No. No, none at all. I want you to stay. I want to talk to you again. I've missed you.

She was a little startled by the unexpected sappy forthrightness of his pronouncement.

—Well, I've thought about you too. Like I said, I've been real busy.

Her apparent lack of sincerity surprised Apollo. She was blowing him off. Such actions by a member of the female gender were simply incomprehensible in Apollo World. He was shaken aback by her seeming disinterest in him. And for just that reason, he found her enchanting.

271

Everyone evacuated the backstage area, moving in the direction of their appointed stations. Mak the Bear stumbled along behind them, spellbound: a honey bear caught with his paw in the cookie jar. Apollo turned to Cassandra and offered.

—You can stand over at the side of the stage with Mak, if you want.

—The bear?

—Yeah, Mak's the bear. Hey, Mak, will you, like, hang out with Happy while we're playin'?

It was like a dream fullfalling true. He could not believe. She. Her so beautiful. Her body—a vessel of ripe fruit. Nipples of cherries perched upon perfect passion fruit. Relaxed melons split and warming in the sun. Skin like expensive soap. A face, shipless launched. His breath. He could not catch his. Breath. Her eyes were stalking his soul. He could not speak. But with all his strength, he summoned words.

—Yeah, yeah. Sure. I can. Hang out. I haven't got anything. Else to do.

—Poppy? Are you sure you're okay? You're, like, actin' really fuckin' weird.

As best as he was able, the bear sobered from the tangle of his hormonal iniquity.

—Yeah. I'm fine. Fine. I just got a little stoned back there I guess.

—But you didn't even take a fuckin' hit, Pop.

—Maybe it's the heat then. No air. Oxygen. I'm just. A little woozy. I'll be okay. Sure I'll hang out with—what's her name?

He was speaking as if she were not present for the conversation, or standing right next to him. It was nearly impossible for him to acknowledge the actual existence of that gorgeous creature. In reality, it was he who was not present. His feet were barely touching the ground.

—Happy? Where'd she get that name? No. Don't tell me. You need to get up there.

He pointed toward the stage. Apollo agreed, and after giving Cassandra a small awkward kiss on the cheek, he strode to his place behind the microphone in the middle of all the crazy activity. The center of his own solar system. The sun king.

Apollo fiddled with his guitar, tuning the B and E strings, even though Mick the Dog had just tuned it with a chromatic tuner. It was a nervous tick. Happy made him nervous. That was a sensation Apollo had not had to address in the past. Others got nervous around him. So that's what it felt like...!

Cassandra asked of Mak the Bear.

—So Mak...It's Mak, right?

The bear bobble-lolled his head in the affirmative.

—What do you do in the band when you're not a bear? Are you part of the security team? You seem well-*suited* for that.

She smiled to herself at her clever pun. No response. She soldierly trooped onward. Tough crowd.

—Although you don't seem aggressive enough to be a bear. Maybe you should have been the dog...You're security then or...?

Mak the Bear did not immediately reply. He was hardly able to indicate that he had heard her. Finally, fully formed syllables began to escape his lips.

—I'm, like, the manager of the Gods, actually.

—What does that mean? Are you like Reuben Kincaid in the Partridge Family?

—No, not exactly. Out here, Angie's doin' all that.

—Who's Angie?

—He's the guy dressed like Moses.

—Moses. Yeah. I should have known. Moses. So what do you do as manager, when you're not a bear in Jersey City?

—Back home, I book shows for the band. This is what their shows are always like, back in Portland.

Blowing a whistle of air passed pursed lips, Happy was duly impressed.

—So he wasn't bullshittin' me about that.

—What? Anyway, I handle all the money. Negotiate for the band. Represent 'em. Keep everything organized and runnin' right. I let them worry about the music, and I take care of the business end of things.

—So you *are* like Reuben Kincaid then! Do you get to drive the bus?

—Naw. We don't have a bus back there. Our soundman Billy Dreier has a van. And Angie's got a van out here, and he hauls all our shit around.

He was so earnest. She sighed to herself. No one was understanding her sense of humor. Everyone was taking her literally. She was quite frustrated.

—All right, all right. How's everybody doin' tonight?

A roar of positive feedback.

—Yeah, yeah, yeah. I'm Apollo the Sun King, and we are the Unreal Gods. We think if people dressed like this all the time, there'd be peace in the world. Wha'd'ya think?

Barely contained mayhemery.

—I see three or four of you dressed like the Ayatollah. That's what I'm talkin' about. Say what?

More boisterous approval.

—This is a song about bein' Happy.

Apollo's attention darted sideward toward Cassandra, as the band slid into a soul-ish groove for "Don't Be Sad." The chord progression for the song was similar to the Pointer Sisters' song, "Fire," written by Bruce.

Steve Cropper was probably Colonel Sanders' stylistic model on guitar; Bud the Urban Cowboy and Luke Skywalker chugging like Duck Dunn and Al Jackson underneath. Christian the Vampire, though no Booker T., filled up musical space with occasional burst of chiming organ pads.

—Coz when Happy gets sad
It's the worst experience you've ever had
So if you're Happy for me
Then I'm happy for you
Don't be sad.

At the top, he fell in with the rest and began to sing.

—I saw you in the market
Man you're lookin' kinda crazy
I know you won't come back
And always comin' back for more
Where you'll end up we're never sure
Don't you know I can't help that.

At the turnaround, they veered into a two-chord riff, reminiscent of the Kinks' "Set Me Free."

—Roger's just a wiener-schnitzel in the butcher shop
Workin' for his dad
I never packaged meat before
But one thing that I know for sure.

Apollo dropped into his lower-register Elvis croon

—I carry a real big ham
And if you're happy for me then I'm happy for you.

To the chorus, where Colonel Sanders and Luke Skywalker joined in like Paul and George in harmony behind him.

—Don't be sad
Don't be sad
Don't be sad.

The solo section found Colonel Sanders emulating Elliot Easton—throwing blues riffs into a straight-ahead rock display, as on the Cars' "Just What I Needed."

It was a short song. A reprise followed the solo—a stanza comprised of edited lines, cross-pollinated from each of the previous verses, then an extended fade on the chorus.

Upon the power chord that concluded "Don't Be Sad," Bud and Luke Skywalker pivoted sharply into the hyper rocker "When The World Comes Crashing Down," Colonel Sanders adding big, shifting chords, reminiscent of INXS, with Chuck Berry jamming along. Christian the Vampire contributed a droning, synth-string high A note. Apollo intoned.

—This song is dedicated to my old band the Malchicks and my brother Denny. I'm dedicating everything tonight.

Yeah I made it to the big time
A real rock 'n' roll mess-sigh-yuh
Then the world come crashin' down
Yeah the world came crashin' down

Yeah you threw me by the wayside
You just threw me away-ee-uh.

Expertly, Apollo hiccupped ala Buddy Holly.

—But you never ever saw my face
My smile was out of place
Livin' in the old days
Just livin' in the old days
When the world came crashin' down
The world came crashin' down.

Colonel Sanders ripped through another scorching solo, eliciting drunken yawls and screams from the clientele. The band's energy was in high gear, propelling the momentum of the song into pandemonium overdrive as Apollo rejoined the fray.

—Uh-livin' in the old days (livin' in the old days)
Just livin' in the old days (livin' in the old days)
Then the world came crashin' down
Yeah the world came crashin' down

Livin' in the old days (livin' in the old days)
Yeah livin' in the old days (livin' in the old days)

Till the world came crashin' down
When the world came crashin' down.

The boys concluded the venture with a slowly unfurling accident scene: Colonel Sanders imitated the familiar cry of a British emergency siren approaching with great haste.

The crowd loved it—tripping out to the sound effects: Apollo kicking his amp so that the reverb would thunder and crash, while Christian the vampire applied a thick, organic keyboard sludge to the presentation. Bud, the Urban Cowboy, added whooping bass slides to bolster the overall sense of confusion. Everything unwound into a slow, dense mire which concluded the song.

Almost immediately, the Gods jumped into the urgent "Used to Hang Around," a song with a theme similar to its predecessor—love and friendship gone awry. People acting in strange, desperate ways. Crazy.

—I used to hang around
With all the other boy boys
We went to all the crazy places
We made all the same noise
Me 'n' Billy boy boy.

Apollo made a sound like "nyah-nyah, nyah-nyah, nyah nyah"

—We used to love the same girl girl
I remember one night
We loved her from the wrong side of town

What happened to you now?
You used to be my friend
C'mon Little Queenie
Let's get together again.

A psychedelic Ferris wheel of a solo followed; electric lights blinked and blanked in that wild room of human insects enswarmed. The Colonel fried up another expositional duck. Eleven herbs and spices. Finger lickin' good.

—We used to hang around
We went to all the funny places
We made all the funny faces
We went around and around and around...

As with "Boom Chuck Rock," Apollo referenced his muse, John Dailey—and the difficulties John was having in his marriage to Donna.

—We used to hang around
And I remember one night
I come over to John's house
I found him cryin' on the back steps
Don't cry no more.

Mak the Bear stood vacant, with his paws hanging limply at his side, transfixed—not by the music he had heard at least one hundred times, but by the scent of Cassandra standing next to him. She smelled exotic: of sandalwood and vanilla, lilac and clove. Of cinnamon and honeysuckle. Playdoh and autumn air.

Just the smell would have given him an erection had he not already had one since the moment he first saw her sitting in the green room. For that, he was actually glad he was wearing the bear costume. He kept checking himself to see if he was dreaming. He wanted to be casual and tell Cassandra band tales. He wanted to explain to her the backstory to every song.

Instead, he was mute. Mute and paralyzed. Mute and paralyzed and hardly breathing. With all the energy he could muster and without saying a word, Mak the Bear left Cassandra's side and headed for the entry door at the front of the room. He really needed nicotine. Bad. And he needed oxygen. Almost as badly.

Standing in the chilly Jersey City night, Mak the bear blew nervous great bursts of smoke high into the air above him. He hurriedly chain-smoked three cigarettes before he was even aware of himself or his location in the world. He was totally and completely freaked out—as never before. He was toast.

It was only after the three cigarettes had been consumed that Mak the Bear realized he had been standing next to Anthony Hudson, the leader of Moby Dickens, the whole time. Apparently Anthony had been intent on speaking to Mak the Bear, although he had begun to feel that he was being shunned. Mak the Bear stared at Anthony, and reared back from him in surprise.

—Shit. Anthony! How long've you been standin' there?

—Pretty much the whole time, actually. How're you doin'? It's Mak, right?

—Yeah, Mak. Hoh-lee shit. I am so fucked up. I think it's, like, this bear suit or the crowd. The heat or somethin'. I can't fuckin' breathe. I know that.

—Maybe it's that killer Oregon weed you guys travel with.

—I haven't even had any of that shit tonight, and nothin' to drink either. I don't know what the fuck is goin' on, man.

Cassandra stood next to the stage, watching Apollo closely. He was very handsome. Gorgeous. His blue eyes and long blond surfer hair. Mouth a broad smile of many teeth. Cleft chin. Tall and lean and lithe. She was sure he was going to be a big, big star. He had all the necessary attributes.

His band wasn't bad. Not great, but they were a good bar band. They knew how to entertain. The songs were okay. A little on the light side, but they had decent hooks. She could not predict how the band might ultimately fare, but she had no doubt whatsoever that Apollo was going to be a star someday.

Still, though she was deeply attracted to him, she knew that she could never sleep with Apollo. She was only a temporary figure in his life and she longed for permanence.

He was too much like her ex, Reynold. With Rennie, the band always came first. There really was no room in his world for anyone else. Cassandra was pretty sure Apollo was of the same breed. An ego too big for two. Ego for one, your table is ready.

She needed someone who would pay attention back. She had hopes and goals, too that were just as reasoned and rational as anyone else's dreams. She knew she was a good songwriter and a good singer. And Paul was a very good tutor. Unlike all his predecessors, he actually worked with her and he did not try to feel her up or get into her pants or any of that crap.

And if the singer-songwriter thing didn't work out, she could always go back to school and get her degree. Only another year and she could teach literature to adolescent children. No matter what happened in her life, she knew that someday, some way, she would be a teacher. Now or later, that was what she was really meant to be.

Mak the Bear reunited with her as the band was reeling out "I Like Berrys."

—Well, there you are Mister Bear. I was beginning to think you weren't coming back. I thought maybe someone had bagged you and made a rug out of you. And that I'd see you one day, stretched out in a luxury hotel in Amsterdam.

Mak the Bear gaped stupidly at the goddess.

—Guh? *Bagged?*

—Yeah. You know. You're a bear, and I thought someone might have shot you. You're a bear. Remember?

She was right. He had forgotten he was a bear. Upon his return to Cassandra's side, all he could think of was her naked body glistening under the colored lights of the strip club. He was a cramped, constricted muscle. He was a bear in heat. The worm of his desire was on fire—crawling in flames toward an earthen mound of merciless frustration.

—I like chuckleberries
I like strawberries
I like raspberries
Almost every time

I like chuckleberries
I like strawberries
I like blueberries
Almost every time

I knew a girl once
We were in love once
We had some fun once
She's fuckin' up my mind.

Colonel Sanders' twining guitar, Christian the Vampire's simple string fills and upstroke organ chops, worked well against Bud the Urban Cowboy's thumping bass lines. But it was a rather repetitive song, with no real chorus or bridge. It's place in the set was mostly to burn up a little time. A holding pattern.

—I like chuckleberries
I like strawberries
I like a good book
And a fine red wine.

Cassandra turned to Mak the Bear, and through a cupped hand, she shouted in his ear.

—So who writes the songs in the band?

Mak the Bear was strangely quick to respond.

—Billy. Billy pretty much writes 'em all. Everyone else invents their own parts to the songs, y'know...the *arrangement*. But Billy writes 'em.

—So *he's* the one to blame

She said it sarcastically, which went right past Mak the Bear.

—Blame for what? You asked if he wrote the songs. There's no blame. It's credit really.

—I'm sorry, Mak. It was just a bad joke. How long has the band been together?

—Just about two years now. Two years in February, I guess.

—That's a long time in band years!

He didn't get it. She smiled at him. In his mind, the atmosphere around her began to wither and shrivel like the heat above an incinerator.

As the band concluded the song, she continued.

—So what's that song about?

—'Like A Berries'...? I don't think it's, like, about anything, really. He just threw the words together, I think. They come up with a lot of their songs while jammin' on stage, actually. It probably means somethin' to Billy. You'll have to ask him.

As if to answer Cassandra's question before it was asked, Apollo announced.

—This is a song about someone I used to know. It's called "High School Degree."

His tremolo turned up to ten, Colonel Sanders created the foundation for the song on guitar, the waves of vibrato setting the swaggering Boom Chuck tempo for Luke Skywalker. It was a fat, wobbly sound—not unlike that of a helium balloon meandering tuftedly across the ceiling of a ballroom. The band leapt into a standard I-IV rock format, the V not coming until the chorus.

—I saw you in the club
Just the other night
It's been five long years
Since we had that fight
Now baby
Where have you been hanging out lately?

Yeah you gotta brand new house
You got a playboy spouse
With just your high school degree
Makes no sense to me
No no no no.

The full room was so constricted, no one could move. One could only writhe in place—sweating so slickly, each tethered to a neighbor by a sticky coat of humid gloss.

—Well as the years tick by
Do you ever wonder why
You left me all alone
Left me in the cold
Now baby
I was Johnny-come-lately

Yeah, I know it's been a while
You really changed your style
You threw away your jeans
Now you ride in limousines
But baby
You don't look happy to me.

Colonel Sanders swung into a fitting rockabilly style for his solo, with a Carl Perkins element playing out.

—So I went back to school
Re-read the Golden rule
Coz you told me
High school is what I need
But baby
It don't work out like that

Because the company said
I can't work for them
With just a high school degree
Makes no sense to me

Yeah, the company said
Billy can't work for them
With just a high school degree
Makes no sense to me

Yeah, you gotta brand new house
You got a playboy spouse
Was it your high school degree?
Or just your warm body?

Cassandra knew it was impossible, but she sensed that some of the songs, or perhaps the way Apollo was singing them, seemed directed toward her. Then again, maybe it was just her imagination.

—All right, all right. So hey, I'm Apollo the sun king and these are the Gods of Music and the Angel Goddesses of Fun. Dig it.

Turning, he swept his hand across the stage toward the rest of the ensemble and the crowd slipped into overdrive.

—And this'll be our last song of the evening.

A collective groan. Squeals and shrieks of bitter disapproval.

—Mirror, mirror on the wall
Who's the biggest nightmare of them all. Yeah!
Ayatollah, I heard somebody say Ayatollah. I don't know.
This one's called 'Even Your Nightmares Come True.'
It's a theme song tonight, okay? All right.
I once dreamt I was delivering newspapers for Patty Hearst. I woke up dreaming and I said:

Am I dreaming (no!)
Even your nightmares come true
Even your nightmares come true.

Bud the Urban Cowboy veered into a vibrant, funky, soul-fashioned, rolling bass line, while Colonel Sanders flanked him with a jagged, updated Chuck Berry-style intro guitar solo.

—I was bound and I was gang raped
By the love-starved female inmates
Of a women's top security prison

The warden sat there laughing
When she noticed what was happ'ning
All her inmates got their rocks off on me

Am I dreamin'? (no!)
Even your nightmares come true.

281

Sighing softly to herself, Cassandra became wistful. Apollo's songs really were not very good. In fact, they were sort of dumb. The band was first-rate at what they were doing, they knew how to keep a crowd worked up. They had great energy. Fun.

And Apollo was so attractive, so charismatic that apparently nobody had really ever noticed that the material was trite and trivial and that it basically sucked. Yes, if he was going to have a big career, he was going to need songs from outside sources. Ultimately, that was going to be his big decision down the line.

She had mulled those thoughts earlier, but they kept re-circling through her brain.

—Is it fantasy or nightmare
I can't really tell the difference
Here I've got another one of you

You were standing on the corner
With your high-heel shoes on
When the boys drove by, they had to whistle at you

Am I dreamin'? (no!)
Even your nightmares come true.

Luke Skywalker and the Colonel provided pleasing, falsetto background vocals—echoing the Temptations in the late sixties- in response to Apollo's call, singing "Even your nightmares..."

Drifting away from his post at the monitor board, Mick the Dog slid up next to Mak the Bear and Cassandra. He was ready to turn on the charm and take his shot at the beautiful babe, especially while Apollo was occupied. Mak the Bear protested.

—Hey, Mick, don't you, like, have a job to do?

—Aw, they're almost done. This is the last song. I haven't touched the board since the beginnin' of the second set. They're on fuckin' autopilot.

Staring directly at Cassandra's tits, Mick the Dog eventually looked up toward her eyes and flutter-blinked to flirt. She was used to guys staring at her tits. It was how she paid the rent. But from time to time, there were guys who gave her the creeps the way they looked at her when she was naked. And Mick the Dog was quickly homing in on that territory, and she had her clothes on.

From behind the main board, Billy D. the Duck, noticing the activity around that beautiful girlfriend of Apollo's, waddled away from his station to go look at her. Meanwhile, from the stage, Apollo could see what was happening, and he did his best to bring Cassandra's attention back to him, where it belonged.

—Am I dreaming? (NO)
Happy days with you again (Even your nightmares...)

The skies above are blue again
Let us sing a song that's new again (Even your nightmares...)
Happy days with you again
(Even your nightmares come true.)
Is everybody Happy? (No)
(Even your nightmares come true).
We're Happy together
(Even your nightmares...)
How is your weather?
(Even your nightmares come true).

Though she was entirely accustomed to having lustful males ogle her—and though the idea seemed entirely appropriate—she was a little unnerved by the fact that they were dressed as animals. Especially the Duck that was heading their way.

—Hey, guys. What's happenin'?

Mak the Bear was still mostly speechless and Mick the Dog was back to drooling (almost literally) over Cassandra's snake-entwined boobs and the low, low cut of her sleeveless tunic. Billy D. the Duck received no reply.

—All right. That good!

Dressed as a giant yellow baby duck, he looked more ridiculous than everyone else and Cassandra began to laugh out loud.

—I don't know about the others...

She said

—But I was just watching this giant duck shuffling in this direction. It was quite a show. You should have been here.

Like the others, Billy D. the Duck had already lost awareness of his surroundings and was openly gawking at poor Cassandra. She was glad the set was coming to an end. She was ready to get out of the Trappe D'Or.

Apollo called out through the PA as "Even Your Nightmares Come True." was coming to a close.

—Hey, Mick, can I get a little more of my guitar in this monitor.

Mick the Dog moved back over to the board and boosted the gain on Apollo's guitar. For unknown reasons, his actions made the mains start feeding back, so Billy D. the Duck rushed back to the big board. Both Apollo and Mak the Bear were much relieved at their departure.

The band broke into an open jam on the Motown groove of "Even Your Nightmares..." Apollo broke into the Partridge Family theme song.

—Hello girl, here's a song I've been singin'
I'm gonna get happy
A whole lotta lovin' is what I'll be bringin'
To make you, Happy.

The band held to the riff as Apollo swung into the minor-key bridge of the original song.

—I got a dream we go somewhere dark together
And spread a little lovin as the evenin' rolls on
Somethin' seems to happen when we get together
We get a funky feelin' when we're rockin' along.

The audience was more or less catatonic. Having been unable to move, or even breathe in a room so thick with smoke and the exhalations of a thousand hot, sweaty bodies dressed in strange, exotic costumes. All were held spellbound in delusional rapture. Apollo turned and looked directly into Cassandra's eyes.

—Hello, girl, hear the song I've been singin'
C'mon now, Happy
Gotta whole lotta lovin' to you I'll be bringin'
I'll make you happy
C'mon now, Happy.

Like a snake, Apollo swirled his tongue around slippery lips.

—C'mon now, Happy
Get happy
C'mon now, Happy
Happy Happy
Get happy, Happy Happy.

Feeling that he was, in a rather immature way, trying to seduce her, Cassandra felt her heart sink. No. Not. Him. She smiled uncomfortably at his efforts in coming up with all the songs that mentioned the word happy. But, unbeknownst to him, his campaign to "get Happy" was falling flat.

—Happy Happy Happy
Gotta get Happy
Gotta get Gotta get
Happy
Happy Happy Happy
Unh unh unh.

Finally, Apollo wound the band down to very low volume. The frenzied throng was moving up and down as a single organism.

—We wanna thank all of you for coming down to the Trappe D'Or tonight. We've had a great time and we hope you've had a great time too. We'll be here next weekend. Friday and Saturday.

284

A small rush of a cheer.

—C'mon out and see us. And for those of you with nothin' else to do, we're playin' at the Peppermint Lounge. Yeah the fuckin' Peppermint Lounge, on Wednesday night. C'mon down and see us. We could use your support.

Apollo flicked his head backward, and the band instantaneously turned on a dime into the chorus of "Gloria."

—And her name is Glow-rious.
H-A-P-P-Y (Glo-or- rious)
H-A-P-P-Y (Glo-or- rious)
Yeah yeah yeah yeah
I'm gonna scream it all night long (Glo-or- rious)
I'm gonna shout it everyday (Glo-or- rious)

So good alright
Yeah so good all night yeah.

Into the final orgasmic chord shakedown, the Gods gave every ounce of dramatic effort, with the intention of leaving the crowd sated. Thus, the band would not have to play an encore. The gambit succeeded. A large portion of the audience only wished to go outside, to catch some oxygen. A final E power chord.

—Thanks everybody. I'm Billy Granger and we're the Unreal Gods. We'll see you next time.

The response was only half-hearted, as the room was evacuating with amazing rapidity. Mak realized that the door money was probably already being counted and skimmed. He thought he had better be in on the calculating, lest things get too far out of hand between Larry and Angie. With such huge door receipts, greed was bound to reveal its repulsive head. He turned and shyly engaged Happy.

—Well, I guess I better get back to the bar and check the gate.

—From what I saw, it looks like you guys did really well.

—Yeah. Me too. That's what I thought. And I'm going to try and keep it that way. It was nice to meet ya', Happy.

He held out his hand to shake hers, but she gently hugged him instead. Happy smelled so good. Her skin was soft and he could feel the full firmness of her breasts pressed against his furry chest. He immediately got another erection under his costume. With great difficulty, Mak limped away.

Shutting down the monitor board in no time, Mick immediately headed in Happy's direction. Billy D. noticed and quickly began to shut down his equipment, as well.

It did not go unnoticed by Billy what was transpiring. He grabbed a white bar towel from the top of his amp and hastily made his way to Happy's side. She was his property, after all, and he was not about to let those assholes fuck up his shit. He had plans. A conquest, perhaps.

All three of them arrived at the same time, surrounding Happy.

—My, my. *Three* sweaty guys. How nice.

Acting the bandleader, Billy, spoke up.

—C'mon, you guys. Why don't you leave Happy alone? She's mine all mine, anyway.

Grinning broadly, he tried to hug her, but she avoided with great reticence his sopping presence as it encroached into her personal space. She pushed him away.

—Ew. No. I hate sweaty things. It's like snakes. Slimy. Slithering. Ick.

She shivered involuntarily. Billy reared back, shocked, engaging her with a hurt, quizzically surprised expression.

Back at the bar, Angie and Larry abruptly cut short their conversation as Mak approached.

—Hey. Have you guys counted up the gate yet?

They gaped at him as if he were a pack of attacking wolves. Larry replied.

—Nah. We was just gettin' ready to do that. Ya' wanna come back to the office and we can check it out? I know it was the best fuckin' door we've ever had, but I dunno how much it's gonna be. But a lot. That's for fuckin' sure.

Larry, Angie, and Mak retired to the back office behind the bar area to make their calculations.

Billy stood, gawking, trying to figure Happy out. She certainly wasn't like the other girls in his life. Well, Carrie, maybe a little. He was unable to decide if he was even going to get to second base with Happy, or whether she was just testing him—playing hard to get. He knew lots of girls like that. They needed proof. They had to be sure.

As the room began to empty out, Happy began to feel a chill. Eyeing her carefully, Billy tried to plot his strategy. How would he approach it? He knew the group would be leaving soon, as they were planning on leaving their equipment at the club, so that they could run through the sets for the Peppermint Lounge gig.

Angie would drop the second tier off at Mrs. Belladro's place, they would be heading back to the apartment. Billy began to hatch a plan. Maybe Annie could help.

—So, Happy, you wanna come back to Angie's apartment with me? We can drink some beer and smoke some weed and unwind. A little one-on-one time.

—What do you mean?

—You know what I mean. Time to get to know each other a little better. I know I'd like to know *you* better.

—Well, that's all great, Billy, but how much can you get to know in a night?

—C'mon, Happy. Ya' gotta start somewhere.

Annie approached the couple looking as if she had been drug around the room for three hours—which is essentially what had happened.

—Jesus Christ, what a night! How're you two kids doing?

—We're doin' okay. What did you do tonight?

—That guy Angie followed me all around the club, trying to get me drunk. He really wanted to get into my pants in the worst way. Which is what it would've been—the very worst way. I think he's finally gotten the message though and given up.

Missing the obvious parallels between her situation and the one he was experiencing with Happy, Billy spoke up.

—Let's hope so. Man, that would be like a pretty shitty combination. Jeez. Hey, Annie. I've got a favor to ask. Do you think you could, like, give me 'n' Happy a ride back to Angie's apartment?

While Annie pondered the question, and her response, Happy shot Billy a hard glance.

—Billy. I didn't say I would go with you. I really just need to go home to my place.

Sensing that a skirmish was about to ensue, Annie excused herself. She wandered back to the green room to check in on Candy and MJ.

—C'mon, Happy. What's the big fuckin' problem anyway? Don't you like me?

—It's not that I don't like you. I do. But I'm just not interested in getting involved in a short-term thing. I told you that before.

—Yeah, yeah. I got that. But how do you, like, know that I'm just a short time thing?

—You know as well as I do, Billy that when you guys leave town, I'll never see you again.

—How do you know that?

—I know, Billy. I know men and I know musicians, and I know you—a little bit anyway.

—You don't know shit about me, Happy.

—Look. You don't have to get mean about it.

—I'll get mean about it if I fuckin' want. Fuckin' skanks.

Happy was shocked. His demeanor had turned ugly and abusive in an instant.

—Fucking skanks. You know all about that, don't ya', Happy? Showin' all the boys your tits and ass and gettin' 'em all fuckin' worked up, and then you, like, walk away. I've seen your type before.

—What type is that, Billy?

—Cockteasers. Sluts. You know.

—I know I don't like the tone of your voice, and I don't like what's coming out of your mouth. And I think it's time for me to go home, now.

—Yeah. Sure. Go ahead and run away, Happy. Fuck you. Fuck you and the fuckin' bike ya' rode in on. Bitch.

Incredulously disappointed and deeply wounded, though not entirely surprised at the outcome, with teary eyes, she turned, and with great resolve, walked away from the rock star. Billy never saw Happy again.

# XXVI

—Seventy-two hundred and change seems a little light to me, man.

Larry was unprepared for Mak's protest.

—Light? I fuckin' told ya' it was the best night we ever fuckin' had. Seventy-two is the biggest night by a long shot.

—How many people did ya' comp at the door?

—I dunno. Probably, like, fifty 'r seventy-five. Ya' understand, man, we gotta a lot of fuckin' *friends*, y'know. People that keep ya' open the rest of the year.

Mak nodded though unconvinced.

—That's cool, I got no problem with that. But even seventy-five comped at the door only amounts to, like, seven hundred and fifty dollars. I was figuring on more than ten grand, to tell ya' the truth.

Larry and Angie looked at each other guiltily, but neither of them said anything. Angie spoke up.

—No, man... Mak. If Larry says it's seventy-two, then it's seventy-two. He's not gonna, like, fuck ya' over.

Mak knew they were fucking him over for about a third of gate—right off the top—and he knew there was not a damn thing he could do about it. He knew he was going to owe Angie his "commission." That was going to be another seven and a quarter off the top.

The band was only going to come out with around sixty-five hundred dollars for the night. That was just enough to feed and house them and keep them in the studio for a couple of weeks. They really could have used that extra three grand.

Unsure what the hell he was going to tell Billy, Mak slunk in his sagging bear costume back to the party in the green room. When he arrived, everyone was drinking beer and smoking weed. Everyone except that girlfriend of Billy's. She was missing.

—Where's your friend, Billy?

—My friend? Oh you mean Happy? She's no fuckin' friend of mine, Pop.

—What happened? I was only gone, like, a half an hour. Did she leave?

—Who fuckin' gives a rat's ass, Pop? Chicks like her are a fuckin' dime a dozen.

Crestfallen, Mak plunked down with a thud on the bench in the same spot where he had been sitting earlier in the evening. She was gone. Only her absent shadow remained. And even her shadow radiated palpable warmth that Mak could sense. Panicked, he asked.

—But, what happened? Did you guys get in a fight? I thought you guys had like some kinda thing goin' or somethin'.

—Yeah? Well appearances can be fuckin' deceiving, Mak. She was playin' me for a sucker and I told her to go fuck herself. I don't need that shit.

Everyone in the room sat silent. A collective hush. Motionless. No one wished to invite Billy's wrath. And it was clear that any such incursion—even the most innocuous of comments—could easily ignite his fury given his temperament in that moment.

Temporarily breaking the tension, Candy coughed with a horrible rattling chest. A wrathful sense of self-pity and genuine concern for Candy scrawled upon his face, Billy concluded.

—Maybe we should get outta here and get Candy to bed. She's fuckin' got pneumonia.

Mick volunteered his own evaluation.

—Or maybe the plague.

Candy randomly kicked at him.

Billy turned his attention toward Mak.

—So, Poppy. How'd we do at the door?

His face and ears turning raspberry red, Mak stuttered.

—Th-they s-said it was only s-seventy-two hundred dollars.

Again, unease rose up again within the room.

—Seventy-two hundred? Are ya' sure? They said seventy-two hundred? I thought ya' were thinkin' ten grand.

—Seventy-two's what they told me. And after Angie's ten percent, and paying for the PA and gear, we only come out with sixty-five hundred.

—Mak, man. That's not right. That's not fuckin' right at all. I thought we'd pulled at least nine. We had a thousand people in here tonight. I know it.

—That's what I thought, too, Billy. But they said seventy-two hundred, and there wasn't much I could say. Ya' know?

Billy nodded grimly.

—I just took the money and came back here. I think we got ripped off.

As if on cue, Angie entered the room in a robed Mosesian flourish.

—Hey, what's happenin', everybody?

He wormed his way between Billy D. and Annie.

—Are we ready ta party?

The room fell dourly sour, yet again. Billy volunteered a reply.

—Naw. We were thinkin' that we need to get Candy into bed, because of her pneumonia.

—Plague.

—Yeah. Okay, Mickey. Pneumonia or *plague*, I guess.

Angie appeared slightly shocked at the reference to an infectious disease in context with Candy—whom from the start he had deemed as a total fitness buff. He did not pick up on the tittering and sniggering that was going around the room. He put his hand on Annie's knee as he stood up.

—Well, then, I guess we better get her home. Whatever the fuck she's got.

Wanly, Angie smiled in Candy's general direction. Candy did not acknowledge him in the least. Nor did Annie, who, with great consternation, puffed unruly bangs away from her forehead.

—So what time'r'ya' plannin' on rehearsin' tomorrow?

A communal shrug greeted Angie's question? All eyes turned toward Billy.

—I don't know. Wha'd'you guys think? Three? Four?

Deciding the question deserved an answer, Col spoke up.

—Four sounds good to me. We can practice for a couple of hours. A couple hours a night and we'll be ready for a couple sets on Wednesday. Don't ya' think?

The members of the band seemed to think four sounded good. So it was decided—four.

Angie ran the Belladro house regulars back to Mama's and then it was on to his apartment. Annie gave brief thought to following them over to Angie's, but after due deliberation, decided that she would avoid any further hassles with the lecherous Angie. She ended up driving back to her brother's apartment instead.

It was an Indian summer in the area around New York City. The weather remained quite warm, in the low eighties. The autumnal golds and reds, and browns of the trees and foliage sharply contrasted the intense blue sky. It was strange to see people still in sandals, shorts, and t-shirts at the beginning of November.

Rehearsals went well for the band. They perfected the material they planned to play for the showcase at the Peppermint. They also had the opportunity to further hone the remaining songs they intended to record in the studio.

They completed the arrangement to a Christmas song called "Happy Santa Claus," which Billy had been working on since they first arrived. They decided to record that song in the studio, too, in order to have a single to release as soon as they returned to Portland.

On Sunday at both Angie's apartment and Mama Belladro's house, the peripheral members hung out and did nothing. Candy was so sick she hardly woke at all. MJ spent the day watching TV and reading. She read *People* and *Rolling Stone*, *TV Guide* and through most of Angie's impressive collection of *Penthouse* and *Hustler* magazines. It was quiet for a change, and she enjoyed being temporarily free of the constant tension that was beginning to enfold the band.

She had decided that she would accompany Candy back to Portland on Thursday, provided they were able to get their ticket arrangements straightened out. She found being a dancer in a rock band far from glamorous—and mostly unforgivingly strenuous.

With Candy feeling so bad, for almost the whole time they were in Jersey City, she really had no one to talk to. Annie was nice, but she was Candy's friend. Or Billy's friend, actually. Besides, it felt like the era of the Unreal Goddesses was over, though she was uncertain why she felt that way.

While the band was vainly attempting to seriously rehearse at the club, Mak, Mick, and Billy D. spent Sunday drinking beer, smoking weed, and watching old movies on TV. They said very little to one another throughout the course of the afternoon. There was very little to say. They were wasted, and their talents were being wasted in New Jersey. They were unable to do their jobs. They had no purpose and each of the trio felt that desolation in a different way.

On Monday, Mak decided he should check in with some of the key scene components back in Portland. He phoned Tommy and spoke to him for more than an hour. He called Jonathan at Euphoria and talked to him for twenty minutes. He reached Stan of the Cowboys and Jimmy Lee out at Lung Fung.

Contacting his confidantes in the press he shared sanitized versions of the events transpiring. He knew the band needed to remain in the news. He understood that it was his job to keep them there. Fans back home would want to hear tales of their adventures. What was the band doing and when would they be coming home? Blah. Blah.

Mick and Billy D. simply continued to hang out; they really did not have anything to do, and they had given up trying to come up with something. Without some guidance and direction from Billy, they were helpless.

MJ and Candy had made plans for Monday. Annie came by at mid-morning and took them to the airport in Newark to get their flight plans settled. It was a big relief for Candy to know that she could go home in three days. She had her ticket. Though she would not admit it, MJ was relieved to be going home, as well.

Taking the Holland Tunnel into the city, they had a nice lunch at a little café in Greenwich Village and then spent the remainder of the day exploring little stores and shops in the surrounding area.

For a while, anyway, they didn't care about the band and they were able to enjoy themselves as young women in the big city—and not mere appendages.

Tuesday was a whirlwind as the band and all tangential parties made ready for the big gig at the Peppermint Lounge on Wednesday. By phone, Mak secured the location and time for load-in and sound check. Billy D. and Mick accompanied the band to the Trappe D'Or, helping each God collect his gear and lug it out to Angie's van.

When they were finished, Billy had Angie play a cassette, on the car-stereo, for Mick and Billy D. It was a partial version of "Happy Santa Claus"—recorded off the board at the Trappe D'Or—and the two roadies were accordingly impressed. It was a fun song with a genuine professional sheen about it. It was all new to the pair and they were pleased to hear the band making progress.

Once everyone had been settled in their appointed quarters and the foursome were back at the apartment, Angie invited Billy into his office for consultation. Gilly tried to tag along, but Angie brushed him off.

Col really did not care about any of it. He knew that Angie was a schemer and Billy was a gullible dipshit just waiting for someone to take advantage of him. Angie seemed the likely contender.

Col preferred to sit back and watch it all play out in front of him. It wasn't going anywhere anyway. Angie didn't have a chance with the Gods. It was like a stupid game. And Col enjoyed things like that.

—Look, Billy, I wanted to talk to ya'. We need ta figure out this manager thing.

—What manager thing?

—You know, like I said before, you need professional management. I can do it for ya'. I could, like, do a fuckin' great job. But if ya' don't want me, I know a lotta

293

people could handle you guys in the right way, ya' know what I mean?

—Yeah. I know what ya' mean. But I don't know if we, like, fuckin' need a new manager. Poppy's been doing fine.

—Like I told ya', he's done a helluva job for ya', and maybe he should be yer road manager, or somethin' like that. But you guys need someone representin' ya' who knows the business. To keep ya' from bein' fuckin' screwed. It happens all the time, ya' know. All the time.

Billy liked the idea of Mak maybe being the road manager. That was a new angle to explore. It would still give him plenty of responsibilities and lots of up-close interaction with the band. But maybe Angie was right about the next level and everything. Angie could see his words having some effect.

—I mean, Billy, man, fuckin' look at it. I got ya' all yer gigs at the club, and that Annie chick got ya' this gig at the Peppermint. Mak ain't done jack shit. Sure, he gets ya' all yer gigs back home, but how long're ya' fuckin' plannin' on hangin' around Portland, anyway?

Upon hearing Angie's full pitch for the first time, Billy thought he made a lot of sense. There was much to consider. Angie was definitely right about Mak: Poppy didn't know any more about the music business than Billy did.

It was still early on Tuesday night, so Billy thought that he would try to reach Carrie on the phone. His relationships with women had been upside-down ever since he had arrived in Jersey City. He felt uncharacteristically vulnerable. He needed reassurance. He needed support. He needed to confide in someone. Carrie.

The phone rang forlornly three times. Carrie answered. Billy sighed. Relieved.

—Carrie. Carrie! You answered.

—Yeah. Hi.

She was cool though—still more distant than the last time they had spoken.

—How are you? Have ya' been doin' all your school stuff?

—Yes, Billy. I've been doing all my school stuff. A lot of reading. I've been really busy trying to keep up. So, I'm studying quite a bit. In fact I thought you were my study partner, Leena. She's supposed to be calling.

Disappointed, Billy asked.

—Well...do you have to go? Should I hang up?

—No. No. It's okay. She'll call back if the line's busy.

—Good. Good. I wanted to talk to you. I've missed you, Carrie. I've missed you a lot.

—I've missed you, too, Billy. It's been pretty quiet around here.

—It's been busy here.

—Yeah? You've been busy?

—We had our Halloween show on Saturday and it was huge.

—A lot of people came?

—Oh, yeah. A lot of people. But it was weird, too.

Realizing that he was actually preparing to tell his girlfriend about his strange encounter with a stripper named Happy, Billy wisely swerved around the frightened squirrel of a subject standing frozen in the middle of the road of their conversation and was able to resume driving.

—Weird? Weird how?

Fortuitously, he was primed with an alternate tale.

—All those people in weird costumes crammed into the Crap Door—it's really the Trappe D'Or, but we've started callin' it the Crap Door. Anyway, it's just a big box of a place, and there were probably twice as many people in there as there's supposed to be. Probably almost a thousand. And it was hot and smoky and there was no air. Candy made all of our costumes for us. I was Apollo, the Sun King.

At first, a confused silence greeted his account.

—Apollo the Sun King? Billy, I think Apollo is…

—Yeah, yeah, I know he's like a God or somethin'. But I don't want to be a god. I just want to be a king…like Elvis.

—So are you going to change the name of the band to the Unreal Kings then?

They both chuckled at that, and it helped to break the tension that had been circuiting between them for nearly four weeks.

—Yeah. So, anyway. We've been in the studio, y'know, like, every day that we're not playin' in the club. We've finished one song so far—'Police Told Me" and we're all set to record a new one I wrote since we got here, a Christmas song called 'Happy Santa Claus'. We're y'know, like, plannin' on releasin' it for Christmas this year. I think the plan is to ship the tape out there to Tommy and let him get it mastered and pressed.

—One song. Is that good? It seems like at that rate you guys won't be back for another month.

—It could take that long.

—Another month? Do you really think so?

—Yeah. Maybe. Doing these recordings isn't easy. It's a lot more technical than the stuff we recorded in Portland. And it sounds like it. It sounds like the big leagues. It's good.

—Fit for a king.

—What do you mean? Anyway, tomorrow night, we've got a showcase at the Peppermint Lounge. We're going to audition for A. Cousins Vetter. He's, like, the owner of Rough Edge Records. That's huge. Major label. If he likes us, we're off to the races.

—That's good, then?

—Yeah, it's great. That's as good as it gets.

An awkward quiet descended.

—So anyway, Carrie. I've been thinkin' a lot about what you said last time.

—What did I say?

—About not trustin' me, and all that.

—All that? You have such a sensitive way of putting things, Billy.

—C'mon, Carrie. Why're you gettin' on my case? I'm not tryin' to start anything.

—It's just that I really don't know what you're up to out there. It's hard for me to believe it's just recording and playing in the club.

—Up to? Wha'd'ya mean *up to*?

—What don't you understand, Billy? I don't know what you're up to out there. I don't know if I can trust you. If it's going to be another month until you come home, then it will have to be another month before we can iron this out, because it's not going to happen over the phone. Maybe it won't ever happen. But every time we hang up I feel sick to my stomach.

He started to feel sorry for himself, moping softly.

—Well. I don't want you to be sick. I guess I better go, then.

—Okay, Billy. I hope everything goes well for you at your show tomorrow at the Peppermint Lounge. It sounds like a pretty big deal.

—Okay. Thanks, Carrie. I hope your studyin' goes well. I know that's important for you, too. I love you.

—I love you too, Billy.

They hung up. Billy was not consoled by their conversation, but only more troubled still. He was in uncharted interpersonal waters. It was like the Cars song. "All Mixed Up." All fucked up.

After another eighty-degree day, it was still in the high sixties when the band loaded into the Peppermint Lounge at six. Mak met with Benjamin, the club's stage manager. Benjamin told the band where to set up and showed Angie, Billy D. and Mick the main and monitor boards. Billy D. gave the main board a cursory glance and then made his way back toward the band, where he helped the guys hoist their gear onto the stage and get it arranged.

Surveying the area, MJ and Candy plotted their positions in relation to the orbit, arc and trajectory of the band members. Despite being so dreadfully ill, Candy was still the consummate trouper. If it was to be her last night in New York—and possibly her last night dancing with the band—then she wanted to go out in style.

Like MJ, Candy had been sensing that the Goddesses had outlived their usefulness within the band's stage presentations as their music evolved and permutated. She wasn't sure if the members of the band had consciously given any thought to dispensing with the girls. But she knew it was only a matter of time. The Unreal Gods had outgrown the Goddesses A Go-Go.

And the Goddesses had outgrown the Gods. Candy was tired of dancing and she knew MJ was too. It was all working out for the best. She looked forward to a life away from rock and roll. She had grown very tired of being treated as an object.

With Billy D's sizeable contribution, the band quickly set up their amps, tuned their instruments, and were ready for a sound check. With equally precise haste, Angie and Mick had their boards relatively dialed in and ready for the boys to hit it. They ran through a few songs, including "Police Told Me" and "Made in Hong Kong." They sounded tough, hot. Ready. They were on a roll.

It was only a little after seven when they concluded the sound check, so they hatched a plan to look for a restaurant in the neighborhood where they might find an inexpensive repast.

They walked west on West 45th Street, from the Avenue of the Americas to 7th Avenue, then north to West 47th Street. They decided to try Famous Dave's near the Palace Theatre—mostly because they liked the name- though they couldn't imagine who Famous Dave might be.

Billy guessed David Bowie. Angie thought of Dave Winfield. Candy suggested David Brinkley. Gilly, David Gaffen. Col and Daw simultaneously hazarded David Cassidy. Mick said the guy whose show followed Johnny and the Tonight Show, David Letterman. At that point in the speculation, they were inside the restaurant, more than ready to dine.

By the time they arrived back at the Peppermint Lounge, it was nearing eight-thirty. Inside, Annie sat at the bar, smoking a cigarette, and waiting for them.

—Oh, good. There you are. I got here and the place was empty and I had nowhere to go, so I figured I'd wait—that you'd be back eventually. I figured I'd have a drink, smoke a couple of cigarettes, and you'd be here. And here you are. How're you guys doing? Is everybody up for the show?

She was greeted by blank stares. Behind black-masked eyes, Candy shrugged, while the rest of the band did not respond at all.

—That good! Great.

Billy finally spoke up.

—Aw. Nah. We're doin' real good. We sounded real good for, y'know, the sound check. I guess we're all, like, a little, wiped out from eatin', and I gotta say, I'm even a little bit nervous.

The others agreed with simultaneous nods. Col piped in.

—Yeah. I'm wiped out, too. I think I need a joint to get my head right.

Again there was agreement in simultaneity, so the bunch of them migrated to the dressing room behind the stage. They fired up several rounds of joints, and choosing from the vast array provided by the club, each popped open a bottle of beer. They sat on facing couches and chairs, a dark walnut coffee table demarcating between.

Billy thought to himself how all the dressing rooms on the face of the planet were essentially identical. Each was a small, dingy room, with bad light, painted some variation of a gawd awful landlady color, usually puke green; the walls were scrawled with some of the most vile and pointless graffiti ever to be manufactured by the childish collective mind of the male of the species.

The band members stared at one another, or, more precisely, stared through one another, individually contemplating the night ahead. All were looking forward to the challenge. Each fretted over his particular role. None were especially worried about a negative outcome. They were a good band. They knew it and they were going to prove it to whomever wanted to know.

Annie and the Goddesses huddled together, to gossip and kibitz and outline strategies peculiar to their gender. After a while as the first sounds of an audience began to sift into the stuffy room, Annie alertly declared.

—Well, I should get out there and meet with Jordan when he arrives.

She stood up and wandered toward the door. Mak rose with her, and twitching nervously, his head the color of a plum, he escorted her out.

—I should go, too. I wanna, like, keep an eye on things, y'know?

The others hardly looked up when the pair left the room. Annie and Mak walked to the front of the building, where they grabbed a booth near the entry so that Annie could watch for the arrival of Jordan Archer. It was a good spot, as it had a great sightline to the stage. They ordered a round of drinks from the waitress. Upon her departure, they each lit a cigarette.

Slowly, people began to file into the club. Mak tried to figure out who they were and why the hell they were there. Or how they had heard of the band. He recognized a few of them from the Trappe D'Or. He surmised that some of them had probably brought along friends for whom the band was new.

He figured, too, that the intense postering effort by the Unreal Phonepole "Power Trio" might have accounted for a few Jersey City residents in attendance. For some the Trappe D'Or was, perhaps, a few levels beneath their station in life. He rubbed his irritated left eye and absent-mindedly sneered slightly at the clientele.

By the time the band took the stage, at around nine-fifteen, the room was about half-full, with a crowd of around two hundred. Mak was happily surprised by the turnout, pleased that Jordan Archer would not be seeing the Gods playing to an empty house. The bar staff seemed happy, as well, so there was a good vibe in the room.

—Hi, everybody. I'm Billy Granger and we're the Unreal Gods and Goddesses. We're from Portland, Oregon. And we're here to deliver the news—Go-Go boots are comin' back. Yeah. They're comin' back.

As they steered the song with expert accuracy, Candy and MJ took to the stage, in skintight gray jumpsuits, covered in pink-sequins, fluffy pink boots, elbow-length pink satin gloves. Both Goddesses wore black masks across their eyes and cat's ears on the tops of their heads. They swiveled from hip to hip scratching at the air like angry kittens. Mee-owww!

The Gods merged into "Upstroke Down" pogo-ing energetically as Billy told the tale. From there, they kept things stupid, light, and fun, maneuvering into "My Girlfriend's Drawers," "High School Degree," and "Boom Chuck Rock." With hardly a break, they ran through crisp versions of "I Like Berry's" and "Don't Be Sad." From there, they slid into "Rockabilly Queen," and finally "Rasta Rhythm." The intention being to conclude the set at that point.

At precisely ten o'clock, Jordan Archer appeared in the doorway. Flawlessly attired in a white shirt, blue sports coat, and light-gray slacks, he immediately spotted Annie, waving frenetically. Following behind him was an old man who was accompanied by two handsome young businesswomen, one at each side, and a step behind him—as if to rein him in.

Nudging Mak to attention, Annie hailed the quartet of newcomers over to their table. She excitedly rose to greet them. Mak shook free of some far distant thoughts and stood up next to Annie. While shooting a finger gun in Mak's direction in an acknowledgement of recognition, Jordan extended his hand and shouted slightly.

—Annie. It's good to see you again. Is this your band playing now?

She nodded.

—Wonderful. Wonderful. I want you to meet Cuz.

He turned and faced the old man, shouting.

—Cuz, this is Angela Fisher, she's the daughter of some very close friends of my family.

The old man's neck was so furrowed and creased it looked like a skin ascot. His receding fine white hair was combed straight back and he was well tanned, which nicely set off a crisp white shirt and light gray suit. He extended his left hand in a European fashion.

—A. Cousins Vetter, my dear. Delighted to meet you.

Voraciously bald, Vetter had a beakish face, with the remorseless unblinking brown eyes of a raptor. His hands were wrinkled and leathery, with long bony fingers that resembled nothing so much as talons. He had the crooked smile of someone accustomed to getting his way. Or, his prey.

Vetter turned sharply in the direction of the chestnut-haired young women behind him. He pointed.

—This is Kimberley Fields, my personal assistant.

He turned around the other way, gesturing with his thumb over his shoulder toward a pretty, honey-haired girl, with the oversized brown-framed glasses.

—And this is Kindred Swain. She is one of my talent coordinators. These two ladies are the foundation of my operation. My right hand and my left and I would be absolutely lost without them.

They greeted Annie warmly and looked quizzically at Mak, who stood shifting shyly next to his friend. Annie shook her head, embarrassed.

—Oh, Mak. I'm so sorry.

She massaged the poor blushing fellow's shoulder.

—This is Mak Poppin. He's the band's manager. You remember Jordan of course.

Mak shook Archer's hand and reached out in Vetter's direction.

—Mister Vetter. It's a real honor. You're, like, really famous in our circle.

Again Vetter extended his hand in the European fashion. Kiss the ring. Holding out his hand further, Mak smiled warmly at Vetter's assistants, politely shaking their hands as well.

—Kimberly. Kindred. It's a real pleasure to meet you.

Mak remained standing as the guests seated themselves between he and Annie. Awkwardly looking around at them, he mumbled.

—I hope you guys won't mind if I excuse myself for a few minutes. I'll be back right back.

He bowed obsequiously and took his leave, heading as fast as he could in the direction of the band. As he approached, Mak waved his hands in Billy's line of vision, drawing his fingers apart in the universal sign indicating the necessity of extending the length of the set. Stretch.

Perplexedly squinching up his face, Billy noticed Mak's frenzied gesticulations. As Billy bent over, Mak rushed toward him and shouted into his ear.

—They just got here. Ya' better play a few more songs. Good ones!!

Catching the gist, Billy casually wandered around to the other Gods to explain the situation and develop a plan, all the while maintaining the skipping reggae beat of "Rasta Rhythm." Billy conducted the band to the song's finale, shouting into the mic.

—Yeah. Yeah. Yeah. We're the Unreal Gods. If we were the Real Gods, then we wouldn't want to be hangin' around here with *you*—now would we?

Returning to the gathering in the booth, Mak winced with visible discomfort at Billy's crack, smiling weakly. Oh, that crazy Billy. He returned to his seat next to Kindred.

Observing Angie and Billy D. at the main board—Kindred wondered where the Jersey looking dark-haired guy fit into the picture. He seemed out of place. Despite his efforts to avoid interaction, she asked of Mak.

—I noticed the one soundman. He's really a big guy. What is his name?

Mak sincerely replied.

—Oh his name's Billy too. Billy Dreier, but we call him Billy D.

—He sort of resembles the singer. Like a larger version.

—You're not the first to mention that. He's the best soundman in the business. He's like another member of the band. In fact, that's why Billy makes sure he gets paid like he's a regular band member. He gets, like, a sixth of the band's take. It's too bad he's not doin' sound tonight. They'd sound a lot better.

301

Impressed, or seeming so, Kindred pursed her lips and exhaled sharply.

—Wh-why isn't he doing the sound, then?

—Aw, it's a long story, ya' know? The other guy up there at the board, Angie, he's the keyboard player's brother, and he's kind of, like, muscled in on things a little bit while we've been here.

—Is he from New Jersey?

—Yeah. Just across the river. How'd you know that?

—Oh, one acquires a sixth sense about these things.

Nodding confidently, Mak said.

—Billy D.'ll be back at the board when we get back home. He really is the best and we all know it.

Meanwhile, a gaggle of girls had gathered around Billy, staring up from the floor into his swimming pool blue eyes, and his Rumpelstiltskin golden straw hair—a long silk scarf—of dark paisley blues and reds trimmed in yellow, wrapped around his forehead. He wore his beloved leopard skin David Bowie jumpsuit, along with black, relaxed-velvet ankle boots. A Hugh Hefner gypsy pirate.

—Now, we're gonna slow things down here for a minute. I wanna tell you a little story. It's about my girlfriend. She's thousands of miles away.

As Col plucked out his familiar dramatic riff, Gilly chimed in—his soundtrack strings sadly singing.

—That's right. She's back home, thousands of miles away, and I'm missin' her. Missin' her real bad. And when I try to talk to her on the phone, she doesn't understand. She just hangs up on me.

The girls standing at his feet moaned sympathetically.

—Oh-oo.

—That's right. That's what I mean. So I say to myself...
I'm walkin' down a rocky road for you
That's all that you have left me to...

And the girls soon swooned, as he crooned the mournful tune.

Back at the table, Vetter cocked his neck to view the band. He opined to no one in particular.

—Well, they certainly are a good-looking bunch. What's their name again? The Unholy?

Seeking confirmation, he turned in Jordan Archer's direction. Archer answered.

—No. No. It's Unreal Gods. Unreal...?

Concurrently, Annie and Mak answered in the affirmative.

—Unreal Gods.

—Yes. Unreal Gods. Well, this is a catchy number. Very evocative.

Annie ventured.

—I know this one is very important to Billy.

Vetter observed.

—I like his energy very much. He has a lot of charisma. He's good in front of a crowd. How is their material?

He looked at Archer, who had thoroughly reviewed their recorded output.

—Oh. It's all right. They play well together. Nothing great. But good enough to be a reasonably successful national act, I'd say.

—I agree. With work, they could do well.

—A little spit and polish and I'd think so.

—Perhaps we could bring in outside material.

In did not slip past Annie nor Mak that Vetter employed the word "we." They saw that as a very positive sign. The wheels of promotion were already beginning to turn. Vetter tossed a sidelong glance at his assistants.

—What do you ladies think? Have we got a star in the making here?

Spontaneously, they reached vigorous unanimous accord. Kindred said.

—Oh, yes. He's great. The band's good, too. But I can't take my eyes off of him. Billy...Angel?

Again, Annie and Mak answered at precisely the same time.

—Billy Granger.

Kindred raised an eyebrow and smiled sarcastically.

—Billy Granger. It sounds like a name from a book. It doesn't sound real. What do you think, Kimmie? He's got it, don't you think?

—Definitely Kin. He's definitely got something special. It's boyish innocence or west coast sunshine. Or, I don't know what. But he's very appealing. Look at all the girls up there.

She waved in the direction of the stage.

—They all just want to take care of him.

Everyone chuckled at the irony of a rock star requiring a mother. It seemed that all the good ones did: Morrison, Elvis, Lennon.

—He appeals to motherly instincts. He's very charming.

Annie could hear a tone in Kimberly Fields' voice that she had heard countless times before in the voices of many other young women—a tone she had heard in her own voice. Everyone had a crush on Billy. It was that simple. It was that instantaneous. Yet indelible.

Their reactions did not escape the notice of the ever astute A. Cousins Vetter. For that was precisely the reason Kim and Kindred were his assistants. He could always trust them to provide honest appraisal. He could read them better than they could read themselves. They were his barometers.

The band quickly slipped from "Rocky Road" into the intro of the next song.

—All right, all right. Yeah it's a rocky road. A rocky road. And I need somethin' in my life, somethin' to keep me square.

He formed a frame with his hands. And, nearing the top of the beat, he hollered.

—Somethin' perfect now. I need some symmetry.

The boys exploded into the song, the upstroke ska rhythm pulsing intensely beneath the seemingly random-noted theme that bounced between Col's guitar and Gilly's synth.

—I need some symmetry symmetry symmetry
In my play in my play
I want it perfect in my theater now
Perfect in my theater, symmetry in my play.

Noting that Vetter seemed to be truly enjoying the Gods' performance, Mak tried to unobtrusively attract Annie's attention. She looked at him from across the table, and he raised his eyebrows, motioning with his eyes. She smiled. Again, Vetter spoke aloud to no one in particular.

—They're a very good band. Really good. Great sense of fun.

—Coz I'm watchin' the best show
That I ever seen

But the leading Bozo
Drives a real Boraxo team.

Screwing up his face, Vetter inquired of Annie and Mak.

—A real Boraxo team. Is that some sort of drug reference?

—No. No drugs.

Mak lied. The Boraxo team was a suitcase full of coke that Dealer Walt brought backstage once for the band to see. Billy called him a Bozo, but they had all gladly partaken of the Boraxo, like a real team of asses.

—No. He's talking about his girlfriend, the symmetry. And the Boraxo team is like Reagan and twenty mules, you know? Billy's surrounded by all these stubborn people. And he wants the band to be perfect, just like he wants his relationship with Carrie to be perfect. He's a perfectionist.

Dutifully impressed by Mak's succinctly inane explanation, Vetter's estimation of the band's lyrical depth increased somewhat. Mak thought it was one of his best evasive actions ever, taken only out of desperation. But he was good at thinking on his feet, and he relied upon that quality within himself to escape from otherwise unpleasant consequences.

He rubbed his watering left eye with his index finger and dabbed at it with a napkin. Perhaps some mote flung from afar... He had no time to give it any thought.

—I want the two notes that I play on my guitar
to be so perfect now perfect now
Watch me now hoo-hah.

Billy massaged his simple, but effective guitar solo, while Vetter—his lips pursed in insouciant delight—smiled amusedly at Mak. Kimberly and Kindred bobbed their heads enthusiastically. From the top the lads ran through the song again, wrapping it up with a quick four bar figure after Billy's second solo. Seamlessly, they embarked into "The World Came Crashing Down."

—Yeah, this is a song about havin' a hard time. When life is dealing you a bad hand. That's when you find out who your real friends are. The others? Well, they never were friends, now, were they?

—I made it to the big time
A real rock 'n' roll Mess-sigh-yuh
Then the world come crashin' down...

Back at the booth, Vetter and Jordan Asher powwowed earnestly, while Kimmie and Kin plotted highly-important, extremely technical potential strategies, relating to what they felt, with a high degree of certainty, was the emerging nascent stardom of the young man they were in the midst of witnessing.

Meanwhile, Mak and Annie mutely watched what transpired with a sort of bemused bewilderment. They were like caterpillars trying to comprehend a butterfly world.

—Yeah you threw me by the wayside
You just threw me away-ee-uh
But you never ever saw my face
My smile was out of place
Livin' in the old days
Just livin' in the old days
When the world came crashin' down
The world came crashin' down.

After more than an hour of playing, the Gods wrapped up their third extra song of the set with attendant gusto and panache. Snickering, Billy narrated into the microphone, in a low, imperfectly delivered, resonant Elvis drawl.

—Thang yuh. Thang yuh veruh mush laydezh and ginlmn. Ahm Billeh Grainjuh and wur the Unreal Godzh. And we all'll beh rat back aftuh thus briff innamission.

Power chording the song's finish, they abruptly vacated the stage, taking a direct and immediate route in the direction of the green room.

Seeing that, of his own accord, Billy was not going to come back to visit with their illustrious guests, Mak again excused himself and maneuvered through the milling crowd, toward the backstage area. He burst into the green room, where Billy and the clique were indulging in beer and marijuana.

—Billy, man. C'mon. Ya' gotta come up and meet A. Cousins Vetter and Jordan Archer. This is a big deal.

—Hey look, Poppy, I'm all worn out from playing. If they're all hot to meet me, they can come back here.

Horrified by what he was hearing, Mak engaged Billy in aghast astonishment.

—Billy? Jeezus Fuck, Billy. Why the hell are we here, man? I thought we came to New York to record and make contacts. Well, two of the fuckinest, biggest fuckin' fish in the whole fuckin' business are out there and they fuckin' want to meet *you*. They. Want. To. Meet. *You*. Dig it, Billy. Now c'mon out and meet these people.

Pouting visibly, Billy took a long swig of beer from a green Rolling Rock bottle and, violently throwing the joint he was holding against the wall, stood up with a loud, exasperated groan.

—Okay. Fuck it, Poppy. Okay. Let's go meet these fuckin' assholes and get it over with.

Only partially relieved, Mak led Billy—a white towel draped over his head and around his shoulders, like a prize fighter—to the back of the room to meet the

VIPs. As the pair moved through the club, people interrupted their conversations to gawk at the tall, handsome, very Nordic-looking young man as he passed by.

Mak and Billy approached the back booth and various discussions of voluble augury and vast significance were abruptly discontinued. Smiles befell the strangers' faces. Mak volunteered.

—Hey, everybody, this is Billy Granger. Billy, this is Kindred Swain.

Billy smiled and modestly bowed his head in her direction.

—And Kimberly Fields.

And they exchanged warm smiles.

—Ladies...

—That's Jordan Archer there, next to Annie. He's the attorney I told you about. He's the guy responsible for putting this together for us.

Billy reached across the table, grasping a firm handshake.

—Great to meet you, Jordan.

Proudly, Mak announced.

—And, Billy, this is Mister A. Cousins Vetter.

Extending his right, Billy was met with Vetter's left hand for the European handshake. But, Billy was having none of it. Instead, he merely shifted his grasp and shook left-handed, in the old-fashioned, straightforward, widely accepted All-American manner, only backwards. Momentarily, he gave thought to give him a brother handshake, but he quickly abandoned the notion.

Vetter smiled warmly—as if he were meeting a distant relative for the first time. His hawk-like eyes narrowed into concentric crater-valleyed wrinkles. Billy shivered. An ineffable frost of ghost malevolently hovered above them.

—Good to meet you, Billy. I truly enjoy your band. Very tight.

—It's really good to meet you too, Mister Vetter. You're a real legend to musicians everywhere.

Slightly embarrassed by the platitude, Vetter redirected the subject.

—So how long have you been together?

Shifting his weight uneasily, as he stood before the landed gentry, Billy mumbled.

—About a year and a half, I suppose. Somethin' like that.

He grinned adorably toward Kindred and Kimberly, and the women twittered like pre-teens.

—Me and the bass player have been workin' together for about four or five years, now, I guess. But the Unreal Gods have been together for...well, goin' on two years in February, actually.

—Do you write the songs?

Suddenly reticent, Billy humbly replied.

—Well...yeah. I guess I do. But all the guys figure out their own parts and they add to the songs. So I guess we all write 'em. Y'know?

—Yes. Of course. That's typically the way it works. I understand you are here in New York to record an album of some sort? Is that right?

—No, it's just a four-song demo, really. That's all we can afford.

Billy was nothing, if not an inveterate opportunist, and he saw his opportunity to hit up A. Cousins Vetter for a loan or a contract or all of the above.

—We're recording over at the Power Station. We'll be done in another two or three weeks. We pretty much have to be.

Nodding, Cousins again guided the topic in the direction of his own implicit interests.

—Well, I would very much like it if you would send a copy of that recording to me when you're finished. My assistants will give all my information to Mister Poppin. I am really looking forward to hearing your demo. Maybe we can work together in the future.

Speechless. A very rare occurrence. Billy's gaze tennis-balled between Vetter and Jordan Archer, as he attempted to assimilate the magnitude of the moment. He smiled feebly.

—Will do, Mister Vetter. Will do. We're just getting' ready to record a Christmas song that I want to release in Portland by Thanksgiving. I'd love to get your feedback on that one.

—Oh, that's right. You're from Aw-rih-gawn. That's very nice country. I've been to Portland many times. I've looked at a few properties out there.

—We love it. It's home. I don't think I'll ever move away from Oregon, no matter how far away I travel.

A wistful hush descended.

Sensing the moment, Billy scrub-dried his sweaty hair and said.

—Well, I better get back there and rendezvous the troops. It was really great meeting you all.

He raised his hand, in a happy trails wrist wave, turned and walked away.

The hush subsided into a collective sigh. Not unexpectedly, Billy had acquired four new fans. He disappeared into the copse of bodies and smoke, and a strange expression crossed Vetter's face. He asked Mak.

—Did he say they were recording a Christmas song?

—Yeah. I think they're gonna get it rollin' tomorrow. It's called 'Happy Santa Claus'. As soon as it's recorded and all mixed, we're gonna send it to one of our associates back home.

Vetter smiled slyly at Mak's explanation. An enterprising bunch.

—And Tommy'll get it mastered and pressed for us. And if everything goes right, we should have it on the radio and in the stores by around Thanksgiving. I think I figured out that we have, like, three weeks to pull it off. That's calling it pretty close, y'know? But it's not impossible. We can get it done.

Caressing the smooth skin of his freshly shaved face, Vetter took in the atmosphere of the room.

—Well, as I told Billy, please get my contact information from the girls, and we'll get yours, and we'll certainly keep in touch. He's a very exciting personality and a real teen heartthrob in the making.

Cringing, Mak gulped, choking down his gag reflex at the term "teen heart-throb."

—I don't know, Mister Vetter. I don't know if Billy really wants to be a teen heart-throb exactly. He wants to be successful. He's gonna be successful. We all know that. A star.

—Being teen heart throbs didn't hurt Elvis nor the Beatles, so there is something to be said for that status. It sells a lot of records. A lot of records.

Mak nodded agreeably. He was not about to tiff with A. Cousins Vetter over whether or not Billy had teen appeal. Conveniently, Annie chimed in.

—He's a star in Portland and we think he can be a star anywhere. The underage kids love him out there.

She engaged Vetter's assistants with a positive posture of sincere delight.

—He's got star power.

No one said a word. But it was settled all around. He had star power.

The Gods retook the stage and quickly unwound the intro to "Made in Hong Kong," one of the new songs the band intended to record at the Power Station.

Over Col's insistent, chunky guitar, Gilly stated the central theme in three or four different synth voicings, supported by Col's liquid riffs—the band sounding tougher and more mature than on any previous material.

Skipping into his vocal, Billy chanted.

—Made in Hong Kong by a Japanese woman
And I don't know where
Don't know where I'm gonna turn up next
I don't know where I'll turn up next

Buy you flowers in the flower store
And my love can't give you any more
But I don't know where we'll turn up next.
I don't know where we'll turn up next.

Except for Jordan Archer, all at the table lit cigarettes. A dense, choking veil of smoke hung just above the booth. Vetter chatted with his associates as they assembled between them the necessary materials for Billy and the band, while Archer and Annie discussed matters of great consequence.

A foul, fuming cigarette jammed in the side of his mouth, Mak fished around in his billfold for a couple of business cards he could give to Kindred and Kimberly. After what seemed like a great deal too much effort, he was finally able to secure a couple of stale, dog-eared cards. He neatly stacked them on the table.

With the cigarette still smoldering severely between his lips, his eye began to water furiously from the hot, polluted emissions funneling into it. He cleared the tears with his index and forefingers, sliding the cards toward Kinnie and Kimmie with his other hand.

—Here's my card. We all live in the same house back home. So whoever answers the phone can probably give you some kind of help. But me and Billy can both be reached there.

The two young women each secured a card in identical black leather pocketbooks. Kim pushed business cards and other sheets of paper in his direction. He inspected the data briefly, folding it carefully together into a little packet, which he slipped into his shirt pocket.

—Saw you shakin' on the silver screen
Yeah, your love is like a jellybean
But I don't know where we'll turn up next
I don't know where we'll turn up
Made in Saigon by a Vietnamese baby
And I don't know where we're gonna turn up next
I don't know where we'll turn up next.

310

Vetter noticed the lack of a definitive chorus in the song and wondered if he might not need to send his young protégé to "songwriting school," in order to learn some of the more sophisticated techniques of the craft. The idea seemed quite reasonable.

Upon the song's conclusion, the band neatly finessed into the sprightly spaghetti western of "Coca Cola."

From the tear-blurred corner of his runny red left eye, Mak could see a commotion stirring near the entry of the club. A hubbub. A clatter of people clustered near the doorway, scurrying frantically—like angry fire ants stirring around an anxious mound.

Suddenly, a scruffy, dark-haired man of average height, wearing a black leather jacket, black t-shirt, faded blue jeans, and beat-up black motorcycle boots emerged into the room, commanding attention from every corner. It was Bruce Springsteen, escorted by a roadie-looking guy, who was carrying a guitar case.

Bruce spotted Jordan Archer and swiftly approached the table. He was surprised to see A. Cousins Vetter sitting at the table with him.

—Hey, Jordy. What d'ya know? Cuz! This is a surprise! How long has it been?

—I think it's been nearly two years.

—Two years? Jeezuz. Man, time's flyin'.

—These two brilliant young women are my private assistants Kimberly Fields and Kindred Swain.

Bruce graciously greeted Kimmie and Kinnie. Kinnie nudged Mak, and they and Kimmie slid out from their positions in the booth in order to allow him to slip in next to Cuz. Playfully wrestling with his old friend and mentor, the Boss knuckled the top of Cuz's head, mussing his carefully fashioned coiffure.

Leaning over the table past Cuz, Bruce asked Jordy.

—So these're the guys you were tellin' me about, right?

—Yes. The Unreal Gods. Billy Granger and the Unreal Gods—and the Goddesses A Go-Go, of course.

Hesitant, curious laughter all around.

—They sound good. A lotta fun. I like 'em. Tight.

—Oh. Say. Bruce...

Archer beckoned toward Annie.

—This is Ann Fisher, she's an associate of the band and our families are very close.

Courteously half-rising, Bruce smiled warmly as he grasped Annie's with his own firm hand.

—And that is Mak Pippin.

As Mak half stood, he corrected.

—Poppin. Mak P**o**ppin

—Mak Poppin. I'm very sorry, Mak.

The Boss playfully waggled fingertips with him, and then he gave Mak an officious two-finger scout salute as they returned to their seats. Bruce, Jordan Archer and Cuz engaged in friendly crosstalk, while Kimmie and Kinnie mapped out a complex stratagem.

As they stared off into the distance, Mak and Annie were not quite able to assimilate the enormity of the events that had transpired in the past few hours.

The huddle between the big three broke up and Jordy spoke up.

—So, Mak. What would you say to having Bruce sit in on a few songs with the band?

His mind swimming in an eddied undertow, Mak sat stunned for a moment. Then he snapped free.

—Jeez, I'll sure ask 'em. When?

—Well, tonight, I would say.

—No, no. I meant right now? In fifteen minutes? Next set?

Jordy turned back to Cuz and Bruce and discussed the options. He swiveled back in Mak's direction.

—Anytime would be fine. Whenever the band would feel comfortable having him come up to play. Whatever works.

It slowly dawned upon Mak just where he was and with whom he was sitting and having that conversation. It wasn't as if he was palavering with Norm, the Cowboys' manager. He was negotiating with Jordan Archer, A. Cousins Vetter and Bruce Springsteen about Bruce sitting in with the Unreal Gods. That was fucking crazy.

He excused himself and lit a cigarette as he moved, cutting through the audience toward the foot of the stage. From his vantage point, Billy could see him bounding through the crowd. Must be something important.

—Coca cola.
Every night. Every day.
That's what I want.
That's what I say.
Coca. Coca. Coca cola.

Billy pulled away from the mic and Col took over with a stinging highly reverbed solo. Slightly exasperated, Billy again leaned down to receive the latest transmission from Mak.

—Billy, man. Fuckin' Bruce is here. Fuckin' Bruce Springsteen. The Boss! Bruce!! He wants to jam with the band.

His face not necessarily lighting up, Billy bit his lip contemplatively.

—I don't know, Mak. Lets talk about it at the break. We're doin' okay.

Having made his point, Billy backpedaled and returned to the protective coven of his bandmates, who were coming down the homestretch of "Coca Cola."

As if by lightning struck dumb as a stump, Mak mutely stood, his mind reeling in a strange combination of bewilderment and embarrassment. The bewilderment was familiar enough, but the embarrassment was not at all typical.

He was embarrassed that he might be forced into a position where he had to represent the band and snub Bruce Springsteen. Mak decided he would wait until the break and see if he could convince Billy to jam with Bruce, if merely for the publicity it would generate back home, but more importantly, for the possible camaraderie that could be forged from playing a few songs together.

Mak was determined that Billy follow through, as it was Annie's friend Jordan Archer who had organized the entire evening at the Peppermint, inviting Vetter and Bruce to the show. It was one thing for Billy to shit on Mak and the band— and their professional integrity. It was quite another to humiliate Jordan Archer in front of his famous friends.

Suddenly standing in a black and white world—cold, short breaths of sad gray desperation crept through his pale, tremulous body and down his spine, to the bottoms of his feet. Flop sweat formed above his brow. Nervously, Mak lit another cigarette from the remains of its predecessor.

Surreptitiously, he tossed the spent butt to the floor, crushing it with the toe of his black dress shoe. In disheartened exasperation, he kneaded his eye with the palm of his hand and, turning at the waist, peered out across the crowd to the booth at the table by the door, where he could clearly see the band's future slowly receding in the dim smoky light. He quickly ran and hid in the green room, where he smoked a third consecutive cigarette, unsure what he should do.

The band blew through hot, smart takes on "English Boy," "Neutral Stomp" and "Stereo Area" before stopping to guzzle beer and catch a sweated breath. They followed with "Madilyn's Rough and "Used to Hang Around." Then Billy said.

—Well, boys and girls, by my watch, it looks like it's almost midnight. So we're gonna take a short break, and we'll be right back to fuck ya' up real good.

They wham-bam thank you ma'ammed the finish before hustling from the stage toward the haven of the dressing room. The rush of them blew in to find Mak sitting opposite the door in one of the gold satin, overstuffed armchairs—a nervously baffled expression on his chowder-white face.

As everyone filtered in, Candy and MJ shared the other armchair. Mick sat on the arm of Mak's chair and the rest spread out upon the two matching purple velvet sofas that faced each other, separated by a dark-brown wooden coffee table. Joints broke out all around as bottles of Rolling Rock were liberally dispersed.

Dripping in sweat, Billy was the last to enter the room. He instantly caught Mak's distressed gaze the moment he came through the door. He shagged one of the joints from Billy D. and took a huge hit before passing it to Col on the opposite couch.

—That was a good set you guys. Hopefully it was good enough for our famous guests.

Suddenly irate, Mak erupted.

—What's up with you, Billy? What *is* this bullshit? Are you, like, tryin' to fuckin' sabotage everything we've tried to do for the past two years? Are you, like, uh, *afraid* of success or something? What's the fuckin' deal?

—Look, Poppy, we don't need these guys. We're doin' just fine on our own without them.

—Have you fuckin' lost your mind, Billy? That's fuckin' A. Cousins Vetter out there. Rough Edge Records? He's here to see *your* goddamned band. Not fuckin' Billy Joel or somebody. And his buddy, fuckin' Bruce Springsteen is here to jam with you, and you just want to blow them all off.

Having not been previously advised as to the events taking place up to that point, the members of the assemblage pooled great aghast-stricken questioning eyes in Billy's direction.

—We don't need to, like, sell out to make it in this business, Pop. We can do it on our own terms.

—So. What? We're gonna, like, form our own fuckin' label? We're gonna, like, fuckin' reinvent the music industry wheel here? Why the hell did we come to New York, anyway? Why are we recordin' at the Power Station? I thought it was to like try 'n' attract label interest. We've got fuckin' Rough *Edge* interested in us. We've got Bruce Springsteen here and he wants to jam with the band. C'mon, Billy! What more do you want?

—We haven't rehearsed any stuff he'd want to do—except maybe 'Gloria', who wants to fuckin' do 'Gloria'?

Like a dirty old man, Col muttered.

—I'd do Gloria any time.

—We've never jammed with anyone before, why should we fuckin' start now? I don't care who the hell it is. We don't need anybody to come in here and try to steal our thunder.

—Steal our thunder? Shit, Billy. Fuckin' listen to yourself, man. You're goin' against everything you've ever said about the band. Jammin' with Bruce would be huge news back home.

—Pop. What do we want to jam with Springsteen for? What good is he to us? He's the competition man. We gotta think for ourselves here. Bruce Springsteen. He's the seventies, Poppy. We're the eighties. No wonder he wants to meet us. He needs us. We don't need him.

Mak was speechless.

Too stoned and uninformed to really give a shit, the rest of the bunch resumed relaxing.

Into the scene strolled Angie, who had been back at the board, deep in conversation with the house soundman, regarding the merits of the new digital delay technology.

—Hey, guys, what's up? Feels like somethin's goin' on.

His inquest was met with stone dead silence. He threw his hand at the lot of them.

—You guys smoke too mucha that fuckin' weed. It's rottin' yer brains out. Ya' know that? Right?

No response. It fell to Billy to update him.

—Aw, fuck, man, Poppy says Bruce Springsteen wants to jam with us and I don't think it's a good idea.

—Well, man, if you don't think it's a good idea...I ain't arguin' wit cha. It's yer fuckin' show. Yer fuckin' show.

Mak buried his face in his hands. There was no hope.

—Okay. Okay. I'll go tell Bruce to go fuck himself. And I'll go tell fuckin' A. Cousins Vetter to go fuck himself, and I'll go tell Jordan Archer to go fuck himself and I'll go tell poor Annie she can go fuck herself too.

Using Mick's shoulder for leverage, Mak hoisted himself up from the chair.

—You got it, Billy Boy. Whatever you say. You're the fuckin' mastermind. You're the leading Bozo. It's your goddamned Boraxo team. I'm just the fuckin' messenger.

Storming out, Mak slammed the door behind him. Resolute, Angie pounded in the final nails of the coffin he had been constructing for the past four weeks. He muttered.

—Man, you guys need to dump that asshole. You've fuckin' outgrown him. You don't need that shit. I told ya' it wuz too early. Ya' need to ease into this rock star thing. There's a lot to learn.

Frustrated and mortified, Mak plodded toward the booth at the front of the club. He didn't know what he was going to say. He didn't want to ruffle any feathers, but that outcome seemed inevitable.

Behind him, the band stormed the stage, after only about a ten-minute break. Without delay they fell into a fanciful arrangement of "Uptown," Col's tremolo guitar springing around the intro like a rabid rabbit. For Mak, that meant that trying to explain things to the guests would be rendered even more difficult.

—I'm the uptown boy and you're the uptown girl
I'm just an uptown toy in this uptown world
I was an uptown baby baby
Walkin' uptown streets
Goin' uptown crazy crazy
I better move my feet.

Dejectedly, Mak squeezed into the booth next to Annie. Her smile of expectation turned quickly chilly, as his mood was easily read. Hoo boy.

Col took his solo, while Billy chanted.

—Duke duke duke took my girl duke duke
Took my girl duke duke took my girl.

Broken, Mak glanced at Annie with brittle-knitted brow. They both knew Billy was only getting started.

—Duke duke. Yeah. Duke duke.
Hey Duke.
My uptown girl
Glow-rhea
My uptown world
Heyyyyy!!!!!!
Meet the new boss
Same as the old boss
I said Glow-rhea...!

He didn't really just say that, did he? Oh shit, oh fuck. Springsteen abruptly rose from his seat, motioned for Kinnie and Kimmie to get out of his way and he headed straight for the door. He traded no goodbyes. He wished no one well. He was outta there.

His guitar-toter, who had been solitarily stationed at a single table normally occupied by a doorman, abruptly sprang to his feet. He followed the (literal) Boss out of the building to his shiny yellow, top-down, convertible Corvette, which was parked in the No Parking zone out in front of the club.

The toter carefully lay the guitar down in the small storage area behind the front seats of the car. He gingerly hopped into the passenger seat, as Bruce revved the engine and swerved away in a great, gray cloud of immolated tire rubber.

# XXVII

Thursday morning, Mak awoke with his left eyelid a vivid shade of puce—the color of a freshly butchered beef brisket—swollen completely shut. His eyeball itself was candy apple red. Throbbing in pain, it itched unbearably. He lay in his sleeping bag on the cot in the room with Billy D., in the house of a woman who was the mother of a guy he didn't even know. Well, he knew Gilly, but, as it was turning out, not very well.

He lay in his sleeping bag on the cot listening to Billy D. snoring and farting in the bed across from him. The band had been in New York for nearly a month already. They had accomplished very little, save for a somewhat successful Halloween show—which easily could have been dwarfed by a comparable performance back home.

He mulled fate and fortune beneath a fog of ominousness from which he could not escape. At least things couldn't get much worse.

Without warning, Billy and Angie suddenly burst into the room. Billy fanned his hand in front of his face.

—Jesus Christ. What died in here? Open a fuckin' window or somethin'.

Billy D. stirred but did not awaken.

—What the fuck is up with your eye?

—I dunno. It's infected or somethin'. It's all runny and it burns and itches.

—Well, don't get any of that shit on me, man. It looks fuckin' contagious.

A look of distaste and horror crossed Billy's face.

—Mak, man. Get dressed and come on out here. We need to talk to you.

Hopping up from the cot, Mak pulled on his socks and pants. He grabbed the blue, plaid flannel shirt that was draped over the chair at the desk and hurried into the hallway.

—What's up guys? What's goin' on?

—We've been talkin' and...

—*We*? Who's we?

—Me and the band. We've been talkin' and, well, y'know, I think you need to go on back home—y'know? To, like, preserve the continuity of the band? Take one for the team?

—Fuck, Billy. You tie my hands and tell me to fight, and then ya' kick the shit out of me. Wha'd'ya want me to do? I've tried everything I can think of.

—That's just it, Poppy. We don't really need ya' to, y'know, like, *do* anything. It's all, like, set up. We're booked in the studio and we've got the gig set at the club. We don't really need a manager here.

Billy impatiently paced around the hallway; as Angie leaned against the wall and said nothing.

—We just really need to do what we need to do to get done in the studio. And I'm thinkin' we need to pare things down, if we're gonna have enough money to get it all done.

—Well, Billy, if you're not gonna let me manage the team anymore, can't I at least be a base coach?

—You can do a lot more at home than you can here, Mak. You can get gigs set up for when we come back. And you can get the wheels turning on 'Happy Santa.' You can get everything organized. Then we won't need Tommy to do it. One more person out of the chain.

—Well what about the girls? What about Billy and Mick? Are you fuckin' gonna send them home too?

—Yeah...

Billy hem-haw huffed.

—Yeah. That's the plan. The girls, they're already, like, headin' home. It's just you three that we had to, um, decide on.

—Okay, Billy. Okay. If that's what ya' want. Then fuck it. Okay. I'm not gonna argue with you. Like I said last night, it's your band.

It was in that very instant that Mak remembered that the band was not at all a democracy, nor had it ever been. That was what Billy had made clear at QP, way back when the band was first getting together. It was his band and he made the decisions. He would consider other opinions, but the final say was his and he had made up his mind. Tier two was going home.

As Mak stepped back into the bedroom with Billy D., Billy whispered *sotto voce*.

—Let D. know what's goin' on. We'll have to get all the arrangements together for everybody's trip home. And you oughta get that eye checked out, man. It looks fuckin' terrible.

Mak nodded obediently.

—Yeah. When I get back to Portland, I guess.

Angie and Billy made their way into the bedroom that Gib and Daw shared, to tell them they would soon be moving out of Mama Belladro's house, back to Angie's apartment. The announcement was favorably received. The pair then went up the steps to the attic, where they delivered the news to Mick—who was not horribly upset by the disclosure.

Immediately after Billy and Angie left, Mak ran out to the phone table in the hallway. Sliding down the wall to sit on the floor next to the phone table, he called over to Angie's apartment to reconnoiter with Candy. He called, hung up and re-called three times—a signal that had worked before—to find out what Candy knew, if she knew anything.

Candy answered haltingly, her throat as dry and barren as a prairie.

—Mak, honey? Is that you?

—Yeah, Candy. Billy and Angie were just here. Did you know that Billy was sendin' everybody home?

—Sending everyone home? What do you mean 'everybody'?

—Me 'n Mick and Billy.

—Are you really that shocked? It seemed like this has been in the cards for a while. Don't you think?

—Yeah. I guess so. When are you and MJ leavin'?

—We're supposed to board at five-fifteen. So we'll probably leave around three or so. Annie's going to take us to the airport. I was thinking about stopping by over there to say goodbye to everyone before we left. You'll be around then, I guess?

—Where else would I go?

—True. True. Well maybe you should give Annie a call and see what she wants do about riding back to Portland with you.

—That's a good idea. We can figure out a schedule. I'd rather get back home sooner than later.

—Wouldn't we all, Makkie. Wouldn't we all. Okay. Well, I'll see you a little later then.

—Yeah. Okay, Candy. Bye.

He plunged down the button on the phone, disconnecting the call. Then he dialed the number of Annie's brother.

—Uh, Tim?
Yeah, hi. This is Mak.
I'm with the band? Mak?
Yeah. Yeah, Mak, the manager.
Is Annie there?
Could I talk to her please?

—Hello?

—Annie? Hey it's...

—Mak. What's up? I think Candy was talking about stopping over there this afternoon, on the way out to the airport.

—Yeah. Yeah. I just talked to her. That's what she said.

—Okay. So what's up?

—Well, I wanted to, uh, let you know that Billy's sendin' all the, like, *non-essential* members home. So I'll be available to ride the train home with you whenever you're ready.

—That's pretty sudden. Lowered the boom, eh? Well, after last night, I guess you saw that coming.

—What do you mean?

—-You know. You and Billy weren't on the same page at all last night. He didn't want to do what you wanted him to do. It's like a teenage boy defying his dad. He's not listening to you. It doesn't matter what you say. You could have told him there was a solid gold car sitting outside the club, and it was all his. He still would have told you to go to hell.

—Well, there *was*, like, a solid gold Cadillac sittin' in that booth last night, and Billy treated him like a broke down VW. There was a solid gold Corvette parked right next to him, and, like, y'know, a solid gold Mercedes on the other side. And Billy fuckin' keyed all of 'em and fuckin' walked away. I think he takes all this for granted.

—You're right about that, Mak. He hasn't thanked me for my help. I know he never thanked Candy for what she did with the Halloween costumes. That was magical.

—And he hasn't like thanked me or Mick or D. either, for anything we've done out here. It's like we're all just along for the ride. Well, I'm ready to get off the tour bus and head on home.

—I guess if everyone else is leaving, there's no reason for me to stay. It's not like he's going to listen to anything I tell him. And there are things I could be doing at home. I've been here long enough.

—Me, too. I've been here long enough, too. It's, like, uh, time to go home.

—Time to go home. Yes. Time to go home. It sure is. So, Mak, when were you planning on leaving?

—Any time, really. Now? They want to kick us out of this place as soon as possible. This weekend? If we can make it happen. This weekend?

—I could be ready to go by then. You call Amtrak and I'll talk to my brother about giving us a ride to the train station. I think there's one in Newark.

—Okay. I'll call about our tickets this afternoon. I guess I'll see you when you bring Candy over, so we can talk more about it then.

—Okay.

—Okay. Bye.

—Bye.

Again he pushed the phone button down, in order to obtain a dial tone. He fished the Yellow pages out from the stack of phone books under the table and called the Newark Amtrak station.

Eventually, he was able to secure passage for himself and Annie on the 67 Northeast Regional, down to DC; then on the 51 Cardinal—from DC to Chicago; then aboard the number 7, Empire Builder from Chicago to Seattle, and finally, the 513 from Seattle to Portland. One hundred and eleven hours, more or less. Four and a half days. More or less.

The two main lines—the Cardinal and the Empire Builder—had sleeping and dining cars. Mak opted for those deciding that the band would be happy to foot the bill for the extra cost.

Soon after, Mick and Billy D. began to stir and it was up to Mak to thrash out with them the decision. It was time to head home. It was odd: Mick and Billy D. seemed relieved. They seemed happy. They seemed glad that they were to be sent away.

The three of them went up to Mick's attic apartment, smoked a joint and puzzled together the pieces of an explanation as to exactly what had occurred in the month that they had been back East. None among them was able to assemble anything rational—other than to reiterate the contention that there was really no reason why they should have come in the first place.

Confidentially, all three agreed that Happy was hands down the highpoint of the whole trip. Each expressed the desire to have seen more of her. Mak willfully suppressed the overwhelming urge to admit that he actually *had* seen more of her—in fact, he had seen all of her, to be precise.

The trio discussed with Gib and Daw the pending changes. The two of them would be sharing the room at Angie's place that Candy and MJ would be vacating. So, their living arrangements would remain more or less the same, except that they would be in the same quarters as the rest of the band. That would make a lot of things so much easier, as far as going over the day's recording sessions and any issues that might arise.

With the intention of finding something to eat, everyone cleaned up from the grime of the previous evening, taking turns in the bathroom to shower, shave, and prepare for what was surely going to be an interesting day. Mak did the best he could to irrigate his eye. He determined that he would try to obtain eye drops at a drug store, if he were to come across one in their ensuing endeavors.

The quintet then hiked over to the Newport Centre mall, to have lunch at the McDonald's on the food court. While in the mall, Mak found a Newberry's, where he was able to secure a variety of eye products and bandages..

Shortly after they returned, Annie, Candy and MJ arrived at Mama's house to say goodbye to the gang. Hearing the knock at the door, Augie sprinted from his bedroom and dashed down the stairs. His bat wagged and bobbed behind his head as he shouted.

—I got it! I got it, Ma! I got it!

Authoritatively, he swung the door open, astonished to see the three pretty women standing in front of him again. Petrified, not saying a word to them, Augie let them in and quickly ran upstairs to alert the proper authorities. The girls shrugged guardedly, unsure what to make of Augie.

As Mak came down to greet them, Candy could see something wrong with Mak's face.

—Mak, hon, what's wrong with your eye?

—Aw, I think it's like some kinda infection or somethin'.

—I think you've got pink eye. Or in your case, I guess it's a shade of mauve. It goes wonderfully well with the bright red of your eyeball. Oh. It looks terrible. Really bad.

Cringing ruefully, Mak sighed. His shoulders dropped like two blue plaid flannel gunnysacks filled with dirt.

—Yeah, I don't know what happened. It just like all of a sudden started botherin' me last night.

—You know, they've got stuff for that. You should go to the drugstore and get some eye drops. For everyone's sake, I hope is not the infectious variety. If it's a bacterial infection, you'll need to have that looked at by a doctor. Hopefully, it's just an allergy. You should stop smoking for a while

323

—Aw, when we get back to Portland, I'll, like, go see a doctor or somethin'. I already got a bunch of stuff at, uh, Newberry's. I got, like, three different kinds of eye drops. And cotton pads and gauze and adhesive tape. I'm all set with that.

He one-eyed Candy with defensive singularity.

—And I won't be able to really smoke on the train. Maybe in the smokin' car, if they, like, have one, I could.

—Well, I'm glad you're taking care of it. It seems like you've thought it out. That's good. You don't want to mess around with that stuff. You could go blind.

Purring, she smiled at him seductively.

—But, I suppose if you haven't gone blind by now, you never will, eh Mister Hairy Bear Paws?

Mak began to perspire along his hairline. Blushing effusively, his whole head temporarily turned the same color as his infected eye. Mauve.

Impatient, and bored with the conversation, Annie interrupted.

—We should probably get going if we're going to make it to the airport on time.

Candy shook free of her sexy nurse mode.

—Well, I want to say goodbye to Gibby and Daw and Mickey and Billy. I don't know when I'll see any of you guys again.

—You better get going then, Can. We can't stay too long.

Mak led Annie and the Goddesses upstairs, where they hugged the boys and said goodbye. Tears welling in her eyes, Candy was especially emotional toward Mick and Billy D.

They quickly returned back downstairs. Standing at the door, Mak said to Annie.

—Oh. I almost forgot. I got our train schedule set up. But I don't think you're gonna like it.

—Why is that?

—Because it leaves at three-thirty Saturday morning.

—Three thirty? Are you serious? Three-thirty? Good lord.

—Yeah. Do you think, uh, do you think Tim will be okay with that?

—Oh I think he'll be pretty good with getting rid of me any old time. I think I've overstayed my welcome by about ten days.

Concluding his delineation of the itinerary, Mak continued.

—And I guess we'll get back into Portland, like, sometime Wednesday afternoon.

With a certain fevered determination and without a hint of forewarning, Augie came bounding back down the stairs, melodically chanting a portion of the theme from the "William Tell Overture."

—No meat. No meat. No meat meat meat.

Marching up to Candy, he faced her squarely. His eyes met hers directly.

—I wanna give ya' somethin'. A goin' away present.

Rearing away slightly, Candy eventually reengaged Augie's steadfast gaze.

—Oh, Augie. That's so cute. You're such a darling. But you don't need to give me anything. I'm flattered that you even thought of me.

—No, I wanna give you this.

Based on the intense crush he had developed for her the only other time they had met, Augie graciously bestowed to Candy his Reggie Jackson bat—as if it were a fur stole.

—Augie. You're such a doll. That's about the nicest gift anyone has ever given me. That's so swee-eet.

She sang.

—But I couldn't take your bat. Like I said, I'm very flattered that you would even think of me...

She pushed the bat back toward him and kissed him on the forehead, at which point Augie began to sob inconsolably. Grief-stricken, he pulled away from the group and rushed upstairs to his room where he could cry in private. In a half-pleading voice, Candy delicately called after him.

—No meat, Augie. No meat.

# XXVII

From a very early age, she was aptly described as fastidious. In fact, Caren Deeds knew how to spell "fastidious" by the age of six. She could spell words before she knew what they meant. She won the second grade competition by successfully spelling "sesquicentennial" after Robby Ellsworth had struck out on "Antarctica."

She remained the reigning spelling bee champion throughout her grade school years. Her name, legend at Ainsworth Elementary, was invoked in hushed reverence due to the enormity of her achievement. Except for a solitary bump in her career, she was perfect.

Only Anthony Snyder loomed larger in school history, for his incredible ability to add, subtract, multiply, divide, or perform any other mathematical function: all in his head. He would blurt out the (correct) answer when asked. He would simply write it down when tested. Because there was none, he showed no work on any problem. Just the answer.

Her mother called Anthony a "prodigy," a word that Caren had no problem at all spelling. That one was pretty easily sounded out. And, actually, she had learned "prodigious" first and "prodigy" by working her way back. She related to words that way. An algebra of letters, composing precise formulas of sound and equations of meaning. She organized words almost mathematically, in ways similar to Anthony's gift for numbers.

It was not altogether surprising that Anthony was also a prodigy at the piano. He composed his first symphony when he was ten years old. And he began touring the country, playing with orchestras, by age thirteen. Caren Deeds took the more traditional path toward scholastic success.

She never got a B. Not in all her years in school—not even in college. She only received A's in her classes. Every test. Every quiz. It was a point of pride for her. A point of obsession.

Only an A would do. Only an A was acceptable. Only an A. Nothing short of perfection was satisfactory. And Caren realized no less than perfection on every occasion in her scholastic career. Except for once. And that one time changed everything.

It was exceedingly rare for any item within the world of Caren Deeds to be out of place. Since earliest childhood, her bedroom was organized like a museum. Her bed was always carefully made, her stuffed bear and her elephant carefully placed upon the covers at either side of her life-sized golden retriever doll, Captain Kirk.

Tall wooden shelves, dedicated to valuable artifacts, were arranged against the wall next to her closet. She was particularly fond of crystal animals. She also liked horses very much, maintaining an extensive collection of horse-related pieces—crafted from any media, the compilation of which she dedicated an entire shelf.

Her sister, Valerie, younger by fifteen months, was not allowed in the room unless bidden or otherwise accompanied. It was Caren's private sanctuary—only invited guests were welcome. Woe to those who dared transgress.

Caren's father held a seat on the Portland City Council, a position he maintained for seventeen years before retiring. The name Jack Deeds was always in the news, as he proved to be a vocal advocate for the arts, the homeless, and the disadvantaged; he vehemently opposed the proposed Mount Hood Freeway.

While serving on the council, Jack was reunited with Neil Goldschmidt, an old University of Oregon classmate. Jack found an enduring ally in the man who became the mayor of Portland. Later in the eighties Neil Goldschmidt was Oregon's two-term governor.

The mortise locking together the Deed's household tenon was Jean, wife to Jack and mother to Caren and Valerie. Jean was adept at organizing and managing functions. She was considered a grand hostess at luncheons and dinner parties the couple often conducted.

In addition, she was essential to the planning of the annual Catlin Gabel School rummage sale. Jack and Jean had elected to send Valerie to Catlin Gabel, after the young girl had problems with her third grade teacher at Ainsworth. Jean was bright and cheery cheer cheerful, but she was desperately unhappy—feeling frustrated, unfulfilled and unappreciated. Her life played out like a shadow behind a scrim.

And there was Guinea, the Guinea pig. When Caren was eight, she and Valerie kept Guinea in the garage. The little rodent had extremely long gray and white fur. The family were never absolutely certain as to Guinea's gender. They referred to him as a male. He was a quiet pet, typically not typically given to dramatic outbursts—except for the occasional piercing whistle he would emit every so often for no apparent reason.

It was on a sunny summer Sunday afternoon, after the family returned from a trip to Hood River for a short weekend that Caren found Guinea dead at the scene. Though they had only been absent from the premises for about sixteen hours, Guinea found a way and a means to inexplicably expire.

Employing her nascent interest in the fields of medicine and forensics, Caren performed a perfunctory autopsy, prudently inspecting the deceased animal from head to stumpy tail. But she was unable to determine a cause of death. He was found unconscious in the wood shavings in front of his exercise wheel. Caren surmised that he might have died of a heart attack; perhaps from too much exercise. However, she knew too that Guinea pigs were easily frightened to death, just like rabbits. Maybe Guinea had seen something that frightened it.

Not long after Guinea's fateful passing, and despite the unfortunate outcome, Jack and Jean resolved that the girls were old enough to have a dog. Thus Wally entered into the fold. Wally was a mutt—possibly of Golden Retriever and Newfoundland extraction. He was black. He had the feathery coat of a Golden Retriever, but he was the size of a corner bungalow.

Willful, but not necessarily smart, as dogs go, Wally was loyal to a fault. He was also something of a crybaby. Wally bawled in a loud wail at the slightest provocation. He was also massively strong. He once ran out into the street right in front of a delivery van going about thirty miles an hour. The van struck him bumper to right side of cranium—so hard that Wally was spun around completely, smacking the left side of his head on the rear driver's side panel of the truck. Startled, but otherwise uninjured, he immediately ran home and never left the yard again.

In addition, Wally was giftedly availed of a magnificent baritone singing voice, one that rivaled Pavarotti. He seemed to be most responsive to reed instruments: saxophones, bassoons, especially harmonicas. Bob Dylan's songs would set off full, glorious arias. The girls noticed that he howled a particular aria every time in response to a specific piece of music. He had created his own parts. He jammed.

Most of all he was a big doofus. Not getting his way caused Wally great consternation. As a means of registering complaint, he would often initiate a sequence of heavy breathing through his nostrils, which culminated in a vague, pitiful sob. His big black nose would bob on his snout like a giant olive, twitching pathetically. It was very odd to see a dog of around one hundred and forty pounds so full of self-pity. But that was Wally. He was the sensitive sort.

It was in September, at the beginning of the sixth grade, her final year at Ainsworth. On the first day of school, Caren and her teacher, Mrs. Dufer, were surprised to find another Karen in their class.

Over the summer Karen Palumbo's father had obtained a job at Intel in Beaverton. She had transferred to Ainsworth from Ardenwald Grade School in Milwaukie, where she was highly regarded for her prowess at kickball and her experimental relationship with one Amber Bell.

Karen's family moved into a mansion-like estate, located off Patton Road. The Paulson family, of Paulson Furniture fame, had formerly occupied it until Rosemary Paulson ran off with a carpet installer from Marion's Carpets named Rick Vincent. Thus inspired, Rosemary's husband, Alan, chose to blow his brains out in the kitchen of the Paulson family hacienda.

Because the kitchen was done in stainless steel appliances and fixtures, with granite countertops all around, cleanup was quick and easy. The house was on the market within a month. Rosemary's affair with Rick Dixon eventually ran its course. After about six weeks, she saw the error of her ways and checked herself into Serenity Lane in Eugene. She later remarried.

For better or worse, to avoid crazy confusion through the whole year, Mrs. Dufer elected to give one of the Karen/Carens a nickname—allowing one of the girls to keep her God-given name, while forcing the other to permanently cleft her identity, with an uneasy new appellation.

Carrie/Kari was the name Mrs. Dufer devised for the loser. Simple enough, a pleasant stump of the original.

At first, Mrs. Dufer considered having the girls draw for cards, before her better judgment prevailed. Then she briefly considered flipping a coin, but discarded that notion as well. Recognizing her position as an educator, Mrs. Dufer felt the need to provide the girls with a learning experience. Or a learning trauma, perhaps.

A quick spelling bee would do. Mrs. Dufer had to have known of Caren's propensity for the spelled word. It was like a home field advantage. Caren meant to make short work of Karen.

However Karen held her own, through "halcyon" "nebulae" and "remedial." Caren countered with "radii" "kleptomaniac" and "syllabus." Mrs. Dufer did not have that many more words at hand, as she had expected for the contest to have been concluded by then.

Karen effortlessly flew through "obsequious." But, for one brief moment, Caren lost her balance. She stumbled. A-C-C-E-S-S-A-B-L-E. In the fleeting instant that those final four syllables fled from her lips, Caren knew she had made a careless mistake. She tried to correct herself. I-B-L-E. I-B-L-E. A-C-C-E-S-S-I-B-L-E. To no avail.

She had misspelled the word before she had spelled it correctly. Mrs. Dufer had no choice in her decision. Caren had lost. The unthinkable had happened. And her loss was deeper than just the mere humiliation of defeat—she feared she was going to be Carrie for the rest of her life. And she was.

Carrie was popular in junior high and later at Lincoln High School. Lincoln was renowned throughout Portland for being the place where the children of doctors, lawyers and local government officials went to school. Grant on the eastside, Wilson and Lake Oswego in the southwest, all had their bright spots. Nouveau riche. But Lincoln extolled a long-won pioneer family pedigree, which was held far above the stench of any social sniff test.

Given the circumstances surrounding their first encounter, it was not readily foreseeable that Carrie and Karen Palumbo would become fast friends. But they did, remaining so through their high school years. They performed on the dance team together. The two of them excelled at softball.

Karen was pretty, with thick, dark, shoulder-length hair, which she wore straight, with long bangs—Cleopatra style, like that of a model. Her opulent, brown eyes looked like two perfect round cups of coffee, heavily made-up in the mode of Cher. She was a little too curvy to be a model—or Cher, for that matter.

Both of them adored America's "Horse With No Name." They were fond of Gary

Wright's "Dreamweaver;" Seals and Crofts' "Summer Breeze" and "Diamond Girl;" Paul McCartney's "Band on the Run;" and "I Shot the Sheriff" by Eric Clapton.

During their freshman year in high school, they became enamored of the Bee Gees' "Jive Talkin." They sang the song in unison at every opportunity. They would tunelessly chant "Dave Walker," the name of Karen's boyfriend, the poor, hapless schlemiel, who never got to second base with her even in their senior year, after almost four years of committed dating. Dave never figured out for whom she was saving herself, but, he eventually deduced apparently it was not him.

In truth, Dave had been Carrie's boyfriend first, all through junior high school. But though she liked the boy, Carrie had no real interest in him. So in an effort to avert any undue calamity, she attempted to slowly create an ulterior relationship for him, hoping that he would slowly fade from the picture, as a matter of course. Karen was cute and personable. And she was available. In essence, Karen took over from Carrie the role of indifferent girlfriend.

Carrie had a few boyfriends after Dave. During her freshman year she had an awkward, transitory relationship with a boy named Rome Randall. They kissed on the school bus on couple of occasions, and he tried to put his hand under her sweater once. But he was summarily rebuffed and he never tried again. Eventually, he drifted away of his own accord, without requiring any tertiary assistance from Karen.

During the fall of her junior year, she had a brief dalliance with Joshua Lovejoy, a descendant of Asa Lovejoy, one of the city's founding fathers. Josh was a devout Lutheran and never even tried to kiss Carrie. Ultimately, the following year, he would become student body president. He seemed to lose interest in Carrie after about six months. She was pretty enough, but she was simply too studious for an affluent, carefree adolescent boy, of which Josh Lovejoy—despite his lofty station and rigid morals—qualified as one.

In the spring, while traveling with the Cardinal team to a softball tournament at David Douglas High in deep southeast Portland, she met Mark Casper. She spotted him in the stands. He was checking out her ass as she bent over to grab a rosin bag before settling into the on-deck circle. He saw her catch him looking at her butt, and he blushed a bright shade of heady red.

She smiled at him captivatingly. Her green eyes sparkled and her golden brown hair glinted in the April sun. He was handsome, with close-cropped brown hair, a cleft in his chin and pale, piercing eyes. After the game, he stood behind home plate on the other side of the backstop, calling to her to attract her attention. They spoke for a while before the team prepared to load onto the bus to go home.

Writing her phone number down on a piece of notebook paper, he tucked it into the breast pocket of his light blue oxford shirt. Breathing a long sigh, he watched her butt again as she walked away; watched her walk all the way out to the bus in the stadium parking lot.

As their relationship slowly progressed, it became readily apparent to the boy that his girlfriend was obsessively academic. It was hard for him to get her to slow down and unwind. She put enormous pressure on herself to succeed in school. She wanted to be a doctor, maybe even a coroner. Or, maybe a nurse. She was not absolutely certain, but she thought she preferred serving the living. Regardless, in her mind, only being the class valedictorian would do. That had been her goal since enrolling at Lincoln in her freshman year.

Mark found Carrie to be a very attractive girl. He liked slim girls. Carrie was slim, though not boyish. She had small, but full, flawless champagne-glass shaped breasts and of course there was her cute round ass, which especially appealed to him. He thought she was pretty, in a professorial sort of way.

With intensely dedicated adolescent persistence, he made frequent attempts to get her bra unclasped and her pants undone—generally without success. But there were enough occasions when he was able to soften her resistance that he was encouraged to continue his quest. Mark was not without some knowledge of a few techniques relative to the subject of sex.

During his sophomore year, he regularly went all the way with a girl. Calista Lynch. In fact, he only went out with her because it had been confirmed by others that she would put out if sufficiently warmed up and gently encouraged. Mark adequately mastered enough maneuvers to succeed on all counts. Their liaison ended only after Lance Kreiter, a popular senior, became interested in her—consequently diminishing her attraction to a mere sophomore. She had her motivations too.

Carrie and Mark remained an item all throughout their senior year, despite the logistical nightmare of trying to get together while living forty-five minutes apart. In order to meet with Carrie, Mark had to borrow his mother's Chevelle, which was always a nightmare to secure. Mark's mother was an alcoholic and often forgot the agreements that she had made with him. His father had died in a car accident a few years earlier and his mother fell to pieces.

Because of Carrie's constant participation on the dance team, it was mostly up to Mark to attend her events, to spend his time at Lincoln functions. Mark was on the Scots basketball team, but Carrie was never able to attend his games, as she had her own activities to carry out. Though he never complained, Carrie knew Mark was not very happy with the arrangement.

Evidently he was more unhappy than she knew. On a Saturday afternoon in April, near the end of her senior year, Carrie was at the Lloyd Center with Val, shopping for a bathing suit and some new jeans. They were wandering around Morrow's Nut House, trying to decide what they wanted. Carrie was partial to Morrow's butter toffee nuts.

Absently gazing down the counter, out the window toward the esplanade, Carrie thought she caught brief glimpse of him passing by. A fleet flinting glint of recognition. She followed her instincts, out of the shop and onto the walkway— spotting two figures sitting down at Hot Dog On A Stick.

Before she could react, Carrie saw Mark passionately kissing a cute girl with bottle-blond hair. They were making out fiercely, right in front of the whole damn world. Disconsolate, Carrie spied Mark furtively cup, with a massaging hand, the girl's breast through her white t-shirt. Broken, Carrie stumbled back toward Valerie, who was just emerging from Morrow's.

Without uttering a word, Carrie continued to walk in the direction of the stairs, which led down to the parking level. Quizzically concerned, Valerie followed closely behind. The sisters silently made their way home in their mom's Chrysler Cordoba, with Carrie crying softly as she drove. She did not answer Val's increasingly agitated inquires as to her well-being. She merely sobbed and sniffed—snot and tears streaming down her face and into her lap.

Carrie never spoke to Mark again. She would not take his phone calls. She would not come to the door on the two occasions he appeared unannounced at the Deeds residence. She threw all of his subsequent letters into the trash, unopened. Mark did not completely understand the nature of his wrongdoing. He continued to think that his other relationship remained a well-kept secret. There was no bliss in his ignorance.

She did not recover quickly from that betrayal. It is possible that she never fully recovered. She had trusted Mark. She had let him do things, and had done things for him, that she had never experienced before. She thought they were committed. She had already decided not to go to the University of Oregon, but to attend Portland State, just to be near to him while he went to the University of Portland on a basketball scholarship.

The event so troubled Carrie she ultimately changed her plans. That summer, she got a job at the perfume counter in the downtown Meier and Frank department store. Instead of quitting in the fall, to begin her classes at Portland State, she made a decision to remain at her job and take the year off from school.

Because they had high hopes for their eldest daughter, Jack and Jean were understandably alarmed at the turn of events. But they stood behind Carrie's choice, perceiving that she needed time to heal and figure out her life. She was at that difficult age between adolescence and adulthood. There was no rush. And there was no sense in pressuring her. It wouldn't do any good anyway.

A year off from school stretched into three, as Carrie became fond of having money. Still living at home, she paid her parents a nominal rent. With no other debts, she managed to save enough money to buy her own car. She also created a savings account to put away money for school. By the end of her fourth summer on the job, she had saved more than seven thousand dollars.

And though she had been away from school for quite some time—being her class valedictorian, a member of the National Honor Society and having never earned any grade other than A in her entire scholastic career—she had no difficulty in securing a scholarship into the pre-nursing program at Portland State.

She remained unsure as to whether she wanted to pursue nursing, or to become a doctor. In addition to her attraction to the idea of becoming a coroner, Carrie had been giving a lot of thought to becoming a veterinarian.

The veterinary arts program was a challenging specialty to pursue. But nothing in the pre-nursing program would be precluded in the veterinary program, at least not in the first year. So she enrolled in pre-nursing to give herself another year to decide on her profession.

In the fall of nineteen eighty, she moved into an apartment of her own, on Jefferson, just a few blocks from the Portland State campus. And she began her pursuit of a calling in the medical field. Carrie's life seemed to be moving in a natural progression toward a rewarding career and a respected vocation. She more or less had her life planned out ahead of her. She was certain she wanted to be in the medical field. Everything was in order; everything in its proper place.

And then she met Billy.

# XXVIII

—Hello?

—Hey, Pop Rocks. It's Billy.

Though he kind of liked it, Mak had never heard that nickname before.

—Billy?

Confused, Billy tried to illuminate.

—Billy Granger? The *leading Bozo*?

Mak was not sure how to respond. He was not certain as to which Billy Granger he was speaking. Billy the bandmate and friend, or Billy the tyrant. Laid back west coast Billy or uptight Billy of the east coast.

—Yeah. Hey. Billy. What's up?

—I'm just checkin' in, man. So the trip home went okay, then?

—Yeah. We all got back safe and sound.

—Did you get that fucked up eye looked at?

—Yeah. Yeah. It's gettin' better now.

—How about Candy. Is she feelin' okay?

—Yeah, man. She's, like, almost completely better.

—Cool. Cool.

—I got the welcome home gigs booked at Last Hurrah for the weekend after Thanksgiving. It's the Pub Crawl that weekend. Thursday. I think it's the second of December. Thursday, Friday, and Saturday at Last Hurrah, when you get back. Shows at Euphoria the weekend after that, then La Bamba the weekend after that. The weekend after that it's Christmas. No gigs that weekend.

—Sounds like you've been fuckin' busy, man.

—That's not all. I booked Lung Fung for New Years Eve. I just got that today, so I don't have the details together. We'll hafta make it some kind of spectacular.

Maybe bring the Cowboys down, or open with the Consequentials. Whatever ya' wanna do.

—That's great man. Look. Poppy. Some of the stuff that, like, got said out here, y'know. I mean. You're still our manager and all. Like I told ya'—once this whole trip blows over and everything...

Cautious—as his wounds had yet to fully heal—Mak hummed a hushed, unenthusiastic endorsement

—It was just gettin', like, too complicated with everyone out here. Y'know? We were too spread out, and it was too fuckin' hard gettin' everybody on the same page.

Still saying nothing, Mak simply continued to listen to what Billy had to say.

—So. So we've almost finished all four songs now. 'Police Told Me"s done. 'Made in Hong Kong' and 'Too Straight for the New Wave' are almost there, just need a little detailing, and we finished up on 'Happy Santa' a while back. We'll be home by Thanksgiving, no matter what. We're already broke. No matter how many people show up at the Crap Door, we never seem to make any money.

—Yeah. I kinda saw that comin'.

—Wha'd'ya mean?

—Aw nothin'. Don't worry about it. Never mind.

—So yeah. And we had to, like, uh, borrow a coupla grand from Augie to get us through.

—Billy, man. You shoulda called me man. I coulda taken care of that out here—borrowed it from Tommy or somethin'.

—Angie offered, Pop. We needed the dough. We're down to it. And he was like right here. Offerin' it to us. Seemed like the right thing to do at the time.

—So how much is that gonna cost?

—Well. We borrowed five and we're payin' him back six.

—Hundred?

—No...

Billy replied sarcastically.

—Thousand. We're goin' through at least fifteen hundred or so a week, with rent and equipment and studio rental and eatin' and all that shit. You know. I guess it's, like, almost two thousand a week. More. And Angie takes his cut.

335

—You're not makin' two thousand a night at the shows? Like you agreed on with Larry?

Knowing that the expenditures that Billy quoted were reasonably accurate, Mak determined the band was getting ripped off at the door for easily fifty per cent of the receipts after expenses. Billy was defensive

—No, Pop. That's what I'm fuckin' sayin'. That's why we had to, like, borrow it. Even borrowin' five grand, we'll just barely fuckin' make it. The way it's goin'.

Angie and Larry were making a killing off the dumb-fucks from Pumpkinville. Frustrated, Mak did not respond to Billy. He only listened.

—Listen, Mak. Ya' gotta do me...us...a favor. I'm gonna send ya' the master of 'Happy Santa'. I'm gonna need ya' to get it pressed right away. So we can get it out before Thanksgiving.

—Billy, man. How'm I s'posed to do that?

—Oh. Just take it over to Northwestern. Bob owes us, like, a million favors. We brought him all that fuckin' business with *Boom Chuck*.... We didn't have to go to him. We coulda fuckin' gone anywhere to get that thing pressed and re-pressed. People were tellin' us to take it to Bill Smith at Rainbow. Remember? But we wanted to keep it local. Y'know? Right?

—Yeah. You're right. Okay, Billy. I'll take it over to Bob the first thing after it shows up. But hey. So wha'd'ya' wanna do for the flip side?

—Just skip the B-Side. We'll just make it, like, a one-sided single.

—Jesus. Doesn't that seem like a fuckin' waste of money, Billy?

—There's nothin' I can think of that I want to put on the flip side. And besides. I only want the jocks at KISN and KNOW to play the Christmas song. And this way they'll, like, fuckin' have to. We won't give 'em anything else to play. And that way we can put out an EP in the spring with the four other tracks, and it'll keep things going for us.

—All right. Okay. Whatever you say, Billy. Single-sided single. Got it.

—That's great, Pop. Tray cool. Okay, so I got one other little favor to ask.

Mak took a deep breath.

—Can ya', like, send us out a couple of oh-zees of John's skunkweed? We're, like, just about dry.

—Y'know man, that means the band has gone through, like, a fucking pound of weed since the beginning of October.

—I know, Pop. But it's our only form of recreation. You know that. It's not like any of us are, like, gonna go to a museum or a fuckin' Broadway show.

—Yeah, you're right. I know. Okay, Billy. Okay. But that's gonna cost another five hundred or so.

—Just tell John to put it on our tab. He knows we're good for it. He can, like, give you some tips on how to mail the shit out here to us, too. Oh, and one more thing.

—Yeah?

—Could you, like, call Carrie for me and tell her how much I'm missing her and everything? Maybe she'll cut me some slack if she hears it from somebody else.

Exasperated and solemnly rubbing his face with his hand, Mak burbled meekly.

—Okay. All right. Sure. I'll give her a call. I'll let her know.

—Great! Great, Mak. I really appreciate it. Okay then, well call me when you get the master and let me know how things are goin' out there.

—Yeah, Billy. Okay. Sure. I will.

Three days later, the master tape arrived at the band house, and Mak and Billy D. promptly ran it over to Bob at Northwestern Duplication. Northwestern was the only place in Portland where a band could get vinyl pressed. Fred Stone of the Prats had the actual vinyl lathe that turned out the very first copies of "Louie Louie." But it was a mono device and not quite what the band wanted.

For the record jacket, Mak used an old black and white photo of Billy in his leopard-print pajamas, which were tucked into black suede boots, set off by a wide black belt and a jaunty Santa cap. A white Fender Strat was slung from Billy's shoulder.

On the back of the cover, was printed the somewhat thin lyric to the song, which consisted of very little other than an overt drug reference: "I'm a happy Santa Claus when I dream of you. Coz when I think of you I feel like jelly inside. I'm a happy Santa Claus when there is some snow. Coz when I have some snow it's a wild sleigh ride."

Within three days the forty-fives were ready. Still almost a week in advance of Thanksgiving, the timing could not have turned out more fortuitously. Mak sent out promotional copies of the record to the radio stations and placed the remainder for sale in the local stores.

So busy with everything was he that Mak had conveniently postponed contacting Carrie. He didn't know what to say to her. He knew he probably shouldn't mention Billy's dalliance with a stripper named Happy. But over the space of a week, he managed to summon the courage necessary to call her as he had promised.

Dialing her number, Mak's mind spun like a roulette wheel. He still did not have a clear idea of what he was going to say—or what he was supposed to say. After the second ring of her phone, her answering machine came on- "Hi. This is Carrie. I can't come to the ph..."

—Hi this is Carrie. Hello?

—Yeah. Hi. Carrie. It's Mak. From the band? Mak Poppin?

—Oh. Hi Mak. How are you? What's going on?

He could hear a shiver of trepidation chill her voice.

—I'm doin' fine. Really good. I just got back into town from New York, like, a week or so ago, and I wanted to give ya' an update on Billy.

—Did he put you up to this?

—No. No. I just wanted to let ya' know he's doin' okay out there and the band is workin' real hard. Recordin' in the studio and playin' at the club. That's all they have time or energy to do. They haven't even hardly done the tourist thing in the city or anything.

—Well, I'm glad they're working hard, Mak, but I...

—No. No. I just wanted to let ya' know that he's, like, been kind of a wreck back there. He's, like, really lonely. They're all homesick. But he misses you really bad. I know he'd kill me if he found out I told ya'. I've known him a long time and he can be sort of the silent type, y'know.

—Yes. I know. That's accurate. Silent.

—And, well, he's sort of, like, more messed up than I've ever seen him.

He could spin a tale, but he was constructing a freeway of tangled webs. The more he struggled, the more entangled he became in the snare of sticky threads he had already woven.

—I haven't managed to uncover that aspect in our separation. Billy hasn't indicated to me anything like what you're saying.

—I know, Carrie. Like I said. I know him really well. I can tell when somethin' is really buggin' him. And he's more bugged out than I've ever seen him. I'm just tellin' ya'.

Deeply ambivalent, she felt a strange mix of enormous satisfaction and overwhelming concern. Part of her was happy to hear that he was suffering and part of her worried that he was suffering. But, if she had to admit, though, she was mostly happy.

She hung up from her conversation with Mak even more confused than she had been before he had called. She did not know what to do about Billy. She did not nor could she trust him. He simply was not trustworthy. He would have to earn her trust. Regain it. No entreaty from Mak was going to change that. It was all up to Billy.

Coincidently, or not, Billy called Mak only an hour or so later.

—Hello?

—Hey, Pop. How's it goin'?

—Hey, Billy. It's goin' okay.

—Did ya' get the record taken care of?

—Oh yeah, man. It's, like, pressed and in the stores. I sent copies to all the media and radio people. It's covered. I'm already thinkin' we'll have to do a re-press. Probably before Christmas.

—Far out! Well stay on top of that, Pop. Sounds like you got it handled.

—Yeah...

He said matter-of-factly.

—Yeah. I'm checkin' with Terry at Music Millennium, and Don at For What It's Worth, and over at Tower just about every day. To make sure they're stocked. If we get down to around like three hundred, then I'll look at re-pressin'. We've got, like, uh, six or so right now. So we're okay. But it'll really start sellin' after next week. With the holiday and all. So. How's it goin' with you guys?

—Well, first off, we got the weed. Thanks, man. You know how much easier that makes everything go. It came just in time. We only had, like, a couple of joints left. I was startin' to panic. We all were.

—Cool. Great. I'm glad that all worked out and nobody got, like, busted or anything.

—Naw. We're all still here.

Billy returned to the subject at hand.

—So, we got at least all the basic tracks done on the other four songs. We, like, completely finished 'Made In Hong Kong'. And 'Police Told Me''s done, of course. And we've just got the last sweetening to do on 'Too Straight For The New Wave', a couple of harmonies and maybe another layer of keys. We're still talkin' about that.

—Cool. Cool. Sounds like you guys're keepin' your nose to the grindstone.

339

—We're gettin' real fuckin' close, Pop. We recorded 'Apple of My Eye' yesterday—that one we've been messin' with at the sound checks? The basic tracks sound real cool. I'm gonna do lead vocals tomorrow and maybe some harmonies, if we've got time. Then we gig on Friday and Saturday.

—Shit man. That's gonna be callin' it pretty fuckin' close!

—Yeah. We know. We're gonna, like, come in on Sunday and try to have all the recordin' done by the first half of Monday. Then, hopefully, we'll have it all mixed by, y'know, like, Tuesday night. We're thinkin' we might have to do an all-nighter or two in there. Maybe Monday *and* Tuesday if we have to. We've gotta have it all mixed and mastered by Tuesday night, no matter what. We're comin' home Wednesday night. The flight's booked.

—Wow. So you'll, like, be here next week?

—Yeah. That's right. So ya' better get all the fuckin' hookers and dealers and sacrificial virgins out of the house before we get back.

Changing the subject, Billy continued.

—I gotta spend Thanksgiving with Carrie and her family. If I miss Thanksgiving again this year, I'm fucked, man. Fuckin' toast.

Remembering the three days of debauched gigs in Seattle, Mak understood completely.

—Carrie's gonna be pickin' me up at the airport. So you'll probably be seein' her there. Did you talk to her?

—Yeah, I finally got around to callin' her today.

—What'd ya' say?

—Aw I told her you were, like, really missin' her and kinda flipped out about bein' away so long. Stuff like that.

—Great. Great, Pop. Nice goin'. What'd she say?

—Well, she didn't really say much of anything. You know? She kinda, like, just listened to me. What I had to say. I'll tell ya', man. I don't think she's buyin' any of this bullshit. You're gonna have to work it out with her. Me goin' to bat for you ain't gonna cut it. She sees right through that shit.

—Yeah. I know. That's pretty much how it's been the whole time we've been gone. She thinks I've been fuckin' around on her out here. But you know that's not true. I mean I didn't even get to second base with Happy.

Mak was strangely relieved to hear again that Billy had failed in his attempt to woo Happy. To Mak she was a goddess. A *real* goddess and she deserved to be treated like one. Mak was hopelessly in love with Happy, or what he knew of her (which was a great deal, on a superficial level, but otherwise not very much at all. In fact nothing—but for her occupation).

—You still there?

—Yeah. Yeah, I'm still here.

—It just got, like, kinda quiet there for a minute.

—Yeah. I was thinkin' about somethin'. I need to check in with Wherehouse Records, too. I only left, like, ten with 'em out at Eastport Plaza the other day. Y'know, they might be needin' more. I hit Crystal Ship and the Tower Eastport store pretty hard, so I only had, like, ten left for Wherehouse when I got over there.

Having satisfactorily steered the conversation away from what was for him a very delicate subject, Mak attempted to bring the exchange to a safe and pleasant conclusion.

—Okay. So...?

—So, I guess that's it. I'll call ya' sometime next week and get everything set. We'll probably need for you and Mick and Billy to come out to the airport and pick the guys up and all our shit. I think we get into Portland at, like, eleven or so. Like I said, Carrie should be there, too, I guess.

—Eleven at night?

—Yeah, at night. It'll seem like fuckin' two in the morning to us.

—Yeah. I'm still, like, just gettin' over that. I mean, y'know, you wouldn't think like three fuckin' hours would make so much difference. For some reason, it's worse comin' back than it was goin' out. I'm not sure why the fuck that is.

—Well, we'll find out when we get back next week. It sure feels good sayin' that. Okay. Keep the home fires burnin', Mak. We're almost done with this fuckin' son of a bitch.

They hung up. Mak was somewhat worn down from all the intense phone conversations he had just endured. Enough for one day. He decided he would kick back with a joint of his own and consider his obligations and responsibilities.

As Thanksgiving day neared, the Portland radio airwaves were filled with the echoes of "Happy Santa Claus," and the singles were moving out of the stores at a brisk pace—so brisk, in fact, that Mak put in an order at Northwestern for a re-pressing; which would be ready right after the holiday.

With professional proficiency, the band finished in the studio, sustaining a great deal of momentum through the remainder of the project. Although time was extremely tight, it was not necessary for the band to work the overtime hours that Billy had predicted.

The mastering process went quite smoothly. By the time Wednesday rolled around, Billy had the two-inch master tape of their Power Station recordings safely secured in a metal reinforced packing case. It would not leave his sight until he arrived back in Portland.

The rented amps and drums were safely returned to Rick at Sam Ash, with Billy handing him a check for seven hundred and fifty dollars to cover the previous three weeks' rent for the gear.

At the Newark airport, Angie helped the band unload their bags and instruments from the back of the van onto a heavy-duty, red metal handcart. As the bunch of them moved the gear, Angie cornered Billy off to one side.

—I want ya' ta fuckin' think about it, Billy, man. You don't hafta pay me the six grand. I'll take one percent of the band. That's most likely gonna be one percent a nothin' if you guys go like most bands. But I'm willin' ta gamble on ya', I believe in you guys.

As he finished stacking his luggage at the top of the pile on the cart, Billy stood up and engaged Angie directly; saying nothing,

—And if you guys like fuckin' happened to make it somehow, make it big— y'know, like, five million or something'—then it'd only be like what? Fifty grand or somethin'? Fuckin' chump change.

Momentarily weighing Angie's words, and though slightly convinced by them, Billy abruptly maneuvered his train of thought back on its tracks. He had been dazzled by math before.

—That's cool, Angie. I appreciate your wantin' to take the chance on us. But Jack Barnes still has a piece of us and Tommy's got a piece. If we give away too many pieces, there won't be any left for any of *us*. Y'know?

—Yeh. Yeh. I got it. I was just tryin' ta offer ya', like, an alternative or somethin'. I know you guys're, like, strapped for cash and all.

—Well, like I said, Angie, I really appreciate your offer, but we'll just have to come up with the six grand to pay you back. We can probably do that in a month or so, back in Portland.

—Okay, Billy, man. I want ya' to think about lettin' me manage you guys or be your east coast rep or somethin' like that. I know what I'm doin', man. Ya' know I could do the job for ya'. Things went pretty smooth out here for you guys, given all the mayhem.

Billy gazed off at the traffic approaching to unload passengers and baggage at the front of the airport.

—Yeah, Angie. Things went great, they really did. We got everything done that we came out here to do. More. And you did great bookin' the gigs at the club. Ya' did great, man. But we gotta get back home and sort things out before we make any decisions about our future.

—Sure, okay, Billy. I can dig it. But keep me in mind, man. Ya' know I can come through for ya.'

Tired of the pressure tactic, Billy turned to verify where the other members were in the embarkation process. He said nothing.

The flight was three and a half hours late departing. Because of the time variable, the flight back to Portland, though it still took eight hours in reality, took three fewer hours by the clock, than the trip out. The five Gods bubbled at the prospect of finally being home again, while slugging down numerous complimentary mini-sized bottles of Jack Daniel's and Bacardi.

They did not arrive back in Portland until after two. As they drunkenly de-boarded the plane and funneled down the bridge to the public waiting area, Billy could see Carrie and the boys, looking haggard and distraught, over the heads of the other travelers.

Billy dropped his luggage and sprinted toward Carrie, sweeping her up in his arms with a flourish of embrace, kissing her deeply and passionately. The rest of the band slowly tagged along behind Billy, with nothing near so grand of a welcome from Mak, Billy D. and Mick.

Hugging Carrie as if to never let her go again, Billy almost started crying.

—Carrie, baby. I missed you so much. I don't ever want to be apart this long again.

—Yes, Billy. Never again. I missed you, too.

Great glistening pools of tears welled in her wounded weary eyes.

In silence, they held each other tightly at two-thirty in the morning in the Portland Airport, on Thanksgiving day nineteen eighty-two.

Then Billy looked up, wondering.

—So what time're we supposed to be over at your parents' house anyway?

Having only had three or four passing interactions with Jack and Jean, Billy was wary of spending the afternoon over at the Deeds house, dining on turkey and dressing. For despite their somewhat progressive political stances, Billy had good reason for anxiety with regard to Mom and Dad Deeds. They wanted only the best for their daughter. A doctor or a lawyer, or some such was what they had in mind. But at least the sister, Valerie, seemed to like him. That was a plus.

Jack Deeds looked like an actor who could play a parent on television. He wore thick, black horn-rimmed glasses, with a head of short salt-and-pepper black hair; a weary beaten look of resignation plastered on his face. The public servant's life.

—So, Bill. You're a musician, right? Carrie says your band is quite popular. What was the name?

For the first time, Billy was embarrassed by the name of the band. He slowly turned a whiskey sour in his hand, grimacing slightly.

—We're called, uh, the Unreal Gods. The name's supposed to be, uh, like, ironic—a joke, you know?

—Sure, I understand. Like the Mothers of Invention.

Astonished that Jack had even heard of the Mothers, Billy loosened up slightly.

—Yeah. That's exactly right. Like the Mothers.

Jean, who was a sort of mix between Barbara Billingsly and Lucille Ball, wrested the carved turkey to the table, as Carrie and Val carefully trailed behind, bearing the yams and potatoes, the gravy and the string bean casserole.

—Okay you two, dinner's on.

The five of them sat down at the big, elaborate dark antique cherry dining table. A starched white linen tablecloth was draped over the surface, set off by matching white napkins, folded in such a way that they looked like cloth puff pastries. Detailed filigree designs in gold scrawled around the rims of the china, ornate vines and leaves swirled along the edges. The elegant wine glasses. The entire dining room gleamed as antiseptically clean and white as a hospital room.

Jean initiated the serving process, taking orders for turkey preferences—white or dark—sending meat laden plates down to each recipient. Once the meat distribution was properly realized, a conveyor of plates and bowls ensued: dinner rolls, butter, cranberry sauce, a light Caesar salad, croutons; as well as all the items Carrie and Val had already brought out. Carrie circled the table with bottles of wine, a nice pinot gris and a wonderful Beaujolais called Puis D'Amour.

For a time they ate in silence. Billy was feeling enormously uncomfortable. He felt as if he was being inspected, assessed and judged. He wished he could simply pick up his plate and run away. He worried about his manners. One slip and he could be labeled unsuitable for Carrie. He already knew he was beneath her in a lot of ways.

It was Jean whose intense curiosity broke through the quiet like a shovel blade slicing through loose loam. She did not mince words, cutting directly to the chase.

—Um, Bill? What sort of career do you have planned, after your days as a rock musician are over?

—Gee, Missus Deeds, I never really thought about that before. Music, being a musician, is my life. I really can't imagine doing anything else.

A look of obvious horror crossed her face as she was confronted with the knowledge that her daughter might soon be participating in some sort of Woodstock-like hippie affairs, with drugs and free love. Carrie would end up living in a trashy trailer park with dirty crying children and barking dogs. Jean looked helplessly in Jack's direction.

—Our band is going to be famous. Soon. I'm going to be a star someday. Soon. The whole world will know who we are. And we'll be rich and we'll never have to work again in our lives, except to play music. But that's not work. That's why they say 'play' music instead of 'work' music, I guess.

—I think what Jean is asking Bill, is what do you intend to do after you have become a rock star and a millionaire. What do you intend to do with your life?

Billy sensed that Jack was mocking him.

—Well, when we start making all that money, I'll buy my mom a house—and buy you guys a house, too, I guess. A nice place up in Washington Park, where all the old money is.

Having returned the ridicule, Billy drilled Jack between the eyes with an intense glare.

—And me 'n' Carrie'll travel all around the world, and we'll stay in all the nicest hotels .

Humiliated, Carrie and Val directed their concentration to their plates, eating meticulously. Carrie used her hand as a visor, to avert her attention away from the participants in the *conversation*. She had been afraid that her parents might try to interrogate Billy, but she had not anticipated that the grilling would begin so soon into the meal.

Never one to retreat from confrontation, Billy continued his defense.

—Nobody asks Paul McCartney or Mick Jagger what they're gonna do with their lives.

Suddenly it seemed that time itself began to run in slow motion. An indistinct nimbus shadowed around Billy's head for an instant, then disappeared. The temporal world resumed its normal pace and Jack retreated.

—It wasn't my intention to impugn your ambitions, Bill. You seem to know what you want. It's just that we're very protective of Carrie.

Completely disgraced, Carrie said nothing, but she continued to dig through her dinner as if training for a speed-eating contest. She only wanted to escape from the disaster unfolding before her. For similar reasons, and knowing the topic of the conversation would soon revolve to her, Val was close behind, swallowing whole mouthfuls of food without chewing. Jean interjected.

—We're protective of both girls. We only want the best for them. Carrie has plans to become a nurse or a doctor. And that's what we want, just as we want Valerie to pursue her intention to study art.

Just from her stiffened posture and the darkened tone of her voice, it was clearly obvious that Jean was not in absolute support of her younger daughter's aspiration to become a graphic artist.

With a mouth crammed full of red wine and the end of a dinner roll, Carrie bolted from the table in the direction of her old bedroom. Within thirty seconds, Val followed. Billy was perplexed as to his duties in a conflict that was not of his making. It was unfamiliar territory for him.

Jack and Jean abruptly left their seats, in hopes of retrieving the girls, while Billy was left alone at the table to gulp down turkey and mashed potatoes as fast as he could so that when Carrie came back they could make a break for it.

After much longer than it should have taken, the Deeds family returned, en masse, to the Thanksgiving feast, wearing game faces etched in grit and resolve.

Carrie dolefully plopped down in her chair, staring off into space. Billy tried to engage her, but she ignored him. Surely she wasn't mad at him for anything. He'd stuck to his guns, that's all. Under the table, he tapped her toe with his. She smiled at him faintly, then her face resumed its detached expression.

—We're so sorry for that interruption, Bill.

Jean authoritatively addressed the young man.

—We haven't had the entire family together for several months, and it appears there have been a few long-simmering issues that need to be resolved between the four of us.

Shaking free of her state, Carrie suggested.

—If you're finished, I should probably take you home.

With a grim degree of respectful solemnity, Billy nodded in accord, privately elated to be fleeing the stormy familial circumstances.

As Carrie directed her little gray Toyota around Council Crest and down the hill toward her apartment, she apologized.

—Sweetheart, I'm so sorry for what happened. That was horrible. My mom's terrible, but when my dad tries to run interference for her—interpret—they're both unbearable.

—It's no big deal, Carrie. My family gets pretty wired up sometimes, too. I could tell ya' a lot of stories. This was nothin'.

—I'd love to hear them sometime.

—Which fistfight with Denny do ya' wanna hear about? The ones *while* we were on stage playing? Or the ones before and after the gigs? And besides that, when we were growing up, Elaine used to kick our asses. My dad always said she was his best boy. She was tough.

—Do you miss your dad?

—Yeah. I miss him everyday. He was my go-to-guy.

—What's that? What's a *go-to-guy*?

—Aw that's something Johnny Wooden said about a guy a few years back.

—Who's Johnny Wooden? Is he a friend of yours?

Billy laughed.

—No. Uh, he's the basketball coach down at UCLA. It kinda means that he was the guy you could depend on when things got down.

—And you could go to your dad?

—My dad was tough. He didn't pull any punches. He always told ya' the truth, whether you were ready to hear it or not.

—Speaking of which, I have a request of you.

Billy was wary of her requests, given the events earlier in the afternoon.

—A request?

—Yes. I was wondering if you would go to morning mass with me on Christmas day. It's a wonderful ceremony. Very colorful.

Visibly squirming Billy whined.

—Aw, Carrie. You know I'm not very good with all that 'bless me father son and holy ghost' shit, uh, stuff.

Her eyes narrowed reproachfully.

—I'd really like it if you went. It would mean a lot to me.

Billy knew he was trapped.

—Okay, baby. You know I'll do anything for you.

—Oh, Billy. You're such an angel. I love you so much when you let me have my way.

At first, her declaration zipped past him like a fastball over the inside corner of the plate. Then a look of "hey!" crossed his face.

They laughed together for the first time since Billy had returned.

## XXIX

One of the most civically unifying events in the Portland music scene was the annual Pub Crawl, inexplicably sponsored by the Portland Opera Association. The Crawl was always held on the Thursday following Thanksgiving. Dozens of bars took part, each offering some form of live entertainment and drink specials.

The Welcome Home show for the Gods was to be held at Last Hurrah. Located on Alder street, near 4th Avenue, the club was situated below street level. A vague, rustic bunkhouse feel, a remnant of the previous country-rock era, informed the low-ceilinged, meandering spread. Woodsy tables and chairs were slung everywhere in the main room.

It was a split-level affair, with differentiated terraces about six inches in height. Whenever people took to the gym-floor dance floor, nearly the entire view of the plywood stage, which, elevated perhaps a foot above the dance floor, was blocked. Only the tops of the performers' heads were visible. Their faces could not be seen.

A second room, adjacent to the lower entrance, was walled off from the rest of the club. That area, with no view to the stage or entertainment, was used primarily for the copious consumption of alcohol and as a hunting ground for those warriors in search of abundant flocks of pheromone-fatted females. The rut-musk stifled space accommodated the "overflow," as it were.

Any Gods show, but especially after their two-month absence, guaranteed a full house at the Hurrah. That it coincided with the Pub Crawl only added to the dangerous madhouse fire-hazard appeal of the spectacle. Everyone knew it was quite possible that the whole building might burst into flames at any moment.

Thousands of people attended the alcohol-fueled Pub Crawl free-for-alls, most of whom knew nothing of the clubs or the Portland music scene. They were merely along for the ride, lured by the insane exhibition taking place. Many of the newcomers were Opera Association folk who were slumming it for the evening and being swept along in the current of events.

Eric Carus and his friend Jim Finity waited outside Last Hurrah. It had been their intention to catch the Gods' homecoming show. But—even at nine o'clock, as the two of them approached the doorman and the stairs down to the pit, and even with H.E. Carus' impeccable press credentials—they were unable to gain entry. Instead, they were driven back by a dark, heavy pressure rushing out to the street, a thick stench comprised of cigarette smoke, bodily exudations, and an intense cloud of stale carbon dioxide.

Eric had hoped to write a review of the Gods' return performance for Loose

Screws, but he was claustrophobically deterred by the mob down below. On that particular occasion, Jim Finity was not of a mind to abandon him. So instead of waiting in line for a chance to get into the club at some point, the pair elected to sit on the sidewalk, lean against the building, and watch the unfolding show. The two of them had a great vantage point.

An endless procession of jolly yellow school buses, which had been specially leased for the occasion by the Opera Association, ferried countless Crawlers from site to site, all around town.

Confederates among a gathering cluster of idlers loitering outside the doors to Last Hurrah, Eric and Jim Finity observed the Pub Crawl partiers, who arrived or departed upon one of the buses that regularly rolled up every fifteen minutes or so.

Early in the evening, riders observed strict decorum in lining up to board the bus and politely exiting in single-file down the steps to the sidewalk. It was a very proper affair and all seemed well enough.

While the pair sat wide-eyed and chuckling between themselves, a sizeable contingent of ne'er do wells collected outside the Hurrah, milling around, awaiting entry. The doorman wasn't letting anyone else into the club until someone left (which wasn't very likely, since the fuckin' Unreal Gods were getting ready to take the stage).

The room was at capacity. That meant there were probably at least one hundred patrons beyond the capacity of two hundred and twenty-five. Seeing as the place was a shameful firetrap, death hole, any fire marshal surely would have shut the show down.

As the night wore on, Eric noticed that etiquette and convention were slowly being abandoned with every complete circuit of the school buses. Awash in alcohol, incredibly inebriated people noisily sloshed from the puke yellow vehicles. They careened down the steps. They poured drunkenly from passenger windows. They fell blindly from emergency exits, plummeting to the pavement with dull liquid thuds, amid debauched laughter and mindless screams. It was sublime entertainment, to be sure.

Inside, the band took the stage to a tumultuous ovation. Oxygen was confined to a ten-inch space just below the low ceiling rafters.

Billy was simply adorned: a rolled up red kerchief headband, sleeveless pale blue work-shirt and jeans tucked inside a pair of highly scrolled honey-brown pointed-toe cowboy boots. Col, his hair cock-teased above his head, wore a similar get-up—a sleeveless white jeans jacket, blue jeans with colorful scarves wrapped around his knees and calves, and high-top black Converse sneakers.

The others were pretty much in their typical garb: Gilly all in black leather and heavy make-up; Gib in a "fall color" muted tone brown and gold bowling shirt and black slacks; Daw in his customary sleeveless powder-blue t-shirt, tight

350

faded-blue jeans and white high-top leather basketball shoes (laces undone).

The band quickly kicked into their first song, with Col flashing a staccato James Bond-like theme, working across an ominous A minor to F riff on his Gretsch. Beneath that were Billy's jagged, digital delay drenched rhythm guitar dribbles. He stepped to the mic, doing his best husky, full-voiced Elvis impersonation.

—Hello-oo! 'lo everybody. Long time no see. How y'all been?

A loud hoot sprung up from the cramped and sweating drunken onlookers.

—We've been workin' real hard. Back east...recording four or five new songs at the Power Station in New York City and writin' lots more in our free time. We're gonna play a couple for you right now. Yeah. Yeah. You left me...in a *Stereo...Area...*

The musicians fell into a slinky groove, a little more stylish and sophisticated than the sort of things they had been doing before the trip: a bit of an urban feel, suggesting, of all things, Joe Jackson's "Stepping Out."

—Friends wanna know
They always ask me
Where you been
Where you've gone
I don't know why
I always cry
When I tell them
Where you've been
You left me
You left me
In a stereo
Area
Again.

Repeating the thin chorus several times, Billy guided the band through a short, sensible jam—primarily invoked to allow the band to ease into performing again in front of a Portland packed house. Then they abruptly right-angled into the bridge.

—Well well well
You left me...
In that stereo area
Again
Here we go again...

Billy muttered a monotone, while Col flawlessly provided stinging touches, first in a gnarled single note solo—evolving into single string slides, and finally, moving into a more complex solo—somewhat superior to his influences.

They wound through a series of repetitions, a device designed to extend the song

351

as much as possible, with the intention of getting more of the crocked Pub Crawl celebrants out on the dance floor—an effort which proved fully successful. They power-chorded a momentary conclusion, then segued into the next number. Billy continued his patter.

—Yeah, yeah. I'm too underpaid for the new wave
Too underweight for the new wave
I'm too straight for the new wave hoo hah
But I always say...
Mom's apple pie...

With a ghostly organ patch Gilly broke into descending single note arpeggios as Daw accented the beat with gunshot snare hits.

—Colly knows a journalist
A messenger of truth
He writes about absurdity
He writes about me and you
He got a certain intellect
But he ain't got much taste
He's a disconnected author
My time he wants to waste
I tell him everyday
He still don't understand
Much too straight, too straight for the new wave
He's too straight for the new wave
Too late for the new wave
He's too straight for the new wave.

Into a certain Beatles-esque psychedelic drone, the band spun around Gib's pulsing bass with Gilly endlessly repeating his gleaming hypnotic arpeggio. Billy broke into a surreptitious rap.

—Yeah. Well I remember drivin' down the road
To mom's apple pie
I went into Last Hurrah
And I didn't wonder why
Coz the crazy fuckin' pub crawl
That's where it's at.

A boisterous cheer sprung from the roiling bowels of the shit-faced ravers.

—I walked in the door and I took off my hat
And this guys says 'hey man—you're in New York'
And I said 'how do you spell New York'?
And he didn't reply
And I said—you spell New York like this:
A rope, a knife a bottle and a cork
That's the way you spell New York.

Chanting the lines over and over, the band slipped deeper into thick quicksand psychedelia.

Outside, on the sidewalk, Eric Carus and Jim Finity watched in bewilderment as the crunch of sodden accomplices increased to borderline riot capacity. There was loud laughing and squealing, as more and more of the bilious buses emptied their liverish contents onto the street outside Last Hurrah—as if the place had become the final destination for every member of the drink-and-be-driven merrymakers. And none of them could even get into the club.

Cop cars circled the block like worried hens—monitoring the situation with the foxes in the henhouse. With apparent professional composure they hopefully awaited the decision from mother hen to tear-gas the lot of them and start beating heads.

—Yeah my sister is a charmer
She is a real doll
She's always been a winner
I never seen her crawl
She's always got a smile
She's always got a kiss
All these things go by
And there's nothin' she will miss
She's only been around since one nine six oh
But she's got more taste than you will ever know.
She's so great for the new wave
She can't wait for the new wave.

Sweating profusely, Billy began to flagrantly bounce in front of the microphone

—Tell you somethin' right now. I'm gonna play these two notes, then I'll tell you about my brother

Bell-tone harmonics sprang from the fifth, seventh and twelfth frets of Billy's blond-brown Stratocaster. He set the beat urging the crowd to join in.

—Boom CHUCK boom CHUCK boom CHUCK
My brother's a musician
The piper in the band
He's such a fine composer
The best in all the land
He plays the lyre and plectrum
And hurdy gurdy strings
He's a polychordal maniac
He measures everything
His music's a fantasia
A rhapsody in blue
He's got more improvisation
Than most fuckers do-hoo
He's too straight for the new wave

Too great for the new wave
He's too straight
He can't relate to the new wave.

With the potential perps on the verge of becoming unruly, the cops opted for a preemptive assault into the belly of the falling down drunk beast that wobbled around in front of Last Hurrah. In most instances, the unerring wisdom of the Portland Police was never to be questioned, especially in times of social calamity. However, the ambling bunch in front of the club were not so much frightened as they were annoyed, and head-achy and totally unappreciative of the sudden influx of clowns wearing white cop helmets and swinging batons.

Like a herd of inconvenienced cows, the crowd meandered down Alder Street in the general direction of the Morrison Bridge. It was unclear whether they were going to stampede stuporously in some indeterminate direction or merely drift toward the general vicinity of Paddy's, Chuck's, or Geraldo's to recover the buzz.

Ever astute, Jim and Eric had seen the whole thing coming when the cop cars rolled up. They agreed that it behooved them to migrate away from the scene with extreme haste. And sensing the likely direction of the drunken yayhoo herd drive, they scooted in the opposite direction, up Alder, making a quick right turn on 6th Avenue. They stood just out of sight, as the echo of tired and bothered drunk people reverberated among the tall concrete buildings in the cold December night.

Below the street, in the guts of Last Hurrah, glutted with hundreds of sweaty breathless bodies, the temperature was seventy or eighty degrees hotter, but there were no cops with batons. Not yet, anyway.

The Gods carved out a well-hewn set—a couple more new songs with a lot of old favorites. At the conclusion, the band slid into the kitchen behind the stage, which, along with the pantry and the cooler, sort of served as a de facto green room.

Mak had been back in the office, a cramped little room tucked beneath the entry stairway. He had been talking with Michael Montagne, who, along with his brother Peter, owned the joint. Mak regaled Michael with tales of far New York, the great adventures of the Unreal Gods.

Later, upon entering the backstage area, Mak was shocked and disappointed to see Billy snorting up two enormous lines of coke that Dealer Walt had laid out on the top of the immaculate stainless steel stovetop. Billy snuffed up the lines and fell backwards slightly, from the rush.

—Shit, oh dear. It's been a long time since I've done any coke. Two months. This really hit's the fuckin' spot. Wow!

Dealer Walt was extremely proud of the particular product he was dispensing that night.

—Tested ninety-five percent pure Peruvian flake. I got it from the guy who brought it in by private plane.

—It's fuckin' blowin' me away, D-Dub. That is some righteous shit there, man.

Obligingly Dealer Walt pulled from his leather vest pocket the brown pharmaceutical bottle of fun, and with a long switchblade, he drew out two more impressive lines onto the stovetop, motioning to Billy to have another go. Billy sucked down the blow. He felt the numbing drainage in the back of his throat as his sinuses became so swollen he immediately could not breathe through his nose.

Dealer Walt spotted Mak standing startled and motionless in the doorway to the kitchen and he waved to catch his attention. Dealer Walt raised his eyebrows towards Mak and put his index finger to his nose. Mak shook his head no, so Dealer Walt slipped the brown pharmaceutical bottle back in his vest pocket and the switchblade into the back pocket of his jeans.

Mak moved toward the rest of the group, who were standing just outside the pantry, smoking a couple of joints with Incomparable John Dailey. He dominated the conversation, with exaggerated accounts of his latest exploits and achievements, while not allowing anyone in the band to tell of theirs. At every turn, Col kept repeating sarcastically, "Oh, tell us more Captain Boom Chuck. Tell us more," which, rather than dissuade him, only encouraged Incomparable John to chatter on further.

Mak suddenly felt distantly estranged from the lot of them. He had a bad feeling, which he could not identify any more than to recognize that it was there.

Joining them, Billy crowded next to Mak to intercept the joint heading in that direction. Mak elbowed Billy sharply.

—What the fuck're you doin' back there, man? You're gonna, like, fuck up your voice. You know what that shit does to your throat. Jesus Christ.

His adenoids were frozen. With a thick anesthetized face, Billy replied.

—Aaaa it doesn't do anything to my throat. I'm fine. Just a little buzzed. That's all.

He took a long hit from the joint and handed it to Mak.

Unable to talk further, Billy's mind flew around the room swimming six feet above the scene. His nose and throat were frozen thick, immobile. His heart fluttered furiously. His breath was shallow and rapid. Incomparable John produced another spliff and sent it around the circle. Billy took another huge hit and grabbed a Rolling Rock from the ice-filled galvanized wash tub, popping the bottle of beer open on the edge of the counter.

—Fu-uh-uck. I am, like, so-oh fucked up.

Unsympathetic, Col sneered, a cigarette hanging from his slack lower lip.

—Well ya' better sober up fast there, snow boy. It's just about time to head back out.

—Uh...Ya' better give me a couple of minutes. I'm fuckin' chargin' way too hard to go out there right now.

—Okay. A coupla minutes. But ya' better get it together, man. It sounds like the natives're gettin' restless.

—Yeah, yeah. I can dig it.

Twenty minutes later, after a forty-five minute break, Billy had finally come down enough to resume the evening's entertainment. Along with the others, he wandered in the direction of the door to the stage.

Strapping on his guitar, Billy twitched involuntarily as he stepped up to the mic.

—Good lord almighty! How the hell is everybody doin' out there?

The fuddled, but ruly ruck answered with bubbly effervescence somewhat to the affirmative.

—If you're half as fuckin' high as I am, you'll need, like, a sandbag or somethin' to fuckin' hold ya' down on the ground.

Again the mob was inspired to shriek mindlessly in response. From that point on, the course of the evening had been charted. By half way through the set, Billy was hoarse and croaky, his throat dry and brittle—a mess for the rest of the night.

Still, it was good to be back in Portland. Home where the lifestyle was laidback and easy; far away from the grimy hustle of New Jersey. And as the night of the Pub Crawl subsided—the herd of drunks driven to some other liquor barn—a light snow began to fall.

The next morning, still creaky and croaky, Billy accompanied Mak on the short walk from the band house down to the KNOW studios on Macadam. They were scheduled for an interview with drive time DJ Connie Pony, recounting the trip back east and to promote "Happy Santa Claus."

—That was Human League and 'Don't You Want Me'. I've got someone here sitting across from me that you *all* want, baby. Mister Billy Granger from Billy Granger and the Unreal Gods...and the Goddesses...Are the Goddesses A Go Go still part of the show?

—Uh, no, Connie, they're not. Not right now.

—I'm sorry, that was Mister Billy Granger, ladies and gentlemen. Billy's here with the band manager, Mister Mak Poppin. And they're gonna tell us all about their journey back east to record in one of the most important studios in the country. Billy, Mak, welcome.

Billy said.

—Thanks, Connie. It's good to be here.

Mak added.

—Hi, Connie.

Wondering if she might recall, Billy queried Connie Pony.

—Hey, Connie. Do you remember bein' the emcee at a David Bowie look-a-like contest at the Earth? About five years ago or so?

—Yeah, Billy, I think so.

—Do you remember the guy who won? The *Aladdin Sane* kid with the perfect make-up?

—Sort of. Yeah. I think I do. I remember there was a girl. And only one guy who was any good.

—That was me.

—No!

Connie Pony grew silent. A disc jockey struck speechless, even momentarily, was a rare broadcasting experience, to be sure.

—Yeah. I won. I got to go to the Bowie concert that summer at the Coliseum and I got to meet him back stage and the whole deal. I wouldn't be here today if it hadn't been for that contest. It got me into music and onto the stage. Bowie made a big impression on me.

Mak and Billy gave Connie Pony an encapsulated recounting of the events in New Jersey—a story that was already beginning to become tiresome for the pair. Connie inquired

—Okay, so, Billy. Mak. You have a new Christmas record...

Mak took up the lead.

—Yeah. 'Happy Santa Claus'. We sold two thousand copies in ten days. And we just got a new pressing of five thousand more a coupla hours ago.

Earlier that morning, Billy D. had transported Mak up to Northwestern to pick up the five thousand singles—one hundred boxes of fifty platters each.

—That was another one we recorded at the Power Station, Connie. 'Happy Santa' and four others.

—And when can we expect to hear those other four, Billy?

—Maybe in the spring. Maybe. It would be nice if we could record four or five more songs of that quality and make an album out of it.

—That *would* be nice. Do you guys have any plans to record a video for MTV?

Caught slightly off-guard by the question, Billy lied.

—Yeah. Yes we do. We plan to start working on one sometime next month, as a matter of fact.

Sitting next to Billy across from Connie Pony, Mak's ears reddened, the blush slowly creeping down his neck and into his cheeks.

—I'm thinkin' it'll probably be 'Police Told Me'. That's the one that seems the most photogenic, or whatever.

—Well, we'll be looking forward to that. It sounds like you guys are going to have a busy spring.

Billy concurred unenthusiastically.

—I guess that's right, Connie. We're gonna be pretty busy.

—So, Billy, tell us about 'Happy Santa Claus'.

—It's just a simple song. Nothing complicated. Just a message from us to Portland—to have a Merry Christmas.

—And you only put one song on one side of the single. What's the deal with that?

—We didn't want DJs like you playin' the wrong side, Connie. We wanted to make it real easy for you.

—Well I appreciate that, and I'm sure all the other DJs in town do, too. Okay everybody. Let's give a listen to 'Happy Santa Claus' by Billy Granger and the Unreal Gods.

As she had been speaking, she had deftly slipped the tone arm down upon the opening groove, and, holding a single monitor headphone to her ear, cued the song. She hit the power to the turntable and the song took off with the sound of silly sleigh bells reindeering along as Santa Billy steered the happy holiday sled.

While their song played on the radio, Connie Pony ushered the guys from the broadcast studio and out into the waiting room, where they could hear it ringing through nice stereo speakers mounted in the upper corners of the space.

—That was so cool, Pop. That was really fuckin' far out. Wow!

—No shit, man. 'Happy Santa's' playin' all over town. Right now! And by the weekend, all the stations in town'll be playin' it. And if they do, then all the stations in Seattle I sent copies to'll start playin' it, too. Let the dominoes fall!

The two of them left the KNOW studios satisfied with a job well done. They headed back up toward the band house, grabbing coffee and croissants at the Lair Hill Café along the way.

They chatted about the success of the interview, and Mak briefly interrogated Billy concerning the upcoming video production, which neither of them had even considered an hour earlier. Billy spoke in generalities on the subject but with great authority. With no other real choice in the matter, Mak was assuaged by the leader of the band.

Late Friday afternoon, Carrie picked up Billy at the band house to transport him back to her apartment, where she intended to cook for him his favorite pre-show meal: chicken enchiladas. It was a short trip to her place, but not without drama. As Carrie drove, Billy excitedly related the radio studio saga.

—Fuckin' Connie Pony. Man, she was shocked as shit when she figured out it was me that, like, won that David Bowie contest. It fuckin' blew her mind.

A sensitive crease braided Carrie's brow

—You know, I've noticed your language seems much harsher since you've come back.

—Harsher? How?

—There's a hard edge in the way you say things. You swear more. It sounds mean. Gutteral.

Billy was instantly embarrassed.

—C'mon, baby, you know I'm not a mean guy. I guess I'm just, like, a little stressed—or I was stressed—for the whole time we were out there.

Gesturing to the east with his thumb.

—But it's really good to be home. I'm sure I'll mellow out in a week or two.

—I hope so, Billy. I hope so.

—I just need a little time to unwind. That's all.

He could see distress brimming in her eyes.

The Friday and Saturday night segments of the Gods' three-day stint at Last

Hurrah were not as ritualistically pagan, nor as out of control, as Thursday. Still, all expectations were met and the band was able to clear twelve thousand dollars from the extended weekend. That gave them operating capital from which to make payments on outstanding bills and it greased the wheels of progress, getting the band apparatus rolling smoothly once again.

Mak's ten percent would have come to around twelve hundred dollars, which would have allowed him to perform similar functions within his own private life. However the band debt was so dire and so immediate, he was only able to draw the same two hundred dollars that each of the other members received.

But at least the rent had been paid and the electricity remained on at the band house. The hope was that everyone would be able to receive a real payday the following week after the Euphoria gigs. Mak had loans from his parents to pay off. They had given him more than one thousand dollars for living and personal expenses during the month he was in New Jersey.

As luck would have it, his dad got hurt in an accident while on the job driving a Trimet bus, and his mom was laid off from her secretarial position—thanks to Reaganomics. They were not at all a well-off family to begin with. They needed badly for Mak to pay them as much as he could, as soon as he could. He felt guilty and helpless.

Sunday evening, Carrie dropped Billy off at the band house as she was beginning to prepare in earnest for finals. He hung out by himself in the living room, lounging on the sofa, vaguely watching television. It looked like a football game was on, but Billy was sure that *One Day at a Time* was to supposed to be on Channel Six at nine-thirty.

Dragging the long cord behind him, Gilly entered the room from the kitchen, whispering conspiratorially into the big black phone he cradled in his hand.

—Yeah. I know.
Yeah. I will. Okay!
Yeah. Yeah. He's right here.

Gilly pulled the receiver away from his ear and thrust it in Billy's direction.

—Here. It's Angie. He wants to talk to you.

Billy sighed and took the phone.

—Yallo. Yeah. I'm okay, how 'bout you?
Yeah? Yeah, we had a pretty good weekend.
Yeah. Yeah I think that's the plan—to send some cash your way. We talked about it. I know you're busted. You took good care of us when we were back there. We'll take care of you.

The voice at the other end of the line relentlessly interrogated the preoccupied musician.

—What?

Yeah. It's playin' around town on all the stations. We did, like, a radio interview about it on Friday. We ran right through the first two thousand copies and we just got the re-press in the other day.

What? Five thousand copies. Oh, Mak and I think we will. We'll sell 'em.

It was nine-thirty—time for *One Day At A Time*—but the show had been preempted. Instead it was the last minute of the game between the Redskins and the Cowboys. The Cowboys were leading 24-10. An upset Billy answered from a distracted distance.

—Yeah, I know, man.

Billy yawned.

—I know 'Fredo, uh, Gilly and Tommy could do the job.

Yeah. I know you can too, Angie. But, it's, like, why should I replace one guy with three?

Yeah. Yeah. Gilly told me. I know Tommy's all hot to book the band. I talked to him this afternoon.

Yeah. He's got connections too. He could book a national tour.

Yeah. Gilly told me you thought he was skimmin' off the top. I really don't think so, Angie. That's not Poppy's style at all.

Billy shot a wearied glance in Gilly's direction—where the keyboardist stood, feigning intense interest in the football game—the object and rules of which he had not one whit of understanding. But he did know that the Cowboys were beating the Indians again, an irony he found desperately amusing.

—Well...like I told ya' before, Angie, I'll give it some thought. But I'm not ready to commit to anything. Not right now. There's too much goin' on right now. What? No, nothin' new. Just what I told ya'. 'Happy Santa' and we need to think about a video, I guess.

What? Yeah, maybe LA. I don't know.

He yawned again.

—Awwm. Well, once we get some of the details nailed down I'll get his number from ya'. Things're too chaotic right now.

Yeah? Well, I liked 'Turnin' Japanese'. That was very cool. He did that?

Oh yeah? I guess 'Senses Working Overtime' was okay. Pretty much just lip-synched live. How'd he meet up with XTC?

Yeah? Well, I guess that's how it goes when ya' run in those circles. Why's he in LA?

Spiraling the black phone cord around his finger, Billy gazed off to a point approximately fourteen inches above the television—at nothing in particular.

—Interesting.

Okay, man.

Well, yeah. I'll give it all some thought. Ya' got a lot goin' on there, Angie. I'm all, like, whoa, what the fuck? I'm tryin' to get my brain wrapped around it all.
Yeah. Well, I'll let ya' know as soon as I get anything figured out.
Okay, man. Talk to ya' later.

Hanging up the phone, Billy hefted it up toward Gilly, who bore it as if it were a chalice.

—What'd you think, Billy?

—Man. I don't know. I just need for things to settle down for a little while so I can get my head straight. Everything's a little out of control right now.

The following weekend the Unreal Gods were at Euphoria. Though their relationship with Jonathan Dixon was always contentious, Euphoria was the only other club in town besides Lung Fung that could hold six hundred people, legally. Playing Euphoria was clearly going to mean another big payday for the band.

Beyond having to deal with Jonathan, they did not like Euphoria because the sound was typically terrible, unless the place was filled to far beyond capacity, which was not out of the question.

The wide high stage stood at one end of the cavernous hall, which was surrounded by towering brick walls. Heavy broad-beamed rafters supported forty-foot ceilings that arced above the huge space of ten or fifteen thousand square feet. The room was a soundman's nightmare.

The sound from the mains would bounce around the room like a superball, with some lower frequencies being absorbed entirely by cancellation, while higher ranges were turned into shrill, gratingly distorted noise. Music (or any loud sound, for that matter) traveling along the nearside wall gave unfortunate "listeners" the impression their heads were being sheered off.

The monitors were even worse. There was no high-end whatsoever, just a muffled midrange sludge that amplified tone, but not articulation. Like singing through thick swaddles of cotton and gauze.

The anticipated overselling of the club was easily realized on Friday night. The mercilessly unbridled party throng, hardwired and wound up tight, and amped-out on crazy holiday spirit, shone with a gleaming, cocaine sheen. The band, a finely tuned machine, geared to delivering three sets of jetfuel-octane music, ran through their old and new material with the facility of a Ferrari steering a narrow seaside highway.

As the evening came to a close, Mak met with Jonathan Dixon upstairs in the spacious office to tally the door receipts. Nine thousand eight hundred and sixty-four dollars, to be precise. For just one night. With the understanding that all band members would receive their regular share of the take, Mak deducted his ten percent from the pot, which came to nine hundred and eighty five dollars off the top.

It was in that moment that Mak recalled the two hundred and twenty-five dollars he had shelled out from his own stash of cash to pay for the second batch of posters back in Jersey City. He decided to subtract that from the take, too, in order to square the debt immediately. Keep everything painless. That'd be that, and he wouldn't forget about it. He really needed to give his parents some money.

He pocketed the bundle of remaining cash and proceeded to the green room, where another huge backstage party was well under way. Dealer Walt had already loaded up his special mirror with great furrows of coke. With the edge of his switchblade, he carefully crushed the glassy flakes into a fine powder, as the lines exponentially fluffed and lengthened.

And a good time was had by all. Except for Mak, who fretted fitfully that the band was going to lose focus to the siren call of the endless party. He was unsure what to do. He hoped that they were merely blowing off steam, that it was just the relief of being back home, and that things would even out soon. But everyone seemed to be having far too good a time to contemplate any sort of expeditious conclusion to the merriment.

Taking a final long drag, Col crushed out a cigarette on the sticky floor, as Incomparable John Dailey sent the usual series of joints around the growing circle of participants. Mak slipped the door receipts to Billy, bummed a cigarette from Col and quickly fled the scene—concerned, but resigned, that the boys were going to do what they were going to do and there was not a lot he could do about it.

With a determination that his services were no longer required by the band at the club, Mak decided to take a cab back to the band house, where the official "Welcome Home Unreal Gods" party was fully underway, with Bam Bam acting as the de facto host.

That in and of itself was odd—owing to the fact that Bam Bam had become persona non grata around the band abode since Northwest Natural had discovered that their meter had been tampered with—a condition quickly rectified. Though Bam Bam had saved the band a lot of money at a time when they really had none to spare—the blame was placed squarely upon his shoulders when the shit came down.

The residence was crammed with the members of other bands, and their roadies and their girlfriends; as well as the usual hangers on and the regular party crashers—with a select clutch of some of the most gorgeous young women to be seen in the city of Portland, all huddled together like a herd of fawns.

Meanwhile, back at Euphoria, after tallying the take, Billy was deep into negotiations with Jonathan over the door receipts. Billy felt quite confident that the band had earned at least twelve thousand at the door. At least a thousand people paid twelve dollars each to gain entry. Either a lot of people got in for free, or something happened to some of the money. Jonathan pleaded ignorance, which wasn't always that much of a stretch for him.

Curiously, Jonathan attempted to maneuver the subject in a different direction by spontaneously offering Billy a couple grams of coke to ease his worried mind. Not surprisingly, Billy took the coke and left the club with the intention of straightening a few things out with Mak.

It was readily apparent that Jonathan, or his partner Bob, or members of their staff—someone—had skimmed a few thousand dollars off at the door. And even at that, there wasn't as much money in the roll as Jonathan told him there was.

As he entered the drunken merry fray, Billy spotted Mak sitting on the sofa talking to a lovely girl with coal black hair. She said her name was Porsche—and joked that "once you ride in a Porsche, you don't want to ride in anything else," which Mak found to be fairly suggestive and provocative and cheesy and obvious.

She had skin the color and texture of cream and penetrating gray eyes, with blood red lipstick. Her front teeth were ever so crookedly crossed, left over right, adding sexy character to her mouth.

Standing directly above Mak, Billy said sternly.

—Hey! Mak! Let's go downstairs for a second. I need to talk to ya'.

The two of them trudged down the stairs to the rehearsal area. Mak stood in the middle of the room, while Billy strode by him, tossing the evening's wad of cash on the card table unfolded beneath the window wall of the control room.

—So what's up, boss? Somethin' wrong?

With a frustrated expression on his face, Billy pointed to the money on the table.

—What's this shit about?

—Wha'd'ya' mean? It's the door money. Is there some kind of problem?

—Yeah, there's a problem.

In all the time he had known him, Mak had never seen such a look of ferocity on Billy's face, nor heard him speak in such a coldly detached voice. It was intimidating and frightening.

—Where's the rest of the money? Jonathan said it's supposed to be, like, almost ten grand and it's, like, eighty-five hundred. Where's the rest? Somebody stole, like, two thousand bucks right off the top, and then there isn't even as much there as fuckin' Jonathan said there was.

—Oh. I get it. Now all of a sudden you're fuckin' worried about the door. It was okay when Angie and Larry were rippin' ya' off blind, but when I take what I'm owed, I become some kinda bad guy. Is that it?

Billy did not relent but only stiffened his gaze of antipathy.

—I didn't steal anything. Look Billy, man...I took my commission: nine hundred and eighty-five dollars, and I paid myself back for the second batch of posters we printed back in Jersey City.

—What second batch of posters?

—The ones I had to redo after the band got the weekend gigs and the Halloween show at the Crap Door? Remember? The cool color ones I had printed along with the black-and-whites? Remember?

—Yeah. I guess so. But pay yourself back for fuckin' what?

Mak pleaded

—Billy! I used my own fuckin' money to pay for that print job. I was always gonna tell ya' and get it back, but I kept forgettin'. Besides, we didn't have any extra bucks back there anyway. I just remembered about it again tonight and I took it out, so I wouldn't forget. I wasn't tryin' to pull a fast one or anything. I just wanted to square things once and for all. Send some cash my parents' way. I was gonna tell ya' about everything when we were all up and around in the morning.

Unappeased, Billy remained stern and incredulous.

—Look, Mak. I told ya' a buncha times before: you gotta run shit by me before ya' go and do it. This is my band. I'm the boss. I call the shots. You seem to've, like, forgotten about that.

Suddenly defensive, Mak whined.

—Billy. Man. I wasn't tryin' to fuckin' pull anything on anybody. The gate was ninety-eight sixty-five. My ten percent was nine eighty-five, and the two twenty-five from that was twelve ten. Twelve-ten from ninety-eight sixty-five equals eighty-six fifty-five. And that's what's in this pile: eighty-six fifty-five—plus a couple of bucks from roundin' off.

—Yeah. Yeah. Okay. Look. I've come to a decision, Mak.

Billy sighed heavily.

—I've been gettin' advice from too many cooks and the soup's gettin' all fucked up.

Mak stared at Billy, trying to assemble sense from his broken analogy.

—I'm thinkin' it's time for us to go our separate ways.

—What? What the fuck're you talkin' about?

—You know. Like I was tellin' ya' back east. I'm thinkin' we've outgrown ya', Mak. It's like the Goddesses. We've kinda outgrown them, too. Y'know?

Billy's logic was hard to refute. The band were indeed beginning to move into territory that was beyond Mak's professional ken. It was his hope to quick-study the game in order to maintain a place on the team.

—Well, I told ya', Billy. Can't I be, like, the third base coach or somethin', if I can't be the manager?

—No, Mak. I don't think so. That's not how it's workin' out. It's kinda like we're in a rebuilding phase for the team. We're goin' from the minors to the majors. You've been a great minor league coach, but we need to, like, move up to the majors now. We'll make sure you get paid your commission on the rest of the gigs ya' booked and some kind of 'retirement package'. You'll get a share or somethin', ya' know? We'll, like, take care of ya'. You know that.

Saying nothing, Mak stared up at his friend. He slowly lifted the rubberband-bound cash and flipped it over toward Billy, who swiped it from the air.

—You've done so much for us, Pop. You'll always be, like, an alumni or somethin'. Y'know?

Peering through the window into the control room, Mak rubbed his strawberry red face with thick, heavy hands.

—Yeah. I know, Billy. I gave ya' everything I had. I guess it's time to hang up the cleats and head on back to school...get my accountin' degree.

—Pop, it's just we need to get lawyers like that Archer guy and a manager who knows how to talk to the lawyer and then tell us what's up with 'em and the record companies. You know? Translate...?

—Yeah. Yeah. I know. It's okay. I understand. Changin' of the guard. Movin' up the food chain and all that shit. I got it.

Billy put his arm around his friend's shoulder.

—How long've we known each other Mak? Like, ten years now?

—It was junior high. When was that? Seventy? Twelve years I guess. That's what I'm sayin'. Billy, man, you're gonna regret this someday. I mean, fuck, if you can't trust an old friend, who can ya' trust?

As he considered the question, Billy's eyes widened.

—Fuck yeah. Twelve years. We've been through a helluva lot together, playin' ball in school and everything, and then all the shit with the band. It's been a crazy fuckin' coupla years.

Mak nodded resolutely. Grudgingly, he began to accept his fate. He was off the team. Released. His contract was not renewed. Traded for a player to be named later.

—Look. Billy. I wanna warn ya! Don't be givin' the job to Tommy Salami or Angie, man. And fuckin' keep Gilly out of it, too.

Mak spat out the words.

—Those guys are only a sideways move. You can do better. I mean, if you're cuttin' me loose so you can do better—then fuckin' *do better* and don't go movin' sideways with that crew. They'll just mess everything up.

—I really appreciate what you say, Mak. I know you're right. Sideways. We might use 'em temporarily or somethin'. Until we, like, figure things out. But you're right. We need to move up the ladder. We're ready.

—Yeah. We...you...you *are* ready. That's what bums me out man. I wanted to see it all the way through. But I understand, Billy. I really do.

He lied. Mak didn't understand. He really didn't. He moved out of the band house the next day.

# XXX

The following weekend, at La Bamba, was like old home week. Familiar faces, from the band's earliest days, were in attendance. All the employees were in festive holiday moods. In Billy's honor, the restaurant ran a special on chicken enchiladas. With the La Bamba shows, the band felt they had finally returned, as if they had come full circle. A cycle had been completed.

As was to be expected with the final gigs before Christmas, the band earned nearly twelve thousand dollars from their two nights at La Bamba. Tommy was not entitled to a booking commission. That ten percent, almost twelve hundred dollars, rightfully belonged to Mak.

But, avarice being the better part of valor, Tommy deemed that it was officially time for the band to begin to repay some of the money he had loaned them. He gleaned a thousand dollars off the top. It was left to Billy to decide whether, as a result, Mak would lose a hundred dollars from his commission, which he did.

On Christmas morning, Carrie had Billy up and around at five in order to attend the Mass at Dawn at St. Stephen's Church on the other side of town, between Hawthorne and Belmont on 41st. She dragged him through the freezing fog to make the service on time. It was a pleasant, quiet neighborhood church, but Carrie wanted to go to the Mass at Dawn, because her friend Jane Apple was going to sing with a choir which she had recently helped to found.

As they entered the half-full church, a priest in glorious white vestments was intoning a prayer from the Old Testament.

—*Say to the daughter of Zion, 'Behold, your salvation comes; behold, his reward is with him, and his recompense before him'.*

While the priest droned melodically, Carrie and Billy traversed the aisle, stopping at an empty row near the altar, where they slid into the shiny dark brown pew.

—*Lesson from the Epistle of blessed Paul the Apostle to Titus: When the goodness and loving kindness of God our savior appeared, he saved us, not because of deeds done by us in righteousness, but in virtue of his own mercy, by the washing of regeneration and renewal in the Holy Spirit, which he poured out upon us richly through Jesus Christ our savior, so that we might be justified by his grace and become heirs in hope of eternal life.*

As he trapped Carrie's hand with his own, Billy moved against her and softly kissed her cheek. She squeezed his hand and leaned her head on his shoulder.

*—Continuation of the holy Gospel according to St. Luke: When the angels went away from them into heaven, the shepherds said to one another, 'Let us go over to Bethlehem and see this thing that has happened, which the Lord has made known to us'. And they went with haste, and found Mary and Joseph, and the babe lying in a manger. And when they saw it they made known the saying which had been told them concerning this child; all who heard it wondered at what the shepherds told them. But Mary kept all these things, pondering them in her heart. And the shepherds returned, glorifying and praising God for all they had heard and seen, as it had been told them.*

Despite himself, Billy actually enjoyed the ceremony. There was a certain happy solemnity to the event that had been missing from his life: a sense of profound peace. And joy. It was like Christmas. And for a short time, he discovered a deeper and more profound appreciation for the holiday.

The following Friday night was New Year's Eve. It was in the low twenties outside and a dry east wind blew the windchill down to around zero. But inside Lung Fung, a madhouse awaited the evening's festivities.

It was ten-thirty and Seattle's rising stars, Donkey Sho-Tay, were opening the night with a set of their pop-flavored original material, once described as "A New Wave Toto—with a conscience," which was very hard for most people to wrap their minds around. Flamboyant lead singer Reineke Fuchs flounced effeminately across the stage in a white silk suit—a fluffy pink boa wrapped decoratively around his neck—singing with a voice that one pundit compared to "David Bowie on helium." He had candy-apple red hair piled beneath a white Fedora and heavy, almost Goth-ish, eye make-up.

Arrogant in a way that really should have been familiar to the Gods, Donkey Sho-Tay held the swarming Lung Fung crush at bay with a barrage of catchy, well-rehearsed songs. Fuchs was so enjoying himself he (apparently) didn't realize he had gone past the band's eleven-thirty curfew. Backstage, by the time Billy noticed at around twenty to twelve, the rest of the Gods were pretty heavily invested in a New Year's celebration of their own.

Agitated, Billy searched for Tommy, pacing like a big cat behind the stage. Donkey Sho-Tay needed to get off the stage immediately. But Tommy was nowhere to be found. Finally, as the openers concluded their Seattle radio hit: "Till You Hear From Me," Billy bounded up, grabbing Reineke's mic from out of his hands and announced.

—The Donkey Hotays everybody. A great bunch, don't ya' think? C'mon, let's hear it for the Donkey Hotays.

The restless cackle of soused onlookers crowed and hooted. Billy quickly left the stage to field the rest of the band from the green room; whereupon they were soon fiddling around with their amps, Gib and Col tuning up, Daw with his drums, making the typical start-up racket.

It was already a few minutes after midnight before the band was ready to play.

369

Billy was dressed in black slacks and a black dress shirt, undone to the middle of his chest, sleeves rolled to the elbow. Around his neck hung a loosened black and white striped tie. On his head balanced an ornate rhinestone crown; a white silk sash that said "Nineteen Eighty-Three" was draped across his ribs. Although he didn't have one on, Billy pretended to check his watch and shouted.

—All right. All right. All right. Yeah, yeah. It's time to countdown to nineteen eighty-three. C'mon everybody. Nineteen eighty-two sucked. Cyanide Tylenol, Iran invading Iraq. War on Drugs—whatever the hell that's supposed to mean. The *Time* magazine Man of the Year is a fuckin' computer!!

Moaning, the crowd hung on his words.

—A football strike, fer chrissakes. No way eighty-three'll be a whole helluva lot better, so we gotta party like it's nineteen ninety-nine folks. It'll be nineteen ninety-nine soon enough. Let's start the party now.

Strapping on his blond-brown Strat, Billy continued to holler.

—Yeah. We got ten-nine-eight.

The swelling throng picked up the countdown chant

—Seven-six-five.

While the band began to fall together centrifugally, gradually coalescing into the intro to "Symmetry."

—Four-three-two.

The teeming havoc makers slurried in a wilder of unremitting fun.

—One!! Happy New Year Everybody!!!

Col and Gib immediately jumped into the angular riff of the song, as Billy roamed the stage creeping with his knees bent and his elbows splayed.

It was one sloshed anthem after another. The band played effectively, but poorly: awash in a wave of drugs and alcohol. It wasn't a problem—no one was really listening anyway. An Unreal Gods show had become a spectacle. Bread and circuses. The band had become the event and the event was bigger than the band.

By the end of the night, everyone in the troupe was completely wasted, from considerably too much booze and weed and blow. Backstage, Incomparable John Dailey, resplendently attired in a tan polyester leisure suit and a bright orange shirt with a cowboy yoke, supplied torpedo after torpedo of his finest stash. Dealer Walt passed the lines around as if they were rows of potatoes to relieve a famine.

Around three or so, the backstage rampage subsided in a swelling dither of swill.

Billy wandered toward the room in the back of the bar, to sort out the door take with Jimmy Lee, Tommy, and Norm, the Cowboys' manager, who just so happened to be Donkey Sho-Tay's manager, too.

That answered a few questions Billy had. He could not figure out why Tommy had been so insistent on having a Seattle band open the night, when there were any number of Portland bands who would have loved a chance at the exposure.

The door was just short of fifteen thousand dollars. Billy started doing the math in his head. In the midst of the toting, Tommy spoke up.

—Hey, Billy. I told Norm we'd give the Sho-Tay guys a thousand bucks.

Taken aback, Billy could say nothing. It was a gig any local band would have gladly done for a couple hundred, max.

—I mean, ya' know, bein' a holiday night and makin' the trip down 'n' everything.

After getting his cut, Norm left the area in all due haste, with Jimmy Lee following close behind.

Tommy handed Billy a roll of bills.

—There's eleven thousand nine there. I took two grand and gave Norm their thousand.

—It's okay. It's cool. I can dig it, man.

As he stuffed the bundle of bills into his pants pocket, Billy tried to calculate the commission he should give to Mak. In truth, the poor guy deserved fifteen hundred dollars, but in band world, expenses off the top would affect the manager's booking commission.

However, Mak was no longer the manager. And making his way back to the band—who were in the parking lot, loading gear into Billy D's van—Billy wrestled with his dilemma, before determining that he would give Mak twelve hundred dollars. He felt bad about the decision. But the band had enormous debts and big plans and they had to be miserly about expenses if they were going to film a decent video.

The search for a director for their video eventually led to David Spasswitz in Los Angeles. He had gained some notoriety around town, most notably for his production of Dollarshine's video for "Herd in My Heart," which had been in heavy rotation on MTV. Dollarshine's attorney, Jesse James Joyce, had recommended Spasswitz to Tommy.

In turn, Tommy advised Billy that David would be the best choice. Tommy knew him from the late seventies, when David worked as a floor producer for KOIN, occasionally hanging out at the Long Goodbye in his off-hours. Spasswitz's production facilities were located in Los Angeles, but the cost of his services were not out of line, and he was known to have a good rapport with musicians.

After briefly considering Angie's suggestion of Martin Lindstedt—who was also based in LA—Billy, eager to curry favor with JJ Joyce, decided upon Spasswitz. Billy liked the videos that Lindstedt had made for XTC and the Vapors—especially "Turning Japanese," which had a storyline and a plot and good production values.

But he wanted more than that. Billy wanted something new and fresh: different, edgy. David had just finished working on a video production for another newcomer—Bryan Adams, who had gotten calls from MTV about it.

The only real obstacle that remained lay in the actual financing of the production. The band could come up with enough money, maybe ten or fifteen thousand, to fund the trip to LA, their lodging and meals, and weed and coke (all the necessities).

But they were going to have to pay for the actual video and that could cost as much as fifty grand, which they most certainly did not have. Tommy thought he might know of a solution. They agreed to meet at Geraldo's on the first Tuesday of the year nineteen eighty-three.

Geraldo's was sizzling with a crisp coke edge, agitated and grinding its teeth. Greg Brothers was back in the far corner, playing a solo acoustic gig. Jim Finity sat at the bar talking to his girlfriend Lorna, a cellist, whom he had met at the Shriners gig when the Gods had first formed.

Suddenly the frenetic calm was seized by an electric cloud, as a muddled aura surrounded the arrival of Billy Granger, dashing in a full-length brown, camel-hair overcoat, set off by a rust and dark-brown plaid scarf. Unaccompanied, he promptly sat down in a booth, where Tommy Demeola was sitting. Tommy was in the midst of charming an attractive young woman with long, straight brown hair and full, seductive lips that parted ever so slightly when she smiled. She absently smoothed her lips with her index finger as Billy approached the table.

Taking off his scarf and coat, Billy sat down and quickly ordered a drink from the ever-conscientious waitress and engaged in smalltalk with Tommy and his friend. Having seen the young star join the couple in the booth, Jim Finity excused himself—leaving Lorna at the bar—as he humbly approached the sainted table.

—Billy, man. Hi. How are you?

—Hey, Jim Finity! I'm doin' just great. How the hell're you?

—I'm doing pretty good. Pretty good. How was the trip?

—It was good, man. It went really well.

—That's great. Hey look. I don't mean to interrupt, but I was wondering if you could write down the words to 'Rocky Road' for me. I'd love to do the song at one of my shows.

Billy was deeply flattered by the request. He retrieved a pen from the inner pocket of his overcoat, scrawled the lyrics on a snow-white cocktail napkin, and handed it to Jim. As if protecting a Dead Sea Scroll or some other delicate sacred object, Jim gingerly slid the napkin in his shirt pocket

—I've always wondered about that song, Billy. It seems like it's about a real struggle. A struggle between desperate dejection or despair and maybe some kind of resolution.

Mildly amused, Billy smiled.

—Jim, man. You're readin' way too much into it. Fuckin' way too much. Me 'n' Carrie were walkin' on some old railroad tracks up in Washington Park one afternoon. And we noticed there were, like, a lot of rocks on the tracks. They hadn't been used for a long time.

Jim was bewildered.

—And it occurred to me that we were walkin' down a rocky road. I liked the sound of that. Well, that image stuck with me. Me 'n' Carrie had been talkin' about stuff that afternoon, y'know? Havin' a little *tiff* I guess you'd say. Chicks can make any road rocky, I think. So, when I got home I wrote the song in, like, ten minutes or so. It all seemed to fit.

Raising his gaze up toward the blue-eyed Irish Indian who stood before him, Billy concluded.

—But, as far as I know, there's no, like, *deeper psychological* significance to the song. It just came out. I didn't really put a whole lot of thought into it.

Disappointed by Billy's explanation, Jim ambled back to Lorna, who was still seated at the bar. He was glad to have a copy of the lyrics—as the words bore special significance for him—even if they did not for Billy.

After Jim left, Tommy advised his female friend that he needed to talk to Billy privately—and at length—implying that it was time for her to get lost. In an instant she was gone. He turned to Billy and declared that he thought Nez Candy might be willing to loan the band a big chunk of money. Billy brightened. Tommy suggested to Billy that he hang around until after closing and talk to Nez.

Nez Candy and his partners were five of the biggest coke dealers on the west coast. They supplied lesser local dealers, such as Jonathan and Bob at Euphoria, and Dealer Walt, who were kingpins within their own circles of sway. Nez and his partners owned Geraldo's and ran their clandestine operations using the club as a convenient front.

For their part, after Tommy had approached them with the proposition, the five partners saw loaning the Gods a large sum of money as a win-win situation. Not only would they profit from the interest and any additional percentages on the back end, but the loan would also allow them to launder a great deal of cash in a securely furtive fashion.

Around two in the morning, as the clientele began to clear, Nez Candy emerged—seemingly out of thin air. He sat down with Billy and Tommy in the booth, a small, dark brown leather briefcase held closely to his side. Nez appeared to be around Tommy's age, maybe in his early forties.

Small and delicate, bone thin, he wore small, round, wire rim glasses. He had shoulder-length wavy blond hair. He was, understandably, a nervous individual—for oh so many reasons, real and imagined—exuding a fine dew of perspiration from most every area of exposed skin.

Once the last of the patrons had vacated the premises and with only the most trusted of staff remaining, Nez hoisted the briefcase from his side, plopping it down on the thick plate-glass tabletop. He flipped the clasps on the locks and snapped open the case. From within, he produced a finely carved rectangular wooden box, perhaps two by three inches, and maybe two inches deep.

As if opening up a Russian nesting doll, Nez slipped off the top of the box, and produced a golden rock of pure cocaine, the size of a small egg. From inside the little box, Nez withdrew a single-edged razor blade and slowly began shaving lovely, glassy, crystal snowy flakes of fresh driven coke into a glistening mound.

Methodically, he ground the shavings of coke into a fine, fine powder, adroitly drawing the pile into several fat, foot-long lines upon the glass tabletop. Then, as if whipping egg whites, he folded the fluffy heap back together again, meticulously chopping the remaining flakes into ghostly pollen peaks, sliding out the long rails one more time.

Evidently from out of nowhere—legerdemain being an apparent favored pastime, Nez deftly rolled tight a crisp one hundred dollar bill and handed it to Billy. The young disciple sucked the silky particles into his nostrils, and the top of his head seemed to blow off, exploding into shards of shattered mind, split into cold numbing flecks of oblivious stult. Nez did not shilly-shally, but cut directly to the chase.

—OK. So, Billy. Tommy says you need money to film a video for MTV or something. Is that right?

—Yeah. Yeah. We've got a guy in LA lined up to do the production. We've been workin' on ideas. We know what song we want to do.

—How much do you think you'll need?

Seeking Tommy's endorsement, Billy searched his mentor's eyes to no reaction.

—We figure it'll probably come in around fifty grand, if we do it the way we want to do it. Make a world-class video that they'll show on MTV or *Night Flight* or one of those. It's not cheap. Just take a look at the good stuff that's on there now.

—Fifty grand? I think that's a little more than we had in mind. But look. If we lend you this money, what are we going to get in return?

—Well, we'd pay ya' back the money, of course—plus interest. What else would ya' want?

Nez was blunt.

—We want a piece of the action, Billy. We want to buy our way into the band. We're willing to take that risk.

—Man, I don't know Nez—payin' ya' back with interest and cuttin' ya' in on a chunk of the fuckin' band seems a little harsh to me.

—Maybe an either-or kind of thing then. We can work out the details. We're not interested in getting our money back right away. That's why we're willing to consider a cut. That's a risk for everybody, but we think you've got a big upside and could pay off big time—in which case you'll make it big time and we'll make it big time too, right along with you.

Not at all unfamiliar with the line of reasoning being propounded, Billy gave serious thought to the proposal. If the Gods were going to do the video project—and they really needed to do it—then a loan was the only way they were going to be able to finance it.

—How many points were you lookin' at?

—We were thinking five. If you guys make a million and a quarter, then we'll have the principal and the interest covered. We were thinking twenty-five percent interest on the fifty-grand, which would come to sixty-two five. But if you make more than a million and a quarter...well then it was a very good investment for us.

—And what if we don't make a million and a quarter?

—Then you'll just owe us sixty-two five and that'll be that.

Weighing the numbers Nez was throwing at him, Billy again sought approval from his guru. But Tommy seemed to be mostly ignoring the conversation—as if, for some reason, he did not want to influence the transaction. In the interim, Nez asked Lila the bartender for a bottle of tequila, a bowl of limes, and a shaker of salt. Nez, Tommy, and Billy proceeded to alternate shots and lines for the next three hours.

It was six and the sky was just getting light before the conference gave any indication of winding down. Sometime within the last hour, Billy resolved for himself that Nez's proposition seemed reasonable and that it was probably the best offer he was likely to receive. He told Nez that he was in on the deal. And they shook hands. Billy stood up, slipped on his coat and scarf, and left the club. He walked the mile back to the band house, mulling thoughtfully as he made his way through the freezing fog.

Three weeks later, Billy was reclined in a posh chaise lounge, poolside, at the West Hollywood Hotel, a block away from Hollywood and Vine, directly across the street from the Pantages Theater. He wore wraparound Foster Grant shades in the raw glare of a somber gray day. He had just been for a dip in the hotel pool, attempting to lead the life of a rock star, despite the fact that it was rather chilly outside.

The Gods had spent the day in David Spasswitz's spacious studios, blocking out the shots for the video of "Police Told Me." It was not yet altogether clear how the action would proceed, but everyone agreed that key elements would be motorcycles and black leather jackets, fog and wind machines, glaring flares, cop car lights flashing in the darkness—lots of stark silhouettes—with the band standing menacingly around the scene of the crime.

On a purely practical level, they had come propitiously well stocked with weed and blow. There was no sense of urgency at any time, whatsoever. They had everything they needed to complete their (rather expensive) mission.

In the ten days that followed, the band members went their separate ways during their free time, exploring on foot, every shop and tourist trap between Hollywood Boulevard and Santa Monica Boulevard to the south, between La Brea to the west and the Hollywood Freeway to the east.

Individually and in groups, they checked out Hollywood Boulevard—from Grauman's Chinese Theatre to the Museum of Death, from Roscoe's House of Chicken and Pancakes to the Hollywood Walk of Fame and the Laugh Factory.

They made sojourns as far away as the La Brea Tar Pits and the Museum of Art down on Wiltshire Boulevard and the Farmer's Market at 3rd. And they hit every bar along the way. It was one unending party. Living like real gods.

And in that time, they also managed, somehow, to cobble together a stylishly sophisticated video that bore the gauzy sheen of LA and money. "Police Told Me" was very professional and without question worthy of MTV. It was by far the most successful video ever created by a Portland band. It was world class.

For the production, all the band members were heavily made up, and they had been made to look quite a bit tougher than they actually were—each of them decked out in t-shirts, jeans and of course black leather jackets. Dangerous, but bitchy. Cross-dressing street punks from Hell. Not to be messed with.

The entourage agreed it was time and money well spent. From their experiences in New York, they had developed a method to contend with the demands and rigors of assembling a polished product. As a band, they had evolved to another level. The scenery was not that unfamiliar; it was simply a bit more refined.

Upon their return to Portland, the Unreal Gods went back to the trenches in earnest, staging twenty-seven shows in ten weeks. They played all the key clubs in town, while making trips to Corvallis and Eugene to the south, and Olympia, Seattle, and Bellingham to the north. After being out of the picture for almost six months, they intently went about reestablishing their Northwest fan base, which they managed to pull off without any needless exertion.

And in that time they continued to write songs, many new songs—more technical, in a rudimentary fashion, more complex in an uncomplicated way. Always taking Sunday and Monday off, they rehearsed down in the basement on Tuesdays and Wednesdays.

Running through new numbers during sound checks—they would work them into sets later in the night (when people would be too fucked up to know when there had been a screw up). By the time spring arrived, they had developed two new sets of material; two sets that they felt far out-distanced their earlier songwriting endeavors.

They were reasonably content with the results of the finished video, which they received about a month after they got back to town. Spasswitz' production values were first-rate. Visually, it did have a lot in common with Bryan Adams' "Cuts Like A Knife." It was dark and edgy. Oddly enough, the video bore some similarities, too, to the Vapors' "Turning Japanese." Unwholesome girls vaguely pursued through the shadows of dimlit alleyways.

But the song and the sound were pure Duran Duran. They used the take they had recorded at the Power Station. It shimmered and shone. Billy would gulp a muted cry, vaguely attempting to imitate early Bowie, but he nevertheless ended up sounding like Simon Le Bon.

Even with a make up job that made him seem both hardened and effeminate, Billy still bore an ineluctable rebel-next-door quality, a bad boy/choir boy—the kind of boy that parents would warn their daughters about, while their daughters weren't listening.

The next step was to actually get a copy of the video to MTV. But that aspect of the process seemed to baffle the members of the organization, so submission was postponed indefinitely.

Given their conflicting schedules, Billy and Carrie were only able to spend quality time together on Sundays. And even then, Carrie was frequently compelled to study and was thus unable to devote her full attention to Billy. But they were able, however, to dine out. And they often had time to see a movie, or to go out to a club and grab a drink.

Still, their lives moved at different tempos. Hers was fast-paced, but methodical and unhurried: Mozart. His seemed frenetic, chaotic and out of control: Spike Jones playing John Cage. Carrie sensed a crevice widening between them, and she wondered if it was only going to eventually rift into a chasm of too great a distance to navigate. There was a growing unease about their time together, as if they had grown apart, or grown altogether separate. Secretly she feared the worst and hoped for the best.

Following a late Thursday night gig at the Faucet out on Beaverton-Hillsdale Highway—on the morning of April Fools' day—Billy received a call from A. Cousins Vetter's young attaché Kindred Swain.

She registered to Billy Mister Vetter's sincere interest in hearing the finished recordings from the Power Station sessions. Billy had forgotten all about sending Vetter a package when the video was finished.

Besides the video, he had neglected to send Vetter a finished mix from the Power Station sessions as well. That sort of stuff had always been Mak's job and Billy had yet to entirely shoulder the yoke regarding many of the duties he had volunteered to assume after Mak's departure. Oops.

Dutifully, Billy wrote down the necessary information and by that afternoon, he had a package containing an audiocassette and a Betamax videotape going out in the mail to Vetter's office. Though still abundantly cocky, Billy had come to realize the importance of playing ball with the big boys, if the band was ever going to evolve to the level of success he anticipated in his quest to become a star.

Less than two weeks later, Billy received another call from A. Cousins Vetter's office—Kimberly Fields on that occasion—to notify him that Mister Vetter's curiosity was sufficiently piqued. She conveyed to the young musician that Mister Vetter would be visiting Portland at the end of the month, and that he was very much interested in seeing the band perform in their own element, in front of a crowd of rabid hometown fans.

Within seconds, Billy assembled in his mind the procession of events. The band would be playing La Bamba the last weekend of April—the second night of which was a Saturday. That show was sure to be absolutely insane and perfect for Mister Vetter to witness the full onslaught of the Unreal Gods experience. And that was the option he suggested to Kimberly Fields. Kimberly agreed completely.

She was certain that Mister Vetter would be well settled by the time of the Saturday show. He had been invited by friends to stay at their "chalet" in the West Hills and he expected to arrive in Portland early in the evening of Tuesday the twenty-sixth. Kinnie and Kimmie were especially excited to be coming along, as neither had ever been to Portland before and both had heard good things about the city from friends and associates.

Through the next three weekends, the Gods played the Orange Peel, Last Hurrah, and Lung Fung in quick succession, garnering almost thirty thousand dollars, which only barely kept the band afloat. In addition to paying Tommy a fifteen percent commission and making the regular monthly loan payments, they required nearly twenty thousand dollars a month, just to operate.

Thanks to the Reagan recession and the deteriorating cost of living, the rent and bills at the band house, kept climbing exponentially. Creature comforts—booze and drugs, had become a sizeable expense as well. Costumes were also a big expenditure. They had begun renting a small U-Haul truck for transporting equipment to most out-of-town gigs, as Billy D's van had grown too small for all but local appearances and was, moreover, on its last spark plugs. And no one else had any reliable transportation of any sort more evolved than a bicycle. So, for all intents and purposes, the band was broke.

There was general excitement among the group regarding the attendance by A. Cousins Vetter at that Saturday show. But there was also a blasé cockiness that had slowly crept into their behavior. Big fish in a small town. Portland's darlings could do no wrong.

The band was generally under the impression that they didn't really need Vetter or anyone else in order to "make it," deeming they had that special something—the convergence of talent, timing and plain, dumb luck. So, it was left to Billy to remain as objective as possible, knowing he was the only one among them to have any grasp of the reality of their position. What hath the Unreal God wrought?

The rest held the opinion that Billy had been espousing, that it was only a matter of time before they were signed to a lucrative major label contract, whereupon all their financial burdens would be banished in a fabulous flurry of deep drifts of cold crisp cash. Millions. It was right there in front of them. It was their destiny. Someone would bite. They were a sure thing.

Just the same, Vetter's arrival did cause a great wave of expectant excitement within the immediate Gods' community. They looked forward to that Saturday La Bamba show with anxious anticipation, knowing the room would be out of control for their crucial, definitive audition (on their turf) for the label owner. Either he would appreciate the magic or he would not. There would be no doubt.

Pulling up to the club on Friday afternoon, in preparation for the first show of that final weekend in April, the band made ready to systematically unload their equipment from Billy Dreier's van. As was customary, they all went inside to inspect the property, even though they had been in La Bamba, and had played upon the stage, easily a hundred times before.

Once the others had vacated the vicinity, Billy D. carefully plunged the lock on the driver's door of the van, in order to prevent theft while everyone was engaged in the reconnaissance mission. He lifted the door handle as he pushed the door shut. It was in that instant that he remembered he had left the keys in the ignition. Locked out of the van: all the gear was locked inside. Disaster.

Billy D. stared at the door dumb-stricken in disbelief, repeatedly yanking on the handle—to no avail. He glumly patrolled the perimeter of the van, trying first the passenger's side door, then the sliding side door, and finally the back doors. All locked efficiently tight. After precisely completing one revolution around the van, he stood motionless, a confused giant baby duckling, unable to determine a solution. They were locked out of the van.

Panic was beginning to set in. Col wandered outside, lighting up a cigarette.

—What's the hold up, big guy? You look like ya' forgot somethin'. Lock yourself out of the van?

Billy D. turned white as a snow goose.

—Man. I hit it on the first guess. Ya' fuckin' locked all the gear in the van! Way to go!

Sadistically, Col cackled like an arrogant insurgent jackal, smoke fuming furiously from his widened nostrils and smirking mouth. Billy D. stood in stark silent shame, the very picture of utter distraught dejection.

—What the fuck ya' gonna do?

The hulking rueful ghost of a man sighed deeply, unable to reply. Stress furrowed his brow. Desperate, he circled the van again, hoping that perhaps he might find a secret door hidden somewhere. Some unlocked secret door. Somewhere. But no.

It became apparent that they were going to have to contact a locksmith—which would not only delay the deployment of the equipment, but add yet another painful debit to the expenditures column. His state of agitation was becoming intolerable, his breathing frantically erratic.

Just as Billy D. was about to implode, an indistinctly familiar, odd little man appeared from up the street—a curly Charlemagne mane of unruly brown hair framing his flamboyantly mustachioed face. It was Mario. Mario, a fellow sound man who had only recently moved to Portland from Los Angeles.

—Hey, Billy. How ya' doin', man? You look kinda troubled. What's up?

—Oh, I locked myself out of the fuckin' van and all our equipment is in there and it's gonna screw up the whole afternoon...

—Whoa, whoa, whoa. What're ya' gettin' so worked up for? It ain't nothin' but a thang.

Nonchalantly, Mario fished an elaborate Swiss Army knife from his jeans. And with expert proficiency, he quickly threaded a specially-filed blade into the door lock—popping it open with a thunk of resounding relief. He pulled open the door and bowed accommodatingly.

—Your carriage awaits, my liege.

It was all Billy D. could do to keep from bursting into tears.

—Mario. Man! Thank you so much! I owe ya' one for this. I *owe* you!

He grabbed the little elf's hand and began shaking it profusely.

—Yeah. Yeah, It's cool man. It's cool. Don't worry about it.

Signaling farewell to Billy D. and Col, Mario continued on his way.

Saturday night, just before the evening's festivities were under way, Billy and Tommy attempted to find for the Vetter party a private space within the expected brawling mass of fucked up worshippers. Billy elected to enlist Bam Bam to guard the Vetter table. They decided on the far corner next to the sound board where Billy D. could keep an eye on Bam Bam.

With four sheets of plywood, Tommy and Billy D. manufactured a small but capacious platform, elevated about a foot above the floor. They cordoned-off the space, stationing three chrome poles on the platform, a red velvet rope threading through cone-shaped grommets at the top of each. Their efforts afforded Mister Vetter and his party a bit of privacy and a relatively decent line of sight. The sound would be as good as it could get in that room.

Accompanied by Kinnie and Kimmie, Vetter arrived at La Bamba at precisely ten o'clock. Cordially introducing himself as they entered, Tommy led them to their special table over near the sound board. Because it was in a back corner, the table was relatively inauspicious, despite the little platform and the VIP sequestration.

Already manning his post with matchless authority, Bam Bam, dressed in a black suit and white shirt, was intimidating anyone who ventured anywhere near the platform when Tommy led the guests of honor to their table. Once they were seated, Tommy rushed off to field Billy and bring him out, before the band was to go on at ten forty-five.

It was clamorously loud, an asphyxiating cloud of sweaty smoke hovering just above the heads of the wasted gentry, stridently screaming and whooping, competing with the din of Ans y Pense—the experimental troupe playing their own final farewell show.

Through some inexplicable transformation, Jim Goodwin, La Bamba's unassuming head cook, would metamorphose into the flamboyant French lounge singer: Ans. A very tall stick figure, sporting a huge pompadour, and an odd David Bowie-meets-Liberace stage presence. An American-portraying-a-Frenchman, Dada-esque persona, Ans was accompanied by a crack sappy orchestra and an array of gorgeous female backup singers.

Performing in the guise of a stranded French lounge act—ostensibly traveling from town to town in search of a way to secure the necessary funds to finance their way to Las Vegas, or even Reno—the horn section of the Ans y Pense troupe typically wore red-striped, nautical shirts and fake moustaches.

Their evenings were often theme oriented, and for that night's performance the theme was "The Casualties of War." Sixties protests songs abounded, all delivered in quasi-French lounge band arrangements, with the same, identical turnaround on every verse of every song, a familiar figure that was an Ed Sullivan Show staple—ditta dit dit da da.

On that night all the troupe members were wearing military attire: uniforms and helmets from various eras of American battle; rifles slung on shoulders. Two of the girls were dressed like battlefield nurses. Each wore a dark wool cape with a Red Cross emblem emblazoned on the back. The capes were draped across their white cotton blouses, starched white linen dove-hats perched upon their heads.

Kinnie, Kimmie, and Vetter smiled simultaneously as Billy approached their table, nimbly hopping up on the platform, wearing a shy grin, which the two young women absolutely adored. He extended his hand to the old man. As before,

Vetter tried to shake with Billy in the European fashion, with his left hand, and again Billy simply shook it the American way, but left-handed. Already nearly a tradition after only two meetings.

—Mister Vetter. Kimberly. Kindred.

He bowed in the direction of the girls.

—I'm glad you could make it tonight. It should be a crazy show.

Vetter looked around the room and sighed warily.

—Yes. I'm sure it will be. When do you go on?

—In about fifteen minutes or so, I'd say. This is pretty wild, don't you think?

He pointed in the direction of the stage, where Ans y Pense were running through a breezy version of Dylan's "Masters of War."

—Yes. Very outside. *Arty*. Their sense of humor is very dry and sarcastic.

—Ans y Pense is real popular in Portland. They don't play very often, so people always show up to see 'em. They always come up with some theme for their shows. Ans goes to Woodstock. Ans goes Hawaiian. I think tonight's 'Protest Night,' or somethin'.

Billy sensed that he may have overstated things a bit.

—But this is our crowd. No doubt.

Looking down at Tommy, who was standing below him, on the floor, next to the platform, Billy inquired.

—Wha'd'ya' think, Tommy? Five hundred tonight?

—Yeah. It sure as hell feels like five. Easy. It's never been this crowded in here before. This is a new record, for sure. By a landslide.

Billy said nothing, but proudly stood alongside his guests, his back straight, shoulders squared—making every effort to look the part of a rock star. To look like a god. The girls, especially, gazed up at him as if he were. He interjected.

—We've got a set of new songs just for you. Second set. I think you'll like 'em. We'll do a couple of the songs from the Power Station recordings and some newer stuff. So don't give up on us too soon.

His humility seemed slightly feigned. There fell a pregnant pause, which veered perilously close to being superlatively awkward. However, summoning up his best good judgment and sense of timing, Billy excused himself.

—Well, I better get back and get ready for the show. Tommy, why don't you open a tab for our guests, get 'em whatever they want, and I'll take care of it at the end of the night.

Tommy had already intended to do just that, but, despite the indignity, he allowed Billy the opportunity to be the gracious host. He smiled and nodded in obedient humility, as Billy walked away, moving through the thickening, madhap milieu, which unfurled deliriously within La Bamba.

Back in the green room, things were totally out of control. There were nearly fifty people jammed into a space that was uncomfortable at twenty occupants. There were mirrors galore being passed around with great hillocks and hummocks of tufted coke. There were ten fat joints in continuous circulation, with more being rolled as backup. There were bottles of Jack Daniel's, Wild Turkey, Sloe Gin, and Southern Comfort circling the room. Beer everywhere.

As he peeked in, Billy realized that out of the entire cast of unruly characters and undesirables, he only knew his fellow band members and just a few others—Dealer Walt, Incomparable John Dailey, and one or two more. With claustrophobia beginning to set in, he wanted to clear the room, to center himself for the show that they would be performing in just a few minutes. But he knew such an effort would be futile and would probably only draw ire and antagonism.

Instead, he crowded onto a bench next to Col, seized the rolled up dollar bill and mirror from his hands and took a long slow hit from the longest line of the bunch. He gave the mirror back to Col and snatched at a passing joint, taking several long drags, burning up nearly the entire thing.

Grabbing back from Col the mirror and rolled up bill, Billy snorted another lengthy line, before downing as a sort of chaser three hard swigs from a fifth of Wild Turkey as it went by. Within five minutes, he was royally ripped. Blasted.

Ans y Pense wrapped up their set with a stirring rendition of Sergeant Barry Sadler's plushly saccharine, patriotic opus "Ballad of the Green Beret," followed by a thought-provoking take on Barry McGuire's rant "Eve of Destruction"—ditta dit dit da da. Ditta dit dit da da da-da—at the conclusion of which, the tall, thin Ans bent down upon one knee.

He resembled nothing so much as a coat hanger twisted in such a way that it appeared as if Ans was just an empty suit with padded shoulders, hung at oddly skewed angles, or draped haphazardly across the back of a chair.

—Non, non you don' believe, ve're on ze eve of zestruction.

Straightening upright, Ans strode slowly from the stage, effeminately waving and blowing kisses with both hands. As he left, the crew concluded their performance with a series of whacky Raymond Scott-like instrumental solos, culminating in a grand silly crescendo. Upon the song's conclusion, the band politely left the stage in an orderly fashion.

Back at the board, as Ans y Pense withdrew from the stage, Billy D. brought up a break tape in the mains, while sliding the fader for each individual channel to the levels marked with magic marker on pieces of masking tape. He had manned the board at La Bamba for so many shows, he could do the sound for the band even if he were deaf—which he knew was a likelihood, were he to maintain his rock and roll lifestyle.

As he toyed with the knobs and levers, Kindred Swain abruptly appeared below him. Out of the corner of his eye, Billy D. caught sight of her, and looking down, he smiled uneasily in her direction. He recognized her from somewhere, but such data meant nothing to him. It was his estimation that he pretty much recognized everyone, by that point.

—Are you Billy D.?

Unsure who she was and if he should respond, he shrugged aloofly, vaguely assenting.

—I'm Kindred Swain. I'm here with Mister Vetter.

She looked over her shoulder toward Kimmie and Cuz sitting at the table, on the platform behind her.

—I just wanted to introduce myself.

Still saying nothing, Billy D. wagged his head, indefinitely to the affirmative, with guarded suspicion.

—Where is Mak tonight? I haven't seen him around. He told me your were the best soundman in the world.

His head falling into his hand, Billy D. replied.

—Uh. Mak left the band around New Year's.

—Oh. I hadn't heard about that.

—Yeah. He wanted to go back to school or somethin'.

She was confused, but continued her interrogation.

—You know, I was wondering... Are you related to Billy? Are you cousins or something like that? You look a lot alike. Related.

Laughing, Billy D. said.

—Nah. But sometimes people call me Triple Billy, because of my name. It's German...

She looked at him quizzically.

384

Just then, Kimberly strolled up, inquiring.

—Kinnie dear, Cuz wants to know if you'd care for another Greyhound?

Slightly unsettled, Kindred looked up at Cuz, who was sitting at the table smiling in her direction. Holding aloft his empty drink glass, he shook it inquisitively. An impatient waitress stood at his side, waiting for him to fucking complete his god damned order. Jesus Christ! Kindred nodded to Cuz and returned her attention to Billy D.

—Well it was nice speaking with you, Billy D. I would imagine we'll meet again at some point.

Coyly, she lowered her head with a coquettish expression on her lips. She held out her hand demurely, fluttering.

With awkward self-consciousness, Billy D. grasped her hand as if it were a packet of guitar strings, gently moving it up and down, so as not to be perceived as rude.

—Well, well, well. It's La Bamba world. Hey D., can you hear me?

Thankfully, Billy D. was forced to direct his attention to his appointed tasks. While bringing up Billy's vocal on the board, he quickly chirped into the talkback mic.

—Yeah. You're right there. How's the monitors?

Billy began to strum his guitar authoritatively.

—Sounds pretty good. Just a little more of my vocals maybe, Mick. How's my guitar?

—Right there. Daw, let's hear your kick.

Daw began the tedious procession of mic checks for his individual drums and cymbals, culminating in balancing the complete kit.

—All right, then. Hey! How about that Ans y Pense, everybody?

Indistinct applause clamored up from the half-drunk room.

—Yeah. He's my favorite Frenchman. Right up there with Marcel Marceau.

—Gib. Let's hear your bass. Ok. Got it. Gilly.

Gilly ran through a series of settings and layers, fingering pieces of different riffs.

—And Ans is a far better singer than Marcel Marceau. So, here we are. Another beautiful night at La Bamba.

—Col?

Col fired up his new Les Paul.

—Me and my brother Denny had a little band called the Malchicks and we played here a few years ago, right after this place opened up.

A smattering of applause sprung up from the distracted minions.

—And we knew, even back then, that La Bamba was gonna be the best club in Portland. And now...here we are for, like, the fiftieth time. Fifty ya' think Tommy? Sixty?

Billy shouted out, not really expecting any reply.

—Where're we at D?

—Let 'er rip.

—Okay. All right. This one's dedicated to our mentor, Mister Incomparable John Dailey. Ya' out there, John? Yeah. There he is. You know what this called, it's called a 'Boom Chuck Rock' now.

They bolted headlong into the song, at full speed.

—Wella Boomchucka rocka it's a rockin' sound
You hear it in the country and in every town...

The sound was impeccable. Both Billy's and Col's vocals floated above the instruments, each clear in the mix. A. Cousins Vetter felt the immediate impact of the band in their element. They had tightened up considerably, even in only the four or five months since he had last seen their act.

From Vetter's perspective, the mix in the room at La Bamba was world class. He tried to think back—it seemed to him that the big, placid fellow at the board was not the same technician who had manned the position at the Peppermint Lounge. From the very start, the performance was infinitely improved, with a percussive punch that was new (to Cuz, anyway) and very persuasive.

—Yeah, yeah. Here's another goldie oldie you'll probably recognize.

Without the slightest hesitation, the band launched into "Used to Hang Around," slickly sliding through the manic reverie that the song inspired. Cuz leaned over, and covering his hand, he shouted into Kimmie's ear.

—What do you think?

—Oh, they're real exciting. Very tight. Don't you think?

Compelled to yell herself, Kimmie transferred her attention to Kinnie, who nodded in profuse accord.

—Yes. They're much better than that last show. It's obvious that this crowd really loves these guys. Much different than the Peppermint Lounge. It's electric in here. Exciting.

In deep contemplation, Cuz stroked his chin and cheek. His voice remained raised.

—I'm still not sure about their material though. It's a little thin, I'm afraid.

Kinnie protested.

—Well, he did say that that the second set would be all new material—so maybe we should withhold judgment until we've heard that.

—Oh there *there* now Kindred, let's not get pissy. All I said was that I'm not sure about their material.

—And all I said was let's wait until we've heard their new songs—to see if there's any growth or maturity there. The songs they sent us sounded good.

—Touché.

Cuz squinted at his assistant with a bemused expression upon his face. He greatly enjoyed the opinionated wordplay swordplay spar, though Kinnie did not. The Gods reeled through their set with professional ease—the smoky, over-filled room teeming with a crazy, drug-induced, alcohol-fueled fury. There was no air to breathe. There was no latitude for lateral movement. Undulatory upward thrusts were the only alternative.

Except for the Vetter table, the entire asphyxiated flock of frolickers seethed with an idiot rabie, tantamount to dithering blither—sloshing uncontrollably, laughing salaciously, wide-eyed, and politely dangerous. Vetter and crew were loving the experience—so vastly different from those they typically endured back east. The mood and atmosphere were real and free from the usual artifice without surcease. It was charming.

—All right then. I'm Billy Granger and we're the Unreal Gods, and we've got a set of newer stuff comin' up next. So get a drink, try to get some air and we'll be back in just a little while.

At madcap breakneck ska pace, they burst into a sprightly take of "Upstroke Down," musing upon the bravado and bluster required to succeed in the world of rock and roll—and upon the greater planet at large.

—Sittin' in a bus stop in downtown LA
So many funky people, I don't know what to say
I've got a little record I want to show around
You Hollywood producers, I got my upstroke down
Yeah, then I knew I really had it made
I got my upstroke down.

387

Sweat pouring down their faces, Col and Gib mugged behind Billy, moving in tandem unison, like real rock star posers.

—Well I've seen the rotten apple, the city of decay
Let me tell you somethin' gorgeous, don't believe a word they say
Ya' know New York they got the Yankees, the red white and the blue
It's a decent place to live aside from a muggin' or two
The mayor said we'll all have it made.
We get our upstroke down.

The song ended upon Col's needle sharp Steve Cropper-like riff, dragging through the groove, drawing to a noisy conclusion, like a nickel-weighted tone arm on a beat up forty-five. Power chord big finish and lights out. The band quickly left the stage.

In the green room, the pot and coke and booze parade began anew, in a robustly boisterous rampage of boundless profusion. Billy D. brought the break tape back up in the mains. Bob Marley and the Wailers, Peter Tosh and Jimmy Cliff. Then he wandered imposingly in the direction of the bar, deftly dividing the choked cluster of beings as he moved.

As Cuz and the girls sat evaluating the band, Tommy appeared, smiling as he unhooked the clasp on the red velvet rope and stepped up on the platform.

—So're you folks enjoyin' the show so far?

As Tommy toyingly twirled his moustache, vaguely flirting with the girls, Kindred spoke up.

—Yes. They're great. Very exciting. We're looking forward to hearing the new material.

—Yeah. It's good stuff. They're sorta headin' in a new direction. Not so mucha this reggae...

Tommy waved his hand with a flourish

—...Uh...stuff. More rock.

—That's good. You know, the Police and all the other *British Invasion* bands sort of cornered that market, and now even they've moved on to something new.

—That's true. Very true. How's about you Mister Vetter?  Wha'd'ya think of the Gods?

—Actually, I was trying to place your accent. It's not Brooklyn...

—Nah. It's Manhattan. Little Italy. You can take the man outta Little Italy, but you can't take Little Italy outta the man.

—Yes. Yes. I suppose you're right.

—I guess. I thought I'd gotten all *Oregonized* by now. So, you're enjoyin' the band then?

—Oh yes. They're good. Great. This crowd obviously loves them. It's crazy in here. I don't think I've ever seen anything quite like this. It's like CBGB and the Louisiana Hayride all rolled into one. Wild.

Somewhat spooked by Vetter's succinctly apposite observation, and aware that he had other tasks to perform, Tommy excused himself and maneuvered through the crowd, elbows smartly splayed, his hands tucked coolly into the high pocket slits of his tight white slacks. His chic, white suit-jacket draped smartly from his shoulders, a white vest buttoned over a black polyester shirt. Saturday Night Fever. A Maltese Tommy Manero with an Italio 'fro and a Zappa-black Fu Manchu.

The din in the room was practically louder than the reggae blare of the PA, as people shouted to make themselves heard, standing next to people who were shouting to make themselves heard. A dense nicotine smog hung above the room in a fine mist of miniature tar balls.

Just as the waitress brought another round of drinks to the Vetter table, Billy D. slammed down the break tape in the mix. The Unreal Gods retook the stage, standing before a withering welter, which writhed spasmodically in response to the commotion.

—All right, all right. I promised you some new songs so that's what we're gonna play. All of these were written in the last six months.

He strummed his guitar absently, as Mick brought it up in the monitor mix.

—So, we're gonna start off with a song that we just finished doin' a video for. It's called 'Police Tol' Me'.

Into the space-aged sounding intro they spun, with Gilly's glimmering keys and Col's skittering guitar swirling through the shimmering galactic span of all perpetuity. Or temporarily so, anyway.

Dapperly dressed in a tight-fitting black suit, with purple and yellow paisley shirt beneath, Col dangled a cigarette from his lip in a flattering imitation of his idol Keith Richards. His hair was a ratted pile upon his head, with mysterious faint white stripes at the temples.

Standing behind him, looking like Dad at a Sunday afternoon cookout with the boss, Gib wore black slacks, a chocolate brown shirt, with black and brown checkered hounds-tooth, tan sports coat. Billy sported a billowy, blousy white linen pirate shirt, tight black jeans tucked inside of burnished brown cowboy boots. His eyes were heavily laden with thick layers of mascara.

From the lower end of his range, Billy sang.

—Police told me
Police told me
Police told me about your plan
It's the same old story
The same old story.

Sliding in behind the second half of the verse, Gilly offered an evocative single note string line, which held across the movement of several chords, creating suspended fourths and minor sixths in their passing.

—So please please hold me
And don't let go of me
Please please hold me if you can.

In the turn, Col renewed the flickering arpeggios that had fluttered around the intro. Meanwhile, Billy solemnly intoned.

—You know what they say
The world will drive you crazy
You know what they say...

Cranked up from the break time festivities, Billy was already drenched in sweat, as he pranced around the stage in a hunched crouch during Col's fiery solo.

Meanwhile, back at the Vetter table, Kim and Kin were transfixed by Billy's every move upon the stage. Cuz diligently observed their reactions and impressions, measuring and gauging them, as if assessing the performance of a muscle car.

Coiled and snaking like a massive slithered serpent, the reptilian poisonous rabble flicked fork-tongues, across venomous fangs and crawled, creepily, towards Billy's feet. The band drove "Police Told Me" down the home stretch toward Col and Gilly's symphonic conclusion, ignoring the tangled mass squirming in the pit below the stage.

As in the opening set, the band spun from the first song to the next without hesitation, riding atop Daw's relentless kick drum, punching a hot and bothered heartbeat.

—Well, well, well. We got another one for ya' right here, it's called 'Thunder and Lightning.'

It was as if a panther dropped from a tree, as the Gods pounced on the song with animal ferocity. Gib's throbbing eighth-note bass pulsed beneath the arrangement, which had been freely borrowed from Billy Idol's "White Wedding."

—Everybody's looking for somethin' exciting
Civilization lookin' for somethin' wild
The stars are bangin' heads with the moon and the satellites

While dangerous friends are just like thunder and lightning
In the sky
Thunder and lightning
So am I I I...

The cinema's fadin' from being an art form
The television's chasing it out of town
The old rule makers refuse to get nervous
The six o'clock news is just like thunder and lightning
All night
Thunder and lightning
Open your eyes.

Squinting, his forehead wrinkled, Cuz winced at the lyric. It was indeed possible that they might have to bring in outside writers. He briefly gave thought to having Bruce write a song for the band. But he abruptly abandoned that notion, recalling the snub at the Peppermint Lounge. Maybe later.

The band swung into a tougher chorus, replicating the feel of John Lennon's "Steel and Glass."

—Thunder-er-er-er-er
Thunder-er-er-er
Thunder and lightning...

An oblivious cluster of amorphous flesh pooled and gathered in sweaty eddies and tides at Billy's feet as he began to affect running in place, a la Mick Jagger.

—Thunder-er-er-er-er
Thunder-er-er-er
It's always exciting
Just like thunder and lightning.

Col warped a tangled solo from his Les Paul, wrenching gnarled notes that moaned and cried. And then they paced through the chorus again and to another verse.

—Everybody's killing for religion
Guess I shouldn't be so damned surprised
It's really nothing—call it human survival
Civilization is just like thunder and lightning.

It wasn't that Billy's songs were stupid. But they were frequently inarticulate and superficial. Cuz knew full well that context was everything with pop idols. Elvis wasn't exactly doing Shakespeare when he broke. And the Beatles weren't reciting "Paradise Lost."

As always, charisma came first. And Billy had charisma in spades. He had charm and innocence. He was sunny. Good-humored. The girls loved him and the guys weren't threatened. It was a good combination. He had the tools to be a huge success. Given the right guidance, the right management, the right decisions, and a little good fortune—it was possible that he could be big star. Certainly bigger than Bryan Adams. Maybe bigger than Bruce. Who knew? There was no telling. Nothing was really out of the question. He was his own biggest obstacle.

At the conclusion of "Thunder and Lightning," the guys quickly toweled off and chugged big swigs from pitchers of beer. Breathless, Billy narrated.

—Okay now. This song is about fidelity. Anybody in here know what fidelity is?

There arose a few whoops and hoots from the clattering clan, but mostly inattention.

—Yeah. I didn't think so. Anyway. This is also the name of a little record store I love up in Seattle. And my favorite Buzzcocks album. It's called.. 'Singles...Going...Steady'.

From the start, the song sounded different from the others Cuz had heard before. Harder. Tougher. He was immediately attracted to the Bolero-like intro, which then broke into a driving pulse. A certain somber sobriety suspended above the song like an incongruous cloud.

—There's a companion some place for you
Who longs for you believes in you
Eventually you'll probably come flyin' through
This night's the same the way you do

Building up the real always travelin' here and there
Now is not the time to settle down
But in a while, you'll see a smile
That is worth a thousand miles
Soon you'll be back in those arms.

Somewhat surprised, Vetter was impressed by the relatively sophisticated melody and the apparent maturation exhibited within the lyrics. It buoyed his enthusiasm for Billy and the band and reinforced his belief that they could ultimately succeed.

—Singles going steady
It feels all right to me
Yes we're singles and I'm ready
I'll show the world who I'll be
Yeah you singles going steady
Well there's a lot more you will be
A lot more you will be.

Over alternating E-minor and F-major seventh chords, Billy and Col—with Gilly's underpinning synth strings, created a dusty, windswept atmosphere in the exotic turn.

It was at that very moment that Billy noticed Carrie standing off to his left at the side of the stage. He smiled, happy that she had ventured from the cave of her apartment to actually attend a show—something she rarely did. But then a troubling unpleasantness cast over the cheer of his demeanor. She was standing next to some guy. Talking to him.

The stranger looked like Elvis Costello—or, more accurately, like Marshall Crenshaw. He wore thick horn-rimmed glasses, jeans, and a tan sport-coat. The guy looked like an executive or something. Sort of slick.

A wave of profound jealousy swept over Billy. He was disgusted. Furious. Who was *he*? Why were they together? Why hadn't she told him about the guy? Billy didn't like the way the guy was looking at his girlfriend. He seemed to be consuming her with his eyes; trying to seduce her. Distractedly, Billy returned to the matter at hand: the song he was in the middle of singing.

—She wants to be a model be a movie star
A sports figure a sad song
And he'll design the cities and she'll paint them
And fly over them and start again

And some song we all sang and long, long we all sang
A million dreams go floating by and they're all meant for you and I
But first we take our rocket to the sky

Yeah, we're singles going steady....

Billy threw Carrie a dark, dirty look. He couldn't understand why she thought it was so fucking important to embarrass him in front of the band, and all his friends, and A. Cousins Vetter. It was his big moment, and she chose it to fuck with his head. She was unaware of his perturbation, she was too busy talking to that guy, which only enraged Billy all the more.

But it was not time to act upon his impulses. At the conclusion of "Singles Going Steady," the band immediately pivoted into "Apple of My Eye."

—All right then. This one's for my Mom, and my girlfriend, I guess.

Again, he scowled at Carrie, and she saw it and could not understand why he was glaring at her.

—And my girlfriend and my Mom...

The band kicked into a jagged reggae riff.

—When I was young with plenty of time to play
Hangin' on your dress in the kitchen I would stay
But now I've grown old and everything has changed
The simple things in life I would not rearrange.

Intentionally directing his concentration in the other direction, Billy did his best to ignore Carrie. He locked eyes with a prettily petite woman. She sort of looked like a slender version of Trudy. Except she had very straight, dark brown hair with long bangs. But she had Trudy's nose and mouth. She was wedged in on the opposite side, near the front of stage. She smiled flirtly up at him and he engaged her with a lost little boy, troubled expression—clearly hurt and in need of consolation.

—Yeah you're the apple of my eye
Why don't you save me just another piece of pie
Sometimes I start to think you like to make the little boys cry
Lost my wings and I can't fly.

He improvised.

—When I see you with another hungry guy.

He scowled over his shoulder in Carrie's direction.

—Sometimes I start to think you like to make the little boys cry
Why don't you spend some time with me
Spend some time with me-ee-ee-ee-ee-ee-ee.

He lowered his chin in an effort to accommodate the descending melody line of the bridge and again aimed sad moony eyes toward the cute brunette. He noticed she had a hot little body on her and that she was trying to offer him the best possible view of it. He appreciated her efforts, nodding in approval.

—I am a millionaire and I just outran my ghost
Yeah, I am a millionaire.

As if he were playing a mandolin, Col flicked a rapid sixteenth-note solo that chittered nervously over the chords of the chorus. Again, Billy made up the words as he went along.

—So I stand around and think of all the times
You and me would go out on the town
Walking in the sun was us everyday
But now there's nothing much more I need to say.

Billy swiveled on his heels and directly confronted Carrie with a menacing sneer as he returned to complete a couple more turns through the chorus. For her part, Carrie was thoroughly mystified by Billy's behavior. She thought that perhaps he was extra stoned or drunk.

But whatever was going on, she was deeply discomfited by his erratic conduct and worried that he might try to make a scene, for some reason. She gave serious thought to departing immediately—to grabbing Peter and simply splitting, but she was afraid that would only amplify Billy's hostility. She didn't know what to do.

The Gods concluded the set, running through another six songs. Billy's mood did not relent, but seemed almost to darken further as he continued to ignore Carrie, while fawning over the cute brunette.

Vetter, Kimberly and Kindred, having only seen the band on one other occasion, were not aware of any peripheral goings on. Kimmie and Kinnie were, however, keenly aware that Billy radiated an intense sexual energy, coupled with a level of anger that they could not have anticipated from him. But they found it to be incredibly sexy.

During the homestretch of "Symmetry," the final song of the set, Billy awkwardly leapt from the stage, to the side of the cute brunette standing below, where he danced with her suggestively, simulating sex as he carried out, yet again, the two notes he played on his guitar so perfect now. The cute brunette was too excited to be self-conscious. Abandoning all decorum, she methodically moved against Billy as he played—rhythmically humping his leg in time to the beat.

Aghast, utterly motionless, Carrie stood next to some guy she only knew from her classes, watching her boyfriend going at it with some mouse-haired bimbo in front of five hundred drunk people. Great! Keep moving folks. Nothing to see here.

Finally, orgasmically, Billy concluded his performance, holding taut his position, as Daw smacked the final splash cymbal. Billy grabbed the cute brunette by the hair and roughly jammed his tongue into her mouth. She kissed him back, and for a moment, it seemed that something illicit might happen right then and there.

The reluctant angels of Billy's better judgment eventually descended upon the shoulders of his neo-cortex and he let go of the girl—who was not necessarily so anxious to suspend the action.

Guiding her upright, he bashfully said hello to the bewildered girl, who had unexpectedly fallen upon a momentary strand of the web of Billy's ever-shifting existence. He was about to make casual clumsy small talk before excusing himself to head back to the green room. But.

Just then, Carrie was standing there next to him. With that asshole. She deliberately interrupted the flow of Billy's conversation with a look of imploring good will. While she had his attention, she addressed him forthrightly.

—Billy. This is Peter Stone. He's in a bunch of my classes.

Peter held out his hand to the rock star, but Billy ignored him.

—Yeah. Hi.

—He'd never seen the Gods, or heard the band, so I thought this would be a good opportunity for him to catch you at your best.

—Yeah sure. Well, welcome to the show. I hope we passed the audition.

Apparently distracted, Billy looked past Peter in the direction of the bar.

—Look, I gotta go see a guy at the bar and I gotta towel down backstage. And check in with Cuz. Good to see ya'. And it was *really* good to see you.

He frenched the little brunette again, in an obvious attempt to put Carrie in her place. To a certain extent, he succeeded. She was properly humbled in front of her guest. She got the message, whatever it was. She clearly saw, at last, the one-way rocky road *she* was walking down. And it gave her a sick feeling. She felt like throwing up.

—Okay, then. Well, we're going to go now. Thanks for being so gracious to Peter.

With a sudden dramatic pirouette, Carrie sternly and stiffly marched away from Billy, a cowed Peter Stone slogging faithfully behind.

# XXXI

—So, I take it Kindred and Kimberly aren't comin' along tonight, then?

—No. Yes. They're staying at the Benson. I've stayed there a few times on my trips into Portland. It's very nice.

—Yeah, I met David Bowie there. I have good memories of the place.

—How did it come about that you met David Bowie?

—Well, it's kind of a long story. Before I even started playin' music—but was thinkin' about it, y'know?

Nodding, the old man flashed Billy an approving expression, encouraging him to continue.

—Well, like, seven years ago or so, a local radio station put on this David Bowie look-alike contest, and I ended up winnin'.

Vetter cocked an eyebrow and smiled wryly.

—And the grand prize was gettin' to meet David Bowie and ride in a limo with him over to his show at the Coliseum, and then hang out backstage.

—That must have been very exciting.

—That was the night I decided I wanted to be a star. I figured it looked like something I could do. After that night I started learnin' about music; me and my brother ended up startin' up a band. And here I am.

A hint of silence briefly breezed between them before they resumed the conversation.

—The house where I'm staying belongs to a friend. It's up here somewhere. Richard, are you okay up there? Are you going to be able to find it again?

Concerned, A. Cousins Vetter called up to the limo driver.

—Yes, Mister Vetter. I'm right on it. We should be there in just a couple of minutes.

Vetter leaned back in his seat, relaxing.

—I'm thinking of buying this place. It's very nice. A great view of the city and the mountain. Mount...?

—Hood.

—Yes. Mount Hood. It's a beautiful mountain.

—Yeah. I guess it is. You grow up with it there and ya' really don't think about it too much. But Oregon's truly a beautiful state.

—From what I've seen, I'd have to agree with you. A lot of different climates it seems.

—I think it's got about everything you could want. High desert, rolling prairies, alpine vistas.

Tunelessly, Billy sang the words.

—There's this verdant Willamette valley we live in, and a rainforest between here and the Pacific and the beautiful coastline.

For someone making such an effort to be so nonchalant about the subject, Billy seemed to Vetter to be the ultimate tour guide. His descriptions sounded as if they had been lifted directly from a travel brochure. And Vetter was not very far from being absolutely correct with that evaluation. A report for Mister Harvey's fifth grade class still maintained a distinct position within Billy's often frazzled brain.

—Portland is really a delightful city. I'm just not sure if I could handle the weather year 'round. All the rain.

—It starts clearin' up around here eventually—usually in May or so. April is tough though. There'll be a day or two that are really gorgeous. You'll start thinkin' it's, like, summer. And then it'll pour for a week.

—It's said, you know, 'April is the cruelest month...'

—What is that? I've heard that before.

—The 'Wasteland'? T.S. Eliot? The poet? Are you familiar with T.S. Eliot?

As might be predicted, the name only vaguely registered.

—He's rather famous.

—I probably slept through that class. My high school English teachers were pretty incompetent. I guess I was too, now that I think about it. Everything was about memorizing. Boring.

—Hmmm...

With his elbow perched on the armrest, Vetter cradled his chin in his hand.

Richard guided the limo up a long, winding, tree-lined drive. Approaching the brightly lit structure, Billy could see that it was huge. Probably built in the fifties: a sort of angular ark effect was created by the converging roofs and vaulted ceilings of the main quarters and the appendaged rooms, which surrounded the chateau on several different levels.

Billy estimated that the place probably had at least ten bedrooms—and who knew what else. He was intrigued, but not all together certain why Vetter was taking him there. He hoped desperately it was not to try to seduce him. He'd had about all the drama he could handle for one night.

Pulling up to the entryway, Richard secured the limo and hopped out to open the door for Mister Vetter and his guest. They convened in the foyer. Vetter explained.

—This house belongs to my friend Alan Palmer. He's currently out of the country on tour with Paul McCartney, serving as bandleader and one of his keyboardists. It's something else, isn't it?

—I don't think I've ever seen a house like this. It's a mansion, but it's sort of like a clubhouse, too.

—That's an interesting perspective. An architect named Robert Green designed it. Alan says that he was a student of Frank Lloyd Wright.

—Frank Lloyd Wright supposedly designed a house in Silverton.

—Yes. The Gordon House. From what Alan has said, Robert Green designed this house using some of the principles Wright employed on the Gordon House. Utonian? Usonian? Usonian. United States. U-S. Yes. I guess he took the design of this house a step or two further than what Wright had in mind.

With a blank stare glazed across his face, Billy zoned. Noticing the situation, Vetter apologized

—Oh. I'm sorry...

Vetter sang in a monotone.

—Too much information...

Billy world was temporarily frozen in space and time.

—Well, come along then. I'll show you some of the high spots.

They took a brief tour of the estate. Billy gawked and marveled.

Leading Billy to one of the lower levels, Vetter presented a large open space with various rooms adjoining.

—As I said, I'm thinking of buying this house...for Rough Edge. And if I do, I want to convert this area here into a recording studio, with living quarters in-house, upstairs. A package, if you will. I would have a gourmet cook and a full staff, on-call at all times. There would be quarters for ten or fifteen people. There's a small swimming pool and a hot tub. All the amenities.

—I could see bands comin' in from all over the world to record here. This is a really nice spot. What's the name of that chateau where the Stones recorded *Exile On Main Street*? Somethin' like that maybe.

—Villa Nellcote? Well, I guess the concept is similar, but I wouldn't want all the debauchery here—and I don't imagine it would really be necessary. I think work could get accomplished. And it seems like there are plenty of activities in Portland.

Billy nodded respectfully, acknowledging to himself that he could understand why no band would want to express entirely the pits of depravity to which they were subject.

—Well, *Exile*'s about their best album ever, so whatever went on there must've worked.

Vetter raised an eyebrow askance, smiling wryly.

—The advantage here is that it didn't serve as a headquarters for the Gestapo during the occupation as the Villa Nellcote did. The downside, of course, is that it's not located on the French Riviera.

They strolled among the rooms and Vetter described his plans for the lower level "basement."

—This open section of course would be the main performance area. I would put vocal and sound booths there and there.

He pointed toward three capacious bedrooms on one side of the space, then wheeled and gestured in the opposite direction.

—The control room would be the master bedroom there. That wall seems perfect for the soundproof windows. And the room is large enough to serve that function, to accommodate eight or ten people comfortably. There is even a restroom and shower attached.

—That's pretty handy.

—And when it's finished, I would like for you to be the first to record here.

—That sounds great. What time should we be here?

Chuckling, Vetter responded.

—Well, it will probably be a few years yet. I hope you will do more recording before then.

—Oh yeah. I intend to. We really wanna finish recording enough tracks to make an album out of the stuff we recorded at the Power Station.

—Not a bad idea. Listen, about that. I would like for your attorneys to meet with my attorneys with the intention of your signing a contract with Rough Edge. Maybe for three or five albums. Something substantial.

Air flushed from Billy's lungs in a sudden rush.

—Attorneys?

—Yes, of course. We'll want to have a look at your books. We'll want to know what kind of load we're taking on, you know.

—Books?

The blood drained from Billy's face, turning him a sickly shade of pale yellow. The idea of *bookkeeping* had never come up in the history of the band—except for dope deals, possibly. They usually just gave money to whoever bitched loudest, managing to keep everything afloat. Even the general concept of *books* was pretty foreign to the Gods. Magazines and television were more their speed.

—Yes. Do you have an accountant?

—Uh, no.

—Most bands don't. I'm not surprised.

—Do you think we oughta get one?

—Yes. I think it's a good idea. When you start getting to the point in your career where you are making a lot of money, you'll need an accountant to maintain your books and taxes for you, if nothing else.

Jutting out his lower lip, Billy blew the bangs away from his forehead and ran his hand against the side of his face.

—Well, I guess I've got a lot to learn. It's kinda like gettin' called up to the majors from Triple-A.

Vetter seemed puzzled by Billy's reference. Billy answered his questioning expression.

—Baseball.

—Oh, I see. Yes. I could see some similarity. I suppose I am asking you to come up to the major leagues.

Billy said nothing. But he smiled as wide as the Morrison Bridge.

It wasn't until the end of June that Billy finally got around to consulting an attorney. After giving the subject significant consideration, he chose to meet with Jessie James Joyce, the well-known Portland music attorney who had helped to engineer Dollarshine's three-album million-dollar deal with Gaffen.

Sitting in Joyce's office, Billy eyed the cute secretary with the light blond hair. He thought she sort of resembled Morgan Fairchild: slender, elegantly beautiful. Her lengthy hair, extensively dryer blown and windswept, had a certain allure in Billy's estimation. But she was better looking than Morgan Fairchild. More fun. Like a cheerleader. Maybe not drop-dead gorgeous—like Happy—but definitely worth a tumble.

Also, he had a keen admiration for her body. She was quite slender, but she had righteous tits going on beneath her sheer white blouse. From her desk, she would occasionally glance in his direction and he would smile seductively, flirting casually, as if for mere sport. You never know—might get lucky.

Her phone buzzed and she picked up the receiver.

—Yes, sir. I will. All right. Mister Granger, Mister Joyce will see you now.

She stood up, smoothing down the front of her black skirt.

—Right this way.

Oh show me the way there slim—Billy thought to himself, as he appreciatively watched her lead him down the hallway to Mister Joyce's office, I'd follow *that* anywhere.

—Misteh Grangeh. Billeh.

Jesse James Joyce stood up from his desk and strode forcefully toward Billy, his hand extended.

—It's good to see you again. Sit down. Please. Sit down. Thank you, Leila.

Smiling broadly, he waved off his secretary, and, with a polite flourish, beckoned Billy toward a chair at his desk, as he sat in his majestic chair. Distracted by Leila leaving the room, Billy stood, momentarily befuddled before he managed to shake himself free from watching her ass. Man, I would...

Charming Jessie James Joyce purred a droll drawl: sweet as syrup poured atop a soft mound of mashed candied yams.

—So, Billeh. To what do I owe the distinct plezshuh of this visit?

—Well, Mister Joyce...

—JJ, please. You can call me JJ. All my friends do.

He oozed a silky charm that caught Billy up short. But he decided to plunge ahead anyway.

—Well, uh, JJ—I've been talkin' to Mister A. Cousins Vetter, negotiating a possible contract with Rough Edge, and he started askin' me questions about the business side of the band that I couldn't really answer.

With a frank nod of familiarity, JJ replied.

—Yes. It often happens at this staige, for many ahtists. You'uh used to taikin' all the money you maike and usin' it to pay off yoah debts; then splittin' what's left between the membehs of the organizaytion. The *spoyals*, as it wurh. Afteh that thehs nothin' left.

—That's about right. We've got a lot of expenses. And everybody's got their own bills to pay and stuff like that.

—Yes. I undehstand. It's the naichuh of the music industreh. A majoriteh of the bayunds in the wuld simpleh toil away in relehtive obscuriteh and theh neveh reach aneh level of succayess much above maikin' a livin' out of theyeh endevehs—if theyeh luckeh enough to do even thayat. It's sayad but true. No one's gotten rich just plaiyin' the clubs fohreveh.

Shifting his weight in his chair, JJ Joyce drummed a pen on his desk.

—So how may I be of surhvice, Billeh?

—Well, I guess I need you to help me figure all this out. I know ya' did a good job for Dollarshine, y'know, negotiatin' their deal with Gaffen, and I figured maybe you could help with us. And I guess I need help findin' an accountant who can look at our books—or help us to make up books we don't have.

—No one has been doin' aneh bookkeepin'? Foh how long has *thayat* been goin' on?

—Forever. We never needed to do bookkeeping'. Like I said—there was nothin' to, y'know, *keep*?

Chewing on the pen, absently gazing at the ceiling, Joyce swiveled playfully in his brown leather chair, slowly rocking forward and backward with each succeeding rotation. He halted his movements at the conclusion of a forward thrust and engaged Billy with a pixilated expression.

—Okeh then. I just needed to know if you had yoah financial hayouse in oahdeh. But I can see I'm pritteh much gettin' in on the gray-ound floah heah.

—Yeah, I guess you could say that. We gotta be over way fifty thousand in debt.

Not at all fazed by Billy's disclosure, Joyce summed up the gist of their conference and then made a request of the young man.

—Well, Billeh, theh *ah* a few things I need foh you to do foah me.

A certain fatherly concern befell JJ Joyce as he proceeded to lay out for Billy a rigorous plan for providing his associate accountant with a reasonable estimate regarding the band's income and expenditures. He instructed the bewildered musician that he should locate the band's calendar for the previous two years and attempt to calculate how much they had earned in that time. Then he asked poor Billy to average out a list of regular expenditures.

Fully aware that a great deal of the band's money was used to fuel their relentless coke and weed habits (a deduction he was unable to fully address with Mister Joyce), Billy expressed concern over assessing accounts for items such as stage clothing and other necessary *stuff*.

Joyce, cognizant as to what Billy was alluding, suggested he just maintain a column for "miscellaneous" expenses, which could include things such as gas, food, lodging, gratuities, laundry and everything else the band could possibly factor into the mix. Recording? Posters? Printing costs? You bet. Fishnets for the Goddesses? Make-up for Billy, Gilly and Col? No doubt. Van repair? New Tires? New van? The list of possibilities was endless. Everything was in play.

Relieved, and generally more comfortable with his assignment, Billy left JJ Joyce's office with a confident sense of growth and maturity. Things were moving along quite nicely and in the proper direction, in his opinion anyway.

Passing through the waiting area Billy narrowed his eyes suggestively as he ambled past Leila. Complicit in the temptation dance, she widened her lips seductively in return. Billy would have loved to have seen her naked, spread across her desk like cream cheese. If JJ would only step out for coffee... He shook free of his fantasy, gave her one last glance over his shoulder and closed the door behind him.

It took about six weeks for Billy to cobble together a pile of assorted papers that was meant to serve as the "books" for which there seemed to be so much demand. In reality, it was just a bunch of stuff that Billy had the other members jot down, at random, on scraps of paper.

For the higher ticket items, Billy D. managed to produce an array of receipt books, from which were elicited counterfeit ring and valve jobs for the band van, as well as the repair of a blown head gasket, a transmission overhaul, brakes, and a wheel-bearing job.

In addition, the band actually had a few legitimate receipts. And then there were all the loans they had out. The loans alone were more than ninety grand—thirty-five thousand just for the video production of "Police Told Me." They were in deep.

After dawdling a brief dalliance with lovely Leila gatekeeper at the front desk—an interlude filled with delicious sexual tension and smolderingly nuanced innuendo—Billy's subsequent meeting with Jesse James Joyce was a bit of an eye-opener for the naïve young musician.

Upon briefly perusing the books, such as they were, JJ quickly arrived at the conclusion that the band should seriously consider bankruptcy. Immediately.

A wave of immense discomfort washed over Billy; his face withered at the mere suggestion. He did not feel comfortable abandoning his benefactors—in one particular case it might mean abject physical harm to his person and belongings. That possibility was imminent and immensely worrisome. He was not indebted to banks. He was beholden to friends and family. Big difference.

Brooding, Billy sat motionless in his chair across from JJ Joyce, as the lawyer stood up from his desk and began to pace intently around the room.

—You know, Billeh. I've been givin' a lot of thought to yoah situaytion, and I wanted to tell you that I have been considerin' comin' out of retahment to represent you in yoah negotiaytions with Rough Edge. What do you think of thayut possibiliteh?

—Wow, JJ! That's amazing. I don't know what to say. I mean, I know what ya' did for Dollarshine. It'd be great if you could do that for us.

—Well, that's just it, Billeh. I'm not realleh int'rested in actin' on behay-uff of the rest of the bayund. I am most int'rested in managin' yoah careeuh. Gaddin' yoah pay-uth.

Dazed at the suggestion, Billy babbled a reply.

—Gee, man, I don't know, JJ, we've, uh...we've been through an awful lot of...a lot together. I'm not sure how I'd feel about just desertin' the others in the middle of the stream, especially when we've almost made it to the other side.

—I completely undehstayund, Billeh. You fellas ah no doubt like brothehs to each otheh. That's the life of bayundmates.

—I mean, I appreciate the offer. I, I mean we could really use your help.

—Well, Billeh. It's just that I honestleh don't think the band is vereh good. Thayuh ah a lot of obvious weaknesses.

Frowning at the critique, Billy did not respond.

—I would like to put you togetheh with a new suppoahting cayast, maybe of a little higheh oadeh of musical sophisticaytion. Pehaps find a musician oah two who could help with the soangrattin'.

Offended, Billy felt cut by the unexpected jab.

—Well, it's always seemed like people like our material. Like the band. I've never heard anybody complain or anything.

—No, no, Billeh. Don't misundehstayund what it is I'm tran' ta say. Yoah songs ah vereh catcheh. But I believe they could be a little moah musicalleh developed. Moah complex. Just the presence of new blood would cehtainleh help to accomplish thayut goal, too. New directions.

—I think we're evolvin' pretty nicely on our own JJ. It got us where we are. I wouldn't feel right headin' off on my own. Not now.

Sensing the negotiations to be at an impasse, JJ Joyce sighed.

—Allrat, Billeh. If that's the way you feel, I won't trah to chaynge yoah mand. Not rat now anyway.

Parting amicably, they shook hands with firm resolution. Billy was all the more convinced of the invincibility of his belief in the band. Jesse James Joyce reaffirmed to himself that all musicians were oblivious fools.

Like so many others, the Gods were not well suited for the music business: they were all music and no business. It was the rare musician savvy enough to understand the nuances of the business end of things.

Not altogether displeased by the outcome of his meeting with JJ Joyce, Billy coolly drifted down the hallway in the direction of Leila's desk. As he approached, he whispered to her.

—What'cha workin' on there, gorgeous?

She spun around in her seat, pertly pursing her lips; slightly crossing her eyes.

—A contract. Is it for you?

—Naw. Not today. We've got a lot of contracts to consider and we need to put just the right team in place.

With a deep and abiding sense of curiosity, she inquired politely.

—What do you do?

Surprised, and rendered suddenly somewhat modest by her unfamiliarity with the band, he said.

—I'm a musician. I'm in the band the Unreal Gods?

No sign of recognition; perhaps, even, a look of slight antipathy.

—We're pretty well known around town. We play all the popular clubs.

—I really don't go to clubs very often. I don't drink. I guess you might say I'm something of a religious prude.

Billy's face dropped, disappointment visibly written in a dark, cursive frown of ill-fortune.

—That's t-...

He started to say "that's too bad," narrowly avoiding the faux pas.

—That's t-errific. Really.

As was common for her, she was instantaneously aware of the solicitously callous tone in Billy's voice, and she promptly began to dial him out of her field of awareness. A veil had descended. The pair were left with nothing to say, no innocent flirtation. Only the sensation of naked anxiety.

Waving ineffectually, Billy turned and got the hell out of JJ Joyce's office. *Weird chick. All pent up. Mushrooms would probably do her good. Get her out of that repressive thing. Set her free. Make her get all wild and crazy. Boy, I bet that would be a fuckin' fun time. It's always the prim, proper ones...Wham bam thank you ma'am. Turn all black-leather sado on your ass. Hot. I'd like to be around for that. Eee-haw.*

Vetter returned to Portland, without Kimberly and Kindred in tow, for the band's Labor Day extravaganza weekend at Starry Night. Against Tommy's wishes, Billy booked the shows at Starry Night. Tommy and the owner of the venue, Barry Hurrvitz, had a long-running feud that began not long after La Bamba first opened.

Considerably more roomy than La Bamba, and even Euphoria, Starry Night had a capacity of around fourteen hundred (maybe sixteen hundred, under the right conditions—conditions which generally included the possibility of dollar signs and zeroes). Barry was known to keep all windows in the building closed, even on the hottest nights—under the impression that people would be more thirsty and would likely drink more under those conditions. People fainted a lot at Starry Night.

It had once been a Longshoreman's meeting hall, down on Northwest 6th Avenue about eight blocks away from Tommy's little empire on the other side of Burnside. In Barry's opinion, his rival was siphoning off valuable trade, not only by drawing three to five hundred customers away from his club. But, in addition, it was a well-known fact around town that La Bamba was the preferred spot for cool, touring bands, emergent acts, such as Adam and the Ants, Bow Wow Wow, and the Divinyls. It irked Barry to no end.

Shortly after the club had opened, Hurrvitz directed a Starry Night flunkie to blow up a porcelain urinal in the La Bamba men's room with an M-80. In retaliation, Tommy repeatedly and frequently called the fire marshal, turning Barry in for exceeding his room capacity.

The fire marshal would enter the room and straight away order the PA shut down until Barry had cleared three or four hundred people from the room, which was not easy and sometimes impossible.

The necessity of administering refunds was far more than just an inconvenience for Barry, the loss of income tore at his very soul—or it would have torn at his very soul, except for the unfortunate fact that he really did not have a soul. Barry was motivated by money alone. Money was the substitute for his heart. Money was his blood. Money was the object. Objects were the only finite things in life.

In retribution for Tommy's indiscretions, Barry would dispatch a flock of minions to spread counterfeit twenty-dollar bills at La Bamba concerts, which caused Tommy no end of run-ins with Portland police detectives.

Not to be outdone, a vengeful Tommy paid underage young girls to obtain fake I.D.; which would allow them to gain illegal entry into Starry Night, whereupon Tommy would report the violations to the OLCC: who were frequently wont to investigate the infringements immediately. The outcome of the probes often led to Starry Night being shut down for several weeks at a time. During those hiatuses, Barry would fume and plot. Plot and fume.

Still and all, in booking the Labor Day weekend at Starry Night, it had been Billy's intention to offer Vetter a different view of the band in a larger, more nondescript hall—more resembling those in which the band would likely play when touring in support of an album. Of course, they would be happy opening for Bowie or the Stones. But the realities of the business were not entirely lost on the Unreal Gods. Opening for the Divinyls was more like it.

Along with a couple of friends, A. Cousins Vetter attended the Saturday evening portion of the Labor Day Weekend events. He was both pleased and impressed. Billy and the band had again grown, incrementally it seemed, in the four months since he had seen them last.

In Cuz's estimation, the band seemed more sophisticated. And Billy, especially, appeared more rugged. Tougher. More masculine and attractive. Mature—or heading in the general direction of maturity, anyway. Cuz's friends agreed that the Unreal Gods were a good band and that Billy had real star power. Looks and charisma. The Elvis.

The following evening, just after seven, Cuz picked up Billy at the band house in a long white limo, impressing immensely the members of the band who happened to be hanging around the place at the time. With all due dispatch, Cuz and Billy hied across the Morrison Bridge, traveling up Belmont on the inner eastside, to the renowned Genoa restaurant, located at Southeast 29th.

There, seven-thirty reservations awaited them. They anticipated an evening dining on Genoa's famous five-course classic Italian meal. The atmosphere was quietly reserved and dignified, though not stuffy or pretentious. Cozy and inviting, though with a faint air of formal propriety.

The low, rectangular brown brick building that housed the restaurant, was decorated to look like a beloved grandmother's parlor and dining room, with dimly lit antique chandeliers hanging from the ceiling over each of the tables.

A traditionally dressed waitstaff scurried efficiently between the tables, preparing the patrons for the two and half hour food production that was to follow. The reservation times for each party had been staggered slightly to allow the staff to tend to the immediate needs of the latest guests without ignoring those who were preparing to receive their first or second courses.

Cuz and Billy were seated at a secluded table behind a small partition at the farthest corner of the room, providing them the privacy they desired for their negotiations over dinner. A prim server named Mary hurried to fill Vetter's wine request, as the two of them perused the scant menu.

Only the main course and the dessert allowed for any alternates at all, and that was a choice between only two or three dishes for each course. With so few options, Mary easily memorized their main course selections. She took their menus and once again hastened off.

The meal began with "Terrina di fegato con tarftufi," a terrine of chicken and duck livers garnished with Oregon truffles and served with a radicchio marmalade and persimmons and quince mostarda.

As they leisurely poked at their plates, Cuz and Billy sized each other up, like two wrestlers preparing to grapple in earnest. Pouring Billy a glass of wine, Cuz initiated the exchange.

—So, Billy, my friends really enjoyed the band at Starry Night. And they were quite impressed with you.

—That's good to hear, Cuz. I really trust your instincts, and I can't tell you how much we appreciate your interest.

—Now, you had a meeting with Jesse James Joyce last month. That's correct, isn't it?

Billy bobbed his head in agreement.

—Yeah. We met.

—And how did that go?

—Not very well. We really didn't see eye to eye. We, uh...couldn't get on the same page.

—How so?

—Well, he advocated some things I could never go for.

—Such as?

—He thinks we should go bankrupt. That would be just fine if we had taken out a big, hundred thousand dollar loan from a bank or somethin'. But we borrowed it all from friends and family—pretty much everybody we know. We can't screw all of them over. If we hit it big, it's gonna be a pay off for everybody. They're bettin' on us like we're a horse.

—I see. Yes.

—I mean we still owe Jack who recorded our first album and Daw's dad and Gilly's brother and Tommy and another local bar owner... They've all invested in us. If we tried to blow 'em all off, our ass'd be grass in this town. We'd never live it down, man.

The pasta course arrived: Casonsei—traditional ravioli with roasted beets and a house made ricotta cheese tossed in poppy seed butter with Satsuma mandarin oranges.

In an instant the conversation hung suspended, as Dvorak's familiar *Ninth Symphony* softly played through the house sound system. Cuz lifted his head as if detecting a familiar, favored scent. Informatively, he said.

—*The New World Symphony*. Dvorak. You know Decca Records wanted to create an album that combined rock music with a symphony orchestra. They wanted to explore the possibilities of stereo, which was still a rather new technology at that time.

Mellowing nicely on a second glass of wine, Billy was actually interested in Cuz's account, and listened attentively.

—Decca thought that classical music better lent itself to richer stereo recordings than rock did. The Moody Blues and their producer sort of walked into the project. Decca wanted them to put lyrics to classical pieces. But once they were in the studio, the band decided to go in a different direction.

His back stiff, stick-straight, with his hands awkwardly folded in his lap, Billy smiled at the suggestion that a band might lie to a label in order to record whatever the hell they wanted once they got in the studio.

—It's my understanding that they would record their songs and then they would immediately turn them over to a fellow who would quickly arrange them for orchestration and *he* would gather a small company and they would record the symphonic parts behind and around the Moodies songs.

Billy nodded with a bemused smile. He interjected.

—Y'know, I always thought 'Tuesday Afternoon' was a blatant rip-off of 'A Day in the Life'.

His lower lip jutting, Vetter's face wrinkled in concentration, mulling Billy's assertion

—The melody of the verses of 'Tuesday Afternoon' is just a compressed version of the verses of 'A Day in the Life'. Think about it. It's just compressed down, but it's

410

the same structure and the movement of the tune is almost identical. 'Tues...day. I read the news today. Afternoon. Oh boy.'

Silently singing to himself, Vetter began to bob his head in affirmation. Billy feigned George Burns, scat-singing pale melodies.

—And the middle part—'I'mlookinatmyselfreflectionsofmymind'—man that's the same chords and feel as—'Wokeupgotouttabeddraggedacombacrossmyhead'. It's the same thing, just changed around a little. 'Tuesday Afternoon's' probably a better song for the radio. But John Lennon wrote the original.

Billy savored the final mandarin slice on his plate, satisfied that he had stated his theory—succinctly he thought, and very well supported by the evidence.

Seeming to agree, Cuz's eyes brightened as he saw Mary bringing another bottle of that wonderful fifty-eight Barolo Fontanafredda. As she opened the bottle and poured, he inquired

—Would you happen to know how many more bottles of this Barolo you have in stock?

She gathered up the dishes from the pasta course, and answered with great efficiency.

—Two, I believe, sir.

—Oh, that would be perfect.

—I'll be back with your salads, and I'll find out what our Barolo supply is.

—Yes, would you please. It's really quite wonderful.

The wine negotiations concluded, Vetter returned his full attention to his young protégé. Billy thought of another Moody Blues connection.

—You remember the Moody Blues' Threshold label?

—Yes. Certainly. They remained with Decca, but they got their own imprint. I think they might still use the Threshold logo. I'm not sure.

—Well, one of the first bands they signed to that label was a band called Providence. They were from Portland. It was, like, about ten years ago or so.

—Oh, I remember them. They sounded just like the Moody Blues.

Mary, with the wine steward in tow, returned with their salads. The steward assured the patrons that the restaurant actually had two more bottles of the Barolo still remaining, information which brought great joy to Cuz.

Their salads were comprised of fresh Dungeness crab and grilled polenta-like panatella, dressed with a Meyer lemon and roasted garlic vinaigrette, and accompanied by panettone one-eyed susans made with red and green peppers and pine nuts. With their plates properly arranged and their glasses refilled, Billy steered the conversation back in the direction of Providence.

—Well, yeah, Providence had some similarities to the Moody Blues, I guess. Kind of mystical lyrics...I know the guitar player, Andy Guzie and Bart Bishop the singer—he played keyboards, too. I met 'em after they broke up. Seventy-six? Seventy-seven? Somewhere in there. Andy still lives in town. I think Bart moved down to LA.

—They seemed to be quite talented. I remember that album they did for Threshold. Strings and harpsichords and such. Very versatile.

—Yeah. And they got Mount Hood on the cover, too. They played at my high school when I was a junior. That was the only time I ever actually saw 'em. They're a little older than me.

The conversation lulled, as the pair parried and thrust at their salads, spearing shards of crab and attacking the spongy panatella with gastronomic gusto. Satisfied that the wining and dining was going satisfactorily, Vetter decided to get down to business.

—Now, Billy. Let's talk about you and Rough Edge Records, and what it will take to have you signed to a contract by the end of this conversation?

Briefly stunned by the question, the dizzy young man attempted to collect his careening thoughts.

Uhhh. Um...I don't know, what did you have in mind?

Like an eagle, convinced of the oblivious indifference of its quarry, Cuz slowly circled in for the slaughter. His pinpoint instincts honed to multiplicative resolution, he homed in upon his prey.

—Well, I have several ideas, actually. Some concern you alone. Others apply to you and the band.

Curiosity piqued, Billy brightened at the prospect of an imminent proposition. He beamed broadly, inquisitively.

—What I would like to suggest to you, Billy, is this. I am very interested in your future and I want to play a part in developing that future, long term, over a period of many years. That is my specialty: developing the careers of promising young artists.

A bemused, fanciful expression crossed Billy's face. Promising young artist.

—I would like to sign you to an individual contract, a six-album contract.

Raising his eyebrow, Billy aimed a sideward gaze at Cuz. Vetter continued with his customary circulatory spiral. He narrowed in.

—I would be willing to compensate you generously, of course. I was thinking in the neighborhood of five hundred thousand, give or take, whatever you think you need.

—Dollars?

—No. Five hundred thousand trout for your fish farm, of course.

Billy's head reeled. Vetter cooed.

—Yes Billy, five hundred thousand dollars. And I expect we would pay your existing debt, so that you could get a fresh financial start. Maybe finance a small studio for you, so you can work on new material.

Pretty sure he was having either a mushroom flashback or some other form of auditory hallucination, the lad shook his head incredulously.

—That sounds great. I think I could go for that.

—And for the band, I would propose perhaps one hundred thousand dollars in a developmental deal of some sort, and we would finance a four-song EP to launch the band on the national level.

Confusion seeped into the grandeur. Billy tried to weigh the offer Cuz was making, but it was complicated and the wine was having its effect.

—Wha'd'ya mean? It sounds like you're talkin' about a coupla different deals.

—Yes, you're right in a way. It's a tiered sort of arrangement. Your contract would be separate from that of the band. And the Unreal Gods would be under contract to record one album—an EP—for Rough Edge. We would pay off all your debts. Square you up. We would pay for the recording of the EP and any subsequent album. And we would assume all distribution and promotional responsibilities for your record.

Desperate dense fog surrounded Billy as he attempted to assemble his rapidly fractalizing thoughts into some form of rational coherence. As luck would have it, Mary reappeared on the scene to retrieve their salad plates in preparation for the main course. Somewhat relieved, Billy was afforded a little time to assimilate all that Cuz was proffering. It was almost too much for him to grasp.

But after a minute or two, it began to dawn on him that he was being tendered an agreement separate from that of the band. The band would have their own contract and get their own payday. Everyone would be happy. In his mind such an accord seemed tenable. He could justify the disparities with only a modicum of solicitous rationalization. He was going to be rich.

Before he could voice a feeble reply, or even a flimsy opinion, Mary fortuitously returned with their dishes and another bottle of Barolo. Cuz had the cod, poached in olive oil. merluzzo e baccala. It was served with salt cod croquettes, accompanied by a sunchoke and fennel puree; paired with a salad of shaved fennel, oranges and black olives.

Avoiding anything exotic, such as the goose cooked two ways—Duo d'Oca, Billy did not stray far from his roots, opting for the Italian take on Beef Wellington— filet mignon enfolded with paste-like mushroom duxelle and lean prosciutto in a puff pastry. It was complemented by a truffle infused demi-glace generously ladled over wilted spinach.

Not to be deterred—and not wishing for Billy to get too entirely distracted before the deal was closed—Cuz moved the negotiations inexorably forward.

—Do you understand where I'm going with all this?

—Yeah. I think so. It's all a lot for me to comprehend, y'know?

—Yes, I understand. It's a lot to take in all at once. That's one reason why it's a good idea to have an attorney retained.

—But I trust you, Cuz. You've been around. You know what you're doin'.

Cuz reflexively lifted a finger in corroboration.

—Y'know, when I was in high school, I had major league scouts—baseball— checkin' me out for a while. And I always let my dad handle the business end of things. He had experience. He played professional baseball and he'd been around a time or two. I trusted him. And I trust you.

It was exceedingly uncommon for Vetter to encounter such ingenuousness. In a way that was rather unusual—for him—he was genuinely touched. He was refreshed and charmed by Billy's intractable wholesomeness. He sensed a wave of real altruism wash over him. But eventually that tide ebbed.

Vetter envisioned the easy millions to be made from marketing Billy Granger dolls to pre-teen girls. He began to calculate the millions in residuals to be garnered from promoting the Billy Granger line of young men's clothing. Posters. TV commercials. Television guest appearances. The Tonight Show. Johnny would love this kid. The all-American boy. Red, white, and blue all over.

—I'll do everything I can to guide you, Billy, but I really do think you should secure some sort of legal representation.

Halfway through a big fork full of the Wellington, crumbs dribbling from the corners of his mouth, Billy replied.

—I really appreciate that, Cuz. I'll see about findin' a lawyer ASAP. But I'm really lookin' for your guidance. I mean, you're, like, a legend in the industry.

Vetter modestly averted his eyes.

—I want to sit at your feet and learn the ins and outs of the business from you.

It appeared that Billy's unintentional flattery got him everywhere with Cuz, who was again suffering from the outrageous slings of fortune's piercing arrows. Oh, and there was an outrageous fortune to be made, most certainly.

The lad was destined to be a bad boy teen idol, like that hot young Matt Dillon. In fact, they even looked a little alike. Perhaps Billy might have an acting career ahead of him. The possibilities were endless. If the deal took a million dollars, it was worth the investment to sign him. Worth every penny.

—That's very nice of you, Billy. I'm honored that you think of me like that.

—It's true, Cuz. A lot of the people you've worked with are heroes of mine, like Springsteen and Patti Smith. And to think that I might be workin' with the guy who guided their careers. Man, that blows my mind. It really does. I really can't believe it. It's been a long strange trip, Cuz. A fuckin' long strange trip.

—Oh. It really hasn't been *that* long, has it, Billy?

—Well, it's been goin' on six years since me and Denny started the Malchicks, and almost eight since I decided I wanted to be a star, after meetin' David Bowie.

—Was that really what inspired you to become a rock star?

Vetter smirked, sensitively.

—No. Not a *rock* star. Just a star. I wasn't sure what I was gonna do. I just knew I was gonna be a star.

—You're finding your way fairly well, I'd say.

—Yeah. I'm...we're doin' great. But it's not like it's overnight success or anything.

A complete scan of his thoughts and recollections necessarily required Vetter to conclude that five years in the music industry was nothing. Considering the abbreviated length of the typical musician's "day," five years was, essentially, overnight success. Cuz agreed with Billy anyway.

—No. Of course not. You've probably played hundreds of shows in that time and you've certainly mastered your craft. That's evident.

—Thanks, Cuz. We've put in our time. We have. The Gods have done four or five hundred gigs. Easy. Probably even more than that. A lot. The Malchicks didn't play that many gigs. Maybe a hundred. But, I'm tellin' ya'...Shit, Cuz. This wine is fuckin' me up.

A. Cousins Vetter neatly crossed his knife and fork upon his plate. Like a wizened eagle, wings volant, he extended entaloned claw in Billy's direction.

—Billy, I've truly enjoyed getting to know you over the past few months and I'm confident that we are going to do great work together.

It was Billy's turn to grin. And it was time for dessert.

# XXXII

After concluding their meal with a tacit gentleman's agreement to Vetter's contractual proposition, Billy had Richard drop him off at Carrie's apartment. Departing from the back of the blizzard white limousine, Billy peeked his head inside, his arms draped across the door and roof.

—Well, Cuz. It's a pleasure doin' business with ya! I think you're right. We're gonna do some great things together.

—Yes, Billy. I'm sure we will. I'll have Kindred draw up a contract and we can go over the fine points then. But for now, I will begin to develop a plan as to how we are going to market and promote you.

—I'm lookin' forward to gettin' started, Cuz. I can't wait. Just give me the word and we'll get these doggies rollin' on makin' a record for ya! We'll give ya' somethin' great. I can promise ya' that.

To Vetter, Billy's bravado seemed quaint and endearingly naïve.

—I'm going to hold you to that promise, Billy, I assure you.

Nearly shrieking Vetter tittered stridently.

Billy stood on the sidewalk staring at the limo as it flurried away. He liked riding in limos. It suited him. He wandered over to the plexiglass double doors at the entrance to Carrie's building. With the little phone in his hand, he buzzed her apartment, leaning against the wall next to the bank of buttons.

—Ye-es?

—Hey. Baby. It's Billity Bobbity Boo.

—It's what?

—It's me. Your lovuhboy. How do you call your lovuhboy?

—Billy? What are you talking about?

—Buzz me in 'n' I'll come right up an' tell ya' alla bout it.

A hum and a click he was inside the building. Up the elevator he went to the third floor.

Carrie's apartment was scrupulously neat, thoroughly spotless, meticulously fastidious—not a thing out of place. Compulsive orderliness. All her books were organized precisely—by subject, arranged alphabetically, by author—on the shelves across from the couch in the living room.

The bathroom and kitchen were antiseptically clean. It was exceedingly rare for any item within her world of to be out of place. Since earliest childhood, she organized her bedroom like a museum. Her bed was always carefully made, her stuffed brown bear and her fluffy gray elephant carefully placed upon the tan goose-down comforter, at either side of her life-sized Golden Retriever doll, Captain Kirk.

At the back of the bedroom, against the wall opposite the head of the bed, a tall stand of wooden shelves, devoted to her most highly prized treasures, were arranged next to her closet. She was particularly fond of crystal animals. In high school, she relentlessly read and reread *The Glass Menagerie*. And she identified with poor lame Laura. "...nowadays the world is lit by lightning ! Blow out your candles, Laura —and so good-bye."

But she liked horses most of all—maintaining a detailed collection of horse-related pieces, including a stirring portrait of Seattle Slew, a horse she dearly loved, which was situated at the zenith of an elaborate altar. Two entire shelves were devoted to an array of all things equine: a compilation of artifacts crafted from many media. Several photos of Seattle Slew, in action, hung on the narrow wall, on either side of the closet.

With his fingertips, Billy rhythmically rapped Ringo Starr's *Abbey Road* drum solo on her door, then leaned against the wall. Somewhat drunk he was having a bit of difficulty maintaining an upright position—without staggering in blatant disequilibrium. Vision impaired, his eyes were crossing. So inclined, he buried his head in the crook of his right arm and continued drumming with his left hand until Carrie finally arrived at the door to let him in. She was visibly irritated, but Billy did not notice.

Just inside, he firmly pushed the door closed. He pulled Carrie close and crudely slid his hand inside her pajama top, across the smooth skin of her belly, grabbing and squeezing her bare tits, roughly pinching her nipples. He tried to mouth a sloppy wet tongue kiss. But she pushed him away in disgust. Sneering.

—What's wrong with you? Are you drunk?

—Yeah, a little. There's no law against it.

—Well, I don't like to be treated that way. You know that.

—Yeah, yeah. I know. I was just tryin' to spark things up a little.

—Drunkenly manhandling me is probably not the best means of seduction, Billy.

He looked back at her blankly.

—Yeah. Okay. So guess what?

Still angry and agitated she replied curtly.

—What?

—I'm halfa fuckin' millionaire.

—You're half of a what?

—Millionaire. Half-a-millionaire.

—So it sounds as if you came to some sort of agreement with the record producer?

—A.... Cousins.... Vetter. *Thee* A. Cousins Vetter. Half a million. Wham bam thank you, ma'am.

—I wish you could find another phrase that could serve as summary to your observations. Wham bam thank you ma'am has really gotten on my nerves.

—It's a fuckin' Bowie song. 'Suffragette City'.

—Yes. I know. I've heard all about that. But it still annoys me.

—What's eatin' at you tonight, Carrie? I'm tryin' to tell ya' we're rich.

Billy stood, wobbling precariously, as if even the slightest shift in the earth's axis might throw him violently to the floor.

—We're fuckin' rich.

—I don't care about that Billy. I've told you. I don't care if you're rich or poor. I just want for you to be a good man.

—I'm a good man.

He whined indignantly.

—You can be. Someday. Maybe. But I think you have a lot of work to do.

Unexpectedly, he unbuttoned the fly of his jeans and withdrew his cock. He grabbed her hand and wrapped it around the shaft, methodically guiding it up and down, as he fell back against the door, pulling her along with him.

—I've got some work for you, too, baby.

He immediately sprung to life and she almost gave in to him, just to get him to stop being such an asshole. Reflexively, she started to move her hand with a certain practiced expertise.

419

—Yeah, that's it. Yeah. You know how...

She was just in the midst of really working him up, massaging and stroking, when it occurred to her that she could be anyone. She could be that one at La Bamba that night. Or anyone else. Her hand could be his own, for that matter. She was just a substitute for that ultimately, no doubt.

If he could find a female version of himself to screw, he'd probably be in utter bliss. They could admire themselves and each other—and each other and themselves, for admiring themselves and each other—in a perfect mirror reflection of circuitous admiration. *Yeah, that's it.*

Much to Billy's immense displeasure, Carrie abruptly stopped beating him off.

—Hey. What's the deal? It was just startin' to get good.

—Good for who, Billy? Good for you? That's it, isn't it? As long as everything's good for you, everything's good.

—Well, yeah. That's how it is.

—No it's not, Billy. That's not how it is. There's a whole world out here, outside that world where you live, in your head.

—Look, Carrie, this world's gotten me pretty far, so far. Look where I am.

—Where are you, Billy? That's a good question. Where the hell *are* you?

—I'm on my way to bein' a star, Carrie. Just like I told ya' I would. And most girls would be proud just to be standin' beside me. There's any number of girls who'd love to take your place.

—How do you know *that*?

She asked sarcastically.

—'Cuz they tell me. I've got ten or twelve of 'em at every show. I could have my pick of any of 'em. All kinds of girls.

He was trying incite her jealousy, but he only succeeded in fueling her rage.

—You don't get it do you, Billy? You really don't get it. Has life been that easy for you? Really?

—No, Carrie. We've been strugglin' for years at this. You know that.

—You call what you and your band do *struggling*? That's a laugh, Billy. You have such a warped, insulated view of life.

—You're sayin' all this because why? Because girls like to hang around and I like hangin' around with them?

—I'm *'sayin' all this'*,

Mockingly, she scoffed.

—Because you live in a world of girls, not women. I don't want to be a girl anymore. I want to be a woman. I want to be a veterinarian. I don't want to be a girl. One of your *adoring* girls.

She eyed him derisively from head to foot.

—And I don't want a boy, Billy. I want a man. A *real* man. And I'm afraid that's something you just can't be right now. A real man.

Angrily, he jerked her to him, crudely grabbing her ass with both hands, his erection poling against her abdomen, he tried to hump her.

—I'll fuckin' show ya' a real man.

Pushing herself away, Carrie was nearly overcome. But her resolve in having the issue out prevented her from acceding to her physical instincts.

—That's the problem. You think that just because you have one of those...

Accusatorily, she pointed at his gradually intumescing dick with an air of unmitigated loathing.

—...that you've got all the answers. That's not the answer, Billy. If you don't know it now, you'll find out someday. A real man is more than just an erection. Any *teenager* can get one of those. They do. Everyday. Just like you. But they're not men and you're not either.

Shamed, Billy indignantly tucked his turgid member back in his pants, buttoning up with his head bowed down.

—Billy, this isn't working out?

—What's not workin' out?

—Us. This. It's not working out. It's like we're on two different trains heading in opposite directions. Fast.

—I don't know what you mean, Carrie. I thought you'd be excited about half a million bucks.

—Honestly, Billy? I just don't care.

—Well if ya' don't care...

Implying something.

—No. It's true. I don't care. Go ahead and be a rock star. That's all that matters to you. Go do it. You don't need me to do that. In fact, I'm probably standing in your way. Holding you back.

—No, Carrie, you don't get...

—Yes I do, Billy. I do. It's all perfectly clear. It's time for us to split up, don't you think? After that fiasco last spring. And then this.

Fiasco? He couldn't remember a fiasco. She gazed at him with an imploring look, nervously fingering her hands in dismay.

—Don't you think?

—Carrie, I. I don't wanna.

—Yes you do. You just said it. You want some girl who will be happy being a fox on a leash. The babe on your arm.

—Ya' make it sound like a bimbo.

—No, Billy. I don't know what it is. But it's not me. It's just not me. I think you better go now.

Under more sober conditions, Billy might have made greater effort to refute her assertions and to protest her edict. However, as it was, he could only admit to himself that she was right. He liked girls. All of them. They were like flavors, like colors. Each one was just slightly different from the next.

Maybe he wasn't ready to settle down. But he didn't want to lose Carrie. He'd put in so much time with her. Like an investment. He didn't want to lose his investment. She was important to him. He just couldn't say how, exactly.

Maneuvering him out of the way, she pried open the door and steered him out. Before he really knew what was happening, Billy was standing in the hallway, disoriented and indecisive. Now what?

Within a month, A. Cousins Vetter, returned to Portland, a retinue of accountants and attorneys herded behind him like baby elephants. An array of legal forms and documents, contracts and ledgers in triplicate, awaited Billy's approval and signature.

As much as he would have preferred to simply sign away the next ten years of his career without a great deal of deliberation—to just take the money and run, instead he pored over each contract with as much due diligence as he could muster, pondering every point and detail with the rigorous vigilance of a rock musician. He was confident that he had it all figured out. All figured out.

With contracts signed and checks in hand, Billy opened up two separate bank accounts. For the band's portion of the take, he deposited the agreed upon one hundred thousand dollars, to which he generously added eighty thousand from his own account. That amounted to one hundred and eighty thousand dollars for the band to split.

He decided that Mick and Billy D. should each receive twenty grand, while the band members would get thirty-five each. A good payday for everyone. Plus, it would leave him with one hundred and seventy thousand dollars. And two hundred and fifty thousand more to come, after the first album was finished. Pretty good numbers for a leading Waldo on da real kine team, mon.

Though the band was mightily irked at not being party to the actual contractual negotiations (by Vetter's decree), the process would have bored them anyway, and would have made them more suspicious of the things Billy was telling them.

But they were all happy to know that their enormous debts were to be paid by Rough Edge (a development especially welcomed by Daw) and that the label would foot the bill, as well, for the EP recording venture—which was scheduled to begin in LA, the week after Christmas. The band would spend the month of December rehearsing for the project, scheduling no gigs after Thanksgiving, in order to sharpen their material.

The first thing Billy did with his newly acquired affluence was to order up a brand new *Pac Man* machine through the local vending company that had helped get the machines fixed for his run in at Sack's.

He had the delivery team set the game up against a load-bearing wall across from the staircase, in the empty dining room—which became the gaming room with the advent of that alteration. In any spare moments, Billy could be found, eating Pac dots and avoiding Blinky and the boys; monsters and ghosts.

The contract allowed for the Gods to finally move their practice space out of the basement of the band house and over to a small warehouse across the river— inner east side, on Belmont at 23$^{rd}$, not far from Genoa up at 29$^{th}$. They bought the necessary gear and set up a decent control room in what had been the office, with the idea of recording future demo projects and possible one-offs.

With ten weeks to kill before the project's commencement, and only the prospect of six weekend gigs around town to consider in the interim, the band was afforded the opportunity for a lavish, extended debauch—in which all members of the Unreal Gods organization heartily participated with all the hardy enthusiasm of stereotypical rock stars, in the city of Portland.

Through October and November, the groupies never left the band house, a constant parade of illicit pulcher: all shapes and shades, at all hours, in all conditions, from somewhat sober to almost comatose. Something for everyone. A potpourri. The band split the cost on an ounce of Dealer Walt's best coke and a couple ounces of Incomparable John's finest bud. The investment was a bargain at four grand, split between the seven of them. The best money they ever spent.

Especially enjoying himself, Billy was taking full advantage of his newfound freedom, skimming la crème de la crème. Cherche la femme. But, of even greater significance, no one in the entire household had seen Col in days. He was holed up in his room in the company of a punky pretty girl with night-black hair named Lori.

At first there was some concern within the community that the couple had possibly overdosed or something drastic. But the initial distress subsided, once it became apparent, every three or four hours, that Col and Lori were very much alive and fucking like minks.

As a result, in an attempt to drown out the relentless pumping and squeaking and moaning and grunting consistently emanating from Col's room, at all hours, Mick turned up the stereo phasers to "volume stun." A continuous jet roar rattled around the expansive living room, resounding throughout the entirety of the structure like a PA speaker in a grade school gym.

However, Mick's actions induced a domino effect, where, to compensate, everyone else in the house turned up the stereos in their own spaces, creating within the dwelling an unyielding blaring din, night and day. Though the houses on the block were situated fairly far apart from one another, the neighbors were fully aware of the events transpiring. So were the Portland police, for that matter.

By Thanksgiving, coke and weed gone, girls worn out and gone, the boys were a tad tuckered out, but thoroughly sated, every one. Only Col remained missing in action, although there had been some sightings of both he and Lori from time to time.

And he did manage to participate in all the band's weekend performances, always with Lori standing at his feet, fondling her breast, thumb and forefinger encircling her nipple, as she enticingly pulled down her lower lip with a lingering finger. Col maintained a perpetual hard-on. Show over, the two of them were gone, immediately, and back to the house and Col's room, to resume the erotic death march.

Everyone knew that their relationship would not end well. Eventually they would run out of mojo and pheromones, and the fires that burned would be tamed and extinguished. It seemed to happen all at once one morning. Half-dressed and shoeless, Lori indignantly stormed off into the gray December day, never to return. And, wearing only a pair of Levis himself, a cigarette dangling from his mouth, sneering from the foul fumes, Col slammed the door behind her. Good riddance, bitch.

It wasn't just the neighbors and the cops, and half of Portland's female population under the age of thirty, who were taking notice of the Unreal Gods' newfound sense of royal entitlement. The rumor swirling around Portland music circles was that the Gods had signed a major contract, which the music press had no trouble scrutinizing and analyzing with very little available information.

Battle lines were drawn. Other bands either loved the Gods for their success and for the attention they brought to the local music community, or they hated them for precisely the same reason.

Slouchy stout Bick Muckler, editor of *Loose Screws*, snagged an interview with Billy for ten in the morning, the first Friday in December. It was Muckler's obligation to the public to interrogate Billy, and expertly extract choice tidbits of meaty information and the flavorful suets of gossip and innuendo. Delicious frontpage soup!

He had on his desk a poster that someone had brought into the Loose Screws office, taken from a phone pole in Northwest Portland:

**Billy Granger**
**Pathetic Looser**
**Schlock Rocker**
**Your a Piece of Shit**
**Give It Up**

Billy sat across the desk from Muckler, who leadingly asked what had been going on with the band. Billy did not hesitate to get to the point

—Well, we signed a contract with Rough Edge records and A. Cousins Vetter. It's just a one off deal for now. I'm not gonna get into the details. I found out about Mister Vetter, that he is definitely a man that puts his two cents worth in. He's the owner of his company and I'm the leader of mine. But we're workin' together.

Muckler solicited response as to reports that Rough Edge was demanding line-up changes.

—The one thing that's been established already is that the band will stay the same. I know there's been a lot of talk around town about personnel changes. That's not gonna happen. No way. I could probably change personnel like other bands around here have done. But it would leave me with the worst feeling in my body.

Earnestly, Billy continued. He flicked back from his face long strands of blond bangs, his chin held high, eyes tracking up from Muckler's desk toward the ceiling.

—And that would take the whole point away from what we're all about, because we are a band and that's what I'm proud of. In fact, our crew has pretty much stayed the same through it all—Mick Noyes and Billy Dreier. You've got to be reciprocal with people that are givin' you that much love or blind faith, or addiction.

Easing back in his chair, Billy tucked his hands behind his head, elbows pointed out away from his ears.

—And the label's been kinda hintin' about changin' our name, like Dollarshine changed theirs from Dogfood Papa and all. We don't want to do it. We are who we are, you know? They want us to work on our material and presentation.

Bick pursued the topic. Billy responded.

—Mister Vetter wants us to establish our identity out of the gates. And the one he sees for us is serious rock. Modern rock. That kind of bores me though. 'Rocky

425

Road' is one of his favorite tunes. We're going to end up re-recording it, maybe with a new bridge.

Bick picked up the poster and tossed it at Billy, who looked it over for a moment, frowning bitterly.

—This poster is pretty sad. It's actually pretty funny. I'd like to see the guy puttin' the poster together. I mean it looks good! Or better than most of *our* posters. I think this is kind of an unfair thing though. When we first started, we didn't have a gig. We didn't have anyone to help us. And he didn't even spell 'loser' and 'you're' right!

Crumpling his face, Muckler remembered the Gods early history somewhat differently than Billy. Seemed like they'd had a little help along the way. But okay... keep talking.

—And maybe that's the reason for this poster. I'm very confident in our band and very proud of our band's originality. 'Shlock rocker'? Punk bands hate us. As far as punk bands go...

An air of cynical arrogance descended.

—You could classify a lot of new music in one ugly pile. I think it's real easy to jump on the punk bandwagon, paint your hair the same color as everyone else; or jump on the heavy metal thing. That's a sickness that's possibly the worst one to find yourself in, creatively.

Randomly twirling the wedding ring upon his tubby finger, Muckler asked in what way.

—To be somethin' you're not. You know? To have to pose in order to make it. I want to be true and real to our ideals. Real. We may be corny, which is one of the main complaints, I guess, but I think we cover the spectrum from serious to light-hearted and corny. I don't think there's anything wrong with that.

The editor nodded, not so much in agreement, as to encourage Billy to continue his free-associative dissertation. He directed the interview toward the creative process.

—My creative spark comes from frustration, hope, a little bit of anger, and maybe a little bit of depression—those things that make you feel like 'what's it all about Alfie'? It can be an everyday kind of pain that everyone goes through. The key to the spark? I don't know. That's a tough one. If I knew, I guess I'd be a millionaire by now.

Pencil in hand, scribbling, dollar signs inside of cubes on a legal pad while his cassette recorder whirred, taking dictation—Bick Muckler asked about a familiar complaint voiced among local club goers that the Gods charged too much at the door.

—Yeah, I've been hearin' it through the grapevine that we charge too much for our show. I think if a band wants to play for free, they should move to communist China or Russia. Then they can do all their shows for free, under government supervision. I think people are ignorant of what makes the United States go around. It's a capitalistic society. I don't think it's right to be criticized for puttin' your product out there and havin' people pay for it. I've taken flak for it and I think it's the biggest pile of shit. I have a real baby face. I think I can be a teen idol for maybe the next ten years. That's a pretty small window, really.

In his imagination, Muckler pictured a printed page filled with all that Billy was putting forth, as he continued to scrawl upon his tablet. He felt almost like a shrink.

—You know, I don't think there's anything wrong with confidence or arrogance, if you do it in a humble way. Sure, we have to be arrogant, but if it's in an innocent way, who cares about it anyway?

And the deal?

—As far as our deal is concerned, well Bick, I'd say it's very lucrative as far as marketing goes— the commitment from Rough Edge. All publishing rights are ours. They're not gonna touch that. We're lookin' at thirteen points right now, after the first hundred thousand albums sold—so they can recoup their investment, you know? Thirteen points is what Bruce Springsteen and Duran Duran get.

And recording?

—We're headin' down to LA at the end of the month. West Lake Studios. It's one of the best studios in LA. Vintage Studer two-inch tape machines. Twenty-four tracks. Forty-eight channel automated board. State of the art.

And who will produce the album?

—John Maclan is going to produce—he just finished up working with Men at Work on their second album. When John was producing Men at Work at West Lake, Michael Jackson was recording *Thriller* right across the hall. If it's good enough for Michael Jackson, it's good enough for me.

And when can we expect the recording project to yield fruit?

—They're thinkin' April or May for the release. They might end up releasin' an EP, then, wham, right behind it they'll release an album. And when and if we get airplay, chart action, then they've said we'll get tour support. They haven't really gotten to know us that well, yet. What we have to do first is show them we're professionals in the studio. It's a big gamble for them. It's three hundred grand just to market it nationwide, to put our album in every store. With everything else, it's hundreds of thousand of dollars they're sinkin' into us. We'd better deliver.

The interview, it seemed, was a means by which Billy could persuade himself and convince anyone who read it in *Loose Screws* of the inevitability of the band's promise and the validity in their signing a huge contract with a major label; ultimately a far larger contract than Dollarshine had signed with Gaffen.

Any misgivings Billy and the band may have had about working with Maclan—who preferred to record the band live in the studio, with a minimum of overdubs—were to be overcome with an intensive schedule of actual rehearsals of the five songs they intended to record and three others they could substitute if one or another didn't work.

In the early evening that Friday, after the interview with Bick, Billy and the band began a rigorous rehearsal schedule: five hours a day, every day. They reviewed every part of every one of the eight songs they intended to have ready for the trip to LA. During their spare time, they woodshed a number of ideas, committing all to the new Tascam eight-track machine they had newly obtained. It was located in the recently constructed control room in their new rehearsal space.

John Maclan came up from LA on three separate occasions during the band's three-week rehearsal stint to make suggestions regarding arrangements. He documented tempos, timing, phrasing and the placement and execution of solos, tweaking individual parts with the intention of having every song build to a simultaneous emotional and musical crescendo, without everyone playing all the time, all over each other.

The guys had entertained such notions in the past, knowing what they needed to do, but they never managed to generate the discipline necessary to actually implement any of their ideas. Besides. Why tamper with success? People loved them and would pay anything to see them play, just as they were.

Just the same, in those three weeks before Christmas, the band whipped into top shape: tough, lean, and tight. Ready for the challenge. With the assurance of not having to use rental equipment for the new project, they carefully packed all their own gear into Billy D.'s brand new van.

Billy thought about giving Carrie a call. They hadn't spoken in almost three months. But he didn't know what he would say to her, or how he would say whatever he finally managed to come up with. He missed her. A lot. But he didn't miss the tension. The stress. To himself, he flippantly referred to her as the "High Peace-Stress of Love," immensely proud of the pun.

Billy figured the time off was probably doing them good. And if it wasn't, then they weren't meant to make it anyway—a mode of rationalization that suited his ambivalence well. He who doesn't hesitate gets bossed.

It had been miserably cold in the middle of the month with a little snow in the days leading up to the holiday. Christmas fell on a Sunday, Billy D. and Mick left Portland on a wretched, sleety Monday, for what was sure to be a tension-filled two-day adventure just in navigating the unpredictable Siskiyou mountain range at the Oregon-California border. Trekking treacherous I-5 through Yreka, Weed, and Mount Shasta, it was a long, icy slide through northern California down to Red Bluff in the last foothills on the other side of Shasta, leading to the long, desolate wasteland that lay ahead, all the way to Sacramento.

For the trip to Los Angeles, a mere thousand miles away, the plan was that, if they did in fact survive, Billy D. and Mick would rendezvous with the Gods at one in the afternoon on Wednesday at the Westin Bonaventure Hotel near the Dorothy Chandler Pavilion.

It was thirty-eight degrees when the five Gods flew out of Portland, at ten-thirty Wednesday morning. It was almost eighty degrees in LA when they landed three hours later. They took a cab from LAX to the Westin Bonaventure, arriving at around three. Gib, Gilly, Daw, Col, and Billy toted their bags though the hotel to the elevator and up to their rooms on the eleventh floor.

Rough Edge had reserved four rooms at the Westin for the entourage. It was determined that Billy would take one to himself. So Gib and Gilly shared one, while Col and Daw grabbed another. As for Mick and Billy D.? No sign of them.

From the balcony of his room, which faced southwest, Billy could see MacArthur Park shimmering in the distance. A distinct bronze gray haze rose above the black lake at the Park's center. The lake glinted and glared the far reflected silhouettes of innumerable swans, as the hot orange sun traced a low, slow path toward the brown horizon.

Someone had definitely left that cake out in the rain a long time ago. Whatever Jim Webb's vision may have been, all Billy could think of was Mrs. Havisham in that Dickens...her old moldy wedding cake disintegrating on the table in the dusty cobwebs of her dining room. He could still remember Mrs. Havisham's bitter monologue, which Miss Pierson had strangely required everyone in freshman English commit to memory. Was that *David Cop...? Great...?*

*I'll tell you what real love is. It is blind devotion, unquestioning self humiliation, utter submission, trust and belief against yourself and against the whole world, giving up your whole heart and soul to the smiter—as I did.*

Standing there, inhaling the faint fragrance of ocean and desert, smoke and smog, Billy unaccountably recalled the other quotes Miss Pierson had forced upon them in freshman English class. He was certain he would never forget Portia's soliloquy from *Merchant of Venice*. Its familiar lilting cadence tortuously lulled unforgettably in his mind.

*The quality of mercy is not strain'd,*
*It droppeth as the gentle rain from heaven upon the place beneath:*
*it is twice blest;*
*It blesseth him that gives and him that takes:*
*'Tis mightiest in the mightiest: it becomes the throne-ED monarch better than his crown;*
*His sceptre shows the force of temporal power, the attribute to awe and majesty, Wherein doth sit the dread and fear of kings;*
*But mercy is above this sceptred sway; it is enthrone-ED in the hearts of kings,*

*It is an attribute to God himself, and earthly power doth then show likest God's*
*When mercy seasons justice.*

That was the way she taught them to memorize it. In chunks. So that it made some sort of sense. But it didn't make any sense. Not to anyone in the whole class. But, God damn it, they remembered the damned thing for the rest of their lives, like little hamsters turning on the wheel of literature. And that was what was important.

Billy thought to himself, Miss Pierson, wherever you are, I will always be your slave. Your fucking treasured quotations are branded in my brain forever. He tried to recall Hamlet's soliloquy but could not get past "To be or not to be..." He never could get that one nailed down.

But another compulsory quote sprung to mind. Kipling. He recited to himself the sing-song rhythms and rhymes of "If" and decided they could make for decent lyrics. Corny, maybe. But hey, he was a corny guy.

*If you can fill the unforgiving minute*
*With sixty seconds' worth of distance run,*
*Yours is the Earth and everything that's in it,*
*And–which is more–you'll be a Man, my son!*

He often pondered that quatrain, imagining it coming from his father. He wondered if his dad would think he was a man. What he would think of the band's success? Would he be impressed? For the briefest instant, Billy contemplated a deep, dark dull pain. But, as quickly as it had arose, like a slipshod secret, it ineffably slid away.

Just in that very moment of uncharacteristic introspection, someone bashed powerfully on his door. Startled, Billy rushed from the balcony, past the bed and squinted through the peephole. It was Billy D. and Mick.

He opened the door to find the two miserable hulks standing forlornly in front of him.

—What took you guys so long?

Sweating profusely, both from the heat and from the ordeal of the harried drive, Billy D. slowly gathered together an answer.

—Uh, well, it was a solid sheet of ice from Medford down past Redding. That took us a while. We only almost got fuckin' killed...three times?

Billy D. turned to Mick, who despairingly imparted a dejected corroboration to his assertion.

—Yeah. Three.

—Yeah. Only three times. So we got a little slowed down with that, ya' see.

Exasperated, Billy D. had turned uncharacteristically sarcastic, before resuming his woeful tale in a more apologetic tone.

—That first day we ended up stoppin' in Red Bluff. We were beat. Then yesterday. Let's see we got a flat outside of Stockton. And then we started overheatin'. So we got as far as Bakersfield. New water pump—I kept the receipt. And today...here we are.

Satisfied with the details of the report, it occurred to Billy that perhaps the lads would like to get into their room and freshen up a bit. Stolidly striding next door, he hailed Daw and secured for the weary roadies the key to their quarters. Billy then bade the tuckered travelers farewell, their welcomed ablutions to perform.

The following day John Maclan and the band met at West Lake Recording Studios, on Beverly Boulevard, to review the plan for their recording mission. Maclan was nothing if not idiosyncratic. Though he liked to record a band live in the studio, he was spectacularly fussy about how the band was to be recorded. He was renowned for using fifteen channels of a board just for the drum mix alone.

In fact, his only reservation about recording the Gods at West Lake was that forty-eight tracks might not be a big enough board to capture everything he wanted on the first pass. The plan was to mix that initial input down to twelve dedicated tracks on the Studer—leaving twelve more open for "syrup," as he called it sometimes—or "love."

Maclan booked the band into Studio A for six-hour blocks, five days a week, for four weeks. Studio A was the classic room where Men at Work had recorded their albums with Maclan. An amazing list of other musicians, going back to the early seventies, recorded in that studio, as well. Tom Petty and the Heartbreakers recorded *Long After Dark* in that room, a fact that, for Billy, seemed a good omen.

Studio A featured a comfortable recording area. It was acoustically magical. Classic reverb effects were available via the "variable decay isolation room," a real echo chamber, approximately ten feet wide and thirty feet long, with marble tiled surfaces at the far end of the room.

In addition, Studio A had an expansive tracking room, a well-appointed private lounge, and a separate restroom. There was a very comfortable, lived-in feel to Studio A. Clean, but well worn, like an old pair of jeans.

Without overdoing it, the band celebrated New Year's Eve by renting a car and driving up and down Sunset Boulevard. After that, they retired to Mick and Billy D.'s digs, where they hung out on the balcony smoking a generous quantity of Incomparable John Dailey's killer skunk weed, and snorting enthusiastic lines of Dealer Walt's best coke. They ordered several bottles of champagne from room service and partied appropriately, given their locale and the holiday.

New Year's day was a Monday. They all slept in and hung around their apartments for the day. On Tuesday they showed up at West Lake at ten in the morning, ready for business.

As was the case in New York, it became patently obvious from the start that there would be nothing for Mick and Billy D. to do really, other than to get in the way. They understood that going in, so neither of them had any great expectations. It was a free vacation down to the land of sun and fun, as Col put it. Rough Edge was paying for it, why not?

And Maclan, seemed reasonably receptive to the presence of the two roadies in the spacious control room—something that Billy D., especially, most appreciated. He was looking forward to watching a real producer work with the band in the studio. Gods at Work! You bet. Sounds good.

But.

—Take me all around
Lift me off the ground, lets go
I'll do anything
But share your wedding ring—you know
I've been there before
But I never could be sure
Where it would flow
Chances are our love might fade
But it might just grow-woo-oh, woo-oh, woo-oh,
Chan..........

Suddenly the click track disappeared in the headphones. The recording had been halted. Over the shoulder of the engineer, Matthew Rose, who was futzing around with track placements and levels, Maclan hit the talkback mic.

—Hey, you guys? How'se about ya' c'mon in and we'll talk over a coupla things.

The Gods laid their instruments aside and dejectedly trudged back to the tracking room—yet again. They had been making that trek on a regular basis, as Maclan seemed mostly unhappy with pretty much everything they were doing. The band had begun to question their readiness for the kind of pressure Maclan was applying. Maybe they weren't as good as they thought.

With a great deal of trepidation and not a little annoyance, everyone congregated behind the sound board, some sitting on the couches against the back wall, others propped up against various effects racks. Col wandered around the room, impatiently perturbed, awaiting the next installment of criticism and bad vibes.

—Guys, I'm not feeling any punch in your playing. Your energy seems lackluster. There's no zest. No snap, crackle, and pop. You know?

He turned, looking through the glass at the band's equipment situated all around the burnished brown wood-paneled hall.

—You're just going through the motions. That's not gonna work. You're pretty dead in there. Ya' gotta liven it up a little bit.

Irritated and despondent, Billy was tempted to say something to their producer, something rude and unkind. But he held back, partly because of Maclan's authority and lofty position within the recording industry, but mostly because he did not want to jeopardize their recording opportunity. He didn't care if it was Hitler standing back there. Maybe it was.

Instead, Billy gravely inquisited of the displeased tyrant.

—Well, John, man, tell us what ya' want us to do. We're all ears. It's not, like, ya' know, we don't want this to be any good or anything. It's not like it's a joke. We're not fuckin' around here.

—Okay. Here's the problem as I see it. The songs just don't make any lyrical sense. They just don't hold together. And some need melodic or arrangement help... development, ya' know? A bridge here, a key change there, a dramatic rhythm/ tempo break. 'Chances Are' has key changes, but the bridge really sucks. And it doesn't really fit in with the rest of your material.

A gathering sense of agitated aggravation descended upon the disappointed musicians. Billy tried another tack, with hopeful reservation.

—Okay. Okay. So, maybe you can just tell us a thing or two you like, and we'll try to build on that.

—Well...You guys play real well together. You're well-rehearsed. Tight. A lot of your songs have good musical ideas.

Awkwardly buttressing himself against the tall back of Matthew's massive black desk chair, Maclan fingered frustrated furrows into his wavy orange-blond hair.

—But, like 'Singles Going Steady'—the lyrics don't make sense. It's a good song but it needs lyrical help. What's that verse? 'Eventually you'll probably come flyin' through, this night's the same the way you do'? That's it, isn't it?

Blank faces.

—That doesn't quite make enough sense to hold together. It almost means something, but not quite. And I think the choruses of 'Singles' and 'Apple of My Eye' sound too much alike to be on the same EP. But I really like Col's solo on 'Apple of My Eye'. That's very tasty.

A thick creeping cloud of outright anguish began to descend. Still, Maclan forged ahead with his evaluation.

—The band's performances are tentative. And Col and Gil, especially, seem to lack focus. I would really like to see you guys move in a heavier direction. Maybe sorta like Bruce, or Bob Seger. Stripped down and a little mean. Big sound, like Journey or Boston. Thirty-Eight Special. Billy Idol. Nothing major, just a little more meat with the potatoes and gravy. You guys've got the gravy. More meat and potatoes.

It required some effort to knife through to Maclan's point. Defensively, Billy fought the suggestions.

—But, John. We're not a heavy band. And I'm not mean, like Billy Idol. And we're definitely not like the bands you're talkin' about. Thirty-Eight Special? That's not us at all.

Salvaging the session was going to be no easy trick, but Billy was going to make the attempt. He changed course.

—Look, so what can we do to make the songs better? Should we rewrite them? Or start over? Or what?

—Your material is almost there. There's a lot to like. But it needs a little help, a little punching up. That's all.

Wary and weary, the Gods eyed each other with narrow brows of worry. Consternation and confusion crossed Billy's face in ripples and swells. The whole situation was starting to make him sick.

—Now, I've got a suggestion. But I'm not sure how you're gonna take it.

Maclan grinned grimly in Billy's direction and resumed his speech.

—I have a friend named Mark Lantz. He's known all around Hollywood as the 'Song Doctor'. Mark is gifted, truly gifted, at writing bridges. His bridges can transform a song from pedestrian to timeless in eight or sixteen bars. He's also a master at dressing up choruses, and he could help with some of the lyrical dead ends.

Sitting rigid on the sofa, his torso as stiff as his indignation, Billy replied.

—Jeez, John. Why're ya' bringin' all this shit up now? You heard our songs. You heard us up in Portland when we were rehearsin', and ya' never said anything. We coulda talked about all this shit then and worked things out.

—Ya' know, Billy, sometimes it takes a while to get a feel for the direction a band should go in. There's no way Men at Work are a reggae band. And 'Down Under' certainly wasn't a reggae song when they brought it in. But we reworked it. In fact, Mark helped with a few of the lyrics. We reworked it and look what happened. Gold record. You want to listen for what a song needs. It'll tell you.

Billy softened in his seat only slightly.

—What're our songs tellin' you?

—They're telling me they need a little work. Some rivets to hold things down. And we need a little outside perspective on these songs, and I think Mark can do that for us.

Oh, him again.

—We're too inside of all this. Mark can be an objective voice. He's the grandson of Walter Lantz? You know the name Walter Lantz?

Group shrug to searching eyes.

—Walter Lantz was the creator of all those cartoons, like Woody Woodpecker and Chilly Willy. Andy Panda?

The entire Gods' contingent brightened at the mention of fond childhood cartoon characters. But the prevailing relevance of all that remained a subject for dispute.

—I think Mark can help. We can bring him in and see if he can add anything. Nothing to lose.

They looked at each other inquisitively. Billy spoke up without hesitation.

—We'll have to talk about that, John. We respect your knowledge and experience. But we have to decide what's best for us.

—I can dig it, guys. I understand.

Later, back at the hotel after assembling in the bar, the confreres conferred their concerns and sentiments. Billy, especially, was most voluble in his discontent.

—We've been down here over a week and we've hardly gotten *shit* done. We keep goin' over and over the same fuckin' songs, but somethin' always fucks up. We haven't got enough hot dogs or buns. Or fuckin' mustard. Always somethin'.

A cynical tirade ensued.

—It's like the tape breaks, or somethin' goes wrong with the goddamned deck, or shit...falls...off ...the wall! Man, that fuckin' *freaked me out*! It's like the goddamned ghost of Janis Joplin was flyin' around in there. Scared the shit out of me.

He was not nearly finished.

—And then that asshole, Maclan. The guy's, like, drivin' me fuckin' bonkers. He is completely neurotic about little pissy things.

He sneered snidely

—Like perfect mic placement and perfect time.

Impudently.

—Jesus Fuckin' H Christ. He, like, wants a goddamn click track on everything! It makes it pretty fuckin' hard to be 'live and spontaneous' in the studio...

435

Overtly sarcastic.

—Or 'zesty', or whatever the fuck it is with that damn thing *farting* all over everything. It's fuckin' ridiculous, man. I can't concentrate. I feel like a fucking...robot.

The others shifted in uneasy agreement. They all had begun to chafe at Maclan who seemed too authoritarian and overly critical. They felt burdened by the yoke of his personality. The producer even seemed niggled by Mick and Billy D., for no apparent reason other than the fact that they were there soaking up psychic space, or some such, in the lounge and recording area.

Ostensibly, Billy's rant was beginning to subside. He purposefully took up the task of outlining the remaining grievances.

—I don't even like Men at Work, man. They fuckin' sound like the Police jammin' with Jethro fuckin' Tull. What's that shit? I want to sound like Joe Jackson and the Clash and Simple Minds and Duran Duran—not like Bruce Springsteen and Bob Seger, for Christ sakes. Or Boston or Journey. Journey! We're not the past, man. We're the future!

A call to arms was struck.

In the studio lounge, the following day, they all gathered in chairs around the big white dining table. Billy said.

—We think we should talk to Cuz about all of this.

John Maclan did not react immediately, but seemed to seriously consider the apprehensions being raised. Elbow resting on the table, he cupped a hand across his mouth. He breathed heavily through his nose, concentrating his thoughts succinctly.

—Okay. Here's the deal, guys. All these changes we've been talking about here were Cuz's idea in the first place. It's Rough Edge that wants to hear ya' go a little heavier, more metallic. I'm not sure what I'd do with you on my own, except I'd bring Mark in, no matter what.

A vague tide of terror swept across their collective faces. Oh shit.

—That's not all, guys. There's something else I haven't told you. Cuz made the suggestion that maybe you guys oughta think about recording outside material.

Now that. Again.

Without consulting the others, Billy spoke up immediately.

—Look, John. You guys are suckin' the life out of this band. You've got us jumpin' through hoops like a barrel of monkeys. We're not, like, dancing bears. Our music's gotta live and breathe. You can't go boltin' it down, or racheting it up. We just are what we are.

Maclan looked at them blankly, as if they were a bunch of grade-schoolers, cranky and tired from a long field trip. Deeply inhaling through his nostrils, he clearly suppressed his real reactions.

—Well then, what do you guys want to do?

A little bitterly.

Billy continued traveling down the rail-less trail of his headlong train of thought.

—Well, I'd like for you to record us just the way we are. Like we planned out in Portland. Figure out how fast we want to do the songs. The tempo. Come up with a few cool changes and see what happens. Maybe layer a few things over. Make it, like, *elegant*, or somethin'.

Without saying anything, Maclan leaned forward on the table, arms angled inward, knuckles cradled beneath the line of his jaw. He had the air of a fascinated, doting parent. But mocking and sour. He nodded faintly.

—We think you're a great producer. We really do. You know how to get a real slick, pro sound. And you know how to capture—or whatever ya' call it—our sound. And you know how to make it sound even better. You know how to break things down and build 'em up again. So the sound's all muscle. We don't wanna sound tough or heavy. We're not that. We're just not.

Somewhat touched by the sincerity of Billy's attempt at clarification, he halted his scoffing posture, resuming his previous, more cautious, position.

—But we wanna sound strong and, like, muscular, y'know? That's us man. We're strong. We wanna show off our muscles.

In that instant, Maclan felt like Annie Sullivan. They had reached a climactic breakthrough of communication. They finally understood one another. Water.

—Okay. I got it, Billy. I think I can do that for ya'. We'll see what we can come up with.

He engaged Billy directly in the eye.

—But I'd still like to bring Mark in. He could help. He really could.

Exasperated, Billy sighed. He really didn't want to bring Mark in. He wanted it to be the Gods' work. Nobody else's.

—No, John. Man, we wanna do it all by ourselves. If we're not good enough to make the grade, then at least we'll know it's on our shoulders. We won't be able to blame anybody else.

Maclan could definitely see the logic in Billy's decision. It made sense. And it let him off the hook in a way, too. No matter what happened with the recording session, it was not his doing. Other than the sound and production values, he had no part in the project.

—Okay, Billy, we'll do it your way.

And with that the matter was finally settled.

The desire to contact Carrie had been weighing on Billy's psyche for quite some time. He had tried to reach her by phone on a couple of occasions while the band was down south, but, predictably, all he got was her goddamned answering machine. He never had anything to say to that fucking machine.

There were things he needed to talk to her about—things that only she would truly understand. He wanted her to know that he missed her. He did miss her. He loved her. He had come to that realization over the months since their blowup. He needed her. He needed her guidance and introspection; her love. He was beginning to feel as if he were drowning, and she was the only one in the whole world who carried a life preserver.

With the air completely cleared once and for all—under Maclan's tutelage—the Gods were able to secure very good versions of the songs they intended to record. The only song he had any hand in arranging was a new, updated version of "Rocky Road." It was decided that they would create verses to surround the original song, which was then consigned to serving as a chorus.

The new verses reflected a more cosmopolitan lyrical and musical influence, corresponding in context to what they had done with "Social Will Call." That more mature approach contrasted somewhat disconcertingly with the ingenuous simplicity of the original song. It was not a seamless fit. But the band was reasonably happy with the direction the revamped arrangement was taking. It seemed more contemporary.

The recording process was continually beset by equipment failures and malfunctions. Otherwise acceptable takes were ruined. Repeatedly. The capstan rollers on the Studer intermittently locked up, due to mysterious solenoid issues. On other occasions channels in the heads would unexpectedly short out, either triggering terrible noise or crapping out all together.

Sometimes mics simply stopped working—their diaphragms suddenly blown and buzzing or their line cables causing horrific radio interference. It was an endless, frustrating succession of technical delays. But the band generally met the obstructions with a sense of good-natured esprit de corps.

Still, Billy remained a little remote, a little preoccupied. His comrades noticed, but said nothing, thinking that he was most likely just beginning to concentrate on the nuances of his lead vocals, which he would begin recording as soon as they concluded laying down the basic instrumental tracks—within a matter of days. Col conjectured that perhaps Billy was concerned about Carrie. And the others agreed.

Indeed, it was only a few days and they were finished with the basic tracks. It had been three weeks to the day since the band arrived in LA. The plan was that Billy would lay down his lead vocal tracks then the band would overdub harmonies and background gang vocals. Then Col would dub his leads, and Gilly, a little bit of keyboard ensemble sweetening around the edges and they'd have a wrap. They were getting close to completion. Real close.

On Thursday, Billy made his way through the vocal on "Shortage of Variety." After recording seven, they settled upon the fifth take—cleaning up a few spots and dumping a quick harmony vocal in the chorus. Though they had an hour of time left, Billy said that his throat was getting raw, and they shut down the session early.

The next day Billy captured "Social Will Call" on the third take, then worked on doubling certain lines, layering harmony vocals elsewhere. And again, Billy complained of a sore throat, begging off before their time had been used up. Prepared for the possibility, Col was ready to punch in a strong solo on the song, knocking it out in two shots.

It was a beautiful Winter's day in LA, safe and warm. Seventy-seven degrees. One of those uncommon clear blue sky days, where hills around the city grew rare green. At three o'clock, everyone returned to the hotel. The seven of them decided that within the hour they would convene poolside to take advantage of what was, to an Oregonian anyway, summer-like weather.

Toting bottles of Coors, Billy D. and Mick were the first to arrive, wearing dark t-shirts, cut off jeans and flip-flops. They stretched out on a pair of chaise lounges, taking in the warmth of the afternoon sun. Then Gilly and Gib showed up. Gilly's tight black swimming trunks and white, short-sleeved summer shirt gave him the look of a sixties rock star. Like he was a member of the Stones or the Beatles or the Monkees or something.

Gib more or less resembled a visiting golf pro. He sported a crisp white baseball cap, a blue-striped white polo shirt, tan Bermuda shorts, and cowhide huaraches with soles made from old tires. An obvious tourist. On either side of the two roadies, Gilly and Gib sat in folding aluminum lawn chairs with red and blue American-flag themed plastic webbing.

Before long, Billy joined them. He was dressed in baggy blue surfer shorts, white undershirt and a bright, deep-blue Hawaiian shirt. With the golden daylight glinting off his sunny blond hair, he pulled up a lawn chair next to Gilly.

—Que pasa gents? Como esta?

The four of them stared at him as if he were speaking gibberish. Billy repeated himself, more coherently the second time.

—What's happenin'? How're ya' doin'?

Billy D. replied.

—Doin' okay. Doin' good. Nice warm afternoon. Havin' a Coors and thinkin' about maybe takin' a dip in a while. What's up with you? Feelin' any better?

—No. Not really. I kinda feel like shit, actually.

Gilly inquired.

—So have you got the flu, do you think? Or what?

—I dunno. Maybe. Maybe an allergy or somethin'. I just don't have any fuckin' energy.

It seemed as though Billy was being vague. He reached over to another lawn chair nearby and snatched up a fluffy white terrycloth towel. He set the folded towel in his lap, and rested his elbows atop, as he leaned forward in the chair.

—But the recording sounds pretty good. Don't ya' think?

—Yeah. Slick...

Gilly agreed.

—Slick and smooth. John knows what he's doing. That's for sure...

Billy nodded faintly. Gilly concluded his thought.

—I can see why they pay him the big bucks. I think we sound great.

—Good. So do I. But it's good to hear that you think so too.

Col and Daw appeared at the far end of the pool both more or less customarily attired, perhaps stripped down for the daytime, outdoors in Southern California effect—but otherwise immediately recognizable as being costumed as themselves. Col, a cigarette artfully hung from his lower lip, like Keith Richards' snotty little brother, just liable to piss in the pool at any moment. Daw dressed pretty much as Daw always dressed, with slight variations. Sleeveless powder-blue tee, cut off jeans and ordinary flip-flops.

As they approached up one side of the pool, Billy stood and moved down the other side. He stretched out the towel and lay down upon it. His head pointing in the direction of the rest of his mates. Col noticed.

—What the fuck's up with him? Is he mad at us or somethin'?

Gilly felt the best informed to fill him in.

—I think he's got the flu.

—Well, I'm glad we fuckin' got his vocals done before he petered out on us. He's not goin' all *lead singer* on us is he?

—No. I don't think so. I think he just doesn't feel very good for some reason. Maybe an allergy. That's what he thinks.

—It ain't fuckin' smog. That's for sure. Who ever woulda thought of LA with no smog? Ya; like, see why people want to live down here. It's really kinda nice.

Mick and Billy D. suddenly leapt from their seats, running headlong into the pool, with Gilly not far behind. Gib remained in his chair, stoically pondering an imaginary forty-foot putt for a birdie. Seizing the opportunity, Col and Daw descended onto the vacated chaises. Col lit another cigarette from the butt of the previous one. He looked over at the bass player.

—So, Gib. We're almost done, man. Another coupla days and we'll have'er sewn up.

—Yeah. Won't be long.

—Couple more guitar solos and some layerin' with me 'n' Gilly, some clean-up and we'll be done.

—Yeah.

Billy D. emerged from the pool like a trained killer whale at Sea World. He glared down at the guitar player, who looked bizarre in makeup in the daytime and outdoors.

—Hey. You stole our chairs.

—You guys weren't fuckin' usin' 'em.

Billy D. shook water from his hair, showering Col and Daw with the spray. Irritated, Col brushed water drops from his jeans.

—Hey, hey! Watch it there Scooby-Doo. You're shakin' yer fur all over the fuckin' guests here.

Strangely distracted, Billy D. said nothing as he watched their leader at the side of the pool struggling to sit up, before collapsing back down onto the pavement. An alarmed Billy D. snatched up a towel from the chair and quickly headed in Billy's direction.

Billy was white as ivory, yellow glinting sun liver sick; moon shivering night cold in the afternoon warmth. He again strained to become upright eventually meeting with pained success moaning indistinctly, as Billy D. approached. Vertical. He crossed his arms on his knees and rested his forehead on his arms, peering through at his bare feet. Bilious. Miserable.

—Hey, D. What's up, man?

—Not much, Billy, what's goin' on with you? Gilly thinks you've, like, got the flu or somethin'. Are ya'sick?

—Yeah D. Yeah. I'm pretty sick. I've been real nauseous and pukin' for the past week. Look, you can't tell anybody, man. I'm swearin' ya' to secrecy' about this.

To shield himself from the view of the others, Billy swiveled slightly toward the roadie. He awkwardly pulled his shirt aside, exposing a massive lump beneath his undershirt. It was the size of a softball and protruded hideously from under the left side of his ribcage, like a water balloon filled with Jello.

—Billy! Man! What the fuck is that?

—Shhh! Shhsh! I told ya'. Ya' gotta keep this quiet man. I don't want the others to know.

—Know what, Billy?

—It's the cancer. It's back, D. That thing's a big fuckin' tumor and it's makin' me sicker than shit. It's been growin' a little bit everyday for, like, the last couple of weeks. Two weeks ago, y'know, it felt like a marble in there. Now it's a fuckin' bowling ball.

—Well, what're ya' gonna do, Billy? You gotta get that looked at right away.

—I'll be okay for another week. It can't get much bigger. Alls it's gonna take is a few days to get the recording wrapped up. I can go to the doctor when we get home. I think it's gonna take a while to get this cancer sorted out.

He peered down at the bulge beneath the white undershirt.

—Prob'ly *quite* a while.

Exasperated, and wobbling weakly, Billy surveyed the lapping blue waves that danced frenetically on the surface of the swimming pool.

—It's fucked, man. It's really fucked. But D, like I told ya'. Ya' gotta promise not to say anything to anybody. I don't want this gettin' around when I get back to town. We gotta keep it quiet. Nobody knows. Just me and you. And Carrie. I gotta tell her.

—Okay, Billy. You've got my word. I won't tell anybody. You've just got a bad case of the flu until you say otherwise.

—Thanks D, I owe ya', man.

—I think we're about even, Billy, I'd say.

The big man hopped to his feet and helped his ailing friend to stand. Billy felt old and feeble. Trembling, he swung his arm around his pal's shoulder; the two of them marched resolutely toward the others at the far end of the pool.

# XXXIII

Billy pushed the button, calling up to Carrie's apartment. It was eight-thirty on Wednesday night, exactly four weeks from when the Gods had left for LA. They arrived back to town that afternoon.

Once settled at the band house, his first thought had been to call Carrie, but he knew she probably wouldn't answer the phone. So, in lieu of interviewing with her answering machine, he decided to walk over to her place, shaking from the frigid February air and the dull, dark illness that gathered deep in his being.

—Ye-ess?

She sang.

—Carrie. It's me.

—Billy?

—Yeah. We just got back from LA. I've gotta talk to you. I'm sorry we had that fight. I've learned my lesson. Please let me come up.

She buzzed the doors open, and met him as he emerged from the elevator, and walked uncertainly down the hallway to her door. They hugged and he kissed her passionately.

—Carrie. I'm so sorry we fought. It was all my fault.

Tears began to pond in his eyes and he shuddered involuntarily.

—Oh, sweetheart, come inside. Are you okay?

She guided him into the living room and sat him down on the sofa.

—Can I get you anything? Do you want a beer? Or a Coke?

—Okay, yeah, a Coke. Please.

Carrie moved toward the kitchen, calling out to him over her shoulder.

—So, things were a little chaotic in LA?

Billy's face clouded abruptly.

—Yeah. To say the least. How'd you know about that?

As if she were preparing for surgery, she extracted a red can from the refrigerator, pulled the ice tray from the freezer and set the items on the counter. Then she efficiently fielded a glass from the cabinet, filling it with ice and Coke. Having placed the ice tray back in the freezer, she picked up his drink.

—I have my ways, Billy. I don't live in a bubble. This is a small town. You know that.

—Yeah. That's what I'm afraid of.

She held out the glass to him. He set it on a plastic coaster in front of him on the coffee table.

—What do you mean by that?

Sitting, she snuggled next to him.

—Afraid of what?

Turning, Billy balanced himself on an elbow and began stroking her cheek behind her ear.

—Look. Carrie. I've got a lot of stuff I need to say. But first, I gotta tell you how much I love you.

He cradled her head in his hand.

—I love you! I don't ever want to lose you. You're my best friend. You're my go-to-guy.

—Wait. Wait. Your *what*? Go-to-guy? What's that?

—Remember? It's a sports term? Baseball? Basketball? I've heard it used in both. John Wooden? The go-to-guy? The player you rely on in tough situations? Your backup guy. You're my ace reliever. Like Rollie Fingers or Goose Gossage.

She had no idea what he was talking about. She had forgotten what he told her before and the ace reliever thing totally threw her off.

—Raw Lee Fingers and Goose Sausage? Are those sports guys? I'm confused.

—Aw. It's baseball. They're great relief pitchers. That's all. I didn't mean to change the subject. Confuse things.

—What things? You're not making a lot of sense.

—I know. I know. I'm just havin' trouble…

—Just say what you want to say, Billy.

—Baby, I'm so sorry about the way I've treated you. It was wrong and I know it now. I've been careless. You're the best thing that ever happened to me. I need you. I love you, baby!

He pulled her toward him and reverently kissed her forehead. Then, searching, his lips engaged hers and they made out intensely. The phone rang, disrupting the momentum and Carrie drew away, listening for her machine to pick-up, so she could identify who was leaving a message. Just in case she wanted to answer.

—Hi Carrie. It's your mom. Jean.

Carrie wrinkled her nose and pursed her lips disapprovingly. Because she, of course, would not have been able to distinguish her mother's voice without the proper familial credentials.

—Hon, would you give me a call when you get a chance? Your father and I wanted to invite you and Val over for his birthday party on the Sunday after next. Lincoln's birthday? He's going to be fifty-five. Yes, I know. We're getting so old! Ancient... So call me please. The party's at two o'clock Sunday afternoon...Okay. Bye-eye.

Sighing resolutely, she reached over and erased the message. A bolt of disbelief lightning-etched Billy's face.

—Is that what you did when I called?

She could not conceal the guilt of her betrayal, lowering her head in disgrace.

—Man. Carrie. Baby, why didn't ya' answer when I called?

—Well, I don't know, I must have been gone some of the times when you called. Most times, in fact, probably.

—And the other times?

—I didn't know what to say.

She sighed.

—I was afraid you'd yell at me or pick on me.

—I don't pick on you.

—Well you *have* picked on me at times in the past. You have to admit that.

Billy tilted his head in acknowledgement.

—So whose call were you expecting?

—Kathleen.

—Who?

—Kathleen. You remember her. She's that pretty girl? Part Asian? I think she's Korean? You've met her before. We're study partners?

—Oh yeah, Kathleen. But that's not what you call her.

—No, I call her Leena.

—Okay. Yeah. Right. Leena.

—She's going to be my assistant. Oh. I haven't told you. I found a clinic where I can start my practice.

—Uh...Practice?

—Veterinary? Veterinarian? Me?

—Oh yeah. Sure. I thought you meant, like, rehearsing. Where at?

—At Rose City. It's just at the east end of the Ross Island Bridge.

Vacant response.

—It's just across Powell from the Pancake House. I think it must be Sixth or Seventh?

The light bulb illumined at last; Billy nodded in accordance.

—Kathleen and I were going to go over there tomorrow and look at the office. The guy's still in there, but we just wanted to look at it for a few minutes. So we can plan.

He knew what they were up to. Planning was Carrie's specialty. Most likely it was Leena's, too, and that's why they got along so well.

—We can't move in until May, actually. Doctor Dahl is moving to Kentucky in May. What *stuff* did you need to say?

—What?

—You said you were afraid of something—like a rumor—and had things you needed to tell me. Like what?

He shifted awkwardly upon the couch cushion, attempting to summon together his thoughts and intentions.

—Well. Uh, somethin's happened. Somethin' not very good. Somethin' pretty serious.

446

—Serious like what, Billy? You're talking in circles. Spit it out. You're scaring me.

—I'm tryin' to tell ya', Carrie. It's...

Turning toward her, he hiked up his shirt and t-shirt, thus exposing the hideous bulge that protruded like an overripe cantaloupe from under his ribcage.

—Oh, sweetheart. No! It's a tumor! We need to get you to a doctor immediately.

—No. It's okay. I'm fine.

—You're not fine. That thing could burst. That wouldn't be good at all.

—All right. All right. I'll call Doctor Todd's office tomorrow and see if they can get me in to see him. Or what they think I should do. I'll call 'em first thing.

Elbow against his chest, head lowered, he cupped his palm over his eye and sighed.

—It's bad. I know it's bad. It's makin' me sick. I'm scared. I'm real scared. I'm ready to fight it. I can beat it. But this is a lot worse than last time. I can tell.

Riven, and replete with lachrymation, she began to bawl. Billy soon followed and they bayed in unison like wolves at the bone white moon.

—What are we going to do with you, Billy?

Weeping, she broke into quaking sobs and he almost matter-of-factly replied.

—It's not fourth down yet...

She screwed up her face in puzzlement. He finished the thought.

—So, it's too early to punt.

In flinders flung upon her bed she fell, as cracks webbed the surface of his valiant façade in intricate patterns of untiring fear and thwarted resolve. Together, they succumbed to troubled sleep, wrapped in the frayed reassurance of each other's arms.

Applemom bedwake late for bus. Game after, mitt, dad will try. Two on. Double to right. Two RBIs. Scan stands: faces: no dad. No dad. Dead. Applemom, swimming pool tears. Secondbase a graveyard in the snow. Fathersunwholly. High in the blue blue sky. Angels. Dennydeaddrunk bench laughs. Dugout in sleep. Sleep.

—Billy!

She shook him, but he continued to moan.

—Doctor Carrie applemom an injured wing to heal. Fail fly. Fall. No, fly. Fly far.

447

—Billy. Wake up.

—Whuh...huh? Hmmm?

—You're having a bad dream or something.

—Better call 'em 'n' tell 'em.

—Okay, sweetheart. Okay. I'll call. Why don't you turn over on your side?

—Whose side? I'm on your side.

—Turn over on your side.

She gently prodded him with her elbow, and he eventually surrendered, readjusting his position in the bed.

Bowiebam thank you ma'am. Trudyrudy that was fine. Kiss slop the lollipop. I pop. I pop when you pop mine. Noblesling...Arrow fortune...To sleep... Perch... The rub. This motor oil.

Then deeper still and all deep dark.

In the morning, he felt as though he had not slept at all. His head throbbed and suffered him, swollen—a big rubber band ball wound way too tight. Sweat steeped and seeped through his t-shirt. He shivered from the heat.

Carrie cooked him a ham omelet with cheese; serving him toast and OJ, on a tray as he lay in bed. The food of gods.

Registering a genuine sense of alarm over the phone, Nancy, the receptionist in Doctor Todd's office, conveyed to Billy, in no uncertain terms, that he should head directly to the office without delay. She gave the impression that the situation was serious. Very serious.

Doctor Todd burst into the examination room with a bleak expression on his dour face, compact wire-rim glasses pinched upon the end of his nose. His hollow eyes were rheumy and red, as though he were suffering from an allergy. Puffy dark bags hung beneath his lower lids.

Beset by self-consciousness, Billy sat the end of the exam table, clad only in a pale green hospital gown. Carrie eyed him apprehensively from a chair next to the counter and wash basin at the opposite side of the room.

Taking precise mental notes, Doctor Todd looked Billy over with grim concentration. At every observation of significance he would respire intensely through flared nostrils. With expert hands, he gingerly explored the lymph nodes under Billy's chin and armpits and in the groin area, unconsciously humming to himself.

—All right then, let's see what you have here.

Doctor Todd unfastened the ties at the back of the gown and pulled it from Billy's shoulders. The great shifting viscous mass beneath the left side of his ribcage was monstrous and within the narrow scope of his professional field of expertise quite unique in its size. And it was most certainly extremely dangerous.

—Mister Granger, I would expect you already know what's going to come next in the process.

—Blood tests? X-rays?

Billy and Carrie exchanged rueful glances.

—That's correct. And we'll want to do a biopsy.

Gravely, Billy pinched his lips together.

—Then what?

—We'll just have to cross that bridge when we come to it, eh?

—Is it worse than last time?

—Well, obviously this tumor is of critical concern. I don't like the looks of that at all. It's what we call remarkable.

A little proud to be remarkable, even if it was his cancer, Billy maintained his train of thought.

—Can we yank it out of there?

—It's too soon to say. We'll know more about the possibility of surgery after the x-rays.

—You mean, maybe we can't take it out?

—Yes, there's a chance that the tumor could be inoperable. There are numerous reasons why. But it's much too soon to speculate.

His expression in freefall, Billy mirrored Carrie's countenance of dread.

—We'll really just have to wait until we have all the facts gathered before we start speaking about treatment options. You can get dressed now.

Todd concluded jotting copious notes upon his individually handcrafted clipboard, made of Wisconsin hardwoods—maple, oak, cherry, black walnut, and African pad auk—efficiently locking closed his sporty black Visconti Rembrandt pen and placing it in the left breast pocket of his crisp white lab coat. Brusquely, Todd continued to address his patient with abrupt directness.

—I'll have Nancy get you set up with all the tests and we'll meet again after I've had a chance to go over all the tests.

—What should I do about this?

Exasperated, he looked down at the big bag of syrup bulging at his side.

—Try to keep your activity to a minimum. Don't sleep on that side, of course. Drink as much water as you can. Just try to relax and take it easy.

Billy wasn't about to keep his activity to a minimum. The band had gigs scheduled for nearly every weekend in the foreseeable future, and there was no way he was going to let it be known that he was ailing. Carrie and Billy D. were the only ones who knew and that's the way he intended to keep it.

It was nearly two weeks until the band was to play again: their annual Valentine's spectacular at La Bamba. So Billy underwent the battery of tests that Doctor Todd prescribed without detection or further complication. Blood tests and a round of x-rays, ultrasound imaging, an MRI. EKG. Then a PET scan and a CAT scan were administered over the following week.

During that time, he was able to convalesce. He did very little, carefully following the doctor's orders to remain quiet. It seemed to him that the tumor had shrunk a little. Not much. But a little bit, anyway. And the intense waves of nausea he had endured subsided for the most part, washing over him only infrequently.

One week later on Thursday afternoon, returning to Carrie's apartment after the CAT scan—the final test of the series—they entered to hear her answering machine just clicking on.

—Hello. I hope I have the right number for contacting Billy Granger.

It was A. Cousins Vetter. Carrie rushed over and picked up the phone on the table at the far side of the couch.

—Hello? Hello? Yes. Yes. We just came through the door. He's right here. Just a moment.

—Hello? Yeah, hi, Cuz. Oh, I'm doin' real good.

He lied.

—Oh yeah, the session went great.

He lied again. A litany of prevarications ensued

—Yeah. We got along great with John once we hammered out where we wanted to go with the material. No. I haven't talked to him since we got back home. He said that?

Billy sounded surprised.

—Well, that's real nice of him. We try to act as professional as we can for bein' a buncha hillbilly yokels. John was the best. He got a real clean, crisp sound. Not heavy...but tough. That's what we wanted. You haven't? I've only heard rough mixes.

He ducked down upon the sofa. Leaning back, he combed the fingers of his right hand through his hair.

—He said what? No? I guess he doesn't want you to hear it until it has the full layer of Maclan *frosting* on his musical cake. Yeah. That's right. So, you know the drill then. I'm anxious to hear your opinion when you do hear it. We're pretty proud of it.

Billy wasn't entirely sure what he thought of the mixes he had heard from the LA sessions. But it was obvious to him that Maclan had put up a good front, and he wasn't about to sabotage the goodwill gesture that John was extending to the band. There were a lot of reputations to maintain.

—Yeah, sure. Go ahead. What's on your mind?

He twirled the coiled phone cord like a jump rope.

—No. I can't say we ever decided on that. The Unreal Gods always seemed to fit us, that's all. We never thought it sounded like a punk band. You do? Really? Gee, I don't know, Cuz. I've talked to the guys about this before. They're not really interested. Yeah, yeah, I could see how maybe it would be hard to market in Kansas or the Bible Belt...hard to swallow in the heartland and all that. Man, I don't know. I'll have to talk it over with the band again. That's really a big decision. Everybody in town...in the Northwest knows us as the Unreal Gods. It'd be weird to start all over with a new name.

Looking up at Carrie, he rolled his eyes and shook his head disbelievingly. With his lower lip extended, he blew bangs from his forehead.

—Yeah, okay. I'll bring it up with 'em again and see what they say. I'll let you know. Yeah. I will. I will. Yeah. I wanna know what you think, as soon as you hear it. We think it's real good...or *unreal* good, maybe.

He chuckled snarkily.

—Okay. Okay. Yeah, yeah, you too. Talk to ya' later.

He smacked the phone down on the receiver.

—Well *that* was fuckin' weird.

Carrie sat down next to him.

—He wants you to change the band's name?

He shrugged slightly to the affirmative.

—Yeah, he's brought that up before.

—What do you think of that?

—Sucks.

—What do think the guys will say?

Smirking.

—They'll say it sucks.

Actually, the band thought it was stupid even to be talking about it again.

—He thinks our name won't, like, play in the heartland, that we'd get *banned from the airways* or somethin', callin' ourselves *Gods*. Like we're makin' fun.

Chuckling, Col said.

—Well, uh, we *are* makin' fun. I mean, at least I was when we were, like, talkin' about the fuckin' name in the first place. What the hell's Vetter want anyway?

—Oh, probably something like Journey. Or maybe Loverboy. 'Billy Granger and the Silver Love Rangers'.

They began good-naturedly throwing around a few substitutes for Unreal Gods. Gib earnestly submitted.

—How about The Yearlings? Or the Black Swans?

The others threw up their hands indifferently. Not bad names. For some other band. Lasciviously, Col leered.

—Cherry Bombers! Endangered Feces?

Gilly cracked.

—Flowers of Evil, the Five Wits.

Col quickly quipped.

—How about Neural Dogs?

Billy stifled scorn with his hand.

—Neural Dogs?

Yeah! *Neural Dogs!* Get it? Neural Dogs?

—No, I don't get it.

—It's the letters in Unreal Gods mixed up. You know? To, like, make another word? Whatever they call those things, y'know like a Jumble or somethin'? Y'know those Jumble things in the comics, in the paper? I can't remember.

Authoritatively, Gib blurted.

—Anagram.

—Annan what?

—*Ana*gram. That's what you're describing—like evil and veil? Or live and vile. Same letters. Different order.

—Yeah. That's it, I guess. Annan...?

—Gram. Anagram.

—Annan gram. Yeah. So that's like what it is. An Annan gram. Neural Dogs.

The subject of grams broached, the discussion quickly deteriorated and nothing further was ever mentioned of the band changing their name.

A couple of days later, Billy arrived late backstage for the Valentine's show at La Bamba. It had taken him longer to wrap the bulge than he had anticipated. He used an elastic Ace bandage to firmly secure the swollen tumor beneath his ribcage. The compression was uncomfortable, but he felt less vulnerable with it in place.

He was dressed in black and white checkered sports coat, sleeves rolled up. A pressed white shirt—collar up, wings at the tips, top button open. Black slacks and shiny Beatle boots. He sported heavy eyeliner and ominous eyeshadow on his lids, thick mascara on his lashes. Cheeks severely rouged, lips heart-shaped red rose colored.

It was the typical atmosphere of mischief and turmoil backstage, with band members, friends and a few animated strangers crammed into the little green dressing room at La Bamba. The usual joints, bottles of booze, and mirrors mounded with coke made their way around the room.

Everyone was laughing and yelling and wound up tight as a fist. Billy sat down on a bench next to Gib and pretended to take a hit when one of the joints went by, turning down the booze and coke. He felt ill and ill at ease.

Col had on tight blue jeans, a white t-shirt with the sleeves ripped off—on the front, the image of a heart dripping blood, wrapped with thorns and with a crown suspended above. His mane shot up in a hair-sprayed fountain above his head, colored deep red for the occasion. Not only his eyes were heavily made up, he wore dark red lipstick as well.

The others wore makeup and lipstick too. Even Gib and Daw who had been the stalwart holdouts in the move toward completely tarting-up the band. Gilly had been a proponent of the look all along and the others were coming around to his point of view, though Daw was obviously the least enthusiastic about the decision.

Billy surveyed the area circumspectly. He felt sicker than before, less able to focus. As with the previous bout, he was determined to continue performing, through whatever therapy he was to be subjected. The symptoms dampened his energy and enthusiasm, but not his resolve. No one was to know. No one was to find out.

Band members, however, spend interminable hours together, only a very few of which are dedicated to the actual advancement of their craft. The rest of the time, all individuals involved—as a general rule under the influence of drugs and/or alcohol—are presented the opportunity to explore one another's psyche, to probe for frailties and vulnerabilities. These points of flaw and failing are duly noted, meticulously stored for future use. Band mates rival only lovers for the intrinsic knowledge they possess about their partners.

So it was not at all surprising that everyone backstage noticed, almost immediately, that Billy seemed not himself. Under the weather. Col was the first to raise the subject.

—So, Billy, man. Are you feelin' okay?

—Yeah. Sure. Can't get rid of that fuckin' flu bug I had. Maybe it's like mono or somethin'.

—Yeah? Well, ya' look fuckin' terrible.

Everyone in the room giggled nervously, and Billy met their laughter with silence, displaying an air of sadness.

—I'm not feelin' real great, Col. You're right about that. It's true.

In despair, Billy scratched his forehead, smoothing his eyebrow with the tips of his fingers.

—Are ya', like, gonna be okay to play tonight, man?

—Yeah. Yeah. I'll be fine.

He lied. Still he summoned all available enthusiasm for the task at hand and rose to his feet with a rallying call to the troops.

—Let's go.

Bounding up the stairs, he led the rest of the Gods onto the stage. He grabbed his guitar, strummed it once, bringing up the volume, and stepped to the mic.

—Good evenin' lay-deez and jennelmen—young lovers, whoever you are. I'm Billy Granger and we're the Neural Dogs.

Sounds and noises emanated from the drum kit and the various other amps and monitors on the stage.

—We want to wish you all a happy holiday, Happy Valentine's Day. Happy Tuesday. Happy Ides of February or whatever the hell it is. I tell you what. We all need some symmetry in our play.

And the band kicked into overdrive from the first note. Tight, tough, and perfect now.

None among the jocularly whacked-out attendees seemed to notice that Billy's performance was subdued throughout the show. By evening's end, they were deeply debauched and well satisfied in the depths of their dumb insobriety. They stood in a bunch near the bar, smoking and yakking boisterously over the din of Talking Heads' *Speaking In Tongues*, which blared through the PA.

Quickly toweling off backstage, Billy threw on a charcoal gray full-length wool overcoat, and hustled out front to meet with Tommy and retrieve the band's take for the night. The crowd was thinning out, as Tommy had closed the bar, condemning the stragglers in the room to the remnants of their drinks. Billy stood talking to a couple of cute young girls who were excited to meet the handsome rock star. He did his best to live up to their expectations, humming and purring as he eyed them appraisingly.

Finally, after the ritual routine of cajoling and wrangling had been enacted, the staff managed to drive all the intoxicated patrons off the property, leaving the poor wretches to merrily fend for themselves in the streets of Portland at two in the morning on a Wednesday, in February. Danger probably lurked somewhere.

While the help were clearing tables, sweeping the floors and swabbing the restrooms, Billy bellied up to the end of the bar where Tommy tallied the last of the night's receipts.

—So, how'd we do?

—We actually did four at the door, which blows my mind, man.

—We only charged six bucks. It was a great deal. And we, like, didn't have any competition.

Tommy nodded in appreciation of Billy's grasp of the bottom line.

—Well, we did fifty-five at the bar, which is a fuckin' miracle, for a Tuesday, with all the water we were servin' tonight. Jesus. I swear the Willamette's prob'ly all dried up.

—Nah…Nobody'd ever use the Willamette for *drinkin'* water.

—Yeah. I guess yer right. But, you know what I mean. Anyway, it wound up bein' almost ninety-six total and, *per our deal*, we're splittin' it fifty-fifty. So I owe ya' forty-eight. Sound right?

—Sure. I trust ya'.

Smirking, Tommy playfully tossed Billy a banded roll of bills, which he stealthily stashed in the inside pocket of his overcoat.

—Thanks, Tommy. We needed to start bringin' in some cash again. It's been a while. We got a lot of bills to pay. We're gonna need to, y'know, *reestablish our fan base*, maybe do like a 'Welcome Home' tour of town or somethin'.

—Yeah, probably a good idea. Hey, look, Billy,

Tommy leaned conspiratorially across the counter, hiding his mouth with his hand.

—I gotta tell ya' somethin', man. Frank sold the building and I gotta close the club.

—Sold the building? Wha'd'ya mean? Not this shit again.

—Sh-sh. Yeah, man. He sold the building to a buncha fuckin' California real estate speculators. I guess they're payin' him top dollar. They're gonna make the place into some kinda fuckin' *mini mall* or some such bullshit. I don't know.

—Fuck, man! Close La Bamba. This is just like fuckin' Long Goodbye déjà vu shit all over again! How soon do you have to close?

—Aw. I've got 'til the end April, I guess. Coupla months or so. We'll have a coupla big shows at the end. Do somethin' for April Fools, of course. That's a Sunday night. Maybe a three-night weekend for you guys? Last night'll be a Sunday, too. Maybe three nights that weekend, too. We gotta close up on Monday the thirtieth. It'll be our goin' away party, n'all. Man, I don't know what I'm gonna do.

In that instant, it seemed as though the whole world was gradually winding down. A slow motion sense of imminent misfortune overcame Billy in a bleak wave of shadow. Something, something important and valuable, something ineffably irreplaceable disappeared. A small light vanished. And life was never quite as bright ever again.

## XXXIV

It was early afternoon the following day. Doctor Todd entered the exam room with a flourish, in a flurry. Papers fluttering from his clipboard, he loomed like fog above Carrie and Billy. They were sitting in familiar positions—the same as before. Carrie, especially, regarded the doctor as if he were a minion of Satan. Billy was nonchalant, stoically maintaining his attitude that nothing was going to slow him down. He was young and strong and he was going to beat the cancer. Again. No matter what.

The doctor hunkered down upon a three-legged stool with rollers, and resting his elbows upon his knees, he flipped through the pages collected in Billy's report. He bit his top lip somberly and sighed.

—So. Mister Granger.

—Please, Doc. You can call me Billy.

—Mmmm, Billy. As you may have surmised, your cancer has returned and it is more aggressive than the last bout.

Setting his teeth, clenching his jaw, Billy stared straight ahead at the blood pressure cuff coiled near the corner of the far wall. He said nothing.

—Your cancer is now at Stage Two. There are four stages. When we saw each other last, you'll remember, you had Stage One non-Hodgkin lymphoma. We were able to eradicate that through surgery. Now, unfortunately, the cancer has reappeared.

The doctor rose from his seat, standing erect with his arms cradling his clipboard.

—Yours is currently confined to the left side of your body. It's involving your spleen. I think we're catching this before the cancer has had an opportunity to take hold in your spleen. To metastasize. If that should occur, then we would have to regard you as being at Stage Three E Plus S, E for lymph nodes, S for spleen. That would require more drastic measures.

He calmly eyed his patient with indifferent authority, shifting his weight to his back leg.

—It's my hope that we're catching all this before it progresses that far. So we'll need to be more aggressive in our approach in combating the problem, obviously.

—More surgery?

—Possibly. But first we'll need to get that tumor under control. We need to shrink it down.

—How're we gonna do that? Radiation?

—Yes. Perhaps eventually. But again, we need to shrink the tumor before we can commit to further, more comprehensive therapy.

Carrie took a deep breath, clutching Billy's hand into her lap as he narrowed down his possibilities..

—Chemo. I guess that's about all that's left.

—Yes. We'll want to get you into what's called a neoadjuvant regimen as soon as possible. Hopefully this week. It will help to shrink the tumor. Then we can begin the second phase.

Numbly nodding, Billy's jaw dropped slightly.

—How long will that last?

—Well, the neoadjuvant portion will probably last three months. Maybe a little less if we get good results.

—How often...?

Coolly, matter-of-factly, Doctor Todd replied.

—We're going to proceed with what is called a CHOP program, which is an acronym for the particular cocktail we're going with. We'll have you come in for a cycle once a week, and we'll plan on ten to twelve cycles. We'll check you once a month, after every four cycles. Then we'll take a look at where we stand.

—Will I get nauseous and lose my hair?

—Possibly. It happens. Those are typical symptoms. There also will be issues with your white and red blood cell counts that we will need to monitor very closely. There are effects. Nancy will give you all the information about your program.

His vanity had overtaken him and he did not hear a thing the doctor said after the word 'possibly'. His hair. His hair. Hair silkprecious as goldstraw. What was he to do? Start wearing a cap? A wig? Shave his head now so no one would know later? There was so much to consider.

—But, I might not lose my hair?

—I'd say it's fifty-fifty.

Billy was satisfied with the odds on that crucial issue.

458

—Is this recurrence, like, uh, fatal?

—I'm certain I've told you, Mister Granger, emm, Billy: in medicine, all cases are eventually terminal.

As he always did whenever he dropped that line, Todd grinned faintly, straightening the glasses perched upon his nose.

—Oh, yeah. Right. I remember. But, y'know some terminals are sooner than others.

—It's much too early for a prognosis. We'll have to wait and see what the outcome of these treatments will be. Oftentimes the program determines itself. Each person's response is different. Mostly predictable, but always unique.

The drive home from Providence Hospital was slow and solemnly silent, as the couple pondered their individual and mutual futures. Turning off Glisan at 39th Avenue, they made their way south down to Powell, where they turned right and headed west toward the Ross Island Bridge. Hesitantly, Carrie broke the quiet.

—You know, sweetheart, I've been thinking.

—Uh-oh.

—What do you mean *uh-oh*?

She had taken offense.

—It was just a joke. I was just tryin' to, like, lighten up the mood a little, y'know?

Admitting to herself the reasonability of his explanation, she continued.

—So I've been thinking that maybe I'd put off the vet practice and take care of you during the months you're undergoing chemo.

—Well, that's just plain stupid. Why would you want to do that?

Visibly hurt, she retorted.

—I'm not stupid, Billy!

—I didn't say that. Don't put words in my mouth.

—Well, I only wanted to help. You're going to need help.

She winced defensively.

—You didn't have to say it was stupid.

—I swear, Carrie, words are like landmines with you. We can be walkin' down the road of some conversation and I'm mindin' my own business—and then, all of a sudden, one wrong move and *boom*, I get my head blown off.

—You don't have to yell at me.

—I'm not *yellin'*!

However, he was being extremely emphatic. He wisely chose to deescalate.

—Look, baby. I'm sorry. You're right. Stupid was a bad choice of words. You know that I'm not that great with words. I think we're both under a lot of pressure right now. You're right. I'm probably gonna need your help. But I want you to get your business started, too. Let's just see how the treatment affects me.

From behind the steering wheel she glanced over at him, with a look of absolute dismay on her face.

—I'm sorry too. I might have overreacted. It's just...

She halted herself, to avoid kindling the skirmish anew.

—I know, baby. I'm afraid, too.

Besides weakness and the occasional bout of nausea—sometimes severe—the first several weeks of Billy's treatment passed uneventfully. The tumor shrank by half and he was elated to find that he had not lost any hair, although it had become a little coarser in texture, while acquiring a slight metallic silver hue.

In that time, Billy managed to maintain his mirage of well-being and vitality. Besides the weekend gigs, the Gods even succeeded in rehearsing a day or two each week, even going so far as to record a few rough tracks in the rehearsal studio on Belmont.

Through the course of his recurrence, Billy seriously contemplated his condition, expressing his incipient insights in songs more complex and sophisticated than any he had written before that time. His disease seemed to be slowly making a man of him.

Among many, one album he had been most impressed by over the previous few years was Joe Jackson's *Night and Day*. He admired the cosmopolitan nature of the melodies and the maturity shown in the lyrics and subject matter. As best he could, he tried to incorporate some of Jackson's more accessible ideas into his own songwriting. Duran Duran's *Seven and the Ragged Tiger* had a deep impact on him as well.

The Clash were still among his favorites, more so the sloppy *Sandinista* than the refined qualities of *Combat Rock*. And he managed to incorporate some of their energy. MTV provided a constant stream of new bands to check out. A number of Australian bands he was seeing inspired him: Real Life, Little Heroes, and Ice House had elements that he tried to emulate.

For their schedule of performances, the Gods traversed a familiar circuit—with the usual stops around town: Euphoria and Last Hurrah, a trip down to Corvallis, and an excursion out to the Orange Peel in Beaverton to play for the hair band crowd. For Saint Paddy's Day three-day weekend they made a swing out to foodstamp flats—Tipper's on the deep dark eastside at 102nd and Powell.

They also booked a show on the inner eastside at the new Pine Street Theatre, just off of Sandy Boulevard. Formerly housing a Church of Scientology franchise, the building was a three-story honeycomb of small, run-down offices and larger meeting rooms, which encircled the expansive main hall. The Pine Street Theatre retained a particular quaint majesty, mostly attributable to building owner Sal Alazar's peculiar fetish penchant for hanging things from the thirty-foot-high ceiling. Arcane things, consisting primarily of an amazingly diverse array of swag lamps and chandeliers.

Grandly magnificent chandeliers, quaint, jewel-like chandeliers. Some were simple and plain, mere bulbs protruding like flowers at the ends of uncomplicated vines. Others were ornate: square tube curls lyrically swirling into one another; hand-polished crystals punctuating each curl, dripping from fanatically elaborate brass cups and bobesches; some bearing finely etched sconces, which were uncertainly secured to the lamps in hopeful ways.

All were suspended on modest cables above a room that could comfortably hold seven or eight hundred people—the good fire marshal willing. There were hundreds of chandeliers of all sizes. Daggers and icicles horsehair dangled above a ravening congress of Damocleses far below. Those chandeliers scared the shit out of everybody.

High on the walls, just beneath the bejeweled ceiling were the skeletal remains of former gigantic broad-winged birds—condors, vultures, possibly a few larger species of eagles and hawks. The massive wingspans of the once splendid creatures were outstretched, sometimes nearly eight feet in width.

In addition to the bird remains, Alazar had mounted, in every available free space on the walls, an eerie array of various sun-bleached animal skulls. The dried carcasses, the aviary display and the chandeliers combined to create a nonpareil effect. Salvador Dali met with Georgia O'Keefe.

Billy had seen the Psychedelic Furs play at the Pine Street. The Furs were so loud that the chandeliers swayed menacingly, as if the audience were on board a cruise ship on rough seas. With concert lights flashing, the birds' bones on the walls vibrated to the extent that a few gave the appearance of nearly flying, Escher-like, off the wall.

It was on Saturday, the weekend after the Tipper's gigs, near the end of the long single set the Gods were performing at Pine Street Theatre that Billy nearly passed out. During Col's extended solo, he had been strutting back and forth on the spacious stage, ala Mick Jagger, inciting the crowd to frivolous havoc on the song "Too Straight For the New Wave."

While he was sprinting back to the mic to catch in time the upbeat for his return to the vocal part, he started to faint. Before he fell completely, he was able to extend his hand, awkwardly bouncing from the floor to the mic stand, to which he clung like a scarecrow to a stick.

Breathlessly, he made his way through the final verse and chorus. After the song, stalling for a little time, he wandered around behind the massive stack of main speakers and guzzled down a pitcher of water. The brief break allowed him to collect himself and the set proceeded without further incident. However, he was thoroughly worn out by the end, even though he maintained severe restraint for the remainder of the night.

The following Tuesday morning Billy was back in Doctor Todd's office for a consultation—preceding his four-hour long weekly treatment. Carrie did not accompany him on that occasion, as she and Leena had a meeting with somebody about something. Billy couldn't remember. He sat in the familiar chair in the examination room and leafed through a four-month old *Time* magazine that had George Orwell on the cover.

Whisking into the room with characteristic abruptness, Todd crouched upon his three-wheeled stool, withdrawing his important pen, assiduously flipping through the charts and graphs contained within the thickening file attached to his tastefully understated expensive wood clipboard. He massaged his lower lip with his thumb and forefinger, studying the data intently. Billy watched him with apprehension.

—So, Mister Granger, how have you been faring with the regimen?

He expertly minimized the symptoms, without total nondisclosure.

—Aw, not too bad. I mean, I feel sort of weak most of the time. Y'know, tired? Not as much energy as I used to have. I get a little nauseous sometimes. A little faint, I guess. Sometimes my ears ring. But I don't think that's comin' from playin' music. I wear earplugs and everything.

—Those are the mildest symptoms you're likely to experience, actually. However, I'm a little more concerned about your WBC count. I'm especially troubled by your lymphocyte readings. Your B and T cells seem very low. That worries me a little. Have you had any sort of cold, or other illness? Infection?

—Naw. Not really. My gums feel a little raw these days. But, no. No colds. No infections or anything. Everything tastes pretty crummy. Like chemicals, or somethin'. I guess that's part of it, too.

The doctor nodded slightly, then drew a deep breath through his nostrils. Todd directed the young man to hop up on the examination table. He expertly scrutinized the glands beneath Billy's jaw, underarms, and groin. With an air combined of professional concern and morbid fascination, he fastidiously inspected the shrunken bulge beneath Billy's ribcage, tenderly prodding and probing the mass with practiced indifference.

With a sniff, he narrowed his nose.

—I think I'm going to make a small change in your program.

—A change? What kinda change're ya' talkin' about?

—Nothing major. I just think I'll modify your treatment from CHOP to what's called CNOP. We'll drop doxorubicin from your program. And we'll have you pick up mixoxatrone in its place. We're only switching one of the four drugs you're taking.

—Why?

—Well, I was hoping that your tumor would have shown more response by now. And we'll see if we can improve your WBC numbers.

—Jeez, that thing's only like the size of a cherry tomato now. It was like a cantaloupe four weeks ago.

—Yes. Just so. I suppose I was hoping for pea-size, by now.

Billy thought he detected a slight downturn of disappointment cross Doctor Todd's mouth.

—Well. Uh...so what sort of side effects can I expect with this change?

—They would be approximately the same side effects, but some may be more exaggerated and others more diminished.

—What about my hair?

Breaking into an actual wry smile, Doctor Todd said.

—If you will put as much effort and concentration into your overall well-being as you extend to the condition of your hair, Mister Granger, emmm Billy, you'll have a much better likelihood of success in this process.

It was Billy's turn to grin with obvious unease as he lowered his head self-consciously.

—Yeah. You're right. Better get my priorities straight, I guess.

—Precisely.

With the exchange at a close, Doctor Todd snapped to his feet, nearly clicking his heels reflexively, placing his important pen in the breast pocket of his crisp, white lab coat. He extended a hand to his patient—who grasped it half-heartedly. Briskly, Doctor Todd left the room.

A sense of gloom overcame Billy. Discouragement. After a short time of feeling sorry for himself, he dressed in haste and made his way from the west side office building, to the south building where he received his chemo treatments.

Lisa was there waiting for him when he finally made it into room S137, twenty minutes late.

—Sorry I'm late, Lisa. Ran a little long with Doctor Todd.

—That's okay. Don't worry about it.

She was in her twenties. Tallish. Plump. Plain. Freckles. Shiny tea-colored hair, tied in a pony tail. She wore a cheery light-blue smock over white, hospital-issue blouse and pants. Lisa was friendly. Helpful. Probably in several service organizations in high school. She always seemed cheerful. Billy couldn't figure her out.

He sat down and laid back in the comfortable recliner, extending his left arm in submission to the awareness of the oncoming ordeal.

—So we're gonna be givin' ya' a little different mix this time, right? That's what Doctor Todd ordered up for ya'.

Lisa wheeled a little chrome table behind her bearing a tray that displayed two IV bags full of medicinal poison and, additionally, the necessary tools required to administer them. She hung the first bag from the drip pole next to the chair.

—Yeah, I guess so. I hope it doesn't create any more problems than I've already got.

—Well, you're not really havin' a terrible reaction to the therapy are ya'? Ya' look okay.

—Oh. I'm okay. I'm just whinin'. I'm sure ya' know how that goes.

—I hear my share of complaints, but it's totally understandable. Chemotherapy is very hard on everyone involved.

Billy looked at the young nurse.

—I guess this is probably pretty tough for you too, huh?

—Yeah. Sometimes. It can be.

Wrapping his upper arm with a tourniquet of rubber tubing, she began to assemble, in order, the items she was going to need to perform the treatment.

—When I saw you guys at Last Hurrah a few weeks ago? I really liked your new songs. I think there was one called 'City of Roses'?

—Oh, uh. 'In Tremolo' maybe.

—Maybe. It was sort of Latin calypso and the guitar player was using a bottle to play his guitar.

—Yeah that was 'In Tremolo'. That's one of Col's favorite parts.

—I like that one. And that one kind of dance song. Maybe 'Dressed Up'? Something like that?

—Yeah. That's what it's called. 'Dressed Up'.

—It sort of sounds like David Bowie, like 'Let's Dance' maybe?

—Other people have said that. This local music writer named H.E. Carus saw those shows and said 'Dressed Up' sounded like a disco nocturne. I don't even know what that means.

Sniffing a muffled chuckle, she lightly explored, then inserted a large IV needle and tube into the median cubital vein of his left arm. He winced at the puncture.

—You know. That's the part of all this that I hate the most. I hate that needle. And you're really good at gettin' it in there and all. But I really hate it.

—Better an IV than a PICC, or a catheter. It could be worse. I don't think you'd like either of those at all.

—What are they?

—Well, with a PICC, we leave the needle and tube in place in the arm so we wouldn't be sticking you all the time. We close the IV off, but we don't remove it We wrap it in gauze and tape and send you on your way. Then when you come in, we just plug ya' in. And the catheter's the same process. We put the catheter in a vein near the heart and leave the equipment hooked up.

—That sounds like that would really suck.

—If you were coming in more often, like, every day, that's probably the approach they'd have us take. It's easier on your body in the long run. But since you're only doin' one cycle a week, you get it this way.

—Lucky, I guess.

Billy smirked and closed his eyes in preparation for the four hour roller-coaster ride that was to come.

Partly out of the sheer incongruity, whenever they would meet for brunch, Carrie and Leena always chose Café Lena, a venerable, hot, hip-poet, cool spot, across Hawthorne Boulevard from Leena's apartment.

As she glanced at the new issue of *Willamette Week*, Carrie sipped a calming tea comprised of chamomile, lavender, and lemon balm. Two lime-frosted gingersnaps were tucked on a small plate next to her tea saucer. Leena sat across from her at the small square table next to the window, facing the street.

She had before her a cup of rich, dark-brown coffee and one of those notoriously plump house cinnamon rolls. Leena was pretty, with Asian almond-shaped brown eyes and a big, wide Scandinavian smile; thick, long, shiny black hair. Her pale, pale skin bore the slightest hint of freckles. With short, thick fingers, she thoughtfully grasped her coffee cup. She had a musical voice, sometimes singing parts of her conversation. Anxiously, she began.

—All right, Carrie, so, like, what're we gonna do? We've gotta figure this out. Um, I hafta, decide what I'm gonna do with my apartment and everything.

Her face sagging into a sad clown frown, Carrie sighed.

—I don't know what to do. This is so complicated. Billy keeps telling me to go ahead and get the practice set up. But I've been watching him and he just seems to deteriorate a little bit every week. He looks a little weaker and sicker. I'm worried.

She placed her cup on the saucer and broke off a piece of gingersnap, nibbling minutely.

—The worst thing that could happen would be that we'd do this and then Billy would take a turn for the worse, and we'd have to pull out. It's such a commitment, with that hanging over everything. I'm afraid he's going to need my help pretty soon if this goes on much longer. But I say that and I think, 'wait a minute, this is Billy'. He's strong, he'll pull through this. I'm sorry, I'm just chattering away here.

—Carrie, honey. I understand. I can't, like, even imagine what you're goin' through. Or Billy! It's all so terrible. I wish I could be all objective about this, but like I told you, my unemployment runs out next month, and I've got to get something going or I'll lose my apartment.

—I'm so sorry to drag you into this, Leena. I just didn't see it coming four months ago. I wouldn't have gotten you involved.

—No. No, it's okay-ay. It's not your fault. It's not anybody's fault. It's just bad luck. You've gotta do what's right for you and Billy. That's all that matters.

Leena tore off a piece of cinnamon roll and plopped it into her mouth. Ball in Carrie's court.

—Kathleen, I love you so much. You're my best friend and you've stood by me all along. I hope you'll stand behind this decision too. Maybe I should give up the idea of a practice for now. If Billy gets better, maybe in six months or so we can look at it again. I just don't know what to expect.

Working the gooey roll in her mouth, she nodded in agreement, in lieu of speaking.

—I hope you understand. I know you understand.

Leena washed down the roll segment with a gulp of coffee, dabbing elegantly at the corners of her mouth with the starched white napkin. She swallowed heavily.

—I understand. You know I do. I'll always be here for you. You're going to need support too-oo. This is hard for everybody. I mean, it's hardest for Billy, of course. But it's hard for everyone who loves him, too.

—Sometimes I wonder if anyone else really loves him besides me. I think the band is pretty much just using him. Riding on his coattails. It seems like their words of praise are seldom accompanied by good actions. I don't know if they can be trusted.

—Sweetie, you've got trust hang-ups. To the max.

—Yeah. You're right. I guess I do.

—Well, take a deep breath, sister, and let *nat*-ure work her *won*-ders. You've gotta think positively here. Let go of the things ya' can't control.

She reached across the table and squeezed Carrie's shoulder. Carrie began to cry softly, whispering.

—If this is the end, it's such a stupid end for a story. And if it's supposed to be some sort of beginning, it's a ridiculous beginning. And if it's only the middle, then I just want for him to get well so we can live happily ever after.

Understandingly, Leena said.

—Carrie, let's just wait a few more weeks and see what happens. You don't have to, like, decide to-*day*-ay. I've got unemployment until the second week of next month. Work *would* be good for ya' though, ya' know?

Without saying a word, Carrie sighed in frustration.

—It's not a good idea for you to be Billy's nurse. You need to be able to get away from that, otherwise it'll just eat you alive. The best way you can help him is to, like, follow your bliss. You should only be his nurse part-time, so ya' can be his girlfriend full-time.

In the end, they decided not to decide that day.

The April Fools weekend shows were mostly uneventful on Friday and Saturday. Billy fought off weakness, nausea and faintness. But on that occasion, it did not come as a surprise to him and he was prepared for any eventuality. Just off stage, beneath a card table, was a bucket into which he could heave, if he felt so compelled. On the table above were a stack of fresh white towels and a couple of pitchers of water.

He took to sitting on his amp or on the drum riser, whenever Col would launch extended solos. He learned to pace himself, so that when a moment called for a burst of the old Billy energy, he was able to briefly summon it. If he felt faint, he knew to grab the mic stand and act all loaded and sloshy, which never failed to incite the audience to a strange, inebriate state of fucked-up identification. If they only knew...

Any tensions that may have arisen during the first two nights of the three-night stint at La Bamba, were solely attributable to the Consequential's camp. They had been selected to serve in the coveted capacity as opening band. Friday through Sunday, at that.

The three Consequentials were a surly and slightly punky bunch and always seemed to be at one another's throat over one transgression or another—never entirely clear to the Gods—hanging around backstage before or after the opening set.

Subsequent to the Friday night round of squabble, Gib observed that the Consequentials appeared to be enduring a bout of "Hot Seat." His premise was that ninety-nine and ninety-nine one-hundredths of a percent of all rock bands in the world were not succeeding in the manner to which they aspired. Typically, it was "his" fault, because it certainly wasn't "my" fault and probably wasn't "yours." The person at fault was typically the drummer.

Adhering to that scenario, Consequentials drummer Maxwell Barton seemed to be the member occupying the seat of heat. His actual drumming was quite good. He was rock solid and didn't overplay.

But he was not the least bit reliable. He would be late to rehearsals, or he wouldn't show up at all; he wouldn't bother calling to notify his mates of the news. He would simply disappear.

His intention was easily diverted and he seemed to frequently forget his mission, en route. Fire trucks, rushing somewhere with lights flashing and sirens blaring, invariably attracted his attention—so much so that he was capable of running through stop signs, red-lights, over sidewalks toward unwary pedestrians, across four lanes and a parade. He was unpredictable, to say the least.

So, all things considered, the April Fools weekend went down with only a modicum of disorder. Until Sunday night.

Billy arrived backstage late that night. He stepped down into the crowded green room where there already seemed to be some sort of tumult underway. Consequentials lead singer Harold Meek was pacing around nervously, occasionally stopping to ask of bassist Ben Corber the time, to which Ben would raise his sleeve and engage his watch, replying.

—It's four minutes a-n-n-n-nd forty seconds since you asked last time. It is now nine-oh-two and...twenty seconds.

—Where the fuck is he? We better call him again.

—What good will that do? If he was at home, he would have answered by now. Maybe we should play as a duo like we did at the Met that night.

—No, Ben. I ain't doin' that again. I mean, I'm not goin' out there without a drummer.

He half-turned toward Billy, his jaw-clenched in frustration.

—I don't know where he is, man. We both talked to him around six and he seemed like he was all set to go. He said he was comin' right over. And that was, like, two hours ago. He could be anywhere.

Billy sat down on a bench next to Gib, who had just taken a long, serious toke on a huge joint that happened to be passing by. Pretty much worn out by the previous two nights' activities, Billy had sort of hoped that the Consequentials might be willing to play an extra long opening set, so the Gods could get along by playing just one longish set instead of two of regular length. It was beginning to look like that wasn't going to happen.

—That sucks major, Harold. I feel for you. That's not somethin' we've ever had to deal with.

—Yeah, well that's because you guys are successful.

From the corners of his eyes, Billy connected with Gib, raising his eyebrows slightly. Hot seat.

Meek continued to wander helplessly, his hands buried in the pockets of his black leather jacket, a look of panic riveted to his bloodless face. Passing the joint to Col who was sitting on a folded chair between the two benches, Billy shook off a slight chill and a wave of nausea.

Just then, Tommy appeared at the top of the stairs, exaggeratedly pulling up his jacket cuff to expose his own watch.

—So when're you guys goin' on, anyway? I wanted ya' up and runnin' by nine-fifteen. Ya' ready to go? The crowd's kinda thin tonight. They're gonna walk on us pretty quick if we don't get some entertainment goin'. You guys need to get out there and get everything fired up.

—Aw, we're still waitin' on our goddamned drummer. He's gone fuckin' AWOL on us...again.

—Okay. Okay. We'll give ya' another ten minutes. Then we'll have to go to, uh, like, Plan B.

He disappeared as quickly as he had shown up, nervously scurrying somewhere, in a huge hurry. Harold resumed walking back and forth, as if his career were flashing before his eyes.

Which it was. Because Maxwell Barton had forgotten that he was a drummer in a band. He was somewhere within the city limits, totally absorbed in an escapade that had nothing whatsoever to do with his partners, who had experienced the disappointment of his behavior one too many times.

—Billy man. I'm sorry but we're gonna hafta, like, boag on the gig tonight. I mean, I guess last night was our last gig. We're all done with this bullshit. All done.

Saying nothing more, he stared up at the ceiling, as enraged as he had ever been—which was quite a feat. He was an angry guy even on the best of nights. Billy's jaw dropped slightly. He knew it was coming, but he didn't want to face the fact that the Gods were going to have to play the whole night. He really did not feel up to it.

Tommy again materialized in the doorway, tapping his watch in agitation. Billy saw him and motioned him down.

—Look, Tommy. The Cons aren't gonna be able to do the gig, so we're gonna hafta go the whole night. Let's plan on us startin' at around ten.

—Ten? Billy, man, there won't be anybody here at ten. The natives're gettin' restless out there. Some're already goin' on the warpath. If they wanted to listen to break tapes, they'd be sittin' in their cars. Which I'm afraid they're gonna do. They're ready to take a hike. One guy already asked for his cover back. We gotta get rollin' here or call it off.

Not about to pull out of a show for the first time, Billy stood up a little too fast and nearly passed out. After regaining his equilibrium, he assembled the troops.

—Okay, you guys. We better get out there and put the pedal to the metal. We got a long night ahead of us.

And it was a long night. By midway in the first set, Billy was worn out. The crowd seemed listless, so he was unable to draw energy from them. He felt dizzy and disoriented, forgetting several of the lyrics to "Uptown" and totally botching "Last of the Rockers." They were almost completely through the first eighty-minute set, well into "All Over This Town," when Billy began to faint.

As he had practiced, he grabbed the mic stand and attempted to remain upright. He wobbled woozily, but he did not fall. Temporarily overcome by aphasia, he pretended to be drunk and did his best Joe Strummer rant. Finally he was able to regain his poise and finish that song, and a smart version of "English Boys" to close out the set.

After a half-hour break, the Gods at last returned to the stage. By that time, the sparse crowd had thinned considerably. The band was shocked. They had never played to a room that empty or lifeless. Not in Portland. Col griped.

—Jesus Christ, what a dead fuckin' crowd.

Billy replied.

—Yeah, I'm pretty dead too.

—Let's play a short set and get the flock out of here.

Billy willingly agreed as he strapped on his guitar with a bit of difficulty. They skillfully launched into "Dressed Up," but were horrified to see some people actually heading for the exit. Suddenly, the song seemed ill-timed and out of place. The beat felt artificial, robotic, cold, and cheerless. None of that could have been envisioned when Billy threw the second set together during the break.

They didn't even try to mingle between songs with the sparse cohort, but tore through their set without a pause—one song sliding into the next. No room for applause or cheers. No matter, there were none.

It was the weirdest gig the band had ever played. It was the first time that a crowd hadn't gone absolutely nuts over them. The lack of response was troubling. Billy blamed the Consequentials. The band blamed Billy, though no one said a word.

As had become their custom after a La Bamba show, Billy met with Tommy at the bar. Tommy had long finished toting the night's receipts. It was twelve-thirty at night, and there was no one in the place besides the help.

Pale and drawn, Billy hunched over the bar, exhaling from the side of his mouth in frustration and exhaustion. He lightly pounded the counter, as Bijou, the tiny waitress with long, straight, shiny hair passed behind him.

—Hey, Bijou. How's it goin'? You're lookin' good tonight.

Even bent over, he was a head taller than the gorgeous little brunette. She stopped to flirt, the brown square plastic serving tray balanced on a cocked hip.

—I'm doin' okay. Kinda slow tonight.

She was wearing a purple v-neck blouse and a short black skirt that, because of her size, hardly required any material at all to assemble. Billy was distracted, trying to unobtrusively catch a peek at her legendary perfect tits.

—Yeah...kinda slow. Uh, at least we get outta here early tonight. I hate Sunday shows.

Bijou knew what he was looking at, because every member of the Gods, every other band that passed through the club, every male that had ever been in attendance at the establishment, and several females made, at all times, every effort to capture a sideward glimpse of them.

With practiced subtlety, she provocatively shifted her shoulders, leaning forward, almost imperceptibly, gathering them together for the best show. Billy did not miss a moment of it.

—I like your new songs. It seems like you guys are changin' your sound. I mean...

471

Slightly insecure, he interrupted

—I hope that's okay. Wha'd'ya' think?

—Oh, I like 'em a lot. They're, you know, really good and all. But I sort of miss those crazy songs from the early days. I guess you guys are just kinda growin' up. The new songs are like somethin' you'd hear on an album.

He jutted out his jaw, nodding thoughtfully.

—Yeah, I suppose that's right. We *are* growin' up, I guess. I hope those songs get on an album. Soon. We're not gettin' any younger.

Tommy walked up and rested his hand on Bijou's head as if it were a post.

—Hey, Billy. Crazy night, huh?

Billy shrugged but said nothing.

Tommy lifted his hand from Bijou's head, and she scampered off like a puppy free from a leash. Fishing in his jacket pocket with the opposite hand, he produced the usual roll of bills.

—There's eleven five-forty there. We only did eighteen-ninety tonight. Kind of a disappointment.

Without Bijou near to lift his spirits, Billy indistinctly crumpled into himself, attempting to make some form of sense out of the numbers Tommy was flashing—given that it had been a three-day weekend.

—I pulled five hundred for Harold's guys. We told him seven-fifty for the three nights. I oughta give 'em nothin'. But hey, it wasn't his fault, ya' know? That fuckin' Rex. He's a real piece a work. They oughta fuckin' kick his ass.

Head hanging, Billy only half heard.

—And then I pulled out my ten percent. That's thirteen-fifty. I'm glad you guys got me paid off on the loan. That money's gonna come in real handy. Things are gonna get real tight around here in a few weeks. I got four more weeks and then I'm unemployed. Ya' know?

—I know, man. I hear ya'. We're kinda in the same boat. Rough Edge paid Jack and you off, and Daw's dad, but we still got Nez to pay. A big chunka what we made tonight is going to Nez. A big chunka anything we make is goin' to him.

—Yeah, I guess you're screwed too, in a way. But you guys're, like, a little more *upwardly mobile* than me.

—Aw, Tommy, man, you always land on your feet. You'll be fine.

—Yeah? I hope you're right about that.

He placed his hand on Billy's shoulder and shook it good-naturedly. Billy winced slightly, in neuralgic pain.

—Oh, hey, sorry, man. Ya' sore there or somethin'?

—Well, uh...Tommy, I gotta tell ya' somethin'. But it's just between me 'n' you. I don't want it gettin' around or it'll really fuck things up.

—Yeah. Okay. What's goin' on?

—The cancer's back and I've been on chemo for the last month and a half.

—Well, I figured somethin' like that must be goin' on. You ain't been yourself for a while now. Seem kinda low energy. I don't know.

—And nobody knows about this, except for Billy D., Carrie and now you. I haven't even told the rest of the band. It'd fuckin' freak 'em out: royally.

—Billy, man. I'm pretty sure they prob'ly already know. I mean nobody's standin' around chattin' about it 'r nothin' but it's been pretty obvious to anybody payin' attention that you've been havin' some kinda trouble.

—Fuckin' shit, man. It's been, like, that goddamned obvious?

Without saying anything, Tommy indicated the affirmative.

—Shit. Shit, shit, shit. That's not good at all. Do you think people, like, in the crowd can tell?

—Yeah, I bet the ones who come to every show prob'ly figured out somethin's goin' on.

—Jeezus Fuckin' Christ, man. We're fuckin' screwed.

Ineffably, an invisible fulcrum pivoted an almost indiscernible shift of balance, transferring to load years of effort, leaving only promises and hopes to hang helplessly in the sky.

# XXXV

As Tommy had predicted, no one in the band was particularly surprised by Billy's disclosure when he revealed it at rehearsal the following Thursday. Some were bleak at the revelation, some seemingly unconcerned. Gib was alarmed. Billy D. was relieved. It was Col who wondered the obvious.

—Okay, so Billy, like, what's the plan? Where do we stand on this, I mean, like, goin' forward?

Sitting atop a stool, peering out across the studio space, Billy ran a hand up alongside his head and through his hair.

—I don't know, man. I don't know. I, like, beat this shit before, so I'm pretty sure I can beat it again. If anyone can, I can, ya' know? But this is different than last time. Last time they just cut off one of my nuts and sliced out a bunch of my lymph nodes and that was it: wham bam thank you ma'am.

He slashed the air with a Zorro motion.

—But, Jesus, this goddamned chemo shit really sucks. I just feel shitty all the time. Some days I feel less shitty than others. Those are the good days. But other days, all I want to do is puke.

The others would not engage his searching eyes, but registered regretful expressions, both feigned and real.

—Food tastes like it's cooked in fuckin' Listerine. I haven't been able to get it up in over a month.

Perhaps more information than was anticipated or desired.

—I'm afraid my fuckin' hair's gonna fall out any day. It's like already feelin' all bristly and weird and shit.

The others could not really say anything. They knew Billy was in some deep shit. None of them had ever experienced anything close to what Billy was going through, except maybe Gilly, who had to watch Augie deteriorate. It was different, of course, still Gilly could already see the similarities in the situation.

—But it won't do any good to sit around and piss and moan. So, we might as well get to it. We've still got a couple of new songs to go over. I really want to do 'History' this weekend, if we can. Maybe 'Close to You' and 'In and Out of Love', if we can, like, get the middle figured out.

With a few thoughts left to explore, Col asked.

—So what the hell happened with the new stuff the other night? There were people, like, walkin' out on us. What was that shit?

Billy defended against Col's apparent attack.

—I don't think it was the new stuff so much. The new stuff did okay on Friday and Saturday. Sunday just wasn't going to happen, no matter what.

—Well, we got another one of 'em at the same place at the end of the month, we better, like, fuckin' figure somethin' out—at least for that weekend if nothing else. People were tellin' me they miss the old, happy-go-lucky shit.

Daw agreed.

—Yeah, I heard that, too, from a couple of people.

Some of the others bobbed in affirmation. Billy thought of what Bijou had said.

—Well, here's the way I see it. We've been pushin' real hard to get our new material worked out and solid. And they're right. The new stuff's not that frat boy shit we used to do. The new stuff is aimed at albums and videos and tours. We can't be frat boys forever.

A few cocked heads. Col smirked.

—Speak for yourself there, Cap'n.

—Okay. Well, y'know I don't think Portland's gonna like us as much as they used to, no matter what we do. Those days are fuckin' long gone. And those people want us to fuckin' make them feel good, like that night they snorted a whole gram of coke and went crazy, or scored with that good lookin' blond in the corner.

There was no dispute to his reasoning.

—We're not fuckin' gods.

The group laughed at Billy until he finally got it.

—Okay, not *those* kind of gods, anyway. We're *unreal* gods.

Gib spoke up.

—We're just a hick rock band from Purtlund, Arragawn, Jim. We can't work *miracles*.

—Yeah, that's it, Bones. So we can either, like, try to make some kinda future for ourselves, or we can just keep recreatin' some past that's long gone, like some fuckin' lounge band. I'd rather be right behind than left behind. Y'know what I mean?

They didn't exactly know what he meant, but it had been some time since Billy had delivered a pep talk and they responded, as they always had, with renewed enthusiasm and a more focused sense of purpose.

Billy's Tuesday treatment went as well as could have been expected. He didn't feel any worse afterwards; mostly he maintained a form of terrible to which he had grown inured. Though he didn't much care for the circumstances, he enjoyed his conversations with Lisa.

She was a good listener. More and more frequently, he saw her as a confidant, letting her in on the inside workings of the band: the minutiae, the quibbles and squabbles. He told her about the disastrous gig on Sunday and that he had come clean with everyone, including Tommy, about the cancer's recurrence. When she asked him how they responded, Billy shrugged.

At rehearsals, the Gods managed to accomplish all the detailing they had intended for the three new songs. They were satisfied that they could debut them over the weekend at the Faucet, deep on the west side on Beaverton-Hillsdale Highway. It wasn't like the Faucet crowd was all that discerning—musically or otherwise.

The regulars at the Faucet (the Gods called it the Farrah Faucet) were a pretty strange bunch—a peculiar combination of serious Beaverton blow-dry, of both genders and new wave marginals, white shirts and thin black ties, polyester black jackets with sleeves pushed up to the elbows. There was the hair-band clique who were always holding court at a clutch of tables over to the right. There were the glam metal types of the Poison/Sister/Crue persuasion. The pop metal contingent were generally Leppard, Aerosmith, Bon Jovi, and Whitesnake replicants.

Most nights a member or two from Siquel or Blond & Tan might be hanging out at the bar, abask in the fawning flutter, which the public bestowed with astounding regularity. There were outsiders on the outskirts who really wouldn't fit in anywhere in deep southwest Portland and they didn't fit in at the Faucet either, because such a thing was hard to do, for the uninitiated.

The Gods were never particularly comfortable there either. But the audience was always receptive, if not overtly enthusiastic. And the band felt free to experiment there, because they were unlikely to offend anyone. For one cannot offend those who would not be offended. Clueless, shallow, pretty, and dim. The atmosphere was like some cheap imitation of a video on MTV. Artificial. Vain.

Their first set on Friday night began with a retrospective of some early hits, such as "Go-Go Boots…," "Symmetry," and "Upstroke Down." A version of the earlier, simpler "Rocky Road" especially seemed to bear a deeper significance to Billy than ever before. He almost choked himself up.

Through the remainder of the set, they concentrated on music from their middle period. They effortlessly rammed through "Stereo Area," "Neutral Stomp," "We Used to Hang Around," and "The World Comes Crashing Down" to a modestly robust response, which, in the Faucet, was akin to a riot. To get people to stop talking and actually listen to the music was an achievement tantamount to Moses coming down from Mount Sinai.

A jubilant feeling of victory befell the band as they moved backstage to towel off after the sweaty set. Even though it was drizzly outside, only in the mid-fifties, the humidity was quite high. Billy was ecstatic to be perspiring, even though his sweat smelled like urine, Pine Sol, and rotten meat. He felt better than he had in months. Symptom free.

Assessing the evening to that point, Col said excitedly.

—All right! That's more like it. That's about the best we've played in a fuckin' month or so.

Gilly added.

—Yeah. The timing was on the money. And the energy was great.

Daw and Gib were in complete concurrence, with Billy deeming.

—I guess it's me, then, you guys. If I'm up there fuckin' pukin' and gettin' ready to pass out and shit, then the show's gonna, like, suck, y'know? I mean, I don't know if there's much I can do about that, but...

Col wagged his head thoughtfully.

—Naw, man. We gotta pick up the energy when you're feelin' shitty. We can't, like, expect you to have it every night. We've gotta be ready to cover for you. Take up the slack.

The others nodded in support, as Daw put forth the proposition.

—Yeah. Col's right. There's things we can do to take the pressure offa Billy when he's not feelin' good.

—I can dance...

Gilly began a mock softshoe. Gib spoke up.

—I could read poetry.

Everyone laughed at the thought of Gib standing at the mic reading poems while the rest of them played behind him. Col said.

—We could be like a fuckin' beatnik band. We could all wear black sweaters and little berets and grow goatees. I'm likin' it. The Unreal Ginsbergs. The Unreal Beefhearts.

Smiling, Billy was flattered.

—Hey, you guys. I really appreciate it. I mean you all comin' together like this, y'know, that's what it's all about.

Ever the pragmatist, Col maintained a straight face.

—Hey, man. What the fuck else're we gonna do? You're, like, our fuckin' meal ticket. It's not like I can sing lead. I sound like Mister Ed. Or Gilly. I mean jeezus, Gilly. He'd look like fuckin' Howdy Doody frontin' the Cure. What's that guy's name?

Inquisitively, Col gaped at Gib.

—Robert Smith

—Yeah, Robert Smith. Look, nobody's even fuckin' close to bein' as pretty as you. We'd, like, lose all the chicks the first night.

That sort of talk cheered and inspired Billy and motivated him to give everything he had for the band.

They quickly took the stage for the second set and, without hesitation, moved immediately into "Singles Goin' Steady," setting the tone for the rest of the night. They moved through "Thunder and Lightning," "Apple of My Eye," "Point of No Return," as well as the hits, "Made in Hong Kong," "Police Told Me," and "Shortage of Variety."

It was only after they had finished driving through those first eight songs that the band stopped to take even a short break. Billy felt exhilarated and he energetically threw himself into his performances for the first time since the band had left for LA. He shouted.

—Hey, hey, hey. How's everybody doin' out there?

A sort of deflated whoompf went up, an indication that the attendees were far more deeply involved with the music than on most nights. Typically, unless the band was Siquel or Blond & Tan, such a question from the stage would elicit only a hushed hissing sound, similar to the last of a hairspray can sputtering to diminution.

—All right. That's good to hear. We got a coupla brand new songs we wanna do for you now. This first one's called, 'Close to You.'

As Daw provided time with clicking sticks, Gib's pulsing bass drove the intro. Next, Gilly faded in with parts comprised of squishy synth strings and throaty flute-like arpeggios. Then Col entered the sonic picture with a low, slow, single note riff—wrung with conflagrant zeal.

Billy cantered up to the mic, resembling one of his favorite characters: Alex from *A Clockwork Orange*. He didn't identify with the character so much as with the eye makeup. He had slathered his left eye thick with mascara, a horrorshow melenky malchick leading his droogie droogs.

It was a new type of vocal melody for him—more complex than most—climbing incrementally up an F-sharp minor scale from the sixth in the bass to the sixth an octave above, before descending halfway back down again. An exotic haunting theme.

—Your eyes take me places so far away
Baby this could be the first day of the rest of our lives
I believe that we can break many hearts
Baby take me as your man or you'll tear mine apart
I just want to get close to you-oo-oo-oo
There is nothing I'd rather do-oo-oo-oo.

People began to drift toward the dance floor, not just to see and be seen, but because they were actually attracted to the feel of the song. The whole room felt strange and inside out. The band noticed the change immediately and ratcheted up the intensity for the second verse.

—I've been waiting—I've made up my mind
Coz love takes years of takin' one kiss at a time
I know you know I have seen you thinkin' a lot
In your sensuous smile there's a face full of lust
I just want to...get close to you-oo-oo-oo
There is nothing I'd rather do-oo-oo-oo
I just want to get close to you-oo-oo-oo.

The thirty or so couples out on the dance floor were working themselves into a real Faucet frenzy, wherein the females, apparently staring at some vague chimera in the distance, would clear personal space by shifting their weight from one hip to the other, suggestively swinging their arms and shoulders rhythmically in time to some aspect of the music. A few of them were smoking, hitting possibly chic poses, in order to garner attention from unspecified quarters.

The males, however, were more inclined to stand nearly motionless, bobbing almost indiscernibly up and down. They gawked and craned like parakeets, nervously searching the room to see if anyone noticed how silly they looked

Col ground out a gritty solo, flame-broiled around the edges. Then the Gods slid into a well-crafted bridge, followed by an interweaving of the chorus with the bridge, ending in a long, sultry fade. Surprisingly appreciative applause more or less erupted from the passive wells of the soulless shells standing before the band.

Not about to let what passed for momentum at the Faucet slip away, Daw quickly fell into a solid kick drum foundation, at first on the one beat at the top of the measure, evolving to the one and three. Gilly pitch-wheeled high, whining solitary synth-string notes while Col strummed harmonics at the fifth, seventh and twelfth frets. Billy shouted

—Yeah, yeah, yeah. This is another new one we're debuting here tonight. It's called 'In and Out of Love'.

As the activity on the stage settled into a quiet groove, Billy grabbed the mic and began to sing in a whisper.

—A part of me wants you by my side
But another part just says no
I've run out of places I can hide
I don't know where else to go
To the tip of Baja I might try
Way down in Mexico.

One of the group's best-developed choruses followed, calling to mind an odd cross of Joe Jackson and REM.

—But don't follow me
Coz it's just not right
Don't call for me
Coz you're not that type
No don't laugh at me
Coz I'm cry-y-y-y-yin' inside

I've been in and out of love
So many
In and out of love
So many
In and out of love
So many times.

Again the audience acted as if they were generally interested in the emotions and ideas being expressed: a wonder, given that most of the attention spans present in the room seemed not to extend much past "whut?" The guys glided into a soulfully evocative extended bridge, a bit of an homage to the Four Tops.

—I've been in and out in and out
I've been in and out of love so many times
For a little cheering up I might become a clown
And paint a funny smile on my face
Or possibly a mime pretending to be
Caught up in a lover's embrace
Then I could hold the princess eyes can't see
And she could wipe the tears from my face.

And back to the chorus.

It mostly went unnoticed that the Gods had just played their most ambitious song ever. The chorus and bridge were especially well constructed, exhibiting an obvious musical maturity. Though the lyrics lagged behind the development shown in the melody and arrangement, they still indicated more effort than any Billy had ever before composed.

The night went on to be one of the most successful the Gods had played in months, all the more surprising that it happened at the Faucet in Beaverton, but it was unanimously agreed: such is life.

Physically, Billy did not rebound well. He spent the night at Carrie's and woke up Saturday morning with a sore throat, feeling drained and listless. He stayed in bed all day. In the afternoon Carrie played some of her favorite records, including Cat Stevens' *Teaser and the Firecat*, Blondie's *Parallel Lines*, and Talking Heads' *Speaking in Tongues* soundtrack.

Billy appreciated Carrie's taste in music, even though it diverged greatly from his own. Still, she had introduced him to the post-*Beat Crazy* Joe Jackson and REM and a lot of other music that he would not have otherwise heard. He lay in bed absorbing the chord changes and clever lyrics of Peter Gabriel's "Solsbury Hill."

From out of nowhere she appeared, draping herself over Billy's lounging frame. She kissed him affectionately over his neck and shoulders. He pulled her close and grabbed her girlish round ass, and began to make a methodical pumping motion. Briefly she pulled away and looked at him in mock shock. But then she lay back down and allowed him to continue his ministrations. His cock slowly began to swell. "My heart goin' boom-boom-boom."

He set about unbuttoning Carrie's jeans, while she shed her dark gray sweater. Not able to wait any longer, he stubbornly yanked her pants and panties down below her knees and pulled himself up inside of her, flicking her bra free with a quick twist of his fingers. He roughly massaged her tits and fucked her hard, almost frantically. It was only a matter of minutes until they came together. She collapsed on top of him and they both fell into a deep sleep.

That night, everything about the gig was dead. Billy was worn out from the night before and that afternoon. The rest of the band seemed unenthusiastic, for some impalpable reason. The Faucet crowd was lifeless, resembling a room full of Gap mannequins. The Gods went through the motions and were able to get through the listless night without incident. Though exhausted, Billy played the evening cool and there was no real sign that he was ailing, only that he appeared reticent and remote, which seemed appropriate, given the response he received from the audience that night.

On the Tuesday preceding the three-day bon voyage party at La Bamba, Billy met again with Doctor Todd. The doctor seemed even more detached than usual while looking over Billy's charts, a look of puzzled concern on his face.

—Well, mmmBilly...Your latest tests are still not what I was looking for. Your tumor has shrunk to the extent that we can begin to consider surgery to get that out.

Billy indicated that he understood.

—But I'm a little disturbed, because it appears the cancer might be spreading.

Eyes widened, Billy asked.

—Wha'd'ya mean, *spreading*?

—There is some indication that it's moving into other lymph systems. I'm especially bothered by the results I'm seeing regarding your spleen.

—My spleen? I don't even know what a spleen is.

Always accommodating when called upon to play the role of physician, Doctor Todd explained.

—The spleen is located underneath the ribs on the left side. It's an organ that creates lymphocytes for the reconditioning of old red blood cells. And it serves as a sort of blood reservoir. It supplies the body with blood in emergencies, such as a severe wound, where there is a great deal of blood loss. The spleen is also the repository where white blood cells trap various destructive organisms.

—Like cancer?

—Well, it's not quite like that, but the results are generally the same. Your spleen seems enlarged. That's not good.

With a puzzled expression on his face, the young man indicated the desire that the doctor should continue.

—It's an indication of infection. We'll have to do more tests to see what the source is. But we want to get that swelling controlled. All right then. That's it for today.

Billy wanted to ask Doctor Todd when he would start to feel better, but he knew he would only receive one of Todd's elliptical syllogisms. So he held his tongue. The doctor snapped to attention, tucking his expensive Montblanc pen into the breast pocket of his white lab coat.

—Next month we'll talk about the possibility of removing that tumor. We'll just have to take it one step at a time. I want to see that swelling of your spleen reduced. That's your assignment for now.

—Well, Doctor Todd, what can I do to reduce the swelling?

—Just get lots of rest and drink plenty of fluids.

That was a routine Billy had already been following steadfastly, so from that he was able to infer that Doctor Todd was telling him there wasn't much he could do about his swollen spleen. Pray maybe.

The send-off three-day weekend of shows at La Bamba was met with a tremendous display of affection from the public. John Westman wrote a loving retrospective of the club-closing for *The Oregonian*. A week later he was fired, for his published review of a Tom Petty concert at the Civic that, unbeknownst to him, since he wasn't actually in attendance—had been cancelled. Doubting Westman's further reliability in such matters, the publication promptly jettisoned their chief music writer.

Friday night at La Bamba was a zoo. The club was packed from wall to wall, far beyond capacity, with a collection of all Portland types, including even a few hair spray mannequins from the Faucet and its fellow Beaverton hair lair to the north, the Orange Peel.

Punkers were in attendance—to kick dirt on the whole affair—though some of their mellower brethren were disturbed by the loss of such a great venue, whether it fit their value system or not. Some new-wavers, who were obvious in their concern for the new destination for their scene, walked the floors with blank expressions on their faces.

There were members of easily one hundred bands or more, hanging around, giving Tommy their condolences and getting drunk on cheap beer. Improbably, even Max Barton, erstwhile drummer for the Consequentials, made an appearance.

And there were plain, regular folk from all walks of life, attracted to the carwreck club finale by a series of segments KOIN had run all week on the *Six O'Clock News*, regarding the closing of "a landmark in the Portland music scene." The station reporters conducted short interviews with Westman and Bick Muckler as well as with several top-tier local musicians, most of whom had never set foot inside the place, but were ready to offer warm condolences, breathless platitudes, and prolific well wishes.

That Friday night was a convergence of unparalleled splendor. Every planet was aligned. The atmosphere was by far the best La Bamba had ever seen—and that was going some. The mood was heated, impassioned and stupidly celebratory. A goodwill brawl.

The Gods rose to the occasion. Billy was heavily made up in white face with rouged cheeks and what was becoming his trademark Alex eye mascara. He wore tight black jeans and black Converse, a white t-shirt and a black leather motorcycle jacket. The jacket was mostly to disguise how skinny Billy had become.

The others were similarly clad: black leather and heavy make-up all around except for Daw who, of course, wore jeans, white leather high-top basketball shoes, unlaced, and a powder blue sleeveless t-shirt. Even he took the stage wearing a black polyester flight jacket, which he promptly removed before he sat down upon his throne.

It was a well-lubed crowd. The excessively exuberant ska frat band, the Canny 9s had opened the night, enlivening everyone with an hour-long set of their incessant, horn-laden, good cheer. By the time the Gods' arrived onstage at eleven, the atmosphere was like gasoline awaiting the merest spark to engulf in ignition.

Manifoldly magnifying the intensity, the band appeared, and without hesitation, swung into "Boom Chuck Rock," maintaining the ska feel, before swinging into a tougher, harder set.

Caught up in the serious magic, Billy gave the evening's performance everything he had, with requisite high kicks and running in place like Mick Jagger. He felt nauseous a couple of times. And he felt faint once or twice. But he was able to maintain his perfected drunken stance, holding onto the mic stand, while other times moving to the back of the stage to sit on the drum riser.

It was all carefully choreographed and well executed. The sets were constructed in such a way as to offer Billy the necessary temporal space for quick recuperation; the rest of the band had grown accustomed to covering for him. In fact, they began to look forward to their moments in the spotlight.

As was the case with the three-day weekend at La Bamba at the beginning of the month, Billy's strength slowly deteriorated through the course of the musical procession of events. But, in contrast to the earlier series of concerts, the festive public celebrations did not diminish in the least, but continued unabated right into Sunday night.

So, when the Gods took the stage following the Canny 9s highly charged opening set, there was a rousing assortment of merrymakers, totally committed to going down with the La Bamba ship. Good evening. This is your Captain. We are about to attempt a crash landing.

Anxious about the state of Billy's well being, Tommy hovered around his young friend like a cat-addled mother robin protecting her brood. But there was no reading the stoic star. The show must go on. Tough it out. Rah rah.

That attitude got Billy deeply into the opening set. But his energy began to flag with four songs left to go. He had not been experiencing intense nausea much over the weekend. And it was only a slight wave that overcame him at moments. More severe was his sense of weakness and lightheaded vertigo. He held himself up via the mic stand, which worked well for "Rocky Road." It added pathos to the song the deeper intimations of which went mostly unnoticed by all observers.

But when, without pause, they swung into the more robust tempo of "When the World Comes Crashing Down," Billy was trapped, sagging lifelessly at the mic stand, knowing that if he tried to move around the stage at all, he would pass out and fall.

—Livin' in the old days
Just livin' in the old days
When the world came crashin' down
The world came crashin' down.

With his weight upon the mic stand, he scribed a couple of wide, reckless arcs around his spot on the stage, whirling woozily, before he collapsed to the floor in a thudding clump. He tried to stand, but he could not. The band kept playing through the remainder of the song, with the intention of convincing the onlookers that it was part of the act: "crashing down" and all that. But when Billy failed to get up, they cut short the ending and rushed to him.

From the back of the room, Billy Dreier was at Billy's side in an instant, helping him to his feet and leading him off the stage. Col stepped to the mic.

—We're gonna take a short break and we'll see what's goin' on.

The room fell silent as Billy's little secret was suddenly a secret no more. Something was wrong. Maybe it was his cancer. Go tell your friends. Speculate. Formulate. Postulate.

Soon, everyone who cared, knew. The entire Portland music scene was ablaze with a windy wildfire of rumor, hearsay, and innuendo. Billy was sick.

And, undeniably, he was indeed sick. The band was unable to continue that final night send off for La Bamba. Stalwart pros that they were, the Canny 9s retook the stage and were able to revive the festivities with a long set of whacky ska madness. The La Bamba tribe seemed satisfied with the party, though Tommy was horrified by what had taken place. A regrettable conclusion to a good run.

In an eerie coincidence, the band ended up canceling their shows at Euphoria, scheduled for the following weekend, just as they had the first time Billy's cancer had appeared. However, Jonathan Dixon had already heard the talk around town, so he was not particularly surprised about the last minute suspension of the Gods' calendar. He was cynical about it when Gilly called to give him the news. It was going to be an inconvenience, but he knew a couple bands he could plug in. Not to worry. He'd get by. Helluva guy.

Carrie and Leena trotted the last boxes of loose items and materials into Rose City Veterinary. Doctor Dahl had left the facilities well stocked upon his departure. He knew Carrie would need all the help she could get.

At Billy's unceasing insistence, Carrie followed through on taking over Doctor Dahl's practice. She found another young vet, Ken Abraham, whom she knew from school at PSU, to partner with her on the business. He was young and, like Carrie, penniless, so the arrangement worked out perfectly for him. It worked well for Carrie, too. In the case of an emergency, she could take a leave of absence without having to close the facility doors. Ken could serve as her backup, while Leena worked the front desk.

Through the course of the month of May the Gods played only four shows. A weekend and a couple of single nights. When Billy was up to it, the band rehearsed more new material—songs that reflected Billy's new perspective on music and life. They were mellower songs, maybe indicative of an interest in Stray Cats, a certain swing jazz element creeping in. The others, Col especially, were not particularly stirred by the new material. It seemed sort of boring and mundane.

Because he was scrambling to find another venue in which to slide, Tommy was mostly unavailable. He finally ended up at Chuck's, which was located right next to where Sack's Front Avenue used to be. Chuck's did not offer live music, but because of Tommy's gravity, the room quickly became a late-night hotspot

Still unhappy with the results he was obtaining in Billy's case, Doctor Todd prescribed another eight weeks of chemo. If that didn't work he would consider a more radical approach—possibly a combo of radiation and chemo, in an effort to get ahead of the relentless advancement of Billy's disease. He was especially worried about the worsening condition of the young man's spleen. It was enlarged and not functioning well at all.

Without Tommy to serve as the band's manager, there was no one to book gigs for them. And with Billy's health being precarious, at best, it would be difficult for anyone to guarantee that the band would show up on any given night.

It was halfway through May and with a schedule of only four performances set for June, many of the other members lapsed into lethargy, complacency and boredom. They spent a lot of time jamming in the studio without Billy present. The outcome was a sort of heavy wavy metal. Twisted Sister meets Flock of Seagulls. Riot meets Duran Duran.

During those jams, Col was able to play out his fantasies of replacing Randy Rhoads in Ozzie's band, or of being compared to Yngwie Malmsteen or Eddie Van Halen. Even though his talent was more on a level with that of Rick Nielsen, Col, like millions of other guitarists, clung to the notion that he had the capability to be a far more impressive guitarist than the Gods' music was allowing him to demonstrate. He was being held back.

The others didn't feel the restraints to be as monumental as Col did, but they were willing to follow his lead. There was nothing much else to do without the lead singer present, but to practice the backing parts for Gods' songs. Every once in a while that might be a good idea, to get everything straight and tight. But after a while...monotony would set in.

The Gods finally did return to Euphoria—on the Sunday night climax to a spectacular Memorial Day weekend, which featured six different high-profile Portland bands on each of the three nights, including headliners Dollarshine on Friday and Johnny and the Destructions on Saturday. In a stroke of uncommon good judgment, neither Billy nor Denny elected to attend Dollarshine's show.

Everything went well for Billy and the band. Both were in good form. Having his schedule reduced so drastically allowed Billy to acquire the necessary strength for the shows they did play. His performance on that night was the Billy of old. But there was a vague mood of disquiet clouding the room. The vigor he attempted to project was tempered by an apprehension that he, the band, and the audience shared: that he would keel over again at some point.

And just as the other members had secretly feared, some of the new songs proved to be not as appealing to the fans as was the older, more reliable stuff. Some of it did not have a solid dance beat. Still, most of the newer material went over reasonably well, given that so much of it was relatively unfamiliar. And it was the best received of all of their shows since before Christmas.

Feeling more driven on than a freeway off-ramp, Billy spent the next several days sacked out at Carrie's apartment. Except for his Tuesday chemo appointment he stayed in bed, watching *Price is Right* in the morning, *Perry Mason* at noon, and a couple of soaps—*General Hospital* and *All My Children* in the afternoons. He had a serious thing for Erica Kane. Her nasty disposition intrigued him, and her slender body turned him on.

Meanwhile, Carrie was spending days at the Rose City office, still trying to organize the business with Leena and Ken Abraham between appointments to give care to her animal patients. Some pets were formerly seen by Doctor Dahl, others were new, most attracted by the Free Initial Consultation coupon she and Doctor Abraham decided to run in *Willamette Week*.

After work, Carrie would stop off along the way home, picking up Chinese food one night, pizza on another. Increasingly, Billy was spending most of his free time at Carrie's place, catching rides from Billy D. to the rehearsal studio over on Belmont.

Although worn out herself, just the same, Carrie was nevertheless exhilarated and excited by her new enterprise; thrilled that they were acquiring new patrons and pleasing those that Doctor Dahl had left behind to their care. She was constantly worrying about Billy. But she was better off for her own success. As Leena's counsel had foretold, she paid him better attention during the time she was actually with him.

By Friday morning, Billy felt well enough to walk over to the band house down on Arthur. He needed clean clothes and fresh personal supplies. Trying to shave with the razor Carrie used on her legs was a very risky proposition, as borne out by the various, tiny nicks and cuts on his face.

As he ambled past the basketball courts, a profound sense of déjà vu overcame him. He could hear a bunch of guys caught up in a three-on-three game. One voice stood out. It was Poppy. Billy saw Mak let go with a jumper from the left side of the lane, banking it in. He sarcastically appraised the effort.

—Lucky shot, Doughboy!

Instantly, Mak stood frozen in place on the court. That voice. He turned with a happy, horrified look on his face. Yes. It was... He grinned sheepishly and headed over to Billy, who stood behind the chain link fence. Mak declared.

—We gotta quit meetin' this way, man.

As Mak wiped the sweat from his face and neck with a white towel that had been lying on top of his shirt, Billy quizzed his old friend.

—What're you doin' here anyway?

—I was gonna ask you the same question. I went back to school. Gettin' my accountin' degree in another week.

—Then what?

487

—Fuck if I know. I'll have to get a job somewhere, I guess.

A bright idea formulated spontaneously in Billy's mind.

—Hey, Mak. I was headin' over to the band house. Wanna come with me? I got somethin' to ask ya.

—Yeah. Okay. We can take my car.

—When the hell did *you* get a car?

—Aw, my mom got a new car in January and she gave me her old one.

Mak grabbed his stuff and led Billy to a spotless white nineteen eighty-two Plymouth Arrow parked across the street from the courts. He unlocked the door, hopped in and reached over to unlock the passenger door.

—Jesus Christ. This is her *old* car?

—Yeah. My parents like to trade 'em in every coupla years.

Firing up the perfectly maintained automobile, Mak continued his tale.

—My dad got his job back, at Tri-Met, and mom's working part-time. And they got a big return on some stocks they sold. So Dad decided to foot the bill for my mom's new car, and they decided, what the hell, they'd give me this one figurin' it might get me out of the house sooner, I guess.

—You're still livin' at home?

Exasperated, Mak replied.

—Yeah. I had a full load at school and it saved a lot of money livin' there.

—But how do you, like, have a little get-together with your friends? Or bring a girl over?

—Aw, y'know, I haven't done any of that shit since I left the band.

It was Billy's turn for a mortified expression, guilt creeping up his spine.

—Look, Mak. I'm sorry about all of that. I really am. I had a lot of people givin' me a lot of advice and most of it was, like, really bad, y'know? I mean, I never meant to fuck you over or anything.

Silent for a moment. Mak clenched his jaw slightly, his grip on the steering wheel tensing just a little.

—Hey. It's okay. Bygones be bygones. Life's too short.

He aimed the Arrow down Southwest Caruthers toward Arthur, continuing.

—So what's up? Wha'd'ya' wanna ask me about?

—Well, Poppy. I heard you're bookin' Lung Fung.

—Yeah. I'm kinda doin' that on the side. Book four or five shows a month. Make a little spendin' money. Workin' capital. You know...

—Yeah. Sure. Uh, Pop, I want you to book us a show at Lung Fung for the Fourth of July.

—Well, I got those Donkey Sho-Tay guys from Seattle in there on the Fourth.

—I really want to work with you again, and I really want to play Lung Fung on the Fourth. Be like a reunion or somethin'.

—I'll see what I can do. You know what pricks Stan and that Reineke guy are.

—Yeah, They're, like, real fuckin' assholes. But just tell 'em there's been a little change of plans. If they don't like it, then tough shit.

Mak pulled up in front of the band house. They exited the Arrow and marched up the stairs and into the living room, where Col was making out with some girl—his right arm around her shoulder, while expertly clutching a bottle of beer in his opposite hand, an unlit cigarette pointing from between his index and middle fingers.

He looked up from the business at hand, muttering.

—So, I'm all, like, what the fuck, and he says...Hey! Look what the fuckin' cat drug in. Hey, Pop. How's it hangin'?

—It's swell, Col. Just swell.

—It's swellin'? Yeah, mine is too! C'mon Sushi Sioux. Let's take this upstairs and see what you can do.

Playfully grabbing her by the neck, he wrestled her upright and marched her toward the staircase, near the *Pac Man* machine. As he started up, she broke free and marched down the adjacent hall toward the back bedrooms and the bathroom.

—I have to pee.

—Okay. I'll be upstairs. Don't dawdle now. I got somethin' for ya.

Smiling devilishly, Suzie cooed.

—Yeah. I've got somethin' for you too-oo.

Eventually their commotion subsided, and Billy and Mak sat down on the couch.

—You wanna beer?

—Nah. Thanks. It's too early for me. I got a lotta stuff to do this afternoon. So, Billy. What's been goin' on? I've been hearin' weird shit all over town that you're sick again and that you've been passin' out on stage and shit like that. What's up? Are you okay?

—I'm not doin' that great, Pop. The cancer's come back and it's worse than last time. A lot worse.

—I was thinkin' you didn't look all that great, no offense.

—It's okay. I know. I look like shit. Fuckin' chemo. My hair's all funky, and my skin's yellow and look at this.

He pulled up the sleeve on his shirt.

—I look like I've been on a fuckin' starvation diet for the last five years. No fat, no muscle. Nothin'.

Mak didn't argue. His assessment was similar.

—Tommy's all freaked out about losin' La Bamba, and then, I've been sick. So he hasn't booked us very many gigs. And really nothin' we couldn't book ourselves. But I know he needs the money. So we've only played, like, five gigs or somethin' since the end of April, and I know the natives are gettin' a little restless. But every time we do play a gig, I need, like, a week to recover. It sucks, man.

—So what's the doc say? Are ya' gonna be okay?

—Too soon to tell, I guess. He wants to zap what's left of the tumor I had over here.

He patted his ribs.

—Then...I don't know. I guess we'll just hafta see after that. I guess my spleen's fuckin' up, too.

Not surprisingly, Billy was met with a confused expression of profound nescience.

—So yeah. I really wanna have a big fuckin' summertime spectacular for Fourth of July. Like that other gig we did there on the Fourth. How long ago was that? Two years? Three years?

It seemed like a lifetime to both of them.

—Whenever it was. Anyway, do you think you can pull it off, Mak?

Drawing a deep breath through his nostrils, Mak pursed his lips, a bit put out to be in the position he always seemed to assume in regard to the Gods.

—I'll see what I can do, Billy. That's all I can say. We got a lotta variables here.

—Yeah. Variables. You math majors...Variables. Whatever the hell that means.

Just as he was about to explain constants and variables, it occurred to Mak that Billy wouldn't understand anyway, so he dropped the notion.

Two weeks later, the Gods were booked for Friday night at Last Hurrah. Summer was at hand and all Portland was in bloom, as only Portland can bloom in those days of bloom and blooming. There was an ecstatic charge in the air.

The show went well. It was a packed house comprised of loyal devotees and morbid curiosity seekers. Having not played for two weeks, Billy felt invigorated and inspired, and despite his illness, he actually had fun. The other guys were suitably motivated by Billy's enthusiasm. They played with more intensity and concentration than they had for quite some time. All agreed the evening was a success—although there were some in the audience who were disappointed that Billy didn't die on stage, or at least pass out or something.

As was usually the case, the next morning Billy was completely wiped out. He felt like a battleship run aground. His center of gravity seemed to be located somewhere beneath the mattress of Carrie's bed.

Carrie spent the morning at the veterinary office, working a half-day, as had become her routine on Saturdays. She would typically return home around one. Depending on how Billy felt, either they would go out to get something to eat, or, if he wasn't feeling up to going out, she would prepare a meal for the two of them.

Still sprawled across the bed when Carrie returned from work, Billy lifted his head feebly as she came through the front door. She came into the bedroom and kissed him tenderly. He kissed her back, with as much passion as he could summon in the moment.

—Hi.

—Hi. Not feeling so great today?

—I might've overdone it a little bit last night.

—Billy Granger *overdoing* it. Now there's an alien concept.

Her sarcasm was not as appreciated as it could have been. Billy frowned.

—Oh, come *on* sweetheart. You know you're notorious in this town for overdoing everything. It's just a little joke.

She saw that her explanation was not having the desired calming effect. It only seemed to further agitate him.

—Billy! You tease me all the time, and I try to tease you once and you get all mad. That's not fair.

—I'm just not in the mood for it today. I'm pretty tired. And I feel like crap.

—Okay. Okay. You just take it easy. I've got some bookwork to do, so let me know when you want to eat.

The phone rang. Billy lay on his back and eavesdropped as Carrie answered.

—Hello? Oh yes. Hi, Mister Vetter. Yes...Cuz.

With a start, Billy bolted upright.

—Oh the weather is just gorgeous. This is the best time of year in Oregon. Not too hot. Perfect really. Yes. He's here. I'll put him on.

Towing the long phone line behind her, she handed the receiver to Billy.

—Hello?

—Hello, Billy, it's Cuz. How're you feeling?

Confused, Billy pretended ignorance.

—I'm feelin' fine, Cuz. Fine.

—Well, I heard that you're sick again.

Billy tried to figure out who it was that relayed that information back to Vetter.

—Yeah, I've had a little setback, I guess.

—So you've been cutting back on shows?

—Yeah. A few, I guess.

For the first time in a long time, Billy felt ill for a reason that was not related to his disease. Jutting out his lower jaw, he blew back the bangs hanging over his forehead, addressing Carrie with a look of grave concern.

—Well, when do you think you'll be up and around and back at full speed?

A chill circuited up Billy's spine.

—It'll probably be another three or four months, I guess. Maybe a little longer. It depends on how well the treatment goes. I...

—So it could be six months then?

—Yeah, I guess it could be. It's hard to say.

Vetter was troublingly silent. A little defensive, Billy tried to change the subject.

—We've been workin' up a lot of new stuff, Cuz. I think you'll like the direction we're goin' in.

—I'm looking forward to hearing it, Billy. You'll have to send me a tape.

—Yeah, I'll send one out to you right away.

—You know, Billy, four to six months is a long time in the music industry. It's like dog years. Four to six months is like five years. Styles shift like the wind.

Though he was bewildered by the direction the conversation was heading, seeing as how Cuz had made it sound like five years was nothing in the music business, Billy continued playing dumb.

—We've been at this for over a year now. That's right, isn't it? Anyway, from what you're saying, it might be another year before you're able to get back into gear. My thought is that perhaps, it would be best to discontinue this project until you're feeling better.

The blood drained completely from Billy's face, then from the rest of his upper torso, and then seemed to pool at the soles of his feet.

—And when you're up and around at full speed again, we can work to cut a new deal.

—A new deal?

—Yes. Our agreement stipulates that you will deliver an album a year for six years. From the looks of things, it may be two or three years, or more, before you're actually able to release an album. I think it's in both of our interests to rescind our agreement. Item five in our contract.

Billy drew a long, deep breath. Despite his attempt to take reasonable steps, he had not noticed that stipulation when he signed the papers.

—And as for the money we advanced you on this contract, we can make arrangements for you and the band to pay that back. We won't try to recoup the money from debts we paid off for you. Just the three hundred and fifty thousand we gave you, and to the band.

—But we have the stuff from the Power Station and the stuff Maclan produced in LA...

—Most of the Power Station recordings are unusable. They need to be rerecorded. 'Police Told Me' is a keeper. And you have that great video to accompany it. The Maclan recordings sound very good. There may be an EP there. But we can't

493

release an EP now, until we know you'll be ready to follow up soon after with a full-length album. When you're well again, we'll probably have to renegotiate a contract for a much higher price.

—Gee, Cuz. I don't know what to say. This is all very serious. A lot of the money is spent already. We thought we had a deal.

—We did, Billy. But the terms of that contract have been breached and we need to return to square one. We'll let you keep the West Lake recordings. So if you want to release those songs and the Power Station recordings as an album, you're quite welcome to do so. We certainly won't stand in your way. And as I said, we'll make arrangements for you to pay Rough Edge back the advance monies. It doesn't have to be done all at once. We can work out an equitable payment plan, I'm sure.

(Well whoopdee-do Cuz, glad you're so fuckin' understanding. Good to know you believe in the band. Good to find out where your priorities are, asshole). Billy was shocked. Totally and completely shocked. Shocked speechless. His jaw hung open and he rolled his tongue from side to side in his mouth, looking as if he was going to cry.

Billy called Mak on Monday to see how the Fourth of July celebration was coming along. Surprisingly, Mak had managed to get everything set. He had guilt-tripped Stan into allowing the Gods to headline, by reminding him of all the favors he had done for Stan without receiving any in return. At that point, little more arm bending was required. Stan had to accede.

All weekend, Billy had been dreading Thursday's rehearsal at the band studio. He wasn't sure how he was going to break it to the others that they had not only lost their recording contract, but they were expected to pay the advance money back as well.

It occurred to Billy that Tommy and Jack Barnes and Daw's dad were going to make more out of their deal than the Gods were. At least they had been paid off and were out of the picture. Nez was another story. And as for Cuz, they'd take their sweet time paying that fucking millionaire back.

The others were sitting at their usual posts, near their equipment, wanging and banging, pumping and thumping, when Billy arrived. It was obvious from his grim expression that there was something on his mind and that it wasn't good. As usual, it fell to Col to interrogate the boss.

—Hey, there he is. Billy, man, what's up? You don't look too fuckin' happy. More bad news?

Given the way things had been going, the guys were pretty much prepared to hear him tell them anything.

—Yeah. I'm afraid so. Real bad.

He sat down at his stool in the middle of the semicircle of musicians and sighed heavily.

—There's no goddamned easy way to tell you guys this, but fuckin' Cuz has, like, fuckin' boaged on our fuckin' contract.

Silence. Then Col burbled.

—Wha'd'ya mean *'boaged on our fuckin' contract'*? He can't do that.

—Yeah, Col, he can. The contract I signed pretty much lets him do, like, whatever the fuck he wants. I guess somehow he got wind of me bein' sick again. And now he wants to back out of the deal *until I'm well again*, whenever the fuck that turns out to be.

The other Gods glanced askance between themselves, as if in confirmation of some pre-held fearful conjecture. Billy continued.

—And that's not the worst of it.

—You mean it gets worse?

—Yeah, Col. He wants us to pay the fuckin' advance back.

—What is it? Like, two hundred and fifteen grand? He wants us to pay him fuckin' two hundred and fifteen thousand bucks back? Where the fuck're we supposed to come up with that?

—He said we didn't have to, like, pay it all back to him at once.

—That's fuckin' big of him. Let's see. If we all like come up with fifty bucks a month. Let's see that's, like, fuckin' three-fifty a month we can send him. How much is that a year?

Col looked at Gib.

—Forty-two hundred.

—And how long 'til we like pay it all back?

—Around forty-five, fifty years, I think.

—Jesus fuckin' Christ, that old bird will be, like, dead and rotted before we get him fuckin' paid off. Fuckin' Kin and Kimmie'll be, like, livin' it up in San Tropez 'til they're fuckin' ninety on that shit.

—Yeah right, on our three-fifty a month, You bet. Honestly, you guys. We don't have to worry about that. I don't care if he ever gets a fuckin' dime out of us. A fucking dime. Fuckin' asshole. I do have a little good news though.

Gilly cracked.

—You've found somebody else to give us two hundred grand to pay Vetter off?

—Nah. I don't think we'll bring in that much, but Mak scored us a gig headlining Lung Fung on the Fourth of July.

Unfortunately, that news did not cheer the band much, if at all. Crestfallen, they set about rehearsing for their next show out at the Foghorn in deep southeast.

Three years earlier, U2 played a gig at the Foghorn to a half-filled room. They were touring behind *Boy*. Groupies purportedly purloined from the backstage dressing room a briefcase containing lyrics, ideas, and notes for their follow-up album. Bono acerbically recounted the tale at the Paramount in eighty-three, when they returned to town on the *War* tour. He had to write the lyrics for *October* from memory and that's why that album sucked. It was all the Portland groupies' fault.

Since that night, when U2 had their possessions allegedly pilfered, the Foghorn had become one of the eastside's few legendary venues. And for that reason, all the good bands maintained the Foghorn as part of their regular itineraries. This held tremendous gravity not only for local bands, but for touring acts, too.

Per usual, the Gods elicited a great response from the Foghorn crowd, who were a little more musically erudite and appreciative of something different than most. Open-minded enough to tolerate new music; open-eared enough to listen.

Billy's appointment with Doctor Todd, on the following Monday further distressed his already distraught state of mind. Todd had made the determination that Billy was going to have to have his spleen removed. It was severely swollen. It was in danger of rupturing. Any infection that might arise from that would most likely be fatal.

What's more, Doctor Todd informed his patient that he would need intensive radiation therapy in several spots on his abdomen and that they were going to have to step up his chemo program. His cancer had advanced to Stage Three SE. It was beginning to spread beyond his lymph system. Immediate action was urgently needed.

With great difficulty, Billy was able to convince Doctor Todd to delay the new program for a couple of weeks: until after the Gods played the Fourth of July show. Todd grudgingly agreed—but he insisted that Billy needed to begin his new chemotherapy regimen the very next day.

The new program, ACVBP, replaced the CNOP cocktail he had been receiving— removing the mitoxantrone, returning the doxorubicin, and adding bleomycin to the mix. Billy did not anticipate any earth-shattering changes to his regime.

He and nurse Lisa had become old friends, talking about the news of the day. The upcoming Reagan-Mondale election in the Fall. The McMartin Preschool thing. Terrible. Computers. The new Apple Macintosh. Billy thought they were cool. Lisa wasn't sure yet. She was still learning to learn how to use her husband's Commodore 64.

She inserted the needle into his arm and began to administer the new chemo blend from the IV bag. Instantaneously, Billy felt far different than he had with any of his twenty previous chemo treatments. He felt as if he were on Mister Toad's Wild Ride, hurtling into an oblivion of darkness at an incredible velocity. The room seemed to cave in, and Billy told Lisa he didn't like the new combination. Breathless, he felt as if he were going to pass out.

But he didn't. Instead, he endured four and a half of the most gruelingly horrible hours of his life. The pain was bearable, however the resultant disequilibrium did not dissipate. It only seemed to grow worse as he sat in the waiting room waiting for Carrie to pick him up.

With his elbow crooked on the arm of the chair, Billy rested his face in his hand, trying to regain his bearings. But his unsteadiness remained and persisted even as he rode back to Carrie's apartment. She always acted as his nurse on Tuesdays when he received his treatments. He never felt very well afterwards, but on that occasion, he seemed to be responding particularly badly.

The following morning, Billy had recovered...somewhat. He felt a little better, but his skin seemed even more yellow than before. And when he got out of bed, at around ten the next morning, he was profoundly distressed to discover several strands of hair on his pillow. He tried to put the thought out of his mind, but he could not.

On Thursday, after initiating plans for the celebration on the Fourth, Billy caught a ride over to rehearsal from Mak. He brought Mak inside with him, so he could meet up again with the rest of the Gods and give them details regarding the Lung Fung spectacular.

But as soon as they entered the main space where everyone was sitting, waiting, it was indisputably obvious that something was up. None of the other members even acknowledged Mak's presence, nor would they look Billy in the eye.

—Kinda cold in here, you guys. Not even gonna, like, say hi to our old friend?

Col ventured.

—Billy, man. We've got somethin' to tell you. And you're not gonna like it.

Billy plopped down upon his stool in the middle of the room.

—So, what's happenin'? Doesn't look good. I smell *mutiny* on the fuckin' *Bounty*.

Daw spoke up.

—It's not like that, Billy.

—Then how is it, Daw? You tell me!

Gilly tried to deflect, defend.

—You know, Billy, we've been pretty bored the last coupla months. We're used to, like, playing fifteen times a month, not four or five.

—Well, I'm real fuckin' sorry for havin' a recurrence of fuckin' cancer. I know it's been fuckin' hard on you guys tryin' to get along.

Col rejoined.

—But that's just it man. It *has* been hard. You know the kind of schedule we've always had. And we were just startin' to get somewhere—and then 'poof', and now we gotta shell out, like, fifty bucks a month for the rest of our lives to some gazillionaire who buys and sells bands like fuckin' cattle. It *has* been hard. It would be for you too, if it was one of us down.

Mak stood silent in the doorway, nervously winking and blinking. He tried to make eye contact with Billy D.—but he could not. Billy D. was off at some other location in his mind—probably thinking about the new twenty-four channel automated boards that were coming out on the market. Now that's a piece of equipment!

—So wha'd'you guys wanna do? Break up the band?

Coldly blunt, Col blurted.

—Yeah.

—You mean, after all we've been through, you guys wanna just quit? Just like that? Wham bam...? What about everything ya' said back in April? Coverin' for me and shit, and me bein' the *meal ticket*. What about that?

Attempting to adopt a somewhat more compassionate tack, Col elaborated.

—Look, Billy. We haven't, like, got anything against you. It really sucks that you're sick again. Fuckin' sucks, man. We, like, feel real bad about that.

Daw interrupted.

—But we've got our own careers to think about.

A shocked disbelief entered into Billy's voice, as it gathered in volume and intensity.

—Careers? Careers? What the fuck are you guys talkin' about? Careers. That's a laugh. We're not surgeons, ya' dumb shits. We're fuckin' musicians. The goddamned Rolling Stones have *careers*. They've been doin' it for twenty fuckin' years. They've got ten gold records. We've been doin' this shit for three years. Career. Uh-huh. We haven't done jack shit.

Scuffing the floor with his shoe—as if he were crushing out a cigarette—Billy sniffed indignantly.

Suddenly defensive about the band's accomplishments, an insulted Daw snapped back.

—Hey, Billy. We've done a lot. We've played, like, seven hundred gigs or so. We've been the number one band in Portland since our first gig. And we did sign a contract with a major label. It's not like we're failures.

—I never said we were *failures*, Daw. You're right, we've done plenty. I just figured there was still a lot more we could do. Okay, so what are you guys gonna do with your *careers*?

Still protective, Daw muttered in a near whisper.

—Well, we've been rehearsing on the side, when you haven't been around. We're gonna start our own band.

Billy stifled a giggle.

—That makes sense. I guess. So who's, like, gonna be your lead singer? None of you guys could carry a fuckin' tune with a goddamned wheelbarrow.

Sneering faintly, Col retorted.

—Daw's gonna do the singin'. He's pretty good.

—So are ya' comin' out from behind the kit, or what?

—Nah, I'm gonna sing and keep playin' the drums.

—I don't know, guys. That kinda kills the *visual appeal*, don't ya' think?

Col explained.

—We're gonna put Daw on a riser. Then we'll have me up front and Gib and Gilly on the wings.

—You think a drummer in the back's gonna work?

—Works for Phil Collins.

—Phil Collins was in Genesis for ten years before he, like, went out on his own. So what kind of music?

Col thought for a moment.

—I guess you could call it, like, glam metal.

Folding his arms and stretching out his legs, Billy leaned back on his stool.

—Glam metal? Like Crue and Riot?

499

It was all he could do to suppress a gust of blatant laughter.

—No. More like Night Ranger and Van Halen. Sorta like 'Sister Christian' meets 'Jump', I guess.

Humbled, Col's voice trailed off.

—What're ya' gonna call yer band?

Gib spoke up.

—Sharon Tate.

—Oh yeah. Sharon Tate. She's the chick ya' said Happy looked like. Nice touch. Didn't you say Manson killed her?

—Yeah. But the guys wanted sort of a controversial name. We wanted to use Marilyn Monroe, but some band already has that name.

—I thought *Marilyn Monroe*, like, already had that name.

—Well, you know what I mean. Sharon Tate's more obscure. Yeah, the Manson family murdered her. There is that.

—Why didn't you guys just call yourselves, like, Bundy or Gacy? Cut to the fuckin' chase.

—We considered those names, actually, but we didn't think we were menacing enough for them. Sharon Tate was a victim and she was beautiful. Glamorous. That's what we were after.

—So what you guys're sayin' is, what? The gig at Lung Fung is our last gig?

Confirming, Col said.

—Yeah, pretty much. Our first gig is at Satyricon, beginning of August. I mean, y'know, if ya', like, suddenly get all better, we can talk about gettin' it together again.

—Satyricon? That new club in Old Town? Fuckin' get yourselves killed just tryin' to get into that place. You ever seen what it looks like down there? Battle zone. Fuckin' ground zero for junkies and bums, and you wanna be a glam band there?

Daw reentered the conversation.

—It's a new club and it's a good place for us to work things out. It's not like a ton of people will be there watching us. They don't have a regular crowd there yet. We can get friends to come down—a few others and we've got the main floor filled. It'll be fine

Put out by what he was hearing—and at the attitudes of his bandmates and supposed friends—Billy snapped at them.

—Well, it sounds like you guys've got this all figured out. Workin' on all this for a while. There's not much I can say.

With a forlornly distressed expression on his face, he looked in Mak's direction.

—Okay, Pop. I guess we know where we stand.

Mak nodded ruefully. He decided that he had not missed much since he was drummed out of the organization. It had become every man for himself.

Though the Fourth show was on Wednesday night, Billy inexplicably elected not to change the date for his next chemo treatment on Tuesday afternoon. Perhaps he had not put as much thought into that choice as he might have. Monday probably would have been a better alternative. Or Thursday the day after the show.

As in the previous week, he rode that same horrible, drug-induced rollercoaster through the tunnel of fast enclosing darkness. It frightened him and exhausted him. The experience left him feeling weak and sick. He was sure that he would bounce back from the treatment, but he did not.

It was hot and humid, in the mid-eighties, early that evening as Carrie drove Billy to Lung Fung. If this was to be the Gods' final performance as he had said, she wanted to witness the event. And she was terribly worried about Billy. He wasn't well at all and she desperately feared for his life.

It had occurred to her that Billy probably didn't even know how sick he really was. She tried to tell him that he needed to slow down, but he wouldn't hear of it. He would take it easy after that last show.

She guided him backstage to the dressing room, where the members of Donkey Sho-Tay and the Gods organization were in full-on revel mode—multiple joints and mirrors circulating at a highly accelerated pace. Billy sat down by himself at the end of a bench, trying to gather his wits. Meanwhile, Carrie left him there, hustling herself back out toward the bar to await Leena's arrival. Leena was bringing with her Zoe, their mutual friend from school.

As always, Reineke Fuchs was dressed almost entirely in white: a white silk suit, white socks and shoes, a white shirt with a red tie, a white fedora set off by a jaunty red feather, cavalierly tucked inside a bright white hatband. He was tall, slender, and agile, though he seemed not the least bit athletic. Instead, he appeared mischievously sly and devious.

With a genial smile, he sat down next to Billy.

—Hey, what it is, my friend? How's it goin'?

Billy didn't really feel much in the mood for chitchat, but he didn't want to be rude.

—Goin' okay, bud. How 'bout you?

—Pretty good, I guess. The guys say you're real sick. Cancer?

—Yeah.

—Well that's a shame, man. I hope you get well soon. Myself, I'm a bleater.

—A bleater? What's that?

—A hemophiliac sheep.

Reineke Fuchs laughed heartily at his own joke and slapped his counterpart on the back, feigning a cordial manner. Then, he hastily stood to join his fellow band members in preparation for their imminent performance. Billy was so enfeebled, he nearly fell over from the blow. He felt like a dry and withered leaf, suspended haplessly in the wind.

From a booth at the back, near the bar, on the "adult" side of the velvet rope, Carrie spotted Leena and Zoe as they entered the odd partly converted bowling alley from the far corner of the room. They had to traverse at a right angle, the long aisles at the perimeter of the lanes, instead of heading directly to her on the hypotenuse.

They joined Carrie in the tuck-and-roll black naugahyde booth. She had purposefully selected that particular booth, because of its direct sight line to the front of the stage. She wanted to keep a close eye on Billy.

The three women sat and chatted for a few minutes. As they ordered drinks, they scrutinized the various females among the gathering crowd. In the heat and humidity of the room, many were attired in mere short shorts and tank tops, which was met with some disapprobation from the more demurely dressed trio. All three of them wore light, cotton summer dresses and sensible sandals.

At precisely ten o'clock, Donkey Sho-Tay took the stage. They were a glossy quintet, with the same instrumental line-up as the Gods, except the dashing Reineke Fuchs did not play guitar while singing, as Billy did. Instead he pranced and preened, fanning his feathers like an albino peacock—though a bleater at that.

The other members of the band maintained a wardrobe of drab suit coats and slacks, looking very prim and proper behind their leader's more overt pursuit to be the center of attention. They were Reineke Fuchs' back-up band. There was never a doubt about that arrangement. Ever. The snow fox and his attendant field mice.

The Seattle band's sound was edgy, comprised of components of popular new

502

wave bands. It was good-natured, affable music, clean and well executed. From backstage, the Gods could hear that the crowd response to the band was by far more patently pronounced than the previous time they had played with them. Coming down to Portland on a regular basis was starting to pay off for Donkey Sho-Tay. They were beginning to attract their own loyal following—especially a large contingent of barely dressed underage girls.

Eyes closed, nearly unconscious and incredibly ill, Billy leaned against the wall, which was sticky from smoke and sweat. He could hear Donkey Sho-Tay playing out front and he thought they sounded good. Tight. Good tempos. Catchy songs. They seemed on their way.

The Gods were dressed casually, displaying a certain arrogant lassitude about the proceedings. It was not as if Billy was really going to notice much. He'd be lucky to make it through the first set. Gilly was in his usual black. Col adopted faded jeans, a striped shirt with the arms cut off at the shoulders. Daw was as Daw always was: jeans, light blue sleeveless undershirt and white high top leather sneakers. Gib looked like someone's dad looking for his pipe and paper in the den.

Seeing an opportunity not to be missed, Reineke Fuchs drove his band well past the agreed-upon eleven-thirty wrap, past midnight and through three encores. They finally left the stage at twelve-twenty—nearly a full hour late—the tumultuous dog-whistle squeals of young teen-age girls piercing the dense stuffy atmosphere like lasers through fog machines at a Blue Oyster Cult show.

The Gods did not finally take the stage until almost twelve forty-five. Despite Reineke Fuchs' best efforts, it was readily apparent from the start that most of the audience was there to party with the Unreal Gods—unaware that it was to be their last opportunity to join in such an event.

Billy D. pulled the break tape out of the mix in the mains, and without hesitation, Col broke into the wobbly, tremolo-laden intro of "Uptown." Billy was dressed like Brian Wilson in skintight, brown Sansabelt slacks and a short-sleeved striped Beach Boys-style Oxford shirt. Help me, Rhonda.

Doing his best to hide his disease, he slid into a familiar gait, running in place, his guitar slung low at his hip.

—I know an uptown boy, and you're an uptown girl...

They buzzed through a fine rendition of "Thunder and Lightning" and definitive versions of "Social Will Call" and "Point of No Return." After a rousing take of "Symmetry," the guys took a quick break. Col lit a cigarette, took three deep puffs and jammed the butt in between the strings at the head of his guitar. Billy sucked a deep breath, grabbing a pitcher of water that sat at his feet. He gulped down most of it and poured the rest over his head. He was consumed by fever, overcome by a blithery welter of swither, out of breath and nearly incoherent.

—Thnkyavrymchladiesngnmn. Nowwrgnnado asong thtwevonlydn two?... other times. I wrote it for...my girlfriend...Carrie. She's here tonight...Where are ya', baby?

Carrie hid her face beneath the fascia of her hand.

—Well, she's out there...somewhere. Song's called..."Glorious History" and it goes...like this. Two three four.

And with expert precision, the band launched into a full gallop. Shaah. Shaah! Gilly endowed the intro with a reedy synth-string sound, moaning haunted—as Col contributed a low-string twang theme, calling to mind Duane Eddy. An edge of sorrow in his voice, Billy sang.

—This time things that cannot be
When all these things come down on me
You don't take us seriously
How can I make some history with you?
Some glorious history
Glorious history.

Putting all his effort into singing the vocal as fully and powerfully as he possibly could, he moved to the forlorn second half of the verse

—And I'm tryin' to make it with you
Yes I'm tryin' to make somethin' new
Yes I'm tryin' to make some history with you.

He searched the crowd for Carrie's face, but he could not track her down. Back to the top.

—I love these things, like city streets
And music playin' in the heat.

Gesturing toward the gyrating crowd.

—But now I'm askin' desperately
Won't you make some history with me
Glorious history with you
And I'm tryin' to make it with you...

He thought he might puke, but he was able to maintain as the band swung into the bridge.

—Coz like the Prince Valiant days
Or one of Shakespeare's plays
Or a Roman chariot race—it's true
Like outlaws from Kansas City
In the wild, wild western days
Our love, still sittin' pretty
In the wide bright sights of the open range.

Backed by Gilly's deft orchestration, Col's solo was smart and compact, echoing the genuinely heartfelt sentiments of the song. Despite their waning interest in the enterprise, the Gods were nevertheless able to summon brilliance when challenged, demonstrating they were still the best band in Portland.

Again, they steered back to the last part of the verse.

—And I'm tryin' to make it with you
Yes I'm tryin' to make somethin' new
Yes I'm tryin' to make some history with you
Glorious history...

Nearly in tears, overcome by the significance of the moment, Billy masterfully sung out the chorus to his last breath. Fearing he was going to faint, he said with great haste.

—We're gonna take a short break, everybody. We'll be back in ten minutes or so.

The other band members were caught off guard by his announcement, but they were not necessarily surprised. Billy had clearly expended all of his strength with the impassioned intensity of his delivery.

Ahead of the others, Billy dashed from the stage directly out the rear stage door to the parking lot, where the van sat. His head swirled, sliding toward swoon. His guts churned and boiled. Sagging against the van, Billy tried his best to remain conscious.

In the glow of a single bare light bulb at the club exit, Billy retched repeatedly, before vomiting thick red bile onto the asphalt. He staggered, continuing to heave blood and guts, and sank to a squat with his head between his knees. He could not move. He wanted to lay down and die. But he didn't want to die like that, out in the parking lot. Just need to take a break for a sec. Rest my eyes. A deep breath.

All of a sudden, Billy D. was shaking him fiercely. Wha?

—Billy. Billy! Are you okay, man? Everybody's been lookin' for ya! Have you been out here the whole time?

—Yeah. Just needed to rest for a sec...

He wanted to continue to rest, return to the soft warmth of unconsciousness.

—Billy, man, you've been out here for, like, a half hour.

Billy tried to stand, but he fell to his knees. Had Billy D. not caught him, he would have fallen face-first on the pavement.

—Billy! You gotta snap out of it, man. You're freakin' me out. Are you okay?

—Glrs hstry. M'tryn. Make. Make it.

He passed out.

Billy D. unlocked the back of the van and swung open the doors. Hoisting the lifeless form of his friend up in his arms, he placed him on the platform inside the vehicle and secured him as best he could.

About that time, an agitated Col emerged from the building, a cigarette clenched between his teeth. At once he saw the panic on Billy D.'s face.

—Hey. Did ya' find Billy? What's up with you?

Out of breath from effort and fear, and close to passing out himself, Billy D. excitedly replied.

—Yeah...I found him. Out here. He's totally out of it. I think he's dyin'...You gotta go find Carrie. We need to get him to the hospital right away. See if you can find her. I'm gonna stay here with Billy.

—Izt time ago on? M'cmn. Hold onnasec.

—Naw. You stay here, Billy. Col's gonna find Carrie, and we're gonna take ya' to the hospital.

—Crrie hsptl? We gt a scnd set tdo. Where's Carrie?

She's comin', Billy. You just take it easy.

# XXXVI

*Thur 'e is. Tha's ar boa. Guid lickin spacimen. Yip, he's a rull bee-yewt thet'n. I dud rull guid thet die, ternin thet'n ut. Yip.*

*Allrutty than. Bully Grunjer...? Um Gud Allmutty. Thus har's muh go-to gah, Pete. Say howdew, Pete.*

*Ahm har tuh kanda luck thangs ova 'fore me'n Pete kin latcha in. Thus har's a purty praavit kunda cuntray clib, yuh say. Uh gatedud kum-yunnity, yuh mutt sigh. Yuh gutta pies yer dooz.*

*So whutcha guts tuh sigh fur yerself, boa? 'Ja heaven a guid laff? Innythang spaceshull? Ahm owna nid tuh say yer buck, uhcurse. Buck. Buck. Yer buck a ull thuh guid thangs ya dun in yer laff. Yuh musta dun sumpin'.*

*No buck? O, thus nut guid 'tull. Boas lack yew ind ep in Purrgoturry for a hulluvva lung tam.*

*Is it yuh jist don't gutta buck? Ur aincha naver dun nuh guid thangs? Bug duffrinse thur. Yuh gut innybiddy tuh speck ep fur yuh? Go tuh bet fur yuh? Yuh gut frinds? Femly? Y'muck a let a minny? Yew a bug sacksis in the whirld? Ur purrhops yer leve is cunt-rary to the leve everlusting? That ain't guid nither. Not guid a tull.*

*Yuh gut inny knellidge butt innythang? Bee-yewty in yer laff? Strinth? Prolly no discrushun tuh spick uv thur, woodnt majjun. Kin yuh piss a tast uh wets wit yer fave sinces? Innythang?*

*I giss yuh butter go own beck n sigh whut yuh kin thraw tuhgather. M'own bick ep win yuh gutter, 'n wool tuck it ever than.*

507

# XXXVII

Billy awoke to Carrie peering down at him—an expression of immense apprehension scrawled upon her marble countenance.

—Carrie. Where am I? What happened? I had the weirdest dream...I...

—You're in the emergency ward, sweetheart. Adventist. You passed out. Your blood pressure was only fifty-five over forty. We were afraid you were dying.

In confused discomfort, his face twisted into a coil.

—Well. I'm okay now. Let's get outta here.

He started to sit up, before he realized IV's were stuck in either arm and an oxygen tube was jammed into his nostrils.

—What is this shit?

—I'm serious, Billy. You're very sick. You're not going anywhere. Once you're stable, they're going to take you over to Providence. They're going to want you to stay there, at least overnight

She smoothed his slimy forehead and wiped his dry-caked mouth with a moistened paper towel.

—I just got a toucha the flu. I'm okay.

—Billy! Look at your skin! That's not the flu. You're pale and yellow. You look terrible. You're not going anywhere. You better get used to it. You're going to be in the hospital for a while, I'm afraid.

He tried to protest, but fell back asleep.

When he awoke again, he was in a private room in Intensive Care at Providence. The television was on and Carrie was sitting next to his bed watching the screen nervously.

—What's on?

—Billy! Sweetheart. You're awake.

—Yeah. I guess...Man, I feel shitty.

—You're very sick, Billy. Doctor Todd has been in several times yesterday and today, and he's very concerned about you.

—What is that? *One Life to Live*?

—Yes. It's *One Life to Live*.

He gazed up at the clock across from his bed.

—Two-thirty? Man, I slept all day.

—It's Friday, Billy. You've been out longer than you think.

—Friday? Holy shit. That's like two days! So what'd Doctor Todd say?

—He said your spleen is liable to rupture at any time. So you're going to have to have surgery first thing tomorrow morning to have it removed. He said he's going to remove your tumor, too, and several infected lymph glands. He said he'll know more once he gets inside.

—Jesus. Sounds fucked up. How longa ya' been with me?

—Since Wednesday night.

—You mean you've been with me the whole time?

—Of course, sweetheart. I couldn't leave you.

—Where'd ya' sleep?

—In the bed, next to you. I wanted to hear your heartbeat.

—Well look, Carrie, you've gotta get some rest too ya' know. I don't want you to get sick. Just one of us at a time.

—I'm okay. I'm fine.

She leaned over and kissed him softly as he extended his arm to pull her close.

—Nah. You're a total mess. I think you need to go home and take a break for a while.

—Maybe you're right. Maybe just for a few hours. I should call Leena. I haven't talked to her since Wednesday. I probably have messages on my machine. And I could change clothes...

—There ya' go.

—Well, if I go now, I can probably be back by nine.

509

—Baby, they've got me so pumped full of drugs, I'm not gonna know when ya' come back.

—Oh, you'll know. I'll make sure of that.

Her pretty smile bathed him in careful concern. She kissed him again, on the forehead, then firmly on the lips.

—I'll be back in a few hours, then.

—Okay, baby. I'll be right here.

A hint of dread creased the corners of that smile. Her eyes glistened with the blear of fearful tears as she moved toward the door. Haltingly, she half-turned.

—I love you, Billy.

—I love you, too. You're my world, Carrie.

And she believed him. Just as she was out the door, he called after her.

—Hey. Have you seen my book around anywhere?

Her brows pinched bewildered together.

—I'm sorry, sweetheart, I don't know what you're talking about.

He commenced to explain, then thought better of it. Waving at her vaguely, he whispered.

—Never mind, baby. Just a dream. Just a dream.

The next thing he knew, it was Saturday afternoon. Carrie was sitting in a chair next to the bed blankly staring at the barely audible television.

—*In other news, the nation's jobless rate fell to a four-year low in June, dropping four-tenths of a percentage point from May, to 7 percent, the labor department said. The report, the first broad measure of June economic activity, suggested that growth continued at a stronger pace than the administration had expected. The jobless rate for black teenagers fell sharply, but government analysts said that may have been a statistical fluke.*

Billy stirred briefly.

—*'Law Enforcement and Crime' was the subject of the president's weekly radio address to the nation:*

*'Believe me, we in the administration have been trying to speak up for you, the millions of Americans who are fed up with crime, fed up with fear in our streets and neighborhoods, fed up with lenient judges, fed up with a criminal*

*justice system that too often treats criminals better than it does their victims. Too many Americans have had to suffer the effects of crime while too many of our leaders have stuck to the old, discredited, liberal illusions about crime — illusions that refuse to hold criminals responsible for their actions.*

He started to come around.

*—Famous personalities born on this day: Beatle Ringo Starr turns forty-four today. And renowned baseball pitcher and philosopher Satchel Paige was born on July seventh 1906. Second only to Yogi Berra, Paige had many adages that became part of baseball vernacular, such as 'If your stomach disputes you, lie down and pacify it with cool thoughts'. And, most famously, 'Don't look back—something might be gaining on you.'*

Ringo Beatle Satchel Starr disputes cool thoughts something might be gaining.

*—That's it for Saturday, July seventh, folks. I'm Dan Rather and that's part of our world tonight.*

Billy put his hands to his face and attempted to assemble himself in some rational fashion.

—Jesus fuck. I feel terrible.

From the chair by the window, Carrie flicked off the television and hastened to his side. Closing his eyes, he sighed loudly, then looked down at his bandaged abdomen

—Shit, he cut me every which way.

—Yes, dear. Doctor Todd had you in the operating room for almost six hours this morning. He said things went well. Or as well as could be expected—whatever that means.

—I think I need some more painkillers. What're they givin' me? Morphine?

Then he was out again.

He felt slightly better when he regained consciousness the next morning. Carrie was sitting in her chair, reading the Sunday *Oregonian*. At the sound of Billy rustling in his bed, she sprung to her feet.

—There you are. Hello, sweetheart. How are you feeling?

Eyeing the complex of tubes and devices that surrounded him he replied weakly.

—Trapped. What day is it?

—It's Sunday. Do you want some water?

—No, but I'd love some bacon and eggs.

—Oh, Billy. I don't think Doctor Todd is going to let you eat solid food for at least a few more days.

He frowned unhappily.

—Okay. I guess I'll have some water then.

The nurse within her flooded forth, and she gingerly retrieved a plastic water bottle from the sliding table tray next his the bed. Like an angel hovering over him, she held the straw to his lips. And he sipped cautiously, as if the water might leak from all the holes in him. But everything held. He drifted back into a light sleep.

When he came to again, crotchety Andy Rooney was babbling on about something that was pissing him off. Then the clock ticked toward eight p.m., and Mike Wallace signed off.

—What the fuck have they got in my dick?

Carrie snapped to attention and rose to her feet.

—It's a catheter, darling.

He started to reach down to pull it out, but she grabbed his hand.

—I don't think they're ready to have you sitting up to pee just yet, Billy. I'm sure it's uncomfortable.

—It's like…

Even in his confused state, his better judgment prevented him from completing the simile.

—Let's just say it sucks.

Snorting, she muffled a grin with her hand. He caught the gist of his own wordplay and smirked half-heartedly. An officious looking woman, in her forties, with sandy blond hair walked in.

—Oh, he's up!

She began to check the levels of the various IV bags that encircled him, replacing a few. Then she cleared his PICC lines and lifted his bandages to have a look at his many incisions. Finally, she walked over to a blackboard with various signs and placards taped on either side. She printed her name like a schoolteacher. Molly Miller. Billy liked the name. It worked both ways: Milly Moller. Molly Miller.

—My name's Molly? I'm your nurse for the night shift? I'll check in on you from time to time. Is there anything you need?

—I'd like a steak and I'd like to get this thing yanked out of my, uh, whatzit. You know?

She laughed at both requests.

—Well, Doctor Todd will be in to see you in the morning? And you can talk to him about those things. That's all his decision. Roberta will be in a little later to draw some blood? If you need anything, just push that red button right there and I'll be in.

With that, she exited the room.

—I must be doin' a little better. She didn't hang around very long.

—Well, you're not out cold. That's an improvement, I guess.

—Are you bein' sarcastic? I don't think I'm sharp enough to catch it right now.

—No, sweetheart. I'm just tired. I'm worried and tired.

—You don't have to worry, Carrie. I'll be fine.

In wordless disbelief, she hummed a doubting moan.

—We'll see, dear. I hope you're right. But you're very sick right now and you need to get rest.

—I think I've been restin' pretty good.

—You know what I mean. You just have to stay down this time. Give yourself a chance to heal.

He stared at the blackboard and said nothing.

—I'm going to leave now. I need to go into the office early tomorrow morning and make arrangements for Leena to reschedule some of my appointments and to have Kenneth take the ones that need immediate attention.

Carrie kissed him on the forehead, smoothing his hair.

—I'll be here before Doctor Todd comes in to see you. He supposed to be in around ten-thirty, he said.

—Okay, baby. You get some rest, too.

He cradled her neck with his hand, kissing her softly and gently caressing her ears.

She kissed him again, gathered up her jacket and purse, and started to click off the television with the remote.

—No. It's okay. Leave it on. Maybe I'll stay awake.

She placed the remote on his swaddled chest

—And can you hand me the sports section? I wanna see how the Dodgers are doin'. I don't think they're gonna catch the Padres.

She had no idea what he was talking about. Picking through the unopened portion of the newspaper and fishing out the sports section, she handed it to him.

—Thanks, baby. I'll see ya' tomorrow.

He opened up his arms, expectantly, and she laid her head on the pillow next to his.

—Okay. I'll see you in the morning. I love you.

—I love you, too, Carrie.

As she was leaving, he began to scan the television channels. *F.I.S.T.* was on Channel 2, but he'd already seen it, and he really did not much care for Sylvester Stallone. Then he landed on Channel 8. *The Executioners Song.* It was that guy from *Coal Miner's Daughter.* He played her husband. Some guy from Portland wrote that. His brother or cousin or something.

He began to peruse the box scores and promptly fell asleep. When he next began to stir, cloud-dappled sunlight crept through the window. Carrie was talking quietly with Doctor Todd, who was wearing light blue scrubs and scrub cap, and a white lab coat

—He seems to be responding fairly well to the surgery. No infections. Though his white blood cell count is not good at all.

Billy mumbled dreamily.

—Whybloocount? Smatter?

Doctor Todd turned in his direction.

—I was telling Miss Deeds that the surgery was reasonably successful. But I was about to say that I'm very concerned about some other things I might have seen. I'll know more when the tests and biopsies come back this afternoon. Yes. Your WBC count is very low. But we need to get a handle on your cancer and see if we are able to slow it down.

Billy wasn't entirely aware what Doctor Todd was telling him, but Carrie was.

—Is it spreading?

—I don't want to cause alarm, but I have reason to believe it is. We may want to go back in to do a little exploratory surgery. That wouldn't be until next week. Then we'll decide how we want to proceed.

More important things weighed upon Billy's mind.

—Say, Doctor Todd?

The Doctor engaged his focus directly upon Billy.

—When can I eat some real food and get this thing pulled out of my Johnson? It's drivin' me up the wall.

Without reaction whatsoever to Billy's impertinence, slightly distracted by the condition of Billy's stitches, he answered absently.

—Let's see how things look tomorrow. Once we have all the tests back, we'll have a better idea where we'll be going next.

Billy was as disappointed as he was uncomfortable.

—I want a steak in the worst way.

—I wouldn't get your heart set on a steak. It will take several days just to get you back on solid food. We'll have to see how you respond to that.

—You mean gettin' nauseated and everything?

—Exactly. We'll just have to take it slow. You'll get a steak soon enough.

But the prognosis wasn't good. Billy's cancer had advanced to Stage Four. Tests revealed that the disease had moved beyond his lymph system. Hundreds of malignant tumors were spread all over both sides of his abdomen. Some had been attached to his spleen. Others were beginning to develop on his stomach and lungs. Doctor Todd concluded that surgery would be neither prudent nor particularly efficacious. Instead, he prescribed an intense program of radiation therapy, coupled with a new round of chemo.

Soon after, Billy was moved out of ICU, but he remained at Providence throughout the month of July. The combination of radiation and chemotherapies weakened him significantly. His joints ached as if he were eighty years old, and his balance was so severely affected that he could not walk without support.

His hair and eyebrows fell out and his pallor had the tint of yellow snow. He was paper thin and unable to keep food down, which caused him to lose another twenty-five pounds. He complained that his meals tasted like poison. The bones in his arms and shoulders protruded in grotesque, like a bizarrely folded piece of human origami.

Finally, on the first Friday in August, despite the horrific side effects, Billy was given permission to leave the hospital. But even that presented a problem. Because Billy was out of immediate danger, it was imperative that Carrie return to the veterinary practice, in order to revive it. So it was not advisable that he stay at her apartment. The only other alternative was for him to convalesce at the house in which he had grown up, where his mother could look after him and transport him to Providence for his daily radiation treatments.

Elegant and tall, Ingrid Granger had aged quite gracefully. In her mid-fifties, she was still very attractive, with striking blue eyes and curly blond hair piled on top of her head. She had not remarried after Pierce had died, and she occupied her time doing volunteer work with the Rose City schools, helping disadvantaged children.

She derived great satisfaction in tending to her son, though she was sorry that the circumstances were so dire. She made it her aim to help him to recover and become strong again. Billy spent the first few weeks lying on the couch, watching the Olympics, which were fabulously uninteresting without the Eastern Bloc countries participating.

Every free moment she had, Carrie was at Billy's side. She was able to spell Ingrid as his nurse. And also, without complaint, she loyally acted as his secretary, chauffeur, and all around gofer. If Billy wanted anything, needed anything, required anything, or wished for anything, she was committed to satisfying him. He kept flashing on Alex: if he were to ask, Billy was pretty sure Carrie would maneuver his jaw for him, to help him chew his food. Despite feeling enormously crummy, Billy still relished being pampered and nurtured.

It was Carrie who had no time for herself—no sort of emotional support, not a moment for rest or reflection. She pushed herself to her limits and didn't complain. Complaining wasn't really a part of her character. Nor self-pity. But she had fears. And it was her fears for Billy that drove her so intensely. She believed that between the two of them, they could will him to life, ordain him back to good health. She would not see the situation any other way.

In the afternoon on Labor Day, for no particular reason, Denny showed up. It appeared that he was drunk, high, or both. He and Billy had not seen each other since Christmas. Denny came rolling through the front door of the house, and, without announcing his arrival, strode directly to Billy, who was lying on the couch watching the end of *One Life to Live.*

Looming over his sick brother, he leaned down and knocked on the top of Billy's head.

—Hey! Fuckin' Rock Star! How's the cancer hangin', Rock Star?

Denny plopped down in the rocking chair next to the sofa and began to teeter methodically. Billy said nothing, but stared blankly at the television screen.

—So whatcha been up to lately, Rock Star? Been playin' lotsa cool gigs with the

Gods? Yeah? Fuck yeah! I got a new band, ya' know. Call 'em the Popsquawks. Got Pete drummin'. You remember Pete? He was the drummer in that band...oh, what the fuck was their name? Shit. Oh yeah. He was the drummer in the Malchicks. Remember them?

Continuing to ignore his brother, Billy's fixed his attention on the first scene of *General Hospital.* All summer he had been following the whole story arc of Luke and Robert's pursuit of the Aztec treasure.

—Anyway, so Pete's our drummer. And Notcho Durock is on bass. Pete's been playing with him since...Gee, I think since the Malchicks broke up. You remember them, of course.

No response.

—Yeah, we've played a couple of gigs at Last Hurrah, and over at Tommy's new spot at Key Largo. Fat Rooster. I like that club. It's like a miniature version of Starry Night. That little balcony and everything. We go over real good over there. That eastside crowd likes us. You know, I grew up on the east side of town. In fact, around here somewhere.

Billy tilted his head back, frowning upside down at his frantically rocking brother. Then he closed his eyes in sincere misery, in the warm, warm house; the golden afternoon sun glinting through the dining room window.

—Hey, Rock Star. I gotta tell ya'. Ya' look like fuckin' shit, man. Ya' know, you've really let yourself go lately. Maybe ya' oughta get your ass off the couch and get a little fuckin' exercise or somethin'. Know whut I mean, Vern? I mean, just because you're a big fuckin' rock star now doesn't mean ya' gotta go all fuckin' Elvis on us, man. Next thing you know we'll find ya' dead on the can with a fuckin' fried peanut butter banana sandwich clutched in yer yellow little hand.

—Denny, man.

—Ah! He fuckin' speaks! What's that, Rock Star?

—Denny. What's eatin' you? Are ya' jealous of me or somethin'?

—Jealous? Of what? You don't look like you're havin' such a fuckin' great time.

—I'm *not* havin' a good time, Denny. It sucks. It really sucks.

—Well, now ya' finally know what life's been like for me all these years. Fuckin' sucks. Yeah. You got it.

—Look, Denny, whatever I've done to you, I'm sorry. Can't ya' just let all that shit go? Start over or somethin'?

—Oh yeah, sure. *Now* you're ready to start over. You bet. You fuckin' bet.

—Jesus, man, I can't change what's already happened.

Laughing sardonically, Denny patted Billy on the head

—You can't fuckin' change *anything*, man."

Billy swatted his hand away, entreating his brother.

—Denny, I need your help if I'm gonna get well. Help me, Denny, please.

—Hey Bro', I'll hold your wallet for ya' and you can cry on my shoulder any time. I mean, look how much you've helped me. After all, what's a brother for? Right? But man, I can't help ya' get well. I don't know if anybody can do that.

At that moment, Ingrid entered from the kitchen, a vexed expression on her face.

—Billy. I just spoke to my insurance agent. Oh, Dennis, you're here.

—Yeah, I hope that's okay. It's good to see you too, mom.

—I didn't mean it like that. It's just...I spoke to Allen Schmidt, my agent at Mutual Life. They aren't going to cover all of Billy's hospital bills. They're not even going to come close.

Billy wondered aloud.

—Well, what are we going to do, mom?

—I don't know, Billy. I really don't. Bankruptcy? I haven't the slightest idea. I guess we need to speak to an attorney.

Denny chuckled

—Like I was sayin', Billy.

Sighing, Billy sank into a deep, dark funk and resumed his study of Luke and Robert as they traipsed through the jungles of Mexico. Denny maintained his neurotic pitch in the chair, back and forth and back. Ingrid looked as though she were going to cry.

—I don't...we can't lose the house. Not after everything your father went through to get it for us. The two of you...and Elaine, this is your home. It's been our home. You kids learned to swim in the pool. We've been here over twenty-five years. We can't...

She broke into tears. Billy refocused. Denny stopped rocking and sat in shame like a little boy who just accidentally killed the family cat. Lips pursed, Billy hiked himself up on his left elbow.

—Don't worry, mom. You're not gonna to lose the house. I'll figure out something.

—Billy, Allen thought our part of the bills could be over a hundred thousand dollars. And you're not nearly finished with your treatments. Who knows how much this will cost?

—Jeez. Sometimes I think everybody'd be better off if I just wasn't around anymore.

Ingrid began to cry more deeply.

—Aw, mom. I didn't mean it like that. You know that. It's just that everybody, you, Carrie, are puttin' all your time and energy...and money, into me and there's nothin' I can do to pay ya' back. Two years ago things looked great. I was plannin' on buyin' ya' a new place. Now...

He was overwhelmed at the reality of the situation. Denny stood up from the rocking chair.

—Well, I gotta go. Good to see you guys, as always. Get well soon, Billy. Bye, mom.

He kissed his mother perfunctorily and got the hell out of there, not even bothering to hit her up for fifty bucks, which had been his intent when he came over.

Around six, Carrie sauntered through the front door, into a leaden atmospheric pall. She had just endured four hours with Jack and Jean—and poor Val. It seemed to her that she was walking into an even more complicated family issue.

—Is something wrong?

Billy said nothing, but Ingrid told her. Responding with a curious sense of optimism, Carrie walked across the room and kissed Billy as he lay on the sofa. She sat down next to him on the floor.

—We'll find a way to get through this, too. Billy has taught me that. And I know it's true. We can overcome this obstacle, too. Don't worry, Ingrid.

Somewhat relieved, Ingrid wandered out of the den and back into the kitchen.

—I'm going to make a grilled cheese sandwich. Anyone care for a grilled cheese sandwich.

—Yeah, mom. I'll have a couple please. How about you, Carrie?

—No thanks. I ate over at my parents' house.

—Oh, that's right. Today's Labor Day. So how'd that go?

—As expected, I guess. Mom spent the whole afternoon picking on Valerie and comparing her to me. So it was the usual battle. Nothing out of the ordinary.

How're you feeling?

—I was *starting* to feel a little better, actually, until Denny showed up and then mom dropped the bomb. Now I feel like shit. No. I feel like I might be able to keep the grilled cheesers down. But my head's pretty fucked up after all that.

—What did Denny do?

—He unloaded on me for bein' his older brother. Maybe you know what that's like. Has Val ever unloaded on you?

—No. We're always too busy defending ourselves against Jean to ever pick on *each other*. What did he say, sweetheart?

—He...Nah, I don't want to get into it. Somethin's buggin' that guy and I don't know how much of it's really about me.

—You'd think he would be trying to help you.

—You'd think. But he's got it in for me. He's real bitter about the Malchicks.

—Bitter about what? From the sounds of it, that band had pretty much run its course.

Billy placed both palms upon his eyes and took a deep breath.

—It had. I think he's just jealous that I was in the successful band. That I'm the one with the cool girlfriend.

Lovingly, he massaged the back of her neck.

—I think he's even jealous of my cancer.

—How could that be possible?

—Oh, you know, for all the attention I'm gettin'. I think he's pissed. The way it looks to him, I'm always beatin' him to the spot when it comes to gettin' the attention.

Carrie shrugged her shoulders as she pondered the reasonability of Billy's conclusion.

—Tomorrow is chemo?

—Yeah. Then the radiation blast. Mom's been a real trooper about all of this. Takin' me to all the appointments...

He polished the top of his head.

—I don't know if my hair's ever gonna grow back. And my eyebrows...I'm tired of baseball hats and eyebrow pencil.

—But you're getting better. That's what's important.

—Yeah. At least I've stopped gettin' worse.

Carrie kissed him on the cheek.

—That's what's important, Billy. You have to stop getting worse before you can get better.

As roughly as his strength would allow, which was not very much. He pulled her close and kissed her hard.

—You're one in a million, baby. One in a million. I don't know how or why, but I'm the luckiest guy in the world to have you. I don't deserve you.

—Well of course you do, sweetheart. And I deserve you. We deserve each other.

—I hope you don't regret sayin' that.

Resting her head on his shoulder, she wiped her moistening eyes on the sleeve of his t-shirt.

—Oh, Billy. I'll never regret anything. How could I?

—Well, I regret some things.

He sensed her tensing.

—Not about you! But I made some choices along the way that I regret.

—Like what?

—I regret the way I treated you. Sort of selfish, maybe. And abusin' my health.

—What do you mean?

—I think it was all the goodies that gave me the cancer. I loved partyin' just a little too much, ya' know? If I could do that over...

—You never know, Billy. Maybe the cancer has made you who you are.

He gave that thought consideration.

—Maybe so. But one thing I can say is *party love just doesn't love you back.*

—But real love always loves you back, sweetheart. Always.

They made out as passionately as conditions would allow, just as Ingrid was coming in with Billy's grilled cheese sandwiches.

—Oh! I just...

—Nah. It's okay, mom. Ya' got my dinner there?

—Yes. I hope you can keep it down.

He sat upright as his mom handed him a small plate.

—I've been having pretty good luck lately. I'd say about fifty-fifty. So, I'm confident.

—Well good. I'll leave you two alone. Can I get you anything, Carrie?

—No thanks, Ingrid. I've got everything I need.

Affectionately, she rubbed the top of Billy's shiny yellow head.

As the weeks unfolded, Billy's health improved incrementally, day by day. He was able to sit up for longer periods of time, sometimes for an hour or two. As soon as his strength allowed, Billy was playing his guitar and singing, writing new songs. Though he was but a shadow of his former self, he still relished the opportunity to express his feelings within the framework of a song—as it was his only real emotional outlet.

And the new songs he was writing came from a completely different perspective than any he had written or performed with the Gods. He had been through a great deal in the course of six months, and he was anxious to figure out how he felt about it.

By the end of September, he had responded well to the aggressive treatment. Most of the cancerous tumors were either eradicated or diminished significantly. Doctor Todd declared that Billy's cancer was in remission. He was willing to give consideration to Billy's request to stop the radiation treatments, but he was unwilling to do so immediately. Billy's condition had improved, but it remained an iffy situation.

It was a warm fall afternoon—what would have been John Lennon's forty-fourth birthday—and Billy was sitting on the sofa, working out the changes to the bridge of a new song. It was sort of in the style of John Lennon, called "My Life." The television was tuned to *General Hospital*, but the sound was turned down.

The front door snapped shut and Billy could hear his mother moving from the living room, down the hall to the den. She had the mail in her hand, with a fretful downward curve to her mouth.

—There's a letter here for you from the Internal Revenue.

He abruptly stopped strumming.

—The wha?

—The Internal Revenue. The IRS?

—How the hell did they know I was here?

—I don't think they did, it looks like it's been forwarded from the Arthur Street house.

She handed the envelope to Billy and he opened it with great unease, as though it might contain an explosive. What the fuck do they want? That's all he needed. Shaking, he nervously scanned the contents of the letter.

—Shit.

—What is it, Billy?

—They wanna know how come I haven't paid any taxes for the past five years. It says, *according to their information*, I might owe them some money and they want to know about the band's income. They want to see our books. That shit again. Jesus Christ. Like I don't have enough to worry about already.

—You mean you haven't ever paid any taxes, Billy?

—Mom, it's not like we've really made any money. We took out so many loans to get our projects done, we pretty much owed more than we ever made.

—What about that Vetter fellow? I thought you signed a big contract with him.

—He wants his money back, because I got sick.

—And you owe other people money? Who?

Billy didn't want to discuss Nez Candy with his mother.

—A couple others.

—Well, I'm sure if you show them the band's books...

—Aw, mom, we don't have any *books*. We were just a rock band, not Nike or somethin'.

—I was just trying to help, Billy.

—I'm sorry, mom. I know ya' mean well. It's just that this is another huge problem. Seems like that's all we get these days. But the IRS can send all the letters they want. They can't get blood out of a turnip. What're they gonna do? Send me to jail? They need to get in line with everybody else.

Ingrid laughed as she began to cry. It seemed like it had been one thing after

523

another since Pierce died. She had nowhere to turn.

—You're right, Billy. We can only give them what we can give them. We can only worry about so much at one time.

—Don't you worry about anything, Mom. You're doin' everything you can. And I love you for it.

Putting the guitar down, he stood up and hugged his mother.

—Thank you for everything, mom. Everything you've ever done for me. Elaine and Denny too. You're the one who kept the family together when Dad died. And that was hard on all of us, but most of all you.

Afforded the rare opportunity to let down her mask of invincibility, she wept into Billy's chest as he held her—helpless to give her anything more than useless words.

After a well-received hour-long set of bluesy rock, with hints of reggae and ska, the Popsquawks finished their Key Largo show in a flurry. The band mixed in a few familiar covers: vintage Stones and Animals hits culled from the Malchicks days. But the majority of the material was comprised of Denny's imaginative songs—which typically sounded sort of familiar, like something else. But they were intelligent and original, just the same. They expressed Denny's thoughts and feelings.

In some ways, Key Largo was similar in construction to Sacks—another of those original Portland buildings built in the eighteen hundreds—rumored to have access to one of the old underground shanghai tunnels. The establishment was built from brick: typical brick archways. As much a warehouse as anything else. A checkered history.

The Popsquawks had worked their way up to headlining Thursday nights at Key Largo, as well as securing prime opening slots on a couple of weekend nights. Since the days of Long Goodbye, Tommy Demeola had held a brotherly place in his heart for Denny. Denny was the troubled Granger and Tommy wanted to help the kid, if he could.

Set concluded at Key Largo on their first Saturday night as headliners, Denny stashed his effects boxes in a small tweed briefcase, winding up his cords and placing them in a matching tweed make-up case. As he was wrapping the last cable around his elbow, Denny noticed a cute blond approaching the stage, looking straight at him. Okay by him. He preferred blonds and she was prime, with the precise posture of a dancer. She stood at the bottom of the stage and hesitantly asked.

—Hi. You're Denny Granger, aren't you?

—Yeah, I sure am. What can I do for ya'?

He squatted down to speak with her more directly.

—My name's Stephanie O'Keefe? But my friends call me Babe?

—I'd say that description fits.

Denny was not particularly gifted at the art of flirt, but he certainly wasn't going to let an opportunity, such as the one that stood before him, get away without making some attempt at it.

—What can I do for ya', Babe? Sounds like we're friends already, doesn't it? You can call me Honey.

She smiled angelically.

—Well I wanted to tell you that I really like your band? I was a big Malchicks fan and you seem to be carrying on the tradition. A lot of good energy? Fun.

—That's real nice of ya' to say, Babe. We're tryin', ya' know? Just gettin' it goin'. We've only been together since, like, August. But we're comin' along.

—You sound really good.

—Thanks. Ya' know, Pete, our drummer, he was the Malchicks' drummer, too.

—Really? I don't remember that well. That was a while ago. But I believe you.

It seemed to Denny that she glowed slightly.

—Say, I wanted to ask about your brother.

Balloon suddenly deflated, he diametrically turned cynical in an instant.

—Billy? Yeah? What about him?

—I heard his cancer came back? I hope he's okay.

—Yeah. He's real sick, but he's doin' better.

Denny desperately wanted to move the topic back to the Popsquawks. But for an instant, he realized that he finally had something that his brother might not ever have again. Life. Time. A future. Imperceptibly, his demeanor changed. Softened slightly.

—I only saw the Unreal Gods a couple of times, back when they first started? Then I left town for a couple of years.

Still, seeing an opening, Denny went with that turn in the conversation.

—Oh yeah? Where'd ya' go?

—LA?

—What took ya' down there?

—Well, I wanted to get into acting? I took some classes and did a little community theater. I got bit parts in a couple of commercials.

—Bit parts in commercials. I never thought of that.

—Neither had I, but it was the only work I could get, besides waitressing. And if I was going be a waitress, I could do that up here.

—So, was it waitressin' that brought ya' back to Portland?

—No. I thought I'd gotten a part in a film? Low budget, independently produced. But I thought it would be a start anyway. I hadn't seen a script, but the director told me I'd have a speaking role.

—So what happened?

—Well I got to the *location* and it turns out they were filming a porn flick.

Denny's mind immediately wandered. He'd probably lay down forty bucks to see that one.

—I should have known by the title. It was called *Deep Penetration*? But that director asshole told me it was a spy movie. I guess that was the theme anyway, *espionage*. I felt so stupid.

Just then, a couple of other girls came up. The tall, gawky one, with drab brown hair sounded somewhat perturbed when she snitted.

—Come *on*, Babe. We've been ruddy to *go* for twunty menutts!

In Denny's general direction, she crinkled her face into something that remotely resembled nothing so much as a phony smile.

—Okay. Okay! Well, it was nice to meet you, Denny. Nice to talk to you.

—Same here, Babe. I hope I see ya' again.

—Oh, you probably will...*Honey*. I'll come and see you guys again some time. Soon.

—Great. That'd be great.

He beamed as she and her friends headed for the door. She looked back at him as she stepped through the threshold to the sidewalk outside.

It was in the Monday *Oregonian* that Denny read Stephanie O'Keefe and Amelia

Rodriguez were killed and Ann Winkler was seriously injured, Saturday night, when the car driven by Winkler was sideswiped by a drunken-driver who had run a red light.

Denny was despondent at the news. Bewildered. He had liked Babe immediately and was looking forward to seeing her again. She was special. He wished that he would have asked her to stay to have a drink with him. He could have taken her home. He was shocked and distraught, and overcome with anguish. Those poor girls.

So, with a newly acquired sense of regret and spirit of reconciliation, Denny returned to his mom's house and met again with Billy. Billy was sitting up on the couch in the den, strumming his guitar and watching *Perry Mason* on Channel 12, when Denny came in. He winced slightly at the sight of his younger brother, steeling himself for the next installment of ill will.

Sighing deeply, Billy looked up, his face wrenched in anticipation of the probable onslaught that was to come.

—Look, hey, Denny. I don't wanna go around and around about this shit anymore. Maybe I've made mistakes in my life and I wish I could take them all back, but I can't...

—No, it's okay, Bro'. Actually, I came over to apologize. I'm sorry I've been so rough on ya'.

Waiting for the other shoe to drop, Billy was suspicious.

—*And...?*

—No *and*. I'm sorry, Bro'. I've been an asshole to you for a long time. I probably will be again—coz face it—I *am* a fuckin' asshole sometimes. But, I know you're sick and I shouldn't be, like, kickin' ya' when you're down.

—I'm gettin' a little better, a little stronger every day, Denny. One of these days, maybe I'll be able to kick your ass again.

—Well don't get fuckin' carried away there, Rock Star. You got a long way to go to be kickin' anybody's ass.

Billy chuckled, because he knew Denny spoke the truth.

—So anyway, I came over to make you an offer.

Which got Billy's attention.

—Yeah? What kind of offer?

—I was thinkin' if ya' wanted to, you could maybe, like, sit in with us at some of our gigs—when ya' felt up to it and all.

527

Caught completely off guard, Billy was momentarily speechless.

—Uh...Gee Denny, that's real nice of you. I'd really love to do that, especially if I keep feelin' better. It'd be great to sit in with you guys. Sounds like fun.

—Well, you know what they say: 'fun's where the fair's at'.

Billy's face shrank into a fist of fuddle.

—It'll come to ya', Bozo. So what'ya say?

—Sure. I mean, there's gonna be times when I feel too shitty to show up, I'm sure.

—It's okay, no pressure. We can handle it. We've got enough material to carry off a night on our own. And we're just a trio, so everybody pulls his weight, ya' know?

—Yeah, sure. I'm lookin' forward to hearin' you guys and seein' Pete again, and, what was the bass player's name again?

—Notcho. Notcho Durock.

—Nacho der, rock?

—Yeah, Natcho Durock.

—Where the hell did he get that fuckin' name?

—Beat's me. You'd have to ask his mom and dad.

—Gotcha. Nacho. Is he any good?

—Yeah. He's no Geddy Lee, or anything, but we're not about bein'...uh...*rock stars*. He and Pete play good together. They're pretty locked in.

—That's cool.

—So, we're practicin' over in Pete's garage tomorrow at four. We've got a gig on Friday at Fat Rooster. But I was thinkin' you could, like, make your *debut* on Halloween at Last Hurrah. That'd give you a couple weeks to get in sync with us.

—Sounds good to me. I'm in. Pete still live in the same place?

—Aw, he'll never move.

—Okay, I'll be there. Uh, do you think you could pick me up?

—Yeah, I'll come and pick you up. Sure. Three-thirty.

—Great. I'll be ready.

The Thursday rehearsal and subsequent get-togethers went well. Billy fit right in as most of the cover songs he had performed with Denny and Pete in the Malchicks. A couple of Denny's originals were familiar enough in construction that Billy had no problem picking them up. He sang lead on a few songs, harmony on several others, and simply played guitar on a couple of others.

Neither Carrie nor Ingrid were thrilled with Billy's decision to play with Denny's band. Carrie worried that he would suffer a setback if he pushed himself too hard. And she knew full well that he would do just that. Observing her obligation as a dutiful mother, Ingrid simply worried. However, both knew he was far too stubborn to listen to either of them anyway, so they kept their mouths closed.

Doctor Todd had no opinion on the matter, because Billy didn't tell him about it. He figured, why bother the doctor with unnecessary details. However, the doctor was pleased enough with Billy's progress that he decided to change radiation therapies from a five-day a week regimen, to a single weekly treatment, utilizing a different technique. Billy was happy with the Doctor Todd's prognosis, and hopeful that he could beat the cancer yet again.

Though the treatments were far less frequent, the new radiation routine was more intense. He felt especially bad the following day, as Todd had predicted. With that in mind, Billy scheduled the radiation therapy sessions for Mondays, the idea being that he would have all week to recuperate in time to perform with the Popsquawks the following weekend, should they have a show. He was sick for several days after his first session on the twenty-second, but he remained hopeful that he might respond better the next week and shorten the duration of the negative effects.

Except that Doctor Todd's decision to move to yet another chemo cocktail also had unanticipated negative results. So Billy's general state of wellbeing suffered a substantial setback. He felt worse than he had for many weeks—though not bad enough to discourage him from playing the Halloween show. He wouldn't miss that for the world.

—All right now. Hey, hey. We're the Popsquawks and we hope you'll stick around. We've got a big surprise for you in the second set.

It was a crowd full of Blade Runners and Tootsies, Super Men and Wonder Women, Flashdancers and Spicolis, drinking heavily and being particularly rowdy for a chilly Wednesday night. A thick shroud of gray smoke hung from the low ceilings of the main room. Rumors had spread that Billy might make an appearance, but no one could confirm or refute the reports.

As the Popsquawks trio left the stage and headed back to the dressing room kitchen, they were startled to find Billy sitting on a folding-chair, his head hung over a white plastic five-gallon bucket, puking a golden syrup of sickly bile. Horrified, the band stood motionless at the door until Billy spotted them, waving them to come in. Sure Billy, come in and watch you barf your guts out.

With his foot, he gently glided the bucket behind a counter and placed a ridiculous cartoon-yellow, Goldilocks wig on his gleaming, bald head. He had applied ghost-white makeup to his face, china doll rouge on his cheeks. With a pencil in his hand he caught the eye of his brother and held it in his direction.

—Hey, Denny, c'mere, will ya'? Can you give me some eyebrows?

—Yeah, okay.

Denny slid over Billy's way and applied the eyebrow pencil with a cosmetologist's panache, his enthusiasm making up for what he lacked in skill.

—So, are you gonna be okay with all this? I don't want ya' goin' out there if ya' don't feel like it. Ya' know?

—Nah, I'm fine. Todd's, like, got me on some new chemo program and it's fuckin' me up pretty good. But otherwise I'm fine.

Crooking a brow, Denny said.

—Uh…Okay, if you say so. There you go.

He stepped back a couple of paces to admire his work. Billy stood and checked himself out in a small rectangular mirror on the door to the storage room.

—Jeezus Kee-reist, Denny! What the fuck did you do? I look like I'm seriously surprised, like, fuckin' *Spy versus Spy* or somethin'.

—It was the best I could do, man! I'm no fuckin' *makeup artist*.

There was an air of expectation, mixed with body odor and cigarette smoke, rising from the crowd as the Popsquawks took the stage, with their special guest in tow. But even ardent longtime fans didn't recognize Billy.

Of course the whiteface and rouge, the wig and the light-blue blouse he wore threw some people off. But most wouldn't have been able to identify him in a police line-up. He looked like rickety sticks of spaghetti stacked beneath a mound of melted candy-yellow crayons.

Once everyone figured out that the mystery person on stage was Billy, they drew near to better inspect the ravages that the cancer had wrought. Their curiosity was satisfied by the gaunt, haunted figure, draped upon a stool, with his Strat resting on his leg.

A burst of adrenaline hit him, but that only made Billy feel slightly more energetic. His singing was hoarse and feeble, almost unrecognizable to even his most loyal fans. The Popsquawks were in fine form, providing workman-like support for Billy's cover songs. Denny's harmony vocals helped to fill out Billy's thin vocals on "Gloria," "Time Is On My Side," and "You Really Got Me". Billy's attempt at harmonies on Denny's songs were less successful, and his guitar contributions were negligible.

Still, the audience responded well enough to the performance that Billy was encouraged that he might be able to stage a comeback at some point in the future. He knew he was too weak and out of singing shape to pull off a set of his own material. And he knew he would have to recover enough strength to be able to stand up and move around a little. No more sitting on a stool.

But he sat on a stool for the next gig he played with the band at Key Largo, on a Friday in the middle of November. On the up side, he felt better and his voice was stronger, and he and the band seemed better integrated with each other.

At rehearsals, Billy began leading the band through a few of his new original songs, with the intention of possibly cutting a record, an EP most likely, by New Year's. There were occasions when Denny felt pushed aside in his own band by Billy's domineering drive and obstinate ego. He vowed not to say anything and to let his brother carry on. Life. Time. A future.

It was also the middle of November when Billy moved out of his mom's house and into Carrie's apartment. He no longer required round-the-clock care. He was able to cook breakfast or lunch for himself, and even the occasional dinner for the two of them—though his expertise did not extend much beyond the preparation of stew or grilled cheese sandwiches. And he faithfully took the bus to Providence for his weekly radiation and chemo sessions.

Cutting her days at the veterinary office a little short on Mondays and Tuedays, Carrie would devotedly pick him up at the hospital, after his treatments were finished, in the late afternoons. Usually, on those occasions, Billy did not feel like eating dinner. Often, even the smell of Carrie cooking her own meal would make him sick to his stomach. For that reason, on those nights, Carrie would typically eat a salad at the table in the kitchen.

Carrie's veterinary practice was not exactly thriving, but she and Ken were holding on. They were slowly acquiring new patients and they had lost very few since they had taken over the business from Doctor Dahl in May. She was frazzled, far more at ends than she let on to Billy. But she was holding up under the circumstances. And she was strangely optimistic about the future, though there was little reason for her to feel that way.

Suffering a perilous Thanksgiving meal at Jack and Jean's, with Valerie bearing the usual brunt of the scrutiny—via Jean's unceasing comparisons to her sister's successes—Carrie made it through relatively unscathed. She and Billy made plans to again attend the dawn Christmas service at Saint Stephen's church, as they had a couple of years before. Carrie was hoping to make of it a tradition that they could celebrate at Christmas every year. A family tradition. Their family.

At rehearsal the day after Thanksgiving, Billy began to pursue in earnest his objective of recording an EP of his more recent material during the week between Christmas and New Years. He quickly put into place seven or eight songs he wanted to record. He thought the Popsquawks would work fine as a back up band. As a rhythm section, Notcho and Pete weren't quite up to the high musical standards Gib and Daw had established. But Denny was a superior guitarist to Col. Denny sounded like Mick Taylor, while Col sounded like Chuck Berry in comparison.

To flesh out the production, Billy enlisted the services of a few sideplayers. He sought out the brothers Mejilla, who were an integral part of Gnu Dooz's horn section—Diego on trumpet and Tomas on sax. He also brought Atilla Tancredi on board to play keys. Atilla was a veteran keyboardist, having played in several bands around town. He even looked a little bit like Gilly.

The addition of those three created an ensemble with a layered sound that was more musically diverse, more muscular and sophisticated, than anything Gilly might produce by himself on his keyboards. Atilla's synth parts were precise and creative. He was invaluable in fashioning the arrangements for Billy's songs.

Finally, in order to thicken up the vocals, Billy recruited Merry Renaud, a well-known local back-up singer. She had worked in the studio with Gnu Dooz and Dollarshine and countless other acts, and she was renowned to be a quick study and deadly accurate on pitch and tone.

Through the month of December, Billy mercilessly rehearsed the group—flickering the tyrant of old—alienating Denny, who was more or less a session player in his own band. Except it wasn't his band anymore but something different, some new mutation over which he had no control whatsoever.

In keeping with the reality Denny was confronting, Billy decided to name the new aggregation Skin and Bones. Denny was right. It wasn't even the Popsquawks anymore. In just a couple of months, Billy managed to take over everything and work it in his own image.

Though he was deeply frustrated, Denny could only marvel at his brother's drive and focus. He was in awe of it and wished that he had similar motivation, which he didn't. Still, he was no longer jealous of Billy. In fact he almost admired him. But that would be his secret. He felt sorry for Billy, but not *that* much.

So he relinquished leadership of what had been, only recently, his band without ever saying a word. Instead, he acquiescently contributed sterling guitar parts that greatly helped to enhance every song. And in those moments where he shone, Denny steadily gained confidence that, whatever talents and skills Billy possessed, he was the superior guitarist. And he found great satisfaction in that.

# XXXVIII

Considering the amount of time it took the Gods to record four songs in New York—or even six in LA—Skin and Bones more or less effortlessly maneuvered through the songs Billy had selected to record in the warehouse beginning the day after Christmas. He had whipped the octet into shape by rehearsing them ruthlessly during the first three weeks of December.

He took a page out of John Maclan's playbook: endless preparation—before recording the whole ensemble live in the rehearsal studio, overdubbing the vocals, maybe key solos, and anything else that needed to be fixed or sweetened. The LA experience may not have been entirely satisfying, but Billy had learned that lesson from Maclan and he had come to respect the method.

The expectation was to complete the recording within the week, to mix and master it the following week, and to have the vinyl out on the street by mid-January. Billy had it in mind that he needed to sell ten thousand copies of the EP, in order to pay for the recording and pressing and to come up with fifty thousand dollars, or so, just to begin to budge the Sisyphean boulder of his medical bills.

With the help of Billy D., recruited to oversee the engineering process, Billy requisitioned Rumblesturgeon Studio's mobile recording unit—a converted Greyhound bus. Similar to West Lake in LA, the board configuration was forty-eight tracks and the recorder was almost identical—a twenty-four channel two-inch Studer deck.

And the band blew through the songs without a hitch. They had the basic takes completed after two days. They took four days more to record overdubs and to retake "My Life," which Billy felt didn't flow with the rest of the material. He still wasn't happy with the song, so he chose to abandon it for that session. He decided to replace it with a good first-take they got on Denny's arrangement of the Beatles' "Across the Universe."

Billy and Billy D. started mixing down the remaining seven tracks late on Saturday and they worked all through Sunday and Monday, taking a break to celebrate the New Year holiday on Tuesday. But by Thursday, the mixing was finished and the decision was made to have five of the songs they had recorded mastered at Rumblesturgeon by Dewey Capulet—who was considered to be about as good as anyone, besides Bernie Grundman, of course.

During the week of mixdowns, Billy found free time to design the album cover. Upon an azure blue field was placed a golden yellow cross, a haunting high contrast, life-sized photo portrait of Billy positioned over it all. Just the cross, alone signified a new outlook, but when one set the cover on its side, it became readily evident that the gold cross on the blue field was actually a superb rendition of the Swedish national flag.

By early Saturday morning the master tape was delivered to Bob at Northwestern. He was under strict orders to have five hundred copies of the vinyl EP pressed by Monday morning, as Billy had already pressured Paul at Triad Printing to have the same number of covers finished by the close of the weekend. One thing Billy had not lost in all of his travails was his ability to cajole—his powers of persuasion. By Tuesday morning the records were shrink-wrapped and ready for distribution. The whole process had taken only two weeks. But it was taking a toll.

Trying not to nag, Carrie frequently attempted to invoke her own influence upon Billy. She urged him not to push so hard, but to no avail. He recklessly hurled himself into the endeavor with almost frantic fervor. He got his way— which was customary in Billy world. But it was becoming more difficult for him to accomplish those aims. Still, he persisted.

As news of the album's release was spreading around town, so too was the report that Billy was broke, with many thousands of dollars in medical bills. It was pretty much common knowledge, by that point, that he was not well, fighting the cancer as best he could. Only a relative few people had actually seen him that much since the previous April, and even on those occasions, he did not seem at all healthy.

A change was taking place in Portland. Earlier, in November of nineteen eighty-four, an odd-ball bohemian pubkeep named Bub Marx unexpectedly won the Portland mayoral race over the heavily favored, deeply-entrenched pol, Fred Icancie. By the time the election was over, Marx's campaign debt exceeded forty thousand dollars. He was not a wealthy man and he was not as well connected as the typical politician. The possibility was very real that he was going to have to file for bankruptcy.

It was at that point that a friend of Marx's, the hippie fringe musician, Willie Hiltz, concocted the idea of putting together a benefit to help the new mayor pay off his bills. Offering his own band, the Dead-like Willie Creditcard and the Gringo Poor-Farm Hoedown, he immediately attempted to influence other bands to participate in a fundraiser for the man of the people.

The response was more than anyone could have anticipated. It was so great, in fact, that the mayor's inauguration ball ended up being held at the Memorial Coliseum. It featured more than thirty bands in seven separate rooms, including the main arena stage, which was reserved for the biggest acts, while the others were relegated to the lesser halls in the building mezzanine.

With over ten thousand music fans in attendance, the event generated more than eighty thousand dollars—thirty thousand of which was donated to Oregon Foodshare. In fact, the affair was so successful, that within a week, Tommy Demeola organized a show on Billy's behalf.

Though not nearly of the magnitude of the Mayor's Ball, Billy's benefit was to be staged on Valentine's Day at Starry Night. Mak was going to handle all the promotion. Club owner Barry Hurrvitz and the three participating bands were, ostensibly, to donate all proceeds to the cause. However, when it came to the subject of money and Barry Hurrvitz, one could never be absolutely certain as to the outcome. But all involved hoped for the best. Charity and all.

Once word got to Billy of the affair, he became resolute that Skin and Bones perform a set at the show. Despite deterioration in his physical condition from two straight months of intense rehearsal, he would not let up. He had a new, sophisticated sound that far distanced itself from his former band; he wanted to make sure Portland forgot about the Unreal Gods

On Wednesday, the day before the Valentine's Day spectacular, Carrie took Billy over to the Goodwill store on Southeast 6<sup>th</sup>. It was located just a short distance north of the veterinary office. They went there in search of a suit for Billy to wear at the show.

Carrie's best efforts notwithstanding, Billy selected an abhorrent celery-green plaid polyester ensemble that, if nothing else, went splendidly with his yellow skin. The suit seemed to fit him well enough. But he most resembled a salad portraying Tommy Manero in *Saturday Night Fever*. She knew the bright yellow wig he had secured for Halloween would give him the appearance of a talking dandelion. Carrie was appalled, which encouraged Billy all the more. She appealed to his vanity.

—Sweetheart, why don't you wait and see if we can find you something that makes you look a little more, um…

—No, I like this. I'll stand out.

—Well, yes, you'll stand out. But not in a good way. This outfit makes you look stupid.

She was startled by her own frankness. But, if ever there was a time to be blunt, she felt that time had come. Billy merely brushed her off.

—I want to look stupid.

—Why? Why do you want to look like you're from Mayberry?

—Because I *am* from Mayberry, Carrie. I am. I'm not a big rock star. I'm just a poor dumb bastard from Powell Butte.

—Billy. You're not a poor…

—Yeah. I am. I'm a poor dumb bastard and I've gotten about as far as I can get in this life with what I've been given…

Unexpectedly, possibly for both of them, Billy dropped to his knees and blurted spontaneously.

—Carrie, I don't deserve you. I think we both know that. You've been so good to me. So loyal. You're my guardian angel. My saving grace. And I've just been shit to you.

—No, Billy. You haven't...

—Yeah, I have. Like I said before, I've been selfish. I've always been so fuckin' busy chasin' my headlights that I never took any time to look in the rearview mirror to see what I ran over. And I ran all over you.

—Oh darling, that's not true.

—Yes, it is. It's totally true. I know what I'm talkin' about. You're too good for me. I've always known that. I think you have, too.

She shook her head no, but he continued.

—So I won't be shocked if ya' say no.

He grabbed her left hand with his right.

—But, will you marry me? I want to spend the rest of my life with you.

Disbelief flashed her face lace white. Her mouth gaped open. She couldn't formulate a thought. A response.

—Darling. I...I...We *are* married. In a way, you know? I mean, after all we've been through. I can't imagine not being with you.

—So are you sayin' no then?

—No. I'm not saying no. But marriage is something we need to think about. It's not something we can just jump into. We need to give it some serious thought. Don't you think? *I* need to think about it.

—I suppose you're right. I guess if we got married, you'd inherit all my medical bills and that would sink your practice.

—That's not what I'm talking about, Billy. As I said, we *are* already married. We're married in spirit and that's all that matters. I want for you to concentrate on getting well and healthy. Then we can talk about getting married. One thing at a time.

Standing up.

—Okay. You're the sensible one. You know best. That's why I wanna try and lock ya' up. I need you.

He kissed her hard. Tears eddied at the corners of her eyes.

—I need you too, sweetheart. I'll never leave you, if you never leave me.

Billy smiled.

—Honey, you know it'll take a train to pull me away.

It was in that moment that the two of them became aware of a gathering crowd of hopeful witnesses to, perhaps, a blessed event. But it was not to be—that day.

The hall was packed with onlookers and well-wishers, the curious, the concerned and the steadfast, for the Valentine's Day extravaganza. All eighteen hundred of them had paid twenty bucks apiece to see the spectacle. They were crammed in every corner and crevice, lit like candles and ready to burn. It seemed like a typical Billy Granger show. Nothing out of the ordinary.

A new band in town, Tin Men, opened the evening with a short set of accessible original material, driven by guitarist/lead singer Ron Lundell, and his bassist brother Rob. Ron's songs radiated a certain vaguely carnal boyish longing to which, combined with his brooding good looks, the females in the audience were quick to respond.

Next up was another new consortium—Mein Street, the band that ex-Dollarshine guitarist Charles Jackson had assembled. They were a cutting-edge band with computer controlled synth parts, which were triggered by a highly prized Linn LM-1 drum machine, over which Greig Willis played exotic sampled drum sounds. The ensemble sound was inspired by Peter Gabriel's "Shock the Monkey," the actual live realization of which was quite an accomplishment in a Portland club setting.

Jackson had the look of a former child-star: freckled, a Howdy Doody-like grin, and sad, hound dog eyes. Besides Dollarshine, he had played lead guitar with Attila in the band Bland, who in the seventies were one of the first local acts to release an album on a national label. Their mysterious decision to issue a two-record set, with music on only three sides, the fourth being blank—insured financial ruin and condemned the project to the dustbin of history. And that was the last the world never heard from Bland.

Supporting Jackson on vocals were two cute young backup singers, sisters Meg and Marnie Dunn, who hailed from a highly esteemed local musical family. They were young and cute—in their own separate ways. Meg was pudgy and buxom, with stylish blond hair and a big wide grin. Conversely, Marnie was quite slender, curly brown hair and the vulnerable face of a Parisian chanteuse.

For the discerning males in the audience, the sisters proved to be a great boon for Mein Street, because, as tastes ran, if one of the Dunn sisters wasn't considered an absolute knockout, then the other one most certainly was. The girls' penchant for skin-tight, thigh-high, little black pencil dresses did nothing to diminish their appeal. They danced effortlessly, in perfect synchronization, as they sang.

With anticipation continuing to build in the room, the Canny 9s took the stage for an energetic set of their exuberant ska-band joie de vivre. They hopped around the stage like a bunch of drunk speed freaks. Though never confirmed they all seemed far too academic to ever go near the stuff. However, it's entirely possible that they were mainlining large doses of collegiate frat-boy adrenaline. That was more their "speed."

At last came time for Skin and Bones to take the stage. Billy D. manned the main board and Mick handled the monitors. Just like old times. The stage lights went low and an expectant static charge overswept the premises in a nervous arc.

The band took the stage, intently plugging in and making any small adjustments their instruments may have required. Without hesitation, they broke into the slinky rhythm of "Thinkin' Zebra." The Mejilla brothers' bright, sassy horns bounced like sunlight across the blue lake of Denny's solid rhythm guitar phrasings, creating a hybrid funky, r&b reggae groove.

As the group hit their stride, a backlit, gauzy white scrim, the width of the stage and twenty feet high, exposed a mysterious figure standing motionless behind the screen upon a platform in the upper left corner. A steep staircase plunged diagonally from the scaffold down to the middle of the stage.

Skin and Bones gradually cranked up the intensity. Like a shadow play, the puppet came suddenly to life and, arms askew and legs akimbo, began slowly descending the steps in time to the beat. With each pace, the apparition grew longer and more distorted; approaching grotesquely gigantic proportions. When at last the form had bounced and bopped to the bottom, it abruptly disappeared. Within seconds, Billy appeared at the side of the stage.

He seemed appallingly thin and unsteady, wearing that Jethro-plaid green suit, his silly yellow wig, and several layers of kabuki makeup. He looked much like a wax-figure of himself.

It was wonderfully exhilarating for everyone to see Billy again, playing with an exciting new band; but it was horrible to see him in such an awful state. As best they could, all in attendance tried to make of it a festive happy occasion—though just beneath the surface it was somber and sad.

The Mejilla brothers mimicked the stuttering precision of Earth, Wind & Fire's horn section, as Billy launched into the verse.

—Luck smiled on us tonight, what else can we say
Let's keep the good and throw the bad away

Then to the chorus.

—And on a starry starry night
When the moon is big and bright
And you look into my eyes
I know that love is black and white
I'm thinkin' zebra

And here she comes again
She's all right.

For a fleeting flicker of a moment, he referenced Bowie's "Suffragette City," and then, just as quickly, Merry was echoing a sweet falsetto in the bridge.

—Oh I love you so
Girl I hope you know
Want the world to know
Girl I love you so.

Another verse and chorus and out with the fade. Warm applause and cheers of encouragement replaced what used to be hysterical fanaticism. It was possible that Billy's core audience had matured as much as he had in the previous year—but hardly likely. Still, many were impressed at the quality musicianship found within his new supporting cast.

Their set was great. Denny and the other musicians carried a heavy load. Merry and Denny bore a great deal of the vocal duties. The two of them created a thick, choral cloud beneath Billy's enfeebled breeze of a voice, artfully masking his many shortcomings.

Though he was quite sick afterward, the show went off without a hitch. No one among the spectators, nor his fellow band members, were conscious as to just how worn down Billy had become from two months of unrelenting rigor to get the band ready for that very night. Even Billy himself was not aware, until the show had finished and the weight of his actions began to slowly suck him down into a pool of physical quicksand.

Only Carrie could see what was happening to him. But, though he loved her and respected her counsel in most circumstances, Billy would consistently ignore her entreaties for him to slow down. They both knew he had only one speed. And even though he was running headlong toward a deadly precipice, there was no way that he was going to hold back. It simply was not a part of his disposition. Chasing the headlights.

The benefit raised thirty-four thousand dollars. Billy donated four thousand of that to the National Cancer Research Foundation. In addition, Skin and Bones sold over six hundred EPs at the concert, which brought in another five thousand dollars. Still, thirty-five thousand dollars in the coffers only slightly offset the ever-mounting siege of his financial woes.

The following week he had his monthly appointment with Doctor Todd. The doctor was startled by the dramatic deterioration in Billy's condition. He scolded Billy for not taking better care of himself. Somehow the doctor managed to get through to Billy where Carrie could not. Billy was frightened by Doctor Todd's prognosis. He was not at all optimistic and not at all pleased. Billy had squandered his fragile health yet again. Another round of tests was going to be necessary.

Results of those tests revealed that the cancer had subjugated remission and was on the move once more. His thymus and adrenal glands were showing early stages of tumors. Billy's White Blood Cell count was frightfully low. Once again, he was in very serious condition.

The days inexorably advanced, yet again, toward the Ides of March, blurred by revulsive retch-filled hours spent watching soap operas, lying on his girlfriend's couch. Meanwhile, Carrie's schedule became unmanageable very quickly—rushing to Providence from the veterinary office on Monday afternoons to pick Billy up after his radiation sessions, and on Tuesdays after the chemo sessions. And she frequently shopped for food Billy might eat, preparing meals for him, when it was necessary, running errands and serving as his driver.

Despite his dreadful state, Billy was not about to give up the ground he had gained in getting Skin and Bones assembled. In order to keep the material fresh and the band ready to play, he scheduled weekly practices for Thursday afternoons—the day of the week when he felt strongest and most able to bear up under a couple hours of rehearsal.

In early April Billy scheduled a meeting with Mak at the band warehouse before the Skin and Bones band members were due to arrive for the weekly run-through. He stepped off the bus at the front door of the building and directly met Mak, who stood waiting for him. The area was cold and dark, so they moved to the control room where a space heater would help to warm things up. A couple of second-hand lamps gave the small room a golden glow. The old friends sat silently at the soundboard, peering through the thick glass out onto the main floor.

They had not seen each other for seven weeks, since the evening of the benefit. Mak was startled by what he saw. In his mind, Billy looked sicker every time he saw him. Before him sat a mere husk of the formerly youthful star he used to know.

—So, Billy, what's up? Sounded like ya' had somethin' important to talk about. Are ya' feelin' okay?

—No, not really. Actually, I'm feelin' pretty shitty. Had a radiation treatment Monday and a chemo treatment on Tuesday. Sometimes I think they're worse than the cancer.

—Well, that chemo's supposed to be killin' the cancer, right? Seems like it's probably killin' the good stuff, too.

—That's it, Mak. That's it exactly. It's, like, killin' everything. If the cancer don't kill me then the treatments will. That's a fact.

Distracted, Billy looked over at a crevice between the board and the window frame, where illumined in the lamplight he could see intricate crisscrossed tiers of spider webs. He studied the enclosure closely, noticing that it was bouncing like a trampoline. Mak expressed his frustration with Billy's situation.

—Man. I don't get this. Why's this shit have to be happenin' to you?

—It has to happen to someone, I guess.

Fraught, caught in the web was some sort of bug. It entwined itself tighter as it struggled to escape. Alerted by the commotion, a daddy longlegs appeared from its lair, somewhere below the webs, instinctively responding to the panicked vibrations it sensed. With all due caution, the spider probed its prey, appraising its desirability, before stabbing it with a long proboscis, injecting the victim with flesh dissolving venom.

—But, I mean, you know, where the fuck is God? You wonder if he's even watchin' any of this shit.

Billy pointed to the passion play unfolding before him.

—Hey, Mak. You see that spider over there? It's got a fly or somethin'

—Yeah, I see it.

—That's God, man. That's God.

His eyes widening anxiously, Mak stared at Billy; a peculiar expression of horror mixed with dismay scrawled across his furrowed face.

—Yeah, I guess ya' kinda have to like *question* your beliefs at some point.

—No, Mak. I mean, really. Think about it. If God is, like, the creator of the whole universe, what's he care about a single life on some planet out here in the middle of fuckin' nowhere? It's like—how much thought do *you* give to a single subatomic particle? It's too small to notice, man.

—Then...what can ya' do?

—You have to just keep going. What else *can* you do?

Palms up, Billy shrugged his shoulders, then answered his own question.

—Maybe pray.

In contemplation, Mak splayed fingers across his lips.

—Yeah, I guess you're right. But, I mean, why bother prayin'?

—Because you're prayin' to yourself when you pray. Not God. Not really. You're just another subatomic particle prayin' to itself. A bag of particles maybe.

He laughed at the complete incongruity of what he was saying.

—Man, Billy. Where're ya' gettin' all this shit from?

—Aw, I've been watchin' a rerun on PBS of that Carl Sagan series? *Cosmos*? When you're sick as I am, you think about this shit a lot. There's that too.

Mak nodded, but said nothing. Billy returned to the original subject.

—So, Mak. I wanted to ask you a favor.

—Sure, man. Sure. Wha'd'ya' need?

—I need ya' to put together another benefit show.

—Another one? You think you're in the kind of shape to be doin' another show? I don't know, man.

—Look, I'll tell ya'. I've been able to, like, rehearse with these guys once a week and make it through. I can make it through a show. We...I need the money. All the money from the last show didn't *even* get me caught up with my hospital bills. I mean, they keep shootin' back up almost every day.

—Yeah. I can dig that. You think people will show up for another benefit?

—Well, that's where you come in. If anybody knows how to fill the room, it's you.

—Where were you thinkin' of havin' this one?

—Same. Starry Night.

—Starry Night? I don't know man. I think Barry ripped you off for like about five grand on the last show. Plus he keeps all the liquor receipts.

—Yeah, I know. What else is new? But Starry Night's the only room big enough to make sense. I mean, if we could, like, bring in another twenty-five or thirty grand, I could get out from under these bills. At least for a little while.

—So who're ya' thinking' of gettin' to play on the bill?

—Well, Grant Leeds said last time, when he was designin' the set, that if we did another one, he'd get his band to play for it.

—Okay. Cool. Grant Leeds and who else?

—I was gonna ask Diego and Tomas if they could talk Gnu Dooz into playin'. And then we could round up some other band to open. That's easy enough. That makes three.

—When were you thinkin' of havin' it?

—Maybe in a month or so? I mean, that's, y'know, kind of short notice for Grant and the Dooz, but maybe we can work somethin' out. Maybe they could play early if they, like, have gigs, and we could put the third band on in the middle. Wouldn't matter, really—people would come out for that show.

—Yeah. I guess you're right. Sure. Yeah. I'll help put it together. I know how tough things are. And ya' know I'm always good for helpin' ya.'

—Uh-huh. I know. That's why I asked.

Billy chuckled and massaged the back of Mak's neck.

Starry Night was full to overflowing on the evening of the second benefit. Because it was being held on a Friday night instead of the Thursday Valentine's show, it appeared that there were even more fans crammed into the hall than before. It had been particularly hot for mid-May. Eighty-eight degrees and muggy.

As was his custom, club-owner Barry Hurrvitz kept all windows and ventilation ducts sealed shut, owing to his deep conviction that the perspiratory heat generated in the room increased sales of alcohol and all other beverages. It was suffocatingly humid, somewhere around one hundred and twenty degrees, and from all appearances, his theory bore some validity: there were long lines of sweaty people waiting to get to the bars—upper and lower floors, long before the entertainment had begun.

As Billy had surmised, the Grant Leeds Syndicate and Gnu Dooz had gigs elsewhere in town that night, but both managed to have the opening acts play long sets at their venues. Still, Mak arranged with the remaining act, the Smurf Cowhands that they would go on third, just before Skin and Bones. Cowhands band leader Tom Motto had no problem with that arrangement. Having the Grant Leeds Syndicate and Gnu Dooz open for his band seemed fine to him.

In order to elevate the second show to a higher level, Billy beseeched Daw and Gib to take over rhythm section duties in Skin and Bones. Because Sharon Tate had broken up a couple of months earlier, they were open to play the date. However, after meeting with him and seeing his condition, Daw was especially dubious as to whether Billy should be performing at all.

The Grant Leeds Syndicate was an ethnically diverse funk-rock quintet. The lead guitarist and bass player were black. The drummer was white. The keyboard player was Asian, and Grant Leeds was an androgynous blend of Hawaiian, German, and Cheyenne Indian. With his delicate features and reedy voice he and the band were most frequently compared to Prince and the Revolution.

They played a crisp forty-five minute set. Their highly choreographed stage movements and calculated arrangements drew a great response, given that it was only nine o'clock and most in attendance had yet to get properly lubricated for the whole affair. But the Syndicate grabbed their attention. Lead guitarist James O'Brion drew well-deserved applause for his fiery solos. And, of course, all the girls swooned for the handsome Grant Leeds.

Gnu Dooz had gone through several transformations in the years prior to singer Mallory Knight coming on board. Bandleader Vaughn Jones always had it in mind to create a funky r&b band, bolstered by a large horn section. In the previous incarnation, Vaughn had paired with Solomon Massey to create a sort of Hall and

Oates meet Kool and the Gang soul confection.

Somewhere along the line, Jones' girlfriend Mallory was added as a conga player and back-up singer, swelling membership in the band to thirteen. When Massey decided to leave to become a professional chef, Mallory was promoted to the position of lead-singer. At that point Gnu Dooz took off. Her soft, sultry smooth vocals blended seamlessly with the band's sinuous, sensuous grooves.

Their set put the throng in the proper state of mind, the temperature in the room continuing to rise exponentially. By the end of Gnu Dooz's hour, anyone could have taken the stage and the crowd would have been pleased. Smurf Cowhands filled that bill, with ten songs written by Tom Motto, derived from an early Eagles play Buddy Holly western desperado rock sensibility. Jim Finity served as lead guitarist in the band.

As the Smurf Cowhands left the stage after their set, Jim Finity spotted a skeletally gaunt figure with a horribly jaundiced complexion standing in the wings next to an attractive young woman in a white summer dress. Jim thought he recognized the girl, but the guy seemed unfamiliar. The stranger was wearing a Ken doll wig the color of tarnished silver, a stylish, vanilla-tinted polyester suit and vest, with a brown shirt. His pant legs were tucked into red cowboy boots. Cowboy boots. Jim knew who the guy was.

—Billy! Hey, Billy, how're you doin', man?

Billy was just as shocked to see Jim Finity still within his own plane of existence.

—I'm doin' good, Jim.

He lied.

—Real good. You guys sound great. Except for the lead guitar is a little suspect.

Jim spluttered a giggle, as Billy clapped him on the shoulder and wobbled slowly toward the stage. He took a couple of uncertain steps and awkwardly wheeled around on his heel, a sheepish grin on his face.

—Hey, Jim, man, do you happen to have a pick on ya' I can borrow? I forgot to bring any with me.

As if he were sharing a sacramental host in some holy ceremony, Jim beamed broadly, handing Billy a brown plastic pick. Transubstantiation of the Eucharist. Billy nodded gratefully and again shambled weakly from the wings.

By the time he reached his microphone at center stage, Billy was breathless. He felt as if he might faint. Looking up from his kit, Daw saw and shouted.

—Hey, Billy. I ain't playin'. You're too sick to be doin' this.

He stood up from his throne and began to stalk off the stage.

Billy spotted him leaving, and steadying himself with the mic stand, turned and hollered back.

—It's okay, Daw. I'm all right. Just a little dizzy, that's all. I'll be okay. C'mon. We can do this. We *have* to do it. Please. I can't back out of this now. Please.

Exasperated, Daw returned to his drums, wary that Billy wasn't going to make it through Skin and Bones' set. The other players were just as concerned for Billy's welfare, but were more unwilling than Daw to challenge his authority, even in his compromised condition.

When all were ready, Billy looked to his right and raised his eyebrows expectantly. At the signal, Mak, wearing a white tuxedo, strode toward the mic and performed the duty as master of ceremonies.

—Hey, everybody! How y'all doin'?

He was met with a loud, rowdy response.

—All right! All right. How about the Grant Leeds Syndicate and Gnu Dooz, eh? Two of Portland's best.

The gathering cheered enthusiastically.

—Two of Portland's best. And, Smurf Cowhands. One of our top up-and-comin' bands. Let's hear it for 'em.

A warm, but comparatively indifferent reaction burst out.

—So, I guess we all know why we're here. We're all here to honor and support our good friend Mister Billy Granger here.

A roar of shouts and screams, as Billy lowered his head in acute mortification.

—We all know Billy's been havin' a pretty tough time of it over the past year. He's been runnin' up some major medical bills. And, with your help, we're gonna be able to help him pay down some of those bills. Anyway, some of you have heard the band. Most of ya' haven't...

Sweeping his hand in a grand gesture of introduction, Mak announced.

—Here's Billy Granger and Skin and Bones.

The band swung into a warm, gentle swaying rhythm, with a setting that would not have been out of place on John Lennon's *Double Fantasy*. A classic D-B minor-G-A chord progression. As the lazy lilting feel locked into place, Atilla Tancredi provided a plaintive theme on synth. Billy clutched the mic.

—Thanks, Mak. Thanks so much, everybody. It's really great to see y'all out here tonight. You're all lookin' good.

Billy shaded his eyes, looking out into the crowd, and a thunderous cheer erupted.

—I see a lot of old friends out there.

He briefly lost his balance and listed sidewards. Denny could see that something was wrong with his brother. From across the wide stage, he watched Billy swaying in front of the mic. He saw, for the first time, that all the beauty had been sucked from his brother's body.

And in that moment, he felt profoundly sorry for him. Denny pitied him so deeply because: Billy had lost so much. Everything. He wanted to cry, out of real compassion. But he knew that, under the circumstances, he could not.

Regaining his equilibrium, Billy continued his patter as the band cycled through the intro to "My Life."

—Hey, Tommy. How're ya' doin', Tommy? Incomparable John. All right. Trudy? And Lisa, my chemo tech. Great to see you under different circumstances tonight, Lisa. Let's have a big hand for Lisa, everybody. Bick Muckler. H.E. Carus…

He gazed up to the balcony, where a lot of old friends were sitting.

—Oh, man. Look at you all up there. I see Paul Springer. Bea, get my man Paul a beer. And put it on my tab. There's Louie and Jack 'n' Alice. Better get them beers, too, Bea. Jeezuz. There's a whole buncha ya' up there. D'ja all come on a bus, or what?

Standing at the side of the stage, Carrie was stiff stricken with fear gravely concerned that Billy was going to die right there in front of everyone. She sniffed mordantly. That's probably the way he'd prefer to go anyway. Resigned to the reality that the choice was not hers to make, she despairingly watched her boyfriend expend the last of his life's vitality.

A wave of nausea whelmed over him and he felt dizzy, as Mick approached from offstage with Tele in hand. Billy strapped it on, sweat pouring down his face. He could hardly breathe. He tried to strum the guitar along with the opening of the song, but his hands were spasming, as he attempted to play. His fingers couldn't form chords; his right hand barely able to comp. He deadened the strings, stroking them the best he could. Resuming his banter.

—Man. Michelle. Tim 'n' Sally. Hey, Sally, when's the baby due? Rick, Stevie. Rainbow. Hey, Rainbow. He's our studio plumber, everybody. S'get a big hand for Rainbow, too. There's Lynn Conroy. Good to see ya' Lynn.

He waved tacitly.

—Thanks for comin' out, everyone. I'm really touched. What the hell. Bea, give the whole balcony free drinks.

Daw could see that Billy was getting too amped up by the faint spark of former voltage. Finally, while the band kept cycling through the intro, he stopped playing his drums altogether, refusing to continue because he was convinced Billy was overextending himself unnecessarily. Seeing Daw standing up from his kit, Billy cajoled his friend. Over the mic he begged.

—C'mon Daw. D-*aw*. Don't go. I'll be good. I promise. C'mon everybody, help me out here. Daw don't go. Daw don't go...

The crowd quickly picked up the chant. And Daw froze in his tracks.

—C'mon, Daw. We've got a show to put on. These people paid good money here. I'll mellow out, I promise man.

An approving wail arose from the floor, further sustained by the stomping of those in the second tier. As the band circled to the top of the intro once again, Daw fell in and Billy signaled weakly that he was ready to come in on his cue. The spotlight stabbed his eyes. The stage lights flashed and flickered in multicolor hues.

—This one's called 'My Life'. It's a true story.
My life is a picture book
I know it's worth a second look
My songs have a thousand hooks
Coz my life is changin' everyday.

The room began to carousel before him, faces liquefying beneath the spinning colored lights. Observing something going on with his brother, Denny sidled over in his direction.

—How you holdin' up, Bro'?

—Denny, man. I feel like I'm gonna pass out. Just keep playin'. I'll get it together.

Shaking his head in frustration, Denny returned to his post. As the spotlight bore in upon him, Billy closed his eyes in an attempt to concentrate.

—My life is a comedy
My life is a tragedy
If Shakespeare was alive today
I wonder if he'd say the things that I say.

Suddenly the lights began to fade and he was riding a horse in an open field beneath the hot summer sun.

—In times like these I need a friend
But I knw Igt everythngnyou.
Nyou.
Yrsmilenw...

And the horse from fell he to the ground. Up bouncing on the green soft ground.

Downfallen he, as if in dream. And Carrie was there beside him, dressed like an angel, all in white. She seemed very sad. A sad angel. Don't cry, sad angel. Don't cry. And Mak, in an elegant iceberg white coat. He looked like the captain of the Titanic. He seemed very worried. Don't worry, Captain Titanic. Well all will be, sir.

Denny saw his brother go down and, without missing a beat, launched into a sterling extended guitar solo. The stage lights went dark and the spotlight swiftly shifted, allowing Mak and Carrie to lift Billy from the stage and lead him off.

Billy tried to escape from their grasps in an effort to return to the mic, but Mak and Carrie were not about to let him go, and he was much too feeble to go back out there anyway. He made if off stage and passed out again. Inspired by the moment, Denny led the band through an impassioned series of solos that lasted nearly half an hour—each member pouring out his heart. Then, summoning uncommon composure, Denny moved to Billy's mic at center stage.

—Your smile how it loves to shine
Your thoughts guided just like mine
Your scent makes my spring unwind
I wouldn't be here if it wasn't for you

My dad had a lot of soul
I understood his rock and roll
I hope that when I grow old
I don't regret the day I pass away
His life was an eight ball game
He had a pocket billiard brain
My stroke hasn't been the same
Since the angels came and took him away

In times like these you need a friend....

In his selfless shining moment, he stepped back from the spotlight, nobly disappearing into the darkness as the music slowly wound to a halt around the dimming empty stage. Goodnight everybody.

—Light as snow...

Billy moaned lazily.

—Umm. Whatime isit?

Carrie watched him to see if he would remain conscious.

—Sweetheart! You're with us again!

Before he could speak, he sat up abruptly and frantically looked around the immediate vicinity, grabbing a plastic basin from his bedside table. He heaved up a frothy slop the color of unripe corn. Choking. Gagging and spitting.

548

—Yuhhk. Uhhh. Aww-hhhk. Awwhhk. Uhgull. Uhghoul. Hookkk. Hawwwk. Aaaa. Caw. Haaaw. Haaa!

Gasping.

—Gukk. Yeah I gss so. Gyukk. Hyukk. Whatime isit?

—It's uh, the *afternoon*...

Craning her neck, she looked over her shoulder at the round black clock high on the wall.

—It's two-thirty...

Billy squinted up at the blurred circle. He twitched and blinked his eyes, but his field was hopelessly bouncing; he was unable to fix or focus.

—Aaaak. Hukk. Isit Friday?

She stood, leaned over him and kissed him tenderly on the forehead.

—Yes, dear, it's Friday, but...

—Hnnnh. Uhnnnh. I feel like I've beenoutfor twenny years.

Smiling, Carrie kissed him on each eyelid.

—Well, it *has* been a week.

Still groggy.

—Wdy'a mean? A wwweeeek?

—Yes. You woke up a few times. We had conversations just like we're having now.

She stroked his hairless head, tracing the lines of his absent brows.

—I don't rememmer that.

She laughed.

—That's what you say every time.

She kissed him again and handed him a towel. Removing the basin from his lap she placed it in the sink near the restroom door.

—Do you want some water?

—Yeah. Water. Sure. *Please*. I've been out a weeek?

—Yes, Billy. You're very sick, sweetheart. You pushed yourself too far again.

Smiling, he engaged her worried expression with faded charm.

—Y're my angel. I know i's true. You were there.

She handed him a plastic container filled with water.

—I was there where, dear? Where?

—When I fll off the hrse. I saw you. I know y're 'n angel. God sent you to me t' prove he hears my prayrs.

Bewildered, exhaling through her nostrils.

—Well yes...That's what I've always tried...

—Yeah. I know. Y're right. I was tellin' Mak about the spider. And God hrd me. And he showed me. He snt me nangel and it ws you. It *is* you! My *an*gel. God's not a spider. He's a horse. Hesallofit.

He motioned toward the heavens and she contorted her face into a troubled frown.

Some considerable time later, Doctor Todd stood next to the bed, reviewing Billy's chart.

—I'm still a bit concerned about your abscesses. They don't seem to be healing. Especially the one on your back. So I'm going to order an injection of Neulasta. That will help to stimulate your WBC.

Groaning, Billy complained.

—Oh man, Doc. Last time I had that, my legs and lower back killed me for a week.

Doctor Todd placed his stethoscope on Billy's chest, delicately prodding his neck and underarms.

—Your lungs have been filling with fluid. Your glands are all swollen. We have to do everything we can to fight infection. Infection is your biggest enemy right now. It would be very bad, at this stage, if you were to come down with pneumonia.

—I understand, Doctor, but I've been here five weeks now. I feel like I'm wastin' away. I only weigh a hundred and forty pounds! I used to weigh a hundred and eight-five. And I weighed a hundred and seventy, like, two months ago.

—Your weight loss was not unforeseen. You're very sick. Your program has been far more intensive through this round than previously. We have to get your cancer under control.

—But, Doctor Todd. It feels like the cure is killin' me. I can't eat. If I do, I barf it up. I sleep twenty hours a day. It's like I'm in a coma.

Billy fought off tears of frustration.

—My hands shake so bad I can barely hold a glass of water. My eyes are bouncin' around, so I can only watch *Perry Mason* with 'em closed.

He waved toward burly Raymond Burr, who was speaking to Hamilton Burger on the television—silently, because Billy had muted the sound when the doctor had come in.

—I can't even stand up or walk without help. I'm witherin' away to nothin' here. What's left?

—Mister Granger, ummm...Bill...

He said sternly.

—It's like this. We must get your cancer under control. If we can force it into remission, then you should recover most of what you've lost. But while you're suffering this relapse, we have to use every weapon in our arsenal. I've ordered an extensive course of radiation treatments on the thyroid tumor. It's still growing and we have to reverse that. Immediately.

There was nothing Billy could say. He felt that he did not have long to live, whether his cancer went into remission or not. Doctor Todd left the clipboard with Billy's chart hanging from the frame at the end of bed. As he moved toward the door, Doctor Todd turned.

—I want you to start your radiation therapy tomorrow morning and we'll pursue a four-week program—every day, Monday through Friday—and we'll see where we stand.

—But when am I gonna get out of here?

—We need to give these treatments time to work. Your system has been severely compromised, Billy. We have to get ahead of the disease again. Until we do, we've got to keep you under close observation.

Billy did nothing to acknowledge that he heard what the doctor had just said. Instead he turned up the volume on *Perry Mason* and closed his eyes. As the doctor left the room, he met Carrie coming through the door. They were both wearing white lab coats—looking very medical. Todd smiled dourly—a blank look—as though he had never seen her before, though he had seen her at least a hundred times.

Candidly, she delivered her assessment to Billy.

—That Doctor Todd is a very odd duck. He's on some other wave-length. Some other *planet*.

—Yeah. I suppose you're right.

—What's that mean, sweety? Did you two have an unpleasant conversation?

—Yeah. He said I was never gonna get out of here. Not alive anyway.

A surge of alarm curved across her face.

—Is that what he *said*?

—Well...more or less. He said he didn't know when I was gettin' out of here. And he's orderin' up all these new treatments that're only gonna make me feel worse than I already do. And I'm feelin' pretty shitty. Y'know baby?

Carrie had the soul of an empath and the heart of a healer. She bore the scars of every living thing she touched. For they inevitably touched her even more deeply in return. She knew what Billy was saying. And in her way, she suffered for him almost as much as he suffered himself. Out of instinct, she maintained an air of calm, as she massaged his earlobe with her thumb and forefinger.

—Yes, dear. I know. I'm so sorry. I know you're going stir crazy in here.

—It's not just that, Carrie. All of these treatments are suckin' the life out of me. If I'm gonna die, I wanna die healthy.

—What do you mean, *die healthy*?

—I mean, if I'm, like, terminal, y'know? If I'm, like, terminal, then I want to just die without all the chemo and radiation—that only makes me feel terrible.

—I don't know if that's a good idea, sweetheart. All those treatments are the only thing that can keep the cancer from taking over your body.

—But it has taken over my body. We've killed every white blood cell in my body, and now I have to get a shot to increase my *white blood cell production*. How crazy is that?

—Well, you don't really have an alternative.

—Incomparable John was tellin' me about a naturopathic oncologist that's been pretty successful with cases like mine. Doctor, uh...Beardsley, I think it is. He's got a regimen of wheat grass juice and Vitamin B-17. It's supposed to have gotten good results. John says Beardsley's patients almost always feel better. I just wanna feel better.

—So what do you want to do, Billy?

—I wanna go home. I wanna try somethin' different. It can't be any worse than what I'm goin' through now.

Disconsolately resolute, she knew better than to argue with him.

—How soon were you planning on leaving?

—As soon as we can. As soon as Todd'll let me out.

—He can't hold you here against your will, Billy. You're not in jail. But I wish you'd stick to his plan for a little longer before you try something else.

He thought it over. Carrie was the one with the good judgment. God sent her. Billy knew he was too impulsive for his own good. He was, at last, willing to concede that fact to himself.

—Okay. I'll give it a few more weeks. But I'm tellin' Todd I'm leavin'—right away. Then he can do his worst to me and get it over with. If I know I'm gettin' out soon, I can take whatever he dishes out.

She did not reply, but wistfully gazed out the window at the summer blue sky.

Four weeks later, Billy was sitting on the couch in the den of his boyhood home directing musical traffic in preparation for his next recording project. Surrounding him were the essential players: Denny; Attila; guitarist Dallas Cotton and bassist Sam Holden, who played in Denny's new band, Two Hundred Persent, and Aaron Opperman, who acted as engineer and assisted Billy in programming the Korg DDD5 drum machine.

—Attila, man, I like what you're playin', but the patch needs a little bit of frosting. Know what I mean?

Attila maneuvered the mod-wheel over the marimba/synth sound he had developed, creating a wiggly shiver to the end of each chord phrase.

—Yeah, yeah. That dressed that up. I'm likin' the drums a lot, Aaron. Real Tears For Fearsy. That's what I'm lookin' for. Let's try it from the top.

The boys expertly wove through the intro and into the verse, where Billy jumped in with the vocal.

—I used to cry about the problems at hand
'Bout money and pain' leadin' a band
And then when cancer materialized
I thought my own strength would keep me alive
But all of a sudden, from nowhere he came
A perfect stranger he came up to me
And now the big picture, the big picture
Is comin' in loud and clear on the television in my soul
The big picture. The big picture...

Raising his hand, Billy signaled.

—Wait. Wait. Hold it. Sam. Could you make the bass more of a rolling thing—like the drums? And let Denny, Dallas and Attila handle the reggae feel? And then on the chorus, where it goes 'big picture, big picture' kinda move into a Paul McCartney sort of run, if you can work it in. Duh-duh duh-duh, duh-duh duh-duh...?

Quickly, Sam ran through a couple of alternatives to what he had played.

—Okay. Let's give it another try. Pick it up at the top of the second verse.

—We used to walk in our favorite park
Then play in the city 'til way after dark
And think about choke brain livin' it high
Squandering love, we'd shout at the sky
But those days were unreal those days turned black
The nights were painful and hard to stop
But in the big picture, the big picture
No fear of dying, only love

Billy interrupted again.

—Yeah. That's better. You got the Paul McCartney thing in the chorus. Cool. That's great. Locks in a lot better with the drum machine. Oh yeah, and Aaron, maybe we can get a little roll going into the second verse?

As if he were typing, Aaron tapped out on the various pads a couple of two-bar choices, mixing in various tom runs and percussion tones to give the fill the sound of authenticity.

—Definitely gettin' there. Can you try that one triplet on just the floor tom?

Billy walked over to Aaron's side. He tried to demonstrate to the technician what he wanted, but his hands shook so badly, he couldn't do it. There was no instrument he could play with any accuracy. He could only lead the band and hope to coax from them the arrangements he heard in his head.

It was a slow process. Typically, he would write the lyrics and develop a vocal melody. He and Denny or Attila would work up the chord progressions and the skeletons of arrangements, then take it to the rest of the guys to contribute their own elements.

In addition, Billy wasn't always up to the physical challenge of rehearsing and recording. On many occasions, Denny led the band and took over the vocal duties, while Billy lay on the couch attempting to concentrate.

—Okay, okay. Denny, can you take these guys through 'Chemotherapy'?

—I don't know, Bro! You're the expert on that subject. I've never been shot up with that shit. No thanks.

—I meant the song, smart-ass. Don't be fuckin' with me, man.

Nauseated, Billy did his best to play along. Denny retorted.

—Yeah yeah. I know. Okay, here we go. It's sort of pop-reggae-blues, I guess you could say. Until the chorus anyway. That's more sort of McCartney-ish. We're plannin' on havin' some brass on the intro—we'll figure that out, we've been talkin' to Tom Tibbs from Canny 9s about playin' his trombone. We'll see. It'll be somethin' sweet. And I've got this little riff. Duh da-da da-da baa-unh.

Denny played a majestically haunting sequence of notes on the lower strings of his guitar. Billy joined in the directions.

—Yeah, so it's, like, three parts. Um. The first part, the verse, is reggae. Play the progression, Denny.

Lying on his back, Billy hoarsely sang the verse, as Denny provided upstroke guitar accompaniment. Billy sounded a bit like Bob Marley, or, more precisely, like someone who was *trying* to sound like Bob Marley.

—Until three years ago I was just like you
Looking for love the romancer
Until that day my doctor's office would say
So straightforwardly I had cancer
But I'm getting better and better everyday
Taking my strength from my master
So now it's the game of games for me and you
Making a triumph from disaster.

Searching the others for any sign of response and seeing none in particular, Billy continued.

—Then the chorus is sort of two styles. The top is sort of dramatic. It goes like.

Nodding once, Denny picked up the thread

—Chemotherapy
Look what you've done to me

Then Denny said

—And in the second-half of the chorus goes back to a reggae feel.

Billy sang.

—I don't feel so good
I don't. Feel. So. Good
I don't feel so good....
Then back to the top half

—No more vanity
This wig looks bad to me
I always knew it would
I always. Knew. It. Would
I always knew it would

He broke off.

—And then the bridge is sorta like the McCartney thing Denny was talkin' about.

—Who would ever thought, who would ever thought
This would happen to me- ee-ee …
And we do that four times. Four times?

Billy looked toward Denny for confirmation, which Denny supplied with another slight ascent of his head.

—Then it goes back to the intro, repeat the second half of the verse, the chorus and the bridge. And that's it. Why don't we try it from the top.

Kicking it off, Denny guided Attila, Dallas and Sam through the composition, as, barely audible, Billy sang his parts. Meanwhile, Aaron experimented with patches, slowly constructing the drums for each section.

Abruptly, Billy sat up, stood up and summarily strode from the room with as much haste as he could muster, heading directly toward the bathroom, down the adjoining hallway. Once he finally secured himself in front of the toilet, he threw up violently, spewing blood, bile, and the rest of the contents of his stomach with extraordinary force.

Once he finished barfing, Billy washed his face, rinsed out his mouth, and gargled with Listerine. He looked intently into the mirror above the sink at his hairless head. Seeing himself saddened him and he nearly began to cry. But he considered himself too tough and brave to cry. He reached into his pocket, spearing his canister of Binaca, and blew a couple jets of spray into his mouth. As good as it was going to get.

Just as he swung open the door, Carrie was passing by, moving in the direction of the den.

—Hey there, gorgeous. Where you goin' lookin' so serious?

—Oh hi, sweetheart. I picked up your prescriptions from Doctor Beardsley and a bottle of wheatgrass juice.

—Blech. I'll get to that in while.

—Aren't you feeling well?

—Well, I'm feelin' better *now*.

Squishing the sack she held against her chest, he grabbed Carrie in a bear hug and kissed her repeatedly about her face and neck. He cupped her ass in his hands and kissed her more passionately.

—One of these days, Carrie. One of these days.

She smiled at him—a mouth inscribed with compassion, wisdom, bemusement and total devotion. She wrapped her arms around Billy's neck and sighed softly.

—I love you, Billy.

His face buried in her hair, he said.

—I love you, too, Carrie. You're my life.

He drew away and peered ardently into her eyes.

—Ya' know that don't you? You know you're my life, right? I tell you all the time.

She didn't know how to answer.

—Well you are. You're my life. You're what I live for. I'm nowhere without you. Nowhere. Nothing. I'm nothing.

Her eyes shimmering, she set down the sack on the hallway floor.

—Oh, Billy. You're *my* life too. I'm lost without you. I'll never leave you. I couldn't. I wouldn't...I won't.

He pulled her close again and kissed her with all his passion soul, summoned from a place of metamorphosis, where the temporal world of now give way to all ephemeral space, in always of light. And the lightness of light. No gravity. As light as space. Dark and clear. As bright as all light. Without weight nor scale. Forever. Shone.

# XXXIX

Using the black metal railing as one crutch and Carrie as the other, Billy hiked himself up the steps to H.E. Carus' house. He was meeting for an interview, about his new album, *Here Comes Mister Groove,* and his plans to perform again, a very short run: the *Cement Forest* tour.

—So, do I call ya' H-E, or what?

As Billy and Carrie eased down upon the couch, Eric observed that Billy was bone thin and in obvious physical pain. It appeared that Billy's hair had grown back. It was close-cropped, nicely groomed, but much darker than it used to be. Eric brought them each a tumbler of water. Setting the glasses down on the coffee table, he replied.

—You can call me Eric. My friends do.

—How'd ya' get the name H-E?

—Well, it's kind of a long story. My name's Henry Eric Carus and when I was in college my mom used to send me mail—mostly money—and she'd address it to me as H.E. Carus. I moved back to Portland and decided to use H.E. as my pen name when I started writing.

—How come they call ya' Eric when you're name is Henry?

—I'm not sure.

—You know what's weird? My first name is Joseph, but everyone's always called me Billy. My brother Denny's first name is John. Same deal.

—Well then, you two know the identity issues I've had to deal with over the years. There've been a lot of times when I didn't know who the hell I was.

—I can dig that. Me 'n' Denny had the same problems, man.

—Cool.

As he sat down in the rocking chair opposite the couch, Eric switched on his hand-held cassette recorder, placing it on the coffee table in front of Billy. He grabbed a pen and pad from the table beside the chair.

—I'm just going let you do the talking, for the most part, Billy. Maybe I'll ask you something to steer the conversation. But I want this to be your story. You talking. Not me.

—Sure. Great. I'm a good one for talkin'.

Swinging his arm around her, he smiled at Carrie and gave her a squeeze.

—Okay. Why don't we start with new plans?

—Denny and Attila have really been working hard on the songs I want to do at the *Cement Forest* show. We're shooting for Halloween at Key Largo. You know Attila Tancredi, right? He's a writer for *Tin Dinner*? He's a great keyboard player, too. Played in Bland in the seventies. I've never seen anyone as persistent in developing a sound. He's excited—we're all learning about this MIDI thing. It's something that's not going to go away. We have to recognize that and learn about it. I just got a Korg DDD-5 drum machine? I really can't program it yet. But I see the emphasis on it in the studio, and I think it's important to know how to use one.

Leaning forward uncertainly, Billy secured his glass of water. He settled back on the couch taking a long drink.

—But you know, you still have to have a good song over that drum beat. The power still remains in the song. The melody, the lyric, the hook are still the most important factors. The machines can help to create a mood and maintain consistency. They're great for that.

He bobbed his head authoritatively.

—And any drummer who does not see the importance of drum machines, and how to program them, is going to be a drummer without a job. They're the best ones to program them because they can actually play the drums.

—So what about the preponderance of reggae material on *Mister Groove*?

—I think my personal rhythmic tastes run more toward African, and of course reggae. Reggae's an entity unto itself. It's this beautiful creation that came out of Jamaica. It was the product of American rhythm and blues, the British Invasion, and the calypso style that was prevalent among the natives, whose ancestors had brought the sound over on the slave ships from Africa.

Billy sat forward again, tentatively placing his glass back down on the coffee table. He brushed the top of his head as if to summon his words by friction.

—It's still my favorite form of music, but I'm getting into dub, which is kind of like reggae rap music. But I like the internal rhythms of reggae. The melody lines seem to interweave. Like, a keyboard part will be going doo-doo-DOO-doo, every eight beats, while the lead guy sings a different melody line, the horn guys doin' a little thing, and the guitar does something else, and it all forms a pattern—the melody line flip flops. But, apart from all that, I'm a fan of the hit song, the catchy love song.

Changing the direction of the conversation, Eric brought up the Unreal Gods and their unreleased recordings, as well as the rumored possible re-release of the Skin and Bones project.

—If the money and timing is perfect, we may yet release the tapes of what the Gods did in New York a few years back. And the stuff we recorded for Rough Edge. All that stuff is outstanding and it makes a good representation of the band. 'Made In Hong Kong' is great. I want to release it sometime, on some label. It's going happen, but I don't know when.

Like an unsupported sack potatoes Billy's weight shifted erratically. He was in obvious discomfort.

—There's the new version of 'Rocky Road', and there's 'Police Told Me'. We've got that big-budget video for 'Police...' I'm just real proud of that band. The only thing we ever released was done on a very low budget. And the band was very young when we recorded it. But this particular group of tapes is the real thing, man. It's really not that far away from happening. All the mixes are done. It's just a matter of the artwork and pressing it. There's a lot of red tape and budget work. Everything takes longer than it seems like it should.

His leg began twitching, and with his hand he tried to steady the tremor. To no avail.

—With the Skin and Bones recording, we actually recorded seven songs and only released five. The other two, I want to get a hold of and remix. One is 'Across the Universe', which Denny sings—and it's done reggae style. The other song is 'Party By Myself', which I wrote with our manager Mak Poppin. I want to put out a single with those two songs. The only bad thing with that session was that I was in a lot of pain at the time. The cancer had pinched nerves on my spine and my kidneys were weird. I wasn't eating. I was just wasting away. So I had to start using painkillers by the end of the project.

To Eric it seemed as if his guest was still pretty heavily sedated with painkillers—though not so much as to slow Billy's train of thought or diminish his enthusiasm for the subject.

—I haven't sent *Thinkin' Zebra*, that's the Skin and Bones project, out to any markets. I'm just starting on that now. I'm planning a re-release. They play the single, 'Oh God' extensively on the radio in Seattle. We had five or six months of good rotation up there. They played 'Please Don't' a lot too. I'm going to re-release that EP for two reasons—one, because it hasn't been released in any of the big markets. Rough Edge, technically, I was still under contract to them at the time. They just wanted me to release it in the Northwest, and two, when I was in the hospital, no one was workin' on it. I want to do it right this time.

Eric asked about the lessons Billy may have learned from his relationship with Rough Edge.

—The American approach to music is a sham. It doesn't have to be treated like it's all a business. When you start talking about corporate chess games, it's tough to get a message through. I've had more than a taste of that. I've had five courses. None of them has given any dessert. I haven't been able to release a record. And, as far as my contract with Rough Edge goes, I'm working to get out of that, once and for all. It doesn't seem like that's going to be a real big deal. I think they think

I'll be kicking off any day now. I just know that within the corporate arena, the manipulation gets pretty heavy.

He gazed over at Carrie, who was smiling wanly.

—The follow through on the message of the sixties fell short. Unfortunately, with the emergence of pop music as a vehicle for a message came associations of drug use and other abuses of the power that came with it. Pop music has now reached a place where it can have another level of effectiveness. A staunch awareness can be created and broadcast to the world. We can communicate a message in ways that weren't possible ten years ago—MTV, for example.

—Any new songs?

—Let's see. 'Divine Light'. It's just a rock 'n' roll song but it has a message about what I've seen and learned in the past few years. There's a couple of reggae tunes. And 'Butterflies to Be' is one I gave to Marv Mathis at BMI. That's more of a love song between two people.

Smiling devotedly, Billy looked over at Carrie again.

—Marv hears a lot of Lennon and McCartney in that one and I agree. That particular cut was done on a four-track, just Attila and I. It sounds real smooth.

And what about the cancer? Eric inquired.

—Every person has a struggle that they're dealing with. Wickedness is all around us and it stops us from reaching our potential. Whether it's greed, or vanity, or drugs or being self-absorbed in your own problems, or someone else's. It all undermines what you want to be doing.

His thoughts pivoting erratically, Billy changed the subject.

—You know, in reality, we have apartheid in the United States—Big Mountain in Arizona is an example, with all the Navajos and Arapahos being forced to relocate. The American Indian has been destroyed, as a culture, at our hands.

Billy's eyes searched the room as he attempted to find his point.

—I think we're all prodigal sons. We all make mistakes and we're all learning from them, moment by moment. No one can do it alone. *You* are not *you* because of *you* alone. I'm glad I had help.

Have there been a lot of complications? Eric asked.

—Right now, I don't have any problems. Physically, my arms are numb. I can't do a lot of things with my hands. My legs are numb. These are all from the things that were done to my body. But mentally and spiritually, I'm overjoyed with gratitude and love at being alive. I'm so happy to wake up and look at all the things I'm blessed with, the things I can do. I'm blessed by good people—like Carrie here...

He hugged her and kissed her lovingly.

—We're getting married in April. And being able to do this...I'm really grateful for that. You're helping to get my message out. I'm lucky. I feel fortunate for the lessons I've been given. If I turn to dust tomorrow, I'll die happy. I'm glad to know what I know now. There's a lot of misery that need not be experienced. You don't have to live hell on earth. It could be heaven on earth. It should be. Being on the right road should be the ultimate goal for everyone.

A thoughtful, earnest expression winced his brows.

—Money, success...they are all fruits and justifiably yours—if your intentions are good, if you place love as your goal. Love your creator whether he's Muslim or Christian or whatever. I was kidding with someone the other day that I was a born-again Rastafarian. It may or may not apply to every one of you. But you have to have respect for God. That's the truth. That truth is love. And when love happens, the firing order of the pistons gets right and good things start happening.

With a concerned look, Carrie nudged Billy.

—I guess my partner in crime here thinks I've talked about enough. We'd better go, before I pass out right here where I'm sitting. I want to thank you, Eric, for the opportunity to talk about my beliefs.

—Oh. Sure. That's what I wanted, too. It's all tied in with music and life.

—Exactly.

—Is there anything else you want to say before we close?

—I just want to thank all my mortal friends for all the love and support they've given me. People helping out with benefits. People like you, covering my story. I'm not the only guy in the world with cancer. I just want to say a prayer to everyone with problems.

Reflectively, he squeezed his lower lip with his thumb and forefinger.

—I really want to emphasize my gratitude to everyone in the music community. I'm so happy to be working with Mak Poppin again. He's an old friend, of course, and we've been through a lot. The club-owners. Tommy Demeola. I couldn't be given more opportunities to deliver my message. Everyone has been so kind. I appreciate it from the bottom of my heart.

He brightened with a hopeful grin.
—I'm excited about putting out this reggae sound. It's a real challenge. But the born-again Rastafarian is ready to produce again.

Eric watched the couple as Carrie helped Billy hobble out to her car. It was sad to see the fine-limbed oak tree of a human being reduced to kindling and ashes.

Halloween came and went, but there was no *Cement Forest* show at Key Largo.

There was no *Cement Forest* tour. For six weeks, there was no word of Billy at all.

On a gray Tuesday, in the middle of November, Eric received a phone call from a distressed John Dailey.

—Hey, H-E, I'm at High Tech and you better get over here quick. Billy's recording his Christmas song and this might be the last thing he ever does.

—Is he sick again?

—Yeah. He's real sick. I don't think he's going to pull it off this time. Get over here right away. And bring your synth. We need to get a few more back-up musicians to fill things out.

Eric packed up his DX-7 keyboard and made his way over to High Tech studios as fast as he could. When he arrived, the control room was jammed with people. John Dailey stood in front of his amp, strumming his guitar. Another keyboard player, Jeff Malvini from the funk band C'Olor, Glen Stucky—the "fishin' musician"—on accordion, and bassist Janosz Czeslaw all sat in a tight crescent, warming up.

Meanwhile *Loose Screws* photographer, Biko snapped shots and Bobby Lester, the band archivist, was memorializing the event on videotape. With the help of engineer Jon Linder, Aaron Opperman wired the drum machine into the board. The two of them checked sound levels and made adjustments.

On the couch lay Billy, solemn sullen, sunken, his skin the golden color of a gathering autumn sunset. He was so emaciated, he resembled a pile of yellow pick-up-sticks randomly poking out of a black t-shirt: strewn upon the sofa. His head was propped up on a pillow. And he held a mic in his hand—creakily moaning instructions to the players. Muscles spasming, writhing in pain, he ignored his discomfort in order to facilitate his aim.

Next to him were huddled his mom and Elaine, who was holding his hand. It was obvious that Ingrid had complied with Billy's wishes against her own. She was stricken with fear that he was going to die right there in the control room in front of everyone.

Unable to attend, Carrie was at the clinic. She had been called away at the last minute to perform emergency surgery for a perforated lower intestine on a black Lab named Bobo. Carrie's personal commitments were at odds. She felt she needed to be with Billy, but she had to save that dog. Billy was not going to die that day, Carrie knew it. Without surgery, Bobo would be dead within twelve hours.

Throughout the entire operation, she agonized over Billy's decision to record his new song. He was so resolute about the project, there was no sense in quarreling. But she dreaded the outcome if he were to overextend himself, which wouldn't require much activity at all. With a scalpel, she made a precise incision on Bobo's mid-section, completely preoccupied by Billy's condition.

It was an uncomplicated song, called "Make Love, Not War." The verse and chorus were supported by the same single descending bass line, seemingly inspired by John Lennon's "Mind Games." Billy's vocals on the verse captured a hint of David Bowie singing "Changes," with the essence of Bob Dylan's "Like A Rollin' Stone" floating through, over a simple reggae rhythm.

Forty-five minutes in, the band, such as it was, had mastered the arrangement and were ready to record. It was going to be performed live, with Billy singing directly over the instrumentation. And everyone knew, without a word spoken, that there would only be one take. So keep it simple and no fuck-ups.

They launched into the song, with Jeff Malvini sketching a bare-bones intro out of a marimba sound on his synth. Eric contributed synth-strings, while Glen Stucky's accordion hummed and wheezed beneath everything. Then, body clenched in incredible pain, slurring unintelligibly at times, Billy began to sing.

—Well I used to mess and fool around
Then I thought I'd try to settle down
What a change was there for me
Now the children ask me if we can stay up late and watch TV
But it's so deranged, I don't know what to say...

None of the musicians could look at Billy. They feared they might each break down in tears at any moment. Instead, they cued each other to the changes with furtive glances and focused upon their instrumentation.

—And when they ask me 'Billy what is war and what is crime
and what're nuclear bombs for?'
I shake my head and say
Make love not war
Make yourself some friends
Make love not war
Let us live again
Make love not war
I wanna be your friend
Touch me touch me like a brand new friend.

They soldiered on from the chorus to another verse. Billy fiercely pinched his forehead with his hand, trying to shut out the wracking pain in his body, struggling to somehow concentrate on the lyrics, which was nearly impossible. He gathered all the strength he had.

—Christmas time had the family over to the house
And things were lookin' pretty good
These crazy things in my head
Couldn't justify the piece of bread
That tasted so good
Coz I know we're part of other places
People dyin' the human race is
Not lookin' so very good.
But through it all, I tell you one thing survives
It's ringin' through my ears at night.

He sang the chorus over and over, for nearly eight minutes—as if by repeating the song, he was somehow keeping himself alive. If the song kept going, he would never die. But, he eventually became so weak, his voice reduced to a raspy croak, he finally just trailed off all together.

Startled to hear him stop, Ingrid shouted in alarm, certain that Billy was about to lose consciousness. She rubbed his feet and massaged his calves, attempting to relieve the cramps rippling through his legs. He asked for water and she handed him a pitcher full. He sat up and drained it as if it were a pitcher of beer at the Long Goodbye. Then he lay back down, exhausted.

They all listened to the playback and Billy deemed it satisfactory. He knew he wasn't going to be able to sing it any better—were he even able to sing it again which he wasn't. Then with Billy directing traffic back in the control room, everyone piled into Room A to do a gang backup vocal of angelic oohs and ahhs. All the musicians, Elaine, Incomparable John Dailey's young daughter Jilly, and her friend Iris Moune donned headphones, singing along behind Billy in the choruses.

It was a slapdash affair, everyone too disturbed by the occasion to think rationally. During the vocal overdub, Incomparable John interviewed Jilly and Iris as to the meaning of the song, upon which, being only five and six years old, the girls were not able to shed a great deal of light. At the very end of the song, Jilly inexplicably blurted out "Goodbye everybody."

After Jon Linder completed a rough-mix to Billy's satisfaction, Elaine and Ingrid helped the worn-out young man out to the car and they drove him home. As soon as the Grangers had driven off, everyone in the studio burst into great sorrowful sobs filled with fierce pity, and admiration. His courage had been as overwhelming as his will. Nothing, not even cancer, could deny him. He would not give in.

Billy was back in the hospital the next day. With Bobo on the mend, Carrie did not have to leave Billy's bedside. She slept with him at night and cheered him as best as she was able. He was hooked up to an array of IV bags, though neither he nor Carrie were certain as to what substance any of the bags contained. However, Billy was relatively confident one of them was filled with morphine. He felt no pain.

Though he had plastic oxygen tubes stuffed in his nostrils, he was still very short of breath, unable to fully fill his lungs. Carrie watched him cringing forlornly, his throat a knotted rope that allowed only a strangled gasp to escape. He felt as if he were slowly suffocating. Frequently, he muttered incoherently, becoming lucid only rarely. He didn't feel like eating. He was coughing up blood and suffered from unremitting diarrhea.

Spending most of his time staring vacantly at the television, Billy was very quiet. He seemed not to know or care what was on. He brightened slightly when the *Three Stooges* came on Channel 12 at three o'clock, as they did every day. But he seemed disinterested in the *Star Trek* episodes that followed at four—even though he had always been a huge fan of the show, typically studying each installment with a fastidious fanatical religiosity.

Wrought with worry, Carrie remained stoic. She did not betray to Billy her gathering anxiety. Instead she remained resolutely calm—and as detached as possible. She simply stood by and held his hand, offering him whatever solace she could. She didn't know what else to do. Most of all, she didn't want to disturb him in any way.

It seemed to her that Billy was slowly fading away from this universe, dissolving into some other realm, just a momentary step away. All the color was draining from the frame. But for Billy's sickly, pus-wan, mustard-yellow skin, everything had turned a vague, variant shade of gray: the sky outside, the shadowed room inside. The walls, the *Three Stooges* on television, Billy's bedding and scrub-wear. Cheerlessly overcast and relentlessly bleak.

She wished she too could fade into that other world. There, she would stand with him, in living color, and tell that bright new place what a wonderful man he had become. How he had grown. What strength the slow decay of dying had brought to his life. She would tell of his lucent transformation. He was not disappearing. He was evolving toward some higher space, woven into the fabric of time with threads of pure light.

The weekend after Thanksgiving, a dejected Carrie, the Sunday *Oregonian* in her lap, stared blind at the light gray and dark gray clock on the wall. Meanwhile, Billy lay on his side—curled up in a ball—vacantly watching the *Three Stooges*, when Mak entered the room. He needed to talk business with Billy. He gazed down at his shrunken friend and asked rhetorically.

—Billy. How're ya' doin', man? Are ya' feelin' okay?

—Naw, Maa-kkk...

Billy gulped precariously, not lifting his eyes away from the television screen.

—'m not.

—Well, I came over, cuz' I need to know what ya' wanna do about re-releasin' the Skin and Bones EP and the 'Across the Universe' project. The single. And then there's *Mister Groove*. How do you wanna go? You want vinyl? Vinyl and cassette? Cassette only? And 'Make Love Not War'...

Billy did not respond, nor did he even acknowledge that Mak had said anything. He remained transfixed, by the moving black and gray images and the crude noisy sounds. Mak waited for a reply, but received none. After what seemed like several minutes, he summed up his inquiry.

—So what'd'ya think, Billy. Do y'know what ya' wanna do?

—I jus' wan-na wa-tch *Three Stoo-ges* Ma-kkk. Tha's all.

Tears rimmed Carrie's eyelids. With a helpless expression, she grimaced at Mak imploringly. But Mak, too, was powerless.

—Okay, Billy. Okay. I'll take care of it.

The next day, Ingrid and Elaine and Denny, silent, gathered next to Carrie, who was sitting next to Billy, gently smoothing his forehead with sympathetic hands of kind compassion. She wanted to say something to him, something profound, but her mind was empty, spilling over with sorrow.

Before her lips could manage to move toward the slightest phrase, Billy locked her gaze—gaping more lucid than for days before. He smiled at her lovingly, pressing her hand to his face. Groaning, he softly kissed her palm.

—Oh my darling, Carrie, my saving grace. I'll love you forever, you know.

He flinched in pain.

—I'll be waiting for you. Just over there.

He motioned slightly toward the window. Then he began to faintly sing

—Carrie Deeds
Carrie Deeds
I will follow wherever she leads.
Carry me, carry me,
Carry me Carrie Deeds.
Good deeds
Good deeds
Good good Carrie Deeds

He slowly turned his vanishing attention toward Ingrid and whispered.

—Sorry, mom...

And, happily, out the window. It was...

Snowing! Floating butterflies of snow wafting in the subtle wind. Hovering and shivering soft, aloft in the cold gray air. As flimsy as fog and cold as light. Flimsy and cold. Suspended in the colorless sky, snow descended. Falling gently down. A white light above, a bright love—behind the sky. Floating toward: like falling. The snow. The snow

*We Used to Hang Around*
*Go Go Boots Are Coming Back*
*Boom Chuck Rock*
*Rockabilly Queen*
*Symmetry In My Play*
*I've Got My Upstroke Down*
*English Boy*
*My Girlfriend's Drawers*
*Police Told Me*
*Don't Be Sad*
*The World Comes Crashing Down*
*Like-a-Berries*
*High School Degree*
*Even Your Nightmares Come True*
*Made In Hong Kong*
*Coca Cola*
*Uptown Girl*
*Happy Santa Claus*
*Stereo Area*
*Too Straight For the New Wave*
*Thunder and Lightning*
*Singles Going Steady*
*Apple of My Eye*
*Chances Are*
*(I Just Want to) Get Close to You*
*In and Out of Love*
*Glorious History*
*Thinking Zebra*
*My Life*

Made in the USA
San Bernardino, CA
01 March 2014